BEWARE THE BLOOD

RACHEL SERRIN

Beware the Blood
Published by Serrin Press Copyright © 2023 by Rachel Serrin

ISBN Paperback: 9781736988039

ISBN Hardcover: 9781736988046

To the nineteen-year-old girl who shed tears in a silent church,

We have healed.
And this is your rage.

Table of Contents

Author's Note

This story brought about many ignored traumas and dark aspects of myself. It is intense, angry, rebellious, and filled with grief. As per the last book, most issues in this book are direct correlations to issues within our own world. They do not only exist within the thin pages of this story. When you shut it, please remember those who have been stripped of their freedoms around the world, especially women, transgender individuals, and the rest of the LGBTQIA+ community.

Please take care.

Trigger Warnings: Abuse (Physical, Mental, Emotional, Verbal, Sexual), Religious Trauma, Death, Mental Illness, Human Trafficking, Forced Prostitution, Prostitution of Minors, Sexual Content, Violence, Genocide

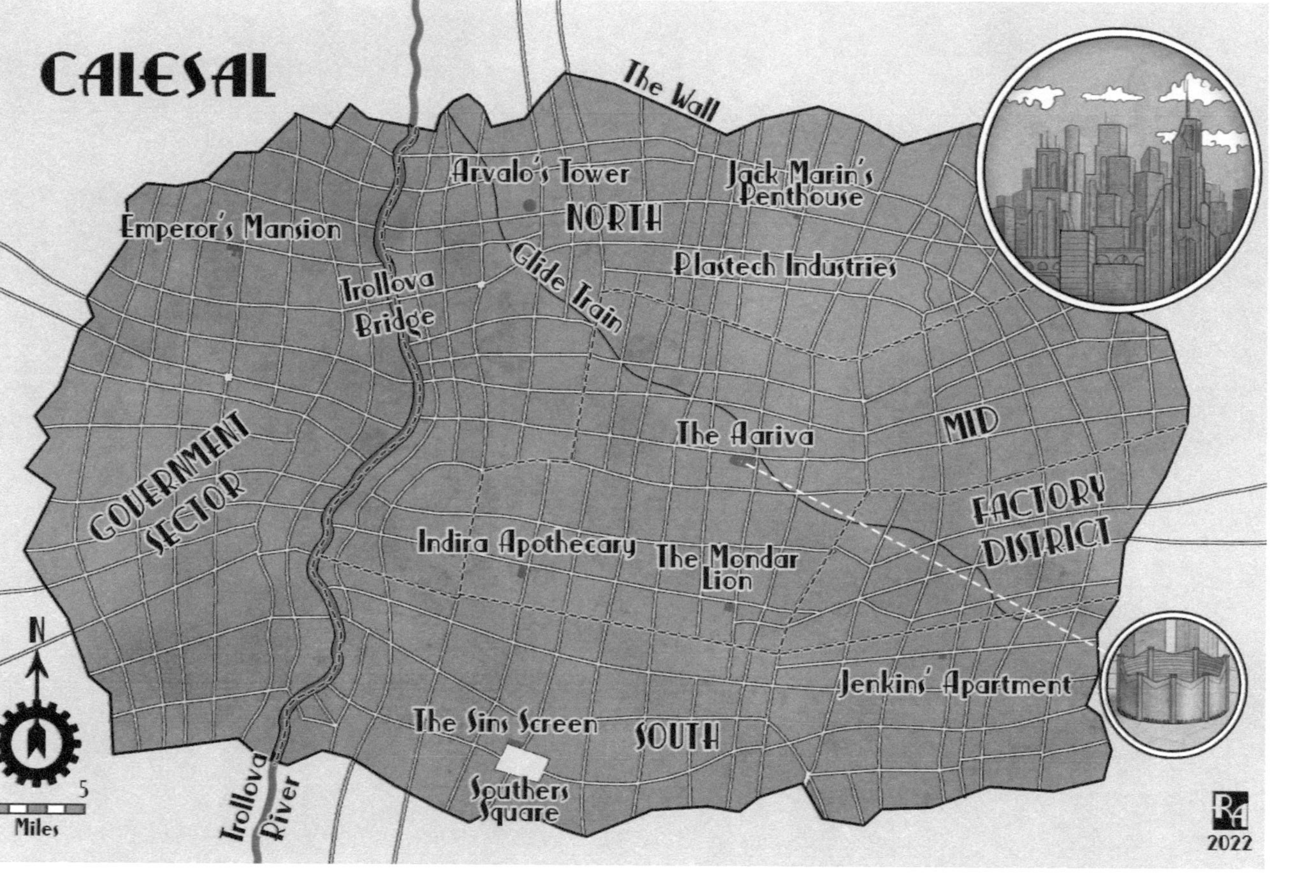

CALESAL
The Wall
Emperor's Mansion
Arvalo's Tower
NORTH
Jack Marin's Penthouse
Trollova Bridge
Glide Train
Plastech Industries
GOVERNMENT SECTOR
The Aariva
MID
FACTORY DISTRICT
Indira Apothecary
The Mondar Lion
Jenkins' Apartment
The Sins Screen
SOUTH
Southern Square
Trollova River
N
Miles
0 5
2022

Prologue

Home always tasted of salt.

Salt bled into the lulling, azure ocean and thrust itself between each grain of pillowy sand. It lingered on the hairy skin of coconuts and crowded the branches of the bowing mangrove trees along the shoreline. It decorated the surfboards, the worn sandals and every pair of shorts his mother stitched, as well as the boogers of his older brothers and the lashes of his father's bright green eyes. Home stretched on for miles, bleeding the same picturesque canvas that Jack Marin loved to wake up to.

The beaches milled on until they were a blur. The islands of other families dotted the horizon. The dense mountains rose above like keen-eyed mothers watching over their creations, and that ever-persistent salt cracked his lips. He loved licking it. Loved tasting it.

It was home.

Jack squatted in the sand, heels buried deep and knees aching from his position. A wilted purple flower lay cupped in his tiny palms as Jack scrunched his nose, focusing on the petals, the stem, the roots, and pushed his will toward the frail thing. A shiver ran through his body, followed by an intense warmth that curled his toes and swarmed his belly. He gazed, without blinking, until the flower began to pucker, filling with life once more. His lips pulled into a toothy grin.

He petted the dainty pillows and whispered, "There, all new again."

Brushing the sand off his cheek, he stood, knees cracking, and padded to the next semi-wilted flower. He called that swirly feeling and pushed it to his palms, just like Mama had taught him. She said to pay attention to the plant's roots—you can never forget the roots. If there aren't roots, there isn't room for creating life. It was the balance.

With no heart, there can be no life.

"*So always make sure you have a heart,*" Mama had said to him days ago. He giggled, watching life return to the second flower. The petals opened, tickling his palms, and the color flourished to a mesmerizing purple. It turned its face to the sun. Jack always liked to think they were smiling after he helped them.

Healed them.

"Jack!" A loud, annoyed voice carried across the sand. "Jack! Come back to play!"

His mood deflated. He tongued the gum where his tooth had fallen out yesterday and decided to ignore Avan—the middle child. Even though Avan was only two years older than Jack, Papa sometimes said Avan would always be a child with how often he wanted to play games. He was the first to rush out of the house in the quiet morning hours, already obnoxious with wiry curls and a toothy grin and brown eyes like Lucien and Mama. Avan whistled to Jack from where he played in the water, but Jack remained before the flower, back to his older brother.

A gargled noise and splash of water—Avan's whine surfaced a moment later. "*Lucien.* That wasn't nice."

"You're too easy," Lucien cackled.

Lucien never backed down from a challenge, but Lucien was the oldest and Jack knew he wanted to put Avan in his place. When Avan won a game, whether it was spearfishing for as many fish as they could catch, or holding a headstand on a wave the longest, Avan wouldn't shut up about it—

Jack squeezed his eyes shut and pinched his knee. Mama said *shut up* wasn't a kind phrase.

—Avan *didn't stop talking* about it for weeks.

"Come on, Jackie! You don't have to be a sore loser." Lucien's beckon was calmer than Avan's demanding one. Jack looked over his shoulder. Lucien waved, his head barely above the water.

"I'm *not* a sore loser—I got too much sand in my eyes from Avan!" Jack yelled. Lucien rolled his eyes and turned to Avan, tackling him beneath the colorful surface. The buttery rays of the setting sun skipped over the frothy water, turning it orange and pink. Jack's stomach gave a low growl. It was nearly dinner time.

Avan huffed a big inhale when he rose, four teeth missing from his smile as he motioned Jack. "You can't pout forever!"

"I'm not pouting," Jack grumbled, standing. He turned to the sea, but his mouth flashed hotly. He tongued his gum again. He lost his sharp tooth yesterday, but it pained him more than usual. Did it hurt this much when he lost his other one? He couldn't remember.

The water hushed along the shore, meeting the crevices of his small toes. Jack wiggled them as his heels sunk farther into the sand. A sudden gasp escaped his mouth and he slapped a palm over his heart, where a stabbing ache formed. It blossomed across his thin chest and along his spine. He glanced down, wondering if a sandmoth stung him—they were nasty sometimes—but it never hurt this much.

He puckered a lip and massaged his chest. Weird. Lifting his eyes back to his brothers, Avan was pointing at him. "It will be fun!"

The ocean turned blurry. Jack lost focus. The pain played with his mind, making Avan's words hard to process.

A giant wave devoured his middle brother's head and Lucien released a high-pitched laugh. "Only fun when you win, stupid!"

They went back to wrestling, and Jack stayed, feet planted firmly on the beach. Rubbing his chest. Confused. Lost. The world seemed to shrink around him. He couldn't spot the distant islands anymore, and when he turned his head to gaze along the shore, the mangrove trees bent a little too much. The sunset lost its luster.

The ocean roar became a chilly whisper.

A rough hand gripped his shoulder. "Why aren't you playing the game, Jack?"

Jack didn't turn to his father. He instead reached up to clutch his chest again, this time to sate both the pain and panic rising within.

"I needed a break," he muttered.

His father sighed. "You know what we said about the flowers… the daylight is too dangerous for that."

Because people would find out and hurt them. Hurt his whole community. It needed to be a secret, but the flower was dying and Jack knew he could help it.

Papa squeezed his arm. "You understand, Jack?"

"Yes," Jack whispered. His lip trembled and he fought the tears in his eyes. Oh, he missed his family so much—

But they were here.

Jack's gaze found his father. Warm green eyes questioned him, dipped to the hand that clutched his chest, then shifted to his wobbling lip. He wore no shirt—only his swim shorts, like usual. His dark curls were held back in a bun, jawline left unshaven—not for very long because Mama didn't like it—and his wide mouth slowly pursed.

"Never mind that. Why did you stop playing with your brothers? It doesn't sound like you." His father's voice was as smooth as the glassy sunrise waves.

Jack always thought the ocean birthed his father, but that would mean he'd have a fin like the fish, slimy skin, or irises as blue as the sea. He walked around their little village like he couldn't figure out how to manage his own legs, but once he stepped into the sea, he swam as fast as the sea turtles, held his breath long enough to dive to the darker-colored corals, and managed to surf the waves with a couple of palm fronds and a dried dorsal fin.

"I just feel…" Jack rubbed at the returning pain. "Strange."

Papa knelt to level his gaze. "Go play the game, Jack. Your older brothers are waiting for you."

"I said I didn't want to play the game." His voice squeaked, demand at the thick of it. They'd been playing for hours, and he wanted to go back in with Mama while she prepared dinner. He'd gotten sidetracked by the flowers and now he was here…

Despite how strange it was to *be* here.

Jack glanced at the hut nestled along a shaded tree line. Papa sighed and turned him to the ocean again. "You know you can beat them. Just because Lucien pummeled you in the first round doesn't mean—"

"He didn't pummel me," Jack snapped. "He just—well, he is four years older than me. And stronger. He has one chin hair, and I don't. And Avan is annoying about games…"

His father snorted. "We each have different roles to play. Your body is strong, but your mind is—" Jack opened his mouth to protest. His father raised a finger. "No, don't interrupt me. Do not compare yourself to your brothers. Do not think about how Lucien is older. How would you go about changing that until you are satisfied? Grow older before this last round so you can match him? No, that's not how it works. It's important for you to know yourself and your abilities, honing even the weakest parts, so you can not only win, but put up a damn fight." Papa tipped Jack's chin. "Now, what are you good at?"

"Games…" Jack pouted, then brightened. "With the mind. Mind games. I always beat Avan. Even Mama."

"If Lucien comes at you with the ultimate water splash, what do you do?"

"Duck into the water and grab his legs."

"And if he kicks you?"

"I'd bite his toes—no." Jack blinked and smiled. "No, I'd get close enough for him to *think* that, then push from the bottom and surprise him with my own splash. Right in the eyes."

"And then you win." Papa smiled. "Be brave enough to know winning isn't the goal. It is about how you play the game. The tricks and the trade. If you always win, you'll never learn." He nudged Jack toward the water.

Despite the elation granted by his pep talk, the ache still gnawed in Jack's chest. He dropped his hand. Refused to rub it. He needed to be strong, ignore the pain, and continue if he wanted to win.

"Play the game, Jack. I'll be right behind you," his father said.

A toothy smile split Jack's face and his brothers beckoned him into the waves. He took a step forward, ready to sprint to them, but his body tensed, and his legs remained still. He frowned. The elation died, the wind growled, and the salt burned his eyes. A sting snaked along his arms, across his shoulders, bit at his growing canines, and even ached in his calves. Jack turned to his father with tears in his eyes. And his tears were like ice.

His voice hovered at a whisper, "This isn't real, is it?"

Those green eyes lost their light. Avan and Lucien stopped laughing. The ocean stilled, the wind gave one last lash, and the world darkened to a bleak, gray haze.

His father frowned. "It is not, my son."

"Because you're dead."

And Jack could see it now. His father's lips purpled, the whites of his eyes reddened, and a horrific bruise blossomed along his neck where the fishing line had killed him. His brown skin paled to that of the buried—someone whose soul didn't exist within anymore.

His father cupped Jack's cheek and brushed the escaping tears with his thumb. "I'm so sorry." His skin was so cold.

Avan and Lucien stood closer to shore—Lucien still bright and alive, Avan shadowed—confused. Lost and abandoned.

Jack's gaze swept to their home made of driftwood and love. Where the clattering of pans echoed, and his mother flitted around inside, humming some tune to her round, swollen belly. He wanted…but he didn't…

He took a deep, painful breath. He wanted to run to her and feel her arms wrap around him. But he didn't want to see the blood along her legs. He didn't want to relive that again.

"I don't think I can play this game anymore," Jack whispered. The tears continued to fall. "I want to be with you."

"You are my strong, powerful, brave boy," Papa said. "But it is not your time yet."

"The world back there is awful. I can't—" Jack's lip quivered, and he shook his head harshly. "I am tired, Papa. I want to go home."

"There is no more home."

The saying intensified the pain. It stretched to a deeper, confusing meaning he could never understand.

"I know." Jack's expression twisted as grief gripped him. "I still want to go home."

"We are dead." His father pressed his cold forehead to Jack's. "But we have never left you. Know that. Please know that."

Jack nodded through his tear-filled vision.

"You have to play the game, Jack," his father urged. "Be smart, be brave, be true to yourself. You are everything I hoped and dreamed you would grow to be. Do not doubt yourself."

"Okay," Jack said. Because he trusted his father. "So, I am not dead?"

"Wake up and see for yourself, my son."

Part I

The Revival

1

NEW AGAIN

JACK MARIN KNEW WHAT DEATH felt like.

It was a contradiction. Peace and paranoia. Sweet and spicy. Light and dark. It bruised and caressed him as he plunged through worlds of the universe. His body morphed from that of a boy to a man. His eyes opened. He glimpsed the lick of flames and the soft rays of a sun, the gentle breeze between blades of grass and the steady lap of water. He saw worlds that weren't his own—ones he had never visited, but ones ready to welcome him. He breathed the brink of existence. The line etched between what it meant to be alive and what it meant to be nothing. They passed on, all creations in an infinite space. He watched as he fell, both calm and panicked.

A continued contradiction.

It was both horrifyingly beautiful and wonderfully terrifying to witness. Images his mind couldn't comprehend. Which was it? Stunning? Awful? He both ached to go and yearned to stay, but he carried on, sailing the stars as the universe debated where to finally drop him.

He lost track of the vast realms. Rivers of lava. Mountains of ice. As if the skies couldn't figure out his place in this universe. Beautiful blue seas called to his heart, and he wanted to cry out—*that one, take me to that one*—but the visions continued, and the next world was bitter and gray.

On and on it went. He was called, then not.

The last contradiction.

Death was both familiar.

And not.

The universe decided. Jack sucked a deep inhale. His consciousness filled with black. The endless galaxies seized and his reality narrowed to a single plane.

When he opened his eyes, he forgot the worlds but remembered the confusion. The contradictions. He remembered the feelings, and it seemed his physical body felt it, too, because he was covered in sweat.

Naked.

Lying on a cold stone floor in a dark, empty metal and stone-walled room.

Jack bolted to his feet, hands out in front of him, preparing for an attack. For something. His head dizzied, and he faltered for a moment. He placed a hand over his thrashing heart. His fingers met a bandage. He glanced down.

A single strip of white lay in the center of his chest. Over his heart. The same stickiness was slapped to his back. Had he been kidnapped? Stabbed? His brows furrowed. Why couldn't he remember anything?

Was he even awake?

The dream he had...it was of his father. His brothers. On the beach. Playing with flowers. He always forgot about those moments, forgot that he could hold a flower in his hand and watch the stem straighten, the petals unfurl. Watch as it came back to life.

No. It was a fantasy. Something his imagination wove into his memories. A trauma response, his therapist used to say. It added something new, something different to his memories to replace the horrific nature of their reality.

He shook his head, his hair brushing his upper back. It was longer than he last remembered. What *did* he last remember? His mind returned to the beach. With his brothers. His father. But he was grown now. No adult part of him knew his whole family. It all ended at the age of seven.

He stared at his body.

And also…damn. He was *totally* naked.

"Subject is awake. Begin testing."

The monotone voice flowed through a speaker in the far corner with a camera attached. A single light illuminated a small door beneath it, and next to that, a giant pane of glass mirrored his reflection.

Focus. *Focus.*

He stared at himself. The gray walls surrounded his skinnier body. He lost some muscle. His green eyes were bleak. Confused. His skin was a sallow brown. His hair a chaos of curls. How old was he—?

The walls groaned. Small, fist-sized pockets opened. He glimpsed the shiny points.

"Fuck," he mumbled.

They shot from the walls and Jack moved. Faster than he could remember. An arrow nearly slammed into his thigh, but he caught it, rolled to the ground, and within a blink, he was on the other side of the room with a decimated metal bolt in his left hand. Split into nearly seven pieces with the simple strength of a fist.

A sharp inhale. Folding it into his palm, he clenched as hard as he could. Opened his hand up. A small mound of dust cascaded between the rivets of his fingers.

He stared at it incredulously. Panic gripped his throat.

"Droanian strength confirmed. Mer reflexes confirmed. Proceed with the next test."

Droanian strength? Mer reflexes?

Jack treaded to the window. Skies, he looked like shit. He ignored his unfortunate appearance and focused on the one-way glass. He knew it was a long shot to see whatever existed beyond the pane, but he pressed his sweaty forehead to the window with his hands cupped around his eyes. He *tried* to see. *Tried* to get a sense of where he was…but the shadow of his dark circles stared back. He knew people were beyond it, but who?

A groan. His attention shifted back to the room. New metal covered the arrow slits in the walls. Across from him, stone scraped, folding into itself and parting to reveal a thick, barred cage. A dark outline prowled behind.

He barely had a breath before two yellow eyes found him and the bars jolted up. The giant cat lunged.

Jack ducked to the side as the massive creature clawed at him. It bounced off the wall and charged again. Jack dodged an outward paw and jammed his hand in its throat. It yelped, huffed a breath, but continued its assault.

He sprinted, barely evading, and the urge to disappear fought at him.

Icy tingles descended his arms, then through his body. It continued to his toes, and just as Jack ducked again, sliding beneath the jumping body of the cat, he noticed his legs were gone.

Not gone. He could feel them. Use them. But he couldn't *see* them.

The cat landed a claw. Pain welled at his side; Jack ignored it. Fury lashed through him. He gripped the icy tingles and yanked on them, disappearing entirely. His vision remained the same, but the more he moved, the more he realized he wasn't necessarily invisible…

The cat stalled, turning its head and releasing a low, angered growl. Arching its back, it pawed at the air.

Jack snapped its neck.

He became the predator.

The cat collapsed. Jack stood over its lifeless body, chest heaving.

"Incinerate feline."

A subtle click of metal sounded from the feline's body, and with a jerk, it burst into flames. Jack raised an arm, covering his face. A moment later, water sprayed from the ceiling, extinguishing the fire. It met his skin despite the invisibility.

He retreated and planted himself along the wall. He struggled to get a grip of his breath, and with that, he lost his hold on the invisibility. His limbs and body rippled back into sight. Water slicked along his skin, mixing with the blood at his side. A gash lacerated his hip bone, but…he blinked, trying to make sense of what he saw. The wound rapidly stitched itself together. The fresh blood remained, but his skin threaded into a whole, untouched piece.

That didn't confuse him as much as the invisibility did.

"Droanian strength confirmed. Endolier camouflage confirmed. Make a note for rapid healing origination—"

A cold, dark voice interrupted. "Association with Mers."

A pause. "Healing associated with Mers."

"What the *fuck* is going on?" Jack sprinted to the window, slamming his palm to the glass. It groaned underneath his inhuman strength. "What is this? Where am I?"

"Heart rate increasing. Proceed with the next test."

The empty cage vanished behind a new stone wall. A line slowly cut into the material, revealing a door.

It opened, revealing a lanky man wearing only a loose sheet around his hips. He looked young. Younger than Jack. Maybe twenty or so. He stepped from the dark and his glazed eyes scanned the room. The door shut behind him. His head tilted, eyes landing on Jack.

A strange aura slunk from the man. Jack had the urge to sniff the air, and when he did, a sharp jolt stabbed his canines.

Jack couldn't shake the icy horror bubbling. The center of his chest panged, his arm still tingled with a cool sensation from the camouflage, his muscles ached, his blood felt warm—Jack's eyes widened, and he gingerly touched his canines. This wasn't his body. No, it couldn't be. But they put him in this room for a reason. They had a one-way window for a reason. So they could watch him, analyze him, and so he could see himself, in the full, foreign form he stood as now.

He couldn't resist sniffing the air, taking in every scent. A bleak musk with a hint of coconut. Tinged with a fiery spice, but it was mellow, diluted like it had been shoved back by the other flavors.

Emotions. He felt this young man's emotions.

Indifference, slight curiosity, and beneath it all…fear.

Jack took a step forward, his mouth salivating. He paused. Shook his head. No, no he couldn't do it…it was wrong. He couldn't *bite* this man.

"It's okay," the man said. "Look into my eyes. You'll know it is okay."

Jack was all kinds of morally wrong, but he knew he should ignore the man. Walk away. Breathe through it. That if he peered into his eyes, there was another test, another way to make him feel even more false and foreign than he already did.

"I'll be okay," the man said again, this time more monotone. "Look in my eyes."

"You won't be okay," Jack replied. He could already feel his resolve slipping. He clenched his jaw. *Come on, hold on a little longer. Don't give in.*

He needed an anchor. He searched his mind for something he loved and landed on Lucien. His brother. Lucien would tell him to be cautious, but offensive if need be.

And he'd pour Jack a strong drink and say, *"Everything comes to an end. The hours, the days, the parties, and life. You have to get through it and eventually, you'll reach the end."*

It wasn't the best advice when Jack stood naked in an observation room while fighting the urge to bite the shit out of this stranger so he could taste his emotions, but it slightly worked. Lucien mainly applied that advice to the parties they had to show face at, but desperation left Jack grasping for anything he could.

He turned to the window, opening his mouth—

"Deliver first punishment."

A shock of lightning seared through him. Jack let out a deafening roar before falling and gripping the stone and metal wall. Unbearable pain blurred his vision and his muscles contracted. He clawed as the electricity took over. Metal shredded, stone fissured, digging cuts into his hands.

The shock stopped.

Jack sucked a deep breath. Lifted his eyes. A gaping hole in the metal stared back. He glanced at his hands—still covered in the occasional water drops, but for the most part, dry. Healed again. No blood marked his skin.

"I'll be okay."

Jack whirled to the young man, who still stood there, completely unbothered. Drugged. It was why that indifference was at the forefront of his emotions, and that tinge of fear was a speck in the back. The drugs numbed him.

Numb, so if Jack ripped open his throat, he wouldn't react.

He snagged his gaze on the man's eyes. Lovely, glazed, brown eyes. Jack searched them for signs of humanness to make him feel better, to make him feel like this was real.

After ten seconds, it happened. And like Jack predicted, there was a reason.

Jack heard a voice as if someone had stuck their mouth inside his ear canal and chattered away. But the man's lips remained unmoving. Detached.

His *thoughts* though…

Make sure you hold eye contact…They demanded I get you to bite me…You're supposed to be powerful…I'm not supposed to die, but their faces when they said it…I might die…I think I will die…

The man's voice pleaded in Jack's head. *Please…make it quick. Make it painless. I won't survive this place if I live.*

Jack broke eye contact.

"Lovuphal mind-reading confirmed."

Calm settled over him. Jack prowled forward. If there was one thing he knew how to do, it was to deliver a quick death. If there was one thing Jack was good at…it was killing.

He reached the young man, who tensed slightly but lifted his arm, displaying his wrist. Jack brought his mouth to it.

"I'll be okay," the man repeated.

Jack's teeth sank into the young man's skin. Every human part of him knew it would take a lot of strength to puncture skin with only teeth, but Jack's canines slipped through the barrier like butter.

He tasted blood, but where it should have repulsed him, it enticed him. He gagged on the indifference, though. There was hardly any flavor. No emotion. He sought after the curiosity, but even that only held his attention for so long. He sucked the blood into his mouth, and after some searching, tasted the fiery spice of fear.

He became aware of the young man's rapid heartbeat, the people watching this interaction beyond the window, and how his emotions digressed into an absurd peace. He pushed that peace into the man. Attempted to calm him.

The young man sagged. When his eyelids drooped, Jack pulled the wrist away from his mouth, blood dripping down his chin.

He beheld the young man. Numbness washed over. He placed one hand on the man's chin and another behind his head.

A quick snap ricocheted throughout the room. The man collapsed to the floor, dead.

It was a moment of silence before that monotone voice spoke, "Aurien ability confirmed."

Jack didn't remember much. He didn't feel right in his current body, but if there was one thing he knew, it was that being observed in a metal box meant one thing: he was an animal, and his captors controlled him.

He *hated* being controlled.

So he let the monster ripple out. He picked up the young man's dead body, and with an easy jerk, tore his arm out of its socket. He turned to the window and chucked it as hard as he could. As much as this Droanian strength would allow.

It smashed the glass, fissuring it with cracks. Jack stalked to the damage and raised his fist, throwing a punch at the center. Then another and another, until his knuckles ripened with blood. Healed. Burst open again. The blood continued to flow. The window cracked more and became a distortion of jagged pieces.

"Are you done with your little experiments?" Jack growled with a lethal smile. "Come on, I'm just getting *started*."

A door appeared to the left of the mirror. It opened. Jack surged toward it—

But what stepped through halted him completely.

Whorls of memories painfully piled to the front of his brain. Hot sand, hot blood, hot pain, hot mouth. And then the feeling of a firecracker bursting within his chest before it all sputtered out. His father's voice, his brothers' laughter, the gush of the sea at his home.

Faces littered his mind, but they swirled and morphed, lips moving—more memories. He didn't know their names. A tiny one with a scowl. A tall one with hair the color of his perfect coffee. A beautiful one with eyes as blue as those ocean waves…

He stared at her now.

His lips moved. He wanted to say her name. His chest constricted. A familiar name. His top teeth bit his bottom lip— *V…V…V…*

He couldn't remember the rest. But it was *her*. She was *there* and in front of him. He remembered her warmth, and it wasn't a comforting fire on a cold night. It was brutal, scalding and dangerous, but he had become addicted to it.

His intuition told him there was no possible way she could be here in this room.

You must play the game, Jack.

He dropped his gaze to his hands.

Familiar.

And not.

He died.

He came back to life.

He has Endolier camouflage, Droanian strength, an Aurien's desire to bite for emotions and truth, Lovuphal mind-reading, and whatever a Mer was.

He was in a game. He had his hand sliced before an obsidian bowl.

The Sins.

But they weren't merely worlds anymore. No. They were ruled by…

Pale skin. Scars. A devilish voice.

Cyran.

Jack recounted his entire time in the Sins. He turned every memory over and over, testing each name, confirming it, then moving on. The burns of Wrath—he glanced to the gnarl of skin at his forearm when he'd shielded himself from blistering heat after that girl pushed him away. He'd been so angry, so mad at her…

But dunes of sand shifted to tall mountains and a blackened, horrific waste of land. The foulness of Gluttony. It was a world etched into his soul—pure, original beauty loved by the Inaj, yet overridden and ruined by the gluttonous desire of the Crale. He remembered her—the woman Crale who constantly touched him, even while he was asleep. Those stark white hands on his body, and his mind then drifting to happier places while that saccharine voice echoed. The groans of those oppressed outside while he curled into a bed, reminded of his life *after* his original home. His eyes watered as he remembered how helpless he had been in that world, how frustrated he was. How much he hated himself for only focusing on his survival until *she* dropped in front of him, and he nearly had a heart attack.

The dangers of Envy. Feelings turned over within the murky jungle. Tired late-night laughs. Robotic animals. The haunting slash of whips.

The desires of Lust. Skin. Moans. Her moans. A head slapping the floor. Deep, thumping bass and smiles of those he cared for— would kill for.

The sharp heat of the dagger going into his back.

You must play the game, Jack.

Jack Marin had played games his whole life. He was just not used to being a pawn in one bigger than himself.

Be brave enough to know that winning isn't the goal. It is about how you play the game. The tricks and the trade. If you always win, you'll never learn.

He lifted his gaze to the girl who should not be here.

His lips formed her name.

"Violet."

Relief flooded her face. "You're alive."

She was a head-and-a-half smaller than him, but there was a confidence in her stance, a swagger, and it always made her seem bigger. Her body was as he remembered—olive skin, athletic build, small breasts, slight curves at her hips. Her simple nose and small, puckered mouth. Then those eyes…those wide-set blue eyes framed with dark lashes and roofed by thick brows. Her brown hair was pulled back into a low bun. Her clothes were simple black pants and a white T-shirt.

She took a careful step forward.

As much as Jack wanted to see her, to touch her, he knew this was another test.

Jack jutted his hand out to wrap around her neck, squeezing hard. "You sure like your victims vulnerable."

A deadly smile curved along her face, and suddenly her body morphed and melted, grew and widened, into the pallid, scarred form of Cyran. He carelessly peeled Jack's hand away from his neck. "I would have been disappointed if you fell for it."

Jack bared his teeth.

"That wasn't a test. Merely fun."

Jack would curse himself for allowing such a thing to happen, but his state didn't enable him to be at his best. He was not the one in control. Exhaustion clawed at him. His blood boiled with new species. The memories and yearning for comfort pained him. Cyran, like any ambitious man, would use Jack's disabilities to his advantage. So Violet was the perfect little trigger.

"Where is she?" Jack steeled his spine.

Cyran mused, "She is dead."

Jack stilled. He glared, searching for a lie on Cyran's amused face. No micro expression betrayed his deception. The truth.

"No." Every bit of Jack's control washed away. He shook his head. "No."

Cyran reached into his pocket and pulled out a small shard. A turquoise thing Jack recognized instantly. Part of Gwen's dagger.

He'd been stabbed in the chest again. He was sure of it. "Where is the rest?"

"Incinerated with her friends in the world of Sloth. It didn't take long for my men to find her shortly after the confrontation in Lust. This"—he held up the piece —"was left behind."

He held it out for Jack. Jack hesitated before taking it. Cyran turned his head and called through the door, "Bring him some clothes. He passed."

He partially noticed the two servants enter the room, holding clothes. When Jack didn't move, they began to dress him. He stared blankly at the wall behind Cyran, unable to form a thought. His chest constricted so harshly he'd rather be electrocuted forty times over.

There was a haze when he thought back to those final moments in Lust. Hounds, blood, kissing her, and fighting the ice that had slithered inside his mind, so reminiscent of the way each Sin worked.

Remembering grew a headache. Every moment after he lost control of himself to Cyran was shrouded behind a veil of darkness. He remembered fiery pain along his body, the snap of his wrist, and the crunch of bones forming together. A turquoise dagger—

Jack lost his composure. "You commanded me to kill her."

"Your bloodbond stopped it." Cyran flicked his wrists and the servants disappeared through the door. "A surprise to me. It's an ancient practice from the Droans. But no matter, I disposed of her after she was Awakened. I can't have a rogue Vanisher cheating my game."

Vanisher…Jack didn't remember much about that, other than it was select people who could teleport from one place, or world, to another. He faintly remembered a bright flash of light and Violet screaming.

Did she…scream like that when the Worldbreaker's men killed her?

Killed. Killed. Killed.

Her death seemed like a far-fetched thing, but Jack knew this game. He remembered it all. There was no luck with Cyran. Only those who are powerful could stand a chance at survival. Violet was a menace with a blade, but she wasn't…

Wasn't…

He pushed down the rising grief. Cyran studied him. A dull roar muffled his ears. All of that—gone. Her…Anaya and Rio—gone.

Cyran said they were incinerated. There'd be no trace of their bodies. Could that make it more of a ploy? A lie? As much as Jack wanted to grasp at the fraying strings of hope, as much as he wanted to believe that Cyran was lying to him, he was only a human. No matter the villain or manipulation, news of important people in his life that have been killed was hard to reason with.

His analysis mixed with his emotion, and his body didn't know how to handle it. He couldn't *fucking* breathe.

"And now you made me into this…thing?" He glanced down at his clothed body. "How?"

"Blood transfusion, DNA manipulation, electrocution." Cyran nodded his head to the door and began to walk. Jack numbly followed. "And the fact you died. It made the renewal process easier. However, it was interesting still to see such tenacity to live from someone born within Calesal. Not many hold that much hope, will, or ambition, especially after entering the Sins."

The walls. Born within the walls. But Cyran didn't know that Jack was born free from a cage. No one knew except the only other soul who shared the same story—Lucien. And that one therapist who unfortunately had expired.

Cyran waltzed through the adjacent room that held rows of computers, analysts, and other high-tech, unrecognizable gear. Pieces of the window's glass splattered across keyboards, along the tables, and even pricked the skin of some. Jack made an absolute mess of something that should, in theory, have taken a plasbomb to destroy. Some workers glanced at him, in awe, as if he were a theatrical display.

Cyran led Jack out of the observation room and into a warm hallway of black marble. Two soldiers straightened and followed them as they made numerous turns. Jack memorized them as much as he could, but the lack of windows and the simple, repeated look of everything made it difficult.

"I was sent to the Sins for my crimes," Jack said. "I lost. There isn't any more ambition left. Especially if she…if they are dead."

"That was the warm-up." Cyran turned to him, eyes gleaming. "Call me impressed."

"Just because I was powerful in the past doesn't mean I'll be of any use to you now."

"Your performance proves quite the opposite." Cyran stopped at a door and a soldier opened it for him. "You are the success." His gaze swept the new room. "These are the failures."

Heat blasted Jack in the face, along with an awful stench that made him gag. Large piles of bodies filled the room waiting to be incinerated. Men covered in hazard suits threw the naked, limp, and mauled corpses into grated compartments, burning to ash within seconds.

Failures.

"Terrible losses," Cyran said. "None of them woke up after we completed the transfusions. Their genetics couldn't hold it, but yours…" A heavy stare. "Yours did."

Jack met his gaze. "I'm sure it was due to my irresistible good looks."

Cyran didn't find the humor. Jack didn't mean to be funny. He…he didn't know how he was supposed to act. His emotions simmered into his belly, coiling low. "Why did you need to kill her?"

"A rogue Vanisher is a danger to themselves and others. It can cause a mess of problems."

"To your game," Jack said. "Not to the people in your worlds. They don't matter."

The soldier shut the door to the failures and Cyran continued on, ignoring Jack. "She was a wild one. A wildflower. I've learned a thing or two from my gardening experience; you merely pluck the weeds."

Jack's throat tightened.

"You will join my ranks and train underneath my best. I will bring in captains to help you harness your abilities," Cyran said. "Zavar will monitor your training closely, as he was the one who threw the dagger into your back. It's the only fitting punishment for costing me great potential."

"No choice?" Jack smirked slightly. "Forced loyalty doesn't linger long."

"By all means, fight the last two Sins and continue, but I will catch you, and I will kill you before you reach that exit."

"Ah, so that's why they always die so quickly in the seventh world."

"I like the chase," Cyran mused. "But no one ever proves to be a challenge."

Jack's gaze hardened. "And if I refuse to work for you?"

The Worldbreaker looked over his shoulder with a side-eye.

The air stilled around Jack. His throat lodged, as if gripped by a phantom hand. His breath halted. He tried, but he wheezed air through his teeth as his blood frosted. He couldn't blink, couldn't glance anywhere but in the Worldbreaker's gaze. Control seeped from Jack and Cyran took it with a delighted smile.

Cyran had this blood control on everyone who was sentenced to the Sins, everyone except Violet. And perhaps Reed.

"There is no refusing me," Cyran drawled, giving no expression to Jack's thoughts. He can't read minds then. "The moment your blood spilled into that bowl it became mine. You are an ambitious man, Jack Marin, and ambition can lead you to great power if you align with the right people. I'm willing to make you a prodigy under my wing as I rule. You can prove to all those who've wronged you, and you've wronged, that you're worth more than an exile into a game."

Jack grew dizzy. The control released. His throat popped open, air pouring in. It burned to breathe and his chest ached. "She has ambition too."

"The word is *had*." Cyran smiled. "Now rest. The soldiers will take you to a room where you can get cleaned up. Nurses will be in to check on you, and you can use them for other pleasures if you wish. They are at your total disposal. We will monitor your progress and get you rehabilitated, then put you in the training room."

A burst of light blinded Jack for a second and Cyran vanished into thin air. The hallway expanded in front of them. He turned, noticing an open door with an attractive maid, bowing her head. A cozy bed lay neat next to her.

Lucien's words descended over him.

Survive, Jack.

The last words his brother said before they'd hugged and Jack left the holding cell to go to the Bloodswearing Ceremony.

Play the game.

A game of what? he thought.

The game of blood.

Jack rolled the turquoise shard between his fingers. Cyran wanted a monster.

But Jack was tired of being a monster. A pawn. A player.

He would be a conqueror.

2

MUTT

THE GLAMOUR OF VIOLET SHOWED up again, then Anaya, then Rio. Over and over, Cyran imitated them. Most times Jack was prepared for it and realized the ploy within moments, but other times seeing those familiar faces caught him off guard, and Cyran noted everything. One day, Jack woke to a version of Lucien hovering over his bed. The version wasn't exact, and while Jack could see through the illusion, he panicked.

Cyran's Lucien smiled as Jack burst up, stuttering, "How did you—"

"Find out?" His brother's dark brown eyes crinkled. So unlike the real him. Malice lingered. "Your new Emperor is quite pliable. He provided one of my Vanishers with a photo of your precious older brother."

"New emperor?" Jack's eyes widened. "Of Calesal? Who?"

"Juss Arvalo," Cyran said.

Deep, icy fear roiled through Jack's body.

It had been a week since Jack initially woke up. He'd since discovered he was in the world of Greed, the sixth world. They were keeping him isolated in a simple, yet plush, room. The single barred window offered a view of a snowy mountainous landscape. Clothes had been lined neatly on a rack, rolled in by a servant a day ago. Fighting leathers, armor, casual outfits, but nothing that gave him any idea of what Greed was like.

The glamours of Violet, Anaya, and Rio were a mockery. A way to poke at Jack's already-pained heart. But now his brother…

Jack sighed and stood, towering an inch over Cyran's Lucien. Correct measurements must have been sent because that inch difference drove Lucien mad.

"You dick, I'm the older one." Lucien shoved Jack into a chair with *a hint of a smile. "You have your power, but don't forget who raised you."*

"You just hate that I can look down at you," Jack teased.

"The only thing I hate is that you never get my drink right."

Jack glared into his not-brother's eyes. "Fuck you for impersonating him."

"At least I know where another of you lay. If I need another Marin."

Jack lunged, taking his not-brother to the ground. He slammed a fist into not-Lucien's face, but only a laugh bubbled out. He gripped his throat, squeezing, but Cyran continued to laugh— then two slits of purple light ignited beneath his eyes and Jack went flying back. He slammed into the far wall with a grunt. "If you want me to stay here, work for you, not off myself, not burn your entire world to the ground, then you will leave my brother alone."

A satisfied smile. Lucien's features rippled away, and the pallid skin of Cyran sucked the dull light from the window. "As expected."

"You have one of us, and I'm the one who can do the most damage if you utilize me." Jack dipped his chin. "Second, I want power, control. I don't want anyone demanding things from me."

"Your brother won't be touched, but you have to prove yourself to earn that power."

"Lastly, if my enemies want to fight me, let them."

"Your training begins tomorrow."

Later that evening, Jack donned his training clothes, flexing in them to get used to the feel. On one set of squats, a motion outside of the window caught his attention.

A flying ship roared by. Made of sleek metal and blinking lights, but in the early evening, ripples of black camouflaged it as it turned here and there.

A foreign world. A foreign body. A foreign life.

The darkness crawled over his shoulder. It cooed in his ear, told him to let it go, that he shouldn't have cared in the first place. Worry twisted his gut and Jack clenched his jaw, hating it.

It laughed at his emotions and shrieked in amusement at his fear. "There was a time," it said, "when you ruled a city. When you commanded fear and pain for the sake of your dream. When a whole world, and everyone within it, bowed to you. If you become him again, there will be no dream out of reach."

The darkness of pride in a world stained with Greed. Pride followed Jack his entire life. The other Sins were basic threats, but pride… It demanded destruction of whatever made him weak, and for him to reach for the bloody stars Cyran held. To be stripped of his rank in front of the city he conquered should have destroyed his pride, yet it left him with shredded ribbons to stitch back together. He was delusional on the Bloodswearing stage and had his hand slashed for a game, but a part of him had been ready to leave the city he'd lost permanently, even if his brother would remain. How selfish was he to keep from Lucien that he was relieved to go? That he failed, and he didn't want to show his face again on those wretched, bloody streets.

The compound where Jack revived settled in a snowy landscape. Nestled between two rocky peaks, Honnrak Castle was the most remote and heavily guarded of all Cyran's fortresses. Only one entrance. One snowy bridge. One landing pad for those flying ships that had to be cleared before breaching the sky miles away. Guards posted at all windows with plasrifles, plasblades, and more weapons than Jack had ever seen before. Bloodhounds lingered in each hallway; the dark, shadowy dogs similar to the ones he'd slaughtered back in Lust. They contained the biological recognition of blood—those allowed within the compound. The hounds, alerted by any intruders' unrecognizable scent, would be ripped apart.

While following a female servant through the hallways, Jack made eye contact with a dog. It sat on its hind legs, pointy ears twitching at each footstep, eyes following his every move. Both alive and not. Nostor made up their paws and teeth—indestructible. The hounds sent to Lust were merely prototypes according to Cyran. Ones to be thrown away. Ones only meant for killing. In Greed, they were exquisite biomechanical beings.

As Jack passed, this particular hound lifted its snout and sniffed the air. Blinked. Processed.

Then it nodded.

Jack straightened his shoulders and stepped between the grand double doors to the outside.

Bitter cold wind slapped his cheeks. Mountains surrounded—glaring, harsh, and completely unclimbable. A flying ship passed, the noise loud and vibrating. Big metal wings stuck out from the sides as it dipped around a far peak and continued into the distance. His gaze flicked to the large, bleak training yard washed with gray stone and pockets of water. Surprisingly, it wasn't slicked over with ice. As he walked to the group waiting for him, the bottoms of his feet warmed in his boots.

A heated floor.

It sizzled up, wrapping his legs then his arms, thawing his clenched jaw and the tips of his fingers. Dressed in fighting wear—firm, hugging black fabric made of waterproof, sweatproof, knifeproof, and fireproof material—Jack felt protected.

The female servant bowed, blonde hair slipping over her shoulder. She wore nothing but a long-sleeve dress. Jack had the urge to command her back inside, but she stepped from the circle and stayed there, eyes cast down. She didn't shiver, didn't even react to the cold. Perhaps a species that didn't feel it.

Jack stepped before their semi-circle, meeting the frosty stares of Cyran and a few of his captains, including Captain Zavar.

Zavar donned his own fighting gear, pitch-black hair a stark contrast to his pale white skin. Single-lidded brown eyes, full pink mouth twisted into a sneer. Straight nose, high cheekbones. He stood as tall as Jack, but with long, lean legs and wide shoulders. The only thing Jack didn't remember was the scar along the left cheek, underneath his eye. A deep one, not from a fight, but from torture. It looked fresh.

"You've recovered well," Cyran said, voice carrying easily.

Jack didn't respond, merely letting his gaze linger on Zavar before flicking to the Worldbreaker.

"Your training begins today." Cyran motioned to the four captains. One other captain struck familiar. Jack couldn't place his name. Deep brown skin filled with muscle and the light marks of scars, a square jaw, a shaved head, the man stood so hauntingly still. Glared. Not a friend. Then it hit him.

Lyla, his most trusted gardia general and comrade's younger brother.

Definitely not a friend after the incidents in Calesal.

Cyran continued, "Captain Zavar will be overseeing your training and assisting as you perfect your abilities. You will study the governments, language, and survival with Captain Yeren Guff." He nodded to the captain with tattoos crawling up his neck and pale-green skin. Inaj. A young one. "Learn to wield every plasweapon expertly with Captain Masar Donnal." The familiar scarred one. "And with Captain Serwa Kinople, one of my War Commanders, you will study battle tactics, techniques, and strategy."

The tall, stoic female glared at Jack. Uneven splotches of white marked her deep brown skin—one along her neck, another peeking from her left hand. Her muscular and taut body matched her hard personality. A shaved head. Wide-set eyes and nose. A spot-free uniform spoke of her organization and cleanliness. By her rigid stance, and the hefty nods along with everything Cyran said, she was another one of his dogs.

Jack would learn war and strategy just by navigating these relationships.

"The servants and guards are the only ones you will have contact with inside this fortress. I will be back to check on your progress, but I trust you not to waste my time." Cyran narrowed his eyes. "If you aren't the captain I need you to be, you'll join the failures in the incineration room."

The corner of Zavar's mouth twitched. Jack clenched his jaw, but gave a short nod. "Yes, sir."

"It's Master," Cyran said. "You may call me Master. All my liege do."

Jack steeled his back, taming his cool fury. *Master*. A word so layered and pained that Jack would normally kill anyone who tried to make him bend again.

Cyran wasn't stupid. He wanted to coil a rope around Jack's neck until he was a loyal dog like Zavar. Even though he ached to rear his hands into fists, he nodded again. "Yes, Master."

Master would only ever hold a meaning if Jack allowed it. He'd separate the word from his pride.

"Say it with a little more conviction next time." Cyran smiled. "Now, I want to see what you are good at."

The servant numbly moved to a rack of weapons and picked up a simple-looking plasblade. It had a beautiful hilt of silver and white metal. She handed it to him and Jack noticed the goosebumps along her hands. He withheld any reaction and took the blade.

He thumbed the hilt and the gleaming silver of the sword sprung out. The translucent tube, as sharp as the blade, hugged the edge. Jack swept his thumb over the second button and colorful energy burst.

It rang yellow. Hummed warm in his hand. The energy, harvested in the multitude of mines far outside the walls of Calesal, twisted and turned within its confines. It writhed with its typical dance of molten bolt. He ached to touch it—he knew the plasma would severely burn his skin, that much was obvious, but he…he…

He wanted to feel. Just to feel something.

She was gone. He was alone.

The eyes of his comrades and Master were on him. He kept his expression blank, concealing his thoughts.

"Zavar."

The captain stepped out and faced Jack. He grabbed the plasblade strapped to his hip and ignited it. It rang a deep blue.

Oh, a fight. Jack twirled the plasblade, remembering how he practiced with it in Lust after they'd escaped with Anaya's collection from Envy. Its weight lightened to match his body, the hilt molding to his grip. *This will be fun.*

Because Jack wanted a piece of Zavar.

"You have five minutes with weapons, five minutes without. All of the captains will judge your skill based on those ten minutes." Cyran stepped back as a group of servants brought him a chair to sit in. The other captains remained unmoving. "No killing."

"Pity," Zavar muttered as he followed Jack into the training circle.

Jack clenched muscles from his arms to his legs to his abdomen. He hadn't used them in so long; a disadvantage. "Going to stab me in the back again, Zavian?"

Zavar loosed a breath. "You'd benefit from remembering the name of your potential murderer."

Too easy. "And you'd benefit from remembering your failure with that scar on your face." Jack tested his left, non-dominant hand with the blade. "How deep did he go? Enough for you to realize you aren't as special as you think?"

Black lightning crawled over Zavar's hands. "I'm going to make this hurt."

"Control your Vaelaur powers, Captain Zavar," one of the other captains called. Jack spared a glance—Captain Serwa. She held her hands behind her back, eyes glued to the circling duo. "Any lightning and it will deter my ability to judge him."

Vaelaur. Vay-lurr. Jack had never heard of such a thing before—

perhaps it was a species to Greed? Memories flashed—the Center Temple, Violet bent over while Zavar's hands skimmed her collarbone. The lightning a brush, a tickle. Her blood vomited on the floor. A brief touch sent her convulsing. What will a full punch of that power do?

Kill. Zavar gave off an aura of being untouchable, and by the number of times he flashed his powers, he needed the reminder. Another trait: Insecure.

Zavar lifted a brow. "Are you afraid, human?"

"I'm not human anymore." Jack released his thoughts and let the cool calm of a fight settle over him. He had the urge to smile—he'd been waiting for a release.

"No—you're a mutt." Zavar's lightning zapped the air around him.

"*Captain*," Serwa warned again, and Zavar drew the lightning back in.

"No worries, Serwa. I'll go easy on him."

And Zavar attacked.

He lunged and arced his blade, the blinding streak of blue plasma following it. Jack met his blow in an array of sparks. He rearranged his footing and twisted underneath, drawing the blade to Zavar's knees. Zavar skipped around him.

Jack parried, bursting up. Their weapons clashed again. They danced in their battle rage. Jack found an opening in Zavar's precise steps and feigned a move. Zavar followed, and when he bowed to meet Jack's blade, Jack swung it around and slashed Zavar's upper thigh.

Zavar exhaled sharply, furious. He became a frenzy. Right, left, right, left, Jack blocked as many blows as he could, but small slashes met his shoulders, his forearms, his legs. It was a minor burn through his clothes, and in the fight, he found himself faltering more, yearning for a bigger slash. He reveled in it. Loved it. Because he *felt* something. The physical pain relieved him from the tormenting memories he sweated through at night—a relief to the bleak future. Jack grunted as he unleashed his energy against Zavar. Power hummed beneath his skin, and when Zavar lifted his blade above his head, vehement, Jack hurled his own blade to the side.

He wanted to use his fucking hands.

A sharp spark of strength clenched his muscles. His fingers wrapped around Zavar's plasblade. They gripped the searing heat, the gleaming metal, and clenched. He pushed into that newfound strength.

And broke the plasblade in two.

Jack tossed one end across the yard and yanked the hilted end from Zavar's grip. Brief shock flashed across Zavar's face. His eyes dipped to Jack's blistering hands, the deep cuts of the plasblade in his fingers. He hesitated.

Jack's burns were already healing by the time the blade pieces clattered to the floor. A half-thought made him realize there wasn't any water around to heal him, but new skin folded over, as if water wasn't a factor like it was in the experiment room.

He didn't care—the burn, the flame, the hurt, the pain—it felt *amazing*.

"Hands now?" Jack teased.

Zavar blinked. His face twisted back into rage. "You mutt—"

Jack tackled him.

He expected Zavar to feel cold, like the ice blanketing the mountains above, but his skin was hot beneath Jack's punches. They wrestled; Jack's hands slipped on Zavar's sweaty skin, Zavar growled as his fingers found the healing burns and scratched at them. Jack seethed, lifted his arm, and pounded again into Zavar's face.

The Vaelaur brought his knee into Jack's stomach. His grip on control faltered and Zavar's fist slipped in, cracking him across the cheek. His vision spotted, his world flipped and Zavar was on top, pinning him, sending punch after punch into his face.

"You think you're something special with these new powers?"

Zavar gritted as he grabbed Jack's collar and lifted him close. "You're a fucking weapon, mutt. That's all you will ever be."

A choking cry split through Jack's lips. Blood dripped into his eyes. "Don't be so scared, Zavian—"

"Stop *calling* me that!" Zavar reared his fist.

Jack's canines tingled, but he shoved down the urge to gnaw. He bet Zavar tasted spicy when he was angry.

Jack yanked on the cooling sensation he'd felt when the camouflage occurred. He caught Zavar's punch with his left hand, squeezing hard enough to feel the crack of bones, and flung his invisible right hand into Zavar's throat.

Zavar coughed. His inhale was a screech, and Jack flung his body off him, standing and wiping his eyes.

"That's all you got?" Jack sucked a deep inhale, rolling his shoulders. "One throat punch and it's over? I thought Cyran's lapdog would be more impressive."

Black lightning flashed from Zavar's hands. The static bit the stone floor in small, lazy spurts. He snarled through another cough. "You're fucking dead."

"You'd be saving yourself a lot of time if you had succeeded." He grabbed Zavar by the shirt and lifted the Vaelaur, bringing his face close until they shared heavy, bloody breaths. "Treat me with some fucking respect and I might consider not humiliating you."

Zavar spit in Jack's face and smiled, his teeth red. "You'll always be the mutt."

Fury roared again. Jack brought his fist back—

Zavar's hand latched around Jack's throat, and a bolt of lightning sprouted from his knuckles, piercing Jack's skin.

His world crumbled. Went black. He felt every spark of that lightning course through his body. His neck burned and burned and burned and a terrifying cry escaped him as his muscles tightened and his blood grew hot. Too hot. His hands grasped at his stomach, his chest, attempting to keep his organs inside. Nothing shredded, but he could have sworn… His heart beat fast—too fast. His knees hit the ground. A metallic taste scoured his mouth. Dying. He was dying. Decaying, if this is what it felt like.

His lips stretched into a smile, and while his body convulsed and seared with pain, Jack laughed. Laughed because he was so used to being the feared one, the bad one, and now he cycled back to his past—a slave to another master. Through his broken cackles, Jack wished for this lightning to take him. He beckoned the pain to become unbearable. To act as his punishment for what he had done. His penance for not saving his friends. Violet. His atonement for abandoning his brother.

A cool patch met the back of his neck and the pain ebbed. His vision went from black to the blurry outline of Serwa. She cocked her head at Jack. "He handled it well, but I said no lightning, Captain Zavar."

Handled it well? It was pure pain. Was there more to Zavar's powers?

Another figure crept into view—Cyran. "Did this fight provide an evaluation for you?"

"Yes, Master," said Serwa.

"He likes the pain," another captain—Yeren—said.

"He owes me a new plasblade," Masar said—the weapons master. Lyla would be proud of her little brother. "Most Droans couldn't snap it in half."

"It was moderate," Serwa said. "And you see his hands—they're already healed."

"Thank the skies for the Mers," Masar muttered, nudging Serwa. Jack put the pieces together. *She* was a Mer.

Serwa gave a quizzical look to Masar and then flicked her eyes to Cyran. Her mouth parted, but Jack caught the subtle shake of Cyran's head while he stared at Jack's healing hands for a long, thoughtful moment. His face remained impassive, rigid, but eventually, he broke his glare. "Set up your schedules. I will return every month to check on his progress. I want him transferred to the cities in three months.

"Yes, Master." They all bowed deeply.

Cyran glared at Jack. "You will do your best."

Jack ignored the blood dripping off his brow bone. "Yes, sir."

Serwa yanked at Jack's hair. "It's Master."

"Yes—*Master*."

Cyran held Jack's gaze before his arms lit up. Bright, twisting lines glowed under his skin and wrapped from the tips of his fingers up his forearms. Two cuts of silver light shined beneath his eyes. He vanished.

Serwa released his hair and Jack sagged forward. Vanisher. While his knowledge was little, he understood that select people could teleport between worlds as he had done with the Iris. But they had free will to choose whichever world, whichever place, and vanish there.

Zavar was one of them, although he was probably prohibited from leaving this fortress; Reed was also one, evident from Envy. Those brown-skinned twins Jodin and Yarrow as well. And a slew of more captains—the Fringe, he remembered.

"Get cleaned up," Serwa said. "You learn weapons tomorrow with Masar."

With a swish of cloaks and a scoff from Zavar, they turned their backs on him and walked through the doors to the fortress.

Jack never thought his ambitions would take him to another world, let alone the game of seven. He'd assumed there was something stopping every candidate from ever completing the Sins, but he didn't think it would be Cyran. A Worldbreaker. A person who pumped him with the blood of other species and molded him into an unwilling weapon.

No tears fell as Jack gazed at the cloudy sky. Snow frosted his lips, blew through his matted hair. He had the decision to make: kill himself and leave this misery or become something greater than he feared.

Retribution sang under his skin. He would kill Cyran, eventually, but he had to let go of his pride and take the Worldbreaker's hand if he wanted to survive.

And Jack Marin always did everything he could to survive.

3

MASTER

Each and every captain was an asshole.

Yeren proved to be his sort of favorite. He was part-Inaj, part-human, and with his now-deceased father bloodsworn into the game, Yeren realized something…

"I could pass through the worlds, too," he grumbled during a break, as if the feat wasn't impressive. "My blood was already in the game via my father, so while I couldn't face the Sins like real candidates, I could pass through, essentially tricking the game."

A roaring fire brightened half the Inaj's handsome face. Dark eyes, dark hair, and full lips, he sat casually fiddling with a page from the textbook in front of him.

Jack was more rigid, unsure how to navigate Yeren's energy. It was like the man was in an entirely different language, if not one no longer spoken.

Jack yearned to break through Yeren's barrier. "And for the other worlds?"

Yeren smirked. "Let's just say some of the Irises I used had a lot of blood on them."

Yeren's ties to Gluttony were minimal, if non-existent. Cyran recruited the rogue part-Inaj, discovered Yeren had Vanisher blood, Awakened him, and now the blood-thirsty man had served the Worldbreaker for nearly twenty-three years.

"I burned one farm down," Jack said.

Yeren leaned back in his chair, expression stoic. He was a handsome man. "That you did."

No relief. No micro smile. No glitter in the eyes. Yeren could have been robotic for all Jack knew. Talk of his home world elicited *zero* reaction.

"You also ruined the oil production. The Stradinths were the top in ahnsa turnout, so His Master wasn't pleased. The Inaj have been rather organized and have since brought down four more farms. They have already taken over oil production in exchange for the exodus of the Crale from their lands. A treaty has been signed with His Master. The Inaj are extremely intelligent."

"And the Master intends on keeping the treaty?"

A shrug. "If they follow his orders and keep up with the ahnsa demands."

Ahnsa—the rich fuel found deep beneath Gluttony's soil—was a primary source of power for these cities, especially Greed. It burned slowly, so it was potent, rich, and perfect for air travel. It reminded Jack of his history lessons on plasma; when the molten energy was mined and manipulated, Calesal found itself in an energy revolution. But plasma didn't have the capacity to sustain air travel—no, it burned too fast for that. Ahnsa, however, could keep a ship afloat for years.

Yeren was a ghost who merged into society with ease. Despite his tattooed appearance, he didn't stand out. His calm aura made it easier to learn the ins and outs of the different worlds and how they operated, as well as Cyran's own body of government. Certain information was omitted, but Jack soaked up every detail he could get, even the ones left unsaid.

"The Fringe are the Vanishers," Jack said. "And they are close to Cyran, some as liaisons to different worlds to oversee operations, others as ambassadors to even more worlds, and others who have more dirty work."

"Like what?" Yeren quizzed.

"Assassins, snatchers, spies, and any undercover shit the Master needs."

"Good."

"So what *is* a Vanisher?"

Yeren narrowed his eyes. "You're not cleared for that information, as you do not hold any Vanisher abilities."

"How do you know?"

"The Master tested you for them while you were unconscious. The bright lines you see around his arms? When they are activated, then placed on an individual's sternum, it either Awakens their own dormant power or does nothing. You did nothing."

Some strange memory, again back at the Center Temple, came to Jack. He remembered fighting the cold control of Cyran, his vision dotting in and out, but he also remembered a striking light blinding him beyond that darkness.

Jack's breathing stopped. Violet. *Violet.* She had been the one with powers?

"It takes a very long time to learn how to wield the abilities of a Vanisher. Nearly every Vanisher needs a mentor, or they are sure to kill themselves. It is an unbearable power to hold without proper training. It is why most need to be judged before being Awakened." Yeren said. "I've heard about her. It is better for her, and for the world, that she is disposed of, but I give my condolences all the same. It must have been jarring to learn that."

Jack's jaw clenched, but he didn't say anything. Yeren's condolences were like being patted on the back by a fork.

"Would you…" It was the most bizarre thing Jack had said before. "Let me bite you?"

Yeren didn't seem surprised. He tugged up the lip of his sleeve and revealed tattooed skin. "At least you're smart enough to see the truth for yourself."

"He could be lying to all of you."

"He doesn't need to. None of us would want a rogue Vanisher alive. It is too dangerous."

Jack reluctantly bit into Yeren's flesh, and his mouth filled with the taste of honey. Truth.

"She is dead, Jack Marin. Along with her friends, the Endolier and the candidate."

The honey taste tickled Jack's gums while his chest sank further into despair. A part of him held out hope that it was all a ruse, all a lie, but this…

Jack pulled away. Wiped his mouth. Yeren drew his sleeve back down and turned the textbook page. "Now, let's visit the remaining Droan clans in Wrath…"

Combat with Zavar was always in silence. They trained four times a week, four hours each day, or until Jack was ready to collapse from spending his new abilities. Droanian strength came the easiest, followed by the cool sensation of Endolier camouflage. His healing ability happened without his command. Jack went through the motions of Aurien and Lovuphal abilities until each sensation became familiar and he had some control.

The Lovuphals—blue-skinned people with tiger stripes from Lust—had a knack for hearing thoughts if they held eye contact for longer than ten seconds. Jack managed to have a servant under a trance once those seconds passed, and the poor girl had shifted forward in her seat, her thoughts muddled with commands and compliments.

He looks so perfect, and his mouth…his mouth could do wonders. I want to lick those dimples, stare into those green eyes…I've never seen a green like that before… And those curls. I wonder if they are as silky as they look… Perhaps he will let me in his bed tonight after refusing me the last four…

Jack broke the trance and cocked his head. She was pretty—brown skin and long hair. Meant to serve in more ways than one.

"What do you hear?" Zavar grumbled.

"She thinks your eyes are too far apart," Jack deadpanned. "And she's happy you are potty trained now."

"*Leave,*" Zavar snarled at the servant. Her eyes darted between them, mouth opening, but she left without calling out Jack's lie.

"Did you graduate to big boy diapers—?"

Jack collided with the wall, Zavar's hand at his neck.

Zavar squeezed and Jack struggled for breath, but still he smiled. "Did I—hit a—*ow*—nerve?"

"Do not disrespect me like that."

"You're too easy," Jack gasped, letting his eyes dip to Zavar's lips. Teasing him. "But also—*easy now*—learn to earn your own respect."

Zavar bristled but didn't pull away. "We are finished for today. Next time you do that, you'll lose a finger."

Zavar's impressive strength hardly compared to Jack's Droanian ability. Jack pushed off the wall, pressing into Zavar's hand until they were sharing breaths. Zavar's eyes widened.

"Like what you see?" Jack teased. "You have a lot of anger within you, do you need some release?" Jack lowered his voice. "I can help *you*."

Zavar's expression blanked. He shoved Jack back into the wall. Hand gone, he turned for the exit, muttering, "That's what the servants are for."

"They must be disappointing, then."

Zavar slammed the door.

Captain Serwa's lessons went as well as Zavar's did. There wasn't a kind bone in the ruthless Mer's body. Jack didn't know if she'd been born that way, or if Cyran had molded her into a cold-blooded War Commander.

Jack met with her two times a week for lengthy, six-hour sessions. The lessons consisted of hand-to-hand combat, intensive workouts that hardly matched the ones with Masar, and significant war strategy using information learned from Yeren. She mostly liked riddles, logic games, and chess.

"There's an uprising in Wrath. The Droans have gone against their kill ban and began bombing their city of Tetro. Food is scarce—a monopoly held by one clan. That means machine and weapon production is down. What moves do you make to solve it?"

Jack pushed his rook up four spaces. Serwa gave no reaction to his self-sacrificing move. "Punish the clan monopolizing the food, then utilize the food as a reward for more machine production. Import food from other worlds—there's an abundance in Gluttony, ensure it works with a Droan's digestion and give it to them as an incentive. Spare lower enforcement ranks to calm the kill-ban—enforcers trusted to not give into the Sin. Create more jobs with the city's rebuilding."

"That takes away from machine production." Serwa moved her horse.

Jack grew quiet, turning over his thoughts as he made a move on the chessboard. "Not all Droans can work the machines, can they? You don't have enough space within that hangar by the Panthon. You'll need more space if you want to increase production because it sounds like you want to do that, but the Droan rebellion is making it hard to keep up the usual numbers."

Serwa hummed as she took Jack's piece. "Perhaps we can give food as an incentive to hire more workers and build another hangar for production."

"You'd be forcing them into a corner. It could lead to a bigger rebellion." Jack took one of her pieces. "You do realize Tetro is the only city the Droans have left, right?"

"You need to think about control, Marin." Serwa folded her hands, elbows on the table. "They clearly lack it, and strict enforcement is necessary. In these scenarios, hurt might be necessary. How would you make it hurt to establish better control?"

"If you want it to hurt, take their leathers," Jack said. "Take their culture. It's what the Master is good at, isn't it?"

Serwa ignored the last part, even though ire flashed across her face. "Interesting choice."

Jack moved his bishop, and Serwa swooped in, announcing, "Checkmate."

"Good game," Jack mumbled, his mouth sour.

He had the haunting feeling the Droan situation wasn't a mere scenario.

With Masar, the hatred the man felt for Jack went into every slice and clang of plasblades they shared. Jack had been itching to take out his repressed emotions on someone who was looking to do the same.

Masar was truly a beauty with a weapon, and the scars proved it. Jack knew who he was now, and the ache in his stomach grew every time he entered the indoor training arena. A month of nearly silent interactions filled with unsaid loathing made Jack snap.

He was dripping with sweat, shirt discarded on the floor, as Masar came at him again with harsh parries. The captain knew when to add strength to a hit, or when to feign, and Jack learned through the unsaid words. Learned a lot, actually.

Banned from breaking plasblades, Jack's temper built. He went on the offensive. He channeled that emotion into his moves, matching Masar's perfectly. Over and over the blades clashed, sometimes so hard plasma leaked from the impact. They were nearing the time they'd move onto arrows and guns, and Jack knew if he wanted a moment, it'd be now in this close combat.

Masar came at him with an upward arc. Jack shifted his weight. Met the blow. Twisted his grip to his other hand and kicked Masar in the gut.

Masar growled as Jack's kick landed. His plasblade was knocked out of his hand, clattering to the ground. But a shimmering purple was at Jack's neck—another blade.

"I didn't know we were allowed two," Jack said.

"There's always a second," Masar said in his raspy voice. "On to guns—"

Jack stepped forward, letting the plasma brush his neck. "If you hate me so much, kill me. Be done with it. Or wound me in some permanent way that will satisfy your fury every time you look at my face." Masar's nostrils flared. Jack rolled his eyes. "Someone like you shouldn't be afraid of someone like me."

"I'm not afraid," Masar snapped.

"You're certainly some level of fearful." Jack craned his neck farther, and the blade burned more. "Is it because your sister *likes* working for me? All that occurred was Reed's little bombing that landed you in the Sins. Do you fear that I never saw you as good enough, and you'd become nothing like every Souther?"

"Shut up," Masar snarled.

Jack's lips curled into a lazy smile. "Slit my throat, Masar. Show your sister how powerful you are now."

"She has nothing to do with this."

"Family makes more of an impact than you'll ever know," Jack said. "Lyla was upset when you were sentenced."

Masar's expression hardened at the sound of his older sister's name. "Your ambition separated us."

"She tried to kill me when you were sentenced," Jack said. "I really thought she was going to, but she was too loyal to cut my throat, so why don't you do it for her? Avenge what I caused between you?"

"Stop that." Masar shook his head, his mask slipping. Pain graced his features. "You're lying."

"She hated me for an entire year before we finally reconciled."

Masar scoffed, "And how did that go?"

"I knew I was going into the Sins, so I told her I'd bring you back." Jack shrugged. "I'd either die or succeed. I said the minute my blood went into that bowl, an eighth of my fortune was hers as long as I had her support."

Masar's grip on the blade tightened, but then he lowered his arm. "So she's okay?"

"She's one of my favorite people. Ever. I would have made sure she was okay even if she hated me for the rest of her life."

"Why do you even care?" Masar rubbed his face. "You could kill everyone who hated you and you wouldn't have to face this retribution shit."

"If I killed everyone I hated, that would only leave fear, and I'm tired of being surrounded by fear." Jack retracted the plasblade.

"Good luck with that." Masar thumbed his own sigil and the plasma fizzled out. "You know a lot of people worked with you because you promised something better than that shit city, and they all got fucked over because of it. I already pummeled Reed because of what he did. Did it within two days of being sentenced—some Droans had to separate us, and Reed was so angry he ended up killing a female Droan with a dagger. He escaped after that and ran off to hide in the desert. I didn't see him until we served our time in Envy at the compound—and even then, I was still so angry. He survived, you were still frolicking in Calesal, and I was paying for both of your mistakes."

Jack kept his eyes on Masar, ignoring the guilt in his gut.

"No good ever comes out of Calesal. I don't hate you for that, Jack Marin. I don't hate you at all—as a person. I only hate that you're bestowed power once again."

Silence sank into the room. Jack opened his mouth, but no words came out. He was…surprised. At the honesty, the revelation—he didn't know. Masar had grown from Lyla's dedicated, but blind, little brother into a wise, strong man who didn't misplace his feelings.

"Why do you work for him?" Jack asked. "Why not fight to go back to the city?"

"Because this is better." Masar picked up a plasgun. "I might have money in Calesal if you are true to your word, but not everyone needs money. Most people are lying to themselves if they think money is all they need." Masar's expression softened. "People need purpose. That's what they all crave. And I have that here."

"What does he give you—all these captains? These people? How…" Jack yanked his bun and his sweaty curls spilled free. "Why do so many follow him when you saw, firsthand, what his curse did to those worlds?"

"That depends on the person." Masar shrugged. "I have a purpose learning weaponry, teaching others, and being respected back in the cities of Greed. It is different there."

The Sin had something to do with Masar's words. There was no twinge of Greed since he'd been here in Honnrak Castle, and he'd assumed it didn't exist at all. But purpose…wealth…respect. A mix of pride and greed. They were the undercurrents of human—any species'—wants. Perhaps Cyran was slowly feeding into that greed, overlapping it with pride, and using it to keep people here. But Masar's eyes were clear—not laced with some undying devotion to the Worldbreaker. So what was it? What made nearly every single candidate stop and stay here? What pushed those few candidates to go to the seventh world of Pride only to be stopped by Cyran within minutes?

The questions circled and Masar was already fixing up the targets—body dummies, bullseyes, and more that regenerated every time a kill shot was made. Jack let the questions simmer. He was too isolated at Honnrak Castle to figure it all out. He needed to make it to the cities, he needed to infiltrate more, and he possibly needed to be exactly what Cyran wanted him to be, to figure out this fucking mess.

❋ ❋ ❋

Jack had finished his silent dinner and wandered back to his room. He passed many doors, but one stood ajar at the end. A steady buzz emitted, and as Jack neared, the servant girl whose mind he'd infiltrated rounded the corner.

She passed the door without a thought, eyes locking on Jack before she bowed her head. He waved her off, wanting to check out the room—

"I meant every thought."

Her soft voice, lighter than that of her mind, drew his attention. She stepped forward with less submissiveness in her gait.

"I'm trained in these sorts of things, you know. How to please, no matter who it is. You're so stiff, and all those thoughts running through your head aren't helping." She lowered her voice. "Let me help you."

She held his gaze. Eight, nine, ten seconds. Then that strange sensation, like a little string he could yank, appeared.

Jack pressed into her mind.

I can tell you things. Things you might want answers to. Even about your home city. But I have to do my job, too, or else they'll know.

Jack stayed silent.

One last thought drifted in: *I'm very good.*

A finger brushed his belt. Tugged on it. She held his gaze the entire time.

Jack bent down, lips nearly grazing hers, and muttered, "I'm very good, too." He broke the trance. "Come to my room later."

"Yes, sir."

He didn't spare her another thought when he stepped into the room. The buzz grew louder—a tattoo gun. A small office with plush chairs, a desk, and a window overlooking the snowy landscape.

Yeren sat in one chair, shirt half-off, bent over the desk, and left hand splayed as he drove fresh ink into the skin of his fingers. Masar lounged on the couch with a dense book.

"What's this?"

The gun paused. Yeren didn't glance up as he said, "Tattoos."

Masar looked up from his book, narrowing his gaze.

Jack ignored him, instead taking another step into the room to gaze at the twirls of ink covering every inch of Yeren. He didn't move to hide it, not even as he turned to catch Jack looking.

Jack's breath halted and he settled any surprise that might have crossed his face. The ink...it was art.

Art of Gluttony.

It was the twin peaks Violet's Gwen had called Srax and Follin. It was the sprawling forests he'd barely glimpsed from the Farm. It was the river, animals, people, symbols, Inaji language, and more. It was his past. Culture. The one he'd left behind.

Yeren had marked his skin with that of his ruined home. During their sessions, he didn't need to tell Jack whether he resented his world or buried his past. It was there, on his body.

It was all unsaid. Everything had to be unsaid.

"How much?" Jack asked.

Yeren scoffed and wiped his hand. He didn't say anything because it was obvious Jack didn't have any money.

"The fallen commander won't want to spoil his skin with the mark of Southers," Masar mumbled.

Jack refrained from rolling his eyes. "We aren't in Calesal, or even that fucking world, no?"

"No," Masar responded. "But you want to go back?"

"If only to give Lyla more money and tell her that her brother is annoying."

Masar huffed and slammed his book. "Funny."

"I know." Jack sat in the chair opposite Yeren.

Yeren cleared his own ink and began sanitizing the space. "What do you want done?"   Jack was a blank slate, born anew. New blood. New world. New feelings. Maybe that was the relief of it all.

Jack shrugged and looked down at his body. "Start with whatever you want, and if I think of something, I'll let you know."

"Covering your past with art?" Masar said with less bite in his words.

"Just don't cover the burn scar on my right forearm. Or the whip lashes." Jack began unbuttoning his shirt, ignoring Masar. "But cover the scars on my hip and back. A *conjua* stabbed me with dinner knives."

Yeren paused his cleaning and his eyes shot up to Jack. A small smirk reached his lips at the foul Inaji word.

Mothercunt. Rio said it was a close translation.

When Jack dropped his shirt, silence met the room. He had his fair share of scars, yes. The whip marks from Envy were all but soft lines now, but the gnarled burn scar on his forearm never healed properly, no matter how many times the bitch Kiane rubbed their low-tech salve over it. He'd grown to like it, though, because it was a result of Violet's furious last act when she kicked him away from the portal in Wrath, leaving him to fend a small bomb before he got his own Iris.

"Come." Yeren beckoned Jack's arm. "Where do you want to start first?"

Jack pointed to his upper left shoulder, where the only tattoo he had was a small flower.

"You already have one and it's a fucking flower?" Masar snorted.

Jack flashed him the middle finger.

Yeren chuffed, put on gloves, and wiped down Jack's arm. "I'll start with some fucking mountains."

Masar snorted again and picked up his book. "Do a penis next."

Jack's smile came easy.

✹✹✹

Jack's upper arm was covered in swirls of black ink by the time he left the room. It had been hours spent in the chair with little talk except to comment on Yeren's artistry. After the detailed mountains reminiscent of Gluttony, Jack had instructed him to tattoo an ocean, followed by mangrove trees and little surfboards.

While there was a big chunk of giant artwork, there were simpler details interwoven in Jack liked. A lemon because he was allergic. Lucien's name backward because he thought it was funny, and his brother would hate it.

As he walked the hallway back to his room, Jack glanced down to his hand where the bloodsworn scar lay. The one with her.

He'd thought about a tattoo for her—an eye, a flower, a middle finger—he didn't know, but he couldn't bring himself to make a decision, nor voice the want aloud. He didn't like the hold she had on him. He could continue on, be the bad, terrible person that destiny constantly wanted him to be, but when she popped into his mind, when some little thing reminded him of her, he paused.

And he didn't want to be so evil.

"Fuck this." He shouldn't care, should have *never* cared, but she…she…

Just *her*.

Her mouth, her taste, her moans, her sass, her smile, her fire. Her roaring inferno had awoken him. But now it was gone. Snuffed out. But why did it still have such a hold on him?

"Sir."

Jack lifted his head. Outside his door, the servant girl stood patiently in simple robes. Pristine, orderly. He didn't know if she'd just arrived, or if she'd been there for hours.

His mood soured. He waved, and she stepped aside, giving him room to open the door. He unlocked it with his bracelet and walked inside. She followed—

Jack whirled, blocking her.

"I didn't invite you."

She pouted. "You asked me to come."

"I changed my mind."

"Change it back."

He held her gaze.

She let him into her thoughts. *I want to see your new tattoos.* Her head tilted. *And more. You're too delicious to look at and not to want a taste. Especially when you're angry.*

She placed her hands on his chest. Slid them down. Dragged a finger along the lip of his pants.

And I can give you information.

"Make yourself interesting and I might change my mind."

The Sin doesn't reach here. If you want to move onto the next world, you must battle Greed within the cities. The Twin Cities. Hallow and Hanhii. His Master will know. He knows when a candidate gets the key to the next world.

The Iris. Jack suspected as much.

"You're not convincing me," Jack said as her hand dipped under his shirt, then slid along his muscles.

Let me help you…I want to make you feel good. This world can be cold, greedy, but it doesn't have to be.

Lips grazed his jaw. Nimble fingers wrapped him below. Jack tried to maintain control, but his eyelids shuddered. It was the briefest spark of pleasure and he simply…let it come. He let her touch him. Her eyes still held onto his, and she pushed another thought, *You can pretend I'm her.*

He slapped a hand on the wall so hard it left a hole.

"No," Jack said, barely above a whisper.

Let me be her. Let me give you pleasure like her—

"Stop it."

Like Violet—

He snapped. Literally. Snapped her forearm in half.

She didn't scream. Tears poured from her eyes.

"Now, choke her."

Cyran appeared from the shadows at the far end of the hall.

Jack obeyed. He wrapped his fingers around her throat while burying his morality. His emotions. His sanity. He squeezed, and she never made a sound as her lips purpled.

"She is a traitor," Cyran continued. "She knows better than to seduce you when you are still grieving. She doesn't respect you. She needs to be punished."

Jack realized the servant wasn't screaming because Cyran didn't let her. A foreign pressure closed his hand tighter around her throat. The pressure built until Jack had no choice but to add to it and put them both out of their misery.

The girl went limp in his hands.

"Bury it, Marin," Cyran said as he circled the scene. "Let the emotions, the grief, the love go. You've suffered through it enough. Now, it is time to give your all into your true potential." The Worldbreaker brushed Jack's fingers that still held the girl's limp body upright. "Let her go."

Let her go, Jack repeated in his head.

And then that girl, that servant, morphed into the bleak, blue-eyed girl who had uprooted his life. Dead. In Jack's grip. Her brown hair brushed his knuckles, her mouth slightly ajar. Not breathing. Not alive.

Let her go.

Violet's neck was cold and delicate in his hands.

Let her go.

And so, he did.

Violet's body crumpled to the floor at his feet. Cyran's cold hand wrapped his shoulder. "You did well, my boy. Now come. There is another assignment for you."

Jack took a step back from Violet—no, the servant girl. His body numbed. He didn't, *couldn't* feel anything.

A blessed relief.

He turned to Cyran, who offered a dangerous smile and touched Jack's hand.

Jack felt a tug on his navel as Cyran transported them to a different location. Bitter wind slapped his face. Cyran stepped away, the flurries of snow never touching him. "You know what a traitor looks like now." He gestured behind Jack.

Jack turned. It didn't take long to discover they were back in Honrrack Castle's courtyard. Blaring lights pointed to the center, where seven bodies kneeled, hoods covering their heads.

Captain Serwa and Zavar moved from the windy shadows of the courtyard, and one by one, yanked each hood off.

"These are traitors," Cyran's voice boomed. "And now you know what to do with traitors who refute their god, disrespect the command of Vanishers, and the union of their worlds under my great empire."

The wind was a warm hug compared to the iciness of Cyran's words and what they meant. Masar appeared and strutted over to Jack, handing him the hilt of a plasblade.

Jack glanced back at the prisoners. Skins of green, purple, black-spotted, white, red, scaly, and sand-colored stared back at him. He searched the plethora of faces, the alien of each of them, and the mix of emotions. Some were terrified—tears poured silently down their cheeks, eyes bloodshot and wide—while the others were defiant, glaring between Jack and Cyran. Tape covered their mouths.

"Kill them," Cyran commanded.

Jack thinned his mouth.

Let her go.

Play the game, Jack.

Survive.

Jack ignited the plasblade. Its red color bloomed on their faces.

He made it quick. Silent. Blood of different colors poured onto the courtyard's snow-covered stone. Their bodies slumped forward. Jack's pulse roared in his ears and only grew louder as he turned to Cyran.

Cyran studied Jack. In the blurring snow, they stared at each other; the final form and the new form. The end and the beginning. Jack saw every bit of his darkest parts in Cyran and knew if he decided, if he chose, he could go down Cyran's path and see the same greatness.

"Satisfactory," Cyran commented. "You still wanted to give mercy, but traitors don't deserve mercy. Finish your training, and I will see you in the Twin Cities for the start of your new journey."

Jack's glare steeled. "Yes, Master."

Cyran disappeared.

4

SLOTH

Three Months Later

A MER BLED IN THE water.

"Grab her!"

Beneath the beating sun's rays, Violet Sutton raced along the coarse wooden deck of the *Lostflower*.

"Don't fall!" Keller warned.

"I won't!" Violet called back to the ship's captain. With a slight smile, her bare feet slapped the gangplank until she leaped at the end. Her fall was brief as the rope between her hands grew taut and Anaya released a loud whoop from above.

The water skimmed Violet's toes as she swung away from the ship. Her belly fluttered with butterflies, the wind brushed her unruly braided hair, and her suntanned hand stretched out to the surf below. The water was a breathtaking blue in the Citran Islands; endless and warm during the day, frigid and depthless at night.

"Here!" Maji called, hazel eyes wide. She extended her arm.

Violet clasped hands with Maji's dark-skinned-splotched-with-white one. The Mer had a steady stream of blood pouring from her long, midnight-blue tail, and if she didn't get out of the water fast enough…

"Now!" Violet hollered to the boat while she yanked Maji from the crystal blue sea.

The rope jolted. Maji yelped in surprise. Violet crawled to give her some room as they began to arc back toward the ship, rising just a little higher above the lolling afternoon waves.

"Aw, shit," Maji grumbled, looking down.

It was a mere shadow at first, but in a blink, teeth the length of an average male's leg blasted through the surface. A deep forest green creature with a long mouth and *two* tails. A myva, the water scorpion beast, was one of the more deadly things one can find in the Citran Seas. It was close enough to touch—

"Not yet," Maji snarled to Violet, who had procured her plasblade.

The myva dove at them just as they swung back toward the boat. Maji whined as the teeth drew close and decided to shift her tail back into legs. "Ugh, I hate these things."

The mvya glared with two laser-like eyes as Violet and Maji put distance between them and the beast. It gave off a blood-curdling screech of frustration and dove head-first back in the water, its long body following.

But the two scorpion tails burst upward at the end of its dive, and they came flying toward the girls.

The rope gave another sharp yank up, and Violet mumbled a prayer to the skies as the bone-white ends of the tails spouted an inky poison in their direction. Still, they ascended, just out of reach, but enough for Violet to take her plasblade and slash it through one of the tail's pricks.

Maji caught the severed piece as blood sputtered and hit Violet in the face like a wet slap. A muffled screech sounded as the myva descended fully underwater, then swam away quickly.

The ship's deck appeared underneath, and Violet let go of the rope. Both girls collapsed to the wood, sticky with the purple goo. Violet coughed, gagged a little, but retracted her plasblade so it didn't burn through any wood. "Skies, that smell is awful."

"Bottom of the ocean rot," Maji said. "The Pirate Queen wasn't kidding about this."

Violet wiped a hand down her leg and watched the goo ooze from her fingers. She wrinkled her nose.

"Hey! Now that stuff is known to have impeccable properties!" Rio stormed from the upper deck and bent before Violet with a jar. He began to scrape it off her. "It might smell like a toddler's diarrhea-filled diaper, but it has been known to mend bones, restore vision, or—"

"Give you a great facial," Anaya interrupted with a smile.

Rio, all brown, sun-freckled skin plastered on semi-muscled long limbs, turned his doe eyes toward the scaly Endolier. Anaya ruffled Rio's thick, nearly black shaggy curls and stared at Violet down the bridge of her strong nose.

Anaya kept her inky hair cropped to her shoulders, but ever since they joined Keller's pirate crew as a safe haven, she'd been wearing low pigtails that stuck out beneath her ears. It was cute, Violet would admit, but cute as in pigtails on a hellish deadly snake kind of cute.

Anaya stuck her hands on her hips, a simple cream tank top and loose, beige pants similar to Violet's normal wear. Her deep brown eyes glittered through their mono-lid shape. "I thought it was my turn."

"I was bored." Violet shrugged. "And this girl didn't leave me with much time to go round to the toilets and ask you during your leisurely dump."

"*Fine*, then schedule it around my quality time, asshole."

Violet stuck her tongue out. Then tasted the myva's goop and gagged. Anaya snorted.

"We've scoured the waters for nearly twenty different myva over these months." Maji stood and wiped the goop off herself. She was wholly naked except for some seaweed along her small breasts. Long braids trailed down her back, decorated with seashells. Maji bent toward her still-bleeding foot and held a hand to Rio. "Salve, please."

"It's funny," Rio said as he shimmied over to clean Maji's wound. "You can kill a Mer and chuck them in any body of water within ten minutes to revive them, but a scratch takes *forever* to heal. I literally don't understand."

"Balance of life." Maji shrugged and hissed as Rio cleaned the wound. "You're not being very gentle."

"You could have made a thoughtful cut."

"Right, next time I'll be more mindful of how I *stab myself.*"

"Great."

"Perfect."

"Skies, can you guys just go make out already?" Violet blurted.

Anaya snorted and a horrible blush crept over Rio's face. "I—that wasn't—that's not—"

Maji patted his head. "Wow, you make anyone feel lucky."

Rio blinked up at her. "You know I—"

"*Up.*"

The command came from the upper deck. Every one of them, Maji and Violet—glop included—formed a line and faced Keller's voice.

Sea Captain Keller.

His dark-skinned gleamed in the sun's rays, followed by the slashes of light brown from his old scars. A gray beard curled tight to his jawline and continued up his sideburns, then underneath his beaten leather hat. His crooked, wide nose had freckles splashed across it, while his tiny eyes always judged from both afar and up close. He was outrageously gay, loved raspberries, and obsessed over most types of cheese, except spicy cheese. He hated spicy things.

There were only two more bodies on board: Warran and Peony.

Warran was a big, burly candidate human with red hair slapped both on his jawline and nearly every other inch of his skin. Anaya had asked him numerous times if she could braid it. He doesn't speak much, so he'd flick her off in response most times. He did a lot of heavy lifting, but Maji, Anaya, and Keller were all there to help.

Peony was the cook, mother, and Keller's niece. She hated most things on land, including people, and was only in a good mood when surrounded by a depthless ocean. *Mother at sea, bitch on land*, is what Keller said.

Keller strutted down the stairs from the upper deck and glared at each crew member. Violet resisted her urge to smirk at this achievement. They did it.

They *finally* did it.

"This was our twentieth myva stinger in the last four months since our small crew accepted these three shits." Keller gestured to Violet, Anaya, and Rio. "And you know what twenty means, right?"

"Pardon!" they cried.

"*Pardon*." Keller smiled, flashing his gold and silver teeth. "Pardon so I can put my feet on fucking land again and get my treasure back from my fucking mother! The pirate queen!"

They all cheered.

"Fuck that bitch!" Keller hollered.

"Fuck that bitch!" they responded.

Violet couldn't wipe the smile from her face. This had been the most restless, exciting, distracting four months of her life. It was something she *needed*, especially after...

She shook her head and fought through the heavy weight of grief in her chest. She always ignored it. It was why she liked to swing on the ropes, to push herself to her limits, she didn't want to think about anything else outside this boat, because it meant she thought of him and...

Her smile faltered.

They all hugged and slapped each other's backs.

Keller clapped. "Warran, gather and secure all myva stings. I want them guarded by you and the scaly bitch until we hit land. No one touches those stings because those are our freedom. She wanted twenty stings for her poisonings, she gets them. I get a pardon, we get the *Lostflower,* and we get a happy life at sea! Break out the seawine—we set sail for Nassren Cove tonight."

Violet hesitated. Stood there as everyone broke rank and went about closing duties. Lingered as Rio and Maji all but dove beneath the deck and the clinking of wine bottles floated up.

"You're leaving," Keller said.

Keller was an observant man, and definitely not a dumb man, either. His eyes burned Violet's cheek as he stared, and she avoided his gaze. His amber eyes were too knowing. She'd spill everything... everything she has held in...

"Was thinking about it," she mumbled. "You were the one who told me the portal was there—in your mother's—the Pirate Queen's courtyard." A shrug. "Why not? I...I like it here, but I have my brother and..."

"I used to be like you, you know."

Violet turned her gaze to the sea, to the setting sun around them. Soon it would be her favorite time of day—the clusters of endless stars in the sky, the four planets, and the giant ring that surrounded Sloth on display from the sun's remnants of light. Violet would hammer seawine and smokes while she stared. Stared and stared and stared until her eyes closed and Keller's strange pet lizard-cat called a cynir would lick her elbows.

"Like me?" Violet said, watching the horizon.

"Depressed, until there wasn't a day that went by when you couldn't be doin' something." Keller sighed and walked over the creaky floorboards until he reached the railing. His ring-laden fingers gripped it. "When you have to keep going and going because for some reason your mind makes ya think if you aren't moping, you gotta forget that you ever *did* mope. That you ever had something to mope about."

Violet glowered.

"You either can't feel anything at all, or you do anything you can to not feel." Keller spat into the water. "And neither solves anything. They just prolong it."

The crew's loud laughter drew from downstairs. Keller turned his head, amber catching Violet's eye with a knowing look. Violet picked out Anaya and Rio's cackles over the others, and more sadness wormed its way into her chest.

"They don't know," she muttered.

"Tell them."

"I…" Violet shook her head. "You saw what it was like."

Keller frowned.

That first week after escaping Lust was exhausting. Cyran's men chased them up the coast of a farming island until they managed to get lost in a fishing town. Fringe members appeared and tried to catch her, but the Sin of Sloth became the best thing to ever happen to them. It was brutal running for ten minutes before the teasing, light voice of Sloth entered their minds.

Come on, take a rest. You don't need to do all of this.

Gosh, you have been running for so long—sit and chill. That sounds a lot better.

What's the rush? What's the panic? Why do you move so much? Why do you worry?

Paired with a heavy sensation in the bones, like weights tied to limbs and constantly tugging down, Sloth made fools out of Cyran's men. She imagined the Sin liked it, laughing at the burly, deadly men who could teleport and kill in an instant, who then decided to lie down on the beach and take naps in between.

The Sin had become an issue for Violet, Rio, and Anaya, but their emotions were torrential after *his* death.

Keller's expression turned mischievous. The man *liked* surprises, challenges, battles, and raising a middle finger to Sloth. He avoided Sloth's grip like a dance, and in turn helped Violet churn distractions so she never slowed or became complacent.

Eventually, that became a problem.

"The enemy ships are pathetic." Keller clicked his tongue. He stuck a smoke between his lips and lit it, taking a long drag. "The Worldbreaker is pathetic."

Violet wished she could believe that, but she had seen the horror. Her hand rubbed at her chest. *Felt* the horror.

"The only thing saving me is this Sin," Violet said. "The constant movement of the boat prevents other Vanishers from teleporting onto it, and he hasn't dared enter this world…"

"Because it creates a ruckus." He exhaled smoke. "I've lived for over fifty years, and he's only come to Sloth once during that time.

I'll never forget that day. I thought the world was ending. The sky darkened out of nowhere, and the sea…the sea was a mess. I thought every boat would capsize." He pointed a finger at her. "He can't enter a world without a show, more or less."

"And he doesn't want a show with me, or else others will know he's looking for something," she muttered.

He snorted. "In Sloth, finding treasure is the most addicting thing."

"I wouldn't call it a treasure."

"No, but the people here are nosey and don't like the Worldbreaker, and he can't take the Sin off the world—do you know how dangerous a fucking myva is without Sloth making it sleep most of the day?"

"A child with a spoon would be dangerous if Sloth were lifted." Violet stepped up to the railing. Keller passed her a smoke and she mumbled thanks. She twiddled the wrapper between her fingers. "I can't stay here. I'm on borrowed time."

"You have your key? The Iris?"

Violet smirked as she lit her smoke. "Had it since the first week. Anaya and Rio know about that one. Rio got another as well."

"Tell them, wildflower," he said gruffly. "Tell them and I'll help ya get to your portal when I deal with my mother. It's their lives, too."

Violet's eyes stung, and she scowled through the emotions. She sucked on her bottom lip. "We already lost one, though."

Violet had been familiar with grief most of her life, but now it was a noose, the rope burning the sides of her neck, the tug steady and waiting for her to slip. To think about him for longer than she had allowed herself to. She refused to remember the nights in Lust; the warmth of his skin and the breathless laughs tickling her neck, the kisses down her stomach, the protective grip of his hands—

A stray tear slipped down her cheek and she wiped it away. She took a long drag, the cherry of her smoke bursting with yellow and orange, a bright light against the dark horizon. She pushed those memories away, even as her throat closed and Sloth massaged her shoulders, whispering, *Don't you worry. Don't get upset. You don't need to give energy to that.*

It was as far as she went mourning him.

She waved Sloth away, and the Sin vanished, leaving a muffled laughter in her head.

"Once you go, there's no coming back," he said.

Violet never quite mentioned that it wasn't true for her. At least…not anymore. Only Anaya and Rio were aware of Violet's *Awakening* back in Lust, and ever since, Violet blamed the sweaty, sleepless nights and the constant tingles in her chest as grief. Anxiety. Bad seafood. Anything to keep the questions away.

She didn't think too hard about what a Vanisher was. She honestly didn't fucking care what it was. She blatantly ignored the few nights she woke up, tangled in her sheets, and briefly glimpsing the glowing lines twisting her hands. It would last only a blink, but then she'd remember her dreams, the way they looked like the realm where she saw the tethers of other worlds.

Keller's comment made her mind go, *no, that's not true.* Violet crushed the thought and merely shrugged. "I just want to get my brother and to make it back home with my friends. That's it. I'm not scared of dying, or him either, but I need to save my brother and give him freedom. He's…" *Been through too much? Haven't I, though?* "Not in the right place, at the moment."

"Save your lies for your own head, not for me," he huffed.

Her brows scrunched. "What?"

"You're good at convincing yourself, I'll give you that." He waved a hand to the water and the giant ship they stood on. "You saw all this, and you thought life was still simple and easy? You thought you could go through the game and still want the same things? You could lose a friend and move on in a blink? You could give shit to Maji for self-sacrificing when you have been doing it all along?"

"Stop that—"

"No, you are on *my* ship. You listen to me." Keller faced her and she shut her mouth. "What do you *want*?"

"I want my brother—"

He laughed. "No, you fucking don't."

She took a daring step into his face. "Don't pretend you know me—"

"People don't stare at the stars like you do and still wish for the same, basic things." His thick finger poked her in the chest. "They don't look at their friends with adoration, then decide to leave them. They don't watch someone they care for die and accept it. They don't do that. You know what does? Sloth. And I have watched you, girl. Sloth doesn't fucking touch you." He blew smoke in her face. "So what do you fucking want?"

Violet slapped his hand away. "I want my brother—"

"*Liar.*"

"I'm not!"

"What do you want, girl?"

"I want him—"

"Liar!"

"I don't know!" she cried. "I don't know what I want. I've never…I've never fucking decided shit for myself until I put my blood in that bowl, until I decided to stay with Gwen and…" A sob burst out and she whirled, turning her back on Keller. Tears burned her eyes as she thought of the Inaj. "And every time I want something, it's taken from me. So I…I don't know what else to want." She furiously wiped her face. "I do want my brother, but I want to pummel him first."

A snort. "Go on."

"And I…" She took a deep inhale. "I want to take a shot with Meema and have her tell me to get it together."

"Who the fuck is Meema?"

"I want Jelan to slap me across the face."

"I can do that."

"And I want to say goodbye to him. *Wanted* to say goodbye to him. Because it wasn't skivvin' fair that he died. It wasn't. He didn't deserve that. And I want to burn that lightning man for taking him away. I want to make it hurt for them like it has hurt for me, and all these worlds, and maybe I want to go for the next world and *be* a nuisance to them. I want to watch their world catch flames. I want them to know what it's like to have that peace, that safety taken away…"

She took a deep breath and tried to fight the forming tears. "I'm so angry at it all. I am. But I feel helpless at the same time. Like I simply let them take him away." *Let the Worldbreaker take control, let Jack stab me over and over in the chest when our bloodbond stopped it.*

Keller's rough hand touched her shoulder. She turned, stepping away.

"You want revenge." He tugged a dirty handkerchief out of his pocket and tossed it at her. "At this game, life, the gods. You want revenge over it all."

She aggressively wiped her cheeks. "How do I get that?"

"You know you're already doing it. Being alive, avoiding death and whatnot," he said. "If you make it to his world, if you upset him, you might die, yes, but that's your revenge. Living long enough to make an impact on his giant world. Especially for the handsome man Rio talked about. What was his name?"

Violet hadn't said it aloud since the day he died.

But she lifted her chin, found her voice, even though it trembled while it tasted the sounds of his name, "Jack."

"Jack." He smirked. Violet thought it looked an awful lot like the teasing smirk Jack always had on his face. "Solid name."

Violet scrunched her brows. "Yeah, I guess."

A sparkle flashed in Keller's amber eyes. The wind fluttered his hat, but the damn thing always stayed on. "Stay alive, wildflower, because that is your revenge. Burn a couple things down, too, for this Jack. But make sure the other shits know, because I guarantee they want the same as you."

"That's right, we fucking do."

Anaya stood at the top of the steps with a wine bottle in her hand, a sharp look on her face as she glared only at Violet.

Rio towered next to the Endolier, but as soon as Violet met his gaze, he strutted over and wrapped an arm across her shoulders. "I mean, we already kind of figured it out, so we would have forced you to tell us anyway, but yeah, we are going to the next world to create chaos, too."

Anaya took a long sip from of the wine bottle as she walked to meet them. "I want to behead the lightning man. Like that Alez dude. It was very satisfying."

"Perfect, so murder, chaos, and blood." Rio squeezed Violet's shoulder. "We do it together."

And Violet knew what that look of adoration was because when she beamed at her friends, a bright, elated warmth rose from the darkness inside. She leaned into Rio, his armpit at the top of her head, his salty smell a comfort she'd find in the sleepless hours of the night. He never said anything about her crawling into his cot, only gave her space, but he would still sneak hand-holding even when she playfully gagged the first time.

"You guys suck," Violet mumbled but accepted the seawine bottle from Anaya, taking a deep swig. "But fine."

"The winds know, girl." Keller nudged her and jutted his chin to the flapping sails. "Nassren Cove, here we come."

5

He's Alive

THE WILD, CHAOTIC SIGHT TICKLED Violet's chest. Nassren Cove reigned in display, especially at night. The massive cliffs churned with undiluted light, stretching from the water's lip to the tips of rock where stone buildings perched precariously on the edge. The capital of the Isles of Citran—the Pirate Citadel in the water-logged world. Ships packed the gigantic harbor, bobbing as the crews dined to swim or take dinghies to the docks.

Violet gawked at the arches above her head, cresting over the entire cove and made of twisted myva bones as protection from the monsters of the sea. Rio knocked her shoulder and pointed below.

Into the water.

It glowed, the lights so bright she squinted to see properly. An extension of Nassren lay beneath, its inhabitants Mers and other fish-like people who preferred to live in the water than on land. Violet dared to dip her fingers into the cool, smooth water as she glimpsed the depthless buildings and the Mers swimming among the massive corals.

A hand yanked hers. Maji tsked. "Some monsters know the smell of humans. And they like the taste, too."

"I thought they became too lazy," Violet said.

"Lazy, maybe, until they snap and eat an entire ship." Maji leaned on the wooden lip of the dinghy as Keller maneuvered them through the traffic of boats. His face was entirely shadowed underneath his giant hat, his tattooed knuckles covered by wraps of leather.

A guard stood on one of the many long docks extending from the shore. He inspected each boat, a smoke burning between his lips as he bent over and looked. Keller would be remembered as the son of the Pirate Queen, but it was too risky to announce his arrival right off the bat. It was why *most* of them wore hats, bandanas, and discreet clothing to not stand out.

Violet liked the pirate ensemble—a breathable, cream long-sleeve shirt with strips of sea lion leather that wrapped her torso like a harness, tight pants with adjustable straps, scuffed leather work boots, and a giant hat that covered her brow.

Their boat sidled next to the guard. He peered in with a bored look. "State your business."

"Trading." Keller patted the stuffed bag on the back of Warran. "Sea lion rubber."

"In which part of the city?"

"Rum District, because we want to indulge, too. Wrestling sea lions is no easy task." Keller tipped his hat.

"That it isn't." The guard gave another final lookover, his eyes lingering on Anaya for a long while. She leered back at him. He looked away. "Carry on. Don't make a mess of docking."

"Wouldn't dream of it."

With the boat situated, everyone clambered out. Violet was last, but before she took the final step onto the docks, Keller stopped her with a small shove.

His eyes glowed in the shadow of his hat. "No funny shit. You are on solid land. There will be Vanishers here, lookin' for you. Even worse, it is likely they'll be at the queen's estate. You make it quick, got it?"

Violet shouldered her way onto the dock. "Got it."

He gave a small whistle through his teeth and his pet cynir, Mango, slithered from his jacket pocket. She was about the length of a child's arm, tail included, with bright blue fur and an orange, lizard-like mohawk of skin running down her spine. Her eyes gleamed green with dark slits, and her tongue was a bright purple. It zipped out, catching a mosquito, and Keller gave her a pat on the head as she settled on his shoulder.

Rio side-eyed Mango nervously, but Anaya beamed. "I still want one."

"You have to catch 'em."

"How do you catch them?"

"Well, you have to go to the island they inhabit, Cynir Isle, and you live there for a week while the cynirs investigate you. They are very predatory and protective over their land, but they are curious. If you force one to be your pet, they'll kill you. Lots of bones on that island. But if one takes a liking to you after that week and swims to your dinghy, you're bonded for life."

Mango gave a scratchy croak and licked Keller's cheek. He beamed.

Anaya huffed. "That sounds like too much."

"A little rum helps." Keller winked.

The minute they reached the shore of glass and sand, Violet tensed. People. Everywhere. Of all kinds. Her eyes darted all over, searching for ones whose gazes lingered a little longer than she liked.

The humid air curled her baby hairs and brought a line of sweat to her upper lip. Violet retained her awe at the disorderly drunks, gambling, men stripping for women, children playing cards, dirtied faces and unwashed bodies pressed together to the beat of drums, and apothecaries sprawling with jarred herbs and drugs.

The corner of Violet's mouth lifted. Rio nudged her as they wormed their way across a packed bridge and climbed the next road. "Familiar, right?"

"A crazy sense of home."

He grinned. "Minus the water and rain."

"And the people with fins, but I've gotten over it."

The Pirate Queen's estate sat above most of the cove. A lighthouse beaconed its location. Keller made the climb with little problem, along with Maji and Warran, but Violet was panting, hands on knees and a tightness to her chest when they finally reached the candle wax-covered gates of the Queen's compound.

Peony stayed with the boat, very much agitated at even being on the same island as her grandmother. Keller himself did not look particularly thrilled. He shuffled on his feet, as if the ground were burning him after his banishment to sea.

His banishment didn't exactly fit the crime in Violet's eyes, but it painted a picture of his mother. He'd lost a jewelry box of rare crystals in the sea. A shark had swallowed them. *That's it?* Violet had blurted. She'd thought he murdered someone, but apparently, murder was low on his mother's crime list.

Pirate guards posted the gates, and the minute an older one stepped forward, Keller removed his hat.

Every guard froze.

Violet's heart thumped loudly. She kept her eyes downturned, watching their boots and their hands for any sudden movements. Anaya tensed next to her.

"Keller."

Keller bent in a mocking bow. "The one and only, Bran."

"She'll kill you." Bran's hand brushed his plasgun. "For daring to step foot on land. It's your body hung over the water by sunrise."

Violet's hand went to the hilt of her hidden dagger. Anaya took a predatory step forward.

"Unless I have myva stingers—"

Bran snorted. "There's no way."

Warran lumbered forward and Bran took a tentative step back as he beheld the giant. Warran dropped the large sack on the ground. Plumes of dust rose. He unwrapped the ties at the top of the beige sack, revealing the first stinger. Bran leaned in, wrinkling his nose at the putrid, slightly poisonous smell, before he scoffed. "You've got to be kidding me, Keller."

Keller shot him a bright smile. "I'm not. Now move. I must kiss the hand of the bitch, or I might be hanged for lack of courtesy as well."

Bran rolled his eyes but motioned for the guards to open the gates.

The dark, wild, and dreary Nassren Cove bled into the Pirate Queen's estate. Black stone and onyx wood marked the sprawling area; walls climbed high and roofs crested like sharp arrowheads. Skulls lined pathways, finger bones decorated overgrown palms. Violet side-eyed a skeleton swaying in the wind, her eyes dipping to the soggy shoes beneath it.

Water sprayed from great spouts on ornate fountains, then drained in small rivets that poured off its own cliff into the city below. Violet welcomed the cool mist on her heated face. The tropical plants created arches and hedges, sporting orange, yellow, and pink blooms that glittered. Eerie music beat.

The juxtaposition of death and bones filling her vision while the scent of jasmine filled her nose left Violet unsettled.

They wove through the gardens before reaching the worn steps that led into an open foyer. Violet side-stepped empty seawine bottles, while Anaya kicked discarded knives out of the way. A large crimson spot stained the floor and Rio whined slightly.

Violet kicked him in the calf. "Keep it together."

"The queen's going to kill us."

"I'll kill you first if you make noises like that."

They followed through long halls that wound like a maze of jungle and black walls. Candles cast a sinister vibe. Bodies began to emerge—live ones, thank the skies.

One drunk stumbled into Violet, his rum-filled breath crowding her. "You're something—"

"Get *off.*" She shoved him into the wall, and the man slumped into the ground, a sleazy smile still on his face.

Everyone gave strange looks to Keller, but he avoided eye contact, head held high as he continued through what was once his home. They passed a room where a group bent over a table and snorted purple powder, and another room where an orgy took place, but everyone was lying down, lazily going at it—

"Keep moving," Keller growled.

Violet hadn't realized she stopped. Anaya collided with her

back, distracted by the scene as well. She sighed and yanked Anaya along with the group, all to Rio's giggles.

Beyond the orgy was the main party room. It was darker, deadlier than the rest of the house. *A witch's den*, Violet thought. Jarred herbs, hanging plants, incense burning, half-naked men…

And at the very center, sprawled across a couch made of bones and gold and velvet, lay Keller's mother—the Pirate Queen. The woman's beautiful Mer skin glistened in the flickering candles; one leg a moon white, the other dark brown, meeting together at her exposed pelvis.

Violet didn't expect to see the hole Keller stretched at birth so soon, but there it was, bush and lips and all, spread before a painted, naked man.

"Mother."

The Queen's eyes lifted to her son. "Bastard."

Immediately, the surrounding guards raised their weapons. Plasguns pointed at the group. Sweat licked Violet's spine.

"You're calling for your death." She tilted her head, and a sly smile teased her lips. "Which I've been wanting for years."

"Because I didn't come out Mer like you wanted?" Keller scoffed. "May the gods forbid you have at least one powerless child among your…what is it now? Nineteen?"

"Sixteen." She rolled her eyes. "You lost me a fortune."

"And a powerful Mer, believe me, I get it." Keller chucked. Mango hissed at his shoulder. "Warran."

Warran threw the sack of stingers onto the ground before the Queen's loveseat. Her…pleasurer took his leave, and she covered herself with the chiffon of her dress. When she stood, Violet had to tilt her head. One tall bitch.

Rio's eyes bugged. She had at least two inches above him, and Rio was typically the tallest in the room.

"Twenty myva stingers, like you deemed my punishment so long ago." Keller unsheathed his sword and slashed the bag open. The white, sharp things spilled onto the marble, some leaking the rare fluid. "I spent nine years catching these, and now I want my pardon. My boots miss the trash on this cove."

She didn't balk at the insult. It was a dirty place, Violet noticed, but there was little to be done under Sloth's effects. It didn't take much time to realize the people of Sloth would be the strongest, most powerful, and most monstrous of all the worlds Cyran had control over. It was probably why he chose this world, why so many of the robotic monster animals generated in Envy originated from Sloth. This world itself would be a threat, and Cyran needed his threats sedated.

"How's my little Peony?" The Queen diverted. "It is rude that she didn't want to say hello to her grandmother."

Keller sighed. "If you banned her from Nassren, she'd throw a celebration."

"Pity, she always had more potential as a powerless than you."

"Grant me pardon, Mother."

Her head cocked. "For twenty stingers? After all these years?"

Maji stepped up, removing her stolen plasgun from her hip and aiming it at the bag. Nearly every guard took a step forward. Even the queen jolted. Anger passed over her face. "Don't you dare."

"The stingers are incredibly flammable. One shot and this whole place goes up in flames." Keller smirked. "If I don't get my pardon, I'll get my revenge."

The Queen's long nails dug into the couch's red cushion. "You threaten me in my own home?"

"This was *my* home, too," Keller growled. "And you took it from me. You knew I wanted no part of this family, but still you humiliated me, defamed my reputation as the best sea captain, and banned me from this land."

Maji shot the plasgun. It blasted into the floor next to the stingers, but the fear was there. A guard threw himself over the Queen, her lover cowered behind the sofa, and a servant dropped a glass of grapes nearby. One rolled to Violet's boot.

"Oh, Mother, why do you entertain him? Just give him the pardon."

The sensual male voice flowed and settled the tension in the room. A younger, taller version of Keller stepped in, but this one fully Mer. Extremely handsome, with a carved jawline, amber eyes, long dreads strung with shells down to his shoulders, and a ring at the side of his lip, he strutted over to Violet. Two men followed him. Candidates. *Vanishers.*

She held her breath. This was not anticipated. She tamed her confused expression as he caught her gaze, the corner of his mouth lifting, and bent before her.

Anaya stiffened, taking the slightest step as if to block Violet...

But he picked up the fallen grape. Looked at Violet and popped it into his mouth.

"Back *up*." Anaya shoved herself between Violet and the newcomer.

He chuckled and stood. "All fun and games, little pirate." He grasped Violet's hand, brought it to his mouth, and kissed it. His thumb rubbed her palm. "I didn't know you had such interesting company with you, brother."

Violet couldn't breathe. Not as his thumbnail stroked the indent of her bloodswearing scar. *Fuck. Skivvin' fuck.*

"Renell," Keller growled in greeting. "I see you are well."

"Back from conquering the Gillan Islands, brother, and expanding our pirate dominance." Renell smiled, and Violet hated how well he used his smile. The man *knew* he was gorgeous, and every line of his face screamed manipulation with it.

The Queen petted her lover's hair. "Renell is—"

"What you always wanted me to be," Keller said.

Renell's smug face didn't lessen. "Grant him his pardon, Mother, and let them stay." His gaze flicked back to Violet. "I think it is time we have a party, especially with our new friends here."

The music grew louder. The atmosphere held a heavy smoke to it. Violet averted her gaze back to the Queen, who judged her bastard son with a long look.

Tensions overwhelmed the room. The Queen stretched it as long as she liked.

"Fine. You're pardoned. Welcome back to Nassren," she said icily.

Keller sagged in relief. "Thank you, Mother."

"You are allowed to stay for the party, but after tonight, I don't want to see your face again."

Keller quirked a smile at that. "Of course."

Renell stepped up and slapped his older brother on the shoulder. "Welcome back, brother."

Keller grunted.

✤ ✤ ✤

Violet found herself an empty balcony as they desperately tried to avoid most interactions in the drunks-packed party. The Queen was inebriated, purple powder staining her nostrils as four lovers worked their way up her body. Keller had been immediately wrapped in welcomes, Warran disappeared, and Maji lingered with her captain, on guard.

Keller had noticed the interaction between Renell and Violet. His brother knew Violet was a candidate by the quick stroke of his thumb, but he had only smiled when she walked away, rigid and unnerved. She didn't dare say it aloud to Anaya and Rio, but one look between each of them said everything—Renell knew. The two Vanishers behind him will know. But no moves had been made. No attempts to turn them over.

Something was brewing.

The portal to the next world crawled with guards. Through the massive gardens, Violet counted at least three as she strolled the outdoor veranda. If they ran for it immediately, they wouldn't make it four steps. If they waited while more became inebriated, while their arrival dwindled and the guards were less alert, then it would become a fathomable escape.

So Violet disappeared, hoping her absence lessened whatever game he wanted to play. They were surrounded by pirates—pirates were not known to work together. Renell found his treasure, and Violet could feel the time ticking as rapidly as her heartbeat.

She clutched the balcony railing and stared down into the massive pool below. Anaya and Rio made themselves scarce nearby. When they came back, they'd make their escape.

Violet had pondered a lot before she came to this point. The shift to the next world would prove difficult.

First, her tracker would switch. Since every planet, even Veceras, was infiltrated by Cyran's men, she had no doubt Cyran would be notified when she stepped into his main domain. That could mean only seconds to act once she landed, but she would be disoriented from the zap to her senses. A risk she'd have no choice but to take.

Second, a thought which shot shivers down to her bones, was that there was a specific place each candidate appeared, and Cyran's croons waited to snatch her.

Third, Reed. Him watching her as she vomited blood, about to be murdered in Lust. Irreconcilable differences separated them, and she didn't know how to navigate their splintered relationship.

Fourth, Jack. Her heart twisted and her eyes burned. It was easy to train herself. When she thought of Jack, she'd bend her pinky finger backward until the pain dulled her thoughts. His death tore a hole through her chest. She needed to avenge him, and that came with lopping the head off the black-lightning skiv.

"You were quite a surprise."

Violet whirled from the balcony, finding Renell with his eyes locked on her. He waved his chalice and seawine sloshed over the tip, splattering to the floor. Slightly drunk. Or maybe it was a ruse. She kept her guard up, hand going to the small dagger tucked in her pants.

"I don't know what you mean," she said.

"Three fugitives wanted by the Ruler of Seven Worlds, and they have never been caught? It was the ultimate treasure hunt. Most rumors consisted of them held captive by a pirate who wanted a reward, but nothing ever came from it. So I thought, what pirate in the Citran Seas would be merciful enough to hide them? Which one would not care about the reward they'd receive for turning them over?" Renell flashed a wide smile. "My brother."

Violet flicked dirt under her fingernails, feigning boredom. "Still have no idea what you're talking about."

"So difficult." His eyes lit with mischief. "Turn your palms over. I felt it, but I want to see it. Just in case it was a ploy."

Violet kept her hands firmly at her sides. "It's all that alcohol in your head, muddling your fish brain."

Renell's face changed. His entire demeanor, actually. The smile dropped, the glittery eyes winked out. The true predator unveiled—

Violet lunged, lifting her dagger. She jammed it at his throat, but Renell dropped his drunk charade and splashed the wine at her face.

It stung her eyes and she gasped. The dagger flew from her grip, clattering to the ground. Renell slammed her into the balcony. She groaned as her spine bit into the stone while she blinked the wine out of her vision.

"You're a real bitch," he said through gritted teeth. "Maybe I'll finally get this damn Sin off our world if I hand you over to him."

He held her throat while his other hand ripped her shirt down the middle, exposing the center of her chest.

In her head, she screamed Jack's name. Desperately called to him, begging him to be there. *Jack*, she pleaded as Renell trapped her. *Please, Jack.*

But Jack was dead. Those arms she called her safe place were gone. Those green eyes she linked to freedom were no more.

"But you could become something more...." Renell's gaze was menacing. "Little Vanisher."

Violet bared her teeth. "Shut your mouth."

"He *never* cares about candidates, unless they are special to him, unless they can teleport, and you obviously can. That's why they're looking for you." A deep laugh rose from his chest. "I could turn over one Vanisher, or I could turn over multiple."

She drew back, throat clogging.

His lips met her ear. "Little Vanisher babies, each one a key to treasure. Each one giving me more. I'm not the only one who has these thoughts. It's why the Ruler is so protective—"

"He wants me *dead*," Violet gritted, pushing at him. "Not pregnant, you skiv. Those Vanishers will snag me first."

"Those Vanishers are drugged up in the orgy room." A sadistic smile. "My mother would finally let me be Pirate King. I'd get this curse removed from our world. I'd finally have control of these people, these monsters, all the while getting more with each little baby you push out."

"You're sick! Get off—"

He slapped a hand over her mouth. "Gods, shut up."

He caged her in, pressing his body against hers. Panic flared and she swallowed her anger. *No-no-no, this wasn't happening. There was no way this was happening.* She was wanted dead—she didn't think about the different ways she could be used when *not* dead.

He bent into her, lips dragging along her jaw as she tried to bite his hand. But he was too strong. All the Mers were too strong—even diluted with Sloth.

"It will be over soon." He removed his hand, and before she could scream, he planted his mouth on hers.

Her body turned to stone. Shut down. She tried to wrench her wrists from his grip, but it was bruising, and she thought her bones were mere seconds from snapping...

"Touch me," he commanded.

No-no-no-no...

He pulled her hand to his chest, sliding it down his muscles over his bulging abs. Lower, to the lip of his pants. Bile rose to her mouth.

His hand rubbed at her jugular. Squeezed.

So unlike the other hands that were passionate, gentle yet strong. Warm yet powerful.

She pushed him. He was unmovable, unfazed. She shoved harder—broke the kiss to gasp. "Stop."

He ignored her.

"Stop," she said again. Her lower back pressed painfully into the railing. She felt the smaller dagger at her thigh, but she was fighting both shock and Renell too much to reach it. Her nails dug into his skin, hard enough that he groaned and sighed. "I like it rough."

Terror flooded through her. She fought between becoming stone or becoming fire. Her body sagged and her fingertips prickled. He held her up. He cupped her bottom. She wanted to scream, but his hand collared her throat, her one wrist pinned behind her, the other hand forced to touch him.

"You are going in your cage, little bird. Because I will do anything for my world."

She panicked. Became a frenzy. Clawed at him. "Get off me—"

"Shut up," he growled, grabbing the back of her hair and yanking.

He gripped her arm so tightly his nails dug in, and when she pulled away, ready to scream, they sliced her skin. Blood welled from the small marks.

She shot out her arm and landed a punch into his eye. He huffed a laugh as the wound barely opened.

"You're cute. You think you can fight me." He smiled. "Amusing you think you can fight anyone in this game."

She remembered green eyes twinkling down at her. The roars of Calesal at her back. Her bandaged hand. The teasing curve of his lip.

It's cute.

What is?

The fire in you.

Her heart thumped out of rhythm. Panic, anger, heartache— it roared within her. A cord yanked from her gut, up her spine, to the base of her skull. A burning sensation grew in her chest, flowed through her veins until it reached the soles of her feet. Her fingertips began to glow. She brushed the hilt of her tiny dagger and released it from its sheath.

She tried to keep a clear mind to fight back, but her body trembled with light and buzzing and fear. She was losing control. Her heart beat too fast, and his hands moved all over her body, sending her into a panic. Light blinded her eyes and her breath shortened.

Stop-stop-stop…

If this was her power, her ability, it terrified her. She disconnected from her body and the heat became unbearable. Sweat licked her skin as the thing awoke in her, lulling from its sleep.

Jack's name reverberated through her mind.

He's not here to save you. He's dead. Human and dead. He would be no match for this.

Lips were at her neck. She wanted to scream.

She managed to raise the dagger as she drew him close.

She slammed it into the back of his neck. The light in her vision winked out. Heat faded. Blood misted her chest. The horrifying sight of silver poked through his neck, nearly meeting the tip of Violet's nose. She twisted it and yanked it back out.

Renell's eyes rolled back, and he dropped to the ground with a thump. Violet collapsed against the railing as nausea roiled through her. Her palms blinked with light and heat scorched in two lines beneath her eyes. Cold sweat covered her. And then it all stilled.

"Fuck."

Violet's head whipped. Maji stood at the threshold to the balcony, smirking.

"I killed…" Violet breathed.

"Not really." Maji shrugged. "This will just keep him out of the way. Can you help me lift him?"

"Why not leave him dead?" Violet clutched her aching throat. "Please…please…"

"The prized son of the Pirate Queen? It would mean no one leaves this party alive. We will throw him into the water. It will buy us some time."

It took a couple of minutes, but with a grunt, both girls hauled Renell over the edge of the balcony, leaving the puddle of blood staining the marble.

They watched his body smack into the pool. He floated for a moment, then began to sink. The water blurred his descent.

Maji wrinkled her nose and helped Violet cover herself. Violet rubbed her throat, stunned.

"What—" Violet shook her head "—just happened?"

"You're okay." Maji attempted to wipe the blood off Violet's face. "You will be okay, but we need to get you guys out of here. Mers usually recover in fifteen minutes."

She and Maji sprinted through the hallways, heads low, avoiding the stumbling people, and darting down some steps until they were on the pool level. Violet spared one glance at the swirl of blood lingering in the water before she pressed forward. They breached giant hedges of palms and lost themselves in the dark maze.

"The guards…"

"Anaya took care of them with her camouflage," Maji whispered. She then whistled a bird-like noise, and a whistle sounded in return. A leaf smacked Violet in the face as they rounded a corner and nearly collided with Rio.

Scales rippled and Anaya's hands were on Violet, teeth bared. "What *happened?*"

Violet shook her head. "I—"

"I'll kill him."

"Violet," Rio gasped. "What—"

"Later," she snapped. "Get out the Iris, we are going. Now."

Rio nodded. His brows furrowed for a moment, but he shook his head. "Ready when you are."

Violet turned to Maji. "Thank you for helping us."

"Of course." Maji squeezed her shoulder. "Good luck. Keller wishes it, too."

Anaya said her goodbyes to Maji and stepped away quickly, her plasblade out. A commotion rose from the house, and the stomping of boots picked up. Someone screamed. A splash sounded.

Rio gave Maji a long hug. "Thank you."

"Until we see each other again." Maji smiled up at him.

Rio kissed her cheek and pulled away. With one last wave goodbye, they parted from Maji, diving farther into the gardens.

Two more turns in the maze and the silver portal table glittered a length before them.

"Almost there," Anaya muttered. "Guard up ahead. I got it."

Rio and Violet stayed back as Anaya dipped into her camouflage. In a flash, the butt of her sword smacked into the guard's temple. He dropped to the ground with a dull thump. She whirled to Violet, "Now, Vi—"

Violet stepped forward, but an arm stopped her. Gripping painfully. She turned to Rio, meeting his wild-looking gaze. "What's wrong?"

"You can't go," he gritted. "I can't…I can't let you go."

Her brows creased. Anaya called, "Now is not the time, Ri."

When Violet tried to yank away, Rio lunged after her, grappling for her arm. She sucked a surprised breath at his strength, the urgency behind it. "Rio, what—"

He fought something behind his eyes. His movements became jerky. "We can't…" He trembled. "*You* can't—"

"I *am*," Violet snarled and ripped herself from his grasp. She ducked as Rio reached again. "And you are, too. No backing out now."

She sprinted toward the portal. Her boots pounded the gravel, Rio's right behind her. To her confusion, he still tried to stop her. Panicked breath erupted from him. Anaya watched, equally confused, from before the portal's pedestal, and when Violet pulled out the Iris, Rio released a panicked breath. "No! It…I can't let you go! I have to stop you!"

She halted before Anaya. Cold terror slid down her spine. She whirled to Rio just as his body slammed into hers, sending them both to the ground.

He pinned her and Violet let him. Numbed. Shocked. Realization flooded through her. There's only one possible answer to Rio's actions…she was too stunned to do anything, even as he got off her and began dragging her by the ankles.

"What are you doing?" Anaya snapped and pushed at Rio. "Stop this! We need to go!"

"Anaya." Violet's eyes found Rio's hand at her ankle. Dirt and grass snagged on her hair, but her shock stopped her cares. "It's happening."

Only one possible answer...the bloodbond to Jack. The one made between them in the last days in Lust. The one that Rio agreed, in all cases, to stop Violet from following Jack, and by proxy, to her death.

"It works?" Anaya said, as stunned as Violet. "Does that mean...?"

Because the active bloodbond could only mean one thing. *Had* to mean one thing. Violet latched onto it, hope soaring within her. It wouldn't...if Jack were dead, a promise like that wouldn't take power. She held a bloodbond to Jack; one that said they couldn't kill each other directly or by proxy. They made it in Wrath, when only hatred existed between them, and it activated in Lust, when the Worldbreaker made Jack slam a dagger over her heart. That same sound—the sound of Gwen's dagger booming against a wall of air above her heart—filled her ears. The picture of it splintering into pieces, one shard still missing. If Jack were dead, no bond would matter to whatever magic harnessed it. His blood would have stopped, and the bond would be null.

Or...that's how she convinced herself.

"He's alive," Violet whispered.

She snapped. Wrenched her ankles from Rio's grip. He immediately lunged at her, sorrow on his face, pleading for it to stop, but he couldn't. Anaya yelled at the commotion, but Violet had newfound energy, and she smacked away Rio's reach.

"Stop it, Rio!" Anaya cried.

"I can't!" Rio yelled back, a snarl in his throat. "Stop me, you have to stop me!"

Rio lunged again. She kicked at him, torn between wanting to pummel him because he was stopping her...stopping her from seeing...

Him.

He's alive.

"You have to stop me," Rio pleaded as he slashed his nails at her arm. "If I don't—feel the bond's power, I can't do anything…"

"What does that mean?" Anaya asked.

"Stop me," Rio begged. "He's alive, Vi. You have to go. *Stop me.*"

"Leave you," Violet said, she dodged another one of his grabs, stepping closer to the portal. He trembled with the frenzy of the bloodbond, but Violet shook her head, tears with it. "I can't—"

"Stop me!" Rio cried mid-lunge.

He crashed into her. They hit the ground hard, the breath leaving her lungs. She raised her arm, keeping the Iris out of reach. Rio's teeth were in her face, as if he were going to bite her and drag her with them—

"I'm not leaving you!"

"Stop me—!"

A loud clang, and Rio slumped atop Violet. Anaya drew back the butt of her sword. "Go Vi. *Now.*"

Violet pushed his unconscious body and scrambled to her feet. "And leave you here?"

Anaya shoved her toward the portal. "Find him. If he's alive, he's within the Worldbreaker's hands. He could be in danger, and we have to—" Anaya shook her head and scrunched her eyes. "Save him, Vi. We'll hide. We have more Irises, we'll be right behind you. We can pretend we didn't know, that you thwarted us, and go back on the boat—"

Violet furiously wiped at her face. Raw emotion flooded her, sparking tears in her eyes. "No."

Anaya shoved her again. "*Go.*"

The sound of shuffling feet snapped their attention to the garden's maze. Guards poured through, plasbows raised.

Anaya nodded toward Violet. "We will be okay."

Violet looked between Anaya, the guards, and the portal.

When she glanced back at Anaya, the Endolier had her hand raised, finger pointing, shrieking, "She tricked us! She's leaving. You're a fucking liar! You said you wouldn't leave us, Violet!"

Violet stumbled back a step.

"Rio, you need to wake up! Why did you hit him? We were trying to help you!" Anaya bent down to Rio, her voice a perfectly poised plea. "We trusted you!"

Violet schooled her expression and went along with Anaya's drama. "I was only using you."

The guards stormed. Violet vaulted for the portal.

"Stop her," boomed a commanding voice—the Pirate Queen. She powered through behind the guards, eyes wild and angered as they landed on Violet.

Behind her, a soaking, bloody Renell stepped up, snarling, "Stop her, now!"

Anaya cried to the skies, the full moon above, tears in her eyes matching Violet's blurred vision. She dipped her gaze to Rio's unconscious form, then back to the Endolier.

The Endolier nodded.

Violet flicked the middle finger to the Queen and slammed the Iris down into its notch. It clicked.

The beautiful flash of light swallowed the Queen's scream of rage.

But another thing followed Violet. Two things.

A flash of an arrow. Pain blossomed in her side. She glanced down to the arrow protruding from her hip, but the bright light melted it away. She cried out, slapping her free hand around the wound.

The last thing she saw was blood.

More blood.

Her blood.

6

Emperor's Mansion

Calesal was a sprawling city. An ancient city in the country of Veceras. But the ancient part was the fine dust layered beneath bricks, and then pavement, and then another round of pavement. It crawled from south to north, poor to rich, shorter, squashed buildings to pristine, giant skyrises. Between the contrasting landscapes was the Mid. Taller buildings, sort-of cleaner streets depending on the proximity, and wider roads. To the west was land. Lots and lots of it. Not farmland or pastures or greenery, but dry bushes, hot asphalt, and massive factory buildings that produced and fulfilled all trade that came from the lands outside of the walls. Then lastly, to the east, past a murky river and across the massive Trollova Bridge, was the Government sector. White buildings, some more modern and made of glass, crested a hill. Flowers bloomed. Trees burst with green. Grass grew.

Calesal had existed for thousands of years, but its history was forgotten. Built and forged with new technological advances, cement foundations of buildings, and the plasma-energy grid—a writhing, colorful molten energy mined within Veceras' lands— the Citadel of Calesal only knew the future.

Only knew its arid climate and hot days.

Only knew the giant beige stone wall that surrounded it.

And now, in the future of a new empire, it only knew that blood didn't look red after an hour in the sun, before a new splatter covered the old.

Jelan Gregory pressed the binoculars to her eyes. She watched the Aariva—the only thing in Calesal that could be considered ancient if it didn't hold a portal going to one world, and a twin portal returning from another. Between the tall, dark metal columns that nearly winked out the sun from her eyes, Jelan watched the giant arena as gray-plated Redders—Red Empire Police—and black-uniformed empire officials gathered yet again to declare a public message. Three layers of a stage jutted out, the bottom holding the Sky Arch Portals and the Bloodswearing bowl between them. Before that bowl, a man with pale skin, a sharp chin, and haunting eyes held a buzzing plasblade to the neck of some unfortunate soul, then sliced their fragile skin.

The fresh crimson splatter replaced the murky brown stains from the last one.

Emperor Arvalo executed yet another treasonous criminal.

"His fourth today," Jelan mumbled. She didn't know why she lingered here or why she cared to watch. She didn't make it for all of them, but there was no possible way she could pace the penthouse and hear the news *again*.

Desensitized, seeing blood looked like any regular fluid at this point. She might see it more often than water. A sad, horrible realization for the dark days they had been living in the past four months. Quiet streets and curfews, massive amounts of Redders, the loss of soul in her city that once had so much of it. She wasn't growing complacent to Arvalos's horrifying regime, but she worried that after watching so many executions, perhaps *something* should be wrong with her at this point. It might be better for her to accept their present day. It might make the nightmares go away, or the stress that ate the lives of her and her friends.

"I wonder if he didn't get his dick sucked properly."

Jelan frowned and lowered the binoculars. Hira sat on the edge of the rooftop, kicking her heels and leaning back on her arms. Her warm brown skin was a little darker, and Jelan noticed the tan line on her neck from the shirt she wore yesterday. She piled her long, uncut hair into a bun, and held her baby hairs back with a bandana. She wore shorts and sandals today, probably to make up for the horrible tan line her socks gave her a couple of days ago, which Jelan made fun of her for. Hira's plus-sized figure basked in the sun, and she watched the execution as if it were an entertainment show. Jelan knew better than to think Hira didn't care. Her friend had a cold, dark heart for most people and things and bugs, but she did care.

Maybe they were becoming complacent.

"I think it's time we head back," Jelan said. "The sun is setting."

"*Right,*" Hira said, jumping up and stretching her hands above her head. "You have *dinner.*"

"Dinner is a weak word." Jelan kicked an old cigarette butt. "I don't even know why he invited me."

"Arvalo requested you. Well, partially. You are the woman who built the plashield. Regardless of the direct request from the Emperor himself, Lucien would have taken you along anyway. You're a safer option, one who isn't necessarily a threat to a room full of threats. Lyla would be too obvious, you know how she makes everyone want to piss themselves. Jenkins is hiding after the Aariva incident since his cover should have never been blown in the first place. Kole, well…it is well known Kole was only sentenced to the Sins by Arvalo, so Kole's father would be punished, but Violet disrupted that plan, so I don't think Kole should go. Poor guy. He's taken up knitting. It's a little weird, but he's very good at it. I requested a hat." Hira smiled, the little jewel in her tooth sparkling. Ever since her job had become exclusive to the Marin gardia, she'd been indulging. Jewelry, a smattering of tattoos on her right arm, some more expensive silks. She liked the finer things. Her skincare lotions now crowded Jelan's bathroom counter.

Even though the woman stayed there only once a week.

Hira continued, "You're a perfect choice. Actually, Meema might be a good fit. She's lucid enough—"

"She'd be killed," Jelan said. "One bad word about Arvalo has people disappearing off the streets. He doesn't want any plans to overthrow him. Meema, no matter how old or slightly delusional, wouldn't be an exception."

"Then you're the one to go." Hira turned Jelan away from the Aariva. "Because you can actually hold your mouth."

"I just don't understand…"

"His brother is dead, Jelan."

Jelan shut her mouth. A dry wind breezed through the area, clinking the new set of beads on the ends of her new semi-blonde box braids brushing her mid-back.

"This is the City Commander's dinner. There's one every year. The last time it happened, Jack was in this world. *Alive.* You're Lucien's support. His rock."

"I'm not denying that, but being invited to the City Commander's yearly dinner party? Across the bridge? In the *Government Sector?*" Jelan rubbed her scarred hands together. "I think the question we should be asking is why I would be useful for such a thing."

"You're useful because you'll keep him calm. Keep him together." Hira tapped Jelan's temple. "Arvalo *will* mention Jack. Might even toast to the fact he's gone. As composed as Lucien can be, he still has Marin blood. Fierce loyalty. You need to be there to make sure he doesn't act out."

"Fine."

"Good." Hira stared at her for a long moment. "Can I get a ride back to the penthouse?"

"I thought you were going home."

"My mother has a *visitor*."

"Fine, as long as you don't mind helmet hair."

"I look sexy with it anyway, so…"

They made their way down the building's fire escape and uncovered Jelan's beautiful plasbike behind a trash can. It was the first thing she'd ever purchased for herself, and while she didn't have too many places to drive it to, she adored the thing. It was sleek, a mix of black and dark gray metal, with leather seats and ridges of white that would ignite in contained rainbow plasma on command. Like a sped-up, supercool lava lamp, Hira had said.

As Jelan shoved the helmet over Hira's head and put on her own, she couldn't resist the smile behind her shaded visor. When she'd shown Lucien her new purchase, even straddling the bike to demonstrate how to ride it, he'd been at a loss for words. She had meant it innocently—she was excited for herself—but she didn't miss his quick glance at her ass, the bob of his throat, or the darkening of his eyes.

That was about all they had between them at this moment: brief flirtations and long glances. Lucien wasn't around much, both because of work and because he preferred the solitude as of late. To lose his only brother…to have never said a proper goodbye. To spend the rest of his life wondering what—or who—might have finally delivered the notorious Jack Marin's death…Jelan couldn't fathom. While she had little feelings for Jack, it did make the reality for Violet a lot more worrisome.

The ride back was smooth. Hira yelped every time Jelan drove a little too fast, weaving between cars and other plasbikes. She made sharp turns and quick stops, a smile twitching on her face the entire time. It made her feel alive, and from the moment her scarred hands met the bars, she was free. The city didn't touch her on these wheels.

Hira had dug bruises into Jelan's ribs by the time they pulled into the penthouse building's garage. Jelan massaged her torso on the elevator ride up.

Hira smiled. "I have an ointment."

"Of course you do." Jelan nudged her, playfully.

Only when the doors dinged open and the familiar, calm foyer of the Marin Penthouse greeted her, did her nerves snap back.

"You're late."

Jelan smirked sheepishly at Lucien, who had a flutter of staff fussing with his hair as he held a tumbler of liquor in his hand. He strutted out of the sitting room, the staff with him.

"I'll be quick."

He flashed her a steely glare. "Why do you watch the executions?"

"You know why."

"Arvalo won't slip up." Lucien checked his phone when it beeped, but continued, able to multitask, "He's scouring the city for things that threaten him now, and when that is completed, he will begin to threaten our entire order. The executions are an ego brush for him." With a lifted brow he commanded, "Go."

"She'll be safe, right?" Hira asked.

Jelan turned toward the staircase. "Hira—"

"Of course, she will be safe, I wouldn't let anything happen—"

Jelan swerved on the top step. "*I* will be fine. I'm quite good with a dagger now."

Lucien's face softened into a smile. "That she is."

❋❋❋

It was strange traveling the Trollova Bridge. It stood like a beacon to everyone in Calesal, but no one could cross it. Crossing it meant challenging the Empire, and well…that didn't happen often. So the people either ignored it or stared at the great, pointed architecture towering above the murky river.

Redders littered the pavement like a line of gray traffic cones as Lucien's sleek, bullet-proof car glided across. Jelan wrung her hands in her lap. Lucien sipped yet another drink on the seat across from her. She felt his gaze drift to her now and then, but she was too nervous, too…*curious*, to care.

"You know the drill?"

"Eat, observe, potentially impress him—"

"You don't need to impress him," Lucien said. "You don't need to be someone else, *but* we don't want attention. In and out. That is all we want tonight."

She nodded and tongued her canine. "He's going to mention your brother."

"I won't do anything. I promise. I'm not as volatile as my brother…was."

The heartbreak, the grief in his voice, drew her attention. Her chest filled with ice, tense and tight. She sighed deeply, unsure what to say. *Was.* An extremely difficult word when you lose a loved one. She remembered the struggle after she lost her mother and brother. One day they were an *is*, the next, a *was*.

"Just don't let any of it get to you," Jelan said. Matter of fact. "He just wants it to hurt—"

"You look beautiful," Lucien teased softly. "By the way."

Jelan's face grew hot. Very hot. He stared at her intensely. Light russet skin dotted with dark, manicured stubble. Chestnut eyes that held an alluring smolder, full lips, strong brows, and rich, black hair that held delicate waves.

Skies, that suit, though. She had the urge to ruffle it. Rip it off. Incinerate it or use it as a damn pillowcase—

"Jelan?"

She blinked. "Thank you."

She was proud of her appearance, but it didn't hold a wow factor. She wore a long, silky dark purple dress that wrapped around her neck and slipped delicately around her waist, exposing a good portion of her back. She liked how well it worked with her ebony skin, and she especially liked the silver jewelry paired with it. Her makeup was simple: eyeliner, rosy lipstick, and a soft shimmer on her cheekbones.

They passed numerous, long stone and glass buildings that housed military operations, the treasury, agricultural and trade relations, Sin operations, and more. Everything that kept Veceras running. The car crawled up the hill the Emperor's mansion stood on. Fountains and waterfalls cascaded everywhere, surrounded by lush, pristine flora. The Government Sector was its own city in itself—but an economically abundant city. The mansion was, to her eyes, not really a mansion, but more of a sprawling, never-ending estate that rolled on for miles, eventually meeting the wall surrounding the entire city. Made of white stone, it consisted of four stories and balconies and soft lighting to highlight its design.

White-gloved servants greeted them when the car pulled up to the entrance. Jelan wore satin white gloves herself. The door opened, and Lucien exited first before turning and holding his hand out for her.

Her heart beat a little too fast as she grabbed it, letting him help her from the car. He brushed a braid behind her ear and smirked at her earring. "Those are fun."

"Hira likes long, dangly ones."

"Of course, she does. I might be paying her too much." He extended his elbow. She threaded her arm through.

"She'll burn every nice thing you own."

"I regret giving her a key."

"No, you don't," Jelan said. "She makes you laugh."

"And you make me smile."

His eyes glittered down at her. She swore butterflies had invaded her body, and she was about to burst into one.

They ascended the stairs. Other guests milled about—government officials, esteemed individuals. Jelan even noticed a few famous people she recognized from movies. Lucien made sure they arrived at this exact time, the cocktail party over, and they would only have to attend the City Commander's dinner. A small table with each commander and their plus one. No chatter or distractions.

In and out.

Just like he said.

Jelan squared her shoulders as they entered beneath the gaping columns that led into the entrance hall. Guards littered the place like trash on the streets in the South. Every eye watched as a servant led them into the dining room. Lucien nodded at a few familiar faces. She avoided gazes. They were given their places at the table.

"Right on time for the most important part, per usual, Lucien."

Alexia Javez, Commander of Health and Biology, smiled from her seat across the table. Her sharp, pointy features were striking against her milky, pale skin. Long black hair shone in the chandelier's light. Her brown eyes flicked to Jelan, she lifted her blood-red wine in a greeting. "Along with your guest. She's a looker."

"She is," Alexia's wife, Venara, agreed. She sat to Alexia's right, a light-beige-skinned woman with hazel eyes and a gold ring on her hooked nose. Her brown hair was pulled back in a long, single braid, and if Jelan wasn't pretty aware of her sexuality and the tension she already had with Lucien, she would be questioning everything. *Everything.* Their gazes were fierce. Very much judging Jelan, but not in a harsh way. More like…calculating.

Jelan offered them a small smile as Lucien said, "Did you enjoy the prior festivities?"

"No, we arrived five minutes before you." Alexia motioned to another commander—Hunt Covokai, Commander of Public Works and Rescue—who was inspecting his fork, a sneer on his face. "He was here before us…"

"By a few minutes, I don't enjoy wasting my time on these things."

"You have other activities? Making sure your septics remain sterile?" Alexia rolled her eyes. "The fork is clean, Hunt. Don't overthink it."

"I have people I want to see, things I want to do, and I don't need to discuss them with you." Covokai rubbed his gray beard. Up close, he had a smattering of old sun freckles along his nose. Similar to Meema's. A common trait of people from the South if they had lighter skin, and especially if they were out in the sun for long days.

"Another man?"

Covokai spared her a bored look. "No. The same man as the last forty years. I apologize that Joel didn't send you a thank you note for the birthday flowers you sent."

"A bit rude."

"Funny thing, he doesn't actually like you," Covokai said. "You're too brash for him."

Alexia winked. "I'll send him another round next week just for your delightful comment."

Heels clacked on the floor, and the last of the current City Commanders walked in with a new woman on his hip. Ellis Pofer, Commander of Transportation and Recreation, grinned at the group and squeezed his attendee's arm. "You all look dashing."

"You're late," Covokai observed.

Lucien snorted.

Pofer looked like he spent too much time in the tanning bed, and not enough time on a treadmill. Not that Jelan wanted to judge, but by the puff of his belly and the stretch of his shirt, it could probably do him some good. His bald head sparkled, blue eyes small and beady. The woman at his hip was not the last he'd been seen with, and Alexia clearly took notice with a side-eye and a curt whisper to Venara.

Another set of doors opened.

Arvalo entered.

His dark aura thrust itself into the room. A pitch-black ensemble draped his thin frame, including a cape with Veceras' sigil on the back. His inky hair had been combed back and greased from his face of hard edges: sharp cheekbones, a pointy chin, and thin lips. His mono-lid eyes immediately surveyed the room.

The ex-Commander of Plastech and Media was flanked by his children; four sons and one daughter. Jelan didn't know the names of each, but she did know Mai.

Mai Arvalo, a striking, short-tempered woman who had a relationship with Violet. Jelan would never forget the abuse Mai put Violet through, but there was a sense of pity when Mai was the clear inferior in the room. Her brothers were all a head taller than her, dressed impeccably, and each extremely handsome in their own regard. All had the same mono-lid feature and dark hair, but their facial structures varied.

"Welcome"—Arvalo lifted his hands. Silver rings glinted at each finger—"to this year's annual City Commander's dinner. I always enjoy these. Little more private."

Arvalo and his kids took their seats at the head, and servants immediately swarmed, decorating the table with food and drinks.

Her hands shook. She fisted her fork. Lucien's touch found her knee and squeezed.

Just hours prior, Jelan had watched Arvalo waltz the Aariva stage amid more blood. Now, he smiled at Pofer as they dove into a discussion at the other end of the table, his sons chiming in.

Mai caught Jelan's gaze and furrowed her brows. Her eyes then dipped to Jelan's gloved hands.

"Is there something wrong with our cleanliness?"

The direct, blurted question shot to Jelan like a plasarrow. Mai's scowl revealed no joke or tease.

Skiv, Jelan thought. She ignored the rising heat of embarrassment. What a shit child. "No, they were simply too beautiful to pass up."

"Who wears gloves in a hot city?"

By now, the other conversations slowed.

"I—" Jelan stuttered. She used her one-prepared response. No one should have cared about the gloves. "Like I said, I—I like them."

Alexia's brows were raised. Venara buried her face in her wine glass.

Mai continued, "It's a hot city. I doubt your hands are cold."

"I—" Jelan flashed a look to Lucien.

Even Lucien was confused. "Mai—"

But Mai barreled on, determined. "Why are you wearing them? Who wears that?"

"Are you trying to start a fight already, Mai?" one of her older brothers chimed in, leering with glistening eyes. "Couldn't even last a minute."

"Eat your food," Arvalo commanded his daughter. Jelan had to remind herself that Mai was twenty-one years old.

Mai bit and refused to back down. "The gloves—"

"I will take them off," Jelan said quickly.

"No," Lucien said. "You don't have to."

"It's fine," she assured. "These hands did create the plashield, after all."

She snapped a look to Mai, whose scowl vanished into a reserved expression. Jelan plucked one glove off and flashed her scarred hand to the table.

A strange smile grew on Arvalo's face. "The one who created the plashield."

"Jelan Gregory," Lucien interjected.

Jelan forced a smile as Lucien squeezed her knee again. His hand lingered there, brushing her dress. Now *that* was more sensual.

"Jelan Gregory," Arvalo said, as if he took a bite from her name and tasted it. His cold eyes drilled into her. "How did you create such a thing? Plasma is extremely hostile."

A tight smile pulled Jelan's lips into a thin line. "Only when it is forced into a container it doesn't fit, sir."

"So you let it free?"

"Only a small amount of the molten energy is needed to band into the wrist contraption. It naturally bubbles into itself, so instead of forcing it to maintain its shape, I simply guided it through certain heat circulations while always holding a small leftover bit within the wristlet that it can suck back into. It took a bit of training with a neutralizing table, but I used enough of the energy that it wouldn't spurt everywhere and would hold its shape. Sort of like…spitting a spider web out of your hand."

"Interesting…" Arvalo's eyes flicked to Lucien. "I have been bothering you about a prototype. We would love samples for our army."

"It is Jelan's patent. She owns it."

That was news. She sucked in a breath and cleared her throat. "They're very basic at the moment…"

"They stopped a massive plasbomb, I can't imagine they're basic," Arvalo said.

"Well, that only has to do with plasma reacting to other plasma and whether other particles come in contact between their reaction. When there aren't any interferences, a plashield covering a bomb would negate any explosions. Destroy itself. As you…saw."

Like when I stopped you as you were beheading the old Emperor.

Arvalo held no animosity. His brows merely raised. He used to be the head of Plastech Industries as City Commander, but he was by no means a legitimate Plastech. One of his sons—Jelan presumed the older-looking one with a feline gaze and feathery bangs—took over the company. She had no doubt Arvalo still had his say, though.

"It is wonderful, I'm sure we would all love a demonstration at Plastech Industries. Perhaps even a deal could be struck on the patent," Arvalo mused. The older-looking son nodded.

After that, each Commander gave updates on their positions and advancements within the city. It droned on, and Jelan only half-listened.

It was bizarre. While each Commander sat at this table and shared curt conversations, they also all had gangs full of illicit activities. Things unspoken when Alexia went on about her renowned surgeons, or Pofer talking about updating the Glide train. Beneath those professional gazes, things unsaid lurked. Lucien's gardia primarily maintained safety and order, Covokai's for security, Alexia's for drugs, Pofer's for a large list of criminal things and laundering money, although they could never quite prove it, and Arvalo, of course, for power. Lucien still had enough going on to point to the literal Emperor having his own gang.

"The open vacancy of City Commander procures my interest." Arvalo folded his hands as the servants cleared the table. "I have been training my second eldest to replace my previous role. Should make the transition easy—"

"Nepotism doesn't look good, Arvalo," Alexia snarled softly. "Let your son do other things."

Arvalo's expression darkened. A different son had looks that could kill as everyone's gazes flicked to her.

A cold, cruel voice emitted from Arvalo. "As opposed to your nephew getting top marks at the medical university?"

Venara stiffened. Alexia's long nails dug into the table. "That's completely different than handing an important, progressive role to your son on a silver platter."

"Is it now?"

"Completely. Different."

"Even when a residency spot at the top hospital in the city has been reserved for him in the last year?"

Alexia exhaled sharply. "He has potential. He is extremely smart."

"He cheated on a test."

"And?"

Arvalo waved to the far end of the table. "And he continues to be a problem, even when there is a gun to his head."

Alexia paled.

A plascreen drifted up from a tiny slot. A video played. It showed the background of a dim, expensive room. It wasn't hard to know it was an apartment in the North—Calesal's lights glimmered in the background. The time was shown on a clock perfectly positioned before the camera.

In the center sat a young boy around Jelan's age. He had Alexia's fair skin, inky hair, but different-colored eyes that Jelan couldn't make out. He was sweating. Shaking.

A man wearing all black held a plasgun to his temple.

Arvalo waved his phone to show the rest of the table the video call. The person holding the gun showed another phone with the same running time.

"I don't care about your nepotism," Arvalo went on. Servants entered the room and placed papers in front of each commander. "I want you to sign off my on my son as the next City Commander of Plastech and Media. The other papers are for military expansion and revenue shifts to increase weapon production for Veceras."

"Stop this," Alexia pleaded. "Stop this or I will burn your Empire to the ground."

"Sign it and I'll stop it. I need the approval of each City Commander to expand the army and weaponry. You will watch your nephew live—"

"This is ridiculous," Lucien snarled. "You can't blackmail—"

"I can't with you, no." Arvalo looked to Lucien. "Because the very thing you care about is dead."

Lucien tensed. Everyone silenced.

Jack Marin's absence suddenly became a giant in the room.

Jelan couldn't keep up, but when Jack was finally mentioned, the energy shifted. Alexia released a mix of a sob and an inhale. Venara rubbed at her temples. Covokai wiped his eyes. Pofer rolled his.

And Lucien…

"Jack Marin's death was a long time coming," Pofer said.

And yet he still garnered a reaction, worlds away. A life away.

"He ruined this city," Arvalo said. "It's only best he is dead and stays dead. Or else he would threaten everything about Veceras."

Covokai clenched his pen. Pofer snorted and scribbled his signature on each paper. Alexia cursed.

Lucien stopped breathing.

Jelan brushed his knee. He didn't blink.

A paper slid in front of her.

"And this…" Arvalo waved his hand. "Is the contract for you to sign over the patent of your plashield to Plastech Industries." He pointed to the screen. "Or else this young man ceases to exist."

A servant held out a pen.

Jelan's entire world began to collapse around her. Her heart thudded against her ribcage and breathing became harder. She'd been so good about her exercises and medicine, but with a lurch, she was reaching for her purse and scrambling for her inhaler.

Lucien was suddenly there, rubbing her back, whispering in her ear, "Breathe. Deep and slow. It's going to be okay. Sign the document and we will get out of here."

"Skies, Arvalo, what have you done?" Covokai snapped.

Jelan sucked in her medicine and closed her eyes. She focused on her breath. Went far, far away from the evil chaos at this table. Lucien continued to rub her back. Only when she calmed down and found a lift in her lungs, did Jelan open her eyes again.

"You…" Alexia shook her head. "You're going to pay for this."

Pofer had already handed his papers to the servants and chugged back his wine. "Stop caring about people, Javez, and life gets easier.

"Well, I'm not surprised by you, since you're bought out by all the fucking plasma industries," Alexia gritted. "You going to buy more women with all that money in your pocket?"

Jelan met Lucien's concerned gaze. "If I sign this, everything I've worked for…"

"We will find a way," he whispered. "I promise we will. For now, I need to get you out of here safely."

Lucien signed each and every paper. Waited. Watched as Jelan's hand shook and she handed over her dream to a sneering Arvalo. Her signature was a messy scrawl. It hardly showed her name. She fought the tears at the back of her eyes.

Once everything was signed, Arvalo spoke into the phone, "Release him."

A loud, relieved sob escaped Alexia as the gun was removed from her nephew's head.

Lucien drew Jelan from her chair. The rest of the commanders stood. Jelan's gaze caught Mai's, and for some reason, the daughter of Arvalo didn't have a scowl on her face. No, it was…pity.

If not, remorse.

As if she'd been through this manipulative shit her whole life, and she was sad to watch it happen yet again.

Arvalo regarded them with an icy smile. "Pleasure doing business with you."

And Lucien returned that gaze, his voice dark. "This means war, Arvalo."

"So be it."

7

The Sixth Sin

Before Violet slammed into the next world, something unusual happened.

She stayed within the portaling realm.

In each transfer between worlds, an assault of bright light blinded her, then it dipped to black. She called it the *zap*—the resetting shockwave to her consciousness that inevitably lessened the load of switching literal realms. It's why her senses took time. Halted. Why she could never breathe in the first moments. Why she never landed on her feet and careened harshly into whatever waited for her.

This time the light didn't fade. The *zap* didn't occur. No resetting of her consciousness—no, she stayed fully aware. She clutched her side, hand dripping with blood as she desperately glanced around. The pain was minimal, but she guessed it was due to this realm. Her body wasn't completely here, only *that* part of her…the Vanisher part.

Was she lost? Did the transfer malfunction?

She wanted to panic, but she couldn't because this realm was warm. Really warm. And comforting. A slice of solitude that was hard to come by nowadays. It was only her breath. Her thoughts. Her thrashing heart.

There was no landscape. It was an iridescent realm without ending or beginning. There was no sky or earth. She merely stood, but it wasn't on ground per se. Nor was she floating.

She didn't hold the Iris anymore. She couldn't walk, but there wasn't anything to walk to.

Deep within, underneath the shedding skin of her old self, the answer became obvious. She'd entered the plane Yarrow had shown her. When he'd pressed that glowing hand to her chest, this realm appeared, but there had been millions of tethers within—millions of worlds and spaces.

She craned her neck. Behind her, a cluster of blue, ever-twisting ribbons stretched into the non-existent sky and down to the non-existent ground. It was more scarce than the last time. She'd guess hundreds of tethers now. Her energy waned. She glimpsed a couple things within different ones; a bright burst of red-orange molten stuff, a marked pad atop a building, a dark road speckled with a few lights, an abandoned square with a well, and a crowded street with brilliant colors and a language plastered on signs she couldn't read.

The next world, but different pockets of it. Violet squinted, and as those tethers twisted, more options arose; as if there were broad points of entry, but if she decided to shift through the blue ribbons and peer into each one, she could detail her drop.

Did that mean she only had the vitality for these places? The logic made sense. She was severely wounded. Her breath shallow. She desperately wanted to close her eyes—

No. She needed a doctor, or at least a room to tend to her wound. Or even just a peaceful place to die.

When she twisted her body and lifted her glowing hand to one of those tethers, it jumped forward, sensing her choice. The small village with some lights. Her fingertips warmed as she brushed the ribbons—a quaint kitchen of wood and dusty pots, a roaring hearth with a rocking chair, the dull window of a shop.

She heaved a great breath and wrapped her fingers around one. Warmth blossomed down her arm.

She pulled.

Her navel jerked and air sucked out of her lungs.

She crashed. Wood splintered. A pop sounded in her ears. Her shoulder flared with pain and Violet bit her mouth, dampening her cry. She hit a hard floor and slid, thumping her head.

An object fell and smacked her throbbing shoulder.

She choked a cry. "Shit, shit, shit, shit." Tears blurred her vision as her right shoulder hung a little lower than the other.

The room snapped her back to reality. The pain in her shoulder and hip became unbearable. Violet tried to sit up, but her bloody hand faltered and collapsed. She grappled for her hip wound, her fingers wrapping the arrow sticking out.

Sweat licked her skin. She looked around the dim room; an office with simple, handmade furniture—one of which was the desk she plummeted onto, now smashed—the picture of a family hanging on a wall, and books scattered everywhere. It was an organized mess. A businessperson? A—a—

Violet tilted her head back as a shallow exhale released. She slumped farther into the wall. The wounds became dull embers. Black dotted her vision. *No-no-no-no…*

I have to see him.

Jack was alive.

But death gripped her.

Violet's lips pulled back as a sob escaped. Salty tears slipped into her mouth. Skies, she wanted to give up. The pain was too much. A shiver ran down her spine. Her heart palpitated.

"We can do this," she breathed, then looked down at the arrow.

Her backpack kept her from crumpling. She adjusted herself, but fire flared within her shoulder, and she bit a cry, slumping back.

No—no, I have to see him.

Her hand slapped the shelf, and she grunted as she hauled herself up. She swayed, dizzy, but straightened enough to let the pack slip off her bad shoulder. She held a cry as it swung, hitting her injured hip. She collapsed with a thump. Dust plumed. She sneezed and sobbed again. Dust? Did that mean this place was abandoned? No one… not anyone to help?

Violet barely held her head up as she fumbled with a zipper and opened the backpack. One bottle of antiseptic, a wad of cloth, a roll of bandages, string, four needles, and a lighter. She desperately wished Rio were here, but in Sloth he'd taught her and Anaya medical care during lazy days on the ship. Treating knife wounds, stitching basic cuts, and beating a fever. Violet didn't know she'd be using those new skills on herself.

With shaky, bloody fingers, she pulled the medical pack out. Then a stolen bottle of rum. She ripped the pack open with her teeth, and the contents spilled free onto the floor. She unscrewed the antiseptic, then tore her clothes away from the space. She grabbed the small dagger—still covered in dark blood from Renell— and placed it across her lap. It took a bit of work, but she managed to disinfect it, then with a giant breath, she poured a little over the wound.

She cried into her lip. Uncorked the rum and chugged deeply. After a few deep breaths, she inspected the wound. Only a sliver of the arrow and its head remained, but she got lucky. The plasarrow didn't burst at the impact, probably because it impaled her just above her hip meeting fat instead of bone. That was probably why, she told herself. She just got skivvin' lucky.

*Fuck this fucking luck and the fucking arrow and the fucking Mers and this fucking world and the fucking Worldbreaker…*her curses made her feel slightly better.

Violet shoved a scrap of her shirt into her mouth, took the blade, and carefully dug it into the wound. Blinking away her tears, growling into her gag, she felt for the tip of the arrow and nudged it up. After a bit of working and powering through the massive dizzy spells that assaulted her, the arrowhead loosened. Her muffled scream bounced around the room. When the arrow was as loose as she could make it, she yanked it out.

Violet blinked out of consciousness for a moment, but when she came back to, she sensed the weight of the arrowhead in her hand. She chucked it to the side and grabbed a wad of cloth to stopper the wound. Her blood had already slowed its course, abnormally fast at that, but she didn't care. She assumed she didn't hit anything important. Huffing deep breaths through her nose, she ran a lighter over the needle and began to stitch.

The needle was nothing. She barely felt it. Another splash of antiseptic there, and mumbled curses and prayers of no infection here, it was stitched, wrapped with heavy gauze, and had minimal bleeding.

Violet took a long, heavy chug of rum. Then she put a cigarette, bloodied from her hands, between her lips and lit it up.

She sighed back, inhaling deeply, and watching as the smoke billowed from her mouth. It trickled up to the wooden ceiling, flowed along, before sliding against the dirty windows.

Her lids closed. A little rest, then she would deal with her shoulder. Sling it until someone could stick it back into the socket. For now, she was content with the warmth of alcohol and the haze of smoke.

The door flung open.

Violet cracked an eye. "About skivvin' time." She took another drag.

A man and woman stared—wide-eyed, white-skinned, and horrified.

Violet knew she was a sight to behold; blood everywhere, hair matted, shirt ripped off, revealing a bra with sweat marks. She huffed a laugh and pointed to her shoulder, her smoke between her fingers. "Can you help?"

The woman muttered in a different language. The man glanced at the broken desk, then toward Violet, shaking his head.

"I just need someone to pop my shoulder back in," she said.

"How did you…" the man spoke in her language, "Where did you come from?"

She adjusted herself and gasped at the pain. "Just help me, I'll leave right after."

The man rushed forward while the woman ran back into the hallway. He assisted her from the floor and to the couch, being mindful of her bandaged hip. "Did you treat it yourself?"

"Yes," Violet said.

He inspected it. "Good work."

"I learned from someone who does better work, but the skiv attacked me, so I had to make do." She gestured to her strewn supplies. "Do you know medical stuff?"

"Our son…" He shook his head. "He passed away, but this was his office. He taught us a lot. Was the first doctor in our town."

"That's nice."

"Yes." The man looked at her shoulder. "It popped out clean, but it will hurt going back in."

"Fine." She chugged more rum. "I'm ready when you are."

The woman returned with a pail of water and fresh towels. She got to work cleaning up the blood, first on Violet's body, then the floor.

"I'll…I have clothes," Violet said as she caught the woman's gaze. "Can you help me change?"

The woman nodded, but her expression shifted. Brows furrowed, she stepped closer.

The man braced Violet's shoulder—

But his wife traced Violet's cheeks, down a line beneath her eyes. The woman saw. Her face plastered with horror, she gasped, "Vanisher."

"No," Violet said quickly, offering a strained smile. "Just marks. Birthmarks. Don't worry."

The man paused. Hesitated. He mumbled to the woman in their language before turning back to Violet. "You will want to bite something."

Violet wadded her shirt and shoved it back in her mouth. The man braced her shoulder. The woman merely held her face, still clearly disturbed. "One moment."

Violet held her gaze as the man shoved her shoulder back into place.

A sickening pop cleaved the air, and Violet's vision blurred. She weakly screamed into the cloth. *Don't pass out. Don't pass out.* Nausea roiled. She swallowed her bile and spit out the gag. "Thank…you…"

"Help her change," the man instructed the woman. He checked Violet's shoulder once more before turning toward the door. "You will leave once you are changed. You swear it?"

Violet swallowed. "I swear."

He left. The woman hesitated but slowly peeled Violet's ruined clothes off, wiped the blood, and helped her dress. It took a lot of maneuvering and groaning, but eventually Violet stood in a mix of clothes from Lust and Sloth. Dark stretchy pants, a simple, loose button-up shirt, a tank top underneath, her knife sheath from Calesal which she filled, a belt, thick socks and a pair of boots. She wrapped Isolo's leathers around her hands and pulled a sweater over her head. She reached into her bag for anything else—

Her heart twinged as she touched the small pouch where Gwen's broken blade lay, a piece missing.

Gone.

"It is colder than that," the woman said. "But…" She shook her head. "No…no… I cannot."

"Cannot what?"

Sorrow grew in the woman's expression. A fight occurred behind her sallow gaze that slowly dilated. The woman's lips curved into a smile; dark, glittering. Violet stopped breathing. The woman lifted a hand, want and yearning slathered across her face—

Fuck.

The woman smacked her cheek. "No." She ran out of the room.

"Greed," Violet muttered. "*Fuck.*"

She needed to get *out*. Having Cyran and his cronies after her was one thing, but in his home world, where the population probably praised or hated or feared him, a prize was still a prize.

And great rewards could come from handing her over.

She quickly adjusted her sweater so it acted as a sling, and limp by limp she hurried out of the room.

Fuck this fucking world, she snarled in her head. Cabinets opened and closed downstairs, followed by sharp whispers. Violet passed an ajar door filled with jackets. She shrugged into a baggy one, shoved a hat over her head and piled her hair into it. Wrapping a scarf around her neck, Violet listened for any movement from the couple, but they seemed to be whisper-arguing, unaware.

The stairs creaked as she descended. She looked for the sturdier spots, and when she reached the bottom, the low glow of light met the rough leather of her boots.

The scratchy language of Greed filled the kitchen next to the stairs. The woman waved toward the ceiling, while the man shook his head, then rubbed at his face. The woman pointed to the window—outside.

The front door, her escape, lay just a few steps ahead. When they turned their backs, she stepped over the light and back into the shadows.

The minute her boots met the welcome mat beneath, the unmistakable sound of barking dogs filled the tense silence.

Violet flung herself out of the house. She stumbled down the porch, her hip flaring in pain, but her panic overrode it. Bitter cold met her cheeks, and she pulled the collar of the jacket up. *It's just wild dogs. Act normal. Don't bring attention.* She needed to find shelter for the night, then she'd be safe.

A few moments to close her eyes.

The man and woman's house extended to a muddy road with tall poles and plaslights dancing in glass atop—like the one she'd seen in the tethers. Gloomy streetlights along an equally gloomy road scattered with quaint wooden homes. Violet whipped her head around, listening, searching. Her fingers brushed her plasblade's hilt.

Skies, it was so quiet. No signs of life, but the dog's barking grew louder, and the air crackled with…

Static.

Dark, nausea-inducing static.

She dove for the side of the house as a bright flash appeared in the middle of the road. A lone figure, tall and dressed neatly in black, halted.

No backtalk. No rages. Now's not the time for revenge.

But Violet's memory slammed into her, taking her back to Lust. Back to when this man—*Captain Zavar*—laughed while Rio screamed. While she vomited blood. While Jack tried to stab her.

She would never forget Zavar's smile, though. In those last few moments, when her eyes had dipped to the dagger tip glistening from Jack's chest, to the haunted, satisfied smile of Zavar. She played it over and over, building her rage when sleep didn't find her. When she bleakly stared into the endless waters of the Citran seas, sipping rum, and pondered all the ways she'd make him hurt. Make him scream. Make him wish he'd never touched Jack Marin.

In the dim light, Zavar turned. His inky hair shifted. Hands in the coat pockets, his mono-lid eyes slid along the road, and his full mouth twisted into that vile smirk.

She jerked, pulse pounding, and clenched her hand to keep from activating her plasblade.

"My dogs will find you, little Vanisher," he crooned, voice deep and sultry. "But I thought I'd do some hunting myself."

Skies, she wanted to lob his head off. Wanted to watch plasma burn that stupid smile.

"I smell your blood," he said, taking a stroll down the road in her direction. She pressed farther into the shadows. "I heard you got a little injury. I am happy the stupid Pirate Queen managed to do her job right this time. Just enough to wound you and slow you down, but not enough to end you, because I'm going to do that."

Ice rushed within her veins. She clenched her shaking hands. They didn't shoot her to stop her, but to track her.

Barking littered the air. The screaming horn of a train sounded in the distance. The little town turned off its lights and closed its blinds as Zavar walked. He paid them no mind. She wanted the wall of the house to swallow her. She hoped the new clothes masked her scent, but the blood from her wound slowly leaked down her leg.

Zavar neared the house, eyes roaming. Brief currents of black lightning littered his shoulders, and her stomach roiled as she remembered what a touch of that power felt like. She looked around, hoping, praying a plan might come to mind—

The train horn grew louder. She whipped her head to the left. Behind the house was a fence, and behind that fence were boxes of goods stacked on pallets. Beyond that, rail tracks.

Violet edged toward them. Her foot creaked on wood.

Zavar paused.

She held her breath.

A smile broke out on his face. He turned in her direction—

The front door of the house she'd escaped fractured into pieces, and a black dog shrouded in dark mist bounded into the mud, a hand in its mouth.

"Good boy," Zavar said. "You found the helpers. They should have known better."

That hand…wrinkly and pale. Male. A hand that had popped her shoulder back in. The dog spat it out at Zavar's feet, and Violet gaped. It splattered into mud. Zavar kicked it away. The dog turned back to the house, growling.

A shriek tore through the space. The woman ran outside covered in blood and gore. The night swallowed her cries. She tripped and fell to her knees as another wail tore from her. More dogs barked from inside the house. The horrible sound of ripping echoed.

Zavar turned to the woman and cocked his head. His devilish smile grew. He sauntered to her. "Look at you, betraying the Master."

"My husband, *my husband…*" Tears stained her face. "They ate him."

"Of course, they did. You two helped her. Everyone knows to report any unusual appearances to the Fringe."

"I—I didn't know."

"Yes, you did." Zavar roamed around her, hands still in his pockets. "Candidates don't show up here, but *she* managed to. And you helped her. If only you'd turned her over, you might have been spared."

"I only cleaned the blood," the woman muttered. "I—"

"I need the fucking blood for my hounds."

Zavar's hand moved fast. It left his pocket, covered in lightning, and wrapped the woman's throat. She shrieked, trembling as Zavar lifted her off the ground. He rolled his eyes. "This is what will happen if you don't turn yourself over! Everyone you touch, everyone who looks at you, who dares help you, will die. Maybe mostly by me, but some even by you."

Black lightning licked his arm, down it, until it collared the woman. She croaked an inhuman sound. A dying sound. Blood leaked from her mouth as her skin turned a horrible shade of purple before her flesh began to slough off her bones, and she crumbled beneath Zavar's grip.

Violet booked it. Limped. Stumbled. Ran. She didn't know. Adrenaline pushed her, and the minute her boots slapped the mud loudly, barking followed.

Zavar laughed into the cold night. "I see you!"

The silver of her plasblade burst out, then flared a brilliant light blue. She reached the fence and cut a hole through it. The barking grew louder, as did Violet's panic. She vaulted for the pallets and slashed. Food spilled out. Firewood.

And then there lay a tank of liquid.

Violet stabbed the sword within.

A strong, oily smell assaulted and threw her back to the Farm in Gluttony. Ahnsa. It spilled onto the ground. She dodged out of the way. Sparks burst from her plasblade.

One flew off.

And ignited the oil. It razed the ground, following the ahnsa. The dogs leapt through the fire, but the minute they touched it, the mist of their coats shrouded in flames, and they burst into canine explosions.

A scream of fury stripped the air. "You bitch!"

She gave a frightful cackle. "So I'm told, skiv!"

The train horn shrilled, growing closer. Its speed vibrated the tracks, the ground. She maintained her footing. A light blared from the front, and within a breath, the first car rolled past. Her legs pumped as she raced along the tracks, hilting her plasblade.

The train passed, and with her last burst of energy, Violet launched herself to it, grabbing a ladder. She held on for her life. Her boots slipped on the bottom rung, and she wailed, swinging, squeezing a bar with her good arm. Sucking a heavy breath, she pulled her body flush with the ladder.

"Shit, *shit,*" she moaned, unbelieving.

Zavar roared into the night. She whipped her head back toward the fiery ahnsa as he waved his lightning and stepped through it. His eyes lifted and met hers. Hair escaped from her ponytail, blowing everywhere and catching in the slight smile pulling at her lips.

He pointed a lightning-covered finger at her. She ducked. A bolt slammed into the car door next to her, turning the wood black. She laughed. Enraged, his arms burned with Vanisher glow, but as he glared at the train, and as distance separated them, he screamed again. The light at his arms burned out. Violet never became more thankful that moveable places were unavailable for Vanishers.

Within minutes, he became a distant blur. A flash of light—he teleported.

The door to the car gaped next to her. Inside was empty, abandoned. With the last of her exertion, she flung herself in. And when she collapsed, she closed her eyes.

And then the beautiful darkness of sleep overwhelmed her.

8

THE TWINS

"**WELCOME TO THE TWIN CITIES,** Jack Marin."

Four whole months of logic, combat, weapons, strategy, powers, and tattoos, and Jack Marin stepped off the gleaming silver ship onto the landing pad of Cyran's main fortress.

The air was bitter, but a warmer welcome from what he left at Honnrak Castle. The slight smell of burning asphalt bit his nostrils. Birds cawed overhead. Night began to descend, and three moons lifted on the horizon while a few clouds dotted the darkening sky. The wind brushed the curls that escaped his bun. His fellow comrades exited the landing bridge with him. Zavar had disappeared the night before, only shoving Jack against the wall when he dared to ask, and vanishing with a sneer. He remained missing, but Jack was thankful for the breather.

Dressed in fine leather uniforms, capes, black boots, gloves, and a scarf, a new air of power graced Cyran's capital. He was aware of the stares—guards, servants, the new-faced captains. One by one, they all fell to a knee. All except Cyran, who stood as a striking statue, the only movement was a breeze tussling his limestone hair.

The sight of him gave the aura of death. The true conqueror and breaker of seven worlds. Jack met his gaze, and once they stepped onto the cement, he fell to his knee.

The ruffle of capes told Jack the captains behind him had done the same.

"Rise," Cyran commanded.

Those on the pad did. Servants hurried into the ship to collect their bags, while guards flanked Cyran. He jutted his chin to the cities at his back. "Your new home."

A cool calm settled over Jack as he stood and lifted his gaze.

The Twin Cities were the pinnacle point, the capital, in the world of Greed. Cyran ruled the entire planet. Five nations made of ice, charcoal, water, lava, and mountains, all pillaged and controlled, targeted and reaped by the Worldbreaker. After five-hundred years, Cyran created his own empire in Greed and expanded it through the Sins. He reigned as emperor. The overlord.

The Worldbreaker.

Jack took a steady breath at the expanse of onyx-glassed skyrises. A futuristic Calesal was his first thought. A *darker* Calesal was the second. The endless cities filled the valley of gray hills, buildings and roads and slivers of parks. Glimpses of gold speckled the landscape: the Order of Avaritia's cathedrals. Airships dotted the skies above, zooming around the buildings and heading to destinations beyond the wall of mountains.

Holding an air of intensity and brutality, the alps were sharp, cut from lava rock and black stone. Roads carved through, along with high-speed train tracks, and then in the farthest distance, Mount Prava stood, bubbling lava down its cracked landscape. That lava and heat generated portions of the city, while plaslights added color, and ahnsa elongated power. Greed was a mixture of all the best things from the other worlds—minus the people, because Cyran didn't like the people. Only the resources. Only things that benefited him.

Hallow slumbered next to Cyran's fortress in the upper left corner, but where Jack stood, some skyrises barely touched. The road was a blur below, holding brief glimpses of colorful motorbikes, gleaming metal, and people who looked like smashable ants. A floating sensation filled his chest. Elation. There was something about looking *down* on people, on a city, on one's creation and watching like a god from above. It called to Jack.

He could be a god, too.

That enticed him. Called to him. Brutalized his dreams and erased the idea that he could want anything else but that. The blue-eyed girl was a blur after the months of training, even though a small part of him still mourned her death.

He brushed the pocket of his lapel and felt for the turquoise dagger's indent. He pressed on it.

Violet was dead.

Along with Anaya and Rio. His life before was gone. There was no next world, no going home, no hope. Only monstrous darkness that he slipped into a little more each day.

After the initial slaughtering of the seven hooded figures, Zavar and Serwa brought their assassination assignments to Honnrack Castle for Jack to kill. He first let them sit in a dark room as he prowled in his camouflage before he appeared. After that bit of terror, he experimented with different murderous ways; squeezing necks so hard they burst into trachea bits and blood, reading their minds as they cried for mercy while he shoved a dagger into their chest.

Jack twisted his hands as a smile quirked his lips.

He was always good at snapping necks.

Masar sidled up next to him. "Impressive, right?"

The city. Not his neck-snapping abilities. Jack nodded. "How many people live here?"

"Oh, nearly fifty million, I think?" Masar pointed to the airships. "Refugees from Zoncolla." The ice nation. "A pain in my side, I'll tell you that. Zoncolla is useless. They got their face tattoos and yeah, maybe they can be shirtless in the cold, but that's about it. It's not our fault they can't get their crime under control. And then there's the Harmas nation." The coal one. The miners who like their knives and can harden certain parts of their body. "Who aren't allowed in the city because the Order of Avaritia forbids their beliefs." Masar elbowed Jack. "Let's go. Your welcoming awaits, oh ferocious one."

Jack turned to the waiting captains.

Anticipation rose at seeing most of his old comrades and enemies from his commander days in Calesal. He was the new and pristine weapon being thrust into their faces. Most probably thought he'd been killed for the gardia wars, never having to hear his name again. But for the past four months, even though he lived in isolation, it seemed the news had spread.

Cyran led the way, black cape billowing behind him. They stood stiffly on a lift, and with a gush of air, it descended into the levels below. Once they were within the walls of his ultramodern fortress, the only sounds were the soft, uniform steps of boots and a buzzing tension. Jack evened his breath and hardened his face.

Greed was a worldly mix of the past and future. As they strutted the halls, Jack was surprised at how clean, open, and neutral everything was. The castle held the same presence of Cyran: ominous yet welcoming. A giant contradiction. The walls transitioned from slate-gray stone to black wooden ridges. Black carpets decorated the marble floors. Plaslight sconces lit the walls—a surprise, considering Cyran had every ounce of ahnsa fuel at his disposal, and plaslights had to be replaced yearly. The lights only gleamed white, and that showed the incredible amount of money and patience Cyran had, because pure-white plasma was mined from the deepest points in the earth and had to be tubed in a specific tempered-glass container. It littered the North—because the North could afford it, but as Calesal trickled from North to the Mid to the South, the plaslights glowed in all kinds of colors.

Bloodhounds stood straight in every passing hallway, eyes flicking at each passerby. No one was an intruder. Certain bloodhounds knew the clearance for particular areas of the castle, and Jack would hear a low growl if he treads close to somewhere he wasn't allowed. Zavar had rubbed that piece of information in his face—he trained them and managed them, on top of his assassination duties for the Worldbreaker.

They continued until the same bitter air met his face as the headaching hallways opened into a massive atrium. Giant columns lined their path, donned with enormous black and gold banners etched with Cyran's symbol—a circle with seven incisions and a star in the middle. It mocked him, laughed at him; a fallen soldier once again commanded by a higher power.

His pulse pounded loudly in his ears. He moved through the atrium to a cresting wall filled with windows.

And as Jack Marin stepped into the bleak sunlight, as he braced himself for this display of authority, his pride sank further. He tightened his expression once his gaze slid from the balcony to the gathering of armies beyond. The sea of obsidian stunned him.

Jack lifted his chin. Primal power flowed in his veins as he remembered what had caused the loss of his family and changed the trajectory of his life. Remembered what stole his innocence and slapped chains on his wrists. What made his memories feel like a fantasy. He circled back when he faltered before his ego—he needed to keep his head up. To play the game.

The Vanisher Fringe lined one side of the sport-field-sized balcony, while the other was made of captains, commanders, and Cyran's trusted followers.

"Welcome, brethren, for today is a glorious day."

Cyran's cold voice boomed everywhere, and within moments the army roared. The Worldbreaker smiled.

"From monstrous animal hybrids to controlled, man-made soldiers, our scientists have manipulated biology in ways no world has done before. I've seen hundreds of realms, and this feat we've achieved could destroy them all."

Keyword: *we*. First step in loyalty. Make them feel like they've contributed. So the armies roared again. They raised their fists and celebrated *their* achievements.

"We will create our own galaxy, our own universe, our own place among the cosmos. Against all other worlds, we will reign true and top. We've shredded mankind and made it our own."

Next, remind them of their ambition, even if the ambition seems out of reach. Incomprehensible. Use big words like *universe* and turn other words into boring nuances like *mankind*. Create a drive for more.

They cheered again. It rippled down Jack's spine.

Cyran lifted his hands. "And now, we've successfully created the first sentient, completely man, biological hybrid of not one, not two, but *five* powerful species combined into one individual." His hands turned to Jack. "Spared from death and given a new, powerful life, Jack Marin is the first of many successes."

A soft thump. Lightning tickled the back of Jack's neck. He spared a glance behind. Zavar fumed. Dirt speckled his chin, while dried blood lingered on his earlobe. He growled, "Step forward, mutt."

Jack's boots were heavy on his feet as he strutted up next to Cyran. The crowd flooded the space and mountains with calls of victory. Clapping ensued.

Cyran turned to Jack. "Now, for your last test."

Two Vanishers appeared. Jack faintly remembered them—the light-skinned twins who chased his group in Lust. Jodin and Yarrow. Jodin had long locs, a wide nose, and a septum piercing through it, while Yarrow carried short locs held back by a leather tie. His small mouth, high cheekbones, and wide-set eyes scowled at the prisoner caught between their hands. Jack stared at him for a long moment as a ripple went through his chest. But even though Yarrow glared at the captive, his gaze was out of focus. He slouched on his left leg, and when he clenched his left fist, Jack noticed the two missing fingers. Bandaged stumps replaced the pinky and ring finger.

They dropped the captive on the floor. Her black hair spilled from its braid. She grasped the stone and pushed up to her knees, lifting her gaze.

Jack didn't recognize the brown eyes or dirtied face.

"While we conquer these worlds, there are still those against us. This one was caught infiltrating our fortress, gathering information on our biosciences for her terrorist group so they can stop our dreams!"

The army booed.

The girl shook, but fear did not reach her eyes. A scar crawled down the side of her face, and he had the urge to trace it with his fingers, wondering what horrible thing she must have seen to receive that.

"Take care of her, Marin."

Jack drowned every sliver of his morality and emotions, until he became a simple vessel of muscle and bones. He stepped forward while calling the cool tingle of his camouflage.

Her brows furrowed as he disappeared. The crowd gasped. She sucked a breath. He drew closer. Studied her while he was safe from the crowd's watchful stares. His finger rose, and he did indeed trace that scar. "Must have hurt."

"Fuck you," she snarled, turning toward his voice.

Jack frowned and dropped his hand.

He knelt in front of her. It became their moment; him studying her every panicked movement, her searching for him. Jodin and Yarrow took steps back.

"We've heard rumors of you," she leered. A smile cracked her lips. "We know you're a monster."

Jack sighed. "This is less interesting than I thought you'd make it." He removed a dagger and let it show.

Her eyes darted to it. She laughed. "Give me one thing. Just one thing before you kill me."

Jack wrapped his other hand in her hair and stood, pulling her with him. He rested his chin on her shoulder as they faced Cyran's endless army. He let his camouflage flare out, and by the gasps, he became visible again. "What thing?"

"Show me your scar," she gritted.

"I can't. It's holding the blade meant for your throat."

"Not your candidate scar," she cackled. "The other one."

Jack froze. The blade weighed heavy and his palm tingled. "Why do you want to see it?"

"Because they're watching," she muttered so low, Jack leaned in. "And they wanted to know."

He brought the dagger to her neck. "Know what?"

She attempted to twist her head. "If it is true—if there really is one person in this entire universe whom you can't kill."

Time slowed. Cyran's gaze burned his back. *Every* gaze burned his skin. Sound ceased, leaving only his pulse crashing in his ears. He paused the blade, dropped it to the ground, then dragged his mouth along her neck. His surprise waned into anger. Protective, primal fury. "I'm going to make this hurt now."

The girl laughed, maniacal. "Pharos will come for you."

He ripped her head from her body. Blood spurted across his face.

Jack Marin felt the last of his skin shed, revealing the true, terrifying monster within. Except this monster was entirely built by Jack himself because…

Cyran pinned a badge to his armor and yelled,

"All hail, Captain of the Hybrid Division, Jack Marin!"

9

ᴘʜᴀʀᴏꜱ

Vɪᴏʟᴇᴛ'ꜱ ꜰᴏᴏᴛ ᴊᴏꜱᴛʟᴇᴅ. Hᴇʀ ᴄʜᴇᴇᴋ pressed against worn wood. Drool slipped from her mouth as she rolled, squeezing her eyes tight against the dull ache in her shoulder and hip.

"Get off my train, little shit!"

A hand wrapped around her ankle and yanked.

The wood slipped from underneath her, and her fingers met empty space. Eyes snapping open, Violet saw the blur of gravel before she smacked into the ground.

"No free rides," the man above her snapped.

She squinted against the sun at his back—grungy looking with his dark beard, torn hat, and long coat with a company insignia. The conductor, perhaps.

She clutched her bad arm to her chest and used the train's wheel to stand. "Sorry. I was kicked out of my house and had nowhere to go."

The conductor was nearly the same height as her, but he still glared down his nose and took in her state. "Did they try to kill you, too?"

"A nice stab here, dislocated shoulder there." Violet shrugged, wincing at the movement. "My father isn't a nice guy."

"Let me guess, tried to sell you?"

Violet plastered a frown. "Yeah, for…"

"Money, of course." The conductor rolled his eyes. "If you didn't look like shit, I bet you'd make a solid price."

Her eyes widened and she took a step back. "Look, I'm sorry for using your train—"

"I'm not gonna sell you, girl." He closed the car's compartment door with a loud slam. "The Twin Cities are that way, but don't go anywhere else but the Navru District. Got it? Lie low, cut your hair, change your appearance, and stuff like that. There are rumors of groups—safe groups—that can help. They'll find you eventually."

Violet furrowed her brows, nearly forgetting her lie based on how casual, how routine this advice seemed to be. "They'll find me?"

He regarded her expression. "Whether you're dead in an alley or locked up by the Order. They can't save everyone, but they'll find you." He frowned. "This world isn't made for women. Not like how it used to be."

Not many worlds are, she wanted to say. "Probably for the better if I end up dead, sounds like."

He leaned against the train. "You either fight and end up dead, or you don't fight and end up dead. Either way, you—"

"End up dead."

A chuckle. "There is a fight going on now—sure you heard about it. War in the Twin Cities…"

Violet nodded, pretending she knew.

"Be careful, it's bad. Stay in Navru and out of sight. Okay?"

She saluted him. "Yes, sir."

He looked at her incredulously.

"Please, my father will be looking for me." She feigned a frown. "Say you never saw me."

The conductor turned and waved. "Stay off the tracks. Turn around, and don't look back. Get yourself lost in the cities— but…" He motioned to the blood. "You can't leave any trace if you want to disappear. Not even a drop."

That seemed impossible for her to do. He didn't spare her another glance as he walked away, slamming the car doors closed and checking for other stragglers. Violet sucked in a deep breath and turned, pulling her hood up. She stepped through an opening between cars, careful with her bad leg. Only when her boots walked from gravel to grass did she lift her head.

Greed was a mountainous region, but different from the beauty of Gluttony. There was a dark allure to this world, embraced by the ragged mountains of black and circling two bright, mesmerizing cities within the middle. A dark-blue river separated them. Far beyond, a larger, more obtuse mountain stood taller than the rest, where blurry lines of red flowed.

Violet racked her brain. Runny red-orange rivulets…what was that? She couldn't remember from science class. The word was on the tip of her tongue…

She'd seen it within the tether before she teleported to Greed. "L…La…" The cold wind ripped through the grass, ruffling her hood. She sagged into her good leg.

"Lava," she breathed. "A volcano."

She wondered why the cities were built here. The volcano was miles and miles away, but one monstrous eruption would demolish this landscape. Perhaps Cyran enjoyed being close to a catastrophic event. Maybe it made his ego feel a bit better as he destroyed world after world, knowing his home world was close to the same destruction.

Violet's lip trembled. Her eyes dragged to the west, where a taller, spider-like structure hovered over the rest of the city. Cyran's fortress, she guessed. The highest, most prominent thing would make sense.

She glared at the dark, beautiful sight; the ragged tips of rocks followed by winking sunrays against the windows, the dark greenery of the plants that weathered the cold, the haunting mix of both ancient and modern, developed solely by the worlds he conquered.

She wanted to hate it. The cold wind bit her watery eyes. Her fingers grew tighter on her wound until pain blossomed. She wanted Greed to be ugly and despicable and villainous, not alluring and calming and provocative.

And as her eyes lingered on the Twin Cities and the first buildings she could reach across the pale plain, she wanted to hate everyone who lived here. To imagine they were all cruel and cunning like Cyran, and that they used others to get what they desired. Perhaps Greed made them that way, but from the other Sins, Violet knew that was a lie. The other Sins had good and bad but…

Weren't they all just victims? Her rational mind said.

She scoffed. The Crale in Gluttony weren't fucking victims.

And yet…there were some who didn't support the genocide and the Farm.

Violet snarled, "Then why didn't they *do* anything?"

Because they were victims.

The lines between good and evil blurred so much that a headache grew every time she tried to figure it out. Why couldn't it be easy? Why did some worlds have to like Cyran? Why was this city so pretty? Why was it all so skivvin' complicated?

Violet unbuttoned her jacket and pulled back the rim of her pants. The bandage covering her arrow wound leaked with blood, nearly all of it red. It had slowed but oozed regularly enough to be a concern. Another thought hit her—

The arrow had poison in it. Mers were adept with poison, although they couldn't necessarily give it to each other since they had a knack for sniffing it out, but on Violet it would obviously work. It wouldn't stop bleeding until she received real medical help.

A heavy sob escaped her.

The dusty room, the cigarette smell, warm hands that popped her shoulder back in, bloody rags, the horrible barking, cold wind, sharp pain, Zavar's taunting words, and the wife's screech.

Violet forced the tears down. The train released a blaring horn and chugged away. Cold wind bit her chapped lips, making her teeth chatter.

Alone. The uncontrollable, little mistake meant for death. Could she walk into this city and risk others? Cyran wanted *her*. He wouldn't care if Anaya and Rio died in the process, so despite the improvised separation in Sloth, she was thankful to leave them behind. Keller would watch over them, Maji included. They could handle themselves.

When she turned her thoughts back to the couple, the guilt faded. It became small. Bearable.

She remembered the woman's fingers tracing the lines below her eyes. Violet rubbed at the same spot, feeling only smooth, dry skin. The conductor didn't mention anything, but Violet still bent down and stuck her fingers in the dirt, then rubbed it on her cheeks.

She needed to be careful about choosing her next place to stay, but if she wanted to truly survive, she needed to heal. To rest. To eat. Change her appearance. And figure out a plan to find Jack and Reed.

Jack. His name was on her lips. *Jack* was *alive.* Her heart picked up its beat, both thrilled and terrified because what did that mean? She lifted her gaze to the city—was he here? Breathing the same air as her?

Why…*why* in the seven worlds would Jack be alive? She had watched his eyes dim. His body crumple to the floor. The life leave. Tears sprang and she furiously wiped them. She *saw* him die. He would have had to be purposely revived to come back.

Why did the infamous ex-City Commander, gardia leader, and pain in her ass remain alive?

She took a slight step forward. Her boot crunched the grass.

It was to catch her, right? But if Zavar is stalking little villages with his gross dogs looking for her, then why would Jack matter? Violet rolled her eyes. It shouldn't be *so* difficult to find her. She only has two working limbs, for skies' sake.

She was not at the top of Cyran's priority list. His regime was ruthless and gigantic, and she was only a speck within it. She hardly knew him, but what she did know with ruling, entitled, arrogant, and powerful people, is that you can only fly underneath their radar for so long. Cyran probably thought her easy. Zavar probably gave her an escape because he liked the chase. She'd play them for some dimwitted Calesal Souther they thought she was.

Until she sat with a cigarette, Jack and Reed by her side, while she laughed and watched that stupidly pretty fortress burn.

"I'm here, you fucker," she said with a smile as she began walking toward the Twin Cities.

❀❀❀

The city looked a lot different within than out.

The first thing Violet thought was that it was similar to Calesal. Tall skyrises, busy streets, a diverse population with cars and motorbikes and more. But each Twin City had its own vibrant districts. On the left, closest to Cyran's fortress, lay Hallow. The right, Hanhii.

She went to Hanhii—the city opposite her enemies.

Ships flew through the air. She stood in the middle of the sidewalk staring up in awe. Looks from others on the street broke her trance. She kept moving, hood nearly covering her eyes and scarf wrapped around her mouth. The roads and buildings extended for miles, but the idea that she could have a corner to pass out in, that there was a group who could help her, kept her going.

Once the streets grew a little dirtier and clothes a little more raggedy, she knew Navru was close. The Navy Rust District, based on the signs. Navy clearly for the river it banked, rust for the tacky orange color spreading along any sheet of metal that made up a building, door, or gutter. That's the meaning she made up in her head, at least. A handful of buildings with giant screens similar to Souther's Square caught her attention. A familiar place. She desperately hurried, limping, while blood oozed down her leg, staining her boots.

The moment she slunk onto the streets, she saw the Sin. It smacked her in the face. Gambling markets, great shows of wealth, and even the flickering videos on plascreens waggled fingers, entrancing the viewers with riches.

Power.

Control.

She passed all types of people, bars, and establishments that fed off the desire for more. She sidled down a sidewalk, attempting to hide her limp as much as she could, while glimpsing the drug exchanges, then the snort and turnaround of a person immediately wanting *more*. A circus-type show beckoned onlookers with pretty acrobats, and they cried for *more*. A man cradled bags spilling with cookies, snarling at others for *more*. A woman sitting on a stoop admired the rings that swallowed her fingers, until, as Violet passed, the woman gasped and pointed to a brief bit of naked skin, and then she stood, clearly wanting *more*. A shop owner shrieked while a thief raced down the street, nearly careening into Violet, a smile on their face. The rush enticed her, too—she didn't blame thievery. But it sucked her into stealing *more*, until she spent one night in a Souther cell and she decided to keep it more lowkey. That was one too many nights spent listening to drunk men piss themselves.

As the streets shadowed with the setting sun, it grew frigid. Violet shivered within her coat. The people milled, but eyes flicked her way every now and then. Paranoia settled along her shoulders, hunching them. She wanted a disguise. Her longing almost convinced herself that her hair had turned blonde, or purple, or black. Skies, she just wanted a break. She wanted food, to heal, her friends, rest, a warm bed she could collapse in, and perhaps a life that wasn't in shambles—

You're becoming greedy.

The cool purr of the Sin bit her ears. Lodged in her throat like she was the one who spoke it. She froze. Bodies continued about. She panicked. Waited for that familiar darkness to descend over her vision and spiral her into the grasp of the Sin.

Turn to the blue storefront. You see those sweets? Don't you want them? Don't you taste them?

"What?" she gasped. The blue storefront rested ahead. A worker flipped a sign, showing that the bakery was closed. Violet ignored the rumble of her stomach and turned around. The sidewalk grew more crowded. Someone bumped her from behind.

"Watch it," a woman said, sparing her a nasty look.

A sweet. Nearly got you with just that. Most are easy. They want books and money and food and jewels. They want the basics. But those are trivial things. Boring things. What truly entices you? What more do you want, young Vanisher?

Wisdom oozed from its voice. An old, cunning tone reminiscent of Cyran, if not more ancient. Violet didn't feel the haze—no, as far as she could tell, her consciousness was still clear. But while she could still see, the voice crowded her thoughts. Made it impossible to escape.

So she played.

I want to disappear. She exhaled, and a cloud of breath puffed out. *No, I want to blend in, to stay hidden.*

And what are you willing to do for such a power? it asked.

A trade. She wasn't surprised. Greed was the most elusive of all the Sins to her, yet the most prominent in life. She didn't know a single person who'd be humble enough to resist. Violet was desperate enough to turn over her pinky finger for a hot meal and a healed hip.

You want to disguise yourself?

She nodded.

Take a life for me, then, and I will disguise you into that person.

Too far. *Way* too far.

You want it? It's yours. But for all greed, there is a price, it demanded.

Violet continued walking. She stepped off the sidewalk and into the four-lane street, not caring about the cars. The Sin remained a hulking weight at the base of her skull. She needed to outrun it.

You want a new identity? A new life in this world? You must take one. I always ask for equal exchange.

And if I asked for riches? she asked the Sin.

I'd ask you for years of your life.

She dodged a passing motorbike, wondering how many people on this street alone had time ticking on their hearts.

Or I'd ask for years of another, it said.

"No," she seethed.

Oh, yes, they all agree to it. Every. Single. One. I give them riches, and they rise to the top, greedy for more. They take the poor, the homeless, the ones who won't be missed—

"Stop it," Violet pleaded. Passersby glanced at her strangely. "Please—get out of my head. I can't deal with this right now."

They probably have no idea their piles of gold suffocate those on the ground.

An expensive car passed, and she glanced through the window, where coins filled the back seat, and someone counted them with a smile that didn't reach their eyes. A motorbike roared, a purse tucked underneath the driver's arm. A man jumped out of his car and yanked the driver out of another, stealing it.

Skies, Violet couldn't breathe.

You're no fun, the Sin said. She could practically see the dark, cunning face of a god rolling its eyes. *Perhaps when you're not so close to death.*

Death. It whispered in her ear, a peaceful, familiar voice. She slouched on her good leg. Her eyes fought for clarity. Breath bruised her lungs. She gritted her teeth and snarled to death, *"No."*

Jack was alive. Her brother was here. She needed to see them.

A horn blared. Violet whipped her head and flicked off the white van. The tint was too dark to see the driver, but she hoped her finger made it up his annoying ass.

"I'm walking!" she snapped, emotions bleeding into untamable frustration. "You can *wait.*"

The van screeched to a halt in front of her.

It sat in the middle of the road, and even as horns honked and people yelled, the moment they realized what stopped them, they turned their backs, silenced. Rolled up their windows and braced their hands on the wheel.

Violet stepped onto the curb and dropped her arm. The busy traffic road continued, along with the crowded sidewalks amid a frenzied dusk. Ice slithered down her spine, and her gut tugged in a feeble attempt, telling her to go.

She stumbled back, bumping into a person. He yelled at her, but as his gaze turned from her confused face to the van, he paled, hurrying away.

Violet knew the driver was staring at her. Was a finger so bad? She wasn't in the best mood after getting shot with an arrow, switching worlds, dislocating her shoulder, nearly getting annihilated by dogs, and submerging her left boot in a piss puddle. But still…

The license plates glowed on the bumpers of cars, and while ninety percent were blue, this one was red. This one created fear. As if the crowds, the cars, the entire damn area knew it was trouble, and no one pulled her away. Not one single person helped. They gave wide berth to her stilled state on the sidewalk.

Cyran.

She stumbled another step. But it couldn't be him…not after all the precautions she took once she entered the city.

Four large, burly men dressed in head-to-toe black and handling plasguns poured from the sliding door. Sunglasses covered their eyes. One lifted his wrist to his mouth. "Located the runaway."

Violet lunged into a limp run, her mind blaring as much as her leg. *No-no-no-no*…but the men were on her, grabbing her, shoving the barrel of a plasgun to her temple. They ripped her hood back and matted brown hair spilled out.

The same guard spoke, "Confirmed brunette, height a match, light eyes—"

"Let me go!" She swung a punch. "My father is expecting me!"

"Less docile than mentioned in notes. Might be on drugs," he continued, and a mumbling, staticky voice came from his wrist. He turned to her. "Your father *is* expecting you, since you ran away from him four days ago."

Violet creased her brows. *No…they must think she was someone else.* "He's dead! I'm going to the graveyard, asshole!" she snarled.

"Lying to the Order is a sin and you know this," he said. He put his mouth to his wrist again. "Morova Nokel found, perhaps drugged by Pharos terrorists."

They tugged her to the van. One man yanked on her injured shoulder, and Violet wailed in pain. Her body burned, and that familiar, yet different kind of warmth grew. She panicked. *Not now.*

But her hands began to glow. Searing lines drew beneath her eyes. But this time…instead of glistening silver, instead of dipping into the Vanisher realm, the light bled purple.

The guards were unaware. They pulled her arms behind her back while another swiped two fingers at the damp spot between her thighs. She jerked, kneeing him. He dodged and ignored. A red spot stained his fingertip. Blood from her hip. He called to another, "Inform the Order to have a medic ready at the meeting point. She tried to hurt the life again."

Confusion breached her. The purple light grew. Wrapped her fists in that filigree…

One man jeered at her. "You really are up for punishment now—"

Many things happened at once.

Violet's hand glowed so bright, that when her punch connected with the sneering guard's face, it sliced a bubbling burn across his cheek.

Gunshots rang out and glass blasted from the van.

Blood misted Violet's face, blinding her. All four men dropped to the ground.

A masked female figure caught her as she fell. She smacked a floral-scented cloth over Violet's mouth.

And words faded as Violet did.

"May your dreams be better than this nightmare of life, wild one."

❀ ❀ ❀

Violet moaned herself awake. Her entire body pained like it had been flung into a washing machine on the fastest load. The room blurred. She blinked through it. A tiny, medical-looking room greeted her first. The cot she lay on did little to help her aching shoulder. She shivered, pulling the sheet up higher—

She froze. Naked. No—she still had her undergarments on, but the first thing she noticed was the translucent bandage wrapping her hip wound. She dragged her fingers over it, aware of the cool, minty sensation it brought, along with the smooth, water-like texture. The same thing wrapped her shoulder, and she could...*feel* it mending.

Her breathing picked up. A tingly, sticky sensation rippled beneath her skin, and the only thing she could think of was stitching. Threading. Her tendons and muscles pulled together in an uncomfortable way that she didn't want to be consciously aware of.

The room bled a simple gray, while a plaslight held a steady glow overhead. A monitor beeped next to her, and when her pulse picked up, it shrilled.

Violet yanked the device off her finger and pulled the needles from her arm. Footsteps echoed outside the lone door. Her movements were a little sluggish, but she flung herself off the bed and whirled about the room.

First, a weapon.

The footsteps grew louder. They ran. Voices barked. Female voices. She grabbed the white sheet off her cot and strung it into a rope.

"We don't know who she is, all we know is she was aggressive with the Order," a calculated, clipped voice said.

"So she's not from here," another voice drawled, annoyance laced within. "Out in the street like that. I had half a mind to leave her there. Stupid idiot. Stay back."

"Be gentle, she might be traumatized—"

"I don't care."

Violet pressed against the wall next to the door. When it flung open, she caught a glimpse of a gun. She moved fast, grabbing the brown-skinned hand that held it and pulled forward.

The girl was strong, grunting with the movement as she tried to remain upright, but Violet already had the sheet wrapped around the girl's throat and kicked out her legs. They flew to the floor. Violet straddled the onyx-haired, ferocious, brown-eyed female.

"Please, no! We are trying to help you!" another woman yelled from the doorway.

Violet tightened the sheet. "I don't believe you."

Instead of being scared, the girl beneath her smiled as her cheeks grew red. "Feisty," she choked out.

"Don't agitate her, Emryn."

Emryn's smile grew brighter. "She likes it, Sasha."

Violet snarled and ripped the gun away. She thrust it against Emryn's forehead. "Tell me where I am, how I get out, and that you'll leave me the fuck alone."

"How about—" Emryn gasped as Violet pulled the sheet even tighter. "I sew your mouth shut instead?"

"Emryn," the other woman—Sasha—sighed at the door. "There's no need for that."

"Oh, is Emryn getting beat up?" A child-like, high-pitched voice sounded from down the hall. "I want to see! I want to see!"

Violet caught Sasha, a light-brown-skinned female with a long braid and pierced nose, leaning against the door frame with an exasperated look. "Bunny, no—"

But whoever this Bunny was bolted into the doorway. Maybe thirteen by the looks of it, with wide charcoal eyes and wild brown-red hair. A gap-toothed smile split her face as she beheld Violet and Emryn. "Oh, Em, you deserved this."

Emryn struggled as Violet pinned her arms down with her knees. Violet wasn't having it. She pointed the gun at the wall and pulled the trigger.

But nothing happened.

"Do you think we'd bring a loaded weapon into a medical room?" Sasha asked. "Put it down, you've had your fun. We know you're scared—"

"I'm not *scared*," Violet defended. "I woke up in a random room after nearly being kidnapped by thugs on a street, then someone told me 'sweet dreams' or something like that. Now tell me who you are, where I am, and—"

Something slammed into Violet, sending her flying off Emryn. Violet fought, but the person pinned her wrists against the wall. Violet's head slammed back, and Sasha sighed again. "Really, Tamu?"

Violet blinked her eyes open and found a dark, depthless eye staring at her, the other covered with an eye patch. With the darkest skin Violet had ever seen, Tamu smirked at her, clearly pleased to have surprised Violet. Her hair was in its natural curls, cut close to her head, with gold piercings littering her ears. Her fingernails—more like claws—squeezed Violet's wrists so hard that she gasped.

"Don't. Touch. My. Girlfriend," Tamu said darkly, raspy like she hardly ever spoke.

Violet retained her flinch, instead baring her teeth. "I. Don't. Give. A. Fuck."

Emryn coughed on the floor, but it turned into a chuckle. "Tamu, baby, nice to see you. How was the trip?"

"I. Will. Kill—"

"We don't need to kill anyone." Sasha stepped into the room, throwing a palm up to stop Bunny from entering. Bunny looked ready to burst with excitement. She covered her face with her hands as if said excitement was too much to bear.

That's when Violet noticed her hands. Mangled fingers lined with deep, but healed, scars. Something about it had Violet sagging against the wall, relinquishing to Tamu, as Jelan slammed into her mind.

She gazed around, and with the chaos calmed, she noticed the thread connecting each of them. The crookedness of Bunny's fingers, the healed scar across Sasha's neck, the slashed cleft lip on Emryn, and then, of course, the eye patch on Tamu.

This time Violet wasn't demanding, she was asking, "Who are you?"

Sasha gently pulled Tamu away, and Tamu retreated to her girlfriend, caressing Emryn's neck.

Sasha's eyes fell to Violet's bandages, but she didn't approach. "We are the remaining hope that this world could be a better place. We are the survivors. We are the fighters. We are the Rescue Division in our sect." With a strong look on a soft face, she said, "We are Pharos."

10

Bryce

Violet didn't get any more answers from Sasha or the others. Instead, she was handed a pile of comfortable clothes and scolded for removing the needles from her arms so aggressively.

And for some reason, Violet apologized to Sasha. Couldn't bear the slight guilt she had in disappointing the woman. She was clearly the doctor; gentle, yet firm. Knowledgeable, yet present. Emryn and Tamu waited against the wall in the hallway, like two panthers ready to pounce if Violet did anything to threaten Sasha. Violet refrained from flicking Emryn off as the girl upturned her nose.

Bunny stayed outside the room, but her eyes were planted on Violet the entire time.

With Sasha's checkup complete, she prepared to give Violet privacy to change as she tapped Violet's palms. The scars lining both. "Don't lie to Bryce about this. They won't like that."

Violet planted her hands on her thighs, saying nothing.

"Are you okay to walk?"

Her hip ached, but she nodded. "It's manageable."

"Those patches are rapid healing. We managed to extract the poison from your wounds that made it unable to clot." Violet refrained from smiling, proud of herself for assuming it *was* poison. Sasha continued, "The work before was a little wonky, but by the time we got you here, the internal injuries were already healing." Sasha pinned a knowing look. "Don't keep that from Bryce, either."

"I don't know what to say about that," Violet said truthfully.

"Just…don't lie. They'll know."

Sasha closed the door softly. No lock clicked.

When Violet changed and twisted the doorknob, the same cadre stopped their chuckles and stared at her. She scowled, shutting the door behind her. "I want my stuff, too. Once all this is explained."

"Well, candidate, you might have to get us to like you first." Emryn shouldered Violet as she passed. Tamu very obviously patted the sheath at her hip and flung an arm around Emryn.

"This way," Sasha said.

They walked numerous hallways, took an elevator, and went down four floors while Bunny beamed at Violet the entire time. Violet awkwardly avoided eye contact, but every now and then, she'd catch Bunny gaping, and the girl would blush horribly, looking away.

Bunny finally said, "Do you know how to crochet?"

"No."

"I love it. It's so fun. Sasha helps me because…well, because of my fingers." Bunny held her hands up. "It's a little more difficult for me, but I finally made my first hat. Kinda made it too big. Maybe I can make one for you. Do you want that?"

"Not really."

"Oh." Bunny smiled. "Well, I'm going to make you one anyway. I do for all our rescues. What is your favorite color?"

"Black."

"That's a boring color."

"I guess I'm a boring person."

"You don't seem like a boring person. You certainly don't seem like a nice person, but you aren't boring. How about black, but with some blue? Like your eyes?"

"Please no." Violet didn't like her eyes. She didn't like anything that was her mother's. Which was nearly all of Violet.

"How about brown for your shit attitude!" Emryn called. Tamu snorted.

"How about a dagger up your hole and you can feel how much of a pain in the ass you are!" Violet snapped back.

Tamu laughed harder and Emryn glowered.

"You're funny. But a mean funny," Bunny said.

Violet looked back at her. "You don't need to make me a hat."

"She's going to make you one anyway, might as well say your favorite color, or else you will get brown." Sasha smiled, and it was such a lovely smile that Violet's shoulders relaxed.

But when Violet *did* think of her favorite color, all kinds of grief and hope and messy emotions arose. Her throat grew tight. She fisted her one hand, the one with the bloodbond to him, and took a shaky breath.

Bunny frowned. "Oh, I'm sorry."

Violet relented. "Just do purple. Purple is fine."

"But it's not your favorite—"

"I don't have a favorite color anymore," Violet said tightly. "Purple will do."

Bunny wanted to press, but Sasha looked back and shook her head. Bunny pursed her lips and nodded. "Purple is a pretty color, too."

They reached a door labeled in another language, with Violet's tongue beneath saying '*Command.*'

Sasha knocked. "We have her."

The door swung open, and Violet's eyes grew wide as she beheld the female scowling before them. "About time."

Violet blinked at the shorter girl. Raspy voice and all, but her bright red hair, the blue-gray eyes with a hint of beady-ness to them, the muscular stature, and reddish skin, all screamed Droan, but not fully Droan.

"Always a pleasure, Grace," Emryn said. "Meretta around? Tamu needs new knives after the last mission."

"She's in the shop. She's got a couple new bikes, too—"

That was all Emryn needed to hear when a smile broke out on her face, her cleft lip nearly meeting her nose. She grabbed Tamu's hand and dragged her away, down the dim hall before they disappeared around the corner.

Grace watched them leave before her beady eyes landed on Violet. "This the girl?"

"The one they mistook for Morova, yes," Sasha said. "I cleaned her up, she'll just need more rest and assimilation to everything. She's a little aggressive when threatened, but docile. No restraints are necessary."

Violet stared between the two incredulously. Bunny bounced on the balls of her feet.

Grace regarded Violet with a long, judging look, before opening the door wider. "Come in."

Violet edged into the room, guard up as she took in the massive meeting-office-command room. Plascreens littered the walls, showcasing different news channels, interactive maps, pictures of men, and then pictures of young girls with listed attributes. Giant windows looked over an expanse of an underground town; four-story buildings washed with old stone and brick, as if descendants of structures from above. People—mostly girls—milled about in the tiny community.

A tall, female-like figure stared through the glass, hands behind their back. A rigidness shaped their jaw. Violet lingered by two worn leather chairs before a paper-covered desk. Shelves were covered in books and trinkets, while one corner of the room had brightly colored carpet and children's toys scattered around.

The figure—Bryce—cleared their throat and turned around.

Violet was not prepared for the attractiveness. Pale white skin, narrowed amber eyes, wide nostrils, round cheeks, and bleach-white blonde hair shaved at the side. And then the skivvin' tattoo. It clawed under their eye, across their temple, and into a buzzed scalp.

"Close the door," they called, voice hoarse and deep. It struck a familiar chord.

They didn't sit in the defined male or female categories. Instead, they floated all over the place, and Violet's cheeks heated. *Damn.* Ridiculously attractive. There was a command there, something a little more sinister than Tamu, but respected like Sasha. Either way, Bryce's energy scattered Violet's defensiveness.

"Take a seat."

Violet sat her ass in the chair. Skies, that tattoo. She couldn't stop looking at it.

"What's your name?"

Reality crashed into her, and the tattoo became a blur. *Don't lie.* When Violet looked over her shoulder, the door was closed, Grace guarding it, Sasha next to her holding Bunny's hand.

"Your name," Bryce repeated.

Sasha urged Violet with a small smile. *Don't lie.*

Violet turned her gaze back to Bryce. "Violet."

Lips quirked. "Violet."

"Yep."

"Last name?"

"I—" Violet glanced around the room again, studying it, trying to gather as much information as she could.

"We saved you, if we wanted you dead, you would be dead."

Violet figured it out. "You killed those guards and drugged me."

"I was part of the team who saved you, yes." Bryce confirmed. "Please, hold all your thanks."

Violet steeled her spine. "I was fine."

"You were going to be snatched by the Order. A lone, injured girl, bleeding down her leg. It would catch their eyes. Now, last name?"

But Violet's tongue grew heavy. She couldn't say it, not when she didn't know what this place exactly did. Sasha said they were a rescue division, but a rescue for what? These girls? *From* what? Did they attack…would Reed be in trouble if she uttered their last name?

"I can't," Violet said. "I don't want to lie, but I can't say it." She flashed her palm with the bloodsworn scar. "This gives you enough information."

Bryce regarded Violet for a long time. "No one has access to the candidate list, so that doesn't help, but we already know. So, just Violet then. Violet the candidate."

She nodded.

Bryce scooted to the chair, body still half-turned toward the window and the town carved into rocks beneath. "You're probably wondering what we are."

"I just want my stuff," Violet said.

"Vain and demanding. You'll get your stuff back," they said. "But first, let me go through protocols for all rescues." Violet crossed her arms. Then quickly uncrossed them when Bryce procured a small dagger. "Do you know what a bloodbond is, candidate? I'm sure you know what a spitbond is, as the Droans do that for leverage in Wrath, which would have happened to you."

"I'm not making another bloodbond."

"Another?" Bryce quirked a brow. "You already have one?"

"No, but—"

Violet's tongue turned bitter. The urge to cough overwhelmed her. She brought her hand to her mouth, a sudden dryness in her throat, and when she pulled it away, blood dotted her fingertips.

Violet jolted from her seat, but two meaty hands slammed her down so hard the chair whined beneath.

"Stay seated," Grace leered.

"She's still healing," Sasha said, concerned. "Be careful."

Violet tried to throw an elbow, but Grace merely slapped it away, keeping her planted in the chair with a firm grip. "I *will* restrain you."

Bryce watched with boredom. "Sasha told you not to lie."

"What…" Violet finally looked back to her hand. "What is that?"

"*Crosnev* serum. We inject it into the patients who are flight risks. It is harmless to everything but lies. It detects the changes in your pulse, and when one lies, it pricks the esophagus and blood leaks into your mouth. It is for any liabilities to our organization, secrets, members, and locations because we must take all precautions. So, who is this bloodbond with? That's clearly a liability."

"It's not," Violet grumbled, not particularly happy that some random serum flowed through her veins. "It only means I can't kill this person."

"Is this person in this world?"

Violet hesitated, before saying, "Yes."

"Are they a candidate?"

"Yes."

"Are they dangerous?"

"Usually, yeah."

"Do they work for the Worldbreaker?"

Silence. Violet rubbed her hands together as she stared Bryce down. They waited patiently.

"I think so." Violet hated her weak voice. "I came here…to see if he was alive."

"What is his name?"

Violet looked down at her hand—the other hand. The one with the bloodbond. She exhaled, "Jack Marin."

Sasha gasped behind her. Bunny stilled. Grace removed her hands from Violet's shoulders so fast, as if the very bloodbond could burn her. She took four steps back, shaking her head. "No."

But Bryce didn't seem surprised. They picked up a paper, eyes scanning the words before they let it fall back to the desk. "I'm happy you didn't lie for that one."

"You know?"

"I have my sources."

She shook her head, anger pouring in. "So then, what's my last name?"

"Sutton." Bryce smirked and waved their hand to a plascreen. Her information popped up. Her height, her weight, her age, physical traits, a crude sketch of her face, and certain details; *two scars, one on both hands. A bloodbond to a prominent figure within the Master's plan—Jack Marin. He was unable to kill her. Two friends she's traveling with; one is a candidate, another an Endolier.* And the list went on. Violet noticed no mention of her vanishing abilities, but Bryce definitely knew. They simply wanted Violet to admit it, like everything else.

Her heart dropped into her stomach. She glanced to the window, then to Bryce, then back to Bunny and Sasha who…

Didn't look frightened.

Violet's brows crumpled. When the woman noticed her Vanisher marks back in the destroyed house, horror smeared her expression. Violet was prepared for that to be the usual reaction, other than the select few, like Renell, who saw an opportunity instead of danger. Bryce's eyes glittered with the same opportunity, but it was subdued. No Greed lingered, but Violet's guard straightened her spine.

Bryce studied her. "I'm not letting anyone within our headquarters unless I know everything about them. If you were a stranger, a rogue, and *not* a candidate, then you'll be in a safe house far from here until we determine every single detail about you. Your bloodbond, your last name—all of it, came from my source. A source who relayed what they witnessed in the world of Lust." A knowing look. "Ever since you dropped into this world, my mission has been to find you."

"Damn, Bryce," Sasha muttered, stunned. "You really kept your mouth shut on this one."

Violet's mind reeled and hope dwindled. There was always a thought, a brief, unadmitted thought that she could never be anonymous again after Lust, but she buried it within the box of things she didn't want to believe yet. Now, with Bryce's admission, it burst open. There was no slinking by while Fringe Vanishers prowled for her, while everyone—

"You're a secret, don't fret," Bryce said. "The Order doesn't know about you. Most of the Worldbreaker's cronies don't, either. The city doesn't care, but according to my source…you are important."

"Who is this source?" Violet asked.

"Nobody to concern yourself with." Bryce kicked their feet up on the desk. "Circling back to your bloodbond with a man whose presence means death, I'm assuming you didn't know he was alive?"

"I…didn't have a confirmation."

"Well, I think by everyone's reactions, you have your confirmation. He is, indeed, alive."

There was a yearning relief. Violet's heart sagged finally after being constricted for four months. But pain loitered—little pinpricks at their reactions. Even though Jack was alive, it wasn't good. They *knew* him, and fear rose. She wanted to ask a million questions, blurt out if Bryce has seen him, if he looks the same, if he *is* the same. The words refused to form. Bryce clearly noticed, patiently waiting.

"It's bad, isn't it?" Violet merely said.

"Carving his spot as one of the Worldbreaker's prized emissaries? It's certainly not good. He's been the talk of the town. But my question is…why do you, of all people, hold this monumental connection to him?"

"It's not *that* monumental."

"Seeing as he's killing members of Pharos but can't kill little you, it seems like a monumental thing for him to agree to."

Violet's gut soured. The news just got worse and worse. "It's not something I want."

"But it does give you incredible protection."

Violet's brows creased. "It wasn't like that."

"Then what was it like?"

Violet clenched her jaw. "Look, does it matter?"

"Oh, she's blushing," Bunny sang. "She likes him."

"He's pretty. But deadly," Sasha clipped. "Doesn't mean he is good. He killed Harriet."

Violet glanced at Sasha, whose fists were clenched. Bryce sighed deeply and flicked a remote. One of the numerous plascreens switched to a video, and Violet nearly leaped out of her chair at the sight. It was grainy, incredibly zoomed in, and clearly hidden within clothing, but Jack stood.

"Harriet knew what she was getting into," Bryce said. "She went too deep."

Tears burned Violet's eyes. She couldn't blink. Didn't want to, for the fear that he'd disappear and she'd never glimpse him again. Hair pulled back into a bun and dressed for war, he stood over a girl. Something about his limbs flickered strangely. He spoke into the girl's ear. She said something. Anger twisted his face, and a breath later, her blood misted him.

Behind him, Cyran leered. As if proud.

Bryce turned it off.

"Harriet definitely taunted him," Sasha muttered, removing her hands from Bunny's eyes.

"Well, she learned about *her,* so." Bryce placed the remote on the desk, side-eyeing Violet. "And their…connection."

Violet's jaw slacked open. She couldn't unsee the mist of blood and Cyran's satisfied face. Petrified anger poured through her. He was *alive* and…

Not the same.

Violet jumped out of the chair. "Fuck your source and fuck the bloodbond." Bunny gasped. Violet ignored it, "Here's my own version; the Worldbreaker wants me because I'm a Vanisher, someone he can't control. He tried to kill me in Lust, but I escaped, and have been avoiding him through Sloth, and now I'm here. The arrow wound is so they can track my blood. Captain Zavar traced me down in a town outside the Twin Cities and tried to kill me, but I made it. I simply wanted to know if Jack was alive, and clearly, he is, doing his best. But that was all I needed." A metallic taste grew in her mouth. Blood filled. Bryce reached under the desk and pulled out a trash bin. They held it for Violet.

Fury rippled. She spat the blood straight on the floor.

"Don't lie to yourself, Sutton."

"Fuck this *stupid shit,*" Violet seethed. "I don't care about any of this, I don't care about him—" More blood welled and she growled in frustration. She snatched the trash bin, hating everything about Bryce's smirking, skivvin' face, and sputtered the stupid liquid into it. She ran the back of her hand over her mouth. "Most importantly, I don't want any fucking pity."

Bryce held their hands up. "No pity here."

Grace snorted.

"You're a Vanisher?" Bunny whispered.

"That makes sense with the healing," Sasha said.

Violet slowly glanced at everyone in the room, prepared for the fear in their eyes, but…nothing happened. They were certainly surprised, but for the most part, no animosity pinned her as this wild girl who was about to blow. She placed the bin on the floor. "You're not…scared?"

Sasha laughed. "You're certainly one of the more interesting rescues, but we'd have chained you if you posed a threat."

Violet glanced at the knife in Bryce's hand and said, "I'm going to have requirements if we do a bloodbond."

Bryce chuckled. "Of course, but first, I just need a few more questions answered. Have you ever worked for the Worldbreaker?"

"No."

"Have you ever worked or been associated with the Order of Avaritia?"

"The people who tried to kidnap me? Absolutely not, and I won't."

"Do you have any other bonds that might jeopardize Pharos?"

"No, just the one."

"Is there anything tracking you here, other than the blood scent?"

"Not that I know of."

Sasha cleared her throat. "Her candidate tracker is still active and alerting the main system for all Sins information back in their world. No other chips were detected in my scans. The blood might be an issue on missions, but from my research, only fresh scents can be used unless the blood is properly sealed, and that's normally for anyone registered within the Order or with the Worldbreaker's

Empire. I don't have much research on Vanishers, so we have to keep the possibility in mind that her energy can attract others. I'd imagine if it is used."

"Then we won't use it," Bryce said.

Violet scowled. "It's my choice."

"Will you use it?"

"No, but—"

"Do you have control over your abilities?"

"No, but I—"

"Then there isn't an argument. New Vanishers are dangerous, so we will keep you off-site—"

"*Keep* me?" Violet stood abruptly. "I'm not a prisoner. I didn't agree to whatever you have plans for."

Bryce cocked their head. "By all means, walk out the door. Go into the Twin Cities and live your life. Grab a bite to eat out in Hallow, but make sure you give your card that shows your Order Commandment approves of your outing, since you are a single woman. Walk alone down the street and get harassed by those who believe you should be locked up and raped. Or how about we put you right back into the arms of the Snatchers, so they can drop you off to the father who has been giving you off to his friends for pleasure…they thought you were Morova, right?"

Violet's jaw slackened. She didn't know what to say.

"Listen to them."

A feminine voice rasped and Violet whipped her head toward it. A girl, a little younger than Violet's age, stood dressed in comfortable pants and a sweater, her horrifically bruised neck in full view.

Brown hair, light eyes, same height.

Morova.

She closed the door with her shoulder and walked quietly into the room. Violet noticed the bags under her eyes, the paleness of her skin. Her shoulders curved inward, lips puffy with a healing gash, and a haunted look that silenced Violet.

Bryce's voice grew dark. "Pharos is an organization that rescues those prosecuted, hurt, and manipulated by the Order of Avaritia—a sect of this nation's Empire that wants to restrict freedom, devalue females, certain males, and people like me, as well as take over the other countries and spread their hateful dogma. They have pillaged thousands of indigenous communities, stripped the ancestries and cultures of this world, committed genocide, and believe in controlling others through blind faith to a god that only, seemingly, listens and supports them."

"The God of Greed—Avaritia," whispered Morova. "They only have one god they fear—Nex. The Dark God. I…they believe it is the Dark Storm."

"Captain Zavar," Grace clarified.

"They praise the Worldbreaker's Empire, bow to Vanishers, steal children from other worlds and make them forget anything that doesn't serve their purpose, and they breed females like they're cattle."

Morova trembled, wrapping her arms around herself.

It just gets worse and worse, Violet wanted to say. The worlds she traveled before flashed in her mind, all filled with suffering and blood. She wanted to vomit. Wanted to cry. Wanted to scream. Wanted to clutch her pouch of turquoise pieces and run to a cabin beneath a mountain peak, where a female would braid her hair and make her feel safe amid the horrors.

She latched onto something. "They steal children from other worlds?"

Bryce bit their cheek. "They have these *schools* that the children go to. Extremely protected schools, but we have some images." They pressed a button on the desk, and one of the nearby plascreens flared with rotating, zoomed-in pictures of light-green-skinned kids in line, dressed in crisp clothing, holding books in her language, guided by white-skinned teachers who reminded Violet too much of the Crale.

Agia. Agia.

Win, agia.

Her hands shook as she fisted them. "They take Inaj children?"

"Anything the Order deems as a lost cause, or different from their beliefs, is worth radically changing to fit their scripture." Bryce flicked off the plascreen. "You don't need to see all of that. We have people for that."

"I want in," Violet said sharply.

"We don't need a martyr." Grace rolled her eyes.

"No martyrs here," Bryce agreed. "*But* we need warriors. Those willing to fight, to help. Extremely skilled fighters, at that, too. But for your predicament, it'll be difficult."

"It's always difficult."

Bryce dragged a finger along the papers. "There will need to be an appearance change. A drastic one. You'll be at a different location along with some of the other street fighters—those who are in action, in the thick of it, and who are on call for missions. Emryn and Tamu are there. You'll be assigned to missions with Emryn to start, but you'll take a week first to heal. Got it?"

Violet wasn't all too happy about being paired with Emryn, but she nodded.

"Good. Now, to the bloodbond." Bryce stood and walked around the desk. They slashed their palm. "Do you swear to never reveal Pharos' locations to anyone not sworn into the organization?"

Violet took the blade and cut over Jack's bond. "I swear."

"Do you swear to uphold Pharos' mission to be a light, a beacon, a hope for survivors and those in need?"

"I swear."

"Do you swear to never utter the name of any member to anyone not sworn into the organization?"

"I swear."

"Do you swear to never utter that you are associated with Pharos to anyone who is not a sworn member? As in, *we* go and find people. They do not come and find us. Got it?"

"I swear."

"And you swear to accept that if you become dangerous, or a liability, we will kill you?"

"How kind of you," Violet said. "Yes, I swear."

"And I swear to you, Violet, that we will offer you safety and protection from those who want to harm you or wish you dead. That we will provide a bed, food, and comfort until you are ready to depart from us, leaving behind no trace."

Violet inclined her chin. Bryce smirked, and together, they slapped their hands and shook.

Warmth bloomed from her palm and traveled up her arm. Bryce seemed used to the feeling, because they pulled away, shook their hand, and wiped the blood off.

"Grace, go get her stuff. Grab Emryn and have her show Violet her new room at off-site twenty-two."

❈ ❈ ❈

Emryn wasn't too thrilled to give Violet a tour, especially when it poured rain outside as they walked a long distance from the main road, and toward a seven-story building smashed in the back alleys of Navru. Emryn punched a code into a semi-hidden door. "Four, four, three. It is changed every three days, but sometimes randomly too."

Violet stepped into a simple, homey place; low-light halls, sitting rooms, a hearth flaring in the kitchen, and other females going about. "About fifteen girls in total. Only three floors are ours; the bottom two and the top. The rest are for an unassuming elderly apartment building." They entered a rusty elevator, and she pushed a button for the seventh floor. The top. "Most of these girls here are survivors themselves, but it takes years before they are ready to face the choice."

"The choice?" Violet eyed the screeching closing doors. It was clearly an abandoned service elevator.

Emryn lounged against the wall. "The choice to either go back out into the world that abused them, or help to rid the world of abuse. Some choose a middle path—taking a safe place and calling it home, content with keeping the past in the past and never stepping foot in it again."

"And you?" Violet leaned against the opposite wall. "You chose to fight?"

A savage smile. "Of course. As long as I take down the Order Commandment that raised me."

"Have you…?"

The smile grew and she flicked her hair as the elevator stopped and opened. "If you ever hear about a burned down church in North Hanhii with four preacher bodies that had all their fingers missing, that was me."

Violet studied her. "Why their fingers?"

A delighted laugh. "Because even in death, I wanted to make sure those fingers never touch a little girl ever again. I always take their fingers. Every. Last. One. I have all the bones under my bed. Helps me sleep at night."

They stopped at a door and Emryn nodded at the keypad. "You make your own code. Put in the number you want and don't tell a soul. It's your space now. Do what you want with it."

Violet nodded, but circled back. "Do you ever think about using those bones, or fingers, as…messages?"

Emryn flicked dirt out from under her nail. "No…" Her eyes widened. "But that is *genius*."

"A thought." Violet shrugged. She used her body to hide the code she punched into the keypad. "Okay, thanks. Bye."

Emryn snorted and waved her hand. "Bye."

Violet let the door shut softly behind before she turned to her very empty room. She shrugged off her bag at the foot of the tiny cot and beheld the towels, blankets, clothes, and bag of hygiene products near the small bathroom door. After brushing her teeth, she collapsed into bed.

A small buzz caught her attention, and Violet found a tiny beetle crawling along the windowpane. Cyran's spider-like fortress and endless Hallow City gleamed through the dusty glass. A sharp pang filled her chest. She rubbed at the bloodbond. She wished she could see him, just once, but Zavar would be prowling the streets. Her identity might as well put a spotlight on her at all times. Hidden in this apartment, it didn't matter, but if Violet wanted to find Jack to discover the person he was now, she needed an advantage, *wanted* something–

A familiar slithering reached her mind.

You want your disguise, young Vanisher? Greed purred. *Give me a life and I will give it to you.*

Violet slid her hand up the wall, groaning as she leaned on her injured shoulder. Her fingers wobbled, but she managed to pinch the beetle in between them.

And then she promised never to hurt another bug again.

She squashed the beetle. The crunch sounded horrifically loud in the room.

There's your life, Violet said.

The Sin cackled. *Well played.*

Violet hugged the dead bug into her palm as a tingling sensation blossomed within the base of her skull. She closed her eyes, and a handful of golden strings appeared, each connected to a different part of her. She plucked one and a choked gasp arose as her nose heated and then cooled.

There's a string to your hair, eyes, skin, teeth, nose, ears, lips, and jaw. Basic things. Think of the changes—as well and detailed as you can—and when you have it, pull the string as tight as it will go. When it is taut, that is when the full disguise is made. Let the string slip? Your real features will peak out.

What if I wanted a bigger ass? Violet asked.

Next time, don't trick me.

And with that, the Sin vanished.

11

TEASE

OVER THE NEXT FEW DAYS, Jack woke in his sleep every few hours, haunted by the Pharos girl and the seething words she spoke. *If it is true—if there really is one person in this entire universe that you can't kill.* As much as Jack believed Violet to be dead, a random freedom fighter to have taunted him with that phrase drew more questions. Questions that failed to let him slumber.

Regardless, no matter how many murders he committed, the Pharos girl's was a regrettable one. It made him sweat, clench his hands, unable to forget the pressure in his palms from the pop of her head, or the warmth of her blood slicking his skin.

But now, he towered over another torture victim strapped to a chair—one of the researchers that made Jack's transition a success, who flailed with fear before the Worldbreaker. It was particularly boring at this point.

"Did you think you could get away from this job?" Cyran cocked his head.

The male captive trembled, nose bloodied and eyes puffy from crying. "I'm sorry, Master. I—I didn't think—"

"Yes, you did." Jack yanked the man's hair back. His chains rattled with every shake of fear. Jack dipped close with a smile. "You thought about every little detail before you tried to escape with the vials of DNA. You knew the security rotations, had an extra key card made under a fake name. You didn't—"

"I didn't want to watch these subjects die!" the man screamed at Cyran into the bare interrogation room. "All these people—they're *people*. But you're making them into monsters. You saw what it did to those failed Endoliers. They *clawed* at themselves because the DNA was so foreign. Their bodies couldn't handle it." His bloodshot eyes turned to Jack. "This man was an exception, and we don't know why."

Cyran's face was blank. The scientist repeatedly brought up Jack's exception, and with each mention, the captive seemed to fear Jack more. Jack was the sole survivor of this manipulation, and even though there was an underlying reason he was the exception, Cyran ordered the hundreds of scientists working in both Envy and Greed to make another one. He wanted his hybrids, his creations like Jack, and the scientists suffered for it because every other subject died. They repeated the same exact process as they had done with Jack; stabbed them, brought them to the brink of death, if not a little further, and pumped them with the same dosage of each species. They thought it was the Mer blood, but so far with that ability, Jack's wounds smoothed over when he washed his hands, and he had a knack for smelling poisons.

"We found that in the animals we combined, the ones with fantastic healing survived. So we use reptiles and others to increase the survival rate, but the only people who harbor reptile-like structures are Endoliers, and they don't survive. You can't up your production, we don't have enough furnaces to burn the bodies."

Jack popped the man's shoulder out of his socket. He wailed into the air. Jack rolled his eyes. "You're spewing nonsense. I'm becoming annoyed. Who else knew about your escape to share this information?"

"No—no one," the man sobbed. "I swear."

"Bite him," Cyran commanded.

Jack sank his teeth into the man's bicep.

And there was the truth.

Once Jack shared a look with Cyran, the Worldbreaker nodded. Jack procured a small dagger, flipped it, and shoved it into the man's spinal cord, paralyzing him, but not killing him. He shrieked, unable to move his legs. Tears flooded his eyes. Jack yanked out the knife.

Cyran pounded a fist on the door and two guards opened it. "Take the captive to a private room in the medical wing. Sedate him first."

A needle went into the scientist's skin, and in moments, his entire body was limp. The guards carried him out, leaving a trail of blood in his wake.

Cyran turned to Jack. "Clean yourself up and—"

"You know why I'm an exception," Jack said, plainly. "I remember your voice when I woke up. You attributed it to the Mer blood. Mers have exceptional healing, but it is not the reason for my exception. The others are catching on."

Cyran gave a humorless laugh. "Stick to your duties. We pumped you with so many things, it could be a cockroach's reluctance to die." His lips curved up. "If we don't have another successful experiment like you, I will turn to the only other person who *would* prove successful—"

Jack lunged, fury taking over his movements. His fist rose, aiming, but Cyran vanished, and Jack cratered the wall where his head had been. Cyran appeared across the room with a growing smile. Jack whirled fast, throwing the bloodied knife, but it embedded into his glowing Vanisher hand.

Cyran curiously stared at the blade. Blood flowed to Jack's surprise, but it was black, demon-like. The Worldbreaker held no reaction as he yanked it out. His hand still glowed. Within moments, the wound healed. His voice held no humor, "Do you think the genetics of a superior species that can teleport through worlds would be so easily felled?"

Jack thinned his lips.

"Do you think you could stop me if I go snatch your brother from the Original City and turn him into a monster like you?" He tossed the knife to the ground.

Jack growled lowly, "I will kill you if you touch him."

"You would kill me if you could," Cyran said blandly.

He turned off his powers and the otherworldly light dimmed. He produced a plasblade. Lit it up. The red glow swallowed the room.

And Cyran sliced his own arm off above the elbow.

He didn't blink. Simply smiled. Watched as his severed limb thumped to the floor. Black blood spurted from the stump.

As if in an immediate reaction, the ground shook. The earth began to rumble—a steady quake that knocked the empty chair over. It grew stronger as Cyran's blood sloshed the hardwood. The deep, agonizing rumble continued until Jack had to lean against the wall, concern rising, but Cyran only stared at him, unfazed.

"Each one of the seven worlds would feel some slightly catastrophic event if I were to be injured. This is an example," Cyran said. "Now, look at me, boy."

Cyran activated his powers again—two bright iridescent slits beneath his eyes, a glow from the soles of his boots, and his uninjured arm. *But* on the other arm, the stump shined, as if registering the wound and fixing it. The bleeding slowed. Stopped. Slowly, that light began to regrow his arm, all the way down to the curving white tips of his fingernails.

The earthquake halted once Cyran stood whole. "Now, this depends on the stamina of a Vanisher and how quickly one activates their powers after an injury." Cyran clenched his newly formed fist. "That isn't an issue with an older Vanisher. They are more adept at it. You must push past the pain and find your power to save yourself. Very difficult for those who aren't used to pain. Now, if your curiosity has increased, then yes, there are Vanishers who don't have certain limbs, therefore limiting their abilities, but..." A shrug. "I'm sure a prosthetic could be created."

"How?"

"Connecting the power to a unique device; however, why go through the trouble of fixing something that is already broken?"

Jack shoved the disgust and fear down. The hopelessness was simple. If Cyran was gravely injured, each world connected to him would suffer. If he were to be killed, they would perish. Everything about the seven worlds, the seven sins, would cease to exist.

Jack still didn't know much about Vanishers to understand, but he guessed what Cyran had achieved was extremely rare. By the looks of his burn and scars, and the fact he completely stopped his bleeding with a thought, it must have cost him part of himself, too.

This was the universe he created.

It brought Jack back to a distant memory. A pain so old and deep, it had Jack averting his gaze. He could hear the wicked crack of those whips from so long ago, and see the steady waterfall of her blood-stained bright blonde hair. The chill of her body, caked in mud. The glassy green eyes peering up at a sunless sky.

A cold, triggered sweat leaked down his back. He gently tucked that memory away. It didn't often surface like that.

"Do not touch my brother," Jack said in a hushed, defeated tone. "I will find you a success."

"You have one week."

Cyran vanished.

❀❀❀

The exhausted grunts of men and women reached his ears as Jack waltzed through the training room doors before dawn. After a restless, sleepless night spent pacing his room and wanting to scream, he pulled his curls back in a messy bun, rubbed salve on his tattoos, and put on his training clothes.

The musk of sweat assaulted him. It was nostalgic, to say the least, of all the times he trained and commanded his own gardia. But these men weren't drilling for street fights or intimidation. They were training for annihilation, brought on by Cyran's promise of a grander life and grander worlds.

As expected, silence descended. Without the shield of the Worldbreaker, Jack lay bare to the hateful glares and scoffs. He headed straight toward the weapons rack of different plasblades, picked one, and entered the ring.

Two men were already at it—mere soldiers by the navy color of their training gear.

"Get out," Jack demanded.

Their parries paused. One paled as Jack ignited his green plasblade and twirled it. "Unless you want to fight me."

They both left the ring in a hurry.

Jack poured every bit of emotion into his movements, channeling his control into fierce, deadly cuts. The plasma hummed and heated. He sliced, lunged, rolled, parried with his Droanian strength until the blade became a part of him, and him a part of it.

She was dead.

Dead. Dead. Dead. And he had no one to blame for her death but himself. He fumbled his control, whether Cyran commanded his blood or not. He should have been better...

Jack snarled as he swung the sword again, his chest tightening and throat closing.

"It's the glorified skiv who ruined the city," a voice drawled.

Jack turned to the man's voice. Someone he wholly recognized. He let out a dangerous laugh. "More of that, Carter? You used to be better with your grudges."

"I've got quite a big one on you."

"Did you beat up Reed on your way here?" Jack asked. "He deserves it more than I do, seeing as I was unconscious while you were captured."

Carter snarled. "You still led us down that road."

"And you still need to get over it."

By now, Jack had the full attention of the room. Only the loud huff of breathless lungs filled the tense silence between Jack and his old comrade. Once one of his most trusted spies. And then one of the many Reed had led to being captured that night long ago.

Carter spat, "How could we *ever* get over it when our lives are now spent here? Our families back at home with fucking Arvalo as Emperor?"

Guess that news had circled the fortress. Not surprising. It pissed Jack off, too.

"You were supposed to lead us to a better city," Carter said as he picked up a plasblade and stepped into the ring. "We all trusted you. Believed we were forging a path to a better life. I can't help but feel some satisfaction knowing you were knocked down from your stupid throne."

The truth hurt. It always did. Jack's dream was to lead the city, the country of Veceras, to a better future. But it had been clouded by the fame and the greed for power he grew accustomed to after rising to the top.

Carter ignited his blade and pointed it at Jack. "You ruined us. About time I fight you for that."

"Ruined you? Come here." Jack's mouth formed an icy smile. "I'll show you just how much I can ruin you."

Carter glowered and lunged. Then swung his plasblade into Jack's with a heavy hit.

Jack's smile widened. "Let's see if you remember what I taught you."

Carter fought well, and Jack picked up the old moves he'd bestowed on the once-young man. But Jack didn't care to entertain. He didn't give a fuck anymore.

He let his Droanian strength slide in with each hit. Carter's eyes widened. He faltered once and Jack slashed a cut against his leather. Another falter. Another cut on his thigh. Jack twisted under Carter's next swing and aimed for the thigh again, the second cut piercing the leather and showing a bit of blood.

Carter fought with anger—his moves became more volatile and uncontrolled. Jack merely rolled his eyes, grabbed Carter's plasblade as it came swinging again, and ripped it from the man's grip.

Shocked gasps echoed around the room. Jack flung the plasblade outside the training circle. His palm bubbled with burns like last time. He threw his own blade to the ground and advanced on Carter. Carter swung a fist, expression concerned, but Jack dodged it and delivered a punch to his cheek.

The old comrade fell on his back. Jack grabbed him by the throat and lifted the squirming man. He pressed Carter into the ring's barrier.

"I do not need my physical abilities to prove I am above you." Jack squeezed his hand, and Carter's face fumbled between anger and growing dread. "I did not earn fear and respect by being able to kill a man quickly. I *earned* it because I fought for it. I ruined the city, I ruined so many lives because of my actions, and I will gladly pay for it over and over again with each person who despises me. But I was sentenced the same as you. I believed in the same goal as you. You did well, Carter, because instead of spewing little hateful words about how I *ruined* you, you actually fucking fought me."

Jack dropped Carter to the floor. He turned to the room.

"If you think I'm going to get on my knees and beg for your forgiveness, then get the fuck out of this world!" Jack lifted his arms. "We have an opportunity to make a better Veceras under our Master, so if you still have a problem with me, fight me. If you don't, then stay out of my fucking way." He grinned. "Because I'm not finished with this skivvin' dream."

Jack exited the mostly silent training room, leaving a groaning Carter clutching his bloodied leg.

The minute he got in the hallway, Masar flashed Jack a smile and handed him a towel. "You really know how to make a scene."

Jack wiped his face, spotting Yeren against the wall. "They brought the scene to me."

"That'll make some impression. Both with the army and His Master," said Masar.

"Great," muttered Jack, he turned to head back to his rooms—

"You need to let loose." Masar slapped him on the back. "You're so tense."

Jack shrugged him off. "I don't need anything like that—"

"You need a good fuck, Marin." Masar smiled.

"A distraction, at least," Yeren said.

Masar snorted. "Definitely a fuck."

Jack agreed with Masar, but he would never admit it. All the training, the constant tension, the lack of sleep. He needed a release that wasn't from anger or nearly every other emotion. But Jack couldn't…the thought of hands on him, lips on him…

He flexed his fists. Perhaps an outing would be fine. "We can leave?" Jack asked.

"Of course." Yeren crossed his arms. "As long as we come back."

"I know just the place," Masar said, his smile growing.

Jack turned, ready to shower and distract himself, but all movement in the hallway stalled as a dangerous roar echoed out of an adjacent, private training room. Black lightning flashed and stone cracked.

Yeren straightened. "Bad news, it seems."

Jack stormed down the hallway, flinging open the door to Zavar's tantrum. The entire wall fissured. The Vaelaur swung his arm again, and the deadly bolts zapped from his hands and into the wall.

"Fuck!" he screamed.

Jack braced himself.

Yeren swooped in right behind, barking at Zavar, "Get your shit together. You know we had to replace the last room only a month ago—"

"I don't care," Zavar growled as he turned. Ink-black hair fell into his face, his eyes burning with fury. Lightning crawled up his arms. His gaze darted to Jack, and more fury seemed to fuel it. Jack flashed him a smirk. He *loved* seeing Zavar worked up.

But Zavar merely shook his head. "Where is His Master?"

"Just returned from a trip," Yeren said. A small frown formed on his face as he regarded Zavar. "I'll put extra salve outside your door tonight."

"Shut the fuck up," Zavar snapped, and with a zap of lightning to the far wall, he vanished.

"He needs a therapist," Masar mumbled.

❋❋❋

Jack thought his tastes were luxurious and fashionable, but the Elite fashion in Hallow's gentlemen's clubs perforated his rich commander days. A black dress shirt freshly steamed by one of his numerous, attractive servants, a snug-fitted dark vest with an intricate silver design, simple slacks, and knee-high, freshly shined boots. His curls were still tucked back in a bun, his jaw freshly shaved, and an extremely expensive cologne wafted from his neck. This might have been the most normal, or put together, he'd felt since Calesal.

They'd ventured here for some peace—a distraction—but Jack's nerves refused to settle. Businessmen, high-ranking officials, and even a few other captains filled the exquisite entertainment society; full of gambling, dancing poles, and extremely attractive people. It was incredibly diverse. And packed. Auriens, Quinams, black-and-white-spotted Mers like Serwa, and the blacks, browns, whites, and even reds of Greed. Of all the colors on the spectrum within the room, it wasn't hard to know what worlds were clearly the more elite. The others, as Cyran's expressions show, are merely for resources.

Droans, Inaji, and Endoliers would not be allowed into this room. As Jack's blood sang with the shots of dark liquor from an earlier bar, it made him frown. Anaya was probably more interesting than any one of them. *And* Jack's most useful abilities were Droanian strength and Endolier camouflage. Perhaps, if there was something Jack could do right, it would be bringing more chairs to Cyran's table.

Jack wrinkled his nose at the waft of smoke around the dimly lit room. He followed Masar and Yeren to a secluded booth in the back, the velvet lining reminding him of his visits to the Mondar Lion with Lucien. Another frown. He wished his brother were here.

Yeren revealed no emotion as he ordered his usual. Masar more excited about trying another drink requested some fruity concoction that was one of the club's specialties.

Jack's gaze roamed the large room again as if he were looking for something. A threat? An interest? He didn't know, but as he moved past another gaping window with a view of the sprawling city below, he *wanted* to find something. He needed a fucking distraction—

His eyes landed on perfection.

Reed Sutton stared at Jack from across the room, an indistinguishable expression on his face. Jack's old friend, comrade, confidant, and someone he had at one point considered a brother.

They'd already had their interaction back in Envy, but Jack still held animosity. It hadn't been a level playing field. It didn't solve any of the tension between them, tension that Reed clearly still felt as he hastily took another sip of the dark liquor, his jaw clenching.

A slight chuckle emitted as a waiter brought over another round of drinks and a plate of smokes. Jack leaned back, spreading his legs, and put one in his mouth. He lit it up. His eyes caught on a female circling a nearby dancing pole; gold bra and underwear sparkling as she twisted underneath the lights. Dark-brown skin, long black hair. Her languid dancing drew his interest, especially the way she balanced on her toes, accentuating her taut leg muscles, the curve of her calves…

Jack cocked his head. *That is a strange color for toenail polish.*

He stilled.

It wasn't just her toenails, but her entire toes. Hardened to silver. Harmas silver. The miners who live on the other side of the planet. They weren't allowed in the Twin Cities, so one word popped in Jack's mind.

Spy.

His smile grew and he stabbed out his smoke, standing and grabbing a drink. "I'm going to have some fun now."

Masar nudged Yeren. "Drunk Marin makes for fun company."

"Drunk Marin will kill you if you repeat that to anyone else." Jack leered over his shoulder. He dropped his lids, and added a little more energy to his smirk as he waltzed over to the dancer's stage. Her eyes landed on him the minute he'd stood, and as she ground the pole, they didn't waver. The old him would have been intrigued by the confidence, but the new him had an agenda.

"You're working hard," he said, sliding a charming smile.

"I always work hard, I'm talented at my job." A sensual smile. A beautiful smile. "Do you work hard?"

"When they deserve it," Jack said.

She abandoned the pole for the stage floor. On her hands and knees, she crawled to him slowly. Sensually. He cocked his head at her.

"You're very beautiful," she said.

He braced his hands on the stage as she drew close, nearly sharing his breath. "Do you want to gawk at my beauty somewhere more private?"

"It will cost you." She rose. Placed her hands on his shoulders. Rubbed them down his chest. "I'm very expensive."

"Since you're so talented?"

"At dancing, yes," she replied. "But I'm especially talented in the private rooms."

He pushed a strand of hair behind her ear. Her smile grew. She leaned into it. He relaxed his gaze and flashed a black card. "Let's see if your mouth lives up to your words."

Her sexual character broke into something more genuine. She took in his body. Licked her lips. "I might give you a discount if your mouth is talented, too."

"Oh, darling." A gentle caress of her cheek. "You don't have to worry about that."

She motioned to one of the dancer's hosts and they booked a private room. Jack let her lead him through the club and past the numerous booths. He glanced around, hoping to find…

Ah, just as planned.

Reed white-knuckled a tumbler from his booth across the room. His companions talked around him, completely oblivious to the murderous expression stitched on Violet's brother's face.

Jack gave him a wink as he and the dancer disappeared behind a curtain.

12

TICKLISH

Jack followed her into a room designed for wild sex. A plush, wide couch—big enough to be a bed—changing curtains, a fully stocked liquor cart, and low lighting. There was even a sliding glass door leading to a balcony where a small hot tub bubbled pink. Toys lined the walls, some Jack recognized, along with a fluffy pair of pink handcuffs.

"Cute," Jack muttered.

The dancer released his hand and strolled over to the liquor cart where she poured him a drink. Jack activated a button on his watch that would beep if it came into a radius where a microphone existed. He took a casual walk, and no beeps emitted. His gaze swept every possible corner or nook a camera might be hidden, but no little light flashed.

He didn't think they'd film in here, but he wanted to be cautious. He wasn't too keen on anyone watching his private activities.

"You can have one, too, if you want," he said as he began unbuttoning his vest and shrugged it off. "I won't tell."

She hesitated, looking to the door, before she smiled and poured herself a glass. "Thank you."

He took his liquor and sipped, loving the warmth he felt. "This can't be an easy job."

"It is certainly easy when the customers look like you," she said, shooting back the entire glass.

"I bet," Jack murmured. He settled himself on the couch, legs wide, arms resting on the top. "So, surprise me."

She smiled sensually. "What do you like? Or not like?"

"Don't touch my back," he said. "I'm rather ticklish there."

Her brows furrowed for a moment, before she nodded and continued with her parade. The music poured softly into the room, giving her beats to move her hips to. She started at his knees, flicking her hair behind her shoulders, before slowly straddling him.

He let his eyes stay mostly on her face, only giving the idea that he was watching her body by occasionally glancing at her knees or elbows or her ankles. She dipped into the right side of his neck, the warm smell of vanilla invigorating him. She licked up, nearly touching the scar—

He tensed, grasped her jaw. "Not there, either."

"Ticklish?"

A tight smile. "Of course."

She obeyed and settled for the other side of his neck. Jack hadn't been in many situations like this where he had to pay for people. Maybe when he was younger and more gangly, less filled out, but by the time he was Gardia and City Commander, he didn't take to paying for sex. He didn't need to. Most would throw themselves at his feet, and in the beginning, it was enticing, but it became old. He liked challenges. Liked those who were unreachable, more forbidden. The daughters and sons of adversaries. The brothers of allies.

The sisters of comrades.

"You can touch me, you know," the dancer whispered.

He snapped out of his thoughts, breathing back, "I will when you impress me."

She pulled away, surprise gracing her face. He watched her pride dwindle just a bit, but she shook it off as he offered her a smile. One smile. It was all it took.

Too easy.

"Can I kiss you?" she asked.

He sipped his drink. "How about this…I will give the orders, and you do them. If there are restrictions, let me know, and I will immediately stop."

She nodded eagerly, a blush rising to her cheeks. "I like that."

"Good," he said. "Now kiss me."

She leaned in, nearly meeting his mouth.

"Here."

He pointed to his jaw. She halted, a flash of disappointment on her face, but did as she was told.

"Here." His ear.

She did. He ignored the goosebumps.

"Here." His cheek.

She did.

"You listen well," he said. "Now look at me. I want to see your eyes."

She locked her gaze with his. Another blush rose to her cheeks, her dark complexion mesmerizing in the faded light.

"You are very beautiful," he said, still holding her gaze.

Counting the seconds.

"Thank you," she said.

Jack searched her eyes. Once he felt that familiar tug, he asked, "Does your Harmas hardening help a talented dancer like you?"

She froze. Trapped.

A satisfied smile split Jack's face. Her thoughts unraveled in his mind.

Harmas…I only use it to help with movements. What—what is this feeling? What is he? I thought we were connecting…

"I'm sorry for the rejection." Jack cradled her face. "I'm grieving for another, but I'm horribly loyal, still. It's a bit annoying, actually."

She blinked. "What are you?"

"Oh, I'm not interesting," he said. "*You* are. So who are you spying for?"

Her breathing grew uneven, but her thoughts raced. *I can't believe this. They said it was safe. Sent me here to eavesdrop on the higher-ups and the Emperor's captains. I only have to relay what I hear since they don't allow earpieces…No, stop. Stop. He's reading your mind, look at his face…*

"Oh no." Jack frowned. "Don't fight it. You have no defenses in that pretty little brain."

I don't want to… Her thoughts tumbled for a second and she shook her head slowly. "I can't—"

"Yes, you can, darling. Answer me."

What is this? I—what does he want? I only hear meeting plans or complaints. That's all the Order higher-ups do is complain. Complain about people like me, nations they don't like, or the new laws they want to enact…it's to fell the Order…because…

She shook her head. "I took a bloodbond. I can't say anything."

Jack tapped her temple. "Say it here, baby."

No…I can't…I need to protect them. They are counting on me…

"You will be fine, I promise, but you won't be if you don't cooperate. I am getting this information one way or another."

*You. It was you. I thought I recognized you from the tapes Bryce played…*Her eyes began to well with tears. *You killed Harriet. They captured her when she rescued a young girl from a church. She was always brazen; I told her to tone it down, but she killed two of the Worldbreaker's men…No, stop…but the Dark Storm found her and she died in front of his army by you…you…I can't—I can't—*

"Yeah, sorry about that," Jack said. "But thank you for confirming your organization. Now, can you tell me more about it?"

*Will I—Will I—*Her breathing picked up, chest moving rapidly.

Jack shushed her, caressed her cheek, then grasped her wrist. "I was hoping you'd drink more so I didn't have to resort to this, but alas, I can't always get what I want."

He held her gaze as he lifted her wrist to his mouth. His fangs elongated and he gently bit into her skin, tasting the sweetness of her fear. He ignored it, even though the alcohol in his system yearned to indulge. Instead, he pushed the cool, minty taste of calmness into her. Slowly, she relaxed into his lap, lids growing heavy. Jack pulled away before she fell asleep completely.

"Now," he said, "tell me about your organization. You won't break your bloodbond, I promise."

Pharos saves the people who are hurt by the Order of Avaritia, who takes advantage of the refugees, then use them for their dirty work in their corporations, and steal their children to manipulate their minds. They…some have killed villages in Harmas, but Harmas people fight back, and that's why the Order hates our people. They call us awful, when we believe in a god as well, but one that is different. But the Order kills for that.

Tears slipped down her cheeks. *We try to save the girls, the ones who don't fit in, because they traffic children and younglings for their games. The higher-ups do. They…sacrifice them to the God of Greed for more control, and that's how villages fall. That's how they take control. But we fight back, we try to save them.* She was sobbing now. *My village, it is gone…my parents are gone…this is all I can do now…*

"It's okay," Jack assured her. "I want to help you."

Her brows pulled together. *Help me? Us? Pharos?*

"Exactly that."

But he works for the Worldbreaker…he killed Harriet…

"I will always be a horrible person, but I want to be the person who does horrible things for good causes." Jack smirked. "So, I will kill, I will maim, I will take down every bit of this world to justify what they took from me. But I have another question… your friend, Harriet, asked me about something very personal that I've only shared with one other. One whom I'm told is dead, do you know anything about that?"

Confusion leeched onto her face. Jack's heart thumped a little harder while her jumbled thoughts shifted into an order he could comprehend. *What did Harriet say? I don't know what this secret is. Bryce keeps things wrapped up so tight, but there were rumors of a newcomer who burned the face of an Order member…"*

"Do you know who this Order member is?"

"They're the guards," she whispered. "They are in the Church District. They are the ones who take the girls and the kids. Snatch them on the streets…" *And they caught a girl, but the girl burned one's face. Everyone was so surprised to hear it, because in this world girls aren't taught to fight back like that…*

Jack stopped listening to her thoughts. His world slowed down. A girl who fights back. Who burned the face of a guard who tried to take her. It couldn't be…but ever since he arrived in this city, his gut nagged at him when it came to Violet. It was easier to believe she was dead, because the hope of her still breathing overwhelmed him with too many emotions.

But there was no way for this Harriet girl to know about the bloodbond unless someone told him. That would leave Anaya, Rio, the Worldbreaker, a chunk of Fringe members, and…

Violet.

It was extremely likely some Fringe members worked with Pharos. There were always people with one foot on both sides, and in a world of Greed, people were selfish, even if a death sentence by Cyran breathed down their necks.

The cruel warmth of hope blossomed in his chest. It flowed through his veins, overpowering the foreignness, and dragged him back to his memories. He trained himself to replace memories of a warm, breathing Violet with a cold, dead one. It was the only way to keep the mourning at bay. Now, each of those memories unraveled into the true form they were always in. Her fire. Her eyes. Her raspy laugh.

The fact she fought back.

Jack grasped the hope. Held it in his scarred palms. Cradled it. He *needed* it for all that was to come. He needed something to fight for.

The woman's thoughts started to scramble, and Jack knew his time was up. "You've been so helpful."

He bit into her wrist again, this time pushing a strong dose of calm. Probably too much, but it wouldn't kill her. She slumped against him, passed out. He lingered, suddenly curious, because he didn't know how to wipe the mark of his bites. He bit into his finger and watched a small bead of blood appear. Opening her mouth, he wiped it on her tongue.

And waited.

Not really to his surprise, the fang wounds on her wrist began to close. Healed. Without water, and with only a drop of his blood.

Also, not to his surprise, he thought back to the dream he had before he woke to this madness—the one where he cradled the flowers and made them bloom.

He tucked that correlation away.

He settled the woman on the couch and flung a blanket over her. Just as he shot back another glass of liquor, the door burst open. Reed stormed in, a yelling owner behind him, but Reed merely snarled at the owner, "You'll get paid for her time."

He took one look at the sleeping dancer, and anger overtook him.

"I thought you'd appear sooner." Jack smiled, a little drunker. "Or were you giving me some time to get changed—"

Reed grabbed Jack by the collar and slammed him into the wall. "Shut your skivvin' mouth."

Reed's arms lit up in those bright, twisting lines, and before Jack knew, they'd vanished. Cool air hit Jack's face, sobering him a little, but he still wobbled to gain his balance.

They were on a rooftop, the bright gleaming lights of Hallow surrounding them. Jack turned to Reed, opening his mouth—

A fist slammed into his face. He toppled back, thumping to the ground. His head smacked the concrete, but where Jack's skull should have split open, only a headache bloomed.

Reed bristled for a moment, but no fear flashed in his eyes. "I'm going to fucking kill you."

"You're going to—"

Reed dropped to his knees and swung another. The alcohol numbed the pain. His face began to tingle. Jack was already healing.

"I'm going to *kill* you!" Reed cried. "For what you did to her! For everything you did to her!"

"You're going to—"

Reed threw a third punch, but Jack caught it, squeezing hard enough to have Reed gasping in pain. "You're going to hurt your hand if you keep punching me."

"I heard about your stupid new abilities," Reed said. "You don't deserve them. You deserve to be dead."

"That's harsh."

"You slept with my fucking sister!" Reed cried, sending another punch into Jack's face.

Jack blew out a breath and smiled, blood on his teeth. "Yeah, yeah, I did."

Reed's growl was straight animal. "And then—" Another punch came, but it was Reed who cried out in pain. "He—*killed* her!"

"Stop that—"

"You were supposed to protect her!" Reed yelled as he grasped his injured hand. "You weren't—you were supposed to keep her safe! From a distance! Not in the same fucking bed—and *then* you take an escort and do the same? In front of my face!"

"I didn't do anything with the dancer," Jack said. "And as for Violet, well, by the time you and I had our conversation in Envy, I'd only kissed her."

Reed's eyes widened. "So, you didn't sleep with her?"

"No, I did." Jack waved his finger. "Just in the next world."

Reed snarled and kicked Jack, landing a hit in his knee. Jack hissed and rolled over. "Okay, that one hurt."

"You're a piece of shit," Reed said. "I watched how you were with all those other women…hell, I had to escort them out after you were done with them, and then you see my *sister* and go and do the same thing? My blood. And you thought that was okay?"

"In the beginning, no." Their memories together ran through his head, and Jack's chest grew uncomfortably tight. "In the beginning…I didn't see her that way. She hated me, and I was just mad she was in the game because I already had so much to deal with."

Reed clenched his fist. "I know who you are, Jack Marin, and I know how you use people. I was okay with you using me, but the line was drawn at Violet. Way *before* her. You were supposed to make sure she didn't starve or go off herself. And now look at this mess."

Jack knew Reed was throwing out insults to make himself feel better. The contract he signed to watch over Violet in Calesal was pretty much null the minute he sliced his hand for the Sins, but he carried it with him throughout the worlds, despite trying to fight for his own life within them as well.

Jack's gut tightened. Looking at her brother—his friend— he knew he failed Violet. He did the bare minimum when it came to the contract, he'd send someone to check in on her and write a report instead of doing it himself. He'd treated her like a meaningless to-do list. Still alive, check. Not suffering from some deadly illness, check. But she *was* suffering, then she snapped, submitting herself into the Sins. It was his job to ensure that didn't happen… but he didn't put in the effort. The reports had come, and he glanced over them. He should have dug deeper. He should have asked the important questions…

Spends time with Jelan Gregory, long-time friend. Visits her guardian on occasional weekdays. Had a run-in with Mai Arvalo, but that relationship has since dissipated. I took a look to see if she does any work, but there is no traceable contract with her name, so if she does work, it is under the table. Enough to pay the bills. Smokes a lot. Drinks a lot. Stares at the Sins Screen most nights.

He should have been more concerned. Her drinking never improved, her habits were the same, but…

But nothing.

Jack failed her.

"Do you understand what you have done?" Reed asked through gritted teeth.

Jack gave Reed an odd look. "She's not—"

"I know her more than you do."

"Actually, at this moment, you don't." Jack wiped his face and stood, shoving his hands in his pockets. "You don't know her anymore, save for her dedication to you. But skies, Reed, how could her entering the Sins to find you come as a surprise?"

"I wanted her to live!" Reed slumped onto his knees, a sob breaking his chest. Tears dripped from his eyes. "I didn't want to leave her! I didn't know any of that was going to happen, Jack. She's my *sister*. My blood. I didn't want—" A deep sob shook his body. "I didn't want to leave her."

Jack's voice grew quiet. "You watched him torture her. You were going to sit back and do nothing but watch her die in Lust."

Reed's tears poured like waterfalls as if he'd been waiting for this moment to finally break. "In some sick, twisted way, I thought letting her die was better than letting her live under the Worldbreaker."

Jack turned away, anger heating his cheeks.

"This game doesn't end with us going home, Jack," Reed said. "It ends with him. We will die by his hand before we ever see home again."

Jack let silence eat up the heartache. Between Reed going through the Sins and slaving under Cyran, and Jack being slapped in the face with the reality that none of their lives were going to end well, it became a pain so unbearable that even Jack's eyes began to sting. He was already struggling to stay afloat, and the only thing keeping him from not spiraling was the desperate string of hope that she was alive.

Reed wiped his face with his good hand. "I can't believe—"

But Jack held up a finger. "Shut the fuck up, Reed. Take off your watch and bring me to this location."

Reed gave him a long, bizarre look, so Jack jerked his wrist and ripped off the watch himself. "I don't want to be tracked for this."

"Who's to say they don't have something inserted in us?"

"I'll deal with the fallout for that, but right now, I'm more concerned with this one guard's burnt face."

An even longer bizarre look. "Are you mental?"

"No," Jack said as he removed his own watch and dropped it on the rooftop. "But I have a feeling, and you should come along with me. Now take us to the Church District's guard house."

❈ ❈ ❈

Reed did as instructed like the good little listener was. Jack smirked, keeping the thought to himself. No matter how much Reed puffed his chest to prove his strength, to Jack he was always so very pliable.

Reed took them straight to the Order's main office in the security tower. It was sparkling clean marble and decorated with gold and fine-threaded furnishings. A young woman sat behind the desk, and when she glimpsed them both, her cheeks reddened. She rose from her chair and bowed her head. "Welcome, gentlemen. It is an honor—"

"Don't make a scene," Jack interrupted. "Wipe the cameras when we leave. This is secret business for the Master."

Her eyes bugged, but she nodded.

"Any officers injured in the facial region in the past few days?"

Her brows scrunched. "Officer Bailey, but it was for a simple traffic stop…"

Jack saw Reed's brows lift in her peripheral.

"Can we speak to him?" Jack asked.

"He's currently in recovery on the seventh floor. I can page you up and let him know you're coming—"

"No worries," Reed said. "We just want to inspect the wound. No need to have him restless in our presence."

She nodded and gestured to the elevators.

Once the doors shut, Reed shared a glance with Jack. "Traffic stop?"

"Did you know the Church steals girls and children off the street for sacrifices, Reed?"

His mouth dropped. "What—"

"Because it seems to me that no one knows," Jack said. "And this particular incident was peculiar because apparently this girl *fought back* and burned a grown man's face with a punch."

Reed paled. "There's no way." He gave a desperate look to Jack. "I can't know—"

The elevators opened, and Jack ignored Reed's hesitant steps out. It was a couple turns, a quick ask at the nurses' station, and they found the injured guard asleep in his bed, half his face bandaged.

Jack turned to a nurse. "Are there pictures?"

She avoided his gaze. "No, um…they went missing."

"Went missing?"

Her averted, shifty gaze said it all.

They were stolen. Or removed. Or burned.

"I'm about to change his dressing, if you… want to watch," she said.

And that was all it took. Reed hid himself behind Jack, breathing heavily, while the nurse carefully replaced the guard's facial bandage. Reed gasped. Jack clenched his jaw.

It wasn't a mere burn from fire. It was…half of his face was gone, and within the knuckles of the punch, little purple iridescent dust glittered.

"Vanisher…" Reed uttered. "But *not*. I've never seen…"

Jack nudged him, shutting him up.

But not.

The nurse's expert hands only gave them a moment to view the damage before a fresh bandage covered it. Her eyes darted to the cameras in the corners the whole time. Jack sighed deeply, but despite the trouble this could land these innocent people in, he couldn't ignore the pounding in his chest. The signs sang to his hope.

"Thank you," Jack said quietly. Reed understood his tone. Within moments, Reed had them teleported back to the gentlemen bar's roof. They picked up their watches and put them back on, and when only the sound of honking cars, the wind through the skyrises, and the muffled music below, did Reed collapse.

His head hung. Tears slipped down. "She's alive."

"We still don't know that," Jack said. "But the signs point to yes. I believe death was supposed to happen, but she's avoided it."

"Jack…" Reed's thick brown hair fell across his forehead. The moonlight highlighted the freckles on his light-brown skin. Those blue eyes were wide and wet. "She's probably terrified."

"Then you really don't know her."

"I…we have to find her. Or fully confirm this. Can you bite Zavar? Or Serwa? They would know."

"Sure, I'll do that when Serwa and I have our next tea party," Jack deadpanned. "Those aren't options, because if we *do* find out the truth, it will become worse. He wants to keep this on the low, clearly, because I'm willing to bet if word gets out that some rogue Vanisher is wandering the city, and the Master is interested in capturing her, the World of Greed will become chaotic. Everyone will be hunting her, hoping to earn the reward that will come with her capture." With a deep sigh, Jack tilted his head to the stars. "That won't keep her safe."

"Then we find her, and I'll take her to a world no one will know to search."

"Skies, Reed," Jack said, exasperated. "That won't fix anything."

"It will keep her safe."

"You keep doing that," Jack snapped. "Doing things that make *you* feel better, but not her. She was going to die back in Calesal after you were sentenced. She can't be helpless. Safe isn't an option for her. She can't go to some world and live a normal life and forget about you. Do you understand that?"

Reed was quiet for a long moment before he said, "Our mother didn't pay attention to her, and she would cling to me. I'd be so annoyed, so I'd go out and get my own friends and do things on my own, and I ended up passing on that neglect, but I—" He rubbed his face. "I just didn't understand—*couldn't* understand what she was going through and how that would impact her later on. I didn't know the impact until I couldn't physically see her anymore. I failed to be there for her. I failed to see her when she convinced herself that she was invisible. I failed to love her to replace all of what our mother didn't give her. Maybe… maybe if I did, she wouldn't have come after me, still begging to be loved, to be seen—"

"Get up," Jack commanded.

Reed blinked at him. "What?"

"Get. Up." Jack stormed over and hauled Reed up by his jacket. "Wipe your tears."

Reed swiped his sleeve over his face.

Jack held him face to face. "Don't say a word. I will track her down. I'll find her. If I don't find her alive, I'll find her body and I will take it back to Gluttony to bury it."

Reed's brows drew together.

"See, you don't know her. You don't know what she has been through in this game. Trust me, Reed. I will take care of this."

Reed looked at Jack, but his eyes told Jack he was somewhere else, deep in his memories. "I really abandoned her, didn't I?"

Jack let go of his collar and stepped away. "That's between you and her."

But Jack wanted to say something different. *We all hurt her*, but even that wasn't enough. *The world hurt her*. Still didn't hit the mark.

No…

This universe was against her the moment she breathed its air.

13

ᴅAD

Jᴇʟᴀɴ ʜᴇᴀᴠᴇᴅ ᴀɴᴏᴛʜᴇʀ ᴘɪᴇᴄᴇ ᴏꜰ scrap metal and threw it to the side. "I remember this place having better pieces."

Kole huffed from ten feet away as he held up a questionable stained cloth. He gagged and dropped it. "You've been here before?"

"New slabs of metal were expensive," Jelan said. "My father and I came here once a week to scour material for his experiments."

"This stuff can't contain plasma."

"No, but it…" She clenched the piece of metal in her hands. "It helps me."

Kole frowned but said nothing. Jelan had made it clear she didn't want to talk about what occurred at the Emperor's mansion. Lucien picked her mood up pretty quick on the silent, tearful ride back where she spent the entire time curled into the door. He hadn't tried to touch her, instead giving her space and comfort. His steady, sorrowful gaze shouted the thousand unsaid apologies on his tongue.

"Can you help me with this?" Jelan muttered and pointed to their scrap-filled cart. She kicked a pile with her boot and caught a small glimmer. A spyglass, usually meant for observing bugs or birds, sat dusty and chipped underneath a slab of wood. Jelan carefully picked it up, rubbed a thumb over the glass, and studied the old, worn silver metal with a careful eye. She judged it to be decades old, at the very least. She peered inside.

Instead of magnifying the metal at her feet, something else was painted—four massive, leafy trees perched on a hill, and in the background sat a sprawling, sparkling citadel.

Surrounded by a wall.

Her head whipped to the side, where only half a mile away, that very wall sprouted proudly. It was a sandstone and steel sort of structure, both seemingly endless, yet confining like Calesal always made her feel. It hurt her neck to stare at the very top. Squinting her gaze, she glimpsed Redders crawling along the lookout platforms, most lingering in the shade to avoid the blaring sun. They were always there, day and night, and it became so constant that no one asked about the walls anymore. Everyone kept their heads down. It was easy to get submerged into the world of Calesal and forget about what lay outside.

Jelan's hand became slick with sweat around the spyglass. Someone *did* see the outside. Painted it. Threw it away like garbage. A once-lived dream now abandoned. It could have been an artistic farmer, a goods transporter, even a Redder, but her gut told her no. Her gut told her whoever did this saw Calesal as something grand with an odd sparkle. It was too pretty to be drawn by someone who was a Vecerian. It held awe and allure, an eye bestowed on something new for the first time before it slowly found the dirtier parts of any beauty.

She pocketed it and turned around. Her chest felt heavy.

Kole wiped the sweat from his forehead and sighed. "It's stupid."

"You didn't have to come."

"No," he said. "It's stupid that he stole the shield from you."

Jelan dropped her hands from the cart. "I don't want to talk about it—"

"Well, I do." He ran a hand through his shaggy hair. "It was *your* work. Purely yours. But this city is plagued by greedy people, and Arvalo doesn't want anyone better or smarter than him. Which *you are.*"

Jelan glanced away. Long moments of silence passed. She could feel his gaze on her, pitying her—

"You know I wasn't just some candidate for the Sins to lure Violet out?"

Her lips pursed.

"It wasn't all a petty Mai thing. Mai can't even think like that—she gets too emotional, believe it or not. She's the outcast and her brothers overshadow her. It was the second oldest—Luka—he was the one who suggested throwing me in…because…" Kole shook his head. "Because my dad wasn't cooperating."

All things Jelan had guessed. There were layers to Arvalo's deceptions. Kole's sentencing to the Sins a while ago, that sparked Violet, wouldn't have had only Mai's tantrums written all over it. There would have been more to gain. "Why are you telling me this?"

"Because Arvalo has always won, and it isn't all him. He's got a little arsenal of cronies feeding him ideas to keep his power, but in that power…in that greed…it isn't compassionate. It's selfish. His sons, his family, they are only loyal to their daddy because dad will hand them keys to power. Not because they care." He kicked a stray piece of metal. "It happened with my family. It happens with everyone."

"So you're saying that fighting any of this is fruitless because everyone has their own agenda?"

"I'm saying that *because* everyone in the Arvalo family has their own agenda, if something better or more…*forced* comes along, then they might stop listening to their father." Kole shrugged. "It is literally the downfall of greed. No loyalty comes out of it."

Jelan glanced across the junkyard to where Ashan and Bronto, their guards, stood watch. Meema smoked a cigarette nearby, to the annoyance of her nurse Fin.

"Family is sad." Jelan frowned. "But you can't pick them, and you can't really exchange them."

"No, you can't. It all changed when I remembered, if not realized, that my mother and father were just as human as me. I wasn't the center of their lives. Other things enticed them. Even though they were obviously horrified for me to go into the Sins, even after Violet saved me and they got me back, it was only a week later, and Arvalo was everywhere, and I didn't exist anymore. It is the same for Arvalo's kids. They only exist when they benefit him. It's why Mai is thrown to the side so much, because she hardly benefits Arvalo except to show a certain dad-daughter love to the cameras."

Jelan remembered Mai's pitied look at the table when all of Jelan's hard work was taken away. *That's how it feels to be used*, Mai might as well have said.

Kole dropped a piece of metal on the cart, the rattle shaking through Jelan. "Mai just wants to be loved. With no strings attached."

"She wants to be free," Jelan said. "So we cut her loose."

Kole winked. "Checkmate."

They dragged the cart through a dusty path, and a sudden commotion caused Jelan to lift her head. Someone yelled. Ashan and Bronto were talking to a figure, who was clearly agitated, while Meema threw a middle finger. As Jelan drew closer, ignoring the alarmed look from Kole, a surprised breath loosed.

"Ahmad."

Her estranged brother pointed her way. "You."

Bronto shoved Ahmad back. "Don't you look at her like that."

"I'm her brother," Ahmad snarled. His dark skin gleamed with sweat as he addressed Jelan. "So you're all mighty with your inventions now, huh? The same kind of things that had father destroying our family…"

Skies, he was high on something. Jelan shook her head, unable to speak.

"I've been looking for you." He stepped up, but Bronto pushed him back again. "You moved out of the South, right? Working with Marin now—"

Meema snarled. "I'll bite your finger off if you point it again!"

"Doing those experiments that *killed* Mama and Calvin—"

Meema shuffled over and jammed a well-aimed hand into Ahmad's neck. Ahmad stumbled back, gasping for air. Jelan took a couple steps closer, witnessing his bloodshot eyes and the scabs on his chin.

"Do *you* think this girl deserves that?" Meema gave Ahmad a kick in the ankle. "Surprising her here all drugged up and angry? *You* abandoned her."

He didn't, but Jelan had still been too forgiving to be angry at him about it. He had abandoned Jelan to drugs until she tearfully escaped at seventeen.

"I was going to find you! I was going to help you! But you went to the *enemy*—"

"The only enemy is the pity you have for yourself." Jelan's hard tone surprised her, but she clenched her fists and stood her ground. Ahmad's eyes fell on her scars. "Clearly you haven't changed since your words are still filled with lies."

That's all Ahmad and the drugs ever told her—lies. About where he had been, about his health, about money and getting food on the table.

"What kind of drugs did Arvalo's gardia give you in exchange for Souther Plastechs?" Jelan tried to tame the anger and hurt in her voice.

"Look, I'm done with him. He got his position, he makes his weapons, sends them outside the walls…" Ahmad put his hands up. "I got money now. I was doing it so I can come back to you. It was just a few. Just a few people, and then we could be happy again, together. Like the good ol' days." A lopsided smile spread on his face. "You remember those, right, J? Just you and me. Us against the world. I got the money now, and I just need to get clean and then we can escape. Travel like you always wanted to…"

Everyone stared at her now. Her hands shook, tears burned her eyes.

"I said I would come back," Ahmad said, almost to himself. His voice rose. "Now I did. Here I am. But you…look at you. You already forgot about me. About all I did for you."

"I made a life for myself, Ahmad. Thank you for what you gave me those three years, but I…" Her throat began to close, and she swallowed through it. "I know I'm not as important as that high. I never will be. Nor will the lives you handed over."

"They were just sacrifices, J. Arvalo needed them. I wasn't the only one. There were a lot of recruiters. They needed bodies, and I was desperate. So I gave them names, and then those people were gone. I didn't know they would be killed in plasma experiments." Ahmad dropped to his knees before Jelan, folded his hands together, and begged with those bloodshot eyes. "I only ever wanted to save you."

Jelan's voice was a broken whisper. "I saved myself."

Bronto and Ashan got the memo. They shielded her from Ahmad's gaze as they dragged the cart back toward the street.

Meema spat at Ahmad's feet. "I wiped those tears, boy. I'll never forgive you for that."

Jelan guessed Meema might wipe more tonight. She'd done it a couple times since Arvalo took her work. It was always a silent, never-talked-about exchange, but Meema did it, and Jelan let her.

As they reached the giant, blacked-out car, Ahmad's voice flowed.

"Father's not doing well! He's dying, J. Go see him if you have any love for your family left in your heart!"

It took every muscle to shut the door and block out his pleas.

❋ ❋ ❋

Jelan, unfortunately, listened. It was time. She needed to see her father.

One look in the rearview mirror from Bronto had her nodding. He nodded back. Within ten minutes, everyone else piled into Ashan's car and drove back to the North.

Only when she was alone with Bronto, did his gravelly voice say something. "Where does he live?"

"Honestly, not far from here."

Jelan gave him directions, and Bronto drove, eyes aware, analyzing everyone on the street in the deep South. It was gross, dirty. Buildings crumbled; apartments hung on by a thread. So many people lay on the streets, baking in the sun, with needles sticking out of their arms. Jelan had only been here twice to see her father and hated it every time. It was a part of the city that was abandoned—all these people forgotten and left with their drug-induced minds and no help, no care, no anything.

The wasteland of the Deep South didn't get any better as Bronto pulled up to the curb before a dilapidated, four-story apartment building with the main door off its hinges. Jelan glanced at the two passed-out women on the steps, then to the flies buzzing around their mouths.

"Sorry you have to see this," Jelan mumbled.

"I grew up in the South." Bronto put the car into park. "My aunt was a drug addict. We rarely saw her until she'd break into our home and steal something of value. Which there wasn't much of."

Jelan took a deep breath.

Bronto stepped out and shut his door, the hulking man in his sunglasses like a beacon on the street. The fact that his face was clean-shaven made him foreign to those here. He stepped up to the two women on the stoop, held a hand over their mouths, and nodded. He opened Jelan's door. "They're alive. Barely. I'll call someone to come get them."

Jelan hated her emotions when it came to this. She was always torn between helping and ignoring. It was easier, almost, to imagine that addicts chose this—chose to dig their own graves and lay themselves in it. But her denial never helped. Addiction was addiction. No one chose it, they simply lived it, unable to leave unless a miracle of will occurred. But even if she were to drop everything and help, she was plagued by the pain of watching those she loved waste away. So she pitied.

She shoved her hands in her pockets and quickly walked up the steps. "I won't be long. Thirty minutes, at most."

"You want me to come in with you?" Bronto asked.

"No, I can handle it."

"I'll be right out here."

"Thanks."

Jelan ducked into the apartment complex. It smelled like rotting wood, feces, and spilled shiva. She dipped her head from a broken ceiling board and walked silently down the hallway. She ignored the open doors, the growing smell of unwashed bodies. Stomping her emotions down, she climbed to the third floor, clearing her face of any expression, and found the door for three-twelve.

She knocked. Twice. She didn't expect an answer, but she didn't want to surprise him. She twisted the grimy doorknob and poked her head in.

"Dad?"

It was a small studio apartment with peeling walls and exposed brick. A metal table with a portable stove made up the kitchen. Underneath was the small refrigerator she had installed for him a while back. The air conditioning whined on the dusty window. A small cot sat in the corner, a rug lay on the floor, and then the plush chair Jelan had snagged from a yard sale and dragged down here in that first year. She'd been fourteen, but she furnished most of the place. Her father didn't touch anything plasma-related after the incident. It would bring on a panic attack. He'd sleep in the dark, sweat through the heat, so she was forced to install most things.

Vaughn Gregory sat in that plush chair, a blanket slung over his lap. The air conditioning was set to a freezing temperature. Goosebumps littered her arms. He watched the small plascreen that featured some old sport where they kicked a ball with their feet. Bottles of shiva littered the ground, and a half-drunk one sat in his hand.

"It's me," she said.

He said nothing.

She walked through the apartment and took in the grimy bathroom with a toothbrush that had mold around it. A deep sigh. "I'm sorry I haven't visited in a while."

She punched the guilt away. He left them immediately after the incident. He saw the rim of a glass more than her face, but she couldn't ignore how his deterioration felt like *her* fault. She was the only sane one left, and *she* let it get this bad.

She turned around, keeping her hands in her pockets. Every time her father glimpsed the burn scars, he'd take a drink.

Her eyes burned even though her chest felt like a gaping hole. Empty. Numb. But she turned around. Faced him. Positioned herself slightly in front of the plascreen so she could look at him fully.

Hollowed-out cheeks on dark-brown skin. A long gray beard, a bald head. A burn scar flowed from his jaw, down his neck, and beneath his stained shirt where it met his armpit. His amber eyes were bleak, but they flicked to her boots, her legs, then, per usual, to her hands shoved into her pants pockets. Then they went back to the plascreen.

"Ahmad found me. He said you weren't doing well."

He huffed. As if to say, *isn't it obvious?*

"I'll get you some fresh food and clean up the bathroom. The toilet looks clogged."

Another huff. *Don't bother.*

She'd still do it anyway. It would make her feel better. Not him, though. *Her.*

Frustration clawed her way in. Look at her, living in a penthouse in the North and forgetting she had a family. Leaving her father, whom she shared the plasma engineering interest with, to this disaster. She thought leaving him alone would help him, that maybe he'd think of her and want to fix himself *for* her. She thought the same of Ahmad, and that was clearly futile. But Jelan was tired—tired of seeing her family like this, tired of feeling the guilt for something that was no one's fault, tired of a world that never gave them mercy, and certainly tired of all this self-pity.

She was fucking *tired.*

"I never blamed you for their deaths," Jelan muttered. "I didn't blame anyone."

Her father's eyes turned her way.

"I blame you, though, for making life stop just because of a tragedy."

His grayish lips pursed.

"If you think you should have died in that fire, fine. Think that. Go do it even." Her nostrils flared. "You are consumed by this guilt that doesn't even belong to you. It doesn't belong to *anyone*. We lost them. That's that. But look, you're still here and so am I. I…" She looked down to her feet. "I'm doing really well. But I work with plasma now and I create things that you helped me dream of, and I am surrounded by people who support me. I didn't think it could be like this, but by some miracle, the world gave me a favor, and now I want to give one to you."

His eyes found hers again. Watched as a tear streaked her cheek.

"I have money now. I live in the North. I have every convenience we could have dreamed of. It won't erase the past, but it will pave a better future because…she'd want us to be happy. The fire was from loose wires that had fallen from the ceiling before you did your experiment. It wasn't anyone's fault. No one could have known. I'm tired, Dad. I'm tired of mourning her and Calvin and Ahmad and you. I'm *tired* of acting like you're dead. I want you back, but only if you *want* to come back. Not for me, either. But for yourself. For *her*."

She could have sworn his eyes watered. He blinked it away.

"I will get you a new place, help, anything you want, but you have to come to me completely sober, and with every intention of wanting to leave all of this"—she nodded to the room—"behind."

And with that speech, she walked up to her father, took his shiva bottle and replaced it with her scarred hands. "I work with plasma with these hands. I faced my fears. Now it is your turn."

He stared at her scars. He didn't squeeze back, didn't do anything but look at her hands with despair. She bent, kissed the top of his head, and let him go.

She shut the door softly behind her.

The way outside felt faster than her journey in. The sun met her cheeks, and she took a deep breath on top of the stoop. Both the women were gone, the stairs freshly swept, and when she looked to the street, Bronto's car was gone, too, replaced by a plasbike, two helmets, and a solemn Lucien.

She stiffened. "How?"

"Bronto."

"Did he tell you directly?"

"Don't be surprised I keep tabs on you," he said with a small smile. "But no, he asked a gardia higher-up for medics to come to the South. Something like that is overseen by Lyla, and it reaches me. Bronto knows, though, that I would hear of it."

Jelan took a step down. "It's dangerous for you out here."

He nearly rolled his eyes. "You think I'm that useless?"

"I think coming all the way down here is a bit useless."

His gaze lingered on the building. "Is he okay?"

"No, but I'll grab him some things and drop them off later." Jelan reached the curb. She sucked in another breath as tears breached her eyes. His face scrunched with pity.

"Don't look at me like that," she gritted. "I'm not embarrassed for the life I was born into, nor the life I lived."

His expression hardened slightly. "I would never pity you. Nor your family." Jelan wanted to scoff, but Lucien held her gaze. "Believe me when I say this, life was not kind to my family, either. I worked for all this after every tragedy imaginable, but I can't change it, so I fight for something better. For *everyone*."

She turned her head, her throat tight.

Lucien's finger was there, tucked under her chin, making her look back at him.

She only nodded.

The tears broke free, silent and hot, and he pulled her tightly into his chest, hand going to the back of her head and fingers threading with her braids.

Lucien had definitely heard about the junkyard, and on this decrepit street, it all caught up with Jelan. Her ruined family, her stolen work. Every hope felt distant from her grasp.

"Let's go for a ride, then we will meet up with the others at a bar in the Mid. We have things to discuss."

She could only nod at this point, but he pulled her back and wiped her face, sparing another glance up to the building where his gaze stayed. She followed it.

Her father was looking down at them, frowning.

There was no bottle in his hands.

Lucien clenched his jaw, but turned to the bike and shoved Jelan's helmet on, fastening it, double-checking, before fixing his own.

"By the end of this, I want you smiling," he said with the hint of a command and a grin.

She looked back to the window, but her father was gone. "So demanding."

He laughed, then said more seriously, "I'll send people to help your father. Get things cleaned. Nothing overwhelming."

Jelan hopped on behind him and wrapped her arms around his waist. He patted her hands before starting the bike. A moment later, they zoomed off, and Jelan found a smile emerging on her face.

❈❈❈

Hira's glasses were lopsided on her head when they arrived at the Neon Glory Bar in the eastern Mid. Her hair was a mess, her skirt on backward, and when Jelan hopped off the bike and pointed to it, she huffed and fixed it. "This better be important because I left a *heavily* muscled man in my bed."

"Tragic…is he new?"

"Fairly new. I left him a puzzle to entertain himself. He looked at it like it would bite him. I'm excited to see his progress." Hira crossed her arms. "Why here?"

"Because I like it," Lucien said as he brushed Jelan's side and walked past the bouncer, both exchanging a knowing nod.

The minute they walked into the dim, empty, low-ceiling room filled with armchairs and end tables, Hira stomped her foot. "It's *closed.*"

Lucien took a seat. "Of course. It's early afternoon."

"But no worries, it's extra attention and free drinks when this handsome fellow owns it."

Jelan's head turned to the voice. Jenkins leaned against the bar where a very reluctant bartender—Lyla—poured him a blue drink. Next to Lyla, a giant, dark-skinned man with gold earrings and a glistening bald head watched Jenkins stoically.

Cairo was his name. Jelan had met him a few times, but he mostly kept quiet and worked outside of the penthouse. Cairo was logistics, math, numbers, and primarily responsible for the trade routes in the city and managing the business deals between the districts. He was the head of Lucien's commandments to the City, and just as powerful as Lyla, who basically ran all security, underground trading, and illegal gardia things.

"It's an important meeting, don't give him the whole bottle," Cairo scolded.

Lyla flashed him the finger. "Jenkins deserves his drink. He's been in infiltration mode for the last three months."

Jenkins smiled slyly. "You're a darling, Lyla."

"Shut up."

It took a minute to get everyone settled. But once they all faced each other in the little armchairs—Cairo penciling the meeting in a language he created that has a ridiculous code and would be impossible to break—did Lucien clear his throat.

"I have nearly five-hundred men working for me both legally and illegally, and you here are the ones I trust out of all of them. It's fairly obvious to point out, but I want you to know that. You are here for a reason, because while this Empire is going under because of Arvalo, it is up to us to fix it." Lucien folded his hands. "Everyone here knows what occurred at the Emperor's mansion. Everyone knows the violent power Arvalo now holds and wants to maintain. It doesn't take much to imagine he wants to create a city that bows to him, in his favor, rather than a government that bows toward fairness and democracy. He plans on jeopardizing our place in this world *and* our world, as shown by his efforts to destroy the

Sky Arches months ago. Arvalo is the number one enemy, and I want him killed within the next six months. No later."

Jelan retained the words, but she was staring at Lucien the entire time. Watching the hardness to his gaze, the rough, sensual tone to his voice. He wasn't the one giving her a ride to cheer her up, he was a commander. He was responsible for a fifth of the city, and something about the way he handled that power had heat drifting into her low belly.

"We need to get ahead of Arvalo in terms of weapon development. Not necessarily create more, but we need to know what he is expediting in production and sending to..." Lyla scowled, as if still doubting it. "To the world of Greed."

It was bizarre to think about. Everyone in the room had the same face—confusion, suspicion. It made it so there was a different way into the Sins, and therefore some other war going on.

"It doesn't take much to presume that Greed is the sixth world," Cairo said. "That is where everyone is stuck. That is where our Jack has fallen. That is *also* where the girl, Violet Sutton, is now, and nearly died once she entered it."

Jelan had a bucket underneath her chin when she watched that. Violet's danger dot, as Hira called it, blinked red for an extremely long time until two *days* later, it was green. Meema had been an absolute mess.

Lyla nodded. "This means the Sins are compromised. Something or someone is keeping everyone stuck in that world, and also has access to ours to benefit from plasma. That is two goals in itself; know what weapons are being sent there, and finding out *how* it is being sent."

"I want two teams, five each, of your best people, and I want them to take a strong dose of one of Hira's serums so we can vet them. They can't have ties to this world. Your most isolated soldiers, Lyla," Lucien said. "I will meet with each of them in four days' time."

Lyla nodded. Cairo scribbled away.

"But..." Lucien turned to Jelan. "We do need a new weapon. A new something. Can be for defense or offense. We need a decoy, and a real thing. Arvalo's thievery may have prevented you from creating more plashields, but it doesn't restrict you from creating enhanced ones or different things entirely. I want a decoy so we can distract him—make him think we are planning destruction or some shit like that, and stress him out a bit. When in reality, we are building another arsenal." Lucien's gaze softened on Jelan, and a small smile lifted her lips. His eyes dipped. Her cheeks heated. He continued, "I know you like working alone, and you still can, but I am requiring you to hire a small team to assist. We will get you a bigger, offsite lab as well."

He looked at her like she was his next meal. What was going on? Why was she so turned on by this? His commands went straight into her, and she dumbly nodded. "Okay."

"Pl*ass*hield—the new and improved." Hira giggled.

Jenkins shot back the rest of his drink that he'd been nose-deep in. "There's 'ass' in there."

"I know, that is why I emphasized it." Hira wrinkled her nose. "It is a fantastic idea."

"It's childish—"

"Plasshield." Jelan tapped her armrest. "Done."

Jenkins rolled his eyes and Hira stuck her tongue out at him.

Lucien ignored the interaction. "Jenkins, I want to speak with you privately about your findings and go over some of the reports you gave me. The general consensus is that Arvalo is making slow, calculated moves to establish his control. Do a couple of things, let some weeks go by so Calesal gets used to it, and then tack on more laws. His kids are also lying low; the eldest is always at plasgun shooting ranges, the second of course has his new role, the third brother is still traveling to the North to get his party fix. Arvalo isn't stupid enough to give him responsibilities. The fourth of course is out of commission from his driving accident a bit ago, and Mai comes and goes."

Lyla leaned in. "We need eyes on the second oldest—Luka. The one taking over Plastech Industries. He's hard to track, extremely secretive, and definitely the smartest of the bunch."

"No," Jelan said, then stiffened at Lyla's glare. "I mean, we need eyes on him, yes, but going after him is too obvious. Not when they just stole the plashield plans. Thwarting Arvalo needs to be as calculated as he is, and I think that starts with turning his *looser* kids against him." Jelan swallowed the lump in her throat. "Like Mai."

"*That* bitch?" Jenkins groaned.

"I think—"

"Mai is Arvalo's forgotten child. Arvalo won't give a shit if she turns."

"What I'm *saying*," Jelan gritted, glaring at Jenkins. "Is that we *make* him care."

"And how do you propose we do that?" Lucien asked.

"We kidnap her," Jelan said.

Hira cackled. "What the actual fuck."

Lyla's mouth opened. Cairo raised a brow. Jenkins chewed on an ice cube, clearly judging Jelan. Lucien looked a little lost, but urged her to elaborate.

Jelan sighed back into the chair. "Well, not *us*. But we hire people to. A third party. Make it public. Force him to show that he wants her back and cares. They eventually find her—we let them—and she goes right back to the mansion." Jelan smirked. "On *our* side and ready to spy on daddy."

"Holy skies," Hira breathed. "That's crazy."

"Risky," Lyla said.

"Impractical," Cairo muttered.

"It might just be perfect." Lucien smiled.

And that smile shot electricity through Jelan.

Lucien turned to Lyla. "I want a detailed plan written up. Let's kidnap the only daughter of our Emperor."

14

I Do

"**AND THAT'S ALL MINE, BOYS.**"

Violet's cig hung between her lips as she gathered her chips and added them to her massive pile. She couldn't resist smirking.

Skies, she *loved* gambling.

She lost quite a few times at first in the last ten days, but her money was borrowed from pockets of the richer folks who shopped at the massive mall in North Hanhii. It wasn't much, but it did provide her a foundation to sit at one of the card tables in Jungers—an infamous underground gambling city that has gotten her really fucking rich. Rich in Navru terms. This wouldn't be able to get her out of the district—not that she wanted to. But it was extremely fun watching the defeated faces of her card adversaries. She was greedy for their disappointment.

So much fun.

Do you want more? The cold, wise voice of Greed whispered to her. Violet's heart picked up. It flipped to her other ear. *Take more—*

Violet fought the urges of the Sin. She clenched her fists that so desperately wanted to pick up another round of cards.

Come on, you like to win. You already won against me. You liked that, didn't you? Like to be on top of things, don't you?

"I think I'll check out, please," she gritted through her teeth. The dealer grumbled as he calculated her chips and handed her a paper card to redeem her money.

The Sin laughed and slithered to the back of her mind. *I'll get you, little Vanisher.*

Nausea soured her gut. Fighting the Sin proved to be a difficult thing after she agreed to the deal for a glamour. As she stood, she checked her strings. Greed's strings. Those little golden lines holding her disguise in place.

"You're a fucking witch," one of her opponents mumbled.

"It's about the luck, my friend." Violet playfully frowned. "And you need to learn how to read. That's a number four, not a two."

"Hey!" He stood in anger, knocking his chair back. "I know how to read!"

But Violet was already hurrying away, calling over her shoulder, "I'm just telling you the truth! You're pretty shitty!"

Violet lost herself in the smoky haze and crowded bodies. The night was in full swing. Music blasted in the grimy, low-lit place, and drugs lay out over multiple tables. She pocketed her winnings card and felt for the little baggy. Dilated, nearly black eyes stared hungrily at either their one chip or hundreds. Others didn't quite care about the money. The winning enticed them, like it did her. They loved the greed of ego, the blurred lines between this world's sin and pride. Others drank heavily, or leaned into a lover, or beckoned more drugs.

"Oh, look at you," Violet said as she leaned on the back of her target's chair. "Winning, finally."

The man scoffed and fished out a bill from his pocket. "I don't pay for smart talk."

"Fortunately for you, that's free." Violet slid the baggy of flintroot into his hand, taking the money, and moved on.

Another client here and a few who winked rather oddly at her there, Violet finally made her way to the redeem booth and got her earnings from the gambles. There was a bounce in her step as she exited down the dark, underground hallway leading to the outside streets. She loosened her strings—blonde hair to brown, green eyes to blue, pale skin to her tan—before she yanked them into another glamour.

Rich black locks shifted as she flung her hair up into a ponytail, followed by brown eyes, a smaller mouth, a nose she really liked—one with a hook and a tiny bump—and a square jaw.

The colors only tingled, but the changes in bone structure hurt the first few times. After repeated practice, it became a strong ache, like a harsh bruise or a worn muscle. Violet took the ascending steps, pulling her hood up, and walked out onto the busy market street.

Next on the agenda: some delicious noodles.

She elbowed her hip, making sure her plasblade remained in position, then headed down the street. Save for the wet pavement after a rainy day, it could have been the South. She wove through the bartering crowds, the neon lights glimmering as boots slapped in puddles. Music blared from a nearby bar. She made her first left, and four blocks later, another right. Cars passed, followed by revving motorbikes.

She rounded a corner through a small cement park, and nearly collided with a red-robed preacher from the Order of Avaritia. Violet bristled as the preacher merely looked over his shoulder, scowled, then faced toward a giant circle of other preachers. Fifteen of them gathered, palms turned up. They began to hum.

Violet scurried around them, hating how her heart raced. Their chants grew louder, praising their god of greed, and soon, it resounded throughout the park, waking drunks and homeless and turning the attention from the bars.

"Avaritia watches over us. He loves us! Those who support him are destined for riches and for the beautiful afterlife! May he strike down those who ignore him, who say his name in vain!"

It was instant. Every person lingering on the street bowed their heads or dropped to their knees. Watched as the preachers screamed their hymns. Violet scrunched her brows.

One preacher pointed at her. "Bow down! You must bow to Avaritia!"

She hesitated between smacking his hand away or punching him in the face, but a woman nearby caught Violet's gaze from her kneeled position and slowly shook her head. Violet bit her tongue and dropped her chin. The preacher huffed in satisfaction.

"*Just bow*," Bryce had said to Violet after checking on her yesterday. "*They are trying to infiltrate Navru, but they've been struggling because of us. It might suck, but when you're alone and not on a mission, just bow. Or else they will mark you.*"

Little by little, Violet edged past the group, and once she was clear, she sprinted down the street. Her hip ached, but after more of Sasha's treatments, and her resolve to get away from Bunny's talking, it was nearly functional. Her arm hurt when she lifted it in certain ways, but otherwise, she'd pop a painkiller and call it a day.

She eyed the noodles restaurant with its bright yellow sign, before someone grabbed her arm and yanked her into a nearby alley. Violet jammed her elbow out, knocking the assailant in the jaw—

"Ow! It's me, you bitch!"

Violet shoved Emryn into the wall. "Could you not start with hello?"

She smiled brightly. "You have good reflexes. How'd you do on your second outing?"

Violet patted her pocket with money from the drugs and the few bags she had leftover. "Fine, just the regular clients and a few extras."

"Well, flintroot is a plant. Makes you all high and stuff, but it's not addictive, and that's what we want. 'Cause we need the money for our..." A wink. "*Services.*"

Violet darted her gaze back to the street, but no one loitered.

Emryn slapped a paper on Violet's chest. "And it's perfect timing because we finally have our first mission together."

Violet's stomach growled in protest. "Can I at least get a bite to eat?"

"Fine," Emryn said and padded the bag on her back. "We have to change anyway, and stop by Meretta's. She's got our fancy weapons."

Violet shoved Emryn away again and stomped to the street. "I want my damn noodles."

Emryn hurried behind her, holding out a smoke. "Probably this, too."

The corner of Violet's mouth lifted. She took it. Dragged a hit. "This shit is smooth."

Emryn cheekily smiled and plucked the cigarette from Violet's hand. She stuck it between her lips, inhaling deeply, then watched the smoke seep from her mouth. She liked to make it sift through her cleft. "I know, right?"

They ventured to the nearby noodle shop and chowed while making fun of passersby. With full stomachs, they carried on through Navru, until Emryn pulled Violet into an unassuming alley.

"So, this Meretta loves daggers, fixes up bikes, and runs drugs?" Violet asked.

"Yes." Emryn sidled up to a metal door nestled between two mounds of trash bags. She rapped three times. Nothing. Another three times. Still nothing. Emryn huffed, "And she likes making people wait. Come on, Ret! Open up."

"I'm *coming!*" The door flung open, revealing a figure that Violet had to drop her eyes for.

Meretta was not what she was expecting. Dark-brown skin, hair tightly coiled into two low buns, large cheeks, and small eyes. But the biggest recognition was something Violet had only seen a couple times in her life. A birth defect, one that caused a certain, recognizable face with a slumped jaw. But the alertness was there, and Violet knew when she was around a person who was not to be messed with.

Meretta's brown eyes snapped to Emryn. "You look like shit." Her eyes shifted to Violet. "You also look like shit."

In the Navru District, after dealing with the heavy rain on the hour-long walk here, Violet didn't doubt Meretta, but based on the way she said it, and the way Emryn didn't blink, insulting at first sight seemed to be a normal trait.

Emryn shoved past the woman. "You got some coffee, Ret?"

"Make it yourself." Meretta turned to Violet. "Who are you?"

"Violet."

"Do you know how bad your breath smells?" Meretta stepped close, sniffing. "Garlic."

Violet tried to take a step in, but Meretta darted her arm out, blocking her. Violet's nostrils flared. "Did you forget to take a chromosome with you when you were born?"

"Ha!" Emryn laughed from down the hallway.

Violet was half-expecting a punch to the face for that one, but Meretta blinked, then burst into laughter. It was bright, cheery, with the occasional snorts. "Stop…ah…wow, that's funny." She looked at Violet. "You're funny. Come in. Get some coffee."

It was a grimy building with tiny hallways and even tinier rooms, but Meretta made use out of the bottom floor of the warehouse. Grace, the scowling Droan, appeared in the kitchen as the coffee finished, and when Emryn and Violet changed into their all-black, lithe fighting clothes, they followed Meretta to a door with six high-tech locks.

Merretta pushed the door open. "I got some new pieces."

Emryn shoved herself into the room, knocking Violet back into the wall. "Holy *shit*, Meretta. You scored this stuff?"

She responded with a satisfied smile. "Modified it, too."

"It's *pink!*" Emryn squealed.

Violet stepped into the room and nearly peed herself. A vault. An *insane* vault. She had to look up first, where rows of weapons hung mounted to hooks, and a ladder wheeled around for access. All things plasma: blades, guns, katanas, whips, tasers, axes, bows, arrows, and more. Any violent device that one could think of lay here, gatekept by Meretta, whose smile didn't dwindle.

There were shelves made for colorful weapons, one a pink plasgun Emryn held. She practiced with it, pressing the trigger, and Meretta mumbled, "They aren't loaded in here."

Violet's eyes landed on the beautiful purple-hilt of a long plasblade. Violet picked it up, noticing the modified sigil—not Plastech Industries' symbol, but a…

"Is that a middle finger?" Violet looked closer. "With a ribbon around it?"

Meretta leaned against the wall. "My own design. A gift to all those who deserve the end of that blade."

Violet quipped, "You're smart."

Meretta tapped her head. "It is what the *extra* chromosome is for, asshole."

Violet snorted, then thumbed the sigil and a beautiful, breathtaking blade sprang out. It was a mix of a thin katana-like sword, but with the crescent-moon curve at the point. Onyx in color, it glittered underneath the lights, a thin line of silver following the pristine metal from hilt to the end's curve, where the line formed a five-pointed star.

"Nostor," Violet breathed. "The metal from Envy." She needed to get Anaya one as soon as Violet dragged them to this world.

"Not entirely nostor, but the outside bit, yes. A full pound of nostor is extremely expensive, not only because it's mined underwater, but because the Worldbreaker's cronies hog it all for their little inventions."

"How did you get this?" Violet asked.

Meretta shrugged. "Those little Fringe Vanishers can be bribed."

"She's a genius, even though she's incredibly insulting. Not to the Fringe, of course, because some work with our male comrades in Pharos." Emryn said as she sheathed another gun—this one bright baby blue—to her other side. She stuck some simpler daggers in the hidden pockets of her pants. "But the males don't get to do the fun stuff like this."

"Are most recon missions this weaponized?" Violet asked. She strapped the purple hilt to her hip, stuffed a black plasgun in the strap at her thigh, then proceeded to find nooks for the daggers.

"Sometimes we need to fight our way out," Emryn said. "But for the Residential School, we shouldn't be going too far in. We need certain information—how many kids, their ages, staff schedules, security, stuff like that. After, we will prepare for the full mission. Save those kids and bring them home with our Fringe contacts."

"It feels a bit unbelievable the Worldbreaker has Vanishers working against him," Violet said.

"It is the downfall of Greed," Grace clarified while leaning against the threshold to the vault. "Everyone wants their own gain. No one is entirely loyal. The ones who do work with us don't do it because they have some savior, warrior streak shit…they do it because we give them the plant drugs."

Emryn cackled. "Easy shits."

"This city isn't the Worldbreaker," Grace continued. "The Order, the schools, all of Greed. It *started* with him, but it isn't him. He doesn't interact with the Order or show his face much in Greed. The people in the Twin Cities just know him by title, and the occasional picture, but he stays away, doing whatever else. The Order has taken over the Twin Cities, and that all started with the line of Chancellors—the current one is an old fuck who sits on his gold throne and calls for the Order's values in every breathing being. Like *every* being. They want to go to every world and strip all the cultures and do more damage to basic life. Even the Droans—my people—fought them, but the Droans won by killing the Order's emissaries." Grace jutted her chin to the mission paper Emryn held. "I'm from one of those schools. Bryce's predecessor saved me. They leave my world alone now, mainly focus on Envy, Lust, Sloth, and Gluttony where the Farms have been demolished by the Inaj and they've taken back their lands."

Emryn stuck her hands on her hips. "But we've heard reports of Order missionaries burning leftover villages in Envy, any other religions in Lust, and of course, conquering more nations in Greed."

Violet finished stocking her weapons and let out a deep, burning sigh. "I can't believe you guys face all this."

"There are levels to Greed," Grace said. Meretta nodded. "The big, frightening ambitions that mean taking over entire worlds, turning populations into followers, and becoming unstoppable. Then there's…more personal things: gaining unfathomable wealth, having a giant house, a big family, influence, fame, or power. Other more comprehensible, but still unreachable things. Greed has you focus on those. It milks your ambitions for all it's worth, until you reach your goal and you're sucked dry. Then another goal spawns.

It's never enough. Greed doesn't stop. It is an incurable virus no one realizes they have."

Emryn stepped in. "*But* while it can be daunting to look at this massive foundation someone built of wealth, you wonder, 'how can I take that down?'"

"So we chip away the bottoms while they focus on the top." Meretta leered. "The small things that keep it moving."

Violet's face twisted in confusion. Grace chimed in, "Do you think the most important position in a restaurant is the owner? The manager?"

Violet pursed her lips. "No."

"It's the dishwasher!" Emryn called through her hands and pumped a fist in the air. "We need the forks! The knives! The bowls! All of it. Or else you can't fucking eat!"

Grace continued, "The manager can schedule who he wants, and the owner can make their money, but their business won't run properly without their dishwasher. The food can't be cooked without clean pots, the drinks can't be served without clean glasses. It is the dishwasher."

"And then the one who mops the floors or even just takes the orders, because those guys make it all look good," Emryn said.

"People don't realize what exists at the bottom of their empires, their wealth, until it's all taken away. And we, Pharos, take it away. We chip at the bottoms of the Order until the foundation is gone and the entire thing crumbles. And you know who is at the bottom?"

"The children." Violet's eyes popped, her voice breathy with realization. "Because if there isn't anyone to pass the teachings on to, then the religion, the power, will go extinct."

Emryn faked a punch into the air. "This one is a big school. It hosts nearly every kind of race from the different worlds, and they indoctrinate these children to continue to spread their message, their hate, their control. So we are taking it down." Emryn fixed her dark eyes on Violet. "Are you ready to take down this freedom-eating, racist, body-controlling, power-hungry institution?"

"One more question," Violet said. "What do you do about the people who genuinely like this religion?"

Emryn cackled. "I don't give a *fuck* about anyone's beliefs. As long as you don't shove it down others' throats, you can believe whatever you want. But once you cause pain based on your dogma, I'm taking you to the dark underworld with me."

Violet smirked. "Then let's skivvin' do it."

Emryn clapped happily. "Meretta! I request a bike, please!"

Ten minutes later, and Violet's vision was concealed behind a shadowy visor of a helmet. Emryn started the plasbike, and it shifted into gear, a soft roar filling Meretta's garage. The little chromy had nearly ten plasbikes all re-engineered to be smooth, silent, colorful rides. Plasma danced in its tubes, little spiky, twisting balls of the energy shifting from green to pink to blue to red. Emryn squealed in delight. "It's so *pretty!*"

Even though Meretta's expression was usually snarky or unimpressed, when Emryn praised her, a genuine smile began to form until she jerked it back into a scowl. "Don't crash it."

Emryn rolled her eyes and closed her visor. "That was *one* time."

Violet clutched Emryn's middle as the girl gunned it, screeched out of the garage, and onto the misty, tight streets of Navru.

"You'll have to teach me," Violet called from behind.

She felt Emryn's hearty laughter. "Sure, I'll take you to the local racetrack."

Emryn swerved the bike so hard that Violet yelped. It dipped toward the street and Emryn let out a holler of glee. Violet's nails dug into her gloves so hard she thought they would break. This girl was fucking crazy.

But a part of Violet loved it.

Emryn zoomed over one of the four bridges connecting Hanhii to Hallow and swerved through numerous streets before she flicked a button and the engine silenced. The bike continued like normal, the only sounds the wet wheels scraping the pavement.

Hallow was different from Hanhii. It was certainly cleaner, but quieter as well. Where Hanhii was rowdy and had a good chunk belonging only to the poorer Navru district, Hallow was comprised of Cyran's skyscraper fortress, businesses, towering bridged buildings, and the city's Elite.

On top of that, it held the Church District. As they edged closer, there were more gilded steeples and the smell of incense. Bright red signs littered the streetlamps, most demanding women dress appropriately and warning that surveillance operated at all times. Hallow was watched day in and day out. Everyone was tracked. The cameras would see them as a small shadow on the screen—two black blobs swerving in and out. But Pharos knew which alleys were out of the cameras' view, so when Emryn jerked the bike into one, Violet finally breathed.

They tugged off their gear in silence. The gloves stayed on and masks went up. A black bandana covered the lower half of Violet's face, but the material was designed in a way that if a picture was taken, the reflective lines would destroy the photograph.

"Ready?" Emryn muttered.

Violet nodded.

"You'll follow me. Remember, we're here for information only."

"Got it."

Emryn tugged on Violet's leathers, her eyes narrowed. "*Information only*. You might see things that make you want to act, but if we want a successful mission, we need to gather as much intel as we can and leave no trace."

Violet shoved her away. "I got it."

"Great. This one is located a little ways into the Church District. We will need to hop the plasma fence." She procured a small, box-shaped device. "Be quick. Plasma burns hurt like a fucker."

"I know that." Violet rubbed her shoulder where she'd been scathed by a plasbullet when she was younger. "Let's go."

They stuck to the edges of the streets. Cars passed, and when they did, Violet and Emryn flattened themselves into little shadowy blobs. It wasn't long until Emryn dragged Violet through two alleys and the Church District's fence appeared. A tall, iron black thing, it had thin, twisting lines of plasma around it. As Violet drew closer, her face warmed. "Is this thing on all the time?"

"Only at night when they have their curfew." Emryn rolled her eyes. "Well, the curfew that only applies to women and children. If the men want to leave to go to the gentlemen clubs, they can. No one will stop them."

Beyond the heated fence, dark-windowed homes and buildings extended until the farthest were a blur. The streetlamps cast an eerie glow to the nearly empty roads. Violet leaned in closer, squinting between the bars, to catch the faint gold of the cathedral steeple glimpsed between tall skyrises.

Emryn shoved her shoulder. "You first." She placed the little black box onto the fence and pressed two buttons on the side, like a reverse taser. Four iron bars lost their power, and Violet didn't waste a breath jumping on them. Emryn held it there, gritting her teeth, until Violet swung herself over the top and landed lightly on her feet at the other side.

Emryn removed the black box. The plasma sprung up around the fence. She tossed it to Violet, and a beat later, Violet was pressing the buttons, removing the energy, and Emryn scaled the iron.

It took a while to find the right alleys that led to the school. Violet buzzed with energy, so she busied her hands by checking her mask, her clothes, her weapons every couple of steps, until Emryn halted and pointed to a gigantic white building with yet another plasma fence.

Emryn turned to her, whispering, "Recon already caught four guards patrolling the grounds during these hours. One usually takes a smoke break, while another has a bladder issue and pees every thirty minutes. They hang together. We wait for the opening, and then we climb the fence. Once we are in, we find the headmaster's office and locate the records."

Violet felt this question might have been too obvious to ask, but she did it anyway. Her eyes stayed on the residential buildings surrounding the school. "Do these people…do people in the Order know about this place?"

Emryn shook her head. "They are called devotion centers to the rest of the city, where kids can go for a rather permanent time to be educated under the Order. Except they don't have kids from the Twin Cities itself, unless they steal them from Navru…which they do. They would have done that to you."

"Taken me to a devotion center?"

"Well, a center specifically for young, able-bodied females who can reproduce, yes." Emryn's cleft lip turned into a snarl. "There's fifty of them in this district alone, but more throughout the city. I escaped through one in North Hanhii. Ran straight to Navru. But the one's here…there's no leaving them, no matter how much you beg, you fight, or you try. They'll always catch you."

Because Greed leaves no room for mistakes when it comes to control. One escape, and the system clenches harder, becomes worse. Violet heard it in the Sin's voice—it valued the game, but it hated mistakes. It hated *her* for thwarting it.

Her brows furrowed. "Does the Order…sacrifice others for Greed? For more control? So they don't have any mistakes or escapees?" She motioned to her hair—

Emryn cut her off. "Your disguise isn't a new thing. Not very popular of a thing, but most of the Order is taught to fear their god, not work with it. If you hear the voice, you bow and say *I didn't mean to want*…stuff like that. The higher-ups are the only ones allowed to work with their god."

Violet's gaze turned back to the school. Through the fence, she glimpsed the two patrols—one lighting a cigarette, and the faint sound of unzipping pants. "Let's go."

They hurried to the door. After some breaths, Emryn pressed a button and disabled the alarm. She used a strong magnet for the lock, and with some jiggling, the back door service entrance was shutting softly by the time the guard stabbed out his smoke.

They were met with bleak surroundings; white walls and gated windows, thick doors and clean floors. Violet wouldn't guess that children lived here. Prisoners, maybe, but not children. She ignored the nausea as she stared at a small, broken crayon on the floor and continued on silently with Emryn.

It didn't take long to find the hallway littered with name-labeled doors, and from there Emryn picked the lock on the headmaster's door and slid in. Violet stepped in beside her, shoulders touching.

Emryn gasped. Violet slapped a hand over her mouth as they stared, stunned, at the scene.

"Fuck, fuck, fuck, *fuck*," Emryn whispered into Violet's hand. Emryn still managed to press the button to deactivate the local security camera.

The small headmaster's office had two closets, a giant desk, a tiny sitting corner, and barred windows that looked out onto a field of pristine grass. But it wasn't the furnishings or barred windows that made them halt.

Violet didn't blink, and the Inaj child before them didn't blink back either. Not dead. He was breathing, but he was also as surprised to see the intruders as they were to see him. His head lifted from his position over the desk, wrists manacled. The position forced him to hunch over. His green skin was too pale, black hair buzzed to his scalp, old tears streaked beneath his wide brown eyes. His tiny lips parted.

Violet held her free hand up. "*Agia.*"

Daughter.

He gasped. His eyes filled with tears, and they began pouring again. "*Agia a Inaj?*"

Daughter of Inaj?

Violet frowned and waggled her hand in a so-so motion.

Emryn darted her eyes incredulously back from the boy to Violet, and Violet felt her mumble, "*What the fuck?*"

"We are here to help you," Violet said softly, removing her hand from Emryn's mouth.

The boy's lip wobbled, and he rested his chin on the tiny table. The chains had blackened his wrists, and as Violet maneuvered to inspect more of the boy, she swallowed her gasp. He had no pants on. No *anything*.

Emryn noticed, too. "I'll grab photos of the papers and

anything else. You get him covered up."

"Are we taking him?" Violet asked. "We can't leave him… He's…"

Violet shared a look with Emryn. *Been touched. By awful hands.*

Emryn fought a battle within herself. Nostrils flared, her hands clenched, and Violet let her go about her process as she darted to the boy and searched for a way to unchain him. His pants were at his ankles, soiled.

"I need you to stay quiet for me, okay?" Violet said.

He nodded. "Always quiet."

She ignored the tightness in her chest as she covered the boy as best she could. She found the keys hanging behind the desk and worked to free him. He silently cried the entire time, little sniffles of snot and the ruffling of paper filling the room. The chains clanged open. Violet gently touched his shoulders. He leaned into her, but when she tried to take him to one of the sitting chairs, he jolted into her body, shaking his head.

Emryn huffed through her nostrils. "We are going to destroy this place." Another flash went off as she took a picture of a document. "There's like two-hundred children here. This is monstrous."

The boy clutched Violet's belt with tiny fingers, but Violet refused to touch him anymore, fearful she may trigger him.

"And this…look at these teachings. It is basically calling every other thought, belief, and more straight up diabolical. To *six-year-olds.* This can make every single child loathe themselves if they explore their body, if they grow differently, if they even have an attraction to someone whom they can't reproduce with…." She released a frustrated sigh. "I hate this place. I hate this so much. I'm going to—"

Violet's head whipped to the door as the handle turned. It pushed open. Too fast to hide—

She shoved the boy behind her and lunged, drawing a taser from her belt and jamming it into the silhouette. The figure gasped and collapsed, but Violet caught them—a female servant—and lowered the unconscious body to the ground.

"Talia?" a voice called from the hall.

Violet's heart thrummed painfully in her chest as footsteps headed their way. Emryn's eyes darted around the room, looking for something…

Violet motioned to the servant. Then the closet.

The footsteps drew closer.

She ripped her gloves and mask off. They undressed the woman and Emryn dragged her, knocking her head against the desk. "Sorry," she cringed. She pulled the body in, and with one last, frightful look, gently closed the door.

Violet whirled. Looked around. She pushed over a table. The Inaj boy jumped. The crash sounded. The footsteps hurried. "Talia? Did you retrieve the boy?"

And the white-skinned, gray-bearded headmaster towered in the doorway, staring at Violet, then the quivering boy holding her hand.

"Talia, what was that?"

Violet watched her pale white hand point to the knocked table. The servant's clothes were loose rags, hiding the leathers and her sweaty skin. Golden-brown hair was in a messy bun at the base of her neck, and she tried to keep her voice high-pitched. "It was so dark in here, I knocked over the table." She bowed deeply, squeezing the boy's hand and hoping he played along. "I'm sorry, Headmaster. It must be the late hours. I will get him to his bed."

The headmaster stared at her in slight confusion, but his nostrils flared. "Clumsy nonsense. Pick it up. You have your shift at the fortress to get to. The airship is in the courtyard. Don't make them late."

Violet bowed again, mostly to hide her rising panic. "Of course, Headmaster."

He huffed and swung around, footsteps retreating down the hall. "Lock my door when you're done cleaning up your mess."

Violet held her breath. She strained her ears until she knew she imagined the pounding of his footsteps. He was gone.

"*Gamsa*," the boy muttered. "Thank you. He is…bad man."

Violet swallowed the bile burning her throat. She bent and picked up the table. Emryn exited the closet, nudging Talia's undergarment body with her boot. "Ugh. Let's get out of here. We can—"

Violet turned to Emryn. "I'm going."

"—bring the boy." Emryn's brows furrowed. "What?"

"I'm going," Violet said shakily. "On the ship. To my shift at the fortress."

Emryn's mouth dropped. She stared at Violet like she'd just murdered her cat. "*What?*"

Violet began to strip her leathers and fixed the servant uniform. "You guys talked about the bottoms of foundations and chipping away at them." Violet tossed a plasgun to Emryn. "They prick their blood for all employees at the fortress, right?"

Emryn dumbly nodded.

Violet pulled out a small syringe meant for recon and stuck it in the unconscious Talia. She drew out just enough, and with a medical kit in the closet, she placed some of the blood in a plastic wrap and used a transparent bandage to attach it to her forefinger. Emryn and the boy stared at her with eyes wide and slacked jaws.

"You'll die," Emryn muttered.

Violet wanted to laugh. "I've been told that my whole life. It gets old after a while. Take the boy with you. And the woman's body if you can." Violet made her way to the door—

"We don't…" Emryn's gaze begged when her words failed. "We don't mess with the Worldbreaker. Not like this."

Violet looked over her shoulder, adrenaline running high. A smirk grew on her face.

"I do."

And she left.

15

Cyran's Fortress

Violet wished she did drugs before this.

Nothing prepared her for the guards lining the walkway outside the school, leading to a small airship where other servants for the fortress waited. The plasguns, the sharp looks, the fact her hands trembled so violently she stuffed them in her pockets. She desperately gripped the little finger tape of Talia's blood as she entered the ship. She wasn't prepared for the deep rumble of the ship as it lifted off, parading through the giant towers in Hallow, while her and fifteen other servants watched silently out the small windows.

The silver metal cargo ship had the basics; simple benches with ropes hanging down for stability. It breezed and groaned, and while Violet fought the nauseous butterflies in her stomach, it still rose higher, aiming for the ominous spider of a city itself.

Despite the destination, she certainly wasn't prepared to see the plethora of scars aboard.

A girl bumped her shoulder, and Violet avoided looking, because a horrifying jagged scar marred half her face. No one apologized. No one said a word. She didn't think anyone was breathing. One girl sneezed, and nearly all eyes darted to her, then went to a buff guard at the airship's door who adjusted his gun. There were at least three girls with eye patches, another with a missing ear, and the last, who opened her mouth to yawn, had no tongue.

So, Violet really wished she had done drugs.

From the window, she watched the residential school's dark lawn fade away, and at the last moment, a blink in a portion of the plasfence. Two shadows—one with a lumpy figure slung over a shoulder—lumbered across the street and disappeared into an alley.

Violet sagged in relief.

It was a tense ride spent tightening her glamour strings and keeping her gaze downturned. The ship vibrated as it landed. Violet clung to the windowsill. With a breath, the door opened, and a landing bridge descended to the pad. The bitter air was cold up here, already making some of the girls shiver in their loose uniforms. The guard lifted his plasgun, and one by one, each girl exited.

The icy wind blasted her cheeks and made her eyes squint. She didn't breathe. She couldn't. Her lungs burned as her too-big boots touched the pristine pavement of the airship pad. She didn't dare lift her head; instead, she stared at the girl's split ends before her. It wasn't until the girl's arm lifted and a soft click sounded did Violet freeze and overthink every decision until now. In her peripheral, the edge of the pad dropped, and she yearned to throw herself into the abyss of Hallow. Perhaps Jack would finally find her...

"Hand."

When Violet met the gaze of a shrewd bald man with a holographic plascreen, she screamed in her head, over and over, that her eyes were not blue. That the glamour held. That alarms wouldn't blare and her blood wouldn't mist the servants behind her.

"*Hand,*" the man said again, irritated. Violet did as ordered, cursing her sweaty palm. She pulled as hard as she could on the glamour covering her bloodsworn and bloodbond marks. He procured a needle-pen and shoved it into the invisible bandage. A small crunch of plastic sounded.

Violet coughed.

"Cover your mouth," the man snapped as the needle was sucked into the pen. A green light glowed, a beep shrilled. Her face—Talia's—popped up on the hologram.

He read a status underneath. "You're on the captain's floor. Get your armband and head to the fourth floor for protocol."

She walked on. Patrols flanked her sides, leading her through the automatic glass doors and into a pristine, black hallway with glistening sconces. She was here. *Here.* In his fortress. Under his nose.

She was *winning.*

Violet was certain her heart was going to beat out of her chest. Sweat dripped from her temple. Her hands trembled. She caught every dark, beautiful detail of Cyran's creation. It smelled of cleaning supplies and jasmine. She was on the top floor—the landing pads—where nearly twenty other doors existed, and all sorts of people came and went. Species of every color, every world, and every rank moved about, some labeled Fringe Vanishers by the twisting vines of their headbands, others labeled captains by their black leathers and silver chokers, and then everything in between. Maybe six, seven ranks.

Small pods made of glass moved to the numerous floors, atriums, towers, or any part of Cyran's city-fortress. The magnitude enthralled Violet, so much so she completely forgot two entirely larger, sprawling *real* cities lay outside of the Worldbreaker's.

Four guards and two other servants joined her on a glass pod, and with a swipe from one guard's wrist, the pod registered their destination. They descended, then moved sideways for a little while, then rose, and Violet was a dizzying vessel by the time the doors opened and everyone filed out.

The Captain's Floor. Tower, really. They had a whole damn tower.

Her neck craned to take in the giant atrium with a ceiling of windows reflecting the sky. She lowered her gaze and it swept the room: a giant purple fountain, cozy chairs with roaring hearths, and a million fucking captains.

A giant gap in the floor showed a training yard. At the far end of the atrium, the rough cut of mountains seared through the glass, while the volcano poured lava in the distance.

A tight-bunned female Aurien—silver-dusted black skin and butterfly ears with rigid horns at her forehead—stood waiting for Violet and the two other servants with a tablet in hand. Violet noted the silver arch they passed through, and a beep sounded. She stiffened, aware of the plasblade hilt along her hip that she forgot to discard.

"Mind your weapons, soldier," the Aurien High Servant snapped. The guard stepped back on the elevator. A metal detector. The butt of his gun accidentally triggered it as the girls exited. She'd never been more thankful for basic stupidity.

They moved to the High Servant. Her eyes caught on a sleek thing. A dog—a ferocious-looking one that glared at each new entry. It was the same image of the bloodhounds that had tracked her to the village with Zavar.

Fuck. She nearly stiffened. *Fuck-fuck-fuck*—

The hounds sat rigid. Ears pointed up. They sniffed. One eyed her.

Then moved its head to let her pass.

She dug her fingernails into her hand. Reed. It had to be Reed. He was in the Fringe, accepted, registered, so she would get through with that.

Violet bowed along with the other servants when they reached the High Servant.

"Talia, Aster, Owen." The High Servant read their profiles. "Good marks. Reliable. You will be cleaning assigned captains' rooms today. Only enter if they allow, or if they are absent. You will report back here to me in four hours' time."

Skies, how did Talia go from the residential school to *this*? The stress was enough to make Violet crazed. The High Servant nodded to a specific hallway, and the other girls set off. Violet followed.

"Did you hear about the new conquest? The *moon*. His Master and the Empire Explorers are magnificent for achieving that feat. I wonder what kind of city they will build there?"

"They'll need to expel the moon people first. Weird, skinny gray things. Put them in nostor mines, it's where they'll be useful instead of playing with their dust."

"Why do you look constipated?"

Violet diverted her attention from passing captains to one of the girls who scowled at her.

They had reached a side door labeled for servants. The other girl sighed as she opened it. "Gods, Aster, do you have to be so blunt?"

Aster ignored the other girl—Owen. "You've looked stressed ever since you showed up. Did the headmaster take the back door again?"

Violet scrunched her brows, but finally processed what Aster meant. She went along with it. "Yeah."

"Weird purity shit," Aster mumbled and turned to the closet, gathering cleaning supplies. "What rooms do we have?"

Owen read numbers off a paper, and Aster scoffed at each of them. But her scoffs, her annoyed looks, were done in the shadow of the cleaning closet. Owen grinned as she read one number. "Oh, I'm getting lucky today. He is so flirty, it's incredible."

Owen was a beautiful girl—light-brown skin, dark brows, honey hair, and a strong nose. But as she beamed at the number, Violet had a horrible, horrible feeling regarding *who* she was talking about.

Even Aster—white-skinned and every feature resplendent of an annoyed bird—smiled. "Lucky."

Violet looked over Owen's shoulder. *Four two two.* "I think the headmaster might have fucked with my brain, too. Who is that?"

Both girls looked at Violet—Talia—with surprise. Owen snorted. "Did Captain Zavar teach you that curse word? With all his…*lessons.*" A wink.

Violet released the deepest, most profound internal sigh of her life.

Skies fucking damnit, Talia.

"Well, you'll see him today. I'm sure he likes dirty mouths," Aster said. "Meanwhile, I have Captain Masar, who never wants to shut up. And Owen has…"

A flick of her honey hair. "Jack Marin. Gods. That mouth. I would beg to have it on me."

Cold, ice-filled envy settled in Violet's gut, and the cleaning basket in her hands creaked. She stuck a pretty smile on her face and turned to Owen. "I heard he's not that great."

Owen cocked her head. "Where did you hear that?"

"The High Servants were gossiping. Something about being… underwhelming." Violet shrugged through her jealousy, delighting in Owen's disappointed face. "Down there, you know? May not even feel it if you let him in your back door."

At Owen's astonishment, Violet lifted her hand in a saccharine wave and darted toward her assignments.

She made her way back to the atrium, ready to play dumb if someone asked her why she wandered. But her emotions ran rampant. Heat splashed her cheeks. She wanted to throttle Owen, even if the girl was completely ignorant to the fact Violet Sutton was wearing Talia's skin. Violet didn't give a fuck. Jack being a flirt, Jack doing this and this and fucking *this*…*Jack* was alive and well, murdering people, being horrible, and sleeping with the fucking servants.

Captains and others darted by her, some laughing, others conversing, no one sparing her a glance. She was happy for it. She made her way to the gap in the atrium's middle to spy the training ground.

One look had her wondering why Cyran wanted her dead. Why did he bother expending energy on her at all? He had all of *this* at his fingertips. Why did he act like she threatened every fragment, every bone, of his operation? *This* was his Empire, and it expanded worlds and a moon and possibly more planets. He was more or less a god, and she was merely one thorn.

One thorn who managed to sneak into his fortress.

Dumb, stupid ideas shifted in her brain as she stared at the training grounds. Soldiers battled everywhere. Two women sparred in one of the rings, the severe clash of their plasblades spraying the colorful energy. One woman, clearly Mer with a shaved head, growled at her opponent and did an impressive move, slashing the other across the stomach. Violet nearly dropped her basket, thinking she'd see guts spill onto the black mat, but whatever the victim wore stopped the plasblade from melting through.

Men walked around with their shirts off. Anaya would scoff at the sight. Violet could hear the noise loud and clear in her head, followed by a cackle and a string of words insulting everyone. She spared one last look at a particularly ripped stomach, and then turned to her assigned hallway.

It was a boring first three hours. Hardly any captain was in their room since it was early morning. Violet was ready to bomb every toilet, every quarter, due to the messy nature of some. There was a different floor for her last slew of rooms, and ones she deduced to more important captains. It was another nauseating lift ride and avoiding weapon detectors before she found herself in a quieter, more private area. She stomped her way to her remaining rooms, but her eyes snagged on one door…

Four two two.

She halted. Judged her decision. Didn't really give a fuck.

So she angrily jammed her finger on the doorbell and waited.

Her pulse pounded. The button blinked with light, indicating the call had been sent out to him. Her hands shook. Jealousy raged. What if Owen was in there? What if Violet were to see… what if… what if…

It blinked red.

Denied.

What if nothing about her mattered to him anymore?

She stepped away from the door, even though she was desperate. She wanted to see him. Wanted to see this monster again who wasn't so much a monster to her. Wanted to see the changed man murdering Pharos members and spreading fear throughout the Twin Cities and across the other worlds.

"Wrong door."

Her boiling blood chilled.

Zavar.

She made sure her glamour strings were in place. He waltzed around to face her, dark eyes studying her features, falling to her lips, before he dragged a finger along her cheek. "You look tired."

If she looked tired, he looked ready for the grave. Up close, she noticed the scar cutting his temple and along his cheek, jagged like his lightning. That wasn't there in Lust.

Violet didn't say anything. She refrained from jamming two fingers into his pretty eyes for trying to murder her.

Talia had relations with Zavar. *She* was expected to have relations with Zavar. *Fucking Talia.*

Zavar scoffed at the door. "He's been getting all the attention lately. Am I so subpar you'd look to *him?*"

She bent her head, forcing the words. "No, sir."

"He doesn't take lovers," Zavar said lowly. Jealousy tinged his voice, and Violet furrowed her brows. Zavar had been the one to *kill* Jack. Why did he notice…or care?

Violet didn't respond to his comment. "I can clean your room now—"

"Good."

He grabbed her wrist and pulled her down one of the many hallways. Violet's heart palpitated between fear and fury. She tried to yank back, but his warm fingers held her in a vise.

No-no-no-no-no…

Her eyes darted around the hallway. Her knuckles whitened on the basket. "I'm…it is that time of the month."

"You know I never minded that."

Violet avoided his stare, bewildered.

Talia, what in the ever-loving fuck.

She had no words, so Zavar took that as a sign and tugged at her hand. His grip was surprisingly gentle, no hint of lightning beneath the pale skin. She willed her feet to move, but her mind went elsewhere. Was she supposed to do this? How…

There wasn't a how.

There was simply no way out of this.

Perhaps Violet's final middle finger to Zavar would be sleeping with him and then revealing herself. Right as he climaxed. That would make her feel better, but it wasn't enough to win. She wanted to *win.* Her body went rigid thinking about it, but if Jack became a monster to survive, she would, too.

Zavar only lived a couple quarters down from Jack, but that was still the other side of the Captain's Tower. He brushed his wrist on the scan and the door unlocked. With a tug, he pulled her inside.

Her body slid into a numbness she recognized. Her eyes lifted to his endless room of soft black. A giant bed, a dresser, a plascreen mounted to the wall, floor-to-ceiling windows glaring north of the Twin Cities.

She couldn't do this.

Everything was undecorated, save for one odd, colorful thing underneath his nightstand; a wooden box scratched with rainbow lightning bolts around it. A sentimental thing. A weakness.

When the door shut, Zavar turned, his eyes heavy-lidded, and a hungry nature swirling in his black gaze.

To Violet, that jerked her. Screamed at her. Renell, Renell. The pirate who wanted to use her. She didn't want to be used like that. Touched like that. Pity overcame her for Talia. It was easy to scorn her for a position she might not have ever wanted in the first place, but that was Greed. The higher-ups had the wants, the controls. The rest had to go along with it.

The rest were merely pawns in their game.

Violet stood in Talia's shoes, finally a pawn, and it was then that she understood.

She would dig Talia out of this hole, because Talia was a victim, whether she knew it or not.

"So this Jack," Violet said. Zavar froze. "Captain Jack Marin. The other servants talk about him a lot."

"I don't like to talk during this."

Violet cocked her head. Talia might not be a confrontational one, but Violet certainly was. "Why? Does *he* bother you?"

An unnamed emotion passed over his face, followed by flared nostrils. "You dare speak to me like that?"

"No one speaks to you ever."

Ah, she poked something. Zavar paced away into his room. "Get *out*—"

"He's not as great as you, in my opinion."

He paused.

"I know that's why you're stressed," Violet followed up. She glided around his rigid body and looked at him through her lashes. "You're so strong, so unstoppable, but he's taking the attention. People are talking about it."

"I don't care about the attention."

Lie. His image was his pride. It was plastered all over his face. The irritation, the fact he didn't care it was her speaking those words. His shoulders sagged while lightning breached his knuckles. She ignored the roiling in her stomach.

Talia *did* talk to him, just didn't poke him as much as Violet did. He seemed rather comfortable around her, so it might have been going on for a while.

"Massage my shoulders," Zavar commanded.

Violet would rather bite off her toenails, but she paraded over to him. He tugged his shirt off, slumping in a chair with ease and comfort.

It took everything in Violet not to gasp at his body. Not to stare. Not to give any hint of what lay on him. He studied her carefully from the moment he showed skin, and Violet would guess if she gave a reaction, he'd fry her.

Scars. Not fighting scars or injury scars, but punishment scars. Ones that must be decades old, others fresher. Like a worn punching bag whose opponent was a knife.

"Relax," Violet said softly, surprised at her voice. She should be satisfied his muscular body was covered in gruesome things, but no fulfillment existed. Instead, her chest deflated. She grasped his shoulders, her fingers running over one long scar that dragged from his collarbone to the apex of his shoulder.

There were certain things she learned about Zavar: he had sentimental things, he was clearly insecure about his body, jealous of Jack, cared about his image, and he was tired. Very, very tired. Used, too.

Lastly, he was lonely.

It truly didn't get any better than massaging Cyran's little punching dog. Violet was winning. Greed laughed in the back of her mind. A small smile came to her lips. *I can use these things.*

A flash of light interrupted her advantageous excitement, and a Vanisher she didn't know appeared. Zavar flung out a blast of lightning immediately, standing. "What did I tell you about teleporting into my room?"

The Vanisher doubled over. Blood poured from the sides of his mouth. He coughed. "I'm—I'm sorry, my liege. The group requests you."

Zavar made sure the Vanisher's eyes stayed on the floor as he dressed himself. He turned to Violet. "Come with me. And keep that mouth shut."

Violet nodded.

Zavar grabbed her shoulder and vanished her.

"What's with the pet, Zavar?"

Violet recognized the cool, casual voice. Before her eyes adjusted to the room, the different air, the altered environment unlike the Twin Cities entirely, she knew that voice.

She remembered it because she chatted with them when she worked at the bar in Lust. One of the twin Vanishers who'd tracked her down.

Zavar released her arm. "I was in the middle of something."

"A slight intermission," another male's voice said.

Zavar turned to her. "Go serve drinks."

Violet whirled. Nearly shitting herself at where they were.

On a cloudy mountaintop staring down at yet *another* city. There wasn't a zap in senses like the transition between worlds, so she believed she still stood in Greed, but this city was made of ice and metal, spreading both above and beneath the snowy landscape. They were in a temple tower overlooking it like a god would his creation. The crescent room was filled with plush chairs, all facing each other. A meeting room? Interrogation?

Violet found the servant door. A man exited, holding a tray of glasses, and placed it on a table along the wall. She hurried over to him, and he said, "Pass out the drinks when the last captain brings the captives in."

There were four others in the room; one of the twins—Jodin, recognizable by his long locs, another brown-skinned man covered in more scars than Zavar, an Inaj with a plaster of tattoos, and finally, the shaved head Mer she'd seen in the training ring not too long ago.

Violet's shoulders sagged, wishing she could glimpse her brother, but from what she knew, Reed mostly worked in Envy, and apparently not with this little cadre.

Zavar plopped himself in one of the cushioned chairs, legs splayed wide. His tense, displeased nature was back. "I don't want this taking long. It's annoying that we are in Zoncolla as it is."

"They're a threat now, Captain Zavar," the Mer-lady said. "They are antagonizing other nations and have killed the king of Harmas. Don't underestimate them."

"Why do *I* have to be here?"

"Because you're the assassin who kills those the captives name," the Inaj drawled.

Jodin snorted.

Zavar grumbled, "That's been overridden by *someone else*."

"Bring us the drinks, please!" called the dark-skinned scarred one. "I am going to need one before seeing whatever state he leaves the captives in."

Violet jolted and darted her eyes to another servant for approval, but they left. Only her and the captains, now. She picked up the tray of dark liquor-filled tumblers and dropped one off to each attendee. The scarred one downed his in a second.

"Slow down, Captain Masar, we will need your proper input,"

the Mer said.

"Serwa, I do not need your chiding." Masar motioned for Violet to bring the whole bottle over.

Serwa rolled her eyes.

Jodin snorted. "You all are the glorified cleanup team for his Master." He nodded to Violet when he picked up his glass. She bristled slightly, shocked by the thanks.

Zavar took his drink without looking at her, and she didn't quite care. He mainly ignored the others and stared out the window.

Violet made it back to the service station, ready to bring the liquor bottle for refills, when a flash of light swept through the room, and two bodies dropped onto the floor. She bent her head, willing her hair to cover her face, specifically the burn along her cheeks.

Behind a lock of hair, she caught a glimpse of two figures who stood over two limp bodies. One—a transporting Vanisher who disappeared again with a flash of light, while the other…brown skin, tattoos, curls.

Her fingers slipped on the bottle.

She whipped her head to the wall. Her heart thrashed violently in her chest.

"Your delivery," Jack Marin said.

She nearly fell to her knees.

The presence. *That* presence. It suffocated her. Consumed her. Every bit of her body became aware of his position, the energy. It overwhelmed her with a dark, dangerous, predatory sensation. This was a bad idea. She didn't skivvin' care about Zavar, or the other deadly captains, or the fact she had a thinning line of an exit left. It was a bad idea because she built up this reunion in her head, over and over, but being in the same room as him left her wanting to run far away, perhaps into the surrounding snowy blizzard, and bury the heat burning along her spine.

"Took long enough," Zavar grumbled. "I was nearly in tears due to Yeren's boring stories."

Yeren—the last one in the room. The Inaj.

"I need a fucking drink, *Zavian*, not your complaints," Jack drawled. Violet could imagine the primal smile on his face.

"Make her bring you one."

Violet's resolve, and her strings, slowly slipped. She clambered for them as her nose began to tingle, and her scalp vibrated. Her hands shook.

"A large glass, please," Jack called, and by a thump, he must have thrown himself into one of the chairs. He sighed deeply.

The others began to chat away with low-balling insults and grumbles. It was a…calm clamor.

Violet didn't move. Gazes burned her back. Slowly, she poured the liquor and walked both the glass and the bottle over to the splayed legs of hard, lean muscles wrapped in black pants. Blood spotted the tip of his boot. She couldn't lift her eyes. She quivered, too afraid that if she met his gaze, every bit of her glamour would melt away. There was a part of her that didn't want Jack to see her…like this. Like some subservient being infiltrating a villain's lair because she was beckoned by the longing of a man. Not because she wanted to win, anymore, but because her actions were crafted out of…care.

Nausea roiled at the word. Skies, she hated herself.

But there was also a small part of her that believed Jack didn't know she was even alive. Didn't *care* if she was alive.

She set the glass on the table and turned to refill Zavar's.

Jack's brown-skinned, tattooed hand snatched the entire bottle. "Even better."

The sudden movement had a disguise string slip. Violet's hand splayed, and to her horror, Jack stiffened. Her eyes darted to her palm. A rigid red mark slashed through the typical lines—the bloodbond one belonging to both Jack and Bryce.

He moved so fast, yet so fluid, that it became their own interaction. His grabbed her sleeved wrist, tugging her forward. Violet stumbled. Her pulse roared in her ears.

She desperately pulled on the strings, clenching her hand into a fist as she did so. "Sir?" She played dumb and pitched her voice high. "Is something wrong?"

"Open your hand," he said, low enough that only she heard. His breath swirled, his scent overwhelmed.

She stopped breathing. Stared at the warm fingers holding her wrist, the strange whorls of a galaxy inked on them, until her eyes followed the arm wrapped in captain leather. The broad shoulders, the curve of a neck where a winged tattoo poked out.

She opened her now-glamoured hand as she took the time to behold his beauty.

The carved jaw.

The soft, dark brown curls.

The dimples.

Full lips.

Thick lashes.

Green eyes.

His name was immediately at her lips. She nearly uttered it.

Jack was *alive*.

The evidence surfaced when Rio's bloodbond activated, but it didn't click until she glimpsed that dimple, those eyes. Wholly alive. Breathing. Before her. Holding her.

The gravity of the situation took away from the glamour string she still held. He saw gold-brown hair. A different nose and mouth. Paler skin. She wanted to let it unravel and say *I'm here… I'm here… I'm here.*

Take me away.

Make me forget.

Make me feel safe again.

But at the same time.

Get me as far away from here as possible.

Look at what you have become.

Have they turned you into a monster?

He shook his head and downed the bottle. His jaw clenched. His hair was longer. He had so many tattoos peeking beneath his captain's uniform. Why did he have tattoos? That was a Souther mark…

He jerked his chin to the bloodied captives. "As you can see, I've introduced them to a few interesting techniques. They've spilled a bit of information. Something along the lines of this whole world preparing to overtake the Master."

Violet glanced at the captives, and she wished she hadn't. They were faceless, covered in fresh and dried blood. One had fingers missing. The other moaned on the ground, lacerations nearly to the bone on his arm.

Jack stared at them in boredom.

He never released her. Instead, his grip moved to her hand, where he fiddled with her fingers. Something about his demeanor turned cold, as if he shoved any warmth he had left down into an unreachable abyss. Violet's eyes darted to Zavar, and the man studied their interaction, gaze glued to Jack's playful touch. A smirk lifted at Jack's mouth. He was *playing* with Zavar.

Jack stopped his teasing. He froze, spine going ramrod straight. Violet turned back again. His bright green eyes were on her like he'd seen a ghost. They darted to her hair—no, her scalp—and grew wider at each passing moment, as if her glamour were unraveling. No tell-tale tingles erupted, but Jack continued to gawk, as if unbelieving.

Violet pulled her hand away. "That hurts," she lied.

"Did she bite your balls, Marin?" Masar chortled. "Why are you looking at her like that?"

"I think I'm seeing things," Jack muttered. "Or I've had too much alcohol."

"Both," Violet whispered.

He heard that.

Annoyed, but clearly still on edge, he waved her away, covering his unnerved expression with boredom yet again. "Go get yourself cleaned up. You look like shit. That's disrespectful in itself for a pretty face."

Fury lashed through her. Yes, she probably looked gross and sweaty and pale with all she had been through today, but *that* comment was uncalled for. Skies, she was going to punch the shit out of her pillow tonight. She gritted out, "Yes, sir."

He bristled for half a second before a calm expression slid over. "Leave the fire in those eyes at the door, too." He waved her off. "She's done for the day, send another since this one isn't fun to look at."

A transporting Vanisher appeared, grabbing her arm. Zavar gave her a long look saying that their previous interaction wasn't over. Jack averted his eyes. The rest didn't give a shit.

Violet clenched her fists as the world turned into bright light.

She landed on concrete. People swarmed around, glancing at her and her Vanisher companion, but continued on. Back in the Twin Cities. The onyx towers glowered at her. The Vanisher pulled out a smoke and lit it. "Go on. I'll make sure you get clocked out, Talia. Get your sleep."

Violet scrunched her brows. "That's it?"

"I don't particularly care to return to the fortress when I'm about to be called to transport someone else." He took a long drag. "And that Jack Marin was about to snap your neck for staring like that. Zavar, too. Best you lie low."

He finished his smoke and vanished.

Violet's ire transformed her little ember into an inferno as Jack's face appeared in her mind.

Skies.

She was going to fucking kill him.

When Violet finally found herself outside the headquarters in Navru, Emryn's fist greeted her face.

Violet slammed into the wet brick of the alley across from the metal entrance.

"You dumb asshole," Emryn snarled and grabbed Violet by the collar. "Do you know how stupid that was?"

"You worried about me?" Violet smiled as blood pooled in her mouth. Damn, Emryn was strong. "That's cute."

Emryn pounded the entrance, waited for it to open, and dragged Violet through the door. "Bryce is pissed. Everyone is annoyed with you. You could have jeopardized so much—" She stopped talking.

Because Violet held a very detailed piece of paper. "I'm sure you'll forgive me after this debriefing."

Emryn huffed, letting Violet go. "I had to carry that woman's body four *blocks*. You owe me."

When the door slammed shut, pitching them in darkness, Violet finally released her glamour. Pain rippled after holding the disguise for so long. She groaned through it, and when she opened her eyes, Emryn had a satisfied smile. "Serves you right."

After that, Violet debriefed Bryce on everything that went down. When Violet mentioned their meeting in Zoncolla—the ice city—Bryce was white-knuckling the papers, nearly ripping them.

"You're from there," Violet stated.

"Those two captives were reported missing days ago," they gritted. "We just want our freedom back."

"So does the rest of the world, it seems."

"We need a plan."

"I want that residential school burned," Emryn said. "We don't have enough manpower to take down the Worldbreaker."

Bryce merely nodded, but turned back to Violet. "Could you do it again?"

Violet swallowed. "I'm not working at the school, only the fortress."

"She has a shift in two days' time. The school shifts aren't until next week. We will have you go in once more, that's it. The real Talia gave us some information, but she is pretty panicky at the moment. She lives alone near the Church District. We'll make some noises in her apartment so the neighbors don't get suspicious."

"Fine."

"We'll have a plan for the school. For now, rest. You made terrible decisions, but you did good." Bryce studied the papers. "Really good."

A knock sounded at the door, and with a call from Bryce, Bunny poked her little head in. Her eyes were wide, slightly nervous, but when they landed on Violet, a giant smile split her face. "I knew you would be here."

Violet stared. "Sorry?"

Bunny stormed in, a crocheted lump in her mangled hands. "I have something for you."

"Oh?"

Bunny strutted up, took the crocheted lump, motioned for Violet to bend, and piled it over her head. It nearly covered her eyes, while the tip of her right ear poked out of a little hole.

Emryn cackled. Bryce smiled.

"See, black, but with a giant purple flower and a little bit of blue in the middle," Bunny said proudly, bouncing on the soles of her feet. "Do you like it?"

Violet patted the snug hat, some holes a little mismatched. She took it off to study the rudimentary flower that covered the crown of her head; indeed purple with blue in the center. Her chest grew tight. "I…"

Bunny beamed, waiting for the answer.

"It's beautiful, Bunny."

She shrieked with glee, ripped the hat out of Violet's hands, and shoved it back on her head, this time covering her eyes. "Wear it all the time!"

16

LUKA

THERE WERE VERY FEW THINGS Jelan became used to in her new world in the North. The coffee was certainly better, the air conditioning was reliable, and she definitely loved clean sheets that Saram so graciously washed once a week. Jelan had maybe washed her own four times in her life. She'd never thought to do it.

These were little things that made her life just a bit easier, but there were still surprises. Like a dishwasher—that was not typically a thing in the South. Or a cook where she could request anything she wanted. Or feeling safe and secure with Ashan and Bronto.

All those things were minimal compared to the surprises of walking down in the early morning, dreary eyed and with coffee on her mind, to find the plethora of papers laid out on the kitchen table detailing a kidnapping.

"Cool, right?"

"Goodness fucking gracious." Jelan startled, throwing a hand on her heart. She turned to Lyla behind her. Jelan was convinced the woman never slept. Didn't need sleep, actually. "You scared me."

Lyla maneuvered around Jelan and dropped two plastablets on the table. "You need better training."

"Do you want me to stab you before we exchange good mornings?" Jelan quirked a brow and waltzed to the coffee machine. "I didn't think I needed reflexes for the penthouse."

Lyla smirked. "No, but even your basic reflexes make you vulnerable."

"Of course. My guard is let down here, where it is safe, but outside I'm better."

Lyla waved a hand. "Let me know if you want training. Just basics."

"I'm not a fighter."

"No, and you're cautious, thankfully, but it's still good to have some skills. You look at plasweapons all day, but when you see the violent ones in use, you clam up. Best to build some skills before the war."

Jelan frowned. She took her mug and sipped, sighing at the sweet relief of the coffee. She liked hers black, whereas Violet would dump half a sugar jar into hers and be wired for four days straight.

Jelan flicked on a small plascreen hanging on the wall and went straight to the Sins Screen. The candidates' names blinked. She checked Violet first—green and doing, okay. Then Reed, who was green, as well, and then to Violet's companion, Rio Gaverra, who was green and had been green for a long while now. Jelan watched the Sins Screen for a bit before she started her day. When she woke up to all green, it was going to be a good day.

"We are initiating phase one for the kidnap tonight," Lyla said.

Scratch that. A kidnapping would sour multitudes of green.

Jelan's eyes dipped to the table. "Today?"

"And you're needed."

"Fantastic."

"There's a political party in the North tonight that we suspect Arvalo's kids are going to. Not all of them—definitely not Luka, the second eldest. He is too dangerous, likes to keep to the shadows. Not that we would send you anywhere near that man anyway. So that leaves three kids. The others are harmless for the most part; Mai, the temper tantrum princess; Bael, the eldest and military-wannabe; and Park, the third, mostly known for his outward personality and being a drunk, but people liked him. He's a charmer."

"Why do I need to be there?"

Lyla gave Jelan a long look. "You? At a political party celebrating Arvalo? No. You'll be at the bar that Mai will hopefully sneak to after the party."

Jelan furrowed her brows. Before she could say anything, Lyla tapped the table. "You have twelve hours. Hira will be joining you. You'll be two girls out for drinks, who just happen to be where Mai is. Hira is strange enough not to make it weird."

"She'll make it totally weird," Jelan grumbled.

Lyla smirked. "As long as it's weird enough to distract Mai, then good enough for me."

❀ ❀ ❀

Eccentric was the only word that came to Jelan's mind when she walked through the doors of the bar in the North. Hira at her side, she strutted through the front doors in a deep purple dress that flared to mid-thigh. After four identification checks with expensive fakes, a five-hundred-coin cover, and judgmental looks at their outfit, Jelan was already tired. But the entrance yawned open, and she beheld the sprawling, two-story underground room that blasted her with artistic pictures of animals she'd never seen in her life.

A giant skull chandelier filled the tiered center space. It was a gloomy lighting, and Hira was already squinting her gaze.

"You really should get checked for glasses," Jelan murmured to her.

"I'm *fine*. I just don't understand why people want to be borderline blind in these places."

Jelan snorted as the curvy hostess moved them to a more secluded area on the second floor. It boasted high booths and small fireplaces in the middle of the tables. For some reason, every establishment in the North liked to pretend it was freezing outside.

Hira and she shared a look. Numerous men surrounded; in business suits with clean jaws and eyes that roamed. They climbed the stairs and Jelan kept her gaze at her feet so she didn't make a scene—

A shoulder bumped hers. Jelan stumbled. A hand caught her forearm, another gripped her wrist, steadying her. The touch tickled her skin.

Hira whirled. "Oh skies, are you…" Hira's words trailed, and she choked.

Jelan's gaze slid from the pale white hand adorned in rings, up the fitted black-and-white-printed shirt with the top three buttons undone to reveal a toned chest, then to the hand's owner.

He wore sunglasses—square ones that accentuated his rigid bone structure and curved nose tip. Black hair fell in tendrils behind his ears, some of it messily pulled into a short ponytail. His full lips parted.

"My apologies," he said smoothly. "Stairs are quite dangerous if you're not looking."

Jelan awkwardly tugged her arm away. "Lots of things are."

"If you aren't careful." He licked his lips. "Enjoy the rest of your night."

"Thanks."

He smiled slightly, those sunglasses hiding eyes that Jelan bet stared too long. His energy was claiming, *draining*, like the world revolved around him, and everyone in it served as side characters to his game. She shook her head, rattling the beads at the end of her braids, and with Hira's beckoning, hurried to their booth.

The minute they sat, Jelan ordered the strongest drink off the menu.

"He was strange," Hira mumbled. Their drinks arrived quickly, and Hira downed hers, calling for another before their waiter even turned away. "Also, there was plenty of room on those stairs."

Jelan chugged, before saying, "That was intentional."

"Very."

Jelan checked her arms, looking for anything unusual. Did he swipe a drug on her? Did he steal from her? She checked all her things, but everything was in the right place. Nothing was missing, she didn't feel any different. Perhaps it was just an accident.

Her gut told her it wasn't. She turned her head and looked at the rest of the bar, trying to find the man in the printed shirt with sunglasses, but it was like he disappeared.

Hira brushed it off once Jelan checked everything, and swung the conversation around. "So how is it with Lucien?"

"There's nothing really there," Jelan said into her straw, frowning. "He's extremely busy."

"You go around looking like *that* and he hasn't made a move… it's fairly ridiculous. I'm about to beat the shit out of him for being so slow with everything."

"Well, technically, I'm an employee." Jelan smirked. "Isn't that against the rules?"

"What fucking rules? There's rules for who you fuck? Absolutely not." Hira smacked the table. "We all know forbidden romances are the best. The sneaky links in the middle of the night when you know the world will explode if they find out. I mean, *fuck*. Gets me hot just thinking about it." She frowned. "I need an enemy."

"Lucien is not my enemy, nor is he forbidden. I just don't want anything to be awkward if something happens. I think he's extremely careful."

Hira tongued her straw. "Beyond opposite to Jack. You'd think those boys came from different wombs."

Jelan furrowed her brows, eyes again glancing to the bottom floor. The political party still had around an hour before it officially ended, but Mai was rumored to leave early, so she could show up at any minute. Along with her brothers.

The plan wasn't necessarily to *kidnap* anyone tonight, but if the opportunity presented itself, Jelan only had to press one button on the watch at her wrist to call in incognito reinforcements. Otherwise, it was simply two friends getting drinks and people-watching. That was it.

Jelan checked her watch for any updates, but the screen was clear.

The waiter approached them. Hira downed her second drink and motioned for another, but the man already had two drinks in his hands.

"From the gentleman below. He sends his regards, and another apology."

Jelan twisted in her seat. Her eyes scanned the growing crowd, and in the midst, she found those sunglasses looking up at her, a sly smile playing on his lips. He gave the slightest of nods and took a sip from his own glass.

Jelan forced a smile. Her cheeks grew hot, a part of her both curious and flattered, but her stomach churned with butterflies. Her mother hated butterflies.

She would say the feeling usually meant danger.

Jelan kicked Hira under the table.

"Ow, fucker—"

"Don't drink that," Jelan mumbled.

Jelan's gaze slid around the room. While at first glance, most looked like powerful Elites enjoying a drink, she slowly caught the individuals who sat with full drinks, twirling the straws, eyes drifting around, then landing on their table. Trained men. She'd be oblivious if she weren't careful, but now, at this moment, she wished she'd taken up training from Lyla.

Hira kept a relaxed posture as she stirred the gifted drink. "You think it's drugged?"

"I think this was a trap."

Hira smiled brightly. They both knew they were being watched. Jelan forced a laugh, matching Hira's energy.

"How do we get out of here?" Hira said with a chuckle.

Jelan twirled a braid. "We will have to be smart. This plan is ruined. I'll send a signal and we will wait it out until rescue comes."

"There are four others here. They'll know by now—"

"You two are really stupid for coming here."

Jelan turned her head. Mai leaned against the side of their booth, her tiny body clad in a pretty silver dress. Her black, inky hair had been cut to her shoulders, a new ring pierced through her nose.

"Ah, the exact person we were looking for," Hira said brightly. She patted the seat next to her. "Sit, we wanted to discuss which of your brothers has the biggest dick—"

Jelan rolled her eyes. "I told you, it's Park. He's asshole enough."

"No, it's the quieter ones. Luka, right? He's all broody in front of the cameras…like he's hiding something. A giant *package* kind of something—"

Mai's nostrils flared. "I'm their sister."

Hira smiled sweetly. "So you would know, honey. Who sleeps around the most? It's what all the tabloids want to know."

Mai scowled and cocked a hip. "They all have their conquests."

"You're surprisingly conversational, Mai," Jelan said.

Mai's cold, mono-lid eyes flicked to her. "You're trapped. Nowhere to run. You'll both be killed by the end of the night—"

"Thank the fucking skies, this life has been a long one and I'm ready to go." Hira jerked her thumb behind her shoulder. "All this fighting has been wearing me out."

Jelan snorted. "A threat here, an assassination there." She turned to Mai. "We are here for some drinks. That's it. Now, sit, Mai, and give us a little attention before your brothers behead us. We want some girl talk. I'm sure you don't get that much." Her smile grew. "I know Violet didn't like girl talk."

Mai stiffened. Her eyes darted over the edge of the balcony and into the crowd. Jelan brushed a braid back, following the direction.

A male figure leaned against a column below, dressed in full black, and a lazy gaze resting on Mai and the girls.

Bael. The eldest, the one who likes shooting the guns, not creating them, and with an ego that was bigger than the skyscrapers. Jelan tapped her pinky finger on the table.

Hira continued the conversation at the signal. "Why are you up here, Mai? Did daddy extend your leash?"

Mai opened her mouth, fury blossoming across her face.

"Don't patronize her. She didn't choose her family, but she has to live with them." Jelan leaned back into the booth. "Indulge us, though. You've piqued my curiosity since Violet got all mopey when you broke up with her."

She had Mai's full attention. "Violet broke up with me."

Hira frowned. "That must have sucked."

Mai's gaze drifted to the open seat next to Hira, but instead she chose a spot near Jelan. She was perched on the edge, ready to run at a moment's notice.

Mai's admission surprised Jelan. It wasn't so much of a breakup at all, according to Violet, just completely insane differences that made their whirlwind relationship a chaotic bonfire.

Pain lingered on Mai's face. She curled into herself for a moment, then forced her shoulders back. "But in the end, that girl was nothing more than a fling."

Hira exchanged a look with Jelan. They both frowned.

And Hira said genuinely, "You know, I tell myself a lot of lies to make it all feel better, but in the end, you are just living with lies *and* pain, instead of just pain."

Mai side-eyed Hira. Hira shrugged.

"Although I'm clearly upset with your father for stealing my work, we don't have grudges against you," Jelan said.

"Although you should apologize for turning Kole over," Hira interjected.

"*But*," Jelan continued, "we don't quite care about your status, about your relations to your father, and all that. Believe it or not, I know what it's like to feel abandoned, too."

Mai glanced toward Jelan. She kept her face hard, unyielding, but those eyes softened slightly. Jelan guessed the girl hadn't had a genuine conversation, or even attention, in a long, *long* time.

Jelan didn't like lying or manipulating. That was Violet. Or Hira. Jelan would rather stay quiet if she didn't have anything authentic to say, so at this moment, everything coming out of her mouth was genuine. She pitied Mai. Despised her for abusing Violet, yes, and that was unforgivable, but she wished the girl was given just a little more love in her life so she didn't resort to anger as her default coping mechanism.

But while Jelan's words were genuine, her feelings were moot. Mai was a means to an end.

"I'm not some sad girl," Mai said harshly. "But I…I shouldn't have treated Violet like that. Or anyone like that."

Hira scowled. "You abused her."

"Yes," Mai admitted, again to Jelan's surprise. "I'm…getting help. If you care."

Mai's eyes darted to Jelan repeatedly, as if Jelan had some telepathic connection to Violet to relay the information. Just as Lyla predicted.

What a woman.

Jelan refrained from frowning. "Good, you need all the help you can get."

Hira's brows raised when Mai didn't get defensive. Instead, the girl sagged more into the booth. "You should both leave, though. I'll give you one chance, then fuck off. You don't need to get involved in this mess."

Jelan's gaze drifted to the ground floor, and Bael was nowhere to be found. She fingered her watch, wondering if she should send a message to alert them of an update.

"Is there a back door?" Hira asked.

Mai nodded, her expression suddenly tight and controlled. "I'll lead you to it. But only this once, as part of my retribution. If you sneak around us again, I can't promise to stop my brothers from doing anything horrible."

A cold shiver shifted down Jelan's spine. She truly believed Mai. They acted as one front, but like their group discussed, each sibling had their own agenda. Lyla played this plan hoping Mai would want to atone for her actions after Jelan detailed the relationship with Violet, and it was working beautifully, in a way hopefully no one would get hurt.

Mai jutted her chin to a dark hallway. Hira eyed her, then the destination, warily, but with a flick of her long hair, she shimmied out of the booth. Jelan followed.

It was all of four steps before a tall figure stepped out of a curtained booth, hands behind his back, and regarded Mai with a cruel gaze.

Bael Arvalo.

"Where are you taking our friends?" he asked. Carrying weapons openly was forbidden by law in the city, but Bael had his plasgun out for the viewing. A bullet would be between Jelan's eyes before she could blink.

He was a lanky, yet muscular man with the same inky hair cropped short and mono-lid eyes. His skin was a bit tanner than the others, lips thinner, nose wider, and a hollowness to his cheekbones that sprouted the difference between the siblings. Half-siblings, technically. Jelan always forgot they each had different mothers.

"For a smoke," Hira said calmly, her gaze roaming him. Jelan internally sighed.

Bael's gaze fell on Hira's voluptuous curves.

"Let them go," Mai said. "There's no need to start a war now."

Bael's heavy-lidded eyes glanced from Hira's generous cleavage, then back to Mai. "Why shouldn't I? We would win."

"Save your violent tendencies for elsewhere, brother," Mai gritted. "The city doesn't need them."

Bael dragged a finger along the holster to his plasgun, but didn't release it.

"Stay out of our territory," he warned before passing through them, aggressively nudging Mai in the shoulder. She snarled, turning.

Hira brushed her arm, playing it off like an accident, but grounding Mai, nonetheless.

Mai took a deep breath, cooling herself off. "He's an asshole. Worse than the others, believe it or not."

"I bet it's him," Hira whispered to Jelan. "*He* has the biggest dick."

Jelan ignored her.

They made their way to the low-lit hallway on the second floor, where a tight spiral staircase lowered itself to the ground floor. Mai went first, Hira next, and finally Jelan. Another hallway extended out onto the main floor, or back to the kitchens, where a clattering of pots and pans reached Jelan's ears. The smell of onions made her mouth water, and she decided on a giant steak for their dinner at the penthouse to celebrate their success.

Mai took a step, turning toward the kitchens, but Hira was fast. She pressed a tiny plasdagger to the column of Mai's throat. "This doesn't leave your neck until our car arrives."

"And then a scope on a plasrifle doesn't leave my forehead until your car is out of enemy territory, yeah, yeah, I've played these games since I was a child." Mai shrugged but didn't relent against Hira's blade. She continued walking, unbothered. "I know you don't trust me. I wouldn't trust me either."

Jelan watched their backs, making sure no one followed. Her eyes caught the semi-alarmed gazes of the servants and cooks, but everyone minded their own business. Hira kept the dagger hidden behind a curtain of Mai's hair and acted like she had the girl in a half-hug. A moment later, Mai was pushing open the metal door to the bar's back alley and the honking horns, the bright lights, and the smell of smoke assaulted Jelan.

The door slammed behind them.

Jelan pressed a button on her watch.

"Which street for your car?" Mai asked.

"To the right," Jelan said. The street was more back-alley, meant for patrons who wanted to access the bars without entering through the main doors. It was policed by its own security and made a lot of money from those who wanted that extra security.

"Typical," Mai muttered. Three sets of heels clicked amid the North's noise until they reached the clean sidewalk.

Jelan's heart picked up its pace. She didn't dare dart her eyes around.

Anytime now.

A pitch-black car pulled up and honked. "That one," Jelan said, trying to keep her voice even.

Anytime.

They reached the car door. Hira turned Mai into a hug, still keeping the dagger against her neck. "It was *so* good to see you."

"You, too," Mai grumbled.

Jelan opened the door.

And the world exploded into dark gray smoke.

It flooded from inside the car like water, pouring out onto the street and lifting to the heavens. Jelan was immediately blinded, and she didn't even have to act this part out. It was horrifying. The sound of the streets muffled, people screamed, the world stopped.

Jelan coughed, bringing her forearm to her mouth. Her hand slapped the car and she followed it. "Hira?"

"Jelan!" Hira shrieked from far away. Growing more distant. "Get—*off* me! Jelan! *Jelan!*"

"Hira!" Jelan cried hoarsely, straining against another cough.

Another scream tore through the smoke, this one bitter and angry. "Let *go* of me, fuckers!" A man grunted. Mai snarled and the faint smell of blood reached Jelan's nose. She rushed forward, arms out, blinking through the haze—

Mai screamed. It was soon muffled.

Jelan's heart clenched.

Then a hand wrapped around Jelan's waist and roughly dragged her back. A groan bit through her mouth. She panicked, throwing an elbow behind her, but the attacker dodged. She was pulled across the street. One of her shoes scraped off, and she gasped as the skin at her ankle tore open. "Please—please, no, no…"

"Shut up!" her attacker growled.

Hira screamed once more and the terror in it had Jelan frantic. Was it real? Fake? Her head was shoved down, body tossed onto the plush leather backseat of a car. She inhaled a clean breath. The door slammed. A hand brushed her forehead.

She bolted up, whirling, and found Lucien.

Wide-eyed concern was plastered over his face. He gently touched her arm, and when Jelan looked down to his lap, one of her inhalers lay there.

"Are you alright?" Lucien asked, concerned.

"You guys could have gone a bit easier." Jelan massaged her ankle in an attempt to hide her trembling hands. "Is Hira—?"

"She's fine." He held up a radio. "Lyla has her in another car. Her screams were pretty realistic. She said she's been practicing." A deep frown. "I'm sorry…we couldn't risk it being too fake. You guys did good. It's all okay now."

Jelan's hands slowed their shaking. She rubbed at her collarbone, willing her heart to slow, but when she met his gaze again, her chest exploded.

She lunged into his arms and kissed him.

He wasted no time tugging her to him. She straddled him, an intense heat flooding from her fearful heart to her core. She angled her mouth closer, while her hands cradled his jaw, fingers dipping into his hair. He bit her lip playfully, and she let out a soft moan. She ground into him, her body electrified with relief and insatiability. There was a sudden need, a hunger, to have everything happen *now*. All the pent-up tension, the flirting, she wanted it undone like his clothes should be. She tore at his shirt, ripping the buttons off. A jerk told her the car started driving. They could drive her straight into Calesal's wall and she wouldn't care, as long as Lucien kept kissing her like she was his last, desperate breath.

He pulled the straps of her dress down, baring her chest. Her nipples were taut, sensitive, and Lucien pulled from their kiss to look at her briefly. "I was ready to destroy this whole city if something happened to you."

Jelan kissed him deeply, then muttered into his mouth. "Destroy me instead."

A soft groan slipped through his lips. His brown eyes darkened. His fingers wrapped in her hair, tugging her head back so her breasts, as small as they were, met his lips. "Gladly."

He brought a nipple into his mouth and she moaned in the car. The driver continued, and with a quick glance, Jelan noticed the wall between them was up. They had privacy.

"Now," Jelan said breathlessly. "I want you now. Fast and hard. *Please.*"

A hoarse, dark laugh tickled her ear. "As you wish."

She dragged her nails down his chest before undoing his belt, then his zipper, before she reached inside and felt him for the first time.

Oh, she will be incredibly satisfied.

One of Lucien's hands went to her rear and spanked. Hard. She moaned louder.

"Fucking sing for me." He sucked the other breast. Her core was pure, wet heat. She was dripping through her panties. Desperation filled each of her breaths. His hands moved her hips, grinding her into him. A moment later, he lifted her up, pushing her underwear to the side and dragging a finger along her center. "You want me this bad?"

"Please," she begged. "*Please.*"

"Then take it."

She was shaking with need as she pulled him out of his pants and positioned him beneath her. Lucien caught her jaw, forcing her to meet his eyes. "Take *all* of it."

Skies, she was going to fucking explode then and there. She felt for his tip. Sat down.

All the fucking way.

He groaned breathily, his mouth parting. Jelan leaned in and caught his lip between her teeth. She began to move. Grind. Ride him through the months of walking past his door, wondering if she should barge in and end the torture. But here, now, as he filled her completely, to the point it was slightly painful, she couldn't resist the animalistic smile that crawled onto her face.

His finger rubbed at that sensitive spot. Jelan arched back, her release rushing to the tips of her toes and fingers. Stars flickered behind her eyes. She had been so pent-up, now she was fucking alive. All it would take was one touch there to make her explode.

He hissed. When she came down from her high, his fingernails scratched her exposed back and guided her into motion, while adding his own thrusts up. Their noises filled the car, her head swam with pleasure, and soon she was reaching another peak, cresting at the same time as Lucien, and together, they fell.

"Oh my…" Jelan gasped, gulping down breaths. She whipped her head to the seat beside them and snatched her inhaler, sucking in.

Lucien laughed. "There are plenty more inhalers at home."

Home. Her cheeks warmed. She slowly clambered off him and he cleaned himself up before fixing her underwear and dress.

She smiled and shook the inhaler. "I only need the one."

His expression darkened, eyes a teasing glitter of promise. "We aren't leaving the bedroom tonight. Nor for the rest of the day. You'll need more."

Sitting next to him now, she had half a thought to tell the driver to leave when they got to the parking garage and go for round two, but when Jelan opened her mouth, her world exploded.

Literally.

One moment she was sated, hot and happy next to Lucien, the next the car screeched to a stop. Crunched against a barrier. Glass shattered. She vaulted forward, only to have her arm roughly pulled into Lucien. The rear of the car flew up and then slammed down, making Lucien's grip release and Jelan collide with the door.

It was a couple moments of silence before Jelan groaned and shifted herself. A bolt of pain met the side of her head. She glanced at Lucien who was on the car's floor. She reached, glass pinching her arm—

The side door flung open, and she collapsed into a set of arms. A familiar shirt.

A black-and-white-printed shirt.

Jelan blinked through the pain in her head as she tried to look up, but her vision blurred.

"Sorry about that, the driver wouldn't stop for me."

The familiar voice.

She caught the black blobs of sunglasses.

A roar filled the wreck. When Jelan looked back, she saw the car had t-boned another at an empty intersection. The man continued to drag her away before he stood her up and hugged her back to his front.

"But you stole my sister, so I need collateral." He inhaled deeply through his nose. "Also, I thought that perfume was you. It is incredible."

Jelan's eyes bugged open. She fumbled with her stance, one heel on, the other barefoot. The man slid his glasses to the top of his head and revealed a beautiful set of mono-lid eyes.

Silver. His eyes were *silver*. An alluring gray burned with fury. Beheld her. Terrified her. She parted her lips, finally recognizing him.

Luka Arvalo.

"I really didn't want to hurt you, but when my sister's blood splatters the street, I have a hard time rationalizing things," he said drily, voice deep and hoarse.

"*Luka.*"

Jelan whipped her head back to the car. Lucien stood out of the wreckage, looking surprisingly fine with glass fragments in his hair. A gash tore through his shirt. Blood welled, staining the material, and dripping off his fingers. "Release her now and I won't shoot you where you stand."

His voice was frightening. Luka didn't even flinch. He actually laughed, the chuckle reverberating into her body.

Jelan's gaze darted back to Lucien's arm, wishing she could stop the blood, but the longer she looked, the more it seemed to clot. She blinked.

A giant onyx car screeched into the intersection, and before it braked, Bronto and Ashan were out, thick vests covering their torso, two plasguns in each hand with plasblades strapped across their backs. Both immediately bolted to Lucien, protecting their commander.

"There will be no publicity about this," Luka demanded, ignoring the new arrivals. "An even, successful trade. You give me my sister back in three weeks' time, and I will hand back Ms. Gregory. Deal?"

"I don't make deals with Arvalo's spawn."

"And here I was thinking you were smarter than your brother." A click sounded and Lucien lunged with a growl, only to be stopped by Bronto.

The cool metal of a plasgun gently rubbed Jelan's temple. Black-clad figures rushed from the shadows of the street, guns pointing at the three men. Jelan bit her terrified gasp. Luka, to her surprise, began to rub circles around her waist, as if trying to calm her.

His breath met her ear. "You have nothing to fear."

Lies. Lies. Lies.

Luka spoke up. "Both will be in complete health by the time we handle this trade, got it?"

Her eyes darted to every gun pointed at Lucien. Panic gripped her throat. "Do it," she pleaded. "Do it!"

Lucien began to shake his head. He stood up tall, shaking out his injured arm. "I can't—"

A gun clicked.

"I'll do it!" Jelan cried, trembling. "Three weeks. I promise. Please, please. Just let them go safely. *Please.*"

Lucien battled, but Bronto muttered something in his ear. Lucien seemed to cave at that moment. He straightened himself, clenched his fists.

"Three weeks."

Jelan felt Luka's smile on the top of her head. "Amazing."

A car raced to their side and Luka opened the door. He jutted his chin and she reluctantly clambered in.

Luka climbed in after. Jelan crawled to the farthest side, curling into the door. She glanced out of the window to see Lucien's frustrated silhouette. Luka's soldiers retreated.

"You did well."

She didn't turn to him.

"But please, for the love of the skies, know better when you step into my territory."

Jelan turned her head fully. Luka lounged at the opposite end, legs spread wide, a watch dangled from an outstretched finger.

Her watch.

She glanced to her wrist. The watch was still there, looking the exact same...

"I actually don't like plasma," he said, humor in his voice. "But I like technology and keeping it to myself. One little tap and the data, the appearance of the watch, can be exactly replicated. It's what I did to you on the staircase."

Her lips parted. She was unable to speak.

It wasn't a long drive. Blood crusted the side of her head and at some point, Luka slipped her alcohol pads and gauze, then mumbled something about a medic at the apartment. She slowly went numb, unable to comprehend exactly what was happening.

Blink.

The car stopped.

Blink.

Luka guided her into an apartment building.

Blink.

They entered an elevator together.

She stared at him while the elevator doors closed. He pressed the top button.

"Do you care about your sister?"

It was the only thing to slip on her tongue. She was…frankly, she was surprised. Otherwise, it would have been a public battle for honor, not for Mai's spilled blood.

"She needs a bit of freedom, anyway. Father is suffocating."

Jelan's brows furrowed. "Is this his game?"

"My family plays their games," he said. "But I play my own."

Not quite an answer. Jelan backed up against the elevator wall. The fast rise made her stomach roil. She flattened her sweaty palms to the metal while ignoring his hard gaze.

"This isn't for your father, is it?" she dared to ask.

Skies, his eyes never left her. They were brilliant, alluring shades of silver. It terrified her. She tried to ring in any ounce of courage she might still have, but it fluttered out with her shaky breaths.

Luka smiled, and it was a dangerous, genuine thing. "No, this is personal."

Personal? She opened her mouth. Closed it. The elevator reached the top floor. Dinged. Jelan thought her heart was going to beat right out of her chest as it opened to a dark concept design. Homey was her first thought. Comfortable was her second.

Dungeon was her third.

"You will sleep in the guest room down there." Luka nodded toward a hallway, where a door lay ajar, revealing a cozy bed. Jelan turned her head, spotting a hallway sprouting from the other side of the joined living room. That door was firmly shut. Luka's room. "Breakfast is whenever you want. Coffee is always available. No one else is allowed here unless I approve. Even my father must notify me."

Her knees trembled. She was having a hard time processing her night's adventures. Her head pounded.

Luka's silver eyes drifted there. "Do you want a medic?"

Jelan's fingers brushed the slight bump. She didn't suspect she had a concussion. "I can wrap it myself."

His jaw twitched, but he continued on, "You are my collateral. No one knows you're here, and no one will know."

"You said this was…personal?" She bit her lip. "Is this because of Mai?"

A glitter in his eye. "On top of kidnapping my sister, I need your help."

Her brows furrowed.

"Gloat all you want," he said with a teasing smirk. "But I need help making the plashield."

Her jaw dropped.

"We start tomorrow."

And then he went down his hallway to his bedroom, while Jelan remained dumbfounded in *his* living room.

PART II
THE BLOOD

17

MED CORP

JACK WATCHED AS ANOTHER SUBJECT took his last breath and went limp.

"Time of death…"

Not wanting to hear more, Jack turned and walked out of the medical room.

He'd lost fifteen other subjects this week, most of them Endoliers whom his Vanisher Transporters picked up in Envy. The entire grisly ordeal had been hard to watch, and half the time Jack put them out of their misery himself. It was the briefest sense of morality, of control, he had while Cyran breathed down his neck. Some of them were so deteriorated their faces were unrecognizable, but Jack requested the Endos anyway. He didn't want to hear them talk when needle after needle pierced their skin, didn't want to hear them scream when they contorted their bodies different ways, trying to see if their muscles reacted to the Droan cells. Every experiment happened the same though, and Jack's options ran thin. After each subject's death, the scientists stared at him longer, wondering why *Jack* survived.

It was to drive him insane. To distract him from the control Cyran slowly weaved. No matter if Cyran could blood-control Jack, it wasn't the same as pure fear and loyalty. Even now, Jack's chest was tight, his breathing shallow, as he made his way to his office. The pain never faded. It consumed him. He's buried his morals his whole life. To get the jobs done. To survive. But Cyran was *destroying* the morals itself.

He dreamed of his brother in all kinds of petrifying situations; Cyran ripping his head off. Cyran feeding Lucien's extremities to a pit of robotic lions. Cyran tearing out his spine and tying it in a knot.

It was only a matter of time. This was the bit of freedom Jack was being tortured with. Captain meant nothing, the control meant nothing, because when Jack couldn't complete this impossible task, Cyran would strap him to a table and drain his blood, until Jack begged for the briefest breath of freedom that he used to have.

It was horrifying.

It was brilliant.

Before he entered his office, Jack whirled to his lingering assistant. "I want more healing serums. Anything you can find. Anything that can be produced in mass quantities."

The man bristled. "Sir—"

"I want to go outside this damn tower and see if there is something else that can make these subjects survive."

"I—we have restrictions with Med Corp in the Cities." He pulled out his tablet and showed Jack a lengthy form. "The CEO wants more money for the supplies."

Jack scoffed. "Doesn't this CEO know I'll kill him?"

The assistant frowned. "It's…"

"Greed, I know."

"I'll send his files. You can take a look for yourself, sir."

Jack nodded, entered his office, and slammed the door behind him.

Jack had sixteen floors in one of Cyran's towers to work in, including a ridiculously large top-floor office. He flung himself in the nearest chair and watched as the files on Med Corp's CEO appeared on the plascreen before him.

He didn't take it in at first, as his mind bled back to the earlier parts of the day. Serwa threw on projects like no other. All ultimately meant to distract Jack. To tire him into never thinking Violet could be scouring this city.

He had begun to see Violet everywhere. In the brown braids of servants, in the lips that smirked at him, in the small touches some dared to give. One female, a low-ranking captain working under Yeren's division, flirted with him far too often, and even went so far as to brush his hair back from his face during training once. Jack had snapped and literally broke her wrist in the process.

Not many touched him after that.

It wasn't until Serwa instructed him to hunt down two Zoncolla fugitives and bring them to the Ice Tower that Jack knew he was going crazy. That one servant—with too white of skin, brown eyes, golden hair, and a rounder face—began to *transform* before his eyes. Her roots leaked to brown locks, her irises melted to blue...

Then she pulled away, breathing that he'd hurt her. But there was a small, little rasp to her voice that he caught. Thought about. Turned over.

It couldn't be true.

But Jack *swore* when he took the liquor bottle there was a long red mark on her palm, a palm he'd kissed before, that he'd made a promise with. Then it was gone. He hadn't seen her since. The servant's name was Talia, and she mainly serviced Zavar and a few others.

Then Serwa piled on more meetings, Yeren gave him tasks, Zavar distracted him, and other commanders flung assignments left and right, so Jack forgot about the occurrence.

Jack's meetings earlier today were mostly boring. Attend a coffee appointment with four women in Hallow to discuss progressive educational opportunities such as building colleges and elite universities. Greed infused the spit of their mouths. The only problems brought up were the physical amenities of each place, how big and plush the classrooms were, and getting the best technology for their kids. It was only for *their* kids. When Jack brought up Hanhii and lesser-privileged schools, it was like their minds blanked. As if they couldn't comprehend a world existed beyond their wealthy bubble. He even brought up an empty lot for a new school right outside the Navru, and one of the women asked if Navru was a stop on the airship lines.

It both fascinated and terrified Jack. He couldn't believe it.

They didn't get much done, as two of the women had spiked their drinks, the touching started, and Jack was forced to leave.

Right after that was production, which Jack had a stake in back in Calesal. However, here it was the most exploited mess he could think of. The people in the room sipped their drinks and made jokes about their teleported vacations within this world, all the while they signed off increasing production on different foods, one of which came from farms seven hours of flight away. A unique nut that took nearly a month to harvest, peel, dry, and manufacture. It was a fad in the cities, put into smoothies and drinks and whatnot. One assistant slid a paper that would approve the use of a fertilizer to rush the growing process.

"What is the list of ingredients?" he asked an assistant. "I want a description of each one."

The assistant relayed them. None of the ingredients were purely natural, and based on another question, they had poisoned the land's waterways.

"And you think using it again is beneficial?" Jack asked.

"They want what they want," the assistant said.

"It's a nut."

The assistant's fingers trembled as he reached for the paper from Jack. "I don't ask questions."

"No, that's what I do." Jack turned to the Hallow's Overall Production Manager. "What are you paying the people who harvest these?"

The manager blanched. "How am I supposed to know that?"

"This fertilizer is poisonous, and if the people harvesting these nuts are going to be handling it, they should be paid accordingly."

His shoulders lifted in a bored shrug. "We give the farm managers money, and they give us our supply."

"Do these farm managers live on the farms?"

"Not that I know of."

Jack ripped up the paper. "Your nuts will remain in typical production as normal. Find an alternative for your smoothies. I will only entertain rushed production if you can provide me with each harvester's compensation. I also want every farm manager's information by next week."

"Why is that?"

"Because I have a hard time believing the money given to the farm managers—who don't live on said farms—is being allocated to the workers they don't see," Jack snapped. "I'll be expecting the reports next week."

And with that, he left.

He then lost another subject and was now here, in his little Captain of the Hybrid Division office, shooting back a shot of liquor and hoping it absolved his growing insanity.

He finally took a look at the files on the Med Corp CEO. The more numbers he reviewed, the more the glass creaked in his fist. Anger chilled his veins. He was so *fucking* tired of this shit. The glass succumbed to his rage, cracked, then shattered, shredding his palm, but Jack was already out of his chair and pressing a button for a Vanisher.

The Vanisher appeared in an instant. Jonathon was his name. He took Jack to most of his meetings.

"Where do you want to teleport to?" Jonathon asked.

"The hospital entrance, please." Jack offered his bloody hand, and the Vanisher accepted it without betraying his thoughts. It was healed a breath later. "I want to see the bottom first before we discuss with the top."

❋❋❋

Jonathon accompanied Jack as they walked through the Hanhii hospital's sliding glass doors. It wasn't part of the richer districts, but more middle-income and lower-income servitude.

One of the receptionists abruptly stood. Jack was dressed in his captain's uniform, so it was natural for silence and fear to accompany his presence. He showed the palm of his hand in a peaceful gesture.

The receptionist bowed. "Good evening, sir. How can I help you? I wasn't expecting…well, we don't ever get captains in this side of the city."

Jack offered a smile. "I'm only here on business. Do you have any available nurses I could speak to?"

She frowned in response. "Well…we are very short-staffed today. I can see if someone is on their break."

"Don't remove anyone from their break," he said. "Is there someone local who doesn't mind me bothering their work?"

"I'm sure I can find someone suitable," the receptionist said. She picked up her phone and dialed a number. A rather ancient system for Greed. The hospitals in Hallow had ear-pagers and holograms and more. "Hi, yes, is Nurse Becca around? She is assigned to the pharmacy today, right?…Okay, good. I have a guest here who's requesting to speak with a nurse."

Jack brightened his smile.

The receptionist blushed deeply. "Perfect. I'll send him up." She put the phone down. "You can follow me."

She took them up two flights of stairs, her cheeks reddening further, but this time from embarrassment. "We'd take the elevators, but we haven't…" She shook her head. "I'm sorry I'm making you take the stairs."

"Not a problem," Jack said. Jonathon nodded. "Are there no elevators?"

"Most haven't functioned for a couple months now. They allocated technicians to fix ones for the operating floors, and that's it."

"Who is in charge of fixing those?"

"The managers. But…they don't come around much, and can be difficult to get ahold of. I think they are based out of Hallow, so we are pretty low on their list."

Jack resisted laughing. Oh, he was going to have so much fun tonight. Jonathon flashed him a curious look.

"I will have technicians here to fix them within the hour." He nodded to Jonathon, and the man pulled out his phone.

"Oh—thank you, sir." She flashed him a bright smile and turned her gaze toward a door. "This is the pharmacy station. The nurse packs the bottles and dosages for patients."

"Isn't a pharmacist supposed to do that?"

"Like I said, we are short-staffed."

She opened the door and stepped aside. Jack waltzed in, taking note of the organized shelves and the antiquated filing.

In Hallow, they had robots. A funnel delivery system. Rapid-response blood testing.

"Let me know if you need anything else." The receptionist bowed and exited. Jonathon stayed outside, flicking the peeling paint on a wall before he made eye contact with Jack. Jack nodded, and Jonathon made yet another call.

Jack shut the door to the hallway and turned. A nurse sat at a small table. She wore glasses, with her dark hair pulled into a low ponytail. She finished shifting through a round of pills, capped the bottle, and turned to him. "How can I help you?"

"I have questions, and I was hoping you could give me answers. Honest ones."

She lifted a brow. "Honest ones?"

"I won't name you." Jack took a seat and crossed his legs. "I'm a little curious about the lack of information when it comes to ground-level healthcare work. So I have questions I want a nurse to answer." He tilted his head. "Someone who isn't influenced or prepared for it. I only need the truth."

She cleared her throat and settled back in the chair. "Okay. What are your questions?"

"I heard you're short-staffed today, is that normal?"

"Typically, yes." She paused. Looked at the door. Pursed her lips. "Most of us work overtime. Don't get paid for it, either."

"Is your salary enough?"

She shrugged. "For a single independent, sure. But it's a salary for a nurse's job. We don't get paid for running food, taking vitals, cleaning the rooms, doing treatments beyond our job descriptions. All of which should be done by another person…but they quit, and the hospital hasn't hired their replacements."

"And why's that?"

"Probably because they know they can put it on us," Becca said and rubbed her eyes. "We say yes for one thing and they add more and more. Also, probably because they don't have to pay more salaries. Not when we do it for free."

"So they take advantage of you."

"I'm not supposed to be doing this." She motioned to the pills. "But my patients need their medicine, and no one is here to cover it. That leaves me to do it. And then if we do something wrong, since we are literally doing everything, we get sued."

Jack grew silent before taking a deep breath. "I have a question about the pills. And their prices."

She shook her head. "I don't know much about the bills, but…"

"There are some ridiculous charges for a hospital that mainly caters to middle and low class. Why are they up-charging nearly every medication, even if it's a simple painkiller?"

"Because they can," she said. "Because people need medicine, and it will never go out of demand, so those in pharmaceuticals take advantage of that."

"What is that medicine next to you? The one in the vial?"

"Oh, this?" She picked up the vial of clear liquid. "Losan. It regulates blood sugar."

"Who produces Losan?"

"Med Corp. The company that produces ninety-three percent of all pharmaceuticals in the Twin Cities, sir."

Jack could hear Alexia Javez's loud, cackling laughter in his head. Calesal was by no means better when it came to healthcare, but it was a giant city, and Alexia was only two years on the job. She was the best he'd ever seen, and she had been actively trying to improve it, especially for the South.

However, Calesal did not allow private companies to maintain total capital over necessary drugs. There was a cap, in which Alexia regulated it by laws, but allowed private companies to develop medicine.

"Med Corp has a capital on the drugs, does the hospital get anything from this? Is that why they control so much?"

"Honestly, I don't know the specifics, but in terms of pain meds…" She paused, but that little smirk came back. "If patients report that they still have pain, then the hospital doesn't get funding. So that means we are over-prescribing medications. It has technically created an addiction."

"You don't get basic enough funding to fix your elevators."

She threw her hands up. "Whatever funding we might get, the hospital doesn't see it." Her voice dropped to a whisper. "There was a rumor last year that the CEO of the hospital used the funding to give himself a bonus check."

Jack nodded. "Those checks are millions."

"And they are handed right to the CEO," she gritted.

"Becca," Jack started. "Are you aware that one of those vials costs four dollars to make, but is priced at nearly four thousand?"

She nodded.

"And how many vials does a regular user need a month?"

"About six, sir."

"So that is an estimated twenty-four thousand a month for a basic blood-sugar medication for a middle-to-low-income patient. Correct?"

She rubbed at her eyes again. Jack had noticed the tears pooling, but unfortunately, he wasn't here to pat her on the back. There were things he was willing to do, but a hug was not one of them. He wasn't that nice of a person.

"And this markup goes for most medications, correct?"

Tears spilled down her face as she nodded.

"What do you do to combat this?"

A sob broke through. "I watch them die. They can't afford it, so they die." She took a long look at the medication, and her mouth twisted in disgust. Tears dripped off her chin and onto her scrubs, which had frayed hems.

Jack had enough. He stood, patted her on the shoulder, ignoring the tingle in his fangs. He could smell her emotion. Sadness, pure misery. It wafted like fresh rainwater, tinged with lemon. "Thank you for your help. Things will change soon."

She wiped her eyes and blubbered, "Thank you, sir."

Jack opened the door and stepped outside, shutting it softly behind him. Jonathon finally closed his phone. "I made a lot of calls. Renovations will begin tomorrow."

"Good, thank you," Jack said. "Now, let's go to the top. I want to speak with Mopper."

❋❋❋

Angus Mopper, CEO of Med Corp, arrived at his skyrise office late. Jack stared down at Hallow City beneath him, hands behind his back. He felt that familiar icy calm course underneath his skin.

The calm that came before someone died by his hand.

"Ah," Mopper said, strolling through the glossy double wooden doors. "You're already here."

"You're late," Jack said.

A portly man, Mopper was shorter than Jack, but large enough to put up a fair fight if Jack didn't have Droanian strength. His black hair was crested with gray, white skin showing signs of wrinkles. For being worth a billion dollars, he could have at least made himself look more appealing.

He took off his glasses and loosened his tie. "Want a drink, Captain Marin? I only have the best in this office."

"I am alright, thank you."

"Please, have a seat." Mopper gestured to the twin chairs facing his desk. Jonathon glared from the far corner. "I have been looking forward to our meeting."

Jack only turned back to the window, shoulders straight. "How was your vacation at the southern beaches?"

Silence. Then, "Excuse me?"

"Your vacation. Your private airship docked an hour ago. The logs aren't secret. You've been there for a month. How was it?"

"Fine… just fine."

"How much is a vacation like that?" Jack turned his head, looking at the confused Mopper in his peripheral vision. "It must be quite expensive. Private airship, private villa, security, personal chef, boat trips and more."

"Excuse—"

Jack turned to Jonathon. "How much would you guess?"

"Around two million for that, sir."

"And how much do nurse scrubs cost?"

"Twenty to thirty dollars each, sir. For basic ones."

"Captain Marin," Mopper said lowly. "What is this about? I'm here to talk medical advancements with you—"

"The only thing you have been advancing is the percentage cut from your markups of necessary pharmaceuticals."

Jonathon strutted to the desk and dropped the stack of papers onto it. Proof. Wire transfers to his own accounts, abysmal funding for the hospital they'd just visited, and then a re-transfer to the CEO, who then wired it back to Mopper. Being Captain of the Emperor didn't make it hard to get information. A few bats of the eyes and running his hand through his curls made it all the more easy.

"These markups are necessary."

"To oil your airship?" Jack finally looked at the man. "To host women at your villa?"

"How dare you." Mopper stormed around his desk. "You are insulting me in my very own office, in *my* city! You have no right to do such a thing—I will be contacting your Emperor—"

"The Emperor gave me this responsibility," Jack said. "The operations of the cities are beneath him at the moment."

Mopper pressed a button on his tablet. "I want an assistant in here now!" He turned to Jack. "I'm leaving. If you have any further questions, you can direct them to my assistant."

A young, ginger-haired man with a round face and full figure stepped in, bowing low. "Mr. Mopper, sir."

"Answer any questions Captain Marin has, I'm retiring for the evening." Mopper picked up his briefcase and tablet, shoving it in. He huffed in anger, and when he took only a step toward the door,

Jonathon appeared in front of him.

"Now, now, Mopper." Jonathon smirked. "You're going to stay here, with us. Okay?"

"You can't force me!"

"Do you always act like a child when you've been called out?" Jack strutted past them, addressing the assistant. "I want to see the labs. The one that produces Losan. Please."

The assistant didn't bat an eye. Just bowed and held the door open. "Yes, Captain. Right this way."

"You can't do this!" Mopper yelled.

"Shut up, you're not being left out," Jonathon said.

Mopper owned one of the nicest buildings in the Twin Cities. Marble floors, sleek metal, working elevators, chandeliers in every foyer. Jack followed the assistant through every ridiculously expensive room, down seven floors in the elevator, then into an advanced laboratory.

"This is absolutely ridiculous, I'm calling security—"

"Security is comprised of soldiers from the castle, Mopper," Jack drawled. "Who I also command. Now, give me a tour."

Jack flashed a charming smile and Mopper's vacation-tanned skin paled. Just enough so Jack knew Mopper was fully aware of the lethal monster that lurked beneath.

Jack cocked his head. "No tour?"

"No tour," Mopper drawled.

Jack clapped his hands. "Then let's commence with the questions. How much do you charge a pharmacy for Losan?" Jack cocked his head and looked at the papers. "It's actually quite interesting. You not only produce the medications, but you also own the pharmacies selling them, and then you're on the boards of most of the city's hospitals. You really used that brain to think, 'oh, how can I make as much money as I possibly can?'"

Mopper remained quiet.

His assistant answered, "The recent price of Losan was three-thousand four-hundred thirty-two dollars and fifteen cents."

"Where is this little vial? I want to see it for myself."

The assistant approached a glass security door and scanned his wrist. He procured a tray of vials. "Here they are, sir."

"Such small things for such large prices," Jack said. "And to think that Losan was first developed nearly fifty years ago with only a couple recent transformations. What is the production cost of one unit?"

The assistant kept his face blank, but there was a light in his eyes. "Fifty-two cents."

"So, there's very little in the way of research, easy distribution within a city, and a huge demand for the medication. It's a money-making scheme."

"You don't know what you're talking about," Mopper gritted. "We live in a city of greed, and I built my business from the ground—"

"Actually, you had a pretty hefty trust fund," Jonathon said.

"And I was the first to patent it, to give this medication to the people to help their health—"

"I just came from visiting the hospital in Hanhii, the one north of Navru. I spoke to a couple people there, even the nurses." Jack dropped his calm demeanor and let his predator filter through. "A nurse sobbed while she talked about her patients dying because they can't afford the medications they need to live. As far as I can tell, people poke their greedy fingers into the healthcare system to take advantage of it, so by the time it gets to someone who desperately needs it to live, they are the ones paying the price." Jack's gaze bled into Mopper's. "Did your private airship ride make it worth it?"

Mopper paled further. His face morphed from fury to fear.

The emotions of someone who was caught.

"Fuck you," he growled.

"No, thank you. Jonathon, my wallet, please," Jack said. Jonathan bowed and disappeared with a flash of light, returning another tense minute later. Jack took the leather bound wallet and threw twelve thousand on the table.

"I'll take three," Jack said.

The assistant's brows scrunched. "Sorry?"

"I want them."

"You can't do that," Mopper snarled.

"Can I not?" Jack waved another hundred-dollar bill. He placed one after the other until Mopper licked his lips. "I want what I want."

Mopper drooled at the money. His irises dilated. Fingers shook as he gathered the bills close to his body. Hugged it.

The assistant took out three vials and Jack frowned. "How much for the big syringe?"

"Thirty, sir."

Jack gave the assistant a long, heavy gaze. The assistant understood, his eyes wide, but he filled the syringe with all three vials and handed it to Jack. In the background, Mopper was muttering to himself, his eyes wholly black at this point.

"Three doses are lethal, correct?" Jack asked.

"Yes, sir," the assistant said.

Jack turned to Jonathon with a smirk. "Good deal."

Jack flicked the needle, watched as a bubble of liquid came out of the tip, and wandered over to Mopper, who paused his gathering of the money. Mopper lifted his gaze to Jack's.

And within that darkness, a peek of realization fought the greed. He knew.

"Pleasure doing business with you," Jack drawled.

He stabbed the needle into Mopper's neck. Pushed the cap all the way in until every bit of the medicine was gone.

Mopper stayed upright for a moment before he collapsed to the floor in convulsions. Jack took a step back.

The assistant didn't even blink. Only opened his mouth to say, "Woah."

"Indeed." Jack wrinkled his nose. "This might be one of my less-messy deaths."

"I didn't like his voice," Jonathon grumbled.

"Precisely why I killed him," Jack grumbled. He kicked Mopper's body. "Who gains his assets?"

"I can look for you, sir," the assistant said.

"Good. Jonathon, please inform the Relations Divisions at the castle that there has been a casualty, and that by law, any death of a reigning owner of a privatized business will be handled by the Empire before finding another suitable replacement to head the company." Jack disposed of the syringe in the hazardous bin. "I want all paperwork on my desk and temporary duties for Med Corp to my team by tomorrow. We have a lot of work to do."

"Yes, sir," Jonathon said with a smile.

Jack turned to the assistant. "I'll have someone clean up his body within the next thirty minutes. You will be working for me now. What is your name?"

"Colin, sir."

"I want reports of his assets and investments. I want every name that money from this company has been sent to. Every business. Everything that you can get me." Jack straightened his collar. "I want to appropriately raze them to the ground."

❀ ❀ ❀

When Jack returned to his office, Cyran was there. Gazing out the window. A creator looking down at his creation.

Cyran devoured emotions from the room. It was a frozen, senseless environment around him, and Jack had noticed he never felt any tingle of emotion from the Worldbreaker. No irritation, no fury, no anything. Just a blank slate.

"Master." Jack bowed.

"You killed Mopper," Cyran said evenly.

Jack bowed his head. "He sent a contract to increase prices for this facility."

Cyran stared at Jack, long and hard. Jack's pulse pounded. Vision blurred. *This is it. This is the beginning of the end of my freedom.*

He took a step back. Cyran's eyes darted at the movement.

"I thought you'd do it yourself," he said. Cyran clasped his hands behind his back. "There were tables, needles, bags, an entire lab dedicated to you. I thought you'd *want* to help me make more."

Jack said nothing.

"I gave you your survival. I gave you hope and power and a mission. You knew what you had to do, and yet you didn't sit yourself down, extract your blood, and try." Cyran's eyes darkened. Jack's muscles grew tight, his blood heating. Cyran's control wormed its way in. "I really didn't want to have to hurt you."

Jack fell to his knees. His lungs spasmed. Breathing stopped. A foreign darkness crawled up his spine, flicking the cords. He tried to fight the pain, but with each touch, a tortured gasp left his mouth.

"I don't know…why…"

"You don't know why you survived?" Cyran strutted toward him. "A pity." His scarred hands wrapped around Jack's throat. "That means I will have to find out."

They vanished in a flash of light. Brutal, bitter wind slapped Jack's cheek. He collapsed to the ground, unable to move his limbs. A desperate plea left his mouth.

"Handle him," Cyran commanded.

A jolt of nauseating lightning caressed his cheek. Boots scuffed the gravel of the platform. Surrounded by the tips of mountains, high enough to touch the clouds, Zavar materialized. The wind whipped his black hair in all directions, his eyes remaining blank. Jack searched his face, but the Vaelaur merely lifted his brow as his lightning maximized.

"This is why you go out of your way to do things for me." Cyran's voice sank in Jack's ears. It reverberated through his skull. "I don't like forcing you."

The lightning came. Paralyzed Jack. There was a thin frown on Zavar's face.

"I want bags of his blood ready by the end of the night. New subjects will begin tomorrow."

"Yes, Master," Zavar said.

Jack's world bled into pure pain.

The wind swallowed his screams.

18

THE BONDS

Violet petted the dog. **"Oh,** you are such a good boy. Or girl. Not sure."

The dog wagged its bushy tail, one blue and one purple eye staring happily at her. Its tuft fur coat lay a light brown on the back, while white covered the belly and trickled in spots down to the paws. Violet felt bad that it was slightly matted by the constant drizzle of rain, but every time she came to this spot, and the dog padded up to her, she tried to brush it out with her fingers.

Its tongue lolled out. Completely unaware of Violet's blood that now covered the crocheted collar Bunny made.

"You will do just fine," she said. "If they find you, they won't be able to resist you—oh, yes, they won't. Definitely not."

The dog howled excitedly, and Violet fed it another chunk of meat from her rice bowl. She turned to the assault of plascreens in a square in Navru.

Jack's face stared back at her.

Jack was a celebrity now, apparently, and not just in the Twin Cities. He was promoted on all different nations' news, and his stupid handsome face littered everywhere. It was the same as back in Calesal—no one knew that he bloodied and killed so many, but instead, the media showed him as an eligible new Captain within the Grand Emperor's military. He showed up at movie premieres, galas, events, all the while posing with other important figures. He flashed his smirk, his dimples, and to Violet, it felt like the whole city obsessed over it.

The dog whimpered and licked her face. Her disposable fork snapped in her hand. She stabbed what was left of it into her food and angrily shoved a vegetable in her mouth.

She wanted all ties to him severed.

❋❋❋

When darkness descended over Greed, Violet disliked herself for how much she liked it. The rivulets of lava from the mountain cascaded like a steady, glowing river in the distance. It ignited the haze of clouds above. Mount Prava—the volcano—stood a powerful, healthy length away from the brilliance of the Twin Cities.

She stormed through the belly of Navru; a dingy place filled with tight, crowded streets that had numerous steps to underground corridors, which led to very illegal things. Somewhere, blocked off from the rest of the public wander, Pharos' resilience lay. She wondered how it was kept a secret, but amid the consistent greedy chaos and the sweep of distractions in Navru's gut, she wasn't surprised it remained invisible. After a day of drug handling and fuming about Jack, Violet was supposed to go straight back to the safehouse and work with Emryn on the plan for the residential school, but she had an errand to run.

She tried a library, but the books were wet and gross and mainly fiction. She might find her answers in the upscale neighborhoods, especially Hallow, but no part of her wanted to venture close to the Church District or Cyran's fortress. Her boots splashed in a puddle as she passed a vintage pawn shop riddled with antiques. She paused. An antique store? Here? In the poor section?

Without a thought, her hands were on the doorknob, and a soft bell rang above as she pushed it open. It was a messy, disorganized place filled with artifacts she knew were very expensive and not from this world. She'd wager a lot of money that they were stolen.

"I'll be there in a moment!" a gruff, male voice called from the back.

Violet didn't respond. She stepped around a tall shelf stacked with books that looked ready to collapse. Animal bones hung from the ceiling, while more shelves were piled with jarred objects. She wrinkled her nose and continued.

The arrival bell rang behind her. She tugged her hood up, turning to peek at the new entry.

She stiffened. Cold sweat laced down her back.

Jodin. One of the twin Vanishers.

She hid herself into the shadows next to a tall, antique cupboard. Her curiosity rose. *Interesting.* Her glamour was the black hair, tanned skin, hooked nose, and brown eyes look. He wouldn't recognize her. Not when their only interactions were drinks at Madam Zona's in Lust and him trying to kill her, then subsequently trying to teleport her.

Skiv.

He wore a long, ratted coat that fit with Navru. His locs were tied back, hands gloved, and a scarf wrapped around his neck. He glanced around the shop with sharp eyes, and she darted behind the open cupboard door, peering through the gap.

She knew the look. His presence was a secret.

"Is it only you?" the male owner called as he filed his way to the front. His wrinkled white skin sagged his cheeks, but a pointy gray beard shaped his frail jawline. Gray, hooded eyes sat below bushy brows. He set a stack of books down on the front desk and crossed his arms. "I thought I heard another."

"Do you have my order?" Jodin grumbled, voice raspy. He sounded tired.

"I told you that kind of tonic is difficult to come by. It takes a while to make."

"I can't wait around forever, Varik."

Varik pursed his lips. "I can't make it brew any faster. How is he?"

"Not well," Jodin said. "He's spent from all the assignments the Master puts us on. His memory isn't any better, either."

Violet's brows scrunched. She vaguely remembered the first interactions she had with the twins in Lust. Yarrow, the other twin, had said something about his brain not being quite right. Was the tonic for him?

"I'm sorry, but like I said, if you want the right medicine, it needs to brew a while longer."

Jodin rubbed at his face. "It already took forever to get the ingredients."

"*You* took forever to get the ingredients."

"Because I had to venture to five different worlds, and that requires rest after each. On top of that, I have assignments. Duties. Don't blame it on me," Jodin said.

"I know you are worried about your brother." Varik checked a paper. "It will be ready before the weekend. Come that day, eight pm."

Jodin sighed, "Fine. I'm afraid I'll need another. He's struggling. His memory goes in and out. The yearly transitions are taking a toll."

Varik frowned and glanced at the door, then dropped his voice. "You know Zoncolla has access to cayna in the ice mines. That serum is incredibly potent. Two drops would help him recover faster."

Jodin poked a string of bones. "I'm not interested in dealing with Zoncolla."

Varik stepped around the desk, drawing close and dropping his voice. "The serum is as close to aether as you could get."

"Don't say that word here," Jodin gritted. "You know how much trouble you would get into."

"*Aether* is what Yarrow needs," Varik whispered. "You know it. He's reaching his limit. Vanishers need aether, especially if they are doing as much as you are."

Jodin towered a head over Varik. His wide nostrils flared in a way that Reed's used to when he was irritated. "I do know it. But…" Jodin shook his head. "It's not possible to get that. It's… you know that cost. Not now. The Emperor would know. I'll see you for the medicine, Varik."

Jodin turned and disappeared out the door. Varik watched the door shut before sidling behind the desk. He picked up a book, loosed a stressed breath, and cursed. His fingers clenched the hardcover, white-knuckled, and she caught a flash of silver on his pinky. Not a ring, but a…tattoo?

She didn't care. She tiptoed to the farthest section of the shop, far enough that it would have been impossible to hear their conversation, and nudged an elbow into a thick tome. It slammed down onto the hardwood, pluming dust into her eyes. She cursed.

"Who's there?" Varik cried.

"Sorry!" Violet exclaimed, rubbing her lids with her sleeve. She picked up the book as Varik marched to the back corner. "I was reading and it slipped."

She glanced at the title. It was in another language, but Varik took it from her. "*The History of Mushrooms?*"

Violet smiled. "I love mushrooms."

He gave her a wary glance and placed the book back on the shelf. His hand dipped into his pocket where the indent of something showed. A weapon. She brushed the hilt of her plasblade.

He waved a hand. "Get out—"

"I want to know about bloodbonds," she blurted.

Varik bristled, eyes bugging. "About what?"

"Bloodbonds."

"I don't know anything about that."

Violet pointed to the front door. "If you tell me, I won't go blabbing about that conversation. I have a loose tongue, you know." She spat in her hand. "And, if you also give me the information I want, I'll make a spitbond to never relay your traitorous words to another's ears."

He wrinkled his nose. "Get out."

"I don't think you want me to."

"You're a street girl who has no business being in here and asking about promise bonds. Get out of my store."

"I'll get you that Zoncolla serum, too. What was it called? Cayna?" She pushed her hood back. "You really need to work on your whispering. Might as well have given you a microphone so the rest of Navru can hear."

"You little—" Varik stepped forward, procuring a knife.

Violet flashed a fiery smirk and released her glamour.

Varik paled as her hair sloshed into brown. Her eyes tingled and her nose cracked as it changed. Within moments, she stood before him in all her Violet Sutton glory. Her smirk that pissed a lot of people off remained the same, as did her swagger. She was winning this round.

"You," Varik breathed. His eyes shifted to the door, then back to her. "*You.*"

"Me." Violet pulled out her plasblade hilted and twirled it. "I'm sure if Jodin's discussing aether and cayna and whatever else that could land you with heads on a stick, you've definitely heard about little ol' me. Now, I'm giving you quite a lot of bargains for a bit of information. I want to know how to destroy a bloodbond, and also more about the bonds. Spitbond, bloodbond, and the others. Why they even work the way they do, too. In exchange, I will make a spitbond with you—"

"You can't make a spitbond if you have a bloodbond," Varik groused.

"Ah, you're smart." Violet flashed her teeth in a smile. That much was evident to her when her spitbond with the Droans was overrode her blood one with Jack. "You caught me. But I can get you that serum. You'll just have to trust me."

Varik flashed an incredulous look. "You have plans to spend months in the ice mine in order to get the serum?"

"No." Violet leaned against a shelf. It wobbled. Varik gasped. She straightened with a sheepish look. "I'm sensitive to the cold. Makes me sneeze for some odd reason."

Varik rubbed at his face in frustration. "No wonder they all want you dead."

"Yes, I'm annoying," Violet said. "What do you say?"

"How do I know you'll show up with the serum?"

"Because I'm not shitty enough to let the man who Awakened me die," Violet said. "He saved my life, and apparently, he's suffering now. It would only be fair."

"You're a lying shit." Varik studied her. "But if you can get me the serum by next week, I won't spill that you can disguise yourself."

"It's a deal." She held out her hand. Varik merely looked at it and strutted back to the front. She followed. "I do keep my promises. Sometimes. But this one is important."

"Jodin will kill me if he knew you know," Varik sighed. "Damnit."

"Jodin has more important things to worry about."

Varik ambled around the desk and began shifting through the book stack. "Why do you want to know about bonds?"

"How many are there?"

"As far as I know, four in total." Varik rubbed his pinky—the one lined with tattooed silver. "Spitbond, bloodbond, deathbond, and amana bond. The spitbond is fairly self-explanatory; make a promise and swap spit in a handshake. It contains the DNA of each person, so the world knows an oath was made and that it cannot be broken, unless there is an action to be done in order to break it."

Like Violet had been forced to do with the Droans. She had to win one fighting ring, then she could leave Tetro. When she tried to run right after making that bond with Arafat, an invisible wall had stopped her from leaving city limits. "And what governs a bond? Magic?"

"Life," Varik said. "The worlds. The universe. It was an ancient thing done by Droans long ago. They mainly used spit and bloodbonds to make pacts between their clans, or even for marriage. In Gluttony, though, the deathbond was discovered. The amana bond, however, has been seen in history multiple times and in multiples cultures—many different worlds, really. The amana is the most universal."

Violet drew a finger through the dust on a shelf. "What is the amana bond?"

"A soul bond." Varik's voice grew soft. "It is a bond between souls. Most call it the love bond, but it is deeper than that. You make a promise with another, recite a declarable oath, swap blood in a ceremony, and bond yourself to them via your souls. For the rest of your lifetimes."

Violet wrinkled her nose. "That sounds terrible."

Varik snorted. "To some, yes."

"So, is there a hierarchy between bonds?"

"Technically, no. The only one that proves a problem are the spit and bloodbonds. The spit isn't really binding, so the bloodbonds always override them. Spitbonds are like basic promises, but in history, it is said that if you made a bond with a stronger part of your DNA, aka blood, then spit becomes null. You can't make another spitbond again, since you already promised something far greater and of more value. The next is a bloodbond, which typically prevents any actions from being made that threaten or defy the bond. Deathbonds are simply bonds that if one dies, the other does, too. So, in theory, you're promising your life, and that overrides any bloodbonds you've made. In history, many worlds used to force deathbonds as a source of torture. For one ruling queen, the conquering king forced deathbonds between all seven of her children, then stole one child. When she didn't listen to his decrees, he killed the one child, and subsequently killed the remaining six. They dropped to the table at dinner. It created a mess. The queen's blood smothered her potatoes a moment later. It was rather smart. Other than that, deathbonds are typically rare and unused."

Violet side-eyed Varik, wondering how he knew about all of that. The man was old, yes, and clearly held a plethora of knowledge throughout his books, but...the way he explained history made it seem like he was there...*in the room*. She tucked it away.

Varik shook his head and stacked another book. "And, of course, with an amana, you are promising your soul."

Violet walked over to the desk and flipped her palm up, revealing her scar shared with Jack. "I don't want to make a death or amana bond, so how do I remove this bloodbond?"

Varik's lips twitched. "Having a rift?"

"I just don't want the nuisance of it," Violet said.

"Well, it's a fairly simple answer. You and another person promised something to each other, and both signed it in blood, so if you want to remove that promise, you both must revoke it in blood again."

Violet's mouth dropped. "What? I can't just do it on my own?"

"No." Varik tucked her fingers into her splayed palm. "Not unless one of you dies."

Violet glowered and waved her hand. "I can't kill him because of this."

"Then you're stuck with it." Varik shrugged. "Either that, or get someone else to kill him."

"Literally no one else wants to see this guy dead. Everyone loves him." She rolled her eyes. "I guess it's up to me."

"You want to kill him?"

"Yes."

"Why?"

"Because he is dangerous."

"Dangerous because he can hurt a lot of people? Or dangerous because he is loved by so many, and he left you behind?"

Heat rose to her cheeks. "Smart mouth."

"You showed off first." Varik folded his hands together. "If he made this bond with you, then he meant it. Maybe not in a good way, but if he is dangerous, then maybe the bond isn't so bad."

"You…you don't know."

Varik rubbed his pinky again. "No, apparently, I don't."

Violet jutted her chin to the silver mark. "What is that?"

He hesitated, but then gave in. He lifted his hand, tugging the sleeve of his sweater down. The silver gleamed in the shop's soft light. It was a fine line that wrapped around the base of his left pinky and circled beneath his wrist bone, like a strange figure eight.

"An amana bond," Varik said.

Violet recoiled from the soul bond. "Again, that sounds horrible."

"That's all the information I know about bonds." He tugged his sleeve back down. "I expect my vial of the cayna serum by next week. You know the consequences if you don't."

"Fine." Violet scowled as she made her way to the front door. "Thanks."

"Violet Sutton."

She turned her head.

Varik nodded. "It was nice to meet you. Even if you are a piece of shit."

She couldn't resist the small smile on her face. She tugged each string, and her original glamour was back up. "See you soon, skiv."

The minute she was on the street, she glanced at her hand where the scar still lay. She hesitated before putting a glamour over it. She didn't want it. Being connected to Jack like this both bothered her and scared her. If she dared to ask Jack to remove it, he would laugh in her face. Varik was right. Jack would say, "*Isn't it better I can't kill you?*" It saved her life in Lust. And then the serum…

Violet huffed. This was difficult on her own. Keeping up with her little schemes that she had no idea whether they would work or not.

She desperately hoped they did.

19

Pretty Lips

Violet was slightly more prepared for her second shift at the fortress.

Armed with information from the real Talia, Pharos dropped Violet off at another designated airship location where her identity was checked, the nausea came and went, and she was immediately herded with the other girls into the fortress.

Rotation of services happened infrequently, but it was meant to keep all servants on their toes instead of growing used to repeated jobs. Violet thought it was more because servants ended up sleeping with captains, lieutenants, and even the desired commanders, so managing officers kept shifts from stagnating.

Today she was on an airship cleaning with her past partners, Owen and Aster. It was nearing hour twelve of her sixteen-hour shift, and Violet was surprised her jaw hadn't cracked with how hard she'd been clenching it. Every time Owen passed, she flipped her honey blonde hair, and Violet's eyes were glued to the dark hickey peeking from her collarbone.

She was *showing* it off. Violet knew it, even Aster knew it. In front of any higher-up it was covered, but the minute they weren't being watched, Owen would undo her top button and flash it to everyone, displaying her little trophy bruise.

"Are you going to throw it at her?"

Violet turned to a curious-looking Aster. The girl's eyes dipped to the sanitizer bottle. Violet's hand was white around it.

"Because that would be fun," Aster said. "But you will get punished for it."

Violet merely continued cleaning one of the pots in the onboard kitchen.

"I myself can't decide if it is worth it or not. She won't shut up about the captains she sleeps with. It's like one of the men's sports games: you score enough, you win a prize." Aster rolled her eyes. "Her prize is going to be the kitchens. No High Servant wants their command learning of a loose girl—"

"Shut the fuck up, Aster," Violet snapped. "Your jealousy is giving me a headache."

Aster fumed. "Excuse me? Your clear jealousy when Owen mentions Jack Marin is enough to give a migraine. It's pathetic. All you servants dropping your pants for any bit of attention—"

Violet's anger flared. "I am a person with a hole that sometimes, when things go in it, *feels* good. I'm allowed to fucking feel good. Even Owen can, too. Shove a cucumber up there and maybe you'll stop ruining my day every time you breathe."

She threw her rag into a bucket and scurried off the ship to prepare for the next incoming one.

Aster and Owen soon followed. Aster barely glanced at Violet, still red-faced and irate. Owen buttoned up her collar before they stood in a rigid line outside the fortress entrance. The sounds of the city at Violet's back filled her head, and she couldn't resist glancing behind.

The endless onyx and bursts of colorful light sucked her gaze. Elation bubbled in her chest. The faint smell of oil and smoke carried its way, even up to this vantage point. It probably filled Cyran with incredible satisfaction to look *down* on his main headquarters, especially for how endless and expansive the Twin Cities were.

As much as she wanted to hate him for it, there was enticement. A snake of power slithered throughout her body, making her mouth part, and she could taste the addiction. She had a brief flash of imagination: herself dressed in dark, commanding leathers, an aura of death and danger surrounding her. Being untouchable, unstoppable, feared by seven worlds and possibly more. A prominent pawn in an enigmatic game.

She dragged her eyes away from the view, and turned toward an airship as it descended on a landing pad. This one was less bulky as the others, more sleek, a little darker gray. Owens and Aster stiffened on either side of Violet. Guards poured out of the elevators and posted around, hands on their guns. A couple of captains and Fringe Vanishers followed. A welcome party.

She refrained from shivering as the ship drew in wind. A roaring whine sounded when its feet landed. Steam blew out the rear. A door opened and a platform slid down to the ground.

Four soldiers exited, a fifth figure braced in the middle with a bag over their head and hands cuffed behind their back. Blood leaked down their leg.

Two figures marched down the path behind the soldiers. Both startled Violet.

Jodin looked dreary as his long coat bristled. He carried himself differently than the exhausted, exasperated man she eavesdropped on in Varik's antique shop just a day prior.

Beside him was Reed.

Skin browner than hers, wider nostrils, fuller lips; a face only partially like their mother's, but with a bigger display of whoever their father was. Thicker brown hair blew in the wind, and those blue eyes flickered, twin to hers. Jodin and he stood the same height, both a rigid stature to their shoulders.

Her knees wobbled, and one of her glamour strings slipped. Her nose tingled. She yanked on it, hard enough that a strained gasp came out of her mouth, and her hand involuntary rose to her face.

Eyes shifted her way. Everyone had a stone-like posture, and any movement was a magnet for attention. Her cheeks heated, even as her brother's gaze flashed to her.

He only lingered on her face. His temple pulsed. Annoyed. Not mad—no, Reed's ears got red when he was angry. Not at her, either, but she became a distraction. He rolled his eyes, a way of him brushing off things so it didn't continue to bother him. He did it a lot when they were children. Her heart ached to see it.

She took a deep breath, composing herself.

Then nearly vomited at who finally exited.

Cyran stepped out, pale white with those grotesque scars climbing his neck. His snowy, limestone hair was combed back, those dark eyes a haunting, dead gaze. Dressed in impressive leathers, muscled in a way that shouldn't be possible for a supposed five-hundred-year-old, Cyran chilled the air even further.

Violet's heart raced. Goosebumps littered her skin.

His eyes landed on her, then narrowed.

She realized why. Everyone was already dropped into a deep bow.

Violet blinked and followed suit. Her stomach roiled so bad she bit her tongue. She could feel his gaze on her back.

Cyran scoffed. Violet didn't dare lift herself up. Not until the scuff of his shiny boots was out of hearing range. Not until every guard and captain followed the Emperor into the fortress, leaving only the servants to continue their work.

Many eyes glanced her way. Aster yanked on Violet's arm. "Do you *want* to get killed?"

"Hurry, get to the airship, act like it didn't happen—" Owen started, pure fear in her eyes. Her gaze tugged on something behind Violet's shoulder, and she paled further.

"Talia."

High Servant Silva, the one who gave her the assignments on the first day, called not-Violet's name.

Owen's face slipped into sorrow. With a soft look, she squeezed Violet's arm and whispered, "Don't ice it right away. You'll want to, but let the bleeding stop first."

Violet's hands began to shake. She didn't know how to process that information, so she just stared at Owen's fingers and wondered if Owen did certain things because she was trying to survive this cruel world, not because she liked it. Or maybe both.

Both was okay.

Violet turned and saw rigid fury in Silva's eyes.

Violet had nearly killed them all.

Her feet were heavy as she made her way over. She tried to predict the punishment during the entire elevator ride that took them to the lower levels where servants primarily worked. *Whipping? Burns?* Violet would have to grasp her glamour with everything she had. Silva led them through the corridors. It was barren in the bowels of the fortress; no room for color or even light, just places for positions that were transactional. Silva's pace made Violet's heart thrash; she was slow, deliberate, every step a show of how she would take her time.

"I'm disappointed in you, Talia," Silva said exasperatedly while she unlocked the door with her wrist. "You were always reliable, but this is completely unacceptable."

The door opened. Violet didn't enter right away. "Are you going to kill me?"

Silva tutted, and a smile split her crow-like face. "That's too easy."

Just face it, Violet. Sasha can heal you.

Silva's office was a bleak setup with a desk, one small window, and padding on the walls. *Silencing* pads. Silva shoved aside a chair and pointed to the marble floor. "Kneel."

Violet reluctantly obeyed.

Silva went over to a large cabinet and unlocked it. She used the door to block the view inside, but a moment later, a long, slithering black thing lay in Silva's hand, while a dagger was in the other.

"Bite the desk, if you must."

Violet stared at the line of wood before her. Ridges ingrained within—nails marks and teeth grooves that others must have used to face the oncoming pain. Cool sweat braced her brow. Violet thought about unraveling it all, screaming that Cyran would want to know it was her.

Violet squeezed her eyes shut, memories flooded back. Her mother's too harsh grip on her wrist. Those judgmental blue eyes. The way Violet would be dragged into the house and tossed onto the stairs, a command to go to bed and to not make a fool of herself in school. The only times her mother was…lively. Those were the times Violet clung to, because even if it meant a slap on her face for being in the way, at least her mother *saw* her.

She gripped the edge of the desk. Silva took the knife and sliced it down Violet's back, ripping her clothes. As the imminent pain drew near, Violet descended into her memories. The room blurred. She wished for a distraction, and amid the past, there was one thing she uncovered. Something she had never remembered before.

A man. Light-brown skin, full lips, a hat that always covered his eyes and he shoved his hair up into. Violet must have been young, very young, but for some reason, in this moment, she remembered this man would hang out at a bodega down the street from her old home and would give her little treats. There was one evening Violet was left alone, while Reed was comforting their mother during a crying spell about their nonexistent father. Violet escaped through her window and ran. Ran as fast as her little legs could take her. She didn't want to hear the wails. She'd rather hear the rush of wind as she sprinted to something better. She found the man. He gave her a chocolate bar. It was minty. He said he liked mint, and she said she liked it too. His laugh was warm.

So Violet ran as Silva ignited the plaswhip. Violet found that man and tried to taste the little chocolate peppermints he'd given her. He'd brush her wrists, her cheek, or her hair and say he was sorry, and that sweets always made it feel better. She never understood why he was sorry. He made her happy. There was nothing to be sorry about.

Silva's voice was cold. "Four lashings for the seconds it took you not to bow to your Master. Remember these."

The plaswhip cracked across Violet's back.

Violet clung to her glamour and tried to taste chocolate peppermint. Tried to remember the face of the nice man who brightened her cold childhood. But the whip's heat seeped in, and she sank her teeth into her lip as the white-hot pain seared her back.

Silva didn't wait long for the next one.

By the third, Violet was dizzy. Blood flooded her mouth and dripped along her hips. She sagged against the desk. Her breathing grew shallow...

No, she growled in her mind. *Don't get like this. Don't give up.*

You want a lot of things, young Vanisher.

Greed purred. Teased. It was so different, this Sin. It came to her like some twisted comfort, treated her like a child and it had a basket of candy. Chocolate peppermint candy.

What's the price of wanting Cyran's death? She breathlessly thought. Silva readied the whip for the final lash.

Your own, Greed said without its usual lilt. Almost as if it were sad.

The door burst open, and the whip cracked against the ground.

"I requested her *ten minutes ago* and you ignored it."

Violet froze, then turned her head slightly.

Silva was against the wall, her feet dangling, as Jack held her by the neck and pure, icy, unrelenting anger masked his face.

"She...disrespected..."

"Does it look like I give a fuck?" Jack sneered and gathered close to Silva's face. "I explicitly told you whips and knives were banned from punishment."

Silva struggled for breath, her cheeks reddening, and Jack let her go with a disgusted look. She crumpled to the floor, knocked unconscious. Jack wiped his hand on his pants and turned to Violet.

No-no-no-no...

But he was walking toward her.

Violet struggled to stand. She had a drastic realization that her glamour, no matter how hard she held the strings, would crumble when he touched her. *He sees through it. Is this part of his rumored new powers?*

Violet stumbled. Jack caught her around the forearms. Her clothes covered his touch, but it burned. She keeled forward, overwhelmed with the desperation to be wrapped in his arms, but this reality was not like that, so she put pressure into her knees and stood as right as she could.

Jack's eyes darted to the whip on the floor, and Violet swore she saw fear flash through them. It reminded her of the whips in Wrath, how Jack shied away, as if afraid. And in Envy when he was whipped himself and he wasn't right after…

Jack shook his head. "This is going to be weird for you, but you're going to do it anyway."

Violet's eyes bugged.

He grabbed the knife off the table and sliced a portion of his forearm. Red blood welled. He took a small breath, as if he were telling himself to keep going, and grabbed her. Yanked her into his chest.

Her mouth into his wound.

Violet gagged at the metallic taste, but Jack held her there and said one command, "Drink."

She reluctantly did.

A moment later, she was off him, backing into the corner of the room and wiping her mouth. She genuinely never thought she'd ever be *that* close to Jack. He stared at her, eyes a bright, curious green, before he gave another command. "Turn around."

She turned around to show him. She could already feel the effects. His new abilities were endless, apparently, and this one was healing her. Stitching her lashes back together. It was the strangest sensation, but it produced a tingly, warm feeling that made Violet want to go to sleep.

"Look at me."

A game. A game. Just play the game.

But with Jack? After all they had been through? After he had seen the most vulnerable parts of her? Kissed her, touched her, heard her moans?

Her heart beat out of control. She thought she might faint. There wasn't enough oxygen in the air to sate the panic rising in her. She couldn't unravel herself to him—she didn't know where he stood. He had spent four months under Cyran's control and command. She didn't even know if his mind was the same—if it was even *Jack* at all.

She was the most wanted person in seven worlds, and here she stood in front of the very person who could make her lose it all.

She tried to cover herself and turned around. Lifted her gaze. Skies, he was remarkable to look at. The tattoos, the semi-messy hair, the glow to his skin, the broadness of his shoulders, the veins along his hands.

He took her in. "Are you okay?"

She bristled, and he took notice with a twitch of his lips.

"Yes," she said, keeping her voice squeaky.

He nodded. "I requested you."

"I didn't know."

"Obviously." Jack sighed. "Given the situation, I would like you to go home. Rest up. Your next shift is in two days. I'll see you then."

Her brows crunched. "See me then?"

His demeanor turned playful. A dimple showed. "You'll be on my service from now on. I thought we could…get to know each other." He extended a hand. Violet refrained from jerking away. His smile increased.

His fingers brushed her cheek, then pushed a lock of hair behind her ear. His thumb rubbed her skin, and when he pulled away, a drop of blood smeared the pad of his finger. She backed up a step. "I should be—"

He put his thumb, stained with her blood, into his mouth. She choked on her disgust, but he merely stared at her through his heady gaze.

"You have very pretty lips, Talia."

Would Violet admit she added a bit more plumpness to her normally small lips? Yes. She accepted the compliment of her handiwork. "Thank you."

"Next shift, come to my room and I'll teach you how to use them."

Her smile strained. It took all of Violet's energy not to punch him in the face.

"And that's an order," he called. "Jonathon."

A young, bored Vanisher appeared. "Yes, sir?"

"Her shift is over. Teleport her to the servant's airship main station."

"Yes, sir."

Jonathon grabbed her arm, and Jack winked as light blinded her. Jonathon quite literally left her there, and a breath later, she was stomping down the street while using scraps of her clothes to cover her back.

Fuck.

Him.

If Jack so much as brushed the zipper of his pants, she was going to bite his dick off.

❋❋❋

Violet didn't go back to her room. She needed to decompress. So she took clothes she stashed in a random bin, changed both her outfit and appearance, and walked around Navru for hours. She liked to eavesdrop on random conversations, so she followed two women who bitched about their husbands, then some teenage boys relaying grotesque things they saw online, and then two large-jacketed men who had bulges of weapons in their pockets.

Violet was in a mood, so she immediately followed them.

"The girl was pretty young, they were happy with that selection."

"Couple more of those and we can score some big bucks."

"You'll find the right ones if you go to the right places; playgrounds, ice cream shops, places where they can get lost from their mother."

"The Order only wants them before their bleeding, sometimes afterwards though, so make sure you know."

Violet halted. She couldn't breathe. She scanned the low-light street they were on; a few people milled silently ahead, the buildings in this corridor had their shades shut, and to her direct left, looming like a beacon, a church for the Order glimmered gold. The men passed it.

One man continued his explanation, and Violet's mind screamed.

Scouts. Scouts for the Order. People who located these children for them to be stolen. She noticed the earpieces, the muddy boots, the way that she *did* see men like this on the regular and never questioned it. She should get a profile of them and tell Bryce, but her gut screamed no. Walk away.

She was out of her zone. Wasn't in her right mind. She'd go home and debrief Emryn, and maybe they could talk to Bryce about another mission. Post Pharos people at these certain locations. Violet took a retreating step. Her boot caught a jutting brick, and she fell into a bush, crushing it, before rolling over and careening into a statue. The stone foot knocked her lower back and she hit the ground. She scrambled. Not just the ground, but the flowery, bushy lawn of the church.

"What was that?" one of the guys said. "Is someone there?"

A metal click. Boots slapped the pavement, growing louder. Violet groaned and rolled over, her hands caked in mud and flower petals. She glimpsed the statue—an ugly man with a foot stomping on a...

A snake?

A woman kneeled beneath the man, clutching at his muscled leg while tears poured down her face. Pleading. Begging. There weren't many churches in Navru—typically on the outskirts. She didn't realize she'd wandered so far.

Violet bolted behind it as the two hooded men lumbered up to the sidewalk. One held a gun at the ready.

"Search the premises."

Violet crawled her way to the side of the building, using rose bushes and more grotesque, man-loving statues to hide herself. The crunch of grass had her hurrying. Before long, she dove behind a row of rain-slicked bushes lining the church walls, but the men were being thorough as they checked, waving their guns into the shrubbery, searching.

Violet reached the church's front steps and hauled herself up. The wooden door was cracked. She squeezed in, holding her breath. A musty incense overcame her. Carpet rubbed at her fingertips before they met smooth marble. She crawled through the brief foyer and into the small worship hall.

Pews stretched, halting before a gold-swathed altar and a giant statue of yet another fucking man being praised by others. Violet spared an eye roll, rushed to the nearest pew, and dove behind it.

As she listened for the men's footsteps, a quiet sob echoed through the room. She poked her head up, curious. A tiny figure sat a few rows ahead of her, head bowed between trembling palms. Another sob shifted the lone girl's long, dark hair.

It was well past midnight, and a girl was here. Crying. Fourteen or fifteen by the looks of her. Violet stared awkwardly, taken aback.

The girl was muttering under her breath. Violet leaned in—

"Please," the girl quietly begged. "Please don't let anything come out of this. I will be good. I promise."

Violet wrinkled her face in confusion.

"I can't…I can't have it."

Violet's eyes popped.

"Please, I will do anything to make it stop. I'm so sorry. I'm so sorry for letting it happen. I can't stop him, but *please* don't let anything come out of it." A louder sob. "I'm so sorry. I'm…I'm… *sorry*. I won't accept the drinks anymore. I will be careful…"

There were quite a few things to digest, but the most alarming statement was *I can't stop him*. Her gut tightened with each sob that broke through the quiet, empty place. The girl spoke no more words, but instead let tears become her pleas.

The men still rustled outside, growing closer to the door.

Violet stood and tiptoed as quietly as she could. When she reached the front doors to the church, she found a gold bowl, the inside stained dark.

Violet knew what blood stains looked like, especially in a bowl. She'd stared at one months ago, and while filled with fresh blood, it looked like a resplendent carbon copy of the bloodswearing bowl. She bent down and sniffed it. Gagged on the telltale metallic stench.

The girl whirled, standing. "Is someone there?"

The guys outside stilled. "Is someone in there?"

Violet stomped in frustration. "This world is fucking weird."

The girl gasped, eyes widening. Violet caught the shadowy ring around one of them. A black eye.

The men stormed up the steps, and Violet winked at the girl. Then she tested the bowl's weight—doable. The door burst open. She swung the metal thing straight into the first guy's face. He slumped to the floor, unconscious.

"Get down and cover your ears," Violet commanded the girl.

With a squeak, the girl dropped behind a pew.

The other guy stormed up, gun raised. Violet tossed the bowl and ducked. The gun fired, bullet bouncing off the curved metal and hurtling down the church's aisle. It slammed into the crotch of the statue. He breached the foyer and Violet grabbed his wrist. He fired the gun again, but it shot the ceiling of the church. She twisted underneath, jammed her elbow into his eye socket, and at the same time, wrenched the weapon out of his hand. She kicked his legs out.

He crumpled to the floor, whining. She shoved her fingers in his hair and yanked his head back, so one eye peered at her face. Her real face. A snarl breached her mouth, "I hope you see me in your nightmares, bitch."

She shot him in the thigh. He wallowed into the air before promptly passing out next to his buddy.

Violet only had a few short moments before someone would come running at the sound of the shots. She ran down the church aisle while shoving the gun into the waistband of her pants. She motioned to the girl. "Come. Now."

The girl obeyed. Violet guided her over the men's bodies and out of the church. Doors slammed nearby. She ran the girl across the street, dipping into an alley, and pressing her against the wall.

Robed, sleepy men ran to the church, guns in hand. It was a few moments before one bellowed a cry. "They dare forsake our precious church! Our sanctum!"

"Oh no," the girl whispered, as if knowing what was going to happen next. "The preachers are going to—"

Two shots fired out.

"Hang them as a sign."

The girl didn't seem surprised when the group of preachers dragged the two now-dead bodies out and, as if it were routine, found rope, flung it over designated hooks at either side of the entrance, and connected the nooses to the men's necks. They were hoisted. Hung like sloppy, bloody flags.

It all happened so fast that Violet didn't have time to react. One moment it was a pretty worship space covered in gold and weird statues, the next—the glamour unmasked. The hooks high above the doors, the lengths of red and gold ropes, as if there for this exact purpose, the preachers wielding guns, and blood-stained bowl now being brushed off by one of the men.

What was once beautiful was now revealed to be gruesome. Violet was very thankful she dragged the girl out.

But when she turned around, the girl was sprinting down the street. Violet bolted after her, but shouts began to rise from the church. A gun pointed in her direction. Fired.

It bit into the brick and sediment smacked her face. Violet released a frustrated sigh and took off in an opposite direction, leaving the girl to her sad little world.

20

Reunited

BRYCE GAVE VIOLET A LONG, silent look from across the desk.

"You need cayna?"

Violet nodded.

"For your friends?"

Another nod.

"And you want me to just…give it to you?"

Violet shrugged. "I mean, yeah."

"That is a serum sacred to my people. It comes deep from the ice in Zoncolla, it's then blended with herbal magic from the earth." Bryce rolled their eyes. "I'm not going to hand over two vials because you asked. Not even nicely, might I add."

"I told you about the snatchers on the streets, about the girl I found there, *and* I'm going into the damn fortress, shitting my pants every time, and telling you all that I learned." Violet squeezed her knees, palms sweaty. "I think I deserve this."

"Deserve?" Bryce snorted. "*You* were the one who snuck into the fortress in the first place. I simply monopolized on that stupid decision. You nearly compromised Emryn, and our entire mission. The snatchers are something we've known about, but their identities are kept secret. Giving basic white-men descriptions doesn't help. But you did save that girl."

Violet waved a hand. "So…can I get the cayna?"

"Double your drug quota, and I'll give you one vial."

"I need two."

"Sell first, then we'll talk."

Violet huffed, standing. "*Fine.*"

❀ ❀ ❀

It was a frustrating evening, and Violet made worse money than usual. People didn't want to get high and smoke their little harmless plant tonight. No, the universe wanted them to focus on the booze and lowball her prices.

Violet stormed down the rainy streets, defeated. She so desperately wanted Anaya and Rio with her that her chest ached, and her eyes burned. She beelined straight toward the offsite hideout, mind only on throwing the sheets over her head and praying for a better day tomorrow.

She stomped down the hallways and took the stairs two at a time. She punched in the code for her room and slammed the door behind her. Her eyes dropped to her backpack filled with the only personal items she had. Her bed was unmade, sheets twisted from last night's restless sleep, and suddenly Violet didn't feel like collapsing and forgetting about everything. She dropped to her knees and dug through her things until she found the little pouch she was looking for. She dumped the contents onto the floor.

Gwen's broken dagger lay in bits before her. One shard still missing. Violet brushed a finger over the beautiful obsidian hilt, still intact, then the jutting turquoise that snapped an inch later. Four other pieces stared at her.

Four pieces that nearly stabbed her.

Tears slipped from her eyes. Sharp nails gripped her heart. She wanted to be stuffed under a handmade quilt in a little cottage in the mountains. She wanted to run the meadows and hills. She wanted to let those strong, green fingers play with her hair. She wanted that peace, that safety, the comfort that she didn't need to be anywhere else but in that moment.

She wanted Gwen back.

A gnarl of leathers caught her eye. The Droanian leathers Isolo wrapped around her hands. Proof of her journey, proof of—

Proof.

In the world of Greed, proof of the most wanted girl can come with a reward.

※※※

Violet took a long step back from the door after knocking. It flung open immediately, and the small Droanian girl greeted her.

Wearing a typical scowl.

Violet learned Grace liked to fix things. Electronics, cameras, daggers, plasblades. She worked with Meretta a lot, and Violet wanted to use her skills to her advantage.

"What?" Grace snapped.

"You got a camera?" Violet asked. "One of those fancy things that takes pictures?"

Grace spared her a short look. "Why?"

"If you can take some pictures of me out on the street and help me set up a fake hideout, I have a dagger that you can fix." Violet shoved her hands into her jeans pockets. "And I'll buy your dinners for the next week. The pancake, fermented cabbage thing that you like."

Grace perked up. "What are you planning?"

"I need money," Violet said.

A long pause. "What kind of dagger."

"A special one." Violet pulled the pouch from her bag and displayed its contents. Grace balked and took a step forward.

"I've never seen anything like that before." Violet swore Grace's mouth watered. "Where…where did you get that?"

"Gluttony. It's broken. There's a piece missing, actually. But I want it fixed and I know you and Meretta can do that."

"I can't weld that dagger without good material," Grace stared at the hilt, then back to the blade shards. "That turquoise shit is different. I've never seen anything like it. I'll need something virtually indestructible to piece it back together."

Violet didn't hide her smirk. "Oh, well, *that's* easy."

Much later, in the late hours of the night when the streets were quiet, Grace and Violet had a photoshoot. She unraveled her glamour and threw off her hood, posing with just enough accuracy to make her recognizable, but not staged. She rummaged through trash for food. Carried a bottle of liquor that could only be purchased at a store in north Navru, far away from the safehouse. She found the dog she liked to hang out with that unfortunately had her blood staining the collar at the neck. She was a little pissed it hadn't been picked up yet—Zavar was lacking.

She staged a picture of her entering a rundown warehouse, and when Grace put her camera away, they headed up the rickety stairs and set up a false place that Violet was hiding out in. Violet smeared her fingerprints everywhere, took out stray hairs and let them fall, even peed in a corner to make it realistic.

"I need something from another world," Violet mumbled. "To prove it."

She fished in her bag and pulled out one of the few things she had; the two wrapped leathers that fashioned as Droanian gloves. Grace gasped.

"Where did you get those?" Her features reddened. "Did you *steal* them?"

"No." Violet frowned. "I was gifted them by a Droan who died because of me."

"Those are sacred."

"I'm only leaving one," Violet said.

Grace stomped up and folded Violet's hand back over the leathers. "If someone gifted you these, you can't use them for your little plan. It's—"

"I don't have any other choice," Violet breathed. She noticed how Grace jerked away when she produced the leather ball. Refusing to touch it. "I don't have anything else to prove—"

"These are *sacred*," Grace repeated, her face turning all shades of red. "The lifeblood for Droans."

Violet stepped back. "I know—"

"No, you don't know!"

"I—"

"You go through my world, and one of my people gives you these? And you're throwing them away!"

"I'm not throwing them away! But I *want* to win this thing. I want to win! I need it! I need more of these wins so I can get my friends back and get some peace. I want this. I *need* this."

"Stop saying those words!" Grace snarled. "These are part of my people! I won't let you leave them, not even one."

Win, agia.

"I need to *win*," Violet said, voice a little harsher than she meant. "This will get me closer. This will get me what I want—"

A voice ripped through her mind. Her vision blackened.

I've got you now, the Sin cackled.

A large force tackled her. She was pinned to the floor and a cry bit through the haze, "Please! Please, don't leave it!"

Violet shoved back at Grace. "Get *off* me!"

"I will stop you! Chain you to Meretta's bike!"

Grace was too strong for Violet to fight, but half of Violet was fighting the Droan girl, and the other half, the Sin. Greed tugged at her muscles, gnashing its teeth into Violet's body. She yelled.

Violet pushed at the darkness. The Sin bellowed a teasing laugh. *You think you can fight me? You've been building this need to be ahead of the game. You want to win against your despairing odds. You won at the tables, won in the fortress, won against the pawn shop man, won in fooling Jack. You want to keep winning, and now here, you want to win this deal with Bryce and the world—*

"Wait," she croaked. She couldn't see Grace anymore. "I—I—"

You like the feeling of winning, young Vanisher, Greed said. *Not wealth, not possessions. Winning.*

It was so subtle Violet had no idea she was falling into the Sin. She just liked besting people. Using her words, her mind, her actions, and watching as they agreed to her. She liked getting away with things. She always had.

"Don't do it!" Grace cried. Violet attempted to push her off again, but Grace held her down. "I won't let you win!"

Greed never pushed her. Greed wanted to watch how far she would go until it became unbearable to stop. No one knows they are being greedy the first few times. Only when it becomes them.

Only when there is no going back.

"He didn't die for this," Violet whispered to herself. And then she pushed the heavy, encompassing Sin out of her mind. It reared back, poked the pain at the center of her chest, and laughed. *I'll be back for more,* it said.

She clenched her fist. Her bloodsworn mark seared.

Exhaustion sagged her to the floor. She stared at the leathers. Remembered how Iso wrapped them gently around her hands.

Only the Sin wins.

She touched her face. Her body. *Sacred. Sacred.*

Violet was ready to throw it all away for her greed.

Tears bubbled in Grace's beady eyes. "Please don't leave the leathers."

"I—I—" Violet couldn't even believe she was holding them. How could she be so ready to part with something special? They were not only sacred to the Droans, but sacred to her. Iso wouldn't approve of it…he wouldn't have died for her to throw his memory away. "I won't. Of course, I won't. I'm so sorry."

The near heartbreak was real across Grace's features, and Violet's chest panged. "Can you get off me?"

Grace stood and Violet pushed up after her. She didn't think as she stepped toward the Droan. "That was…my bad."

Grace wiped her eyes. "I lost my leathers. My mother and I were taken to this world against our will when I was eleven. Then she died. And I…I lost mine. So don't lose yours." Grace burst into a sob and threw her arms around Violet, bruising her with a Droanian strength hug. Violet choked a breath, but didn't complain. Instead, patted Grace's back. But what she did do after some moments was pull away, grab one of Grace's hands, and began to wrap.

Tears poured like a waterfall down Grace's face. Violet fought to keep her own in her eyes. Grace's hands were scarred and burned from all the metal and wires she worked with. Violet's fingertips drifted over the rough edges as she wrapped one of Iso's leathers.

"I don't have any sacred things from where I'm from," Violet said softly. "I didn't know there were such things as culture deep enough to mean life or death. Not until I stepped into your world."

Grace sobbed.

"I don't need both." Violet offered a small smile. "So, I offer you one of my leathers, Grace. Because you fought me and won. You earned it."

When Violet finished, Grace wiped her nose and caressed her wrapped hand. She stared in awe at the piece of her home, and a crooked smile pulled at her face. A whisper, "I earned it."

"Now let's go get these photos processed and some food," Violet said.

❋ ❋ ❋

A couple days later, Violet slapped her drug earnings on Bryce's desk.

"This isn't double," Bryce said.

Violet tossed the photos, the proof, of her whereabouts. "This will get you more money than drugs."

Bryce stared at the photos for a long time, flipping through, their frown deepening with each one. "This disregards your safety."

"I need the cayna. Two vials. Sell it to whoever you want. It means that Captain Zavar will get closer to me, but I've covered my tracks as much as I could. Slip them this information with your contacts and get your money. Zavar will run into some trouble, so it should still keep him off my trail for a while longer." Violet tapped the desk. "No photos reveal Pharos. Only Navru. Which I'm sure he suspected."

Bryce grunted.

Violet held her breath.

And from their pocket, Bryce procured two glowing green vials and gently put them in Violet's hands. "You're extremely dumb for this."

"Probably, but I need my friends. They can help you."

Bryce shook their head. "Your one and only mission is the residential school, then our work is done. You move on. Once this proof is released, your time with Pharos and this world starts ticking." They glared at Violet. "I can't afford to put Pharos at risk if the Worldbreaker turns his eye this way. Captain Zavar can only be fooled for so long."

Violet's heart dropped at the prospect of severing ties with Pharos, but she knew the outcome when she concocted her plan. She didn't want to continue to put them at risk. The minute Anaya and Rio entered this world, that will speed up the clock ticking on her heart.

And Pharos didn't need to go down for that.

"The school mission is in a week's time. Study the plans with Emryn. We are getting every child out of there."

Violet nodded and turned. Stopped. She glanced at Bryce over her shoulder. "How do you plan to end the kidnappings from other worlds altogether?"

The exhaustion showed on Bryce's face. Even their tattoo seemed gray, pale, like the stress was slowly devouring the ink. "That requires someone to kill the Order's Vanisher accomplices."

As Violet left the headquarters, she tried to ignore the answer to that problem. The one person on her mind capable of that kind of thwarting. That kind of killing.

But that was only *if* Jack was still the same person whom she shared a bed with.

A little voice of doubt told her no.

❋ ❋ ❋

When Violet arrived outside the pawn shop later, she inhaled deeply to expend her nerves and waited in the shadows of an alley.

Like usual, the street was busy this time of night. The market was in full swing, filled with all sorts of bodies, and Violet studied each of them until Jodin's familiar worn face appeared. He tucked his coat in tightly, looked around, and entered.

She slid in right behind him. The bell jingled only once. She slipped to a row of shelves on silent feet and held her breath. Skies, what she would give for Anaya's camouflage at this moment.

"Who's there!" Varik called.

"It's me," Jodin replied.

"Lock the door." Varik appeared from the back, books in his hand stacked with a wrapped package on top.

Jodin did as instructed. Violet edged into another row of shelves, still hidden from the front desk. She peered through a crack in the wood.

"I have your medicine," Varik said. He patted the package. "You know the dosage. He should see improvement within two weeks. This should be enough to last a month."

"And then he declines yet again." Jodin rubbed at his face. "I'll need another round shortly after that."

Varik hesitated, but sighed, "I might have access to cayna."

Jodin perked. "Cayna? Really?"

"It hasn't been confirmed. Some girl was in here asking about bonds and said she could get me cayna in exchange for the information. She…" Varik paled as he shared a long look with Jodin. "Overheard our conversation. It's probably useful to tell you that she is—"

"Me." Violet dropped her glamour, flashed a saccharine smile, and lunged for the front desk, a dagger in hand.

Varik bellowed in surprise. He pressed himself against the back wall—"*You.*"

Jodin was quick in his reaction. His arm knocked the package to the floor. The glass clinked, rolling across the dusty wood. She elbowed Jodin in the gut and reached for it, but his strong arm wrapped around her stomach and held her back.

She swiped her dagger behind, catching him at the arm. He grunted, and when he reached for her wrist, she stomped on his foot. He buckled into himself, but he still kicked behind her knees, ruining her balance. She went flying toward the floor and slammed into it. Pain ricocheted off her bad shoulder, but Violet gritted her teeth, arm still reaching for the package inches away. Her fingertips brushed it—

"Come here, you little bitch," Jodin snarled.

She twisted and kicked at him. Missing his face but her boot connected with his shoulder. His free arm reached within his coat. Pulled out an object…

A plasblade illuminated.

Violet panicked. Jodin swung the weapon expertly. She rolled out of the way and sent a kick to his groin, but he parried it with his arm. She crawled, aware of the plasma heat along her leg—

She took the hit to her calf. It sliced through her jeans, blood blossoming. She cried out as the fiery pain flashed through her body. But she gritted her teeth and whirled, flinging her dagger at his shoulder.

"Stop!" Varik cried.

It embedded outside his clavicle. His plasblade arm sagged, but when he switched, ready to fight her with the other arm, he froze.

She was standing on her good leg as her other bubbled with plasburns. The package was in her hand, arm stretched as high as it could go. Jodin took a step forward.

Violet jerked her arm. He halted, then thumbed the sigil. The plasma fizzled out.

"I will throw this on the ground as hard as I can and it will shatter," Violet said, breathing heavily as her blood leaked onto the floor.

Jodin shook his head and dropped the plasblade. His hand moved to where her dagger stuck out, holding pressure. "You'll damn him."

"I have a proposition," she gritted. "I'll give you this medicine in exchange for what I want."

"It's for his brother!" Varik yelled as he held up a book, eyes darting between the two. "It's for his health!"

"You're only digging your grave further," Jodin taunted.

Violet faked a throw and Jodin took a desperate step. She cocked her head. "My grave has been dug since I was born. You think death scares me?"

"You want to damn my brother?" Jodin asked, bewildered. "The one who Awakened you and saved your life?"

She shrugged. "Don't take it personally. Get me what I want, and I'll give this medicine."

"What do you want?" Jodin seethed.

"I want you to pick up my friends." She smiled. "They've been vacationing in Sloth and I miss them dearly."

He shook his head. "I'm not doing that."

"Why? I'm lonely."

"I don't give a fu— stop!"

She frowned, halting her arm mid chuck. "I want you to get my two friends—Anaya and Rio—and bring them to Hanhii to the coordinates I give you. They should be on a boat, but if my timing is correct, they will be in Finnport and resupplying during their monthly land excursion. If they aren't there, then check the Pirate Queen's estate. And if you're that unreliable and *still* can't find them, you and I will return together. Once they are safely here and unharmed, I will give you this medicine."

"I will turn you over to the Master."

"Then when he shoves a plasblade through my chest, I'll make sure it hits this package first. I'm not giving you another option," Violet said. "Going once, going…"

"I will kill you myself."

Violet smiled and then swung her arm as hard as she could. The package flew to the floor, shattering on impact. A soft, gray liquid oozed through the paper and into the lines of the wood.

"No!" Varik screamed. "Do you know how long that takes to produce?"

Jodin released a dangerous growl and lunged at her—

But she merely put her finger up and flashed another vial. The cayna serum swirled within. Jodin stiffened, eyes going wide.

"That medicine means nothing compared to this," Violet said. "Right? Two drops of this and your brother will be significantly better."

"How did you…how did…" Varik stuttered.

"Never mind that," she said. "If you get my friends and follow my instructions, I'll give this to you."

The revulsion on Jodin's face flickered, revealing something short of relief. Violet ignored the pang of guilt in her gut. His gaze on the vial was pure, unfiltered hope, and she held it between her grimy fingertips.

Tense silence passed through the room as both men stared at her little treasure. Violet could practically hear the thoughts racing behind Jodin's dark eyes. He battled within himself. She could see the process: *assist the enemy in exchange for my brother's life or continue on with blind loyalty.*

Violet didn't want to damn Yarrow. She would say horrible things to get what she wanted, but she meant what she had previously said to Varik. Yarrow had saved her life by risking his in the weird, strange way he did.

Her heart thrashed in her chest. But as Jodin didn't move, didn't say anything, she lifted her arm and the vial. "I'll go down for this, I know that. I don't even give a skiv if you turn me over after all is said and done. I just want them safe, here, with me, no different from what you want for your brother."

It was another long round of silence, and Violet, with a heavy heart, jerked her arm—

"Fine."

Her eyes widened. She searched his gaze for a lie. But he merely nodded and sagged against the counter. "I can have them here by midnight."

Her heart soared. Eyes stung. "Really?"

He gave her a long, weird look. His eyes flickered around his face. His brows scrunched and he shook his head, as if shaking away whatever thought was in his mind. "Varik, get me a healing patch and get this knife out of me. You—" He regarded Violet. "Will not leave this shop until I bring them back. They will come straight here, and you can hide them after."

She lowered her arm. "Fine."

"You will leave the serum on the counter. No one will touch it until I return. This…" Jodin sighed. "This will stay between us. I don't care about His Master's wish to harm you, just as I do not want anyone to know that my brother is suffering."

Varik disappeared into the back of his shop with soft steps.

"You swear?" she asked.

"I'm not making a bloodbond with you, girl." Jodin huffed a laugh. "The last thing I want is a connection to you."

"Fair enough."

Varik returned and helped Jodin strip off his jacket and shirt. The dagger was yanked out and a healing patch replaced it. The patch glowed as it sucked up the blood, and by Jodin's exasperated sigh, began stitching the wound.

"I do not like the Endolier," Jodin said.

"No one does," Violet agreed as she poked an antique statue and Varik cursed at her.

"I will need proof that you are safe and agreeing to this in order to avoid being maimed by her."

She nodded and Jodin held up his wrist with the glowing watch. "Now." He pressed a button.

"Hey, guys, it's me, the one and only. I haven't died yet. I'm not captured either. I have Jodin here with me because I sort of blackmailed him into retrieving you. He's bringing you straight to me and then we will be even."

"You'll want to say something more personal. Something that couldn't be fabricated."

"Jack's alive and is a captain. He is still annoying. I'm planning to kill him."

Jodin rolled his eyes. "You have the balls, girl."

"Actually, it's a vagina and it can take more hits than balls, but I understand the meaning."

And that's when Jodin ended the recording.

Once he was patched and had a long chug of some energy drink, he pointed to the counter with a glowing hand. "Once I'm gone, it goes there. Varik, don't hesitate to shoot her."

Varik winced but tucked a plasgun into his belt.

Violet glanced at the time. Ten-thirty in the evening. An hour and a half. She was…slightly confused on how he would manage the traversing an entirely different world and returning so quickly, but Jodin seemed unbothered by the adventure. He'd probably done enough work for the Worldbreaker that his stamina was through the sky.

"I will see you at midnight." Two small strips of light slashed beneath his eyes. He took a moment to stare around, his arms rising and cutting, as if he were shifting through the tethers, then with a huff, he yanked one and vanished.

Violet slapped the serum on the counter and plopped herself in a nearby chair.

"That's antique." Varik eyed the chair.

"So are you."

He poured himself a large glass of liquor, sighed, then poured another. He gave it to Violet. "You care about your friends."

"I saw an opportunity and took it."

"That's how you win this game, young Vanisher." He took a long sip and sat in a chair next to her. "You almost have me rooting for you."

"For what? For me to get back to my city?"

"For you to upheave this cruel universe," he said softly. Then laughed. "Just kidding."

"I'm not responsible for that."

"No, you're not, but you are in a position to do so. You have two options: ignore it all and move on with what little life you have left, or do something about the cruelty."

She grew silent, her voice uneven when she muttered, "I'm not a savior."

Varik chuckled at that. "Skies no, you are not." He caught her gaze, sadness in his eyes. "But you can be a warrior."

Violet ignored him and downed her drink.

The time passed slowly. She stared at the clock as Varik dozed off next to her, jerked awake, and poured himself another drink. It was three minutes until midnight when Violet felt a shift in the room.

She burst from her seat at the same moment light appeared. Two thumps shook the floor.

"Your shit friends," Jodin said as his Vanisher lights flashed out.

A high cackle and a groan.

Tears sprung to Violet's eyes.

Rio and Anaya lay sprawled on the hardwood. Anaya surged up first, swinging a blunt butter knife which Jodin whacked out of her hand. "You're a tw—wat."

"Yes, you've said that to me forty times."

Rio gazed at Violet from upside down. "Skies, Vi, you look awful." Rio hiccupped. "But you're alive."

Jodin snatched the bottle of liquor from Varik, took a chug, then pocketed the serum. "They're drunk." Violet thought Jodin would swiftly leave, but he merely slid down the desk and sat on the floor.

Anaya stumbled a step, waving her fist before she realized her knife was gone. She scrunched her brows. "What—"

But Violet lunged at her, wrapping her in a tight hug. Anaya's warm, spicy scent enveloped her, and that was when Violet's tears began to fall. They dripped down her friend's neck.

"Vi?" Anaya whispered.

Violet nodded her head.

"Oh—*oh*, Vi." Anaya's arms came to wrap around her. Her grip bruised Violet's ribcage.

"I've missed you," Violet blubbered. "So much."

"Well, I want a part of this." Rio lumbered up, stumbling into a shelf and knocking a book off. "Sorry." He swathed both girls into a hug, pulling tightly. Their breaths mingled and Violet's nose shifted from Anaya's scent to the unmistakable smell of Keller's rum stash. Rio planted a kiss on the top of Violet's head.

"They are in no shape to go out tonight, it will draw too much attention outside my door." Varik's voice broke into their circle. "I have a spare bedroom upstairs. They can use it."

She tried to pull away, but at this point Violet was merely a crutch for her drunk friends. She twisted within their grips and ignored another slobbering forehead kiss from Rio. She ruffled through her coat pocket and pulled out the other cayna serum. "I need more time. Can you get me it?"

Jodin eyed the second vial. He then released a loud, unbelieving laugh. "You're fucking nuts."

"How did you…" Varik rolled his eyes. "Never mind."

"I also need a slab of nostor. The nice metal from Envy—Iveyrez."

"Nostor?" Anaya mumbled. "Love that stuff."

"I'll buy you time, but I can't promise anything." Jodin opened his hand. Violet tossed him the vial, amid Varik's horrified gasp. "Varik can get you nostor."

Varik glowered and ran a hand through his hair. "Fine."

Violet turned back to her friends and buried her head in their embrace. Tears poured freely.

Just a little more time.

21

EAVESDROP

JELAN HATED THESE MOMENTS. THERE had only been two of them, but it boiled her blood. At both her captor and the emperor who had no idea she hid in said captor's clothes closet.

Arvalo's gravelly, annoying voice filled the space she sat in. One of the arms of Luka's many sweaters brushed her cheek. She flicked it away with a scowl.

"The quota is not being met," Arvalo went on. It was a video call this time—the emperor rarely stepped foot in the city, it would mean something is wrong. "You're stalling, Luka. Why?"

"Stalling?" Luka's rough voice remained calm. "We had a lag in mining shipments. I cannot produce your weapons without plasma. I told you the quota needs to be adjusted for the riots in the mines."

"The riots are not a problem, and you know this."

"They aren't a problem to you, father, because you would have everyone killed, but who else am I supposed to send now that your little experiments were found out by Marin?"

Jelan sighed. Another drop of information. Luka was incredibly smart for the way he did it.

"Send the entire South for all I care," Arvalo crooned. "Those riots need to be quelled—"

"They sleep in bunks and sweat their skin off and live with new plasma burns every day. I want to help you, Father, I really do, but there needs to be a little more humanitarian standards for your plasma mines. Word can slip and get out in the city. People want to know more since the change in crown. I'm covering your tracks from the last fifteen years." Luka sounded exasperated, like this conversation had circled numerous times. "You gave me this responsibility, but you also gave me a plethora of problems when you turned your sights and fought for the throne."

A long, steady silence. Luka's slight fear might as well have been seeping into Jelan, it was so palpable. He'd suffer for these words.

Good, Jelan said in her head. She had no intention of feeling sorry for any of Arvalo's children, especially the child that was rumored to suggest her plashield be stripped from her hands.

"Give me the weapons quota for this week and we will discuss improvements in the mines. I want more plashields—"

"That takes the most amount of plasma, father, along with the engineers that have yet to master the work. It takes five just to complete one prototype, and even then, it doesn't act as the girl's did."

"That bitch did it on her own."

"Probably because she warmed Marin's bed and gets substantial riches from him. You know they treat their help with revolting rewards."

"You haven't yet produced a full-fledged shield. You know the consequences. I want it by this week. If I don't, you know who suffers."

Silence. Jelan was basking in the glory of thwarting Arvalo with her intelligence for only a moment before she frowned.

She was surprised by how Luka kept his cool. "I understand."

"Speaking of, where is your sister? I sent her out to please that horde of businessmen and she has yet to return. She's typically quick about her duties."

This time, Jelan caught the tense quip in Luka's voice. "She's spending time with Park. Partying her whore-ness away."

Arvalo scoffed. "Avoiding me. Per usual. If she doesn't return in a week, I'm sending Damian."

Another tense silence. Luka cleared his throat. Seemed he wasn't expecting this *Damian* to make it into the mix.

"Understood?" Arvalo urged.

"Understood."

And the call ended.

It was a couple more moments in the closet. Jelan lowered her forehead to her knee. Took a deep breath.

The door opened. Light flooded in.

"The sweaters don't bite," Luka mumbled passively. He stepped aside. Jelan stood, avoiding the plethora of wool and polyester, and exited the closet.

"Why do I have to hide in there?"

"Would you rather eavesdrop from the balcony?" Luka asked.

"No, I…" She frowned. "Why do you let me listen?"

"Because you need something to relay to your little toy." A shrug. "And because I'm tired of these games."

"Do you not like your father?" *Are you not like him?*

The simple answer was no. Luka wasn't like Arvalo. That was purely based on human configuration and environment and the lack of scientific advancements in carbon cloning. But Jelan couldn't swallow this act. Yet she heard it. Heard all of the little irritations in Luka's voice when Arvalo condescended everyone and everything. It was astounding to witness, but even though Jelan's understanding of Calesal's higher politics shifted, it didn't mean she was supposed to suddenly like the man that car crashed her and Lucien and held her hostage in his extremely comfortable apartment.

It had been a week. One week. Part of her almost accepted this. Part of her *wasn't* surprised. This was a dangerous world—city—after all. Luka didn't seem to want to change this world for the better, but he didn't follow in his father's controlling footsteps either.

She thought she'd test him a bit more. Just for the fun of it. "How does your father have a connection to the world of Greed?"

He was slightly taken aback by the last word. His eyes widened and his gaze dipped to the plascreen mounted to the wall in the office adjacent to his bedroom. "You know about that?"

"How does…how do things get there?"

"Can't disclose that." He placed his hands behind his back. "Even if I knew."

"But you…" She frowned. "Okay, well, what are your father's future plans for the city?"

"Can't disclose that, either."

She blanked her expression. "This is unhelpful. Why can't you just tell me? You already let me hear the conversation with your father. That revealed a lot. I didn't know there were riots in the plasma mines."

I didn't know the accounts of people who worked the mines.

I didn't know Arvalo's children were a business transaction most times.

I didn't know Mai was sold off to be a political pleaser.

It wasn't hard to believe all of these things but hearing it aloud didn't stave the surprise. Jelan didn't want to swallow the evil of the world. Losing her ignorance made it all seem darker, grayer, and less pleasant than when it was just the chaotic South and wishful thinking.

"Because I entertain truth and lie detector sessions weekly, and I don't care to explain the change in my pulse when they ask if I have *told* others of confidential issues." His brow raised. "You eavesdropped. That's it. Stop asking me things directly because you won't get them."

He strutted out of the room, tall body lithe and smooth like a dancer. It was different from Lucien's wide shoulders and thick thighs and…

Jelan needed more coffee. And to figure out another way to deter Luka from creating a perfect plashield. She followed him. By the time she entered the living room, he was already on the couch, knees spread, elbows resting on them, and pouring over the copied blueprints from her originals. All the metrics, the components, of her experiment were there, and yet it stumped him. Stumped everyone in Plastech Industries.

Jelan kept deterring, "Was it really you that suggested Kole be thrown into the Sins?"

He didn't look up. "Yes."

His blatant answer dropped her jaw. "Why?"

"Because it was the easiest way to get the guy's family to cooperate." Luka's silver eyes danced across the blueprint. "Not like it worked, anyway. If you'd been thrown in, it would have saved a headache."

Anger flashed through her. "You don't really expect me to help you with that talk, do you?"

"I don't expect anything from you," he said. "You'll help me regardless."

She crossed her arms. "And what makes you think that?"

His eyes finally flicked up to her and then went back to the papers. "You don't need to tell me anything. I only need to observe you." He pointed to a certain equation and tapped it. "So this equation is wrong, right?"

Her chest caved.

He lifted his head, studying her, and then a vile smirk crossed his mouth. "Knew it."

Jelan was magnificently confused. How was he…how was he *reading her*? She bowed to a stoic face and tried to keep her emotions in check…

He was riling them.

And he did it on purpose to get answers from her actions.

"…Would you rewrite it like this? Or this?" He scribbled away. "Oh…*oh*. I see. You decreased the numbers here. You toned it down."

Her eyes bugged. Her emotions whirled; surprise, irritation, annoyance. It flashed and she couldn't tamp it down. *Tone it down.* He peeled every single mask just by being an asshole.

She turned toward her bedroom, heat flooding her cheeks.

"Thank you for that," he called. "I'll bring this to the lab. Be back in a couple of hours."

She slammed her door. Sunk her back on it. Slid to the floor. Her hands cradled her head and her breaths came faster. Sharp. She rubbed at her eyes and crawled to the bedside table where the asshole had stocked an inhaler and medicine for it. She went through the motions, sucking until her spasms settled along with her growing rage.

She listened to the silence of the apartment, barely hearing him shuffle the papers and walk toward the apartment door. He paused—he normally checked the space for around four seconds before he opened the door and locked it—but this time she counted ten. Six extra seconds deterred from his routine.

She turned her eyes to the white-painted bedroom door. She felt his gaze on it. She stared right back.

And deep within her, she knew he was smirking.

He opened the door. Locked it.

Fucking six extra seconds.

Jelan rummaged through his office. She had an inkling he left it deliberately unlocked and stocked with papers that wouldn't reveal too much. He was more calculating than a literal computer. She hated it. *She* was the observant one. *She* was the smart one. She never had such an ego about it until Luka's smirk drifted into her dreams and riled her in ways she didn't understand.

She tossed papers into a neat pile when they provided no information. He had every meticulously labeled; *Plasma Standards, Commander Codes, Weaponry Assets and Finances, Salary,* and more. Things that didn't matter to what she needed to know: Greed. The weapons going there. *How* they were going there.

Even if I knew. His eyes had said it all. He truly didn't know. He'd heard it and knew about its secrecy, probably by being an observant asshole per normal, but she doubted he sat in on meetings about it. She doubted Arvalo had a true idea. Based on what Kole said, people died if they were risks, and Arvalo would make Luka no exception.

She took notice of a severe increase in plasma mining, but there wasn't an indication it came from the regular mines. The number shouldn't have been possible, but it was confirmed, yet Luka had an issue with plasma production in the first place due to riots. It boggled her, but she tucked it away.

She placed the last paper down, halting briefly as her eyes caught Luka's full name.

Jeon Luka Arvalo.

So the man went by his middle name. That wasn't a coincidence, she guessed. Perhaps she'd use his first name to aggravate him as he did her.

She abandoned his office. Whatever Luka knew that he didn't want Arvalo to know, it'd be in a strange place. Possibly the place where kidnapped people were allowed to eavesdrop.

She paused before his bedroom door before trying the handle. Locked. Not an issue. She stalked to the impeccably clean kitchen and searched for a slim butter knife, a screwdriver, or anything, but after opening and slamming most drawers, Jelan gave up and grabbed the paperweight from the living room coffee table. She paraded back to his door and slammed the paperweight into the handle. It bent. She jammed it again. It tumbled to the floor with a clatter.

Kicking the door open, she stalked through his bedroom to the closet. *The sweaters don't bite.* She bit her lip and yanked the closet door open. It was a spacious thing and as organized as the rest of the place. She turned to a particular swath of color-coded wool and began to shift through them, not knowing exactly what she was looking for. She wasn't gentle, and she didn't care. Her beads clinked as her hands swatted one, then another, then another, as frustration blossomed and—

A different kind of clink. She paused. Sucked a breath. Her eyes drifted to the cool, navy blue cashmere ensemble. She poked it. A rattle. She dug a hand into the neckline and felt around.

Her fingertips smoothed across metal. It was nicely tied around the bottom part of the hanger, and with a little jostling, Jelan freed it. She pulled the tiny amber key away, her frustration fizzling.

Damn, he'd be a good opponent in chess.

She whirled in the closet, searching for the place that the key might unlock. Her eyes flickered and landed on his dresser. An antique thing similar to the key. She tried the drawers until she tested a top one and felt for a false bottom. She opened it fully, nearly taken aback by the stack of black boxer briefs inches from her nose. She jerked away. "Shit."

After a moment of surprise, she picked one up, letting it hang from her finger. Even the band was engraved with silver polyester. She scowled and let it drop back into the drawer. After shoving the rest of his boxers and hating it, she felt for the tiny keyhole. Then jammed the key in. Twisted it.

A soft click. The bottom opened. Papers lined her vision along with a thick, leather-bound journal.

And when she opened the journal, laid out the papers, and stared, Luka's secret research boggled. Entranced. Detailed, neat handwriting covered every page, followed by thin sheets of paper where he'd charcoaled symbols and made notes. One symbol held question marks, but the bit that caught her attention was Luka's note: *before the wall?*

It was a cursory twirl of wind, with a small star in the middle. He'd re-drawn it over and over, splattering it through his journals that dove into questions on Veceras' history and the walls and plasma mining—everything that he suspected, he jotted down. Jelan unfolded one paper and was stunned to see a hand-marked map of Calesal, walls and all, but with roads that didn't line up. She stared further, squinting, trailed a finger down one, and tried to determine why it was *so* familiar. Dots marked certain areas, followed by degrees she couldn't make out—

She audibly gasped. "Plasma points."

And the roads trailing their connections: Calesal's sewers. She'd stared at a similar, albeit less detailed blueprint months ago before they'd figured out Arvalo was going to blow up the Sky Arches. Luka took the same map and engraved it with every bit of research he knew: *sewers built before the walls, Covokai documents detail heat points in walls, unable to fortify waste management because of heat—plasma?* She continued trailing a finger until a certain road slithered past the wall and marked another point.

Jelan suddenly thought of the spyglass she found in the junkyard. Someone had been outside of the city before a wall was built, and it was painted a glistening silver. The wind and star emblem gave similar vibes, and slowly, the gears in her mind began to turn.

The sewers in Calesal were apparently older than the walls—which would be more than five-hundred years old. They can't be fortified because of plasma, but Jelan also connected that other strange word to it—*aether*—the same word she'd seen with the first plaspoint blueprint. All of these things existed before the walls and were mapped by Luka into a cohesive understanding that the sewers extended beyond, plasma production increased without being mined, and aether possibly meant the creation of more Sky Arches.

Her mouth dropped. Her eyes trailed to the door, where Luka now stood, glaring down at her but without a hint of surprise on his face. She realized how funny it all looked: his underwear drawer hanging open with boxers falling out, papers and his secret journal held open by her fingers, and the small smile crawling onto her face.

"So *that's* how they're producing all these weapons and shipping them to Greed." She tapped her finger to a particular point in the sewer map—a point that extended beyond the wall. "There's another Sky Arch." Her smile widened. "And the bodies of Plastechs were never from testing—well, maybe some, but from mining *underneath* Calesal to advance production to Greed. Wow, it took a little bit, but…it's genius."

Luka glanced toward his closet. "You figured it out."

"Not all of it, not until I understand what this symbol is." She bit her bottom lip. Luka's eyes snagged on it, then back to the papers. She ignored his gaze. "But this is…beyond me. The fact that there is another way into the Sins without bloodswearing oneself is astounding, and…" Her face dropped. "And…it truly means it is all compromised." She looked back at him. "That there is no leaving it."

Her heart ached deeply. She thought of Violet, still in the sixth world. Of Jack's death and Lucien's clear depression about it. Maybe if she could relay this information to him, they could stop production and—

"My father will put a bullet in the head of everyone who knows. It's futile. That is the accumulation of three years of research, and I've never determined where it is." Luka shut off the closet light that she'd forgotten. "Put it away. We need to go."

"Go?"

"Your father is in the hospital. Mid Sector. I got a message from your lover," Luka said, clearly irritated. "Marin won't be there. Don't get your hopes up about fucking in a broom closet."

Her mouth dropped. "Are you jealous?"

"No." He slammed the door to *his* bedroom.

❋ ❋ ❋

Her dad was in recovery.

She stood next to his bedside, staring dumbfounded at the thinness of his body, but more surprised that the doctor told her he'd been one week sober. It took a toll on his body, though. When one of Lucien's men went to check in and bring another round of groceries, Vaughn collapsed on the toilet, unresponsive. He hadn't been eating properly, mostly drinking the shitty water of the Deep South and suffering through seizures as he went through withdrawal, all without telling anyone.

But he was in recovery.

Her eyes watered. He slept soundly, hooked up to numerous machines and drip lines to provide nutrients while also supporting his organs through the detox process. There had been a dull roar in her ears through most of the doctor's speech—she'd been caught on his sudden sobriety. The fact they found shiva bottles tossed out of his window and shattered on the street. The attempt to cook something on his small stove. The sudden smell of cleaning supplies in his bathroom.

Luka entered the room again and shut the door softly. He held two coffee cups in his hand. He handed her one. "They said he'll be here for the time being but he'll be transferred to a rehab center afterward. Marin will oversee payments for that."

"You don't have to stay." She took the cup. "And I can switch the payments to my account. Lucien doesn't need to do that."

He gave her a long look. "Arrange it with the front desk. Also, I'm not letting my collateral out of sight. I know who Alexia Javez sides with, and some trip to the hospital is a stupid, but obvious scheme."

"Lucien wouldn't use my father as a way to get me back," Jelan said, voice rising. She held his cold silver gaze. "That's insulting."

He snorted. "This is gardia business, baby, and it doesn't follow moral rules."

She ignored the shiver down her spine at the pet name. She let the coffee warm her fingers and relax her grip. The doctor came back in and discussed treatment, but the whole time she digested it, she became acutely aware of Luka tapping away on his little plastablet device. She leaned near him at some point while the doctor gave her details about the recommended rehab facilities, and even though Luka pulled away, annoyed with her peeping, she caught a glimpse of a typed sentence: *seizures likely, visits advised once per week if traumatic symptoms involved with addiction…*

Her cheeks warmed. She averted her gaze, nodding absently to the doctor and glancing at her father, while her thoughts tumbled with reasons. She was collateral, and this was a detail about it. Luka calculated everything in this life down to minute detail. But the more she tried to reason with *why* he was taking notes, the fewer answers she had.

She filed it under, *Ways to Further Be An Asshole*, and left it at that.

When she said her goodbyes to her still-unconscious father and left the room, Luka was leaning against the far wall of the clean hospital hallway, staring at a group of nurses as they wheeled a discreet body covered with a sheet into an elevator. The arrow pointed down.

But Jelan stopped breathing.

Because a hand hung from the stretcher, and it was covered in twisting, bleach-like lines, glistening with a hint of silver dust.

Luka stared, too. "Interesting."

She turned to him. "Do you think—"

"No."

A door opened, swinging wide. A supply room. A doctor exited in casual clothes, discarding her scrubs into a bin. "You don't think at all? That makes sense."

"No, Jelan—"

But Jelan was moving, heart a hammer in her chest, as she caught the closing door with her foot and edged herself into the empty on-call room. Pairs of fresh scrubs lay neatly on a shelf, ready for the other doctors.

Luka slipped behind her as the door gently shut. His warm breath met the top of her head, body heat simmering her back. She jolted away as his hand brushed her hip. "What are you doing?" He grumbled.

"Researching," she said, beelining for the shelf and taking a pair of scrubs her size. She pulled her shirt over her head and Luka let out a choking cough. She glanced over her shoulder, forgetting how Northers were extremely private about changing. "You can turn around."

She ignored how his eyes flared with fire and moved quickly down her body. She knew it looked great. Her genetics never failed to turn heads. She tugged the scrub top on and tossed him a pair. "Are you joining? To make sure your collateral doesn't scheme?"

22

ASHER

JACK HAD BLED A GOOD amount during his life. Injuries were common for a City Commander and one who ran a gardia. He had to be the best, had to prove his worth as the one wielding all the power.

It meant a lot of blood.

Throughout his time in Calesal, he never gave thought to the surprised comments in response to his healing, but it wasn't noticeable unless a singular medic checked on him over and over again. Even then, it was nothing out of the ordinary. Some bodies healed faster than others. His whip injury in Lust debilitated him to the point he was out for multiple days. And then he was back. Healthy. Like nothing ever happened. It was normal for him. He thought it to be his ridiculous stamina or a commodity of healthy genetics. He never realized that a couple of hours to heal a paper cut wasn't normal.

But now, after his transformation, his healing was…magnified. As if whatever ability he possessed had been dormant his entire life, and now it finally alighted. It may be genetics, it may be some secret, unidentifiable power, but regardless, he deemed whatever it was similar to a Vanisher, one who never knows their secret potential unless it was awoken within them.

But he wasn't Awakened. He wasn't sure *if* he needed to be Awakened. Either way, they still nearly drained him dry every day, and by midnight, his blood count was normal.

Another look and his jaw tensed as he stared at the blue material.

"What? Are they not cashmere enough for you?" she blurted, unbuttoning her pants.

A twitch of his lips. "They're missing encrusted diamonds."

"Just tell daddy to have more children sent to the mines."

He huffed with a tense smile before he peeled his V-neck sweater over his head. She pushed her pants down. They both looked at each other; her at his chiseled, lean torso, him at her legs.

A breath. A moment.

They continued changing.

She shoved their clothes into a scrub waste bin and pulled two face masks from a box. They situated them over their mouths. Luka took the scrub bag from her, eyes glittering. "After you, partner."

Alexia needed to up her security a bit, but since it was a Midian hospital, strict measures weren't taken. After snatching two picture-less identifications from behind the nurse's desk, they entered the elevator and the scrubs granted them access to the bottom floor of the morgue. Jelan suspected no one was worried about breaches to dead bodies. Luka strutted next to her silently.

They found the morgue. Then they found another room, where a body-sized cavity shot into a hallway and the smell of sewage drifted through her mask. She paused. Glanced through the darkness where a hazard-suit person rolled bins filled with body bags.

But Jelan wasn't looking at the grotesque sight.

Instead, she stared at the swirling white painted air symbol plastered on ancient brick. So subtle, so tiny, that no one would have noticed unless they'd seen it already.

Luka's arm brushed hers. He saw it, too.

The same symbol scattered across his journals.

"Research partner, indeed," he rumbled.

She hated how his voice alone riled a thrill through her bones.

"How many bags?" One of the medics in the hybrids lab asked.

"Six, but we could probably do more—"

Jack nearly growled. "I'm done for the day."

His head spun. Heart a slow beat in his chest. Jack extracted the needle and, to the protests of the two medics, he stormed out of the room.

"They don't have any advances."

Jack turned to Jonathon, who had become more his shadow and companion than Vanisher transporter for his captain's duties. Jack sagged on the wall and leaned into the man, unable to hold his weight. His vision was a blur of black blobs. "I'm surprised."

"It means he will keep going."

"He will keep going regardless of whether we discover another successful subject. He wanted me desperate for a win, so much so that when he inevitably strapped me down and made me the experiment, I would still want that win. It's a deranged manipulation."

"Deranged manipulation is the Master's specialty."

A deep sigh heaved Jack's chest. "Yes. No one gets this far, with this much rule and power and control, by simply being nice to everyone and expecting them to truly want what you want."

"No, you have to trap them, give them a little freedom and control, and then trap them again, so said freedom and control becomes like candy thrown into your cage."

Jack snorted. "You're too observant for your own good."

"I grew up in Greed, was made into this purposely by the Master's reproduction program for Vanishers, and here I am." Jonathon patted Jack on the shoulder and his hands lit up with his powers. "Where to?"

"Bed."

❃ ❃ ❃

Jack slept peacefully for a good six hours before he awoke in sweat. Always in sweat. His body was still getting used to all the changes.

He worried if perhaps he'd decay and end up failing Cyran after all. But he pushed through, and after a long shower with his forehead pressed to the cool tile, he forced himself to think about his plans.

And implement them.

It all started with Violet.

Jack truly thought he was going insane when he summoned Talia, the servant, yesterday and said those things to her. But he had been insane the moment he realized that bitch of a High Servant was whipping her as punishment. His initial request was to spend some time with Talia, to figure out why the fuck when he touched her, it was as if his fingers unmasked a layer, revealing Violet.

But his gut... seeing that untamed fire as he requested to show her what her mouth can do, sparked joy in Jack. He couldn't... there was no way it could be Violet. But he saw portions of her, and whether he was crazy and his subconscious simply wanted to give him hope amid this torture, he craved more. He found himself desperate for mere reminders, because the more his warming heart was poked, the more he found himself *only* believing that she was alive.

Cyran was gone from Greed attending to business in other worlds, and that was all the information Serwa gave him before she left to have a meeting with the other ten War Commanders. Zavar was supposedly going on assassination jobs, but seeing as Jack took care of most captives daily, Jack suspected it was Zavar's job to locate Violet.

Besides that, Zavar had done an exceptional job at avoiding Jack after his lightning torture. A part of Jack was disappointed not to see him—the teasing lit up his day, and whatever annoyance Zavar used to hold was now gone. He debated bantering the Vaelaur, and for a moment Jack wasn't going to, but he strutted over to his hologram watch, found Zavar's contact, and pressed a button.

To Jack's surprise, Zavar not only didn't tell him to fuck off, but he buzzed his location in the fortress. Jack's chest alighted. This should be fun. Or horrible. He was never sure about the lightning man.

Jack changed and went straight to Zavar's location. He didn't expect to end up closer to the mountains, where fields and grassy training grounds and giant warehouses took up miles of land. He wandered near a giant courtyard and the kennels for Zavar's bloodhounds. He found the Vaelaur sitting on the floor, surrounded by dogs, while leaning against one of the kennels. A bloodhound sniffed Zavar's neck and whined, then whipped its head toward the door, analyzing Jack. Zavar lifted his head, the most annoyed and exhausted expression on his face.

"Did you get your dick bit again, Zavian?"

One look at Jack had Zavar's vanishing powers flaring. He disappeared from his defeated seat and materialized in front of Jack, shoving him in the chest. Jack's lips twisted upward, and he twirled away. Zavar lunged after him, a whip of black lightning launching from his hand. Jack dodged it with a growing smile. Oh, he was mad *mad*.

Before Jack reached him, the hounds began to bark collectively, and in Jack's peripheral, a brown and white blur sprinted across the grass and happily rolled before Jack's boots.

"An assassin job," was all Zavar said. He didn't even try to hide it anymore.

"What did this dog do to require you to murder it?"

"I didn't have to murder the dog." Zavar's expression betrayed how appalled he was at the idea. The man really liked his animals. "But someone else. I couldn't find them. Only found this stupid dog."

"Was it in the city?"

"Navru."

Oh, this was calculated. Jack resisted a smile. "Who'd you have to kill in Navru?"

"Some bitch."

Come on, Zavar. Don't tease me like that.

Jack looked down at the dog. Zavar's eyes flicked to his face. He could feel them. Watching him.

"Can I keep him?" Jack asked.

"Her."

"Okay, well, can I keep her? She's lovely."

"Fine."

"Great."

Zavar eyed him for a long time. "I was going to see if you wanted her anyway."

"Are you..." Jack placed his hand on his chest in false astoundment. "In love with me?"

"I can't wait for Fire Night," Zavar groaned, and his hands began to glow.

Ah, Fire Night, the upcoming event meant for captains where they had a dark hide-and-seek chase with very consensual individuals, mainly women, of their choice. It was held deep in the mountains outside of the Twin Cities in a maze of caverns. Nearly every captain was talking about it. Most commanders wanted to abolish it, but few said it was necessary for morale. The chance to indulge in fear and lust, in a world where everyone was greedy for something. The chance to fuck as many beautiful, voluntary women and men as you wanted amid the growing tension of seven worlds. *Everyone* was excited for Fire Night.

"Why? Do you want to save our first kiss for then?" Jack continued to tease.

Zavar's nostrils flared. "Just keep giving him your blood." His eyes shot daggers at the playful new pup. "Now you have something to annoy that isn't me."

And with that, he vanished.

Jack looked down at the dog, who was now on her back, legs partially in the air and her tongue lolling into the grass. One blue eye, one purple eye, and a mix of brown and white fur. He bent and rubbed her belly. She groaned happily. He made his way up to her neck, where a dark red crocheted collar lay. It was an... abysmal piece, but the thought was there. Jack's fingers slid over it. His teeth tingled...

He stilled.

At that moment, Jack thought he might have been the luckiest man alive.

So, he gently removed the collar, and while petting the animal gift bestowed to him, he licked it.

And two things clicked.

A high, pronounced laugh burst out of him. The dog jumped up on his chest, howling and then licking his face. Jack laughed into her fur.

"Skies, little buddy," Jack said. "I can't believe it."

She barked again.

"It was her all along."

Because Jack had tasted Talia's—Violet's—blood yesterday. He had been curious. Talia—Violet was clearly revolted when he sucked her blood off of his thumb, but the twist in her features, the evident, one-of-a-kind scowl, confirmed even more. The blood was the true test.

And her blood from yesterday tasted the exact same as the dried one on the collar. It wasn't even a coincidence—no, it was a *message*. Maybe not to him specifically, but a slap in the face to Zavar. Yet where Zavar pouted and had a tantrum, Jack typically found a win. He found more than a win, though. This was hope.

Violet was alive. And if Violet was alive, Rio and Anaya were most definitely breathing as well.

Jack held the dog's furry face. "Guess what?"

The dog barked.

"Yes, that's right." A savage smile. "Your mother doesn't know what is about to hit her."

Another elated bark.

"Uh-huh, you definitely take after her with that mouth."

He thought back to Talia—Violet. He had seen that fire in those eyes. He hadn't misplaced the person. While his logic struggled to comprehend, his body knew. Now that everything clicked, he figured it out.

A glamour. She was wearing a glamour.

But…how?

The only time Jack witnessed a glamour being used was during his recovery at Honnrak Castle, when Cyran had walked in wearing the skin and face of Violet, Anaya, Rio, and Lucien. It had been jarring to see, and incredibly realistic at the same time. But Violet…there's no way.

He needed to test the theory first, both for his sanity and the annoying headache this foolishness brought on. Violet had been walking underneath their very noses and under a guise. There shouldn't be a connection between that and Cyran.

Yet, there was.

His questions were overrun by panic. What was she doing? Did she think this was a game? That she could walk into the Worldbreaker's castle and get away with deceiving all of them? Cyran wanted her dead for the very reason that he couldn't blood-control her like he could everyone else…and if he discovered that she also possessed another ability of his—the ability to glamour…

Jack leaned his forehead on the dog. She licked his cheek.

He needed to find Reed.

After securing a kennel for the dog he named Minji and ensuring that she was to be properly cared for—and then subsequently shifting his schedule to make time to play with her—he spent the rest of the day searching for Violet's brother. He tried to contact him, but his communications were off. So Jack ordered soldiers to probe every corner of the fortress, but no one knew where Captain Sutton was. Jack's gut grew tight, and he dismissed each soldier with a fake laugh. "He must have beat me to the party tonight. Go rest."

Only when his members dispersed did Jack find the nearest balcony and indulge in a cigarette. He had kicked the habit for the most part, but his nerves were crackling with anxiety and tension. He couldn't rid the sour taste in his mouth, his chest, his head. He'd found Violet, but he'd had the horrible feeling that meanwhile, he lost something else.

He'd seen Reed nearly every day since their sort-of reconciliation, and now the man might as well have disappeared out of this very world.

Jack paused. His breath stilled. The obvious solution was to check the tracker screen. Only one existed, and it was held in strict security—something Cyran wouldn't dare give Jack. He took another drag, poring through any plans he could make…

Hard boot steps stomped the floors, increasing in volume. "If they are *gone*, I'm going to kill every last one of those stupid Mers."

Zavar. A very, very angry Zavar. Who was about to pass this balcony at any moment.

Jack felt the cool tingle of his Endolier camouflage slide along his arms, his neck, until nearly every centimeter of his skin shimmered with those little scales. Within a breath, his body melted into the background, matching his surroundings. Clothes included.

A flash of black lightning zapped down the hallway, and Zavar followed right behind, throwing another one out of anger. "I want to see for my fucking self. They were on that stupid ship the entire time. How did they make it to this world? I had my men watching…"

Jack followed Zavar up a floor. A floor Jack was explicitly not allowed on: The Vanisher's floor.

Zavar scanned his wristband as a soldier hurried behind. "I'm sorry, sir, I only just heard—"

Zavar flung another bolt that nearly hit the soldier's head. "*Leave!*"

The soldier trembled and ran away.

Zavar flung open the door and stormed in. Jack slipped right behind. The Vanisher's area was cream and black with floor-to-ceiling windows that looked out over the city. It was minimalist and modern, but certainly was one of the best-looking floors. Zavar stormed through the dormitory section, passed a giant lounge with a library, and drilled his way through an enclosed security bridge flooded with bloodhounds. Jack sucked a breath, too late to do anything. But as the bloodhounds lifted their noses and sniffed, then looked around, clearly confused, he continued on behind Zavar, rather chancing his invisibility. They began to growl, but Zavar was in such a rage, and the guards posted were so afraid, that he turned and snarled a command. The dogs shut up and returned to a still position.

Thank the fuck for Zavar's anger.

He continued down a single corridor that was, for the most part, extremely separate from the rest of the fortress. Zavar scanned his wrist and flung open another door. Jack followed, letting it shut softly behind.

Before him was a screen. But not just any screen.

The Tracker Screen.

It was a large headquarters room, where cleared workers milled about at desks and took notes on movements. It was mostly quiet, full of clicking keyboards and the taps of pens. His eyes snapped to the names, breath faltering in his throat. He scanned the sixth world.

Zavar released a furious cry.

Rio's name blinked green. Jack couldn't resist the rising smile at seeing Rio's name. His heart pounded as it landed on another name—Violet. Confusion poured through him. Not Violet Sutton, but...

Violet Asher.

He didn't know what Asher was. Her middle name? But Jack had seen the documents on her, the registrations at school, with her apartment, *everything,* and Violet never had a middle name. She was only assigned Sutton when she was born, along with Reed, because it was one of the few last names that were given to families with an unknown father. It was a common name in Calesal— common enough to throw off any lead between Reed and Violet, as nearly fifteen others in the sixth panel alone had it. In the South, Sutton had a rogue, underlying slang with it.

It meant abandoned.

Jack hated the law that slapped Violet with a bigger reminder of her family's misfortunes, but now was not the time to craft his proposal of amendments to change said law. He'd already drafted a million others out of sheer boredom.

Hope beat through his veins. He stared at her name. His mouth parted. She was *alive*.

He searched again, this time finding confusion. Two things were missing.

His name was not there.

Lucien, he thought. *No-no-no…*

Jack touched his neck at the spot where they placed the tracker. Did Cyran have it removed? Why…

Of course, there was a why. Because Jack couldn't simply die on the screen and pop back up as green without an explanation. It would send a shockwave through Calesal.

And the second thing: Reed Sutton was nowhere to be found. Not in any panel.

Jack stared, dumbfounded.

"Where did the little shit land? Was he with the scale girl?" Zavar asked one of the workers.

"I—Rio Gaverra didn't land at any of the typical points. He… he didn't have the Iris at all," a worker stuttered from his desk.

Zavar grew quiet. Clenched his fists. Took a deep breath. "There's no way she could know."

She. Violet. He was thinking Violet vanished them from Sloth to Greed.

"Is every Vanisher accounted for?"

"Everyone has logged their movements and signed in when they arrived back. I don't have an illicit vanishing out of this world. But…as for the rogue Vanisher, we don't have her set up in the system properly, so no tracker would be able to show that she went *back* a world. A normal candidate is only tracked when they go forward—"

"I *know* this," Zavar snarled. "There's just no way…"

Zavar's expression of disbelief tickled Jack.

The door scanned and opened. Another worker filed in with a tablet. "Reed Sutton is back with His Master. Correct his tracker location, please."

"Where did they arrive?" another worker asked.

"The rooftop."

"Corrected."

"Ensure the change did not appear in the Original City's communication."

"Confirmed."

Zavar drew up his watch and pressed a button. He stalked to the door and flung it open, yelling, "Bring me that fucking pirate now! Renell or whatever the fuck his name is. He was supposed to catch the duo, that piece of shit."

Jack tiptoed behind, wanting to hear more of this conversation… but his heart beat too hard to maintain his composure. He followed Zavar's storm until they passed the silenced dogs, and then Zavar vanished on the spot. Jack continued to the elevator, sliding in with another Fringe member, and when they left the space, he released his camouflage. A gasp of pain and relief escaped his mouth as his skin rippled back to normal. He could never hold it for very long. Thirty minutes at most.

He always gave Anaya props. It was an extremely uncomfortable feeling to keep up with. He smoothed out his expression as the elevator doors opened to his floor, and bolted into his room. Paced. Waited. Digested the information.

Rio, and most likely Anaya, were in Greed. But it wasn't through the typical Iris transfer. Someone *brought* them there.

They suspected Violet, but based on all Jack knew, it was incredibly unbelievable that Violet could have done that. Zavar knew this, too. But…if there were a way, Violet would find it. She'd risk everything for Anaya and Rio.

The other thing was the bright, obvious realization that they manipulated the Tracker Screen in Calesal. So, when Reed went to Envy, or *completely disappeared from the seven worlds*, it didn't show up. Lucien wouldn't notice.

Lucien would also not know that his own brother is well and alive.

Lucien would believe he is the last survivor of their family.

Jack ran a stressed hand through his hair.

I am here, brother, Jack wanted to say. *You may not be able to protect me like you used to for all of us, but I am here. I am with you. We may have lost everyone else, but not me. Not you.*

Never you.

As for Reed's little excursion…Jack checked the time. And then he headed up to the airship deck. If he knew anything about the Sutton siblings, after a hard, challenging day, they wanted to be on a rooftop.

He couldn't shake the feeling as he walked past the airship pad and the hangars and headed toward a series of empty stone platforms. They weren't necessarily places to hang out, but it made for a stretch of space where training occurred during the day. Otherwise, they were empty due to the harsh wind and bitter cold. Jack's nerves made the chill only prickle.

His gut was right, because sitting precariously close to the ledge, was Reed. He kicked his legs with a giant, delusional smile on his face. Jack held back for a moment, observing him.

His arms were covered in cuts. Healing cuts. *Rapidly* healing cuts. When Jack blinked, he could have convinced himself they hadn't existed at all.

But Jack knew better.

Reed's brown hair was wild and untamed, sticking up in some places, matted and greasy in others. When the cuts disappeared, they revealed the spots of dirt, the torn shirt, the lack of shoes. His hands and forearms were bleached with filigree, as if he used his abilities so much it became a permanent part of his skin. Reed didn't show signs of pain; no, he only laughed periodically and pointed to the city, only to chuckle again.

"What did he do to you?" Jack whispered with clenched fists.

Reed tilted his head back. His smile broadened. "Jackie. You look tired."

Jack took careful steps toward his old comrade. His guard flashed up. Just like those cuts, the bleached Vanisher lines began to fade into Reed's brown skin.

Reed seemed to think Jack answered him, so he merely waved to the city. "Yeah, I had a long day, too. But this city is pretty to look at, right? Sometimes I close my eyes and pretend it is Calesal. Makes me feel a bit better." He hiccupped.

"Are you drunk?"

"Oh, I could use some shiva right now. His Master gives me this other drink that tastes really bitter, but makes me feel really good. And look! All the cuts he did, they're gone!" Reed clapped his hands. "He is so nice to do that."

"Where have you been off to, Reed?" Jack lightened his voice. Acted dumb.

"We went to this cool place, but…" Reed's brows scrunched. "I can't remember. I think it was purple? Maybe green, I—this stuff he gave me, it makes me forget. That's what he said but…" Confusion. "I think I forgot."

A steady wind roared across the rooftop, making Jack shiver. Reed was completely unbothered and lifted his face to the sky, his confusion bleeding into awe.

Not awe.

Delusion.

Jack's chest cracked. He lifted his hand to rub at it, but shoved it in his pockets instead, thinning his mouth. "Hey, Reed," Jack said softly. "How have you been?"

Reed frowned and looked deep in thought for a second. "Alright. I think I need to eat more. I get pretty tired after traveling."

"Yeah, you should eat more," Jack said with a smile. "Can I ask you something? Something that you can keep a secret."

Reed laughed. "Everyone tells me to keep secrets. I have a million secrets. It is so funny because I can't remember any of them."

Jack had the urge to put Reed into hiding and take him far away from this world.

"Why did you tell Violet that you couldn't be siblings in this game?" Jack asked.

Reed bristled slightly. His legs stopped kicking. He frowned. "I never hear her name anymore. I can't believe—*no*—I'm not supposed to know that name. No. I don't know that name, but..." Reed cackled a high-pitched laugh. "I can't believe I've fooled him for this long. He doesn't know she is...that she is..." He pointed a finger at Jack. "I won't say it! You can't *trick* me. Ha. You thought you could, but I won't fall for that again."

Jack's eyes stung and he associated it with the wind. "Did something happen—?"

"I'm not connected to *anyone* in this game," Reed said. "Not a single one. Not her, not you. Siblings? I don't have any. Never had any. I'm the only one my dumb mother decided to have."

"Reed—"

"You know, my mother doted on me so much. Loved me, hugged me—was it because she felt bad? And then..." Reed's face turned furious. "She got *nothing*. Because she *was* the mistake. I figured it all out now." A tap on his temple. "I know why she was a mistake. Why our mother hated her, despised herself for having my sister. I know it all. I'm the *only* one who knows it all. He told me it. I'm special. I'm *super* special. But then he throws my memories in a washing machine and I can never—oh! Look at that airship!"

Reed pointed and Jack forced a smile, nodding. "Yeah, it's a cool airship. Reed, can you tell me why you can't have a sibling—?"

"Do you know what it's like knowing that *she's supposed to die?* Reed frowned and tears bubbled in his eyes. "Hearing it all the time? No, no, not because she is some thorn in his ass and he wants to get rid of it. But because she—no, no, I don't have a sibling. Who is *she?* I don't even know what you're talking about." Reed's eyes were unfocused. He laughed. A tear slipped free and he wiped it away, then said to himself, "We are the only ones who know. And now... Oh, Jackie, why are you here?"

"Reed." Jack lowered himself, voice gentle. "Does the Worldbreaker control you? With your blood?"

"Oh, he controls me alright," Reed said. "He tells me to do all these things and I have to. A lot of the time I want to do what he says, and I do. He is very powerful, do you know that, Jack? He has seen a lot. Done a lot. He says I'm special. But she can't feel him…" A tear slipped down his cheek.

"What is supposed to happen to her, Reed?" Jack asked, a tremble in his voice.

"Death." Reed muttered incoherent words, talking to himself, then continued, "Because she…she is the only one who can stop him. The one who throws tantrums and wasn't loved and likes peppermint tea the same way I do and drinks shiva like it's water and smokes like it's air. *Her.*" A cackle. "Her? Who would've thought that the one person who hardly wanted to live is the only one capable of bringing an end to all of this? But…I have a secret." He beckoned Jack closer, and Jack leaned in. "He. Doesn't. *Know.* I know. And I can't let her stop him, because he wants better things and I want them, too."

Jack stayed quiet. Reed talked to himself in mumbles for a little bit. Jack only had one more question, and it pained him to ask it. "Do you share the same blood as the Master, Reed?"

Reed froze. His eyes widened. "Blood will doom you, Jackie." He smiled at the cities. "Beware of it."

Reed's laughs turned into hysterics and Jack slowly stood, the chill in his body not because of the wind anymore.

❋❋❋

Jack couldn't sleep. He didn't even bother to try. So, he seized advantage of Zavar being distracted by whoever this Renell pirate was and ventured.

Jack studied first. He was curious. He'd done more research on Pharos, but it was impossible to find anything beyond speculation. A leader who changed every five years or so, documents depicting pictures of their kills, the women or others who were rescued and disappeared from the world. The missing person papers, the locations of interactions in Navru. He stared at a couple of spots, memorized them, and abandoned the information center at the fortress.

He needed more info. The need clutched at him as much as the simmering anger toward Cyran did. Jack wasn't one to explode. He didn't like acting out. It made him feel clumsy. But Reed's vulnerable predicament triggered him.

He took Minji on a joyride to the Church District. The Order was both impressive and damaging. It astounded Jack they'd created this—that the entirety of the Twin Cities, and most of the world of Greed, seeped into the basic belief that men ruled, women obeyed, and the Sin was praised as a god. He asked for private tours of the churches. Order members were giddy to assist him. They explained that an initiation was given with blood—a prick of the finger when they were a baby—and registered with the Order. Alarms blared in Jack's head while he smiled.

The more information he gathered, the more Jack wanted to burn everything about it to the ground. But it was easy for him to think that way—he saw it from an outside, untainted perspective. Those raised within the Order would struggle to understand the cult that it was.

"You have an easy time acquiring more land, people, and respect," Jack said as he peered into the eyes of a gold statue, one of many that swarmed this particular cathedral.

"We give back, and Avaritia blesses us."

"Mhm." Jack tightened his grip on Minji's leash. The dog was surprisingly domestic and didn't pull much. She stayed by Jack's leg most of the time. "How do you give back?"

The preacher giving him a tour paused. His smile grew, deepening his wrinkles. "We help others find the good and blessings that Avaritia gives us. They see it all and they understand. We try to start young so they know the bad that can send them to the hands of Nex—the God of Death—and while it can be hard for the kids to understand, soon enough they obey, listen, give their praise of Avaritia, and fear Nex. It takes some time, but Avaritia is here to save us in both this lifetime and the next."

After the tour, Jack turned to the preacher, lowering his voice. "This has been wonderful, but I've heard…things about *extra* blessings to those who are most praised by Avaritia." A lie, but not a far stretch.

The preacher's eyes alighted. "Oh?"

"Because I truly believe that women are meant to serve us men in more ways than one. They certainly don't have as grand of minds as ours to think on their own." Jack's grip tightened on Minji's leash. His smile was easy. The preacher stayed relaxed. "And their bodies…well, you don't get bodies like that to not be admired. Or used."

A smile filled the preacher's face. "Precisely."

When Jack was guided to the next place, he was truly surprised. And disturbed.

"Did you want to participate?" the preacher asked.

"Maybe next time." Jack turned his gaze from the plush red room of women, some bleary eyed and unaware of the hands scathing their bodies. His stomach churned, but he couldn't make a scene. Not here, not now.

This *was* beneath Cyran. He let the worlds do as they pleased as long as it didn't interrupt his ultimate mission, nor create question of his rule over the worlds. The Order praised him, and Cyran loved his praise. His pride.

He thanked the preacher for the tour and exited the Church District with an escort. He gathered all the information in his head and tucked them into files, creating a portfolio on the Order.

Then hailed a cab and made the long journey to Navru.

He let Minji lead him around to different spots, analyzing everything. She sniffed long and hard at certain areas that Jack deemed familiar to her. They found a line of crocheted pieces and followed them.

When he turned down a certain alley, something slammed him into the wall. A blade was at his neck. Minji didn't bark. Instead, wagged her tail more.

She certainly wasn't a guard dog.

Jack smiled down at the Droanian girl and her misty red hair. She snarled, "You've been wandering around too much. What's your business in Navru, *captain*?"

"You got a leader?"

She balked. "What?"

Jack pulled out his phone and started to display the photos he took during his tour. "I want to give her this information."

"Them. Give *them*."

"Apologies. I want to give them this information."

The girl sputtered and then mumbled a few code words into her wrist.

An hour later, Jack was tied to a chair, and a figure entered through the doorway. He stared at their facial tattoo as they said, "Captain Jack Marin."

Jack got right to the point. "Don't tell her I'm here. I know she is working for you. Don't send her to the fortress again, either, or I will burn down your entire organization, and make sure you regret ever putting her in harm's way."

"She decides what she wants."

"Fine. Just not the fortress. It's too dangerous there." Jack leveled his gaze. "I'm here because I want to help you destroy the Order."

"Why?"

"Because she clearly wants that. Whatever she wants, I want."

"And what are you looking for in return?"

A sly smile spread across his face. Jack began to explain, and they matched his smile.

"I have to ask, out of spite," they said. "Will she be safe?"

"From death? Yes. Injury? That, too." Warmth slid across his shoulders, down his body in anticipation. "From me? No."

The leader looked almost pleased. "She gives me a headache."

"This should help relieve it. Do we have a deal?"

"You have a deal, Jack Marin."

❈❈❈

By dawn, when Jack arrived back at the castle before most of the eyes woke, he knew something was wrong. He walked Minji, who was exhausted of him at this point, to his room, then went for a coffee.

The minute he sat in a lounge area that Reed went to every morning, Jack knew. He sensed surrounding emotions, the emptiness. He followed his gut to Reed's quarters.

Reed was gone. There was no trace of him. His room had been emptied, and others even forgot he existed. As if his memory had been erased.

Purposely.

It was then Jack knew that he was in deep, deep shit.

23

CHASE

ANAYA AND RIO SLEPT MOST of the next day. Well, Anaya slept with her head in the toilet, and Rio slept with his in a bucket. They were not used to solid land.

They mentioned that their weeks in Sloth were fairly uneventful. It took a little while to escape from the Pirate Queen, who had wanted to keep them under her eye after Violet's getaway, but Sloth made it easy to evade her grip. A night of drugs, a thwack of a sword to a few guards, and Keller and Maji were waiting for them on the other side of the gates.

The moment they were back on the boat, they wanted to ease the tension for a bit before making their way with one of Rio's irises, so they drank. Sailed to uninhabited islands and drank more. Rio and Maji had their little fling, and Anaya got a ridiculous tan. Her scales went from a bluish-green to a shimmering orange.

Renell had been the biggest issue. He chased them through every Citran Sea, but it wasn't until a couple of days ago that Maji and Anaya snuck onto his boat, knocked out his lookouts, and ripped his sails to shreds. Their peace lasted until they were back in Finnport for supply refuel, like Violet had predicted. They had been at a tavern when Jodin appeared, played the recording, and whisked them away with a soft wave from Keller and a bright smile from Maji.

And now the three of them were together. On a rooftop in Navru sharing a variety of noodle dishes packed in plastic containers.

Anaya slurped her soda. "This is amazing. It is all bubbly."

"More of that at home," Rio said.

"Calesal," Violet clarified at Anaya's confusion. "You can get any flavor of soda there. Some stores have nice, fancy ice machines and you can make the soda extra cold."

Anaya beamed. "Really?"

"The best time to sip it is in the afternoon on a curb or stoop. Let your feet bask in the sun while your head is in the shade. Share some chocolate sticks and play cards. It's normal."

"What most Souther kids did after school." Violet smiled.

"School." Anaya sighed and sat back. "Do you…think I could go to school, too?"

Violet exchanged a look with Rio. "Like, children's school?"

"Well…" Anaya frowned. "I can't read, you know. Not your language. Or mine. Back in Iveyrez, we spent most of our time learning plants, our powers, and when to keep quiet. We didn't have resources for a school, but my papa taught me everything he knew by speaking."

"Yes." Violet's smile dropped. "You can go to school, it's just…"

"Very expensive," Rio said softly. "But I'm sure we can find money. We will have won the Sins. Someone will donate or—"

"We'll steal it." Violet winked.

Anaya bobbed her head, her inky hair shiny in the morning sun. "Alright. I'd like that."

"My friend Jelan is extremely smart. She could teach you about these plasweapons. She taught herself it all, and even got a big girl job in it."

"My mother was always pretty strict about our grades and helped us with homework. She knows a lot. She would love to teach you, probably as long as you don't insult her cooking." Rio filled his mouth with noodles. "Speaking of parents…do you think your papa is here?"

Violet's eyes widened. "Good question."

Anaya shrugged. "I dunno."

"What's his name?"

"Rich Whule."

"We will have to get a look at a Tracker Screen to make sure," Violet said. "I know there is probably one in the fortress. The Vanisher's floor, most likely. But…"

"You can't go back." Rio pointed a fork in her direction. "Because they'll know. Jack knows. Even if he is on our side, they will know."

"I didn't even find the portal." Violet pouted.

"So your job at the fortress was useless," Anaya blurted.

Violet scowled. "I know the grounds, schedules, and good times to take action. It means that when the time is right and we have access to both the Iris and Reed, you will also need to sneak in. The portal is definitely in the fortress, guarded by all of Cyran's cronies."

"We will need a distraction for *him*," Rio said. "If we go to the seventh world, every alarm will go off and he'll kill us before we even figure out how to battle the Sin. The most a candidate has ever survived is six minutes in the seventh world. It takes six minutes to even have a conversation with the Sin. We need at least an hour, and we need to nominate a person who is an easy target for Pride."

Violet met her friends' stares, because if there was one extremely prideful person they all knew, he currently wasn't included in their escape. Violet put her fork down, her mouth sour and her appetite gone.

"Can you…" Anaya sighed. "Can *we* talk to him?"

"No," Violet muttered.

"I don't feel good leaving him behind—"

"*No*," Violet said again. "We can't risk it."

"But, Vi—"

"Fine." Violet pointed in the direction of the fortress. "Go talk to him. Walk right up to those heavily guarded ships and request transport to Jack. I'm sure they'll set you up in the tearoom while you wait for the *esteemed* captain. You can take a look at his tattoos while you watch him battle on the training ground with Zavar. Or better yet, why don't you pose as a servant and seduce him like the rest want to do—"

Rio put a hand over Violet's shaking one. "We will figure it out. First, we need to know where the portal is. Maybe Jodin can tell us."

"Maybe if we put a knife to his brother…" Anaya started.

Rio groaned. "Skies, he will actually kill us."

Violet snorted. "Yarrow is the best collateral."

When Rio opened his mouth to protest, a scream tore through the air. All three of them jumped and rushed to the ledge of the rooftop.

They were only three floors above the crushed street markets and a crowded square that a main road cut through. A mill of colored, rusty cars and a cruising white van languidly moved along the painted pavement, all amid more motorbikes. Rio pointed to a circular group of red-caped individuals, one of who was in the middle. Screaming.

Chanting.

"Behold Avaritia! Behold our god, our savior!"

"What the…" Anaya began.

Violet rolled her eyes. "They do this like once a week. Just some absurd call for their religion, and it's really damn annoying…" Violet nodded to the guy in the middle. "They made me stop and kneel after I was done selling for the night. They have cut fingers of those who have refused. Or had the shit beaten out of—"

Violet's Pharos pager rang. Her heart palpitated for a moment. She frantically dug in her bag, tossing random items before grabbing the tiny black metal box.

It had only rung two times before. Violet wasn't at the top of Bryce's on-call list, as the only other times were helping to escort rescued girls *after* a successful mission. The most recent one was last week, where Violet showed up as Tamu and Emryn, covered in blood from hounds guarding young girls from Lust, passed out blankets and instructed Violet to get them to drink water. They had been holed up in a worship center in North Hanhii for at least two weeks, based on Tamu's recon.

Violet will never forget the blank, hopeless stares of the girls as they headed to safety. They'd given up. Given in to a world that wanted to use them. One had fought back, and Violet couldn't stop her eyes from glancing at the girl's long, mottled wounds along her arms.

"Fuck," she breathed, staring at the words. Not even from Bryce, but from another mission commander.

Snatchers on the move. Closet soldier; V.

V. Violet.

Look down.

"Holy skies," Rio whispered, staring at the street below. "It's a distraction."

Another page. *Stop that van. Reinforcements are on their way.*

Violet's eyes flicked up from the pager. She searched the road below until she found the white van. It idled slowly, shifting lanes closer to a sidewalk.

The crowd grew more disordered and lawless. Most fell to their knees and gave their repent prayers, while others yelled back. Screamed. Threw rocks and other items at the preachers. Guards who surrounded the preachers also hounded the oppressors, creating fights. Violet's gaze darted back to the van. It braked at the edge of a square where a group of young, teenage girls looked wary with drinks in their hands.

The van door rolled open.

Three large individuals jumped out.

Each one snatched a girl, clamping a hand over their mouth.

Within a blink, the girls disappeared, and the van door shut. It tore off down the street.

One girl, the one who fell to her knees, turned to wave at her friends, but when she glimpsed the empty spot filled with drink splatters and broken cups, she paled. Stood. Looked from the screaming cult to the empty spot again.

She twisted every which way, searching for her friends, but the van was already prowling along the street. A confused shriek tore from her.

A beat of silence passed over Violet, Anaya, and Rio.

They shared a glance.

"Stay here," Violet ordered as she stood and dug through her bag. She slapped on her weapons, then her gloves, and turned toward the rooftop's ledge. "This should be quick—"

"Shut the fuck up, Violet, we're coming." Anaya rolled her shoulders and followed suit. "I need to stretch my legs, anyway. Been cramped on a boat for too long."

"You know I hate missing out on things," Rio said. "That van won't stop until it reaches its destination. We need another car. I'll hijack one and tail behind."

Violet didn't even bother arguing. Relief flooded through her chest, minty and fresh, and she nodded. "See you in a bit."

Rio flung himself over the ledge and onto a fire escape.

Anaya smiled darkly at the city and handed Violet a plasblade hilt. "We are going to be the worst sinners they've ever met. See you at the end."

"Don't fall behind," Violet said, stepping back.

"Wouldn't dream of it."

Violet bounded for the rooftop edge and jumped. She soared over to the next, not missing a beat as she hauled herself over another ledge and ran.

Ran like she'd done her entire life in Calesal.

When her fingers met brick, she was a child again, barefoot and wild, and the city was her playground. Most of the rooftops here were cloistered together, so it was more up and downs or scaling connecting fire escapes, but some required jumps, and those were always the most fun. She tucked and rolled as she did when a Redder chased her for stealing gum and smokes for Meema. The broken bits of stone and brick pushed her more, and it was around five when she learned to ignore the bloodied fingertips and bruised knuckles. She was a climber, a runner, and a smile pulled at her face.

This is her.

This is Violet Sutton.

And she wanted some fucking vengeance. After the girl begged in that church, after Jack was manipulated to the wrong side, after these strange powers manifested and she couldn't get some damn *peace.*

Anaya kept up with her as they scaled the roofs along the main road. The white van gleamed in the distance, slightly idle in traffic and stuck in a plethora of cars. It reached an intersection.

"It's making a left!" Violet called.

"Rio's got a car! Red, orange stripe on top."

"Got it."

They turned at the intersection and vaulted between the gap in the buildings. The next building was two stories taller than the other.

Violet whined, "Looks like we have to go in."

"Fine."

Violet jumped to the next wall, catching the iron of a grated windowsill. She swiped the fluttering curtain. Her boots met creaky wood. An old woman in a squishy chair gasped. Anaya cackled, following behind. "Nice slippers."

The woman glanced down at her duck slippers and merely gaped.

They ran through the apartment and exited to the hallway. Violet whipped open the stairwell door. Their boots slapped the metal. They climbed. Shoved open the rooftop door.

Violet rushed toward the edge of this rooftop. Glanced at the street. The white van was a block away.

"On top?" she asked.

Anaya twirled the plasblade hilt. "Of course."

Violet's heart thrashed in her ears, a smile teasing at her lips. She couldn't be stopped. She was winning. She hauled her rear onto the ledge, took a deep breath, and jumped, landing on the rickety fire escape below—

And fell straight through it.

The rusty iron fractured beneath her weight. The rest of the platforms and ladders were in ruins, and she crashed through the next. Then the next. A bar smacked her knee. She hissed, twisted herself—

"*Violet!*" Anaya cried from above.

Violet gritted her teeth and released the plasblade, igniting it into a purple color. She had half a mind to tell Meretta how much she loved this blade, once all this was over. Maybe beg to keep it. She jabbed it into the wall of the building and the plasma burned straight through. Sunk deep. It shredded brick, and when she reached two stories above a jam-packed bar, she removed the heated energy and left just the steel. She gripped the hilt with all her might. Her shoulders screamed as she jolted to a halt. Her glamour strings snapped and she lost hold of them. Her blonde hair gusted in the wind, and a blink later, sloshed into her typical brown. Her nose heated and then snapped its bump away. She cursed, fumbling for the strings, but they slipped through the cracks of her mind, and Violet was left hanging above the rowdy bar.

"Are you okay?" Anaya cried from the rooftop above.

"Yeah!" Violet called back.

"Okay, I'm going to find another way down!"

"Okay!"

Violet rested the tips of her boots on a windowsill, and after a few harsh pulls, she yanked the plasblade out, flew backward, rolled onto a tarp cover above tables filled with bar patrons, and stuck the landing.

Her head whipped up. Her brown hair stuck to the sweat along her temples. Fire simmered in her now-blue eyes. The corners of her mouth pulled.

A harsh wave of language met her ears. People cried. Pointed at her.

"Did she just fall from the sky?" someone cried.

"Like a damn angel," Violet huffed, scattering her hair from her face. She took off down the street.

A honking horn caught her attention. Rio waved his hand out of the broken window. "Vi! Four cars up! Pile the girls in here!"

Violet charged toward him. Slashed the blade to stop oncoming traffic in the six-lane congested street, and to Rio's bewildered expression, she bounded to the roof of the car. A loud bang erupted. One look showed Anaya on top of a car, stomping at the flailing hand of the driver. "I'm saving kids, you dumbass."

Violet spotted the van. As a gust of wind whipped through the Navru street of madness, and her vision zeroed in on her target. Rage honed her muscles. An undying vehemence that tightened her grip on the plasblade. She ignited it, and the purple burned like a beacon in the maelstrom.

She didn't want to think, didn't want to plan anymore, didn't care about hiding herself. She wanted to be seen for the disruptive, annoying, rogue Souther she was. She wanted Cyran to know that she wasn't going down without a fight. If she was some small mistake in his damn game, she'd be a *nightmare* of one.

Violet volleyed off Rio's car and onto the rusty metal of another. Anaya followed right behind her. The plasma heat of her blade sizzled her skin. Urged her on.

"I'll take the top! You get the kids!" Anaya called as they hopped to another car, closing in on the van.

"They'll shoot at you."

A loud cackle. "If they can *see* me."

Anaya shimmered into her surroundings. Her shadow vanished. Indents marked her parade, and a large thump noted that she was atop the van. Violet hopped onto another car next to the van's side door as the traffic loosened and sped up. The door slid open. She smiled at the black-covered head poking out. "Can I ask you about your ugly car's extended—"

The masked figure growled, and her saccharine smirk grew.

She swung her plasblade in an arc, and the head of the kidnapper separated from his body. It bounced into the street, immediately lost in the chaos. People scream, gasped.

Gunshots rang from inside the van's cabin. One grazed her forehead, her shoulder, but she slid to the driver's side of the car she was on. Her feet met the driver's open window. She crouched as the bullets rang. The driver ducked and pressed the brakes—

She waved her plasblade. "Keep going!"

The driver—a frightened man—paled but pressed the accelerator again.

A slam on the van's hood. Anaya's bright orange plasblade flashed, then it lacerated the windshield. The van's driver ducked, pulling a gun from the front seat as his comrade's shoulder was severed. The bullets stopped. Violet bounded up on the car, and when another kidnapper tried to slam the sliding door, she wedged the plasblade within.

And then the kidnapper's forearm hardened. Harmas hardened.

Violet's driver sped away. Her blade ricocheted off the Harmas metal. She cried out, falling—

An invisible arm grabbed her. Rippled. Anaya morphed back into being, and with a grunt, hauled Violet atop the van.

"Duck!" Anaya cried, dragging Violet to the front hood. Violet took a moment to look up as a wall of brick nearly knocked her off the roof. A tunnel enveloped them, and Violet's ears filled with loud, whooshing wind. She covered her watering eyes with her forearm. Anaya clung to her arm. They moved underneath the river, heading for Hallow.

The kidnapper driver gunned it, his comrade slumped dead next to him. He screamed a harsh language into a radio and pulled out his small pistol. It was an archaic thing compared to the sleek, new tech of a plasgun. Anaya burst up, jabbed her plasblade through the wrecked windshield, into the driver's gut, and twisted. "You deserve worse."

Violet bolted for the windshield opening as the dead driver

slumped forward, laying on the horn. The van accelerated. The tunnel lightened from the exit opening. Violet ignored the scrapes of glass on her arms as she rolled onto the seat, shoved the dead driver to the side, and slammed on the brakes. They burst through the tunnel at a terrifying speed. Violet maintained control of the van as she swerved into a parking lot, and they screeched to a halt.

"Fuck—"

The door at the center console burst open, and a hand with a gun appeared. She ducked just as it fired, blasting the side window open. She aimed to kick up—

But her driver door opened, and Rio was there, plasblade in hand. He swiped it straight through the gunman's arm.

Violet dropped into Rio's arms. She recovered quickly, feet now on the gravelly parking lot pavement, as Anaya crashed through the windshield with a battle cry, jabbed her sword in that kidnapper, then disappeared into the body of the van to take on the other. One more gurgled bellow, then all went silent.

Rio flung open the van's back door, and four young girls, along with three other smaller children, huddled in the corner with bags over their heads. Blood from the dead kidnappers, one succumbing to his injury from Violet's amputation, pooled and soaked the girls' knees. Anaya stood in the middle, sneering at the headless one. "Nice work, Vi."

"Thank you," Violet said.

"At least they didn't see it," Rio said. His voice grew higher as he addressed the kids. "Hey, guys, we are here to save you. We're going to take you back home."

A muffled answer came back from one. Their mouths taped.

Violet pocketed her plasblade. "We need to hurry, guys."

The girls were trembling, but as Violet gently grasped the hand of one and let them feel her fingers, hear her shushing voice, the one nudged a friend, and they stepped out. Violet made sure they each exited the van before Rio shut the doors softly. They pulled off the hoods and tape, and one by one, piled them into Rio's stolen car.

Rio got into the driver's seat and started the ignition.

"Okay." Violet sighed and wiped the sweat from her forehead. "My one good deed for the day. I want to go back to our noodles and—"

A giant black car screeched into the parking lot. Halted. The doors flung open, and high-tech plasweapons flashed.

"*Rio!*" Violet shouted.

Armed men piled out of the car, the blazing sigil of Avaritia on the chest. They hoisted their sleek plasguns, pointed them at Anaya, and fired.

Anaya collapsed, bleeding. Violet jolted, a scream lodged in her throat. She panicked, then threw herself behind the discarded van. Rio cried their names. The girls shrieked, and the sound of screaming tires and fracturing metal filled the parking lot. Violet fell to the pavement as more bullets rained down, her eyes finding Anaya's body, motionless, across the way. Blood pooled from her belly.

"Anaya!" Violet screeched. Her fingertips gripped the concrete. She crawled underneath the van. Rio yelled again, but the tires of his car moved, and he skidded onto the street, the horrified shouts of girls being sucked away by the distance. Violet ripped her purple plasblade from the hilt and held it in her sweaty palms.

The shots stopped.

"Come out, girl! You might be spared if your body is good enough," one of the guards said. Four pairs of thick black boots kicked at the ground. Two muffled cries. Girls. Two girls snatched from Rio's car.

"Anaya," Violet muttered. The Endolier's body wasn't moving. Pain poured into Violet's chest, gripping her. Her breaths were short. Another van pulled up, and Violet's hope disintegrated at the Avaritia symbol.

More guards poured out. Violet gripped her plasblade tightly. Where were the reinforcements from Pharos? Her eyes locked on Anaya, panic flaring at the growing puddle of blood.

"Guess we will do this the hard way," a hoarse voice grumbled.

A hand wrapped around her ankle and Violet was yanked out

from underneath the van. She whipped her body around, facing the bright, cloudless sky, and the silhouette of the hulking masked man above her. A plasgun was shoved into her neck while he pressed his boot onto her wrist, harder and harder, until she blew a breath between her teeth and released the plasblade.

"Not too bad looking." The man cocked his head. Four more guards circled around the van, guns aimed at her. Violet's eyes watered as the one gun pressed farther into her throat, choking her. "Little older than what they want, but your service will make up for our loss."

"Service," Violet scoffed. "Do they make you capture the girls because your dick is too small for the rape rooms—"

The barrel of the gun smacked across her face. Her jaw cracked. Pain exploded behind her eyes, and blood filled her mouth.

"Filthy fucking bitch," the guard said. "You'd be better off in the ground than pleasing our blessed leaders."

She could hardly see when he leaned forward and grabbed her jaw, squeezing so hard Violet thought he was about to rip it right off. Still, when he drew closer to her face, rancid breath antagonizing her pain, she spat a mouthful of spit and blood into his brown eyes.

"I may not have a place in your world," Violet gritted. "But if I'm going to the next one, you're coming with me, skiv."

She swung her leg up, knocking him in the nether regions, then twisted her body into his ankles so he collapsed. The other guards moved quickly, clicks releasing from their guns and shots firing. Violet pulled at every muscle to haul the fallen guard up and use him as her shield. The bullets piled into his back, plasma heat stinging her cheeks and palms, but Violet squeezed her eyes shut and held on.

"Abomination! Abomination!" the other guards cried.

A spark of that slumbering power reared up, hissing, wanting out. Her hands trembled, and a hot, searing pain slid along her arms. They flickered with soft light. Her eyes flashed into the Vanisher realm. Ribbons of other worlds surrounded her. She desperately wanted to pull on one, and her gut, her soul, screamed at her to do so. As if this was the only way to escape this fate, to protect herself and what lay inside of her. But the silver of the Vanisher realm flashed into purple, and a different ability grew, pushing at her chest. The tethers disappeared, and instead, some higher eye opened, and she...she...

She looked down. Like a god. It was the world she stood in. The world of Greed. She saw her mortal body covered by the guard. A string connected. A blink; she glared at the guard's hairy chest. Another blink; she stared down at the chaos and creation. The totaled van, Anaya's unmoving body, the swarming Avaritia guards...

She didn't understand it all, and at this moment she didn't care to. *Another* realm appeared before her, one of purple and a thousand possibilities. Her hands warmed. She...she could...

Bend it.

Break it.

Manipulate it.

She roared up, her vision a blast of purple. She threw the guard off her with ease and, covered in that glowing light, stomped from her higher, world-bending eye. Bullets went through her body, not touching her. That brilliant light. She hated it. Hated the hurt and the misery. She stomped and stomped and stomped. The van flattened. The guards were thrown. The pavement soiled. She wanted to fracture this world with her bare hands, and she knew the god-like part of her could.

The other side of her—the physical, earthly one—jolted violently. Muffled cries reached her ears.

"Fall back! Vanisher! Oh, blessed, another—"

A crack of light signaled an arrival. A car screeched into the lot and smaller, more lithe figures rolled out, guns blazing. Pharos.

She hung onto the different realm—the manipulating realm— her rage not burnt out. She saw each and every man who had their hands on girls, stealing them, using them, taking every breath of freedom, and she watched them like a god.

Stomped.

Over and over.

They crumpled like flies.

"Come back, little one."

A strange voice to hear in this place. It called to her like an echo from dark depths, something otherworldly. She looked up in her realm and found Jodin standing before her, hands in the pockets of his long coat.

"You did your damage." He glared at the landscape of a ruined parking lot scattered with dead bodies. "Come back."

Violet shook her head. "They called me an abomination."

Abomination. Abomination.

Mistake. Mistake.

Jodin looked sullen. "Aren't we all?"

Tears poured from Violet's eyes. She glanced at her glowing hands. Same as Jodin's. His was filled with the same purple. Their words clanged around her skull, and a sob escaped her lips. Jodin watched. Didn't move.

"Find something good, little Duo, and let it bring you back."

She thought of Meema. Remembered how the woman would scour the parks near school when Violet had fled midday. That was the beginning, when Meema entered their little life. The principal would call Violet's mother, who was terrified of the phone and nearly any stranger. So Meema started showing up. Violet would stiffen when that metal gate creaked. That familiar, annoyed huff would make her jump.

"Now why is this school calling me about you running away?" *Meema tsked. Violet didn't dare lift her head. She knew her neighbor was scary with how many times she told Reed off.*

Violet mumbled nonsense.

"Speak up, girl."

"I got a bad grade on my test."

Meema crossed her arms. "Stand up."

Violet obeyed, chin still tucked to her chest. Her eyes caught Meema's red-painted nails, the worn metal rings adorning each finger.

One nudged Violet's chin. "Look me in the eye and tell me why you left school. Not the thing that started it."

"Because…" Violet swallowed. Her eight-year-old hand was small as she rubbed at her eyes. "Because I stole the tests."

Meema folded her arms and gave Violet a stern look.

She continued, "And lit them on fire at recess."

Meema sighed deeply. "Little wildflower…"

Violet pouted. "I think it's stupid that I have to study when…" She sniffled. "When my mama is…"

"When your mama is what?"

"She screams at night now." There was a wobble in Violet's voice, and she bit her lip to stop it. "She…has bad nightmares. Talks to the walls. Says things…"

"What kinds of things?"

But Violet refused, transferring her teeth from lip to tongue.

"I need to have something to tell the school—"

"No," Violet snapped, finally meeting Meema's dark eyes. "You can't tell anyone. Reed said so—"

"Your brother knows?"

"He says mama is just sick, but I hear her, I hear what she says. She talks about him—our father. Laughs and has conversations, but no one is there." Violet shook her head. "You can't tell anyone."

Meema poked at Violet's collarbone. "When was the last time you ate?"

"Reed tries…"

"Shit on the skies," Meema blurted. "Does your mama not feed you?"

"Reed gets stuff."

"Reed is eleven." Meema ran a hand through her short black hair. "You're coming home with me, got it? We'll get some food in you both. You need a proper meal. But I need to know what your mama said."

Violet took a jittery inhale, relenting. "She just keeps saying that she's going to die. She thinks someone is going to kill her. She says they'll come for her, and then they will find me and know that she made a…a mistake."

Soft hands wrapped around Violet's upper arm. "Come. We are going to apologize to the school and your teacher, and then get some ice cream. Okay? You'll have dinner with me every night, got it?"

"Okay."

"I'll have a talk with your mama."

"Okay."

"What kind of ice cream do you like?"

"Mint chocolate chip."

At this moment, Violet remembered that mint chocolate chip ice cream was the best thing she'd ever had, next to the other minty chocolates the random man gave her. She treasured those moments, even though Meema chain-smoked and catcalled men while Violet happily became a creamy mess next to her. She didn't feel like a mistake then. She felt whole, if not a little loved.

Jodin analyzed her with a strong gaze. He appeared weathered, perhaps a bit sad at the sight of her. As if he had seen it before and had witnessed too much of the chaotic, alternate outcome if she hadn't calmed herself.

"Let's go somewhere safe."

"Anaya," Violet breathed. "Is she—"

"Alive. Endoliers aren't as fragile as humans." He glanced from their godly eye and Violet followed, watching as her own body remained standing, glowing, untouchable. Her gaze shifted to the Pharos members rushing Anaya, and the two remaining girls, into their van, slamming it shut. Jodin's glowing body stood next to hers. He reached a hand. "Now, let's go. Zavar will be coming."

Violet hesitated, but at Jodin's impatience, she grabbed it.

He whisked them both away.

The minute they landed, she collapsed to the floor. He dug through a pocket, pulling out a vial of red blood. He tossed it to her. "Drink this."

She caught it. "What is—"

"Just drink it."

She reluctantly did, and the minute the red liquid touched her lips, she nearly spat it back out. Jodin teleported in front of her and slammed the vial between her lips. "That's wasteful."

She chugged the entire thing and shoved him away. "That's *blood*."

"It's blood that will heal you."

Her eyes bugged. A cold, agonizing pain washed down her spine. She whirled around the tiny, wooden room with a couch, a fridge, and plascreen. Violet touched her throat and stepped away until her back hit the wall. "Please, no—"

"He's not here. And yes, he knows. About everything. I do like him more than you." Jodin gave her a long, judgy look and waltzed to the mini-fridge. He opened it. Tapped his chin. Pulled out a bottle of bubbly and shut the door with his foot. "Yarrow is doing better if you care."

Her nerves didn't calm, even though Jodin seemed sincere about Jack not popping out of nowhere. She rubbed at her jaw, which should have definitely been broken after that gun hit, but it was merely sore, tender to touch.

Jodin opened a candy bag and popped one in his mouth. "Your Vanisher and…" He looked puzzled, and Violet thought she imagined the slight flash of fear in his eyes. "Your powers help you heal if you use them after injury. His blood will add to that, too. But his blood…" He shook his head, as if the words on his tongue were hard for him to comprehend. "Is different, too. Skies, it's just getting more complicated."

"How did you know…"

"You want time, the organization wants time, and I needed some entertainment." He plopped himself on the couch. "They pinged me."

"You work…?" Violet's jaw slacked open. "Really?"

"I need more cayna and I don't want to go through your shit to get it, so I went to the source." He patted the couch. "Have a seat."

"But the…oh skies, Zavar is going to be after me—"

Jodin threw candy at her. "Relax, Jack is taking care of it."

That name sent a cold shiver through her again. Sweat beaded her brow. She eyed the lone door. "I'm going to leave."

"That is precisely the reason why I'm lingering." He popped open the champagne. Smiled as the cork hit the far wall. He pressed a button on a remote, turning the plascreen on. He flipped through the channels, some in her home language, and others in the native. "Oh—I like this one."

Violet's anger dissipated. Slightly. Just slightly. Her eyes bugged and her brows creased in confusion. Two females were yelling at each other, and one threw a glass of liquid in the other's face. They started fighting with their nails.

"Is this a battle?" Violet asked.

Jodin rolled his eyes. "It is reality television. Not everyone is at war like us."

"Do they get weapons?" Violet walked behind the couch, watching closely. "She could smash her glass and find the biggest slice and stab the other in the eye. Or just go straight for the throat, that would be the quick kill—"

"Were you always this perky?"

She shut her mouth.

"They're fighting because one of their partners was caught cheating with the other. I have been meaning to watch the latest episode. In the last one, one's husband got pushed into the pool."

Violet shimmied around the couch and took a seat on the other side, curling against the armrest. She stared at the screen, entranced, as the women were separated by some random men while they screamed profanities at each other.

"Get this…they were *best friends*." Jodin sipped the bubbly alcohol straight from the bottle, then held it out for Violet.

She took the bottle. "Really? How did it get this bad?"

"Well, fucking her friend's husband for starters."

She was intrigued. She downed a large sip of the bubbly, and Jodin tossed her a bag of candy.

By the time Violet relaxed, hours had passed and Jodin's watch beeped, waking her just as she was falling asleep. He sighed and stood.

"Where are you going?" she asked. "Are you supposed to vanish drunk?"

Jodin snorted. "I received my Vanisher license on the first try."

"There's a license?"

"No."

She scowled.

"I'm curious," Jodin said. "You don't seem inclined to know more about *this*." He activated his abilities. Two glowing slits beneath his eyes, and lines twisting up his hands. "You've been Awakened, and you're wanted *because* you're one of us, yet you don't seem to care about it at all. The powers certainly come in handy when your basic humanness won't save you, but otherwise, you despise it. It is all over your face. People would kill countries, worlds—they *have* killed countries and worlds just to acquire this ability. And yet…you sit with it slumbering."

Violet averted her gaze. She didn't have an answer to why she didn't bother learning or even care about this ability. The others used it so freely—even her brother could do it. But her? She didn't know… "Why can't *he* control me?"

He shrugged. "You're not the first. But you're certainly rare and extremely annoying for the Master."

"That doesn't answer my question."

Jodin lingered. Sighed. His watch beeped again, and he hesitated before saying, "Control comes from your blood. The only ones who can't be controlled are the ones who never signed it over to him."

"You mean bloodswore it?"

"Yes, but you did that."

"Yes."

"I wouldn't spend so much time pondering over it, as you're still likely to die at some point during this war. It would just mean you might be related to him." Jodin's gaze didn't meet hers, and Violet took note of it. She didn't sense a lie, but she did sense that the full truth wasn't there.

"Related to him?" A shiver slid down her back. "How?"

"That's the universal question," Jodin said. "How can a little shit like you be related to an immortal man who, for all I know, can't reproduce?"

"Can't reproduce?"

"It's not common knowledge, but I assumed he couldn't. His heirs would be the most powerful things in the universe. But he never had one." He popped another candy in his mouth. "I'm extremely sure he can't physically have one. He's not human."

"What is he?"

He smirked. "A god."

Jodin dug underneath the couch and produced a bag. He threw it at her. "Your next mission. Big one. Get dressed. Another Vanisher will be back and will take you to the location. Keep your powers under wraps—basically, what I'm saying is, don't get too emotional. Might be difficult for you."

"What…already?" Violet protested.

Jodin motioned to the room. "You got your break. It's easy. Serving drinks and getting information. You want to save that school? This is how you do it."

And with that, he vanished.

24

FOUNDER'S NIGHT

ATTACKED DURING A MISSION. SHE is fine. Updates on the way. Will continue as planned.

Jack's jaw clenched. *Fine.* How fine was *fine*? He wanted to have some concern flow through him, but all that was left was pent-up energy. He both wanted to wring her neck and kiss her, wanted to destroy this whole city and save it from hurting her.

Wanted to hate some part of her for consuming his thoughts. It fogged his mind. He needed to release this energy, and there was only one true way he could go back to his calm, stoic nature.

By snapping a few necks.

He let the nice woman with warm fingers finish tousling his hair. She hummed to herself—one of the many church hymns he studied. Her fingers lingered on the back of his neck a lot, also brushing his collarbone a couple of times. His eyes flicked to find hers already staring back at him in the mirror. Her humming stopped and she looked away, a blush rising to her cheeks.

"Do you ever...participate?"

She bristled at his question. They were the only two in this small powder room. It was meant for the higher-ups of the Order, used to prepare themselves for various festivities.

Her eyes flicked to the closed door, then back to him. "Participate?"

"In the fucking."

Shock plastered across her face. Her fingers stopped messing with his hair. "I—I don't know—"

"I'm simply curious. It's my first time. How many partners is one expected to have?"

She swallowed. Another glance at the door. She shook her head. "Can you be one of them?"

Jack knew he was out of line for pulling on his charm, but it was too easy. He felt too volatile—ready to explode, and he needed to poke things to release the tension. He liked her reaction; she stiffened like an animal seconds from losing its life. Her aroma enhanced…fear, lust, anticipation. Fear lingered longest, though, and Jack cursed himself for even saying such a thing.

In this establishment, this woman wouldn't have a positive idea of sex. She'd think…he'd *force* her. Jack let her fumble for an answer, waiting to see if she could salvage this, and to his surprise, she did.

"I—I've seen them have a lot. Maybe fourteen was the most in one night. And I…" She gave him another look and bit her lip before continuing, "If you wanted—"

"To be fairly honest, you are beautiful, but I'm just kidding." He offered her a dimpled smile and she relaxed. "I didn't mean to unnerve you."

"It doesn't matter what I want," she said. "I'm here to make you comfortable."

He finally turned to look at her without the mirror. "You know what will make me comfortable?"

"What?"

"Stay in this room. Don't come out. No matter what you hear." He brought her warm hand to his lips and kissed it. "Because perhaps I might find you later, and I would hate to see you gone."

It is for her own good. But he hated every word coming out of his mouth.

She aimlessly nodded. "Okay."

He offered another smile, stood, and walked over to the door. "See you later."

"Yeah."

Once the door was shut behind him, he shook off that one act and put on another. A Vanisher by the name of Vernon exited his powder room and caught his eye. A bright, crooked smile split his face and he sidled up to Jack, black hair pushed behind his ears, and two hickeys marking his neck.

"I've only participated in one of these because it is extremely difficult to get into. Thank you, *thank you*, Jack, for getting me in."

Jack wanted to wring the man's neck for thinking they were on a first-name basis, but he merely slapped Vernon on the shoulder. "I see you already started."

"Gods, her whimpers. It's more fun when you *take* it."

At that, Jack's smile grew. "Of course. Taking things is the precipice of Avaritia. He wants more, so we want more."

Vernon nudged Jack. "And you know what more I want."

"Lead the way, *buddy*."

Jack stared at Vernon's partially balding head down the red-carpeted hallway that was lit by fire, smelled like incense and vanilla, and lined with at least a hundred doors that slowly opened. Order members and other Vanishers Jack specifically invited clambered out, some having already indulged like Vernon, others merely waiting to start in the main room.

They were deep underground in the Church District. It took quite a bit of sweet talking and Aurien bites to persuade those in charge to give invitations to him and his 'friends' to the elusive Founder's Night—a celebration of high-ranking men in the Order with booze, drugs, cigars, and...to quote, "Freshly caught females. Desired ages can be arranged."

It was different from the captain's party called Fire Night, one Jack was looking forward to more than this aggravating space filled with suffocating cologne.

Jack became one of many filing into a line and walking down the hall. A gong sounded. As they moved, everyone pulled out a unique mask that fitted the upper half of their face. Jack's was simple black lace—he didn't get the memo until the day before.

He tied it behind his head as his eyes found three more Vanishers he had personally invited.

Good, they showed up.

It was difficult determining the Vanishers' identities at first, but some persuasion, and again, Aurien bites, helped him figure out the culprits. It was their hands that grabbed Inaj, Endoliers, Auriens, Quinams, Droans, Lovuphals, and much more from the other worlds to subsequently turn them over to the Order. Their hands that were greedy for the money after the trades.

There was a growing pep in his step. Jack was, by all means, *extremely* excited for this revelry.

Only one person knew he was here, and that one person was bound by a bloodbond to never tell where Jack had been, what he had been doing, and any of the horrid aftermath they would surely see. Jonathon didn't really deserve to be involved in this, but Jack needed a mode of transport, and Reed was still out of commission.

The hallway ended at a cavernous room. Two tiers of balconies looked down on red. Red couches, red carpets, and red drapes leading to private areas. They each took a spot as four preachers walked out, and the Order Chancellor made his unusual appearance. Jack folded his hands behind his back as he studied the man.

The hands of the Order have been passed down within an elite group of white males for centuries. They ruled. On the outside, they preached mercy and praise, wanting to gather more and more for their religion to benefit from the control that the Order demanded.

"Welcome, fellow trustees, to the annual Founder's Night for our elite members!" Chancellor Oren raised his arms, robes loose around his portly body. Jack guessed he was about two heads taller than the man.

A round of applause erupted from the crowd. Some nudged their friends, others shook out their limbs.

"We praise Avaritia for blessing us every day. The sacrifices made in His name honor those who pray to Him, and you have proven your loyalty tremendously. You are here because you deserve rewards, and Avaritia has prepared this one just for you."

Vernon turned to Jack, whispering, "I snatched a couple nice-looking ones from Gluttony a while ago. They have the best bodies. I was a bit…selfish in my choices." The smile reached his eyes behind the gold mask.

Jack smirked. "I'm sure you chose well."

"Even got some Crale, too. They're a little easier to nab. All sad about losing their land and whatnot."

Wasn't their land to begin with, Jack thought. A cold, disgusting shiver passed over him as memories returned—things he tried to bury and forget, telling himself over and over that it was for his survival. He'd seduced one Crale; the princess of the Stradinths. He'd done it out of desperation, but she'd…

His jaw clenched. She'd taken advantage of it. Of him. Touched him when he'd been tortured for information, when he'd seen the working fields of Inaj slaves, or when he was asleep. She made him service her while whispering sweet mumblings of what would happen to him if he didn't. He found himself vomiting after most incidences.

"Let us say a prayer to our beloved God," the Chancellor called. "For giving us the patriarchal power and the obedience of the lesser species meant to bow to us and serve us!"

A cheer was followed by a long-winded, monotone prayer. Jack moved his mouth aimlessly with a slight hum, not knowing the words. Vernon had his head bowed, hands clasped, saying each word with revere.

Hands that snatched. Hands that took. Hands that still wanted more.

Jack sighed. At least the stains left by their blood will match the decorations.

The prayer finished. In the main room below, the Chancellor gave a hand signal, and each of the Order guards lining the walls turned toward pitch-black doors. They twisted the gold knobs and stepped away from the doorjambs. Girls began to file in, heads bowed low in submission, led by older women who had whips wrapped around their forearms. The rows of females were endless, but eventually, the parade of chiffon red robes, hoods covering their heads, finished, and each guard retreated inside the doors, locking them.

The hallway behind Jack shut. Locked.

No one was able to get in. And with Jack, no one will be able to get out.

He watched with a bored expression as the girls followed their leaders and assigned themselves to different positions. Jack noticed the rigidness in their shoulders and the slumped steps of their bare feet. They were sedated, as Jack expected. A few peeked through their hoods, and faces of all colors peered up at the balconies. Jack tried to control the jolt of revulsion coursing beneath his skin. It made him want to lash out. *Wait. Wait*, the calm killer said inside. *The time is not right.*

He instead imagined himself in their shoes. Or bare soles. Unsure of where they were, worlds away from home without the prospect of ever returning, lied to and manipulated and drugged into submission in a foreign world, expected to adhere to a religion they didn't believe in. One that took and loved control. These girls stared up at their predators, slowly becoming more aware that in this room, their lives were reduced to that of skin and bones and holes. They were an object for these men to drool over, a pretty present to be used and abused.

That was how the Order thought of others different from them. *Others* weren't allowed. It was one religion, one belief, and that was it. Everything else was an abomination beneath them.

"Come, my brothers, and indulge in your reward." The Chancellor gestured to the long staircases, and one by one, each man drifted down. Jack's pulse ticked harder in his neck.

He slung an arm over Vernon and dipped his mouth. "Gather the other Vanishers. I thought we could indulge together as one of His Master's humble servants. We deserve it, you know."

Vernon nodded enthusiastically. "Gods, we get the Founder's and Fire Night? I'm going to go crazy."

Fire Night. Jack masked his excitement. Yes, he was *very* excited for Fire Night, too.

Vernon went to each of the other six Vanishers and assembled them into a red-draped area that consisted of plush cushions already occupied by a couple of girls. By the time the curtains shut behind Jack, music began to pour from speakers above. The lights flicked off, save for the glinting sconces of real fire. Jack counted them all.

"Look at you." Vernon brushed the hood of one girl back. The black-and-silver-dusted skin of an Aurien gleamed in the light, her lips puckered and eyes glassy. The girl didn't look consciously there. Jack clenched his fists and realized the other Vanishers had turned to look at him. He'd been standing stiffly for too long.

The girl might have only been thirteen, maybe fourteen. Barely at the age of puberty, if that. Bile cloyed in Jack's throat. He wanted to act *now*, but he needed to wait. Everyone was still aware. The drinks were just being passed out. They were unwrapping their presents.

Vernon took a shot with the other Vanishers and offered one to Jack. "It helps you relax."

Jack refused it. The girls were so still. Skies, what were they drugged with? Through the sheer curtains, Jack glimpsed their woman leaders prowling the floor, whips still clinging to their forearms. One girl in their room eyed them, too, more aware than the others, and when Jack caught her gaze, he nearly gasped in utter surprise.

His mask was on, so she shouldn't completely recognize him, but she still stared a little too long.

Navee.

His lips fell open and he quickly shut them. The fiery Inaj who served the Stradinths and ultimately blew the mines on the mountain in Gluttony, burying the Farm in its debris. How? This girl was not meant for this room, nor this world. She was too fierce to be caught by a Vanisher like Vernon—

Vernon saw her. Recognized her. "You."

Navee's light-green skin still betrayed her young age for an Inaj. Fifteen, at least. While the other girls looked defeated, she had a cognizance in her eyes. It was something familiar to Jack. Something he'd seen before in Violet and Anaya. A glint that told him danger was imminent, and someone's death was on the table.

Fucking skies. He watched as Vernon pulled back her hood and revealed dark hair flowing down her back. "Your hair, in that braid. Easy to grab."

Jack was behind him in an instant, shoving him away. "Find someone else."

Navee stiffened, her eyes glued to Jack and his mask. Recognition bloomed, then fizzled into a scowl. Jack lightly stepped on her toe, and it smoothed away.

"But—" Vernon started.

"Find another," Jack commanded.

Vernon stammered but obeyed. He found a different girl, this one even younger than Navee, and his attention was fully on her once he made the girl remove her robe and reveal her barely grown body beneath.

Jack sat beside Navee. Sat too close, to his disgust, but it was necessary. She leaned away as fear flickered. He held her gaze, counting the seconds.

Her mind pulled him in.

"You look nice," he said with a smile.

A mix of her language flowed into his mind, strung with numerous words he assumed were cursing him out. Her voice held an agitated edge, nervous even though it was loud. His language flickered through. *Conjua. I know him. He helped destroy the Farm, and now he is just a giant liar. What the fuck is this world—*

"This is my first time," he dropped his voice. Behind him, the other Vanishers continued undressing their targets. Vernon moaned. Jack forced a smile through his disgust. "I was hoping you could help me."

Help him? Help him with what? Sucking his—

"No," Jack said quickly and tapped his temple. She furrowed her brows, but Jack drew her gaze to the red velvet couch he patted. "Help me create a little bit more of this color."

It took her a minute. She refused to answer him via her mouth, but Jack guessed it was a rule—no talking.

Inaj flowed through her mind, rapid and indiscernible. Jack tapped his temple again. She stared at him like he had four heads. Called him a conjua again.

He leaned in, not breaking eye contact. "Your mind speaks to me, darling. Don't look away from me."

Oh. What was his name? Ja—Jack. He was typically nice back at the Stradinths. What did he say? He wanted to create the color. The color red? More red?... Her face blossomed in understanding. *Blood. He wants to create blood. He murdered that entire family with a couple of forks and a meat knife. He wants to create more blood... Here.*

Jack's smirk answered. He glanced at the other Vanishers who were busying themselves, not yet taking full advantage of the girls. One already had her top off, though, and Jack looked away. Moans of men trickled around the room. A pressure built in his ears, along his shoulders, until his limbs felt stiff. He glanced at the sconces again and reached into his pocket.

It was a small vial he had procured from Jodin with the help of another man named Varik. It was meant to be powerful when it came in contact with fire.

Jack began unlacing his boots. Within a secret lining glistened two small blades that extended into forearm-sized ones. He drew Navee's attention there.

Her brown eyes widened and a smile pulled at her lips. Little deadly skiv. He swiftly pushed one beneath the chiffon of her robe and slid the other up his own sleeve. He glanced at the nearest sconce again, then the line following them. *Might as well start now.* With a shrug, he stood and stretched his arms. He aimed a throw at the row and hoped for the best.

"What are you doing?" Vernon called.

Jack threw a wink over his shoulder. "What I'm good at."

Confusion flashed over Vernon's face, along with the other Vanishers, but it was too late. Jack used every ounce of his Droanian strength and threw the vial of gray dust. It was an invisible blur, but it smashed into the first sconce, then continued on like a bullet, demolishing the four behind it. The result was immaculate.

Tiny explosions blossomed and charred wood rained down. The lights snuffed out save for a couple of remaining fires he missed across the room. Screams and panic flooded the space as it descended into further darkness.

The best part was the smoke. When the special dust met fire, smoke multiplied and would cover any kind of room in seconds. It also dulled the senses if it met nostril hairs, stung eyes, or poured into ears. Jack wouldn't be able to do much to help Navee as he was really the only one immune to it. It was poison and Mer blood still flowed through him. But when he turned, releasing his blade, she had already hopped into action.

Two of the Vanishers had their throats slit, and Navee was lunging toward the next, who had been in the process of shoving a girl's head down. She jammed the dagger into his neck and sliced up.

Jack took care of the fourth. Vernon was a ball on the floor, rubbing his eyes. Jack hauled him up by the collar.

"Why, why? I thought—"

Jack sliced off Vernon's hands at the wrist. Vernon opened his mouth in a silent scream, torn between bare comprehension of the situation and horror. He stared at the severed limbs, then at his hands on the floor that spilled blood on Jack's polished shoes.

"Hands that snatch, that take, that abuse, are not hands deserved." Jack gave him a deadly smile. "Or at least, that's what my god told me."

"Your god?"

"Well." Jack shoved the dagger into his chest. Twisted it.

Reveled in the smell of his pain and fear. "That god is me."

Jack threw him to the floor. He turned to Navee, who was stripping one of the smaller Vanishers and dressing in his clothes. He stared at her for a long moment, while the panicked screams of the room filled his eardrums.

"What?" she snapped.

"You're…quick."

"I'm not helpless." Navee crossed her arms, the big button-down swallowing her petite body. "You seemed more relieved to have help, so who is the helpless one?"

His expression fell into an annoyed scowl. "Let's get this over with. We kill the men, leave the girls, then I call my transport. Got it?"

Navee shoved past him, and he thought she was a worse version of Violet. "Got it, *conjua*."

His eyes nearly rolled out of his head.

They exited the curtained private area and stumbled upon the smoky, near-blind room of half-naked girls and drunk men. Jack stepped over coughing bodies. Navee had the sense to wrap a random handkerchief around her mouth. He pulled men away from girls and sliced their throats. One by one. They didn't see it coming, and a frown formed at that. While he needed the smoke to be able to kill this many people by himself, he *did* want them to know it was him. Because the poor, horrible thing about this, is that even if blood spilled, they believed their actions were justified. They believed women were lesser, that a bent knee meant prayer, that restricting freedom meant redemption, that control was theirs and only belonged to them.

Jack was no better, but he made a deal with Pharos, and this was him fulfilling it. More than it, technically, but he was sure Bryce wouldn't complain.

"Nex! Nex!" one man cried as he spotted Jack through the smoke. Jack smelled the urine, saw the stain along his pants, and wrinkled his nose. "I repent!"

"Not going to help," Jack said dryly. He snapped that one's

neck.

His wrist began to ache slightly, so he switched the dagger to the other hand. A slash, blood, the crumple of a body. Navee was a little more chaotic than him—jumping on backs, stepping on throats, kicking stomachs and calling them all sorts of curses. She'd lived through her world being stolen, and now her people were going missing here, and she wanted her revenge.

She *deserved* her revenge.

Jack felled nearly everyone who didn't make it out of the center, then moved to the perimeter. He took down each pathetic body banging on the doors. He made them hurt, smiled at their blood that misted his face, judged them when they fell to their knees and begged. He slaughtered them all with zero remorse.

He was the god here.

Only when the room silenced and the men's cries gargled into death, did he take the opportunity to look around. Bodies everywhere; slung over chiffons, missing limbs, and some gruesome slashes to the back from Navee. She yanked the blade out of a chest, and stuck her tongue at the crumpling man. They locked eyes across the room.

"That was fun," Navee called.

"Skies," Jack muttered. "I'm always finding the bloodthirsty ones."

Navee grinned widely, pale green barely seen beneath the swath of red liquid. She tore off a dead man's jacket and wiped her face, before she began to call to the girls and gather them in a corner of the giant room. Jack tapped a button hidden on the side of his watch and sent the notification.

His eyes snagged on one portly member, and he paraded over to the Chancellor. He'd covered himself in his comrades' blood, and had even tried changing out of his robes to hide his identity. Jack stopped in front of him, holding the dagger loosely. Blood dripped down his clean-shaven jaw.

The Chancellor finally saw him. He whimpered, whined, red in the face and fear in his eyes. "Nex," he whispered as he lifted a finger. "You've made us martyrs."

Jack honestly wanted a nap. The preaching was getting old. "You drug and rape young girls, I don't see how that makes you a martyr."

"This is our *reward*—"

"Why can't you give out nice bottles of wine like a normal person?" Jack said.

"We are blessed by Avaritia—"

"I shouldn't even bother." Jack took a step forward.

The Chancellor screamed and held his hands up. "No! No!"

"You are my main target, actually, but I thought it would be more economical to get rid of the rest. The best part about your greed is that it blinds you, so you don't see someone like me coming along to rid you of it." Jack cocked his head and flashed an icy smile. "It's quite the recipe for disaster."

"My god will smite you."

"Stop it with the 'god' shit, it's extremely grating."

And with that, Jack threw the dagger. It landed between the Chancellor's eyes and he collapsed. A moment later, the doors began to open, and Pharos members poured into the room, guns raised. Jack removed his mask and held his hands up as nearly ten red lasers landed across his body.

"He's cleared," Bryce said as they stepped out in full armor. Their eyes narrowed on the bloody massacre. They didn't reveal their surprise, but there was a flicker of fear as their gaze snagged on Jack. "Evacuate the girls."

Blood dripped from his mouth. Jack swiped a thumb, looked at the red stuff, and wrinkled his nose. Definitely not worth his taste buds.

"There's a girl here who assisted. Name is Navee and she is Inaj. Pretty deadly, too."

Bryce's eyes narrowed more, but they merely nodded. "You injured?"

If he was, it would be cleared up with his healing powers by now. "No."

"You have your transport?"

"Already on the way."

Bryce gave a wary look. Jack smelled the fear. "Good work," they said. "We covered the guards. It will take a while before anyone realizes what happened here." Their gaze avoided Jack's. "You did all this…for her?"

Jack offered a smile. "It's pathetic, isn't it?"

Bryce studied him, then turned to blast off more orders.

Jack bowed his head as Pharos escorted the girls from the room. Blankets covered those who were nearly naked, others had to hold onto soldiers as a crutch because they were so drugged. Some stared at him. Their gazes burned. He heard the whispers, echoing those of the Order.

Nex. Nex. Nex.

Yes, he supposed he could be considered that.

The God of Death.

It was a few more minutes after the girls were evacuated before Jonathon showed up holding a pile of clean clothes. He took in the room and bristled, his face paling by the second. He swallowed. "His Master will find out."

Jack side-eyed the Vanisher. He moved them to a private corner, shrugged off his jacket, unbuttoned his top, and dropped his pants. Naked. With a wary gaze, Jonathon handed him a pile of clothes and a damp towel.

"You want a response to that?" Jack said dryly. He began to wash.

"Well…" The fear, the appall, lingered in his ears. This meant death. This meant someone burned pawns on Cyran's chessboard. Jack watched as Jonathon tried to wrap his mind around the actions. "Aren't you afraid?"

"Of death? No." Jack shucked on his new slacks and buttoned them up. "I've never been afraid of death because most who tried are without breath before they reach me. There are the few who have gotten close, but they don't live long either."

"But what of…*him?*"

"Torture doesn't scare me." He frowned at a bit of blood on his wrist tattoo. He wiped it off. He shrugged on his black dress shirt. "Not when you lived through most of it during childhood."

Jonathon blew out a breath. "Makes sense."

"That I'm volatile?"

"That you have a reason." The man frowned. "So then what are you afraid of, Jack Marin?"

The corset went on. Jack adjusted his collar and brushed his curls back as a smile curved on his lips.

"Losing."

25

FIRE NIGHT

JODIN HAD NOT GIVEN VIOLET *clothes.*

It was pure, white chiffon that wrapped around her breasts and her upper arms. Cutouts exposed her stomach, and the fabric hugged her crotch like high-waisted underwear. Strands of it cascaded down her legs and her glamour-pale skin. Blonde hair sat on her head. Brown eyes glanced around. But even though Violet wasn't wearing her own skin, insecurity blossomed so hard that her hands shook.

Maybe it was greed, and every scantily dressed person there wanted to look their best. Maybe it was a fight to the death for *who* looked best. Violet's gaze darted from each beautiful, robust woman, all different skin tones and painted lips and sultry eyes. Goosebumps spilled along her arms.

The Vanisher transport who had given her a long look called it Fire Night, and Violet was there to serve drinks before the festivities began. She held a tray and kept walking around the room, fighting the urge to slam it into the girls' faces who looked her up and down with aggressive expressions. They were sizing each other up, and based on the trickling conversations, Violet realized she'd been trapped in an event where Cyran's captains were let loose on prey for…sexual taking.

"Drink?" Violet gritted to one girl, who stood four inches taller and had the prettiest brunette hair.

The girl took a flute and gave Violet a look before turning back to her pack of stunning friends.

Violet fought the urge to ruin the girl's hair and walked away with a strained smile.

They were piled into an ornate cavern. Light from millions of candles danced on the high ceilings and the stalactites above. Rugs adorned the floors, chandeliers dripped wax onto plates made of gold.

According to one of the other servants, Fire Night had been occurring for nearly eight decades. Each and every person was willing. Prey and predators. The prey were vetted for what they brought to the table, both physically and mentally, and how they would pleasure the infamous captains of Cyran's regime. In this room, where excitement buzzed beneath everyone's skin, captains got what they wanted. Whether it was a chase, to play hide and seek, or to get started with no foreplay.

Said excitement seemed to stem from the callous protocols and oppression seen in the Twin Cities from the Order. Names were dropped, churches were mentioned, and some girls—while anticipatory—slugged back a little more wine while discussing the fact their strict, religious parents could never know.

Violet bet the Order knew about Fire Night, but the utmost identity protection was given to all those who participated.

Or at least, that is what everyone muttered when they received the secret invitation.

Either way, Violet did hear things—names of pastors who were stricter with others, who got weird and had strange events at the churches. She heard very graphic talk from some regular attendees, and discovered the sizes of many captains below the belt. Violet found a dark corner and shot back an entire flute when she eavesdropped on the seventeenth discussion of what two girls had experienced with one particularly depraved captain.

But there was another buzz going around…and that was about the new initiate. The man who should be dead. The one with powers and tattoos and boiling hot looks.

Captain Jack Marin.

"It's a true competition tonight, ladies," one woman with a coiled updo and sparkly brown skin pitched her hands on her hips. "Everyone is going for him."

"He's been elusive, apparently, but it says a lot that he is showing up at *Fire Night.* Like, come on, it is a night for great sex, and I bet he delivers…" A white-skinned girl said. Her cornsilk hair was let loose in waves, and her red-painted lips smiled in anticipation.

Violet had zero control in managing the scowl on her face. *It isn't that great,* she wanted to say. But it would be a lie. A giant, selfish lie.

The woman with the coils smirked. "You don't get lips like that for show."

"You don't get hair like that to *not* be pulled on," the red-lipped girl said.

"Those *eyes,* they could probably make me come—"

"*Drink?*" Violet gritted, interrupting the women. They turned to her, shocked at her sudden arrival, but they each took a flute and clinked them together.

"To whoever catches his eye."

They all laughed and drank. Violet swallowed the lump in her throat and wished she could have snuck in a plasblade to lob Jack's head off. Her bloodbond mark tingled at that, reminding her that she couldn't do lasting damage to the man like she wanted to.

"Everyone!" An event organizer appeared at the cavern's main entrance. "Thank you for attending. You each have been selected for our hardworking, powerful captains. To give them a night they deserve. Now it is time to get started!" The portly man clapped his hands and beckoned to the hundreds, "Let Fire Night begin!"

The group rushed to the entrance, a bubble of excited murmurs fluttering around. Violet stayed back with the other servants, and once it was only them left, the event organizer beckoned them to a drink station. "Keep it pouring. Anyone sloppy is to be reported to me or the guards on call. And remember, if you are desired and *also* have the desire to participate, you only need to say yes. I'll be making rounds after. Everyone will receive a tonic, so there are no…repercussions."

Each of the thirty servants nodded. Violet bobbed her head along. She had the desire to participate—in punching Jack in the face.

❋❋❋

The caverns were endless, oozed in ambiance; sensual, seductive, expensive. Lounges and carpets and loveseats filled every open space, followed by some caverns made of glistening, bright blue pools of hot springs. Some juts had doors for private rooms, while other larger areas welcomed parties of twenty or more. As the stretch of caves went on, smaller tunnels sprouted with darker lights, and squeals of happy shrieks echoed from beyond.

Violet's grip was bruising on the tray. She couldn't abolish Jack from her head. What if he was in there, indulging, and she happened to stumble in on it? Ignorance preferred, she kept her head down as she wandered, approaching most of the action. Some people were already going at it in the hot springs when she passed over the rocky bridges in bare feet. Naked bodies intertwined in private rooms. A captain was splayed out on plush pillows with three women surrounding him. Two men were making out amid a small garden, and in an expansive, main room, most of the captains lounged on sofas, surrounded by men and women and those in between or not at all, indulging. Drugs were passed around as much as drinks. A fellow servant abandoned her tray to lie with a blond male captain.

Violet's pulse pounded in her ears. She looked around, growing more afraid that she would see…

Her gaze snagged on perfect coils. She caught the stunning woman from before. Brown legs were flung over a pair of dark slacks, followed by another pair of white legs and shimmering cornsilk hair, then red lips brushing the scruff of a familiar jaw…

To the winner, indeed.

It was dim in the cavern, but Violet could see the spark in Jack's eyes as he and the two women shared a laugh.

The world stilled. Violet tried to control her shaking hands—her anger. Her breath. Her jealousy. She didn't realize how long she stood there. Her eyes slowly lowered to her empty tray. She hadn't even noticed the people helping themselves to the flutes.

One woman's head buried in his neck. She laughed. The other giggled. Red lipstick smeared near his mouth. His arm came around their waists as he winked to a guffawing captain. Slowly, surely, Jack's sensual eyes swept around the room, past Violet—

They immediately snapped back to her.

Her entire body was frozen, her spine rigid. Her teeth bit down on her tongue.

He stared.

She glared.

His mouth parted.

Violet let her glamour slip.

His green eyes widened slightly, and something flashed in them that she'd never seen. Hunger? Relief? She couldn't place the name. It was so… un-Jack-like. As if he realized he'd been caught in trouble. His hands went limp, falling from the women's bodies. But a breath later, he plastered a demure smile on his face, grabbed a tumbler of alcohol, and shot back the liquor. One woman continued to smile into his neck and tugged a button open on his collar. "Let's go somewhere private."

"Oh?" Jack responded, never taking his eyes off Violet.

"Yes," the red-lipped one purred.

Violet jerked her glamour back in place. She stood for another moment to let Jack memorize her disguise before she turned into the crowd. She deposited the tray on a random table.

The last thing Violet saw was them standing up and walking away together. She turned into a small, dark cave and hurried through it. Her breaths came fast, uneven. She clutched her throat. She should be mad, angry, wanting to throttle him, but instead, her chest squeezed so deeply she wanted to stab it to minimize the current pain. She stormed through caves of crystals and pools, keeping her head down against the growing moans and exposed skin.

There was no information here. Only torture. She needed to get *out*.

Sweat licked down her back as she made her way into a maze of smaller caverns, uninhabited by intercourse. She dragged her fingers along the rock as the caves grew darker, hoping to find a way out—

The crunch of rocks echoed in the caves.

"Oh, little flower! Come out, come out, wherever you are…"

At Jack's teasing, slightly on-edge voice, her knees trembled. Violet picked up her pace, but it was growing too dark to see properly. The smell of mud met her nostrils. Her mouth was dry. The footsteps behind her crunched louder, powerful and…horribly familiar. She turned—

"Oh, you are a surprise."

A stranger. A captain with blond brushing his brow. Another male stood behind him, both nearly naked. "Do you want to join?"

She didn't have an answer. Her emotions—particularly her yearning—were wild. Fear was bleeding into something warm in her core. The captain stepped forward and brushed hair behind her ear. His finger dragged down her neck, across her collarbone, and something about the rush of Jack's chase, the darkness, the touch of the captain, the fear, dizzied her. She felt herself leaning in, imagining it was a browner finger—

Another hand grabbed the captain's and squeezed. Then flung it to the side.

The dusky space rippled.

Jack appeared. From Endolier camouflage.

"Touch her again, and your finger bone will be my toothpick." A dark, icy smile on his face. He was enjoying himself. "This one is spoken for."

The captain stilled and paled slightly. He bowed his head to Jack, who now wrapped his arm around Violet's waist. "Oh."

The captain and the man ran. *Bolted.* Like fire exploded and nipped at their heels. Violet shuddered as Jack's hand brushed her lower back across bare skin.

She darted away, but his hand encircled her wrist, and he pushed her into a wall.

"Skies, I thought you'd make it harder." He dipped his head, breath spraying across her face. There was a roar in her ears. "Coming back from the dead and all that."

A valley formed between her brows.

"Giving me a dog."

Her lips twitched.

His jaw clicked at her expression, and his hand wrapped her throat. Squeezing. Violet's brief moment of satisfaction flooded back into fear. Jack was unhinged. Her eyes caught a speck of red at his jaw. He'd killed someone.

He had his control, his power, taken from him.

He was riled.

He *killed* someone. And then left the mark there for her to notice. Otherwise, it would be gone. There was never a mistake with Jack. He wanted her to know just how furious he was.

"I cannot trust myself right now." His nails dug into her skin. She gasped—whimpered slightly—and his eyes flashed hotly. "So I need you to do one thing for me before I fuck the shit out of you."

Oh, my holy skies. Her mouth dropped. She was *not* expecting that. Fire exploded beneath her skin while the surface surged with goosebumps.

Then his lips were on her ear, restrained fury icing his voice. She caught the sharp points of his teeth.

"*Run.*"

She shot out of his grip and spared no glance back. She blindly ran as Jack's cackle echoed around her. A crack of rock. A choked, distant laugh.

He was asking for an energy release. What did he do before this? This couldn't have been from her, but *she* could have been his push. If he'd believed her to be dead, only to slowly discover that she shared space with him under the guise of a glamour, she could understand why he'd be furious.

But something else was there. There were slight bags under his eyes, a flash of anticipation. This was more than him being on edge and out of control.

"Do you know what I did before this, little flower?" His voice surrounded her. "My pregame of sorts. I watched hands roam glassy-eyed little girls who were too young to know what a violating touch was. I heard them celebrate. I listened to them bow to their God of Greed and thank them for the opportunity for rape, control, and torture."

She stalled at one wall. Part of her wanted to turn around and scream '*what?*' but she was too stunned to hear such a thing. Jack went to the Order? He…saw the horrors? Things so horrible that even Emryn gagged talking about them?

Why had he been there? Why was he even involved? Why… why…

"Eighty-one ugly old men. I killed them all." Jack's voice came, this time with a strain to it. "With help, though. She was a surprise. The reunion between you two will be splendid."

The blood on his jaw.

Bryce's smug gaze two days ago that didn't seem directed at her.

Jodin's involvement in Pharos.

They were all working together.

She clenched her fists. This wasn't some mission for her. This was a *trade*. Her own rage replaced her fear. She was here, dressed stupidly, because Jack requested it since he completed something for Bryce.

And just like that, Violet became a means to an end, yet again.

So she sprinted, lightly on her feet, away from Jack Marin. She needed space. A chance to breathe. This was the setup. *She* was a pawn. Again. And something about it irked her deeper than all the other times she'd been used. She didn't ask for the powers, but she also didn't ask to be left in the dark while everyone played their own game.

She found a fork along the path and nearly veered to the left, but halted abruptly, glancing to the right. A stretch of rock. A yawning opening. Starlight glistened on the dewy grass. Violet bolted for it.

When she reached the cave entrance, cool, enticing air met her lips. She didn't feel the chill against her barely covered skin.

A giant forest, basking under the night sky, expanded before her. Her bare toes wetted in the manicured clover grass. An oasis. Of boulders and lush greenery. Of small pockets of ponds and lily pads. A maze of hedges rolled on one side of the giant clearing, and Violet didn't waste any time bolting there.

A scuff of sediment. She flung herself behind a tree. With a held breath, she glanced over a low branch.

Jack's tall, ominous silhouette appeared at the cave's mouth, but halted.

He stood there for a moment, and then his shoulders sagged. He rubbed his hands over his face. She had the urge to appear. To comfort him. But he was...

"Marin!" Someone called his name. A dark-skinned figure appeared, and with squinting eyes, Violet recognized him as Captain Masar. "I've been looking for you."

"I'm in the middle of..." Jack shook his head. Plastered a smile on his face. "Never mind. Drink?"

"They've started games. Naked games. It's amazing." Masar bellowed a laugh and slapped Jack on the back. Jack paused, then followed Masar into the caverns.

Violet blew a breath, her forehead against the rough tree bark. Heat still coursed through her at Jack's raunchy, callous words. She...hated that she had liked it. Wanted it. But his needs were pent up and fueled by something strange. Something she hadn't really seen on him ever.

But it would be stupid of her to believe that Jack's barely contained emotions were nudged by...fear.

That's what she'd seen when he glimpsed her without the glamour. Fear. But it was a strange kind of fear. Like he built something and knew it was to crumble. Explode.

Regardless, she needed to leave. She wanted a smoke so bad her mouth turned sour and her saliva tasted like paste. She needed a skivvin' drink, too. She dragged herself quietly to the maze of hedges and wormed her way inside. The frigid air was welcome on her skin, and she sighed deeply—

A crack of a branch. Two baritone, whispering voices. Violet's sigh lodged in her throat. She pushed herself into the bushes, letting them swallow her whole, and slapped a hand over her mouth to quiet her heavy breathing.

"How was your mission—?"

A hard shove. One man grunted. "Don't talk about that here."

"*Here* is safer than the fortress. He has eyes and ears everywhere. He can't know we are looking for it."

"*It* is impossible to get to. I don't know how Darien did it. He never said a word to a soul, but he found something out… something that made him desperate and sloppy when running."

Violet squeezed her brows. Darien? The name sounded familiar. She'd heard painful screams of it before and—

Her mouth parted.

Darien Bones.

The smoke and oil smell of the South brought her back to the memory. Darien Bones. The sole name that appeared in the seventh world for barely a minute before he died. And apparently, these men believed it wasn't the mere yearning of returning to Calesal that made him fight his way to the final world. It was something he learned.

There were certainly a lot of horrible things about this world that would push someone to run, but those weren't secrets. It didn't take much to know Cyran was a monster solidifying his rule.

What pushed Darien?

"It's there, I know it is. Darien didn't come back right after he searched, but he said the Iris beacon pointed there. I don't know why he didn't continue on—"

"Because he went crazy. His tongue was all black and blue. Didn't you see that? Couldn't even tell us what he witnessed.

Something scared him from going to the next world. Then when he did, a lot of us were killed."

Tense silence ensued. It went on for a long time, until Violet thought they had left and abandoned their conversation. It was a dangerous one to have, but she needed to know. *Where* was the portal? Where did the Iris's beacon point?

"The volcano—"

"Should not be on your tongue."

Violent, nauseous electricity slashed through the hedges of the maze. Violet dropped to the ground as twigs and leaves erupted around her. Black lightning zapped, and two familiar thumps told her they met their mark. Through the brush, she spotted the incinerated bodies of the men, skin already sluicing off their bones. A cloying, decaying smell reached her nostrils, and she slapped a hand over her mouth, quieting her gag.

A deep sigh. The lightning dissipated. "I want an Aurien testing this week. If anyone has uttered its location, they're dead."

"Understood, Captain," said a random assistant standing above the bodies.

"You're dismissed," Zavar commanded.

A flash of light and the accompanying Vanisher disappeared. Violet didn't move a muscle. Her lungs burned, desperate, but one shift of the plant debris covering her, and she'd be as dead as the men.

Volcano. Volcano.

The portal was at the volcano.

Zavar's boots crunched on the grass. She glimpsed his shiny black hair. He pursed his full lips and kicked the two bodies. "Stupid."

Zavar used both hands to grab part of each dead man and vanished with their remains. Violet heaved a shaky breath. The debris shifted around her, and when she glanced at it, she thought it looked strange. *Very* strange.

What was once healthy and green and perfectly manicured was now decaying. She poked a leaf and it crumbled, nothing but ash.

She lifted her head to the entire maze, and slowly but surely the connecting hedges turned black. Everything dead.

It wasn't a surprise that Zavar's lightning could kill, but it seemed absurd for a killing blow to take out all the surrounding plant life by proxy.

She dragged her body up to her elbows, then her knees, brushing the ash off her. Her heart hammered against her ribcage as she rose to her feet, finding the two imprints of the men's bodies in the grass.

A playful scream crawled from the caverns and Violet hesitated, knowing she should go back and lose herself in the orgy chaos, but cloying fear kept her rooted. She looked down at her clothes, the white chiffon now stained with dirt. She tried to brush it off as best she could, and took a single step forward in the dewy grass—

A flash of Vanisher light. Zavar appeared, hands in pockets, and a cold, evil smile on his face. "Well, you're certainly a surprise."

Violet froze and checked that her glamour strings were in place.

He pulled a hand out, and baby bolts flickered around his lithe fingers. His head cocked slightly. "But you shouldn't have witnessed that."

Lightning burst from his hand.

But she was already lunging to the side. Rolled. Popped up, and began to run. Zavar released an icy laugh. "Oh, you want to make this fun? Fine, then, prolong it. It all still ends in your death."

She pumped her arms, ignoring the jolts of pain on her feet when they met the ridged edges of twigs. Lightning flung past her head and landed on a tree. It stabbed a hole in the trunk, and from that blackened hole, the rest of the tree decayed. She passed it and veered in a different direction.

Another flash of light. Zavar grabbed her by the throat and slammed her into the dead trunk. "Time's up. I want to get back to the party to get my dick suck—"

Violet swung a fist and landed on his nose. A crunch. Zavar's head bowed back, and blood poured from one nostril. She twisted herself from his grip and continued running.

A beat of silence passed. Then a loud, bone-chilling, fury-filled scream.

"I'm going to *fucking* kill you! And I'm going to make it *hurt*."

She cursed under her breath, glancing once at the sky in the hopes a ship would sail down and save her. She clenched her fists as she darted around another tree, jumped over a bush, and aimed for the empty cavern entrance. She could get naked, change her appearance, press her lips on someone and lose Zavar, but…

A fist wrapped around her braid and yanked her to the ground. A branch slashed her shoulder, her breath knocked out of her lungs. She barely had time to suck an inhale before the muddy bottom of a boot pressed at her throat. Zavar glared down at her, eyes alight with rage.

He bared his teeth. Her throat burned. Bruised as he pressed down. He waved his hand, and bolts of black severed the ground. Dirt sprayed her eyes.

But she wasn't done.

She forced a moan between her lips. Zavar's brows crumpled. She let a hand roam his calf, the back of his knee, before dropping down to her breast and squeezing. His eyes zeroed in on her hand. She flicked a nipple, and the whine that left her was…semi-real. Not a ploy. Her body coursed with warmth—with the want to win. Seducing Zavar could give her another win.

He removed his boot and she breathed deeply. "Why'd you stop?"

"You…" He paused. "Liked that?"

She shot him a sultry look from the ground. "Like to be choked?"

A scoff. "You have an ego."

"In this world? Of course." She rose to her elbows and parted her legs, letting the chiffon slip and faintly reveal herself. "It's the only way to grab Captain Marin's attention."

A pause. Electricity licked her skin, and she didn't know if it was from Zavar or her own giddiness. This was enticing. Bad. She shouldn't be enjoying this. She should be scared. Terrified. But where the slight fear pulsed, it only made her more curious.

Then there was lightning.

Around her neck.

Where fear told her to buckle, that she should be vomiting blood and doubling over in intense pain, only pleasure arrived. It was a warm, strong jolt along her skin. Her cheeks flushed, and that heat carried down to her core.

Focus. *Focus.*

He bent and grabbed her arm, pulling her into his chest. He was warmer than she expected. His collar was unbuttoned, revealing a smooth, scarred chest. She remembered his skin—the alabaster mess of it. He stepped into her, pushing her against a tree and pinned her there, clearly forgetting that she punched him, or the blood beneath his nostril.

"They all want him."

"Maybe I want both of you."

His rage completely faded. His eyes flickered hotly. He dipped his head until warm breath danced across her lips. "Why both?"

"If I'm going to be killed, might as well indulge in my fantasies before," she breathed. His hand skittered around her neck. "And I want to find out the truth."

"The truth of what?"

"Of your beauty, your intensity… your excitement." A sinful smile. "I like things that scare me."

"Does Jack scare you?"

She nodded, biting her lip. "It scares me that I know he won't like this."

"Because…"

"Because he likes me all to himself."

And that did it. Confirmed it for her. Zavar licked his lips, and thumbed her jaw. Slid one of her arms up the tree and pinned it there. He *liked* having what he shouldn't taste.

Perfect.

"Touch yourself," he commanded.

She buzzed with heat. She didn't think it would last long before she surprised him, ruined him, made him angrier than ever, but she didn't think…that she'd be excited. He was an exquisite man, all muscle and dark gazes and lithe fingers meant for specific places. She dropped her free arm, dove her fingers underneath the middle fabric of her dress, and found her center.

At that exact moment, he pushed his lightning. *Pleasure* lightning.

Her breath sucked in. She arched back against the bark, her chest meeting his as a moan ripped out of her. Her vision blurred and her head nearly cracked into the tree, but Zavar's hand was there, cradling her.

"Keep going," he said. "You can take it."

She was so overwhelmed with electricity and heat that she forgot how to breathe. Forgot it was a show. Inhaling sharply, she swirled her finger, pressing on that nub. The static was back, but instead of a sharp jolt, it was a low buzz circling her core. She grew wetter by the second.

Zavar sucked in a breath. "Look at you, a mess for me."

Her brows bent into a scowl, and she jerked her fingers away, but Zavar was too fast. He released her trapped wrist and palmed her hand back on her core. "I didn't tell you to stop."

His long, strong fingers pressed against hers. Her knuckles bent. Found her slit. He maneuvered her cresting climax without ever touching her. But he did the work. Held her hand there. Trapped her in electric lust. She lifted her eyes, lip between her teeth as she kept quiet.

His gaze locked with hers, and the corner of his mouth lifted. "You can do it."

Now, now. She was losing her sanity as a heavy fire swarmed her bloodstream. Skies, she couldn't breathe. Her vision grew dark, but still he held her eyes and urged her with an approving look.

She hooked a leg around the back of his knee and yanked him closer. A groan slipped and he dove to her neck, kissing, biting her as she nearly lost control. He ground himself against their hands.

"Stay quiet," his breath skittered her collarbone.

Violet tried jerking her gut, tried to think of dangerous situations that would trigger her power, but the hot, sultry buzz of his abilities made her dizzy. She dropped her gaze to his lips, yearning, wanting…

He stared at her, mouth parted, as he knocked her hand away and slid a finger inside. He pressed a thumb to her nub. "That's it."

"Please," she found herself begging. The forest became a blur. Stars began to dot her eyes. He pushed more of that lightning.

"Is this the excitement you want?"

"Yes," she breathed.

"Take it."

"Oh, *skies*," she threw her head back and whined.

As she unfurled, Zavar stilled. He pulled back, confusion crossing his expression.

Fuck.

"Skies?" he repeated.

Her orgasm dwindled, and Violet thought of every horrible thing said to her, imagined the deadly situations she had been in before, and hoped it elicited her abilities. She guessed it awoke when she was in serious danger—a survival mechanism. Her mind overflowed with memories; running from the Droan's ballistic army, fighting Kiane, the initial fear when being lowered to battle with Navo in Envy, the crack within her chest when Jack tried to stab her, getting shot when leaving Sloth, and all the pain Greed provided.

Zavar watched her, still perplexed, and his eyes flicked downward. To the glow. They snapped back to her face. "*You.*"

"Me." She released her glamour and revealed her natural form. A devilish smile. "Jack still does it better, though."

The Vanisher realm appeared as Zavar's rageful scream filled the space. Bolts flared. She yanked on a nearby white tether. The Vaelaur's hands slipped from her body.

She landed atop a thick branch and stumbled to the next, bark scratching her stomach, but she righted herself just as Zavar flashed with light. She dipped into the realm again. Pulled on another. Landed a little more expertly on a giant boulder within the forest. Zavar followed, but Violet had already moved onto another boulder a distance away.

"Fucker!" he cried. His hand flashed out and a thick bolt seared across the space between them. Violet teleported to another, finding it easier to pull a tether if she hung onto the realm. It was like a buzzing inside of her—she controlled how much enraptured her. Like a door, and when she peeked through, all she saw was a flourish of bright, silver light. Endless. She managed how wide that door went. She kept the powers at bay and her vision would flick back to the current reality, but when she wanted to vanish, she'd open the door a little more and the realm would appear. She placed herself on another rock and flung her braid over her shoulder. "Did you come out of your mother's ass?"

Zavar whirled, lightning lifting the deep, black locks on his head.

She flashed him the middle finger. "Because you're a real piece of shit."

"Bitch!"

She smiled, but she stumbled too hard into her satisfaction, because Zavar vanished with a tiny flash of light, and appeared...

Above her.

He shot a stream of lightning down. Violet dove off the boulder and tried to open that door again, but the knob felt hot. *She* felt hot. Fear pounded with her heart for a moment. The door opened wider than before, and the light at her hands and forearms ignited. But in her desperation, she pulled a random tether without checking the space and landed on the ground. She skidded across dewy grass and mud. Her head thumped a tree root. Pain thrashed and she groaned. Her fingers dug in the ground, but her vision blurred—

A flash of light.

Zavar's cold voice.

His fingers wrapped around her upper arm and dragged. He flung her into an open space of grass. She blinked at the stars and numerous moons and planets above, all little blobs.

A whimper escaped as Zavar knelt beside her.

"A young Vanisher is a danger when they indulge in the silver—the Vanisher powers. You see that silver realm, you play with it, and you get yourself killed." A finger brushed over her forehead, and she glimpsed the blood when he pulled it away. "Silver, silver. The color of a Vanisher…"

"There's purple, too, sometimes," Violet breathed. "Unless you're colorblind."

He scowled, but Violet saw a flash of confusion over his face.

The clear sky filled with starlight were like wings behind him. Dried blood stained his upper lip. His eyes betrayed racing thoughts. "You must have hit your head hard."

She tried to crawl backward, but lightning met her ankle. Nausea roiled. A metallic taste filled her mouth.

"Hurts, doesn't it?" he sneered.

"It tickles." She coughed, glancing at the jagged thing on his striking face. "Nice scar. Wonder who gave that to you."

"It's a reminder of what I should have done eons ago. It ends here, little Vanisher," Zavar merely said. "You don't have to run anymore."

A strange sensation overcame her at those words. She had the urge to be squeezed…in a *hug*. Even though the words were from Zavar, a sob racked at her chest. Her eyes burned while she forced a solemn smile. "Did you ever have a mother?"

His brows creased.

"Well, of course you had a mother. But did she hate you, too?"

He balked. A ripple of fear passed over his face. It was a very beautiful face to be wasted on such a monstrous person.

"Too?" he said plainly.

"Yeah." Violet huffed a laugh. "I know that look." She put up her fist, wanting to bump it with his. "Neglected children gang."

Zavar stared at her incredulously.

"I don't even know why I'm thinking about her. Why would I? I don't think about her that much. But now…" She puckered her lip out. "I never knew my father, so I can't ask him for comfort. But why do I suddenly want a hug from my mother? Right now? Before you kill me? Why do I suddenly care to have that?"

Zavar took out his plasblade and thumbed it to life. A bright, haunting red wrapped it. "Mothers may have birthed us, but it doesn't mean we are guaranteed love. That's a choice. Love is a choice."

"And our mothers didn't choose us."

Some human emotion overcame his expression. His nostrils flared, and he fought a battle behind his eyes. Dark, beautiful, haunting eyes. "I don't know why I care to tell you, but I don't actually take joy in this. You gave me a damn good fight, though, and…got off from me, too. I have respect for that, even though you piss me off to no end." The tip of the blade met her chest. It burned. Flared at her skin. The chiffon began to char away slowly, and she had half a thought that she should cover up. She didn't want Zavar staring at her nipples after she was dead.

"Do it," she said with a small smile. "Then you won't get a matching scar on your face for failing again."

He bristled.

She rested her head on the ground. Splayed her arms out like a cross. Closed her eyes. "I'm going to whatever hell my mother ended up in. And I will spend the rest of my afterlife beating the shit out of her for allowing me to be born."

Silence.

Then, "I'll make it quick."

She felt the briefest flash of unbearable heat in her chest, then it stopped. Violet opened one eye. Zavar frowned down at her.

"Oh, come on, don't hesitate *now*," Violet growled. "This is extremely inconvenient. I didn't mean to trigger you. I just wanted to whine."

"Shut up," he gritted. "I'm taking a moment."

"To *mourn* me?" Violet rolled her eyes. "I'm still here, asshole. Come on. Do it."

"You can't just *tell* me to do it."

"Yes, I can. Do it. I want to be done with this stupid world."

"I've never—" He shook his head. His night-black strands skittered to his cheeks. "I've never killed someone who actually wanted to die. You're crazy."

"Stop being a skiv and do it!"

"*Fine*. Damn, you are annoying." He raised the plasblade—

There was a ripple of air behind Zavar's head. The slightest contour of reality. Two tattooed hands appeared on either side of his skull and clapped the Vaelaur in the temples.

Zavar dropped, unconscious.

And like some menacing, true god of death, Jack Marin appeared behind him.

26

NEW JACK

VIOLET GAPED. HER TRAITOROUS HEART surged at the sight of him. Feelings that flickered between fear and hope. She jerked her heels, trying to scurry back, but every movement made to put distance between herself and Jack felt like stupid effort. A curl slipped across his brow as he studied her.

He looked so different. Powerful. Untouchable, yet *right there*. She both wanted to spring into his arms, mold herself to every part of him, and run far, far away until the lines of his beautiful face, the puff of his sinful lips, and those haunting green eyes hazed in her memory.

He was giving her time to adjust, she knew that much. Was letting her mind catch up to reality in the intensity of his presence. She had a hard time finding her breath. He took it away.

Even though she'd been chased by him briefly in the caverns, it hadn't felt real. They were still wearing their armor and playing their parts. *This* was real. As naked as they both could be. Jack seemed…more settled than back in the cave. He opened his mouth, softness crawling into his expression as he wanted to say something, but then decided against it. The spot of red on his jaw was gone.

Blood leaked down her face. Her chiffon dress was stained with mud and ripped in obscene places. Jack's eyes dipped only a couple of times, but mostly toward the plasburn at the center of her chest, then to her head. She watched him take her in, and every moment beneath his gaze felt like a painful eternity.

Jack's lips parted, his deep, honeyed voice sending a shudder through her. "You look beautiful."

Her brows furrowed.

"I much prefer you with brown hair than blonde." He took a step over Zavar's body. "Blue eyes instead of brown."

Her disguise at the fortress. Talia.

"You're fired from there, by the way."

Her jaw slacked open.

His gaze swept around the partially destroyed forest space. "I thought you would serve drinks, and I'd have fun discovering what glamour you were wearing, which I would eventually tease out of you. But…I lost my head. I shouldn't have been that way. I saw you and something snapped. And even when I left…" A hint of a smile. "You still got into trouble."

She said nothing. Shock kept her mouth open, but her tongue empty.

"You went head-to-head with Zavar, skies." A smile found its way to his lips, but the minute his eyes landed on her head, he glowered. She dug her fingertips into the grass to keep from trembling. "You ruined the dress I bought you."

"It was a stupid dress," she whispered.

A strange relief passed over him. He exhaled sharply. His gaze traveled her body. "You still look good in it."

"It is basically toilet paper."

Jack's lips twitched, but fell. He glanced down at Zavar.

"Jodin," he clipped.

The Vanisher appeared next to Jack, boredom on his face. "Yes?"

Jack nudged Zavar's body with his boot. "Drop him off somewhere, please."

"Of course."

Jodin grabbed Zavar's limp arm and vanished.

Once they were alone, Jack clenched his fists. He sighed deeply. "It was a means to an end, Violet."

It took her a moment to realize what he was talking about, but his lingering gaze on the palm housing their bloodbond told her enough.

Why do you, of all people, hold this monumental connection to him?

Bryce's words from when they first met echoed in Violet's mind. Back in Wrath, it was a stupid pact made to get out of a city. There was still lingering hatred, and even to this day she had the urge to gouge his pretty eyes out. They hadn't known any better. Now, their little connection was a pawn to play, and Bryce used the advantage when they figured out there had been a relationship between the two.

"A means to an end," she said. "All of them Order people?"

"The higher-ups."

"And the girls?"

"Safe."

His eyes went to the landscape again. He wrinkled his nose. "It was so…abysmal."

"Power," Violet said. "Loyalty."

"They do not have loyalty." Jack's gaze flicked back to her. "Only fear. Fear of death, shame, sin. It creates false loyalty. If you threaten someone's existence enough, if you tell them at the young, impressionable, and fragile age of six that they will suffer if they sin, people have no choice but to believe. *Children* have no choice. These pathetic men saw me, with my dagger, and repented, but no god came to save them. So instead, they painted me as their devil, rather than a human stopping their horror."

She didn't know what to say, so she glanced at his tattoos. "Do you…believe in him?"

His eyes raked over her. "I believed you were dead," he said quickly.

She didn't want to think too long about it, because the straight answer hung between them, so obvious that Violet knew she'd been ignoring it for a while.

"I never cared about…him. I didn't care about anything. I thought I had lost. Everything had been taken from me—my body, my blood, my sanity—and so I did what I was good at. What everyone kept me around for. I killed, I teased, I threatened, I flirted, and in the end, I helped bring his captains together. First based on hatred of me, then based on fear of me. People follow me, and he needed someone like that." Jack shoved his hands in his pockets and glanced away. "Among other things."

His jaw clenched when he looked back at her. Studied her. Fury lashed again.

"You're mad," she said.

"I'm trying not to be, because it was better you didn't reveal yourself, but…" He sucked in a tight inhale. "You were there. In the fucking fortress. In front of me, talking to me, in Zavar's room, surrounded by a million pricks of danger." He scratched his jaw and his eyes dipped below her waist. "And you let him touch you."

She bristled. "That was my decision. All of it was. And Zavar… it was worth it to see his betrayed face. Why? Are you jealous?"

"Partially jealous I wasn't invited." Jack's eyes darkened. "Partially astounded you fooled him yet again."

"So there's no need to be upset."

"I'm not upset about that, Violet. I don't…" He steadied his breath. "I don't own you. I don't tell you what and what not to do, and Zavar…he's always asking for it."

Violet studied him. He held her gaze, but the hot spark in his eyes wasn't that of jealousy or protectiveness or whatever. Jack had good bits of all of that in him, but there was something else there. Something she tucked away. Perhaps Jack found a fondness for the man who killed him.

"But I think you liked it." He took a step closer. "I think you enjoyed playing the fool of everyone, even him, even me, under all of our noses. I think that's why you didn't care about the consequences."

"Oh skies, Jack, and what is *your* consequence? Are you going to spank me?"

His eyes flashed. Wind blew through the clearing. A strand of hair caught in her mouth. She reached up, annoyed—

Jack closed the space between them and tugged the strand from her lips. Tucked it behind her ear. She didn't miss the way his fingertips lingered on her skin before falling to his side. "Don't tempt me," Jack warned, green blazing.

Her mind fluttered as her chest did, but a dark thought bloomed through Jack's trance. She glanced to the space where Zavar had slaughtered the two men. Jack followed her gaze. "It's so subtle," she breathed.

"The Sin of Greed doesn't need a voice to claim its victims." His voice smoothed. "Everyone wants more—that is a part of having a conscience. No one in this world is born humble. Greed is power. It is a blind necessity. It is a euphoria and torture. Once someone tastes a win—gambling, a court case, a promotion, followers, or a world—very few, and I mean possibly no one, sits there and thinks just that one win is enough."

Her fingers itched to touch him. His musky scent flooded her senses, along with his obvious irritation at this world. She glanced to his face, where she caught a flicker of sadness. She balled her fists. "It's why the Order has infiltrated this world and now goes to others—they want more followers and control."

Jack shrugged. "There's more to it. *He* is involved, but I can't figure out why."

"Perhaps it's…" Violet shook her head. Realization dawned on her, and her eyes widened. The bowl in the church. The blood staining the bottom. "No."

"What?"

"How does one…enter the Order?" She glanced at her bloodsworn scar. "Is it binding?"

Jack followed her gaze, his brows furrowing. Then his eyes snapped to hers, and they widened as well.

She gave a slashing motion against her palm. Jack solemnly nodded.

"Millions," Violet whispered. "*Millions*."

"The Order has been in existence less time than the Sins," he muttered. "It should have been obvious, but it's…incomprehensible."

The damage to this world, and the rest of them, was done. The crisp night drew her back to her pounding heart, to Jack's watchful gaze, as if their world-altering predicaments drowned in their tense proximity.

"Power…" A light sparked in his eyes. He prowled to her. "Is fun. They created their lists of sins, and condemn others if they fall into them, therefore manipulating them. Should I do that? Should I have sins that I could…punish you for?"

She scowled. "Are you delusional? *Punish* me?"

"Should I push you into a Droanian army like you did to me in Wrath? Give you a heart attack while surrounded by cannibals in Gluttony? Hold a dagger to your neck while I kiss you like you did in Envy?" He drew closer. Her heart was going to jump from her chest. She took a step back. His gaze darkened. "Should I make you wild like in Lust? Tease and torment you as you have done to me? Should I frolic with fish people in Sloth? Make a fool out of you? Show up in a disguise and watch you get whipped while in the very fortress of the man who will kill you in an instant? Give you a dog to take care of? Make your heart beat so bad with the thought that you might be dead?"

Every word lodged in her throat.

His voice became sensual. "If I had my own list of sins, it would be everything you've done to me."

So I need you to do one thing for me before I fuck the shit out of you.

She took a step back. The corner of his lips twitched, eyes marking the movement. "You torture me." His voice was gravelly.

She sinned? She hated the lightness in her voice. The slight pinprick of fear bubbling within her. "If I'm such a sinner in your eyes, why don't you get rid of me like your Master wants you to?" She held out her hand. "Remove the bloodbond. Then we can really punish each other."

His eyes traveled over her with a goading gaze. "So you can kill me?"

"So I can end your torture."

Jack's smile was feline. "Then do it." He took out a small knife, and with a breath, cut into his bloodbond hand. Crimson dripped down the lines of his palm and the rivets of his fingers. His blood stained the decayed grass between their feet.

She swallowed. Hesitated.

"Do it, sweetheart." His voice was a teasing whisper. "Remove the bond. Kill me like you want to. Do it to end your pain." Jack smirked, showing a dimple. "Sin for me."

He circled her, a predator analyzing his prey, until he stood in front and nudged her chin up with his fingertips.

"Come on," Jack mused.

She gazed up at him. Her lips parted. Bloodbond forgotten. Her thoughts formed incoherent sentences, so emotion took over. She clenched her shaking hands as that purple-silver power warmed her chest. She grazed the realm's doorhandle. Opened it slightly. Her hands glowed. Jack watched her carefully.

And his voice grew deep, dark. "Sin for me, baby."

Ferocity filled. She lunged.

Grasped the hand he outstretched and brought them to the Vanisher realm. She turned to a white tether nearby and yanked it.

She landed wobbly, but her anger pushed her back to her feet on the smooth, cavern floor. Rushing water assaulted her ears and a cloud of steam heated her cheeks. One of the underground hot springs, with numerous waterfalls and bright azure pools and waxy stalactites. It was abandoned by any others. A lone entrance flickered with candlelight, while another pocket sported the view of a plush, round bed.

"Fuck," Jack exhaled.

She whirled on him, snatching the knife that he tried to hold out of reach, and jammed it at his chest. It clanged, loudly, shrilling her ear drums.

"*That's* what it felt like," she snarled.

She slammed it again, and it bent into that invisible force of their bloodbond, a breath from where his heart lay.

It hurt. It bruised. It *tortured* her.

She didn't care that Jack had been under the control of Cyran. *He* still did it. He went straight for her heart. After all she went through, she wished the blade had pierced her skin. Stabbed her organ. It would have saved her the misery of having to mourn him.

"You tried to kill me and then you *died*!" she cried. "You died in front of me! You say you're the one tortured? I believed you were dead because I watched it happen. I—I thought I became okay. But I'm not okay. You tried to kill me while under his control, and then I watched you die."

Jack grabbed the dagger and threw it across the cavern with uncanny strength. It knocked into a far wall so hard that it fissured a small crater.

She slammed a fist into his chest. "I want the bond gone. I don't want this connection to you—"

"Do you want to kill me?" he asked evenly.

"Agree to remove it!"

"Do you want to kill me?"

"Jack—"

He snatched her flailing hands. *"Do you want to kill me?"*

"I don't know!" she cried. "I don't know if I want to kill you or kiss you or hate you or save you! I don't skivvin' know! I just want it gone. This pain. It's distracting, and it hurts. I didn't ask for it." She bowed over, both hating and loving the feel of his grip. "Your stupid tattoos, the tortures, the outfit, the powers—" A dry sob clawed at her throat, but she swallowed it down. He stared at her, jaw clenching. "I spent four fucking months mourning you, and I can't just go back. I—I don't want to go back. So there's a part of me that thinks if this bond was gone, whatever happens to you won't hurt me again."

He opened his mouth, then shut it.

She lifted her tear-filled gaze to his saddened one. "I watched you die, Jack. Even though you are standing here, clearly alive, I don't think I ever got over that. Because you didn't come back the same." A thickness lodged in her throat. "Neither of us did."

Her hands settled. His palms slid atop them, and he shifted one to the center of his chest. He held her steady.

Strong hands that had killed. Died. Slammed a dagger over her heart.

But also, hands that felt so familiar. That pressed her into a bed while he made her moan and see stars. That held her snug against his body as they slept, as if afraid to let go.

It had been ripped from the both of them before they'd even settled into each other's skin. He believed her dead. She'd witnessed his death. Then they finally reunited in a world that was collapsing around them, and she didn't skivvin' recognize any of what they had before their final moment in Lust.

She held her breath. His gaze burned.

But she felt it.

Thump-thump, thump-thump, thump-thump.

His heartbeat, a gentle reminder that he was alive and breathing and—

"Is it really you?" she whispered.

"Yes," he whispered back. "This part is me and it will always be me."

"And the other parts?"

"Those died in Lust." He took a deep breath. "I'm not the same person anymore—physically, a bit emotionally and mentally, too. He filled me with blood and DNA of five different species. Droan, Endolier, Aurien, Lovuphal, and Mer. From the moment I woke, I was not the same. I knew I couldn't be the same. I was completely new, different. I even thought you had been a dream, but then he told me you were dead, and with all this newness, I thought I could let the past go and become this monster he wanted me to be. But that monster never happened. I still couldn't leave…and I think he knows he can't influence me in the way he wants to, but as long as I'm there for his experim—" Jack shook his head. "As long as I'm there and I listen, I don't think he cares. He doesn't believe he can be taken down."

She opened her mouth—

"But I'm not removing the bond." He showed his blood-stained palm, revealing a completely healed cut. "I won't agree to that. He won't use me to hurt you."

Strands of hair fell into her face as she shook her head. "Jack, I..."

"It's you." His breathy whisper hugged her cheek. "I was ready to become a monster, but you were a lifeline I was desperate to hang on to. And I despise the way this sounds—" The corner of his mouth lifted. "Honestly, I despised that this was true, but the idea of seeing you again kept me going."

"Ew." His heart picked up its pace underneath her palm, matching her own. "That was gross of you."

"Probably the most unattractive thing I've ever said."

"Was there supposed to be a violin band for that monologue?"

"They called out sick. Something about being terrified of me."

She bit her lip. "That's too bad, it would have made you look even more soft."

"*Soft.*" He scoffed. "I want to rinse my mouth out with rubbing alcohol. There are convenience stores in the city. We can run an errand..." Jack snorted and shook his head. "No. Never mind. That sounds dreadfully domestic."

"We could set the store on fire afterward. That's not very domestic."

His fingers squeezed hers, and he said, "Arson. Good pivot. I like it."

She couldn't resist the smile that crawled to her face.

Jack's eyes danced over her expression, and the green in them seemed to lighten. "There it is."

His intense stare had it falling. A scowl replaced it. "You don't get my smiles yet."

He snorted. "You saved Anaya and Rio? With this?" He trailed a finger along the lines of her dimming Vanisher light.

"I blackmailed Jodin and stabbed him in the shoulder. He brought them here," she said.

"Impressive girl." Jack smirked. "No wonder he didn't mention it. That's embarrassing for him."

"Super embarrassing, he probably cries about it."

His eyes flicked to the wound on her head and his expression shadowed. "Is there more?"

"It doesn't hurt—" she started.

That wasn't the right thing to say.

"My abilities heal—" She started.

"They don't heal fast enough. Open your mouth."

It popped open out of shock.

He suddenly grabbed her and swung her around. Her back warmed from his front. A moment later, a swelling wound on his arm shoved its way to her lips. His blood met her tongue. The same taste as the vial Jodin gave her earlier. Violet reluctantly swallowed. He continued to hold her close, so gently that she melted, remembering this type of touch. Affection that she accepted. His breath met her ear. "My blood heals faster."

She tracked her brain for whatever power it might be, but her thoughts ended when his other hand wormed its way down her side and rested on her hip. Gripping.

A breath later, when he was satisfied, he removed his arm and she choked. "What. The. Fu—"

Jack spun her around, grabbed both sides of her face, and kissed her. His thumb slid over her throat, squeezing, and she gasped at the sensitivity from Zavar's boot. He pulled back, looked down, and his eyes swirled murky.

But all the pain she felt, the cuts and bruises from her battle, began to warm and heal. She placed one hand on his chest and pushed. He finally moved, stepping back to give her some space as her eyes drifted over him.

"How much do you want me?" She tilted her head. The bare chiffon suddenly felt stiff. Tight. The steam spiraled her hair as well as her core.

Jack's eyes briefly dipped to the entrance. When they landed back on her, his expression was full predator. A shiver slithered down her spine, and with a graceful hand, she pulled the first strap off her shoulder. One breast met the broiling space and his eyes flashed. He didn't make a move. Instead, looked to the entrance.

Annoyance flared. "I'm *undressing*—"

"And I'm making sure no eyes lay on what's mine tonight." He drank her in. "No ears hear the sounds I'm going to drag from you. If anyone interrupts this, you'll be moaning my name in their blood."

He said it so plainly, so brazenly, that her breaths came faster. Her chest puffed as she stepped on the cavern floor, bare toes curling. She pulled the other strap off, her chest now bare. The chiffon draped along her waist. Sweat licked her stomach.

"How much do you want me, Jack?" she drawled again.

His lips twitched. He prowled over and his fingers dove into the remains of her dress still covering her lower half. She stopped breathing. "Too much," he purred.

He ripped the chiffon off her body. The scraps fluttered to the floor. She stood, naked, but he made no move to touch her.

He tore his corset off and began to unbutton his shirt underneath. She turned around, ignoring how much her mouth dried at the sight of him. His heady gaze burned her back. Her toes met puddles of water, and her hand lifted to the cascading hot shower pouring from the gaping ceiling. Behind the waterfall, she spotted bottles of soap.

"Did your behind get bigger?"

"Probably." Violet didn't turn. The water met her head, soaking her hair, and the heat coiled with the burn in her bones. She reached for the first bottle of soap and dumped a dollop in her hand. She began to wash, but her movements became lithe and sensual. She angled her head and let the water cascade through her hair, down her chest, where her nipples perked.

The rattling of a belt snapped her attention toward the next soap bottle. Violet filled her hand with a mountain of vanilla-smelling stuff, and when the water spray began to fissure in different directions, when the heat became unbearable because his body sidled close, she turned around and flattened her back against the smooth rock wall. Her eyes caught Jack's. She stared between her lashes, letting her mouth part...

And rubbed the soap over her body. Down and down, until mostly washed off, and without taking her eyes away from Jack, she dipped her fingers between her legs.

Jack, in his naked, tattooed, muscled glory, stepped under the water and watched her with a dark, sinful gaze, until his curls were dripping on his neck. Violet let one of her legs fall open, using the wall to steady, and she pressed into her folds. A whimper fell from her lips, and she bowed her head back.

"How much do you want *me*, Violet?" He breathed, unblinking as he stared.

She held his gaze. "Too much."

Her vision became his impossible beauty. They both searched and studied their new bodies, the same but different, and even after all their changes, Violet still felt herself getting worked up. Her cheeks grew hot. She slapped her other palm to the wall. Rubbed at her center. Jack's green sparkled. He took a step forward as she moved harder and gasped. Pleasure flooded. She squeezed her eyes tight. She kept going, her climax in sight, and when she lifted her lids, Jack crowded around her. He didn't touch her, but his palms were flat on the wall at either side of her head. He watched her fingers and dragged his gaze up her body, back to her face.

"Feel good?" His voice was rough. Restraint rippled along his muscles.

"Yes," she said breathily.

He cocked his head, eyes heavy-lidded. "Have you thought about me every time you've done this?"

"In your dreams," she muttered back. She flicked her fingers again and a full moan escaped. Jack's eyes landed on her mouth.

He dipped closer, lips brushing hers. "False. In my dreams, I have my hand wrapped around your throat as you scream my name."

At that, Violet felt herself nearing the edge. Her vision dotted with black. She clenched hard; her teeth, her core, her heart.

"Almost there, baby," he said.

She bit her lip. His eyes zeroed in on that. The warmth of his skin danced with the warmth of her oncoming orgasm, and with the memory of his hands, his lips, the pleasure she felt entangled with him, Violet moaned her release.

Jack didn't touch her as she came down. When her vision returned, his lips were quirked with a smile, a dimple showing. He looked at her like she was a gift. "What do you want now, Violet?"

Skies, the way her name sat on his tongue. It made her shiver. Her breathing was ragged. She dragged her used fingers and slid them into her mouth, sucking. Jack groaned softly.

"Touch me, Jack Marin," she said. She drew her mouth to his. "Make this world fade away."

A true smile. "As you wish."

And with that, they collided.

She'd forgotten what he felt like. How he tasted. The way his hand sought the nape of her neck, and his fingers wove through her hair. His other hand came to her throat, his thumb tracing along her jaw. It caressed, pressed, angled her to deepen their kiss.

The only thing that filtered through the heady daze was one thought:

This is definitely *Jack.*

His lips were soft. A yearning, breathless groan escaped from his mouth, and in response, she wrapped her arms around his neck, tugging him closer. The water pounded around them. New abilities, new destinies, new worlds. She wanted to explore it all with him. She whined into the kiss, opened her mouth and dragged her tongue across his bottom lip. He matched her ferocity. Insatiable. She bit his lip, and his hand slid down her body, wrapping around her ass. He slapped it gently.

"I'm sleeping on this thing tonight," he grumbled.

She laughed, then dragged him back into a kiss. He pressed her into the wall, but pulled away after a moment and dropped to his knees.

He wasted no time lifting one of her legs up and throwing it over his shoulder. His mouth immediately found her folds. Her clit. She moaned desperately, and Jack sighed, "The rest of your sounds are by me tonight. Don't forget who gave them to you."

"I could—" His mouth was back on her. "*Never.*"

He was soft and gentle. His fingers squeezed her thighs, and he groaned as he lapped her up. She leaned her head on the wall. Her gasps became louder. Jack hummed, and the sound trailed from her core to her throat to her toes and to the fingers she shoved into his wet hair. He flicked his tongue, and she bit her gasp.

Then his fingers slid into her.

One, two. Jack curled and Violet moaned. His eyes, framed by dark, wet lashes, looked up from between her legs, and when she met her edge again, they lightened. Encouraged her. She came down around his fingers, and he gave her a soft kiss before rising.

He grabbed the back of her head and dragged their mouths together. "Skies, I could eat you all day."

Her only response was a whimper. This was Jack's appetizer, and she was already having a hard time standing.

Her slapped her rear.

"Up," he said.

She jumped and he caught her, snagging her lips again. He dragged them from the showering cavern, dipping down once to grab something, and then to the adjacent bedroom. The dark-sheeted bed greeted them. Violet bit her lip, ecstasy coursing through her. She felt on top of the world—ready to be ravished and to forget her name. Ready to be in her safe place. She dipped her head and licked up his neck.

Jack shuddered, then paused. "Have you...been with anyone else? Since me?"

She creased her brows. "What?"

His expression turned sincere. His one hand splayed across her lower back, fingers tightening just a bit. He searched her gaze, and within those irises, Violet could tell he fought something. The next words? This?

"Not that it would matter," he said quickly. "Not like that. I wouldn't blame you for anything—you can do what you want, but it's more for protection—"

"No," she murmured.

He nodded.

Her gut soured and her mouth immediately dried. Skies, she didn't want to, but… "Have you been with anyone else?"

She swore she'd go deaf with how loud her heart pounded. She wouldn't blame him—but it would still…hurt. She bit her tongue. No, it wouldn't hurt. She wouldn't let it hurt. There was nothing *to* hurt. Jack could do what he wanted and as he pleased, and if that meant sleeping with someone else, she…

"No," he muttered. "I haven't."

"Really?" she blurted. Then she shut her skivvin' mouth.

Jack snorted. "Surprised?"

"No—I—"

"A shower and thoughts of a pretty, blue-eyed girl with an awful mouth does the trick." He smirked and brushed his lips along her jaw. "Especially when I remember you bent over before me."

Heat doused her. A horrible blush crept across her cheeks, and she yanked on his curls. "You little skiv."

He answered with a dimpled smile.

She could feel the taut, hard muscles both holding her and his control, and she squeezed them, loving the feel of how tightly he held her against his body, especially the feeling of his hard-on when she ground her hips against his. His tip brushed her entrance. Jack dropped her on the bed and leaned.

"I was going to be…gentle." His breathing tightened. "But you're walking a very, *very* thin line."

"I like walking it," she teased as she kissed up his jaw and tugged on his curls. "You like me bent over, and I like you struggling to handle yourself."

"I'm trying to be good to you, Vi—"

She grabbed his jaw and locked their gaze. His eyes swarmed, the green blazing, and every bit of her wanted to burst into butterflies. His breath was hot on her lips as she said, "I don't want you to be good to me. I want you to ruin me."

Jack held millions of strings when it came to control.

And she witnessed every single one of them snap at that very moment.

He pinned her down and ground his erection into her core. She nipped at his jawline, dragged her tongue down the column of his throat, and bit his collarbone, sucking hard enough to leave a mark.

His grip grew bruising, and she loved it. A moan escaped as he rubbed at her core, pressing in that precise little spot. He smiled at her reaction. He stopped suddenly, bending down and picking up his belt—what he must have grabbed from the cavern. He tossed it to the side of the bed. "For later." He winked.

He dove for her. His hand wrapped around her throat. Squeezed. The other tugged hard at her hair. He ground deeply between her legs. She was surrounded by him, overwhelmed by his control. Yet she wanted him to take it all. His hands gripped her arms, slid down them—

"What is this?" His fingers dragged along the scar at her forearm. Left by a sharp nail that dug into her a world ago. Renell popped into her mind, but she shut that image down.

"From when I entered. They shot me with an arrow, and I was hurt coming into Greed."

He pulled back, eyes raking over her and snagging on the mishmash of a scar at her hip. Flames burst in the green. "They shot you?"

"You didn't know this?"

"I didn't…" He tugged her in for a kiss, ending the conversation. *Didn't know you were alive.*

But Jack wasn't stupid. He clearly had little proof she'd been killed.

I didn't want to believe you were alive, because it felt like torture.

Perhaps they tortured each other. But they were also both used to pain.

Jack dipped suddenly and kissed the plasgun scar on her shoulder. Then the scar at her forearm. His lips continued to find each scar dotting her. He licked and nipped along her skin, replacing bitter memories with pleasure.

His mouth fell upon her breast, and she bowed into it, a whine escaping. Skies, the work of his tongue, the maneuvers and flicks the wretched thing did. Her nails dug into his tattoos. Her breaths grew heavier. He switched to the other one, and her lids shuttered closed.

"Nope," he exhaled against her skin. His hand wrapped her throat. "Look at me."

She opened her eyes, locking with his gaze.

"Watch me as I make you scream my name."

She wanted him to ruin her. To make such a mess out of her that she couldn't dare wash him off. His words, his mouth, his body ravaged her. She was on fire, and she would never, *never*, be able to put it out.

He kissed his way down her stomach.

"Again?" she said exasperatedly.

"Again." He licked her navel. "And again, and again, and *again*."

She nearly drooled at the sight of him—naked, sexy, tattooed, and very, *very* ready for her. It was a frenzied reunion. They were desperate in their kisses, with their hands, and before she could wrap a hand around him, he splayed her out on the bed and dove into her core.

Those magnificent lips devoured her. The tongue flicks, the sucks, she was a canvas, and he was making art. Her hands were stuffed into his curls, pulling hard enough to make his scalp sore later, but she didn't care. She loved everything about it. He tucked her legs over his shoulders and went deeper. Her climax drew in, her heart slammed, and she arched into his sinful mouth.

"Jack," she breathed. "*Jack*, oh fuck. Oh skies."

"That's my good girl." His fingers found her entrance, pushing in. "Beg for me."

She keeled as he curled them. There wasn't one wrong move with this man.

"*Please, Jack*," she begged. Her legs wobbled and she clenched her thighs. He pulled them apart. "Please. I need you."

"I need you to come for me first."

He didn't even demand it from her. He asked it simply, and when his fingers found a rhythm, she was a goner. She used his hair as a handlebar, and she just fucking took it. Her vision spotted with black. Her orgasm smacked into her, leaving her breathless, tight, and a mess.

"I'll do more later, but I am horribly desperate to fuck you now." He looked almost apologetic, and she wanted to laugh. He crawled up over her and collided their lips. "Literal anguish."

He lined up with her entrance, and before she had a chance to say something back, he smirked. "Hold tight."

Violet didn't know whether he meant him, the bed sheets, or her sanity.

And when he slowly pushed in, felt his generous size, she clawed his back. He didn't go slow for long. Once he was all the way in, Jack took a shuddering breath and stared at her, glossy-eyed, before he picked up his pace. He bent down, caught a nipple in his mouth, and sucked. One hand clutched her thigh tightly, the other gripped her jaw.

"Just like that," she said with a nod. "Yes, yes…"

"Like that?" Jack licked up her breast.

"*Please.*"

Jack followed her orders and kept up with his intense pace. It was nothing like Lust, which might have clouded their true passion. This was full of sin; wet and sweaty and pressed against each other with roguish desperation. She dragged her nails down his back and Jack groaned, eventually turning her to the side and burying again. Sweat glistened on his forehead. His hand snaked down the curve of her back before it smacked her ass. He hit that spot, staying there for a moment, before hitting it again.

Her next orgasm slapped her, and she cried in pleasure.

Jack had a dirty, satisfied grin on his face.

He held on for a long while. At some point she was on top, grinding into him, and he bit her nipple. She moaned with a smile. He kissed her and flipped her over to her stomach, gently caressing her ass as he tugged it up. Grabbing her hands, she bit a gasp as he thrust into her, but at the same time locking her wrists together behind her back with a leather...

A deep pitch. A loud uncontrollable, whine.

He tightened his belt around her wrists and fastened it. He kept up his rhythm, breathy grunts escaping. Only when his hand wrapped around her neck and squeezed the sides, did her body tighten. Her toes curled. She squeezed her eyes shut. Stars flickered. Jack moaned and bit her shoulder. "Come on, baby. Fuck, *fuck*—"

Violet choked out a scream. "*Jack.*"

"Like that." He pressed his sweaty forehead into her shoulder. "Come on, come on, love."

He hit that spot, over and over, never breaking pace. She grew dizzy as she reached a peak she'd never been to, the orgasm so strong, so demanding that she felt like she portaled into a new world. Her senses zapped and her climax carried over. "Oh skies—"

"Yeah, they aren't helping you now," Jack drawled. "Another one, baby."

"No, Jack—"

"Yes, you can, you beautiful girl."

Between the hold on her wrists, the strong grip on her throat, the breathy moans they both shared, and the way he kept hitting that *damn* spot, Violet came again. Tears sprung in her eyes at how good and brutal it felt, along with the way he handled her.

Jack lifted off her, snapping his hips three times more before he fully pushed in and stilled. She turned her head.

His body gleamed with a coat of sweat, his tattoos some sexy, nightmarish thing to look at. His curls stuck to his skin, his lips parted as he squeezed his eyes shut and tilted his head to the ceiling, revealing that strong, lickable throat.

He looked like a fucking god.

He shivered with his own release, muscles contracting as he sucked in deep, heavy breaths. "Holy fucking skies."

Violet rested her cheek on the sheets, sleep—no, *death*—singing a lullaby in her head. "That was…amazing."

Jack regarded her with a growing, dimpled smile. "Yes, yes, it was." He unfastened the belt and kissed her shoulder. "You did so well, but there…" He snorted. "I left quite a few love bites on you."

He pulled out. She whimpered and rolled over. Jack immediately fell on his stomach beside her. She glimpsed his back. "Well, I certainly scratched up your back, too."

He smiled into the sheets. "That means I did a good job."

"Are you able to stay the night?" she whispered.

He nodded and brushed a strand of wet hair back from her face. He opened his mouth, as if to say something, but his eyes began to close. He tried to fight the lull of slumber, but Violet eventually watched them shut and his breath evened. He jerked just once, turning, and she bit her yelp as he wrapped an arm around her waist and tugged her flush into his body.

"Almost forgot," he muttered.

Silence passed. Violet remained slightly awake, thoughts running wild as their sex high simmered, and the Fire Night predicament rose. He clutched her harder as if sensing where they ran. "We're safe. I have it all figured out. But…please don't run away, Vi." His lips met her sweaty shoulder. "Not from me."

And then he was out, and Violet wandered into a dreamless land right after.

27

PARTNER

JELAN WOKE. STRETCHED. UNLOCKED HER bedroom door and padded to the kitchen to find a steaming mug of black coffee waiting for her as it always was on the kitchen island. She gave a curt nod to Luka, whose eyes tracked her above his newspaper, and found the remote for the plascreen.

She turned on the Sins trackers. Searched for Violet's name first as she did every morning. Her lips met the ring of the ceramic, and she sighed as she took her first sip. Her eyes landed on her target. A green dot.

Jelan furrowed her brows and pulled the mug away. "Asher?"

Luka didn't look up from his newspaper. "Excuse me?"

"Violet's last name…is 'Asher' now."

No ruffling. No indication of interest. "So?"

Jelan set her coffee cup down gently, swallowing. "Someone replaced it."

At that, Luka's newspaper folded over and his silver eyes focused on her. She steeled her back and held his gaze.

"Replaced it?"

"Yes," she said. "That's not her last name."

"Maybe it is a glitch."

"They can track their blood across dimensions and worlds. I doubt it is a pixel problem."

He went back to the paper. "Maybe someone is having fun. Not everything has to have an underlying reason. Sutton is also a common name in the South, given to—"

"Those who didn't have fathers to the family. Yes, I know the name is everywhere. Fifteen other people have it in the sixth world alone." Jelan sucked a shaky breath. Luka's gaze darted to her lips, then back to her eyes. He lowered the paper to the table.

"You're saying there is an underlying reason," he said, his voice gravelly.

"I'm saying that *Asher* isn't...a coincidence. It's her middle name. Well, sort of." Jelan tapped a fingernail on the table. "It's not registered. Her mother never gave her a middle name. Even Meema—Coco Mathan—didn't know about it until Violet started writing it on her school papers randomly one day."

He quipped a brow.

"She never really explained where she got it from. Meema noticed it first, Violet had refused to give an answer—she'd been like eight or nine at the time—and it wasn't until Reed trailed Violet that they realized Violet would hang with this man at a bodega a couple of times a week. Reed confronted the man. Nearly beat him up actually for only being what like eleven? Twelve? But the man ran down an alley and disappeared. Violet was upset for *weeks*." Jelan rubbed at her temple. "I remember Reed told me this story a long time ago because he and Violet were in the middle of a fight and weren't on speaking terms for like two weeks, and he wanted to rant about it. But it stuck with me."

"So...the man was named Asher?"

Jelan shook her head. "No. It was the name on the candy bars he'd gift her. There was a wrapper left there and it freaked Reed out—"

"So she gave herself the middle name after a candy bar?"

"*No*," Jelan said firmly, reigning in her scowl at Luka's teasing gaze. "It freaked him about because there wasn't a candy bar labeled *Asher's Mint Chocolate* anywhere in the city. Reed spent years with it on his mind, thinking that it was some fancy thing, but nothing like it existed. So Reed, of course, thought it was a drug the weird man was feeding Violet. But it had some metallic, red label and with this glittery stuff that was…" Jelan swallowed, throat tight. "*Otherwordly.* He had said."

Luka stared long and hard, probably searching for the lie in the story. It was a ridiculous story, and Jelan had thought Reed was on drugs when he ranted to her on the curb outside the bar Violet had stormed from. Maybe Reed was upset that Violet kept things from him, but Violet kept certain things from everyone. Jelan hadn't expected one of those things to be the name of a candy bar that didn't exist.

In this world.

"So…" He finally said. "Only so few people know that Violet Sutton once added *Asher* to her name."

"Literally me, Meema, a couple of schoolteachers, and Reed," Jelan murmured. "There's just…no way. Violet stopped after Reed found the man. It was never talked about again."

"And now…" Luka glanced at the screen. Jelan looked with him.

Violet Asher.

"There's just no way," Jelan breathed again.

It wasn't a coincidence. Was it a message? Was it a warning? Jelan snapped her gaze to Reed's name, but his last name was still *Sutton.* It blinked green in the sixth world.

Jelan leaned forward. "Your father knows things. Has access to things. There's…"

"This isn't any of my concern. It's jarring, sure, but it doesn't make a difference to us."

"Something could be going on—"

"Drop it," Luka said firmly. "It's giving me a headache."

Jelan's jaw slacked. "Are you—"

"Serious?" He went back to his paper. "Absolutely. Your focus is on showing me the proper productions for a plashield so I can swap you for my dear little sister. It should not be on your candy-wrapper-obsessed friend who *ran* to her guaranteed death. We made discoveries on archaic things about Calesal the other day, but the further we go, the more people we give a death sentence."

Jelan stood abruptly. Words lodged in her throat. Luka didn't spare her a glance, and she witnessed the uncaring wall build between them. She closed her mouth, grabbed her coffee mug, and stormed out of the room.

When she slammed her door, she pressed her back against it. Her chest grew tight, breaths shorter and shorter. Jelan hurried for her beside drawer and rummage through her tiny notes until she found her inhaler. She slumped to the side of her bed and sucked hard.

Reed's voice clambered into her mind.

"She hasn't had a friend like you. Not one that comes around to the house." *He sagged on the curb and kicked a bottle.* *"I'm…worried."*

"You think the man did anything?"

Reed shook his head. *"No. He was pretty shocked to see me storming up. Must have scared him. I couldn't see his face clearly beneath the hat, and mind you I was also…drunk. But Violet was adamant he only gave her candy bars and she'd seen him like four times, during the day, and he never touched her. So I don't think that's in the question but…"* *Reed sighed deeply.* *"I can't reach her anymore. Not like I used to before our mother passed."*

Jelan glanced to the busy, bar-filled road. Fifteen years old and she already knew the regulars here. Reed was one of them. He didn't even bother chasing Violet down the street after they got into a fight and the bouncer kicked them out. *"Maybe her secrets are just a way of holding on to some control of her life."* *Jelan sipped her beer.* *"Don't punish her for that."*

Reed dropped to the curb. Jelan sat next to him. He nudged her. *"At least she has you."*

"And I have her."

"Maybe some space is good."

"Maybe."

"But…" *He rubbed at his face.* *"I don't want to lose her."*

"Let her have this Asher thing. Let her breathe on her own. Yeah, she'll get in trouble but we all do and that's how she can learn. Skies know we need independence from pesky older brothers."

At that, he laughed.

It was a message to her. *Reed's* message to her.

The Sins wasn't a game anymore.

❋❋❋

Luka left for a meeting with his father at Plastech Industries. He'd been gone longer than Jelan was used to, so when she finally finished her scribbles and corrections, she let out a frustrated sigh. For the past hour, her ears strained on the apartment door's keypad, waiting for the familiar lull of the buttons he pressed. She sat up from the couch and scowled at the door. Where was he?

She bid her time by compiling her notes into organized sections that will never rival Luka's, then went about wiping the kitchen counters. She put the dishes away from her lunch and paced the living room, before turning to the refrigerator and pursuing something else to eat. She was bored. Antsy.

She was waiting for him to come back.

She stilled with the bag of shredded cheese in her hand. *Back. Waiting.* All the words she shouldn't associate with Luka. She did the same thing with Lucien, but Lucien was easier, less rigid, and cold. He would always swing by her tiny lab when he returned to give a soft hello and check in, whereas here…she was waiting for the bare minimum of a man who *kidnapped* her.

Lucien checked in via Luka every now and then, and Jelan wrote back once detailing that she was fine, but otherwise, the communication was minimal. Mai was apparently *relaxing* as Lucien put it; enjoying the amenities of a personal Marin apartment that included a private chef and lots of shows. Mai liked popcorn—something Jelan never thought she'd know about the girl.

She missed the penthouse, sure, but being left alone in an apartment that only one other person shared was…nice. There were no ins and outs of servants and familial people, not that she minded, but privacy became lacking at some points except in her bedroom.

She shoved a hand into the bag of cheese and dumped a swath into her mouth. Took one more bite. Put it back into the fridge and shut the door—

The keypad clicked. Her heart jumped. She moved to the sink and washed her hands, hating how her mind zeroed in on the peripheral front door. It opened. A sleek, shiny leather shoe stepped through, followed by the tailored businessman suit, and ruffled hair.

She paused. Shut the running water off. Looked at him entirely. Ruffled hair.

And a welling red spot on his jaw, right above the crisp collar of his shirt.

"What…" she started.

The silver in Luka's eyes inflamed. "Leave."

She bristled, gripping the counter for stability. She opened her mouth—

"*Leave*," he snarled. The front door slammed as he took long strides to his wing of the apartment. His bedroom door shut, rattling the ceiling fixtures.

She stood in the kitchen for a long moment, gathering her breath and thoughts. The *leave* part didn't phase her; he was a man caught and angered and embarrassed to be seen with a legitimate welt on his strong jawline. Jelan didn't need a lineup to know who committed the act.

She clenched her fists, attempting to settle her racing heart, before she grabbed her notes off the couch and stormed to his door. She didn't bother knocking.

He didn't bother locking, either.

"Do you want him dead?" she asked, standing in the threshold. He sat on the edge of his cool-colored bed, head in his hands and hair even more chaotic. She was so used to it in a tiny ponytail or bun, with only a few tendrils slipping out, that it unnerved her. "Do you…want your father gone?"

"I thought I told you to leave."

She flashed an incredulous look. "I'm not sure where to go, being kidnapped and all."

"Well, you know where the front door is."

"Funny," she said. "I also know where a man's balls are so I can kick them."

He lifted his head, fire ebbing as she shut her mouth and lifted her chin. That was certainly a daring thing for her to say.

"Marin has people outside of the building, always watching. I'm sure if you strutted up and got in their car, they'll take you far away from me."

"I'm not leaving." She padded to him. He straightened, eyeing her warily. She threw her stack of notes on his lap. "There's your plashield. You were missing a few components. I'll come in and build it myself if you want, but before I do that, I need you to answer my first question."

He didn't even glance at the papers. His eyes were daggers on her, dancing around her face, her bare arms, then to her scarred hands that she didn't bother to hide, and he didn't seem to linger on.

"It's complicated."

"It's a yes or no question."

"So demanding," he breathed, lips quirking. "And brave of you."

"Just because you're the son of the emperor doesn't mean you're to be feared," she said. "And I don't fear you."

"Then your self-preservation is abysmal."

"My self-preservation is for worrying about my next meal, not arrogant men who run an entire city."

"You don't have to worry about your next meal."

"Why?"

"Because I'm willing to gamble it's going to be me."

Her breath stalled. She stepped back, accosted. "What?"

He smirked, clearly satisfied he riled her. "Yes, I want my father dead."

Her heart thundered out of rhythm. Playing with her, that's what he was doing. She hated that her eyes had dropped to his sardonic mouth. "Then let Lucien keep Mai and use her to cross the bridge. That's all he needs—collateral, like everyone else in this damn city. On top of that, you have the full plashield." She motioned to his welt. "Use the skivvin' thing next time he raises his fist at you."

Luka stood, towering ominously over her. "And there's one more advantage."

She ignored her pulse at his proximity. "What is that?"

Glittering eyes and all, he drawled, "Do you know of a man named Faroh Blich?"

❀❀❀

Faroh Blich—the elusive childhood friend of Reed Sutton, liege of Jack Marin, and the bane of Violet's existence when he popped up at Souther's Square every now and then to taunt her.

Jelan didn't think she'd be standing in the square again so soon. Yet here she was, beneath the beating, buttery late morning sun, dressed in Souther clothes that were procured and standing next to Luka Arvalo, second son and City Commander of Calesal.

His ensemble was the same incognito version, and he pulled it off well. It boggled her to see him in jeans, leathers, and a simple shirt, along with a cap. He didn't seem so out of place, which made Jelan ask, "Have you been here before?"

"The South is the only place my brothers won't follow me to and my father won't find me in." He shrugged. "Well, I realized that when Park got into some bad business with Marin's gang and ended up around here, drunk as shit. We were only sixteen."

"Your father must have had a fit."

The square milled with its regular chaos, but Luka managed to stall it to a blur around them. He gave her a wink. "He never found out."

She had no doubt Lucien's men trailed her, but this mission was beneficial on both sides. Jenkins had been searching high and low for Faroh, and for Jenkins to fail was unheard of. But Faroh was a shadow; and had laid low since Jack Marin lost the gardia wars over two years ago.

Because, as Jelan found out when she began work with Lucien, Faroh was the traitor. The bug. The leech that took Jack's gardia and handed it straight to Arvalo. He was the reason Reed had to forfeit everything that fateful night, along with the bombs that were apparently placed beneath hospitals and orphanages and Violet's house that forced Reed to surrender.

Faroh was the one that contributed to Jack's downfall and Arvalo's reign. On top of being one of the most wanted men in the city by Marin's gardia, he was also the only man to have held leverage over Arvalo to get out scathe free. Luka believed it had something to do with the sewers and the plaspoints.

Jelan was not only getting an adventure, she was also supplying the man who took Violet's virginity right into Lucien's hands.

"Come," Luka said, jutting his chin to Sobra Bar. Jelan had taken quite a few shots there one night and failed to remember her and Violet hijacking two bicycles that they subsequently crashed into bushes. Luka snorted, "Memories?"

She didn't realize her mouth had quipped. She smoothed her expression. "Something like that."

Her gaze darted to the Sins Screen as they passed over the square, nearly bumping into the plethora of Southers and skirting through the market stalls. *Violet Asher*. Still green. She'd forgotten to check Rio Gaverra's name. She glanced to the fifth world only to realize it wasn't there. A scan of the sixth, and she found him. He'd made it.

They wandered up the un-swept stoop of Sobra and through the dusty door. It creaked into a low-lit, drooped-ceiling bar with soft beats playing out of the speakers. The bar was emptier than usual, but within a few hours, it will be packed. Jelan was thankful for it—she'd gotten used to not sweating consistently and having space in the North.

"There." Luka's hand brushed her back, gently nudging her, and she began sweating. No air conditioner would be powerful enough to cool her. "Back left booth."

And she saw him—Faroh Blich, the same as ever. He looked a little more raggedy this time; stressed, exhausted, clearly on edge as his nose buried in his shiva with his eyes darting about the bar. They landed on Luka and widened, then slid to Jelan and bugged.

He stood, looking toward the door, but Luka's firm face told him that was a bad move. He sat back down, sighing.

They slid into the booth across from him.

Faroh's dark hair fell to his brows and curled behind his ears. His olive skin paled as he shrunk under Luka's hard eyes. "I thought…"

"That there would be a middleman passing the information? No. Just me."

"Congrats on your promotion, then." Faroh's eyes fell on Jelan. "And what are you…"

"His accomplice," she said.

"Fantastic." Faroh shot his drink back and motioned to the bartender for another one. "I can tell my freedom is coming to an end."

"You might still have it as long as you cooperate." Luka pulled out a paper from his pocket and unfolded it. The wind symbol with the star shaded the center. He tapped it. "Recognize this?"

Faroh rubbed at his face. "Fuck. Yes, I've seen it doing daddy's dirty work down there. Why?"

"This was also in the dungeons of the Empire's library, etched before a crushed-in corridor." Luka folded the paper back up and placed it back in his pocket. "I want to know where you saw this."

"And what do I get in return?"

Jelan leaned over the table. "Me not blabbing about you to Marin's gardia."

Faroh paled four shades. His brown eyes shot around the room, then back to Jelan. "I heard you were working with Marin, but this…confuses me."

"Just tell us where it is and I won't put a bullet between your eyes," Luka said casually.

Faroh rolled said eyes. "Fine."

They followed him out of the bar, where he took one more shot and stuffed a hat on his head, then to the alley out back. They walked nine blocks until Jelan's temples dripped in sweat, before Faroh took a turn into an alleyway hanging with drying laundry. He halted, looked at both ends to make sure no one was watching, and moved aside a cardboard box. A grated door appeared. "It's a cellar of an old bar that leads to the sewers. It was how we smuggled stuff, but I saw it numerous times here and well…with daddy Arvalo, too." He sneered. "When he had me meeting with him in the sewers in the North."

"Skies, you really are a traitor." Jelan clenched her fists. "You really ruined it all."

Faroh lifted his hands. "Money pays for loyalty, baby—"

Luka pulled out a plasgun and pressed it against Faroh's cheek. "And a wanted man pays for an apology."

Jelan's brows crumpled, but in her peripheral, figures moved into the alley—ones with Marin gardia emblems. Their faces were masked and she didn't recognize their eyes, but Luka held that plasgun to the incessantly sweaty, knee-trembling Faroh, until two men plascuffed him and dragged him away.

"I thought you said freedom!" Faroh struggled. "I thought…I thought you…"

But Faroh's helpless cries were muffled by a gag. A car door slammed and veered off of the street.

"An apology?" Jelan turned to Luka, lifting a brow.

Luka bent down, and with a couple of harsh pulls, the rusty metal door opened, revealing a cob-webbed staircase into a cellar. Sewage smacked into Jelan's nostrils. Luka pulled out masks and handed one to her. "For crashing his car."

❋❋❋

They descended into the bowels of Calesal. Through the cellar, they found another pair of wet steps that echoed with the thrush of water. Jelan put her headlamp on and the plasma flared red. She spotted the rats, the old, broken bottles of shiva, and the graffiti of past hangs. The fact Luka was a clean freak, he didn't seem to be unnerved by such filth. He pulled out the sewer and plaspoint map. "We would be here, closest to this path that leads beyond the wall. Following the one from the Midian hospital would have taken too long, but I had no idea where to look for the entrance, so Faroh wasn't completely useless for that. However, whatever business with plasma and Greed seems to be pinpointed in the North, but that would be heavily guarded."

"And probably unattainable to breach unless with a small army."

He nodded. "This first step is to determine what these little symbols mean. I'm guessing a pathway? A marking for escapees from something? Either way, it predetermines the wall."

Jelan leaned in, eyes trailing the map. "Maybe it gives answers to 'aether?'"

"The true enigma to all of this mess."

She glanced up to find he was already looking at her. She held her breath, aware of the scratches from critters and the drip of unknown liquid. His eyes barely dropped to her lips, then back up. He folded the map. "Lead the way, partner."

They descended the curving, archaic steps into further swaths of darkness. Jelan slipped at some point and Luka caught her elbow, righting her without saying a word. She carried on until her boots met a puddle of water, and a long tunnel extended before them. Luka had to duck to fully fit.

"Which way?" she asked, glancing to the long tunnel and the adjacent corridors strung along it.

He turned his head, with his headlamp, and looked to the wall. A glimmer of silver caught her eye. She gasped, pointing. "Look."

The air symbol. His light pointed down the sewer where in the distance, another minuscule twinkle beckoned.

He regarded the map and pulled a pen from his ear to mark it. "Left, then."

They continued in silence, avoiding the depressed center of the sewers where rats dove into water and trash lumbered the lazy stream. She thought it must have been hours in Calesal's bowels, every now and then stopping to check the map, then rerouting in the right direction. Her breathing became tight at one point, and she dug into her tiny backpack, pulling out her inhaler.

"I have a backup if you need it."

Her eyes shot to him. Through the red light of her headlamp, and the blue of his, he stared at her hands. She swallowed, "You do?"

"It would be annoying to carry your unconscious body out of this mess."

She scowled. "Shut up."

"If I can ask…" His eyes lingered on her scars. "How?"

"Building fire. Plasma burns." She shrugged. "It killed my mother and my brother. Ruined my family."

"And yet you still face plasma."

"Well, they're gnarly enough as it is. A few more burns wouldn't hurt."

"They are pretty ugly."

She whirled to him, mouth dropping open, to find his eyes alight with mischief. Teasing. She couldn't help the smile rising on her face. "You asshole."

There was no sensitivity crawling in her heart, and no urge to hide them. Instead, she flipped him the middle finger and, in a continuous teasing fashion, he snapped his teeth together, pretending to bite it.

They carried on, switching to other tunnels, until they found the smudge of silver again and again. Soon, the ground ascended and Jelan was huffing. At this point she became more worried about how they'll retrace their steps, but her curiosity overrode the survival. She knew they'd find a way back, but when else would they find a way forward?

"How do you…have this time?" she panted between breaths. "To do these things."

"Crawl through a sewer with my captive?" His velvety voice bounced against the stone.

"*Yes*," she blew in a breath.

"I hired people to take care of everything for me. I need to be there to sign certain things, but my City Commander job is just a face. My father, as you know, still has his foot in there."

She was jealous his breathing stayed even. "So, you just ride the wave of fame and money?"

"Depends on the perspective."

"Do you like the fame and money?"

"The money, of course. The fame also has its perks. I can bring many to their knees without batting an eye."

"I bet you like that."

"Depends on who."

"All the women who chase you? Do they enjoy it or do they leave rather quickly?"

His lithe fingers wrapped around her wrist. She whirled into his chest, her headlamp carving a red light across his high cheekbones and devilish expression. "You want to ask me if I have the biggest dick, don't you?"

Jelan choked. She stood chest to chest with him, lips parted as her brain racked his sentence. She glanced at her wrist—the one he still held. "You heard...?"

"Your conversation with my little sister?" His breath fluttered her eyelashes. "It was very enlightening."

His thumb stroked her skin, rubbing over the beginning of the scarred tissue, but no expression betrayed any true disgust that she expected when people touched it.

She played along, "Did you have an answer, then?"

He patted her hand and moved around her. "Only one way to find that out, baby."

And when she turned, his blue headlamp was on another silver marking, this time on the ceiling and next to a rusted-over grate.

"Ready?"

Not, really. She was still reeling from his flirtation and the fact that she...played *back*. But she shoved that down and nodded.

He turned the wheel on the grate. It didn't budge at first, but with some urging, Luka had it moving, peeling old metal and stone bits from its nonuse. When he reached the end, she brushed forward to help him. On her tiptoes, they pushed and the grate groaned, long and low, until it popped open a sliver. Sunlight seared the darkness and Jelan squinted at the sight of a bright blue sky and the green leaves of a very tall tree. They tried one more shove, but it wouldn't budge.

"Something's blocking it," Luka muttered, finally winded. He peered out, eyes widening as he looked. "Holy shit."

She tried to see on the tips of her toes, but the rim of the grate blocked the entire view. A cloud drifted over. The leaves rustled in the steady, warm wind. A gust dipped under the grate and brushed her cheeks.

"Here." Luka motioned to his back, holding his hands behind. She got the gist and jumped on, wrapping her arms around his neck as he piggybacked her to see the landscape in its entirety. She tried to ignore the warmth of him seeping into her thighs, her chest, or the way her nipples were already slightly hard as they rubbed against her leather straps.

But Jelan forgot all about the rich and famous man holding her the minute she glimpsed through the grate. Forgot about everything, really.

It was the rolling hills.

The wall.

The sprawling city *behind* it.

All of it took her medicined breath away. Luka squeezed her thighs.

"We're beyond the wall," she breathed. "There's…there's a way out."

"Only more to discover, *partner*."

Tears sprung in her eyes.

Only more to discover.

28

LIGHTNING

A BODY WARMED HIS SIDE. Hair spilled across his arm and breath tickled his shoulder. His eyes flashed open, and his heart pounded. It took a moment for him to remember where he was, and even assure himself that the person who slept next to him was real, and everything that happened *did* happen.

He'd felt that before—the jump and cursing of his nightly actions, then he'd quickly leave with a written note. But that was a very young Jack. One who hadn't learned respect and did whatever he wanted. But skies, he slept like the dead, and nearly everything about his life floated away. He had forgotten who he was, where he was, and who he was with.

For a moment he thought his past came back.

But he was different now. Bigger, stronger, more right in the head, and certainly more emotional. More destined for death. He wanted to laugh.

Violet slept soundlessly at his side. Her head rested in the crook of his shoulder, her fingers splayed across his stomach. She normally tossed and turned, especially when they were in Lust, and Jack was a light sleeper, so he was surprised he didn't wake up.

His gaze slid around the cavern bedroom, but there was no indication that someone had discovered them. The other captains and Fire Night attendees would still be rousing, he hoped, but he was assured by Jodin that the day after Fire Night was a lazy one.

People were so spent indulging that no one expected much from the captains.

His watch beeped from somewhere on the floor. Beeped again. A call. Jack ignored it. He had his plans. Jodin knew them, and Jodin passed Jack's trust test.

He cuddled into Violet. Her knee was flung over him, brushing his bottom half, and Jack felt the tingle. The blood rushing. And then all he could think about was holding her tight, with the belt and his hands, while he pounded into her.

He stifled his groan and debated waking her. Would that be selfish? He would make her feel incredibly good, so maybe it wasn't. By his fingers, tongue, and cock, he'd have her coming at *least* five times before he found his own release. That seemed like a good trade-off.

A dark smile grew. He was going to be very, very selfish, and then very generous. He'd let her sleep after.

He turned and kissed her forehead, her cheek, her slightly parted mouth. His fingers skated down her imperfect skin scattered with moles and scars until his hand gripped the dome of her ass and he tugged her closer. "Wakey, wake—"

She grabbed his arm and slapped it back to his side. Her eyes were wide. She bolted up, panic flaring across her features.

He winced but found his voice. "It's okay. You're safe."

"But Zavar—"

"Will not touch you," Jack pressed. He kissed her palm. "I have precautions."

She turned to him, those blue flickering with unease. He smelled her slight fear, then spicy fury, and skies, he wondered what it'd be like to bite her...

"He knows I can glamour myself," she said.

"You're perfectly fine," he assured. "You remember the blonde girl with red lips? The one whom you clearly wanted to murder? You'll disguise yourself as her, okay? As far as Zavar knows, I'm entangled with her—Sofie—and Mariah. He also believes I was drunk out of my mind last night."

Violet scowled at him.

He flashed a sheepish grin. "Now please ride my face."

The alarm ebbed, and a wicked smile split her lips. She rolled over and threw off the sheet covering his lower half. She licked her lips, taking in his erection.

"I'd rather do this." She pulled her hair back and lowered herself to her stomach. His eyes grew wide, and hers, doe-like, innocent. An expression foreign yet purposeful.

"You don't have to—*fuck*," Jack groaned as she licked his tip, wrapping her hand around him. "Vi, what—" He tilted his head back as she took him entirely in her mouth. Worked him, expertly.

She glanced at him innocently. "What?"

"I will not last long if you do that." He breathed deeply. "Or look at me like that."

"Perfect." She smiled sweetly. "Because my jaw will most definitely ache after a while with...*this*." She licked him again. Teased, before she spit along his shaft and just fucking went for it.

He helped push her hair out of the way but *skies*, his control was unraveling. Her warm mouth, the flick of her tongue. His other hand clenched the sheets.

His watch beeped again, and he was tempted to throw it into a pool, but her mouth drew all thoughts out of his head, and all he could do was watch her. Shove her head down enough that tears sprang in her eyes, and she smiled, *enjoying* it. An approving growl rumbled his chest and he released. She swallowed it all. Licked her lips. Crawled up along him, and with a little urging, he was hard again...

She lowered herself onto him.

And then a flash lit the room.

Jack acted fast. He flipped Violet and slapped a hand over her mouth, before tugging the bed sheet over them, covering her with his body, both to hide her and provide some privacy. Cold fury lashed through him. He had every urge to snap their intruder's neck, but with Violet's fearful face, and their compromised position, Jack had to keep his murderous tendencies under control.

Jack pulled at Violet's hair and whisper-groaned, *"Sofie."*

She nodded. Her forehead creased in concentration, and Jack caught the flash of blonde hair and pale skin before he blinked, and a rendition of Sofie stared at him. He tapped at a small alert button embedded behind his ear, which notified Jodin when he needed assistance. It was Jodin's idea, and while the technology was very advanced and expensive, it was useful for communications not monitored by the fortress.

There was only one thing Jack instructed Jodin to do if he pressed the button—

"Nice room."

Jack inhaled an even breath. Violet's eyes grew bigger.

"I'm busy, Zavar," Jack drawled. "As you can see. Let me finish."

Jack heard a slight gasp from the hot springs room, then the pad of feet. "I'm coming back, loves! Holy shit, Jack, my legs won't straighten—"

Mariah—brown-skinned and coiled hair with a sultry mouth—paraded into the room entirely naked and dripping with water. She bristled. "Captain Zavar." She bowed deeply, and Zavar waved her off. A strained smile split her face as she padded back to the bed, and to Violet's confused expression, got under the covers.

"Where is…" His gaze landed on Jack, then flicked to Violet, who appeared at Sofie. His eyes narrowed. But Jack had an alibi. Other than chasing Violet through the caves, he spent his entire time laughing with Masar and nestled with the girls, who were specifically hired to be with him. They knew their duties and knew what their jobs meant. Zavar stared at the girls, wary. At some point, his face smoothed and Jack held a breath, hoping his plans had worked.

As far as Zavar knew, Jack had been seen being flirty with servants, other captains, and various girls, but never to the point he'd sleep with them, obviously. Zavar watched him too closely for that. The Vaelaur's suspicion would rise if he suddenly participated in all kinds of sexual acts, as well as none at all, so Jack had to walk a thin line of proving Violet wasn't on his mind. But Fire Night was his clear temptation. Jack made sure to talk about how excited he was, and even go on a couple of dates with Sofie and Mariah to solidify it.

"By all means, don't let my presence stop you. His Master is away, yet again, and so I have time before my failures come to torture me." The Vaelaur walked to the side of the bed and peered down with glittering, dark eyes. No injury from when Jack knocked him unconscious. "I didn't think you liked the blondes. She's pretty. They both are." His eyes flicked to Mariah, darkening.

Jack released a breath.

Mariah put on her act and kissed Jack on the cheek before crawling over to Zavar. "I can take you elsewhere—"

"I'd rather stay right here," Zavar said.

Jack bristled, regardless, still angry at the lack of privacy. "If you don't leave in four seconds, I will happily finish with them in a pool of your blood."

Zavar scoffed. "You're a romantic one."

"And you're overstepping bounds. I'm *busy*. Get out." Jack was still buried inside of Violet, and while the glamour of Sofie faded away from his eyes due to his Aurien abilities, he hadn't softened for a bit. The intensity of the situation…those in the room…made his heart pound harder.

Violet glared at him, clearly noticing it too. Mariah tried to distract Zavar by reaching for him.

"I've been calling you." Zavar glanced at his nails, ignoring Mariah. He's been painting them recently, and clearly loved their dark blue color. "You haven't answered. I figured you were in danger."

"Concerned?"

"Slightly, because this seems more precarious than finding you stabbed in an alleyway. I didn't expect you to be so…indulgent during Fire Night. Everyone says you'd been excited since yesterday morning. What changed your mind about taking lovers?"

"Needing a release from your constant annoyance."

Zavar snorted. "Well, come on, let's see it then." A cock of the head sent an inky lock sliding across his pale cheek. "I'll wait before delivering the news."

"Get *out*," Jack snarled. "I'm not in the mood to play."

Zavar backed up and turned to an armchair still in view of the bed. Jack was ready to pull out, wrap Violet up in the sheet, and make Zavar regret thinking he could step in his personal space. But Zavar flashed him a teasing smile and something about it, about the spark in the Vaelaur's eyes, made Jack think this wasn't *only* to tease him or upset him.

Zavar removed his long, tailored coat and tossed it across the chair.

Jack stared at Violet, unsure of what to do, but her eyes were focused over Jack's shoulder. Mariah stood, naked, and leaning against Jack's back. She peppered kisses along his neck, then ran her hands up his sides and grazed his abs. One hand drifted to Violet's thigh, and the girls made eye contact. Mariah smiled.

Violet *nodded*.

Mariah slid her hand up Violet's thigh, closer to the apex, while her other hand nudged Jack's lower back. "Let's continue where we left off, shall we?"

Mariah squeezed Violet's thigh. She urged Jack to move. He repressed a groan. What in the actual *fuck*—

Then Mariah flicked that little bud at the center of Violet's thighs.

Violet whimpered into Jack's hand. Her lids fluttered. His lips parted. Jack didn't think he could grow any harder, but he did. Mariah hummed behind him.

"Oh, I heard that," Zavar said. He took a seat, legs spread, a sensual smile growing. "Give her more, Jack."

Jack caught Violet's gaze. She tugged at his wrist, motioning for him to remove his hand from her mouth. He did. Her voice was a little higher than usual. "Go ahead," she said. "Let's give him a show."

Something about the situation had Jack battling between aggravation and…curiosity. Violet flashed a look at Zavar, and while her body was mostly covered by Jack's and the sheets, her head was fully visible. Jack prayed the disguise Zavar saw was good enough.

But Zavar wasn't even looking at her.

No, his eyes were glued on Jack. Fire alighted in them. Some smoldering flame. He had been cold, distant, wary, and on edge every time Jack ran into him. Jack was no fool. Neither was Zavar.

Neither was Violet. And of course, Mariah was paid well for her supreme intelligence, too.

Jack's heart thumped a little stronger.

Violet caught onto the strange tension, and while Jack assumed she would be angry or disgusted at being in the middle of this, she surprised him—as she normally did—and rocked her hips into his. He drew a sharp breath as she purred, "Perhaps we can make him jealous."

Her hand pushed the sheet down just a bit, and when Jack possessively stopped her, not wanting Zavar to see the parts of her that Jack selfishly desired, she leaned up and kissed his neck. Mariah followed suit at his back.

Violet's hand scratched roughly down his arm. "We had so much fun last night, and I just want to make you feel good, *captain*."

"*So* much fun," Mariah uttered.

Jack wove his hand around her neck. "Do you now?"

Her piercing eyes, blue for him, said it all. "Captain Zavar is hot, maybe we should have him join. So I don't get bored of you."

"I'm in need of some fun—" Zavar started.

Jack thrust. Deep, penetrating. Violet shuddered, moaning. She was ridiculously wet.

Was she…enjoying this, too?

"Shut the fuck up," he growled at all of them. At none of them. He lifted her leg, and the sheet slipped off more, revealing her torso. She arched more, putting on a show, pouting her lips, and Jack went feral.

"Give it to her, Jack," Mariah said seductively in his ear. "Make her scream your name."

Violet *did* scream his name. What fucking game was she playing at? She was going on with the show and…liking it. He wanted to demand the answer out of her, but her sassy looks made him pound deeper, harder, enough that it wiped the mischievous expression from her face.

He groaned as he hit deep, her own moan matching. And then she turned her head.

Zavar watched her with a heavy gaze, finger grazing his bottom lip.

Jack grabbed her jaw and crashed his mouth to hers, claiming her with something so ugly and possessive. He wanted to bottle her moans and take them for himself. "Look at me."

He tugged her hair, got a bit rough, and with every whine, Jack continued. He wanted her covered in his kisses, his bites, the imprints of his grip on her hips, the taste and smell of him lacing her every hair. He didn't care to remind himself that to Zavar, she looked blonde and different. But to Jack, this was extremely personal.

Jack slammed his hand into the sheet beside her head. He could feel his control slipping, so he aimed all his extra strength into that hand. The sheets ripped under his pressure, a hole burying into the mattress. Skies, he could smell…taste. His mouth tingled, and he had the urge to bite.

The sweet spiciness of Violet's pleasure mixed with the crackling tang of Zavar's curious lust. His teeth began to ache. Violet gave one nod.

Jack's eyes darted to her neck, but he pulled himself back in. A darker-skinned arm was at his lips. "Do it," Mariah said.

Violet nodded again.

Jack bit into Mariah's skin and tasted the sultry tang of her own arousal. He groaned as pleasure engulfed him. Mariah petted his hair. Jack continued to pound into Violet, sucking deeply at each breath, and when Mariah tugged a little harder at his locks, Jack released her.

Blood dripped from his lips and onto Violet's stomach. She fought to keep her eyes open, her lips sucked into her teeth as her whimpers grew louder. She grew tighter.

Then there was electricity. Black lightning. It lazily trickled from Zavar's fingers and brushed Jack's exposed back.

Deep fear pushed through Jack, but the lightning simply hummed as a strong, pleasurable tickle. Within moments he shuddered, coming, and Violet right with him.

The lightning dissipated.

Violet's mouth opened—

"Don't say a word," Jack commanded.

Jack pulled out, flung the sheet over her, and stood. Mariah stayed put on the bed. Zavar had a roguish expression on his face, clearly satisfied with his little trick. Jack stormed over to him, but Zavar vanished from the chair and appeared again before Jack, holding pants.

Jack didn't care for that kind of decency. "Get *out*."

"You're wanted for a fitting today." Zavar smirked.

"This is what you came here for?" Jack gritted as he took a step forward into Zavar's face. "To tell me about a clothing appointment?"

"I was bored. Upset from yesterday. I wanted to ruin some things." Zavar looked behind Jack's shoulder, searching for Violet, but Jack stepped in his vision. "You're also requested for reparations for Commander Halco."

"What?"

"Captain Sutton is currently under medical surveillance and out of service, given his exhausting assignments with the Master. You're to be his replacement. Now put your pants on, we are going."

Sheets rustled. Violet's heavy breathing stopped. Shocked.

Fuck, fuck, fuck, he was going to tell her about Reed's situation. His breaths tightened. He didn't want Violet to do anything rash…

Jack pushed the Vaelaur into the wall. "Get out." He shoved his pants on. "I'll be at the fitting."

"Well, it is now, so." Zavar grabbed Jack's arm and turned to Violet in the bed. "I enjoyed the show, and might be interested in the next one. I can assure you I'm not nearly as rough as this partner."

"Doubtful," Violet muttered.

Jack's panic didn't ebb. While she modified her voice to keep up her disguise, he sensed her anger. It was a fiery taste at the back of his gums.

"Let me prove it next time," Zavar carried on, unaware, with a wink.

And before Jack could say anything, he vanished them into a bright flash of light.

❋❋❋

The minute they landed on soft carpet, surrounded by the whirring of a sewing machine, Jack tackled Zavar, straddled him, and wrapped his hand around the Vaelaur's throat. "You are fucking dead."

"Well, you need someone to tell you how awful you look, so don't kill me just yet," Zavar sneered.

Seamstresses gasped at the two of them. One woman fell out of her chair. Jack had a jolt of guilt soar through him. One thing after the other. He was spiraling.

A timid seamstress shuffled up to them, and asked, "May we get your measurements, Captain?"

Jack clenched his jaw. Zavar's smile grew devious.

"Yes," Jack gritted.

Zavar stayed the entire time they measured him and fitted him for colors that matched his skin tone. One of the commanders, who oversaw the captain division, liked them to be well dressed, even if they were bound to their rooms. Serwa agreed, and had broken bones if there was a hair out of place. A loose image was not tolerated.

"Have you spoken to His Master, yet?" Jack dared to ask.

"No," Zavar said. "But I'm sure he sends his regards."

Jack snorted. "And requests for more of my blood."

"Well, seeing as the experiments are surviving now, yes. You know your schedule for that. You give your blood, you can leave your room and fuck whoever you want."

Jack ignored the tickle from the measuring tape at his armpit.

He wanted to take advantage of Zavar's lowered wall. "What is His Master planning with that?"

"Probably accelerating the better races of other worlds." Zavar didn't look up from his nails. "Presenting his findings. Roping the advanced species in on his successes, and preparing to work with them. Growing his empire. But you already know this."

But the one thing Jack learned from that was Cyran's pride. *Accelerating the better races of other worlds.* Jack should have realized, but with everything else going on, he didn't think to ask *why* Cyran was doing all of this. Sometimes the simple answer is power, but Zavar provided a more detailed answer…

It was insecurity.

A dagger twisted in his heart. Jack's blood was from the wastelands. He was belittled for a good chunk of his childhood, along with his brother, constantly being told that they were nothing. He could have continued believing it, but instead, he turned that insecurity into proving he was something, and he took over a city by chasing that egotistical pride.

Cyran's steps were the same, except he was much further along. Cyran wanted to *prove* something. Only a person who has lived with no power would chase it this hard.

The seamstresses finished. Jack stepped off the platform and kindly accepted a change of clothes that were fit for traveling. When Jack walked out of the changing room, dressed and slightly more put together, Zavar sighed and stood from the couch.

"Go back to the fortress, rest off your sex night, and I'll see you tomorrow," Zavar said. Jonathon appeared in a small flash of light. The Vanisher had bags under his eyes, but he bowed deeply at both captains.

"You summoned me, Captain Zavar."

"Get some sleep, Marin." Zavar winked at Jack and disappeared in a stronger flash of light than Jonathon's.

Jack's gaze narrowed.

Jonathon grabbed Jack's elbow and whisked them away.

29

No God Existed

THE CHEERS SPREAD AROUND PHAROS'S headquarters, and Violet buried her face deeper into her non-alcoholic drink. It was a bubbly, fruity concoction consisting mainly of sugar, and she had downed four of them. Her leg bounced. She picked at the skin around her thumbnail. Emryn slouched in the chair next to her, a slight, exhausted glare on her face while Tamu stroked her thigh affectionately. Meretta played with one of her knives.

The Rescue Division was a sore sight, but the rest of Pharos—hundreds packed into this underground, untouchable city—celebrated the death of eighty-one higher-ups within the Order.

Soon, most of these girls would be transported to another part of the world by a handful of Vanishers. It was in preparation for the coming missions. They were dangerous ones, including the Residential School, and no one unauthorized to fight was allowed to stay in the Twin Cities. Their safe location was half the world away—and it was a big damn world. In the abandoned mines of an ancient Harmas location, Bryce had built a commune of sorts for more shelter, and after years of recon, they had determined it was safe for girls who wanted to live untouched for the rest of their lives.

There was no safe place in this universe, Violet wanted to say, but she stuck with burying those words in her fruity drink. A sour feeling swirled in her stomach, one she'd been unable to get rid of since Jodin smuggled her out of the Fire Night caverns, and into the waiting arms of Rio.

She'd collapsed there, in Varik's spare room, wrapped in Rio's warm skin, while his whispers grew more panicked. *Where have you been? Are you alright? Jodin said you had a mission, and there were some complications and that you were going to see Jack—*

Violet clenched her glass.

Reed is not okay, she had said. *He's working directly with the Worldbreaker.*

Rio's thick brows had threaded together. His confusion, and then sympathy, made Violet sick. Everything about it made her feel sick. Anaya's scowl had deepened, stuck to the bed surrounded by medical supplies, but she had said, *And Jack?*

Now, Violet enclosed her lips around the straw and pretended it was a bottle of shiva and that she had an arsenal of drugs in her pocket.

I don't know.

Glass clinked, gathering attention. Bryce stood at the head of a long table along with other Pharos members, including Grace, and she waited patiently for the party to quiet.

"Tonight, many of you will travel away from this terrorist city and embark on a life of safety, community, and longevity. You don't have to worry about the cruel eyes of an order wishing to chain you and abuse you. No more living for the greed of another. No more praying to a god who only wants control. No more for you, my beautiful people, because a new life awaits."

The room erupted into cheers. Many smiled, and some shed tears. They hugged. Relief flooded throughout the room, and the more Violet looked, the more her stomach turned sour.

Bryce's face was lit with adoration as they hugged many. Violet wished she could look away, but some part of her needed to watch—needed to see a falter in this saving grace that fought so hard for these people. But Bryce's face remained genuine, and whatever Violet wanted to see never appeared.

"You look like shit."

Meretta turned to Violet suddenly. The little extra chromosome, who had gained a lot of Violet's respect, studied her.

Sort of looked out for her, too.

Meretta's lips thinned. "You're jealous."

"I'm…" Violet wrinkled her nose. "I'm not."

"You *are* an outsider," Meretta said plainly. "You were never meant to find the same peace as them."

Cold fissured into Violet's chest, and she buried her expression back in her drink. That's what Violet didn't want to hear—no matter if she laid her life down and fixed everything wrong with this world, she'd be an outsider to Pharos.

"You shouldn't have gone to the fortress," Meretta continued. "It's why Bryce uses you so much, and yet promises you nothing in return. You are a means to an end."

"You are so affectionate, Rett, has anyone told you that?" Violet grumbled. She stirred her straw. "I don't want anything from Bryce—"

"But you want something."

"I want…"

"Peace?"

"Of course, yeah."

"Family?"

Anaya and Rio popped into her head. Violet even spared a glance toward Emryn and Tamu, whom she'd been semi-hanging out with now and then. It mostly consisted of smoking on the rooftop, sharing the occasional laughs, and insulting people from afar, but it became a normalcy. Meretta was part of that normalcy, too. She'd allowed Violet to tour more of the weapons while she blabbed on about them with words Violet didn't understand. The whole time, Violet thought that Jelan and Meretta would probably weaponize the best army in the universe if they worked together.

"No," Violet said.

"Purpose." Meretta sipped her soda. It wasn't a question. It was *the* answer. Violet wanted a purpose. The realization stabbed her in the chest. Violet unraveled, and by Meretta's satisfied smirk, she knew the little chromy hit home.

"Purpose," Violet tasted the word. Absolutely nothing came to her head.

"You won't find it by sacrificing yourself in the Worldbreaker's fortress, that's for sure, little shit." Meretta cackled, leaving Violet stoic and staring at the girl. "It was stupid of you to do that, and stupid of Bryce to not only agree, but push you to go back."

"I wanted to go back," Violet said. "And I know my decisions are stupid."

Meretta sank into her plushy chair. "My mother worked at the fortress."

Violet raised a brow. "Really?"

"Yes, and she died because of it. Died after escaping, actually. The hounds hunted her down a week after she'd given birth to me. She'd already smuggled me into the orphan system by that point."

"Wha…" Violet's mouth turned dry. "What did she do?"

"It was because she had me." Meretta's eyes darkened. "Because she chose it, and they didn't respect her decision. The moment they knew I was going to be…different—deformed—they deemed me a waste. My mother never took the tonic to get rid of me. She didn't think I was a waste—at least that's what she told me in her letters. When they realized she was still pregnant, she managed to get out on the very night they were going to execute her."

Stone-cold and stoic Meretta softened at that moment. She always held eye contact with whomever she talked to, but for the first time, Violet saw those brown orbs dart away. They grew watery, and Meretta blinked. A heartbeat later, the emotions were shoved down.

"Why…?" Violet's voice was above a whisper.

"Because the man who got her pregnant was a part of the Fringe—a Vanisher. He's since been killed now when the Worldbreaker had his meltdown months ago, but…they deemed me unfit to carry such a power."

Violet's eyes turned to slits. "They're the stupid ones, then."

Meretta glanced at her.

"Because they would have had one of the most powerful weapons masters in the game," Violet said. "Clearly your talents were better used elsewhere."

Meretta snorted. "You look like shit."

A smile. "I know."

"I'm not Awakened, though. Not like you."

"I didn't choose it."

"But that's what I'm telling you—why going into the fortress was stupid. Your purpose was the freedom in choosing to do that, but you've never been free. None of us have. Any freedom is an illusion. There is no true freedom in these worlds, because whatever freedom we get is what people of power dictate." Her face hardened. "They'll snatch it away if you step out of line."

Violet pursed her lips.

"You can grab a cord and escape all of this. That's why I think you're stupid." Meretta's eyes narrowed. "Because you stayed."

Violet had a million words on her tongue, but not one of them escaped. *I stayed because I have friends. Because Jack was alive. Because...*

Because I'm stupid enough to believe there's still hope.

Violet's eyes swept the giant room of girls who *were* escaping. The bright look in their eyes as hope filtered in and pulled wide smiles onto their faces. It was why she was so sour. Why she blamed Bryce and all these other people for keeping her chained down, when in reality, she was caging herself. Locking it all away. Unable to fathom that she had the power to free herself.

But the idea of turning her back...Of leaving Anaya, Rio, Jack, and her brother behind... Of never returning to Jelan...

"I stayed because..." Violet flicked her gaze back to Meretta. "Because I'm tired of running."

Meretta scrutinized her, but after a moment, the corner of her mouth lifted. "That's what I thought."

Violet didn't return the smile. The realization weighed heavy on her chest. Reed. How was she even going to get to him? How was she...

Grace strutted up as all the selected girls began to file out of the room. Violet stared, watching two young ones who looked no older than seven, bounce on the balls of their feet. Their braids swished, smiles beaming, as they giggled about the games they were going to play in their new home. The sleepovers they were going to have—

"Violet!"

Something smacked her cheek. Violet flinched. Emryn cackled and chucked another nut at her. "Grace wants to take a picture."

"Oh, I—"

Grace gave a wry smile and held the camera to her face. "For our rescue squad. Say *fuck 'em!*"

"Fuck 'em!" The women cheered, Emryn being the loudest. Violet kept her mouth shut and turned her eyes toward the lens. She plastered on a small, closed-lip smile.

The flash went off. Tamu cursed and rubbed her lids. "Damn, Grace."

"It's better quality than the last one." Grace lowered the camera.

"The one that caught fire?" Emryn giggled.

"Because you hardwired it to an *actual* lightbulb," Meretta grumbled to Grace. "If you had only let me help—"

"You like knives, not tech stuff."

"I still *know* tech stuff."

"But your experiment wouldn't have been any better."

"At least my knives don't explode."

"Okay listen…that was *one* time."

"Twice." Emryn cackled.

Grace grew redder, and Violet couldn't hide the real smile twitching at her lips. She wished Anaya and Rio were here, but even though they helped Pharos during the one mission, Bryce didn't want newcomers in their main headquarters. Not when so much was at stake.

Grace turned her eyes to Violet. "I have something for you." She reached into a small satchel hanging off her shoulder, and procured a wrapped, familiar shape. She held it out.

Violet tamed her shaking hands. She knew what it was. She unwrapped the bundle, aware of everyone's curious gaze, as Gwen's new-forged dagger gleamed in the underground light. Nostor zig-zagged across turquoise fragments, then finally ended in an onyx tip where Violet had a shard missing. It was new, and deadly, yet the hilt held the same worn intimacy.

"Thank you," Violet rasped.

Grace grunted. "It's a weird blade. There's some different fragile metal within it, but they covered it with the blue stone to secure it. Or well, whoever made it did. The nostor only makes it stronger. It shouldn't break again."

Violet sank into her chair and stared at the blade. Overwhelmed. Heart-warmed.

The room was nearly empty a half-hour later. Violet had felt herself relaxing in the slightest as she listened to Tamu, Emryn, Grace, and Meretta talk. Sasha and Bunny had made their way over at some point, and Bunny immediately plopped onto Tamu's lap. Tamu stroked the girl's hair. Everyone smiled, laughed, enjoyed the company of each other, and the few other Pharos fighters who were scheduled for the school mission as well.

"And then, when I tried to take the drink away from her, we both collapsed into a puddle. *Soaked.* I was so freaking cold. Not drinking ever again." Emryn winced.

Tamu laughed, her voice soft, she said, "You drank the next day."

Emryn nudged her girlfriend with a teasing smile. "*Maybe.*"

As Sasha's high laugh circled and she began telling stories, an alarm rang across the room. Bryce was hugging each and every girl exiting the Twin Cities, so when their watch buzzed, every head jerked toward it. Bryce kept their smile in place, no alarm in their eyes as they paused to answer the small phone.

"*Details?*" Violet caught the one word. Sasha's story paused. Emryn's face dropped.

"*Okay, and what's the other thing?*" A pause. "*Where?*"

Then Bryce's eyes were on their little fighting group across the room. They snapped the phone shut. "Emryn, Violet. Come."

Emryn and Violet bolted out of their chairs. When they neared, Bryce nodded to a secluded corner and dropped their voice. "You're our fastest pair. Take one of the bikes in the garage and go to the coordinates I send you. A scout caught a strange girl wandering the back alleys of Navru—a girl who looks out of place. Find her, get her to a safe place, and we will question her. They reported blood on her hands. Keep it on the downlow."

Emryn gave a nod. "Of course."

"And Violet."

Violet paused. Bryce's gaze was soft. They sighed deeply. "I'm sorry."

Violet's brows pulled together in confusion. "Sorry for what?"

"For getting him involved." They absently brushed the tattoo across their face. "I shouldn't..." They shook their head. "Just... I'm sorry."

Emryn tugged on Violet's arm as she tried to piece together Bryce's enigmatic words. Jack. They were talking about Jack, and probably about his massacre within the Order, but Jack ensured things were fine. That his tracks were covered. So, was Bryce... sorry for using him? There was regret in their voice, so it must have been that.

Violet merely turned her back and hurried out of the room with Emryn.

The sour feeling didn't fade.

✿ ✿ ✿

Emryn gunned the bike and tore out of the garage. It was a cold, misty night, and as the streets grew tighter, so did Violet's breath. She turned all her focus on the girl they needed to rescue. The scout still had eyes on her, but her steps were becoming more erratic. This girl could be a ploy to drag out Pharos members, which is why the scout remained unseen and watched for a little while before notifying Bryce. Emryn had dealt with traps before, saying they normally made some young girl walk around alone to lure Pharos out. But it was typically on a busy road, where vans like the one Violet, Anaya, and Rio had stopped, were able to snatch members.

"I just hope we get there in time!" Emryn yelled. Her map system put them near the last updated coordinates. She pulled a risky turn down a tight alley, startling an elder man, and gunned it another two blocks.

Violet had a medic kit ready for any injuries that needed to be treated at the scene. In her other hand, she gripped the hilt of her purple plasblade. Her palms grew sweaty in her leather gloves. Emryn took a shaky breath.

"There!" Violet pointed ahead, where a hunched, thin silhouette wobbled underneath a canopy of broken string lights. The figure tripped over trash and collapsed.

Emryn slammed on the brakes. The minute the bike slowed to an easy momentum, Violet launched herself off, sliding for balance. Then she ran for the figure. She took in her surroundings, but the alleyway was void of any other bodies.

"Help me," came a small, timid voice. "*Please…*"

Violet reached the figure. "Hey! Hey! I'm here. I'm here to help you." The girl was only wearing a cloak overtop a thin, white nightgown. Violet nearly flinched from how cold the girl was, but she ripped out a special blanket made of aluminum and hurriedly wrapped her. Lips blue, eyes barely cracked, the girl didn't seem to comprehend Violet.

Emryn slid to her knees at the girl's other side. "Status?"

"She's been out here longer than the scout has accounted for. It was only ten minutes since we were notified, but she's…she's been wandering for a while. She's so damn cold." Violet wrapped the girl tighter, praying warmth got into her system. It wasn't until Emryn helped to lift her tiny body to wrap her properly, that the girl's hands slid from her cloak.

Covered in blood.

Emryn gasped. Violet's mouth fell open. They shared a heavy look. Violet nodded. Emryn dared to peel back part of the blanket, and her face paled.

Blood covered the girl's legs and stained the bottom of the nightgown.

The girl began to mumble, and when Violet leaned in close, all she could make out was "*I'm sorry, I'm sorry, I'm sorry...*"

And then there was a soft, final gasp.

The world shuddered around them. Stilled. The light patter of the rain filled Violet's ears. She pulled away and stared down at the girl who couldn't have been older than fourteen.

"No," Emryn breathed.

"I recognize her," Violet said.

The girl from the church. Dead.

Emryn gently shook the girl. She remained lifeless. Emryn started chest compressions—five minutes and nothing. Violet sagged back on her knees. The blanket slid open, as did the cloak.

And across her arm, where her entire sleeve was torn off, a messy scrawl etched from the curve of her shoulder to the thin bone of her wrist. The words were wrapped with dried blood and dirt.

"We go tonight," Emryn snarled softly.

Violet's eyes blurred with tears. She couldn't tear her gaze from the desperate, bloody words engraved into her arm.

No god existed in the room where I was raped.

30

GLUTTONY

"Did you clean the fish for dinner like I asked?"

Jack tongued a loose tooth and whirled to his mother. No, he had not cleaned the fish for dinner, and by his mother's current scowl, she already knew. Knew long before she ventured out of their home, swollen belly and all, to find little Jack stacking seashells atop a surfboard.

"Mama—"

"Jack," she cut him off with a sharp tone. "Avan and Lucien already did their chores for dinner, what has you distracted?"

His bare feet sank into the sand as he stepped in front of his game. "Nothing, Mama. I'm sorry—"

"Step aside from the game, Jack," his mother commanded.

Jack listened to his father as much as he listened to his mother, but where Papa was a little more lenient with the rules, Mama was not. Jack shut up and became very quiet around a frustrated Mama. She scared him, just a little bit, as she did all of them, but it didn't mean she wasn't loving. No, she scared him because she didn't need to yell or scold, but merely stare with an all-knowing face. A face letting him know that she caught him. A look that said she was to be listened to.

Jack admired Mama, but sometimes from a distance, like when she'd scold Avan, who was the biggest troublemaker of the three brothers. Lucien was always perfect, listened and helped, worked with Papa on the fishing boats, while Avan was...

Well, as Mama says, he came out feet first, trying to run the minute he breathed this new world. He caused trouble early on, and still did to this day.

Jack was a mixture of his two siblings, but at the same time, different. Mama hugged him tight some nights, waiting a couple extra moments before letting go. He didn't know why. He tried to figure it out; not by asking, but by observing. But Mama was Mama, and she didn't reveal her secrets.

Her rich, flowing dark hair was pulled back into a braid. Brown eyes narrowed at him. Hands on her hips, stomach peaking between a simple top and canvas pants.

"Come now. You know the rules. Help with dinner and you get to eat it." She turned to their two-story home made of beautiful wood, windows adorned with gossamer curtains, and nooks and crannies filled with seashell ornaments Avan liked to make.

Confusion tugged at Jack.

Avan…why did that name seem foreign to him? Unsaid? But Avan was his older brother. Jack would obviously know, since Avan and he slept in the same room…

Jack's breaths turned sharp. They hurt his chest.

Avan. Avan. Avan.

He suddenly didn't remember what his brother looked like. Like Papa, but with their mother's high cheekbones and soft face and brown eyes. Jack tried to picture it, but he couldn't. Avan was a blob in his mind.

Then he knew.

"Wait," Jack stopped.

"I'm not waiting any longer Jack Shayan Marin. Now come help in the house—"

"The house doesn't…" Jack shook his head, ragged curls falling into his eyes. "It doesn't exist anymore."

His mother spun around. "What do you mean?"

His throat grew tight.

He knew. He knew.

"You don't exist anymore."

She paused with her brows furrowed. But Jack saw it. Saw through it. Her bright, tanned face slowly lost its glow until her lips bruised with a gruesome purple.

"I remember this day, Mama." Jack stepped toward her because he yearned for her warmth once more. "This was the last day. The last night."

His mother forced a smile on her face while blood slowly leaked down her legs. It dripped into the sand, between her toes. "My beautiful, intelligent boy."

Tears breached his eyes. He pointed to her belly. "She is gone, too."

A sad smile. A line of blood dripped from the corner of her full mouth. "Yes, my love."

Hands found Jack's shoulders. Scarred, burned, abominably pale hands. Cyran appeared, gazing at his mother with an evil smirk. "I have him now. He is in good hands."

"He's my boy," Mama said. "My baby boy. He shouldn't have to do all this—"

"He was born for this, Mezcla."

Not Jack's mother's name. No, her name was Sima. Mezcla triggered something in him. He'd heard it before, within his parents' whispered conversations, but it was said like a secret. Jack roared, his child's voice transforming into one of a man. He swung at Cyran, but Cyran vanished. And so Jack turned to his mother, but she…

Jack sprung up from the bed, black sheets twisted around his sweaty body. He shoved them off, hyperventilating. He grasped his throat, his chest, squeezed his eyes shut and wished those dark images from his mind. Naked, he stumbled to the windows, peering at the Twin Cities, and resting his forehead and palms on the glass.

The nightmares happened infrequently, usually when he went to bed without having a glass of liquor. He was good at avoiding them, believing that his past was situated where it should be—in the past.

He shuddered, and the window whined underneath. He pulled back and clenched his fist. A sideways glance showed the torn sheets on the bed.

Lucien was always better at dealing with the past. It never stopped hurting, but Lucien saw a therapist and faced their trauma head on, steadily healing. While Jack staunchly avoided it. Jack was only six that last night on their beach. Pieces were blurred with traumatized fantasies, and he only suffered when he revisited it. So he silenced his mind, ignoring the past and focusing only on the future.

In the quiet, early morning hours in the fortress, it was evident *why* these nightmares popped up more often. When there was nothing to move forward to, his mind upturned the gravel and graves he buried his past in.

He put his thoughts away and went about a routine; exercises with his abilities, showered, brushed his teeth, and made his way to the far reaches of the fortress, where plains met the mountains, and the city was a quiet shrill beyond the constant wind. He picked up Minji from her kennel and walked her out to the rolling lawn.

The sun warmed his face, spreading it to the steady beat within his chest. He was…relaxing, surprisingly. The large, grass-filled fields gleamed green under the cloudless day. Minji barked at him, her slobber covering the small ball in Jack's hand. "You want it back, huh?"

She howled, stomping her front paws.

He chucked the ball across the field and Minji sprinted to fetch it.

The hairs raised on the back of Jack's neck. Sharp metal laced his tongue.

"You need to do something about the dog."

"She's in training," Jack said to Zavar. "And not for job use. I've already submitted it in her paperwork."

"She distracts *my* dogs."

Minji barked at the ball before her bright gaze flashed to the other dogs in the training pen, and she barked again.

"Your dogs are boring, anyway," Jack said.

"They're hunting dogs."

Minji sprinted back to Jack, gave him a wet kiss on his cheek, and then bounded toward the pen. Nearly every dog turned to watch her, and soon their barks littered the air like a cacophony of alarms. They followed her as she ran along the pen, mocking, and when she stopped, they howled.

"She's a tease," Jack said with a proud smile.

"She's terrible at hunting," Zavar grumbled.

Jack turned to him. "Did you touch my dog?"

"I tried to *train* her." Zavar crossed his arms. "Unlike you who thinks it is fine to be covered in slobber and dog hair."

"She is not to be trained by you, nor is she a dog meant for your uses," Jack said lowly. "You already knew all of this, so why?"

Zavar fixed him with a cold gaze. "I'm in charge of the dogs."

"Not this one." Jack stepped up closer. "Did you not enjoy the show I gave you?"

Zavar bristled.

"Have you been thinking about it?" Jack released a breathy laugh. "Maybe in the shower? In the lonely, late hours? Thinking about what I did to that woman, how I made her feel…"

Zavar pushed him away. "No."

Jack smirked. "I didn't know you could make your lightning feel good."

Zavar then did the most surprising thing.

He *winked*.

And said, "You know where to find me if you want more."

Jack's mouth dropped slightly. Curiosity piqued him. *That* was new. "Oh?"

"*Oh.*" He mimicked with glittering eyes.

Jack's heart picked up its pace. He prowled around Zavar. "Did you like it when I pinned her to the bed? When I fucked her until tears sprouted?" His arm rose and he cupped his hands like a collar. "How about when I choked her? Gave her just a little bit of pain to justify all that pleasure? Did you like all that?"

He smelled Zavar's spice of curiosity and the enticing scent of…

Jack smiled. Moved fast. Grabbed Zavar by the collar and pulled him close until they were nose to nose. "Do you want me to do that to you?" His gaze dipped to Zavar's lips. "I kind of want to do that to you."

"I don't kiss." Zavar didn't attempt to shove Jack away. Within those dark irises, Jack thought he spotted relief. A distraction. Something that might give a little more excitement to the dark, tortuous world surrounding the Vaelaur.

"We don't have to kiss."

Zavar smirked. "No, we don't."

Jack was playing. Or he thought he was. His feelings weren't similar to those he held for Violet, but as they stood in that field, alone in a villainous world, Jack noticed a part of him held a soft spot for Zavar. He'd been with men, of course. Topped them, usually. And while most sexual thoughts disinterested him unless they involved Violet, Zavar was a curious thing that Jack wanted a taste of.

The truth shocked him. The idea of it enticed him. It was a *bad* idea.

A dangerous, *dangerous* line.

"You have an assignment," Zavar said, snapping Jack out of his tumbling thoughts. "Maybe later."

Jack reined in his surprise at Zavar's nonchalant attitude to it all.

Zavar was straying away from that blind loyalty. He was blossoming into someone more independent, even if it was the tiniest step out of his Cyran-curated bubble. This…this might be the most surprising little advantage that landed in Jack's lap.

"Where is this assignment?"

"It is time for you to go say sorry and clean up your mess," Zavar said.

Jonathon appeared, still exhausted.

Zavar's eyes landed on Minji, who licked his boot. He scoffed, "Take him. You know where."

Jack never thought he'd return to this world.

It was a harsher teleportation than usual. He lost his breath but fought to keep rigid as a new world snapped into vision. Balmy air flooded his nostrils the moment they landed. Jack had to steady Jonathon, who nearly fell into a patch of dewy grass as his powers sputtered out. On the first breath, Jack knew where he was.

Gluttony.

They stood in a small meadow, but he recognized the curved mountain of Follin, still leaning toward its twin, Srax. It was a little after dawn. Birds cawed overhead, circling the giant pine trees and ravaging rolling hills that bled into rocky cliffs and sharp boulders. His blood grew hot as anxiety wrapped his throat. He glanced at his arm, where the gnarl of fire-blasted skin was circled by tattoos. The last time Jack had teleported to Gluttony, he'd been freshly singed, his chest ached from Violet's kick, and he'd never felt a worse rage in his life. There had only been a couple of minutes of clarity before a pack of Crale scouts circled him. Then tied him up. Then brought him to the Manor where a certain female touched him way too much.

He would never forget that day. The day he finally understood the horrors of the Sins. The day he knew it wasn't a game. It was real. Their lives and conflicts were as real and valid but theirs had been stained by a man who played games for pride.

Jonathon regained enough of his stamina to stand. "I grabbed her, too. Earlier when I was briefed on bringing you here. I thought…you two can make a decision when she is back in her own world. It's why I'm so tired. I told Vanisher Control it was for scouting purposes."

When Jack turned around, Navee lay in the grass, staring at the clouds. She flashed her middle finger without glancing at them.

"Why am I here?" Jack stuck his hands in his pockets, raising a brow to Jonathon.

"Commander Halco has been having problems with the reigning Inaj and remaining Crale that still fight over the ahsna oil. The Crale want an apology from you."

"For helping destroy the Farm?" Jack scoffed. "This land is in better hands with the Inaj. It was never the Crale's to begin with."

Jonathon sighed and plopped on a rock. He rubbed his temples and Jack could see the exhaustion all over his face. "I'm sure part of it is out of spite, but Commander Halco can't have the Inaj being stingy with the ahsna. They are increasing production on a lot of fronts, most of which are classified, so the need is more, but the Inaj are proving to be difficult and not mining fast enough."

"Probably because they now have a say in the politics instead of being colonizer slaves and food."

Navee huffed.

Jonathon spared Jack a long look, and Jack knew what it was for. That it didn't matter about morality or justice. They wanted the oil, and they didn't care how they got it. Which was evident from the centuries of cannibalism that was never fixed.

Jack turned to Navee. "Are the rest of the farms destroyed?"

"As far as we know," she said. "Once we destroyed the Stradinths'—which was the biggest—the rest were pretty easy to ruin."

Jack nodded. "And the towns?"

"We've taken over. A lot of the Crale moved away. Kinda hard to look us in the eye when they looked at us on their plate for most of their life." Navee threaded her pale green fingers through the deep green blades. "But it's better."

"We are rather far away from any civilization," Jack said. "Why here?"

"She likes it here. Instructed me to search for this exact location." Jonathon said. "And we have a place to rest before our meetings."

Jack searched, confused, because it was only nature. He had no problem with sleeping on the ground, but it was a...unique spot. He flicked his gaze from the trees, then back to a giant boulder, and his heart thudded.

Rusted chains lay at the base of the boulder.

In the trees, arrows stabbed the bark.

A small, woven basket peeked through the brush.

"Up there, dumbass." Navee tilted a finger to the crag above them, where a platform peeked, and just beyond the rock, the tip of a cottage stuck out.

"I'm staying down here." Jonathon proceeded to knock out immediately on a patch of moss.

Navee's voice quivered slightly as she continued, "Up there is where she rests."

❋ ❋ ❋

Jack tried to control his breaths on the steep climb as Navee bounded around, unfazed by the exercise. Perhaps that was the Inaj's ability—ridiculous stamina. Navee ran up to one rock and did a flip off it, her smile growing the closer they got. When the path leveled, and a stone arch appeared, Jack lost more of his breath. And it wasn't from the grueling trek.

Violet went into heavy detail about where she stayed in Gluttony. He remembered every bit of it—partially because it was the first time their touch had been…genuine. He'd held her in his arms while her tears licked his chest, and her voice blubbered slightly. She said it was the most beautiful thing she'd seen, and that everything tasted better there. She had been astounded at how *quiet* the world could really be, and that she wanted to fall asleep when the sun went down and open her eyes right when it was about to rise. She'd been sober the entire time, which surprised Jack.

As Navee led him under the arch, a beautiful cliffside home extended before him. The cottage, the creek, the garden, and the unpaintable landscape beyond. Jack's jaw dropped. It was… *breathtaking.*

"There she is."

Navee pointed to the ground a couple steps from the cottage. The sunlight perked up the wildflowers and glisteed against the dew. The stone marking her grave was brushed clean.

Jack shoved his hands into his pockets. His fingertips found the little thing he carried with him every day. He walked before the grave, breath lodged in his throat, as every word Violet had told him wove into reality. It was a sanctuary, a peaceful haven beautiful to breathe within nature and not on top of it. The amity jarred him—so much of his time in the Sins was spent on edge, in chaos, but here, it sailed away in the dancing wind, as if giving him a moment to be present.

Before Gwen's grave, Jack Marin bowed his head in respect. He pulled out the little turquoise shard that had belonged to the Inaj's unique dagger.

"It's nice to meet you," he whispered into the wind, beneath the twin peaks, amid the spring meadows of wildflowers and sweetgrass. His eyes dragged from the dagger piece to the stone grave marker.

The grave was tiny. Buds of flowers poked. Tree bark and woven grass mats lined where Gwen lay. A pile of bones sat near the rock

"It was tradition to place food on the graves so the dead may eat." Navee walked up next to Jack. "Long before." Navee kicked a rock. It hit Jack's boot. She snorted.

Jack glanced toward the cottage. It stood peacefully underneath the spring sun. Weeds formed at the foundation, poking from tiny rivets in the smooth dark wood. The door was shut, the windows dusty, the porch unswept with dead leaves. A way away, a hearth was etched into part of a boulder, the gray rock blackened from the ash of many fires. Two cups sat near it filled with rainwater.

Jack's throat grew tight.

"Is she alive?" Navee asked quietly. "The girl."

"Yes," Jack said throatily. "She is still alive."

"You say that like it's unfortunate."

"In this lifetime, Navee, it is unfortunate for many."

The wind shifted, blowing Navee's long, dark hair back. Jack watched the girl—watched as her fists slowly unclenched and the rage-wall crumbled away. She stared at Gwen's grave, and as the birds sang their songs above, the world pushed and pulled, Navee's tears fell.

Jack's gaze flicked back to the cottage. He took a step. Navee didn't stop him. Another step, and his long stride took him up the rickety steps, and he stood before the door. He bent, took off his shoes, and placed them next to a worn pair of boots that nearly slouched to the floor.

Jack paused. Shook his hand. Took a breath. Turned the knob. Pushed the door open.

He could feel Navee's eyes on his back. He waited.

"She's in grave danger, now. We all are." Jack's eyes fell on the sofa covered in a colorful quilt. A strong aroma of herbs and dust hit his nose. "But I'm afraid she is the only person who can stop him. He's afraid of her. Afraid enough to make her a problem. Not afraid enough, though, to do anything about it by his own hand."

Navee didn't say anything. It was partially to answer all her questions, but also to… in a strange way, update the fallen Inaj whom Violet had loved.

"It's a beautiful place," Jack said.

Navee grunted.

Jack spotted the loft and the unkempt bed, the kitchen in the back that led to a small stream and a cliff garden. His gaze fell back on the couch, where a sweater was neatly folded with a note.

"I put that there," Navee said, right behind Jack now. He didn't flinch. "I found it while rummaging through her closet. She has nice things." She kicked out her legs, motioned to the cozy-looking hunting pants she wore. "My size, too. But that sweater…well, the note is pretty short, but I can't read it, and part of the sweater's sleeve is half-finished, but it does say '*Violet*'—"

Jack stepped into the cottage. He had to duck into the doorway and felt unusually large as he straightened. He walked over to the sweater and picked up the note.

Violet—

For yer jurneeys.

Jack huffed a laugh. Navee leaned against the doorway, smiling, too. "You should give it to her."

"I will," Jack said, folding the note and touching the sweater. It was a simple knit, dyed dark maroon and, like Navee said, the left sleeve was half-finished. "She deserves to have this."

Jack took one long look at the cottage's interior and exited. He shut the door behind. Parading back to Gwen's grave, he stuffed the sweater and the note into Navee's bag.

He showed the turquoise fragment to Navee. "Do you have more weapons with this material?"

Her eyebrows furrowed. "Other colors, yeah, but that one…it's an old one. The elders think it's from before the Farms started, but they never found stone with that much blue. One even said the material might be from another world, but it was molded by Inaj hands to make an Inaji weapon."

Jack glanced at the piece, watching as it shimmered in the buttery sunlight. It was an unusual material—not quite from the earth, but not completely man-made either. Natural, yet not.

"Well…" Jack turned back to Gwen's grave and bent down to dig a small hole at the base of her headstone. He buried the piece there. "Violet will find it when she needs the rest. Now, let's get you back to your family—"

She stepped back, guard up. "You're… *delivering me?*"

"You think you're going back to Greed?"

"But you said—"

"And I take it back. You aren't meant to fight this battle." Jack moved toward the rock arch and ducked. "It's too dangerous—"

"*Everything* is dangerous. I want to fight! Didn't you see how many I killed in that room? I *liked* it. I wanted to see them suffer. I *want* this!"

Jack hardly spared her a glance. She stomped after him. "Because you're a child and things are only going to get worse. Once we talk to Nahele and my business is finished, you can discuss with him what you want to do—"

"I wanted to infiltrate—"

Jack whirled on her. She stopped short and faltered on her words. Annoyance slithered within, and he knew his eyes were dark. Hard.

"You are a *child*," he said firmly.

"And yet I've seen more horrors and lived through them than you." Navee flared her nostrils. "There was no childhood for me, and there never will be."

That struck a chord in him. Her smooth, adolescent Inaj skin was suddenly a little duller. Bags hung under her eyes. She was still on the bonier side, and just now passing through puberty by the looks of it, but the more Jack studied her, the more he could see the way the Farm aged her soul.

"You can have freedom, Navee." He softened his voice. She was *still* young, and only needed a little push…

"I want the rest of them to have freedom." She lifted her chin. "I don't care about me. I don't need freedom. I've already suffered. I've watched my people die. I want to fight, because I know I'm good, and I know *that's* how I want to spend the rest of my breath."

Jack stared down at her. Gave her a blip of his intensity that he wasn't fucking around, and he wasn't the person to fuck around with. She glanced away for a moment, but then forced herself to look back and hold his gaze.

Jack's lip jerked. "Let's go."

They made their way back down the mountain. Jonathon was fast asleep, snoring loudly, but a chipmunk managed to shove a leaf into his mouth. Navee, still sour, crossed her arms and waited.

Jack nudged the Vanisher. It took a few more to finally wake him, but eventually he stirred and squinted into the sun. "Hello?"

"We're going. I'll make sure you get your room right away."

Jonathon sighed deeply and nodded. "All right."

A moment later, they vanished.

31

PLANS

SITTING IN FRONT OF THE Inaj Council turned blood and bones into ice—Jack loved it, it invigorated him. Staunches of green, twelve persons in total, lined a long wooden table, all facing a singular Captain Jack Marin. Only three Crale were present; white-skinned men shaking with restrained fury.

He faced them from the other side of the table feeling like a kid being scolded. Jack held onto his demure smile and took a gracious sip of the heavy liquor they had offered him.

He knew the time had come to get this over with. He turned to the three Crale men. "Sorry about that." He twirled his finger. "The whole Farm thing. I meant to burn them all, but I got lazy."

"You despicable—" One Crale shot forward, face brimming with red. "I'll kill you—"

An Inaj lazily held out a plasblade and stopped him from tackling Jack. "Please, Conrad, we all know the man wasn't solely responsible. He merely doused the place in your stupid oil, but we set the revolution on fire. Let's not get ahead of ourselves."

"If he—"

Nahele—one of the first Tribal Inaj Jack met through little letters on their plan to destroy the Farm—sighed deeply at the angry Crale man, "Please, I told you we should dispose of him eons ago."

"That's what these…*commanders* want. They want to see us retaliate, incite violence. To give them a reason to wipe us off this land," the elder Inaj woman said bitterly. "We are holding on with peace, but this peace does not fix our genocide. They will use any excuse to destroy us. The Worldbreaker only wants his oil—he doesn't need the natives to harvest it. The fact that any of us are alive is simply to spend every day in fear that we are meant to be destroyed."

One Crale shivered, the other upturned his nose, and the angry one merely turned redder. Jack tried to hide his smile.

"So, you want collateral," Jack said.

"We want to guarantee the safety of our people. The Crale were a temporary enemy. There will always be more," the Inaj woman continued. "This world already breathes better without the Crale infesting our lands—"

The angry Crale snapped. "We found them—"

"After we *welcomed* you. Saved you. Fed you. And you turned against us," Nahele said.

"That was the Sin."

"The influence of the Sin doesn't excuse your actions. Your head might have nagged you, tortured you, pushed you, but the Sin didn't move your hands." The woman crossed her arms. "It certainly didn't build the factories, either."

Conrad flared his nostrils but wisely kept his mouth shut. He sat back, fuming, and Nahele rolled his eyes.

Jack took another sip, dropped the cup back on the table, and stood. "I thank you for your hospitality, but I must fetch my Vanisher and return to Greed. There are more things I need to attend to. Tell whatever Crale that I gave my apology so we can be done with it."

"Wait." Nahele stood with Jack. "Might I talk to you separately?"

Jack, aware of the clock on his heart ticking away, only nodded. Nahele bowed to his elders and exited. Jack followed. They brushed through open corridors, the only sounds the soles of their boots and the chirp of birds. It was a lively spring day, and with the glimpse Jack had at some of the Inaj's recent city renovations, this world was only going to grow more magnificent.

"Navee should stay," Jack said as they exited the meeting house and into a flourishing edible garden. "She's not meant to fight in this war."

"No one is." Nahele brushed his fingers along a tomato vine, the flowers nearly in bloom, ready to produce. "But if we want freedom, more than what we've already done, we need to destroy the Sin. Navee is determined to do so, and she's lost her entire family. None of us can stop her decision."

Jack sighed deeply. He'd expected that answer. There was no stopping Navee unless he chained her down, and that was the last thing he wanted to do to someone who has had the briefest taste of freedom. "Fine, I'll keep her." Jack tucked his hands in his pockets.

Nahele turned. Behind him, the new beginnings of construction for the Inaj's growing city sprouted. It was iconic, and rather advanced with technology powered by the sun, but at the same time, their homes still bowed to Mother Nature. "Why hasn't the Worldbreaker destroyed us yet?"

"He is one man ruling seven worlds. The others are cities with millions, if not billions of people, I doubt he thinks much about this one as long as he gets his oil. But to sever the tie from him would mean killing him…" Jack locked eyes with Nahele. "You must know this. It is a secret. Tell no one."

Nahele gave him a wary look.

"I won't bother with a bond, because if you tell others, the knowledge marks their death. You'll know how to handle that information," Jack said firmly. "You cannot kill him. No one can. If you do, all worlds die with him. He has created a…soul connection with each."

It was a long, serene silence as Nahele contemplated Jack's words. The air weaved through the garden, rustling the plants, and bringing with it the syrupy, earthy smell from the surrounding fields of sweetgrass. They stared at each other. Then Nahele stood straighter, sighed deeply, as if he needed to inhale the information.

Jack turned his head. The white face of a mountain towered in the distance. Mostly rock, with a few scattered dry brush and pine here and there, it was strange looking. Jack squinted, bringing his hand up to shield the sun.

"Are those faces?"

Nahele scoffed. "Indeed."

Jack's eyes caught the ridge of a curved, bulbous nose, along with four others. Carved with precision, four very Crale men were etched into the alp. He had the urge to laugh. "Is this for real? Did they really do that?"

"Apparently, defacing rock was essential to their rule."

"It's pathetic," Jack snorted. "Statues, paintings, a fucking mountain—a man who has nothing of substance will slap his face everywhere to convince the world he does."

"Men are so fragile in their ego they need to ruin earth to prove their power." Nahele rolled his eyes. "I don't understand the point."

"Do you need to bomb it?"

"We've already installed mines, it should be down by the next full moon."

Jack nodded, his back turned. "Have you received the plasweapon shipment?"

"Yes. A kind gesture from you. I've already begun training my people on the uses."

Jack noticed his answers were getting more clipped. His eyes flicked to the windows of the surrounding buildings. A movement appeared in one. Jack forced his senses to heighten. His ears pricked. A warmth—eagerness—hummed beneath his skin. "I have arranged monthly shipments. Defense is your best ally, as well as land."

A soft, near soundless whine. The creak of wood. An arrow being pulled. Jack's shoulders tightened.

"Understood," Nahele said.

Jack's eyes caught movement within the garden. He took a deep breath, smiling, and turned to Nahele.

Nahele released the arrow. Jack stepped out of the way, catching it, then camouflaging. "I was hoping you would give me some fun."

Nahele dove into the garden, disappearing into the greenery just as well as Jack's abilities. "You can't leave this world alive, Jack Marin."

Jack cracked his neck. Another whoosh, and he twisted away from another arrow. It embedded into the dirt, right where his foot had been. "Are you grounding me?"

A high laugh. "Perhaps, yes."

A rogue Inaj rolled into the clearing and jammed a spear near Jack's abdomen. Jack fell into his camouflage. He evaded the spear, released his invisibility, and grabbed the wood, snapping it in half. He tossed it aside to the Inaj's great surprise.

"That's bone."

"Okay, and?"

Another arrow shot from between the tomato vines. Jack narrowly stepped out of the way, but it grazed his shoulder, warm blood leaking in its wake. He dodged again, but then Nahele burst from the brush and chucked a glimmer of silver.

Jack caught the dagger inches from his right eye. It sliced into his palm. His smile dropped, as did his arm. He crushed the dagger to pieces. "Are you done?"

Nahele's eyes widened. He took a fearful step back. "So, it's true."

"Was there a reason for that?"

"He *made* you." Nahele shook his head. "It's…unnatural."

"Don't make me read your mind. I hate doing it. Too many sexual things."

Nahele gasped, as did his comrade when he motioned him back. Two other Inaj stepped into the clearing, arrows pointed at Jack. "What are you?"

"Different. *Unnatural.* He put the genetics of different species into my body, and I survived. He's using my blood to create others like me."

"And you let him?"

"I don't have a choice."

"Your blood—" Nahele nodded at the drip of red from Jack's hand. "—is not human. Not as human as we are." Jack kept his expression tight, stoic, as Nahele took a step forward. "I...I had to take a chance."

"So, there was no apology?"

Nahele shook his head, expression grim. "The rumors about you were horrible. Things that sounded like a dream. It is an abomination of our souls—"

"I'm still the same."

"No, you are now the Worldbreaker's weapon."

"Perhaps, yes." Jack's lips pursed. "But I don't imagine I'll be allowed out of my cage for very long. My end is coming."

Nahele weighed the words, and Jack offered his hand while letting his canines sharpen. "I can prove the truth. If my actions are ever to hurt you or your people, it is by the Worldbreaker controlling me. I would rather die than let that happen."

Nahele warily stepped forward. The bows creaked, a slew of harsh Inaj sounded with warning, but Nahele watched Jack. After a moment, he put it hand up to halt the others. "Show me."

Jack gently grasped the Inaj's wrist and bit. Nahele tasted bitter—wary, defensive, strong. But Jack pushed the truth of his words—his true feelings—into the Inaj. Nahele's eyes widened and he ripped his wrist away. "I never thought you to be a sad one, Jack Marin. Nor scared."

"Scared is a stretch." Jack wrinkled his nose. "But my end is here. I've...disrupted too much for the Worldbreaker. I'm too useful to kill, but my loyalty will never be to him. I've..." He swallowed. "I've lost too much and became revengeful too young."

A young girl's scream. Blood soaking his hands. His brother's desperate pleas. The cold mud. So much mud. The smell of rancid fish and wet metal. The throat of the guard.

"Jackie…Jackie…" Her body so tiny and little. Her hair stained burgundy.

"I've got you, just hold on."

"Are we going home?"

Deep, nauseating pain stabbed the center of his chest. Her eyelids drifted lower. His tears met her cheeks. "We're going home, Lily."

Nahele's voice snapped him back into the present. All of his repressed memories were coming back. A cold sweat slithered down his spine and he stumbled, just a fraction, before righting himself and plastering a smile.

"—and your shoulder isn't bleeding anymore. The fact you are still standing proves to be unnatural. You should have died with that arrow. Instantly."

"I should have died months ago, anyway." Jack tipped his head. "Good on you for trying again. I need to be humbled."

Nahele's lips twitched, but he nodded to Jack's shoulder. "The poison coating the dagger and arrow should've left your insides torn up, like it did to us."

Ada. It was the poison the Crale used to paralyze and shred the uneatable parts of the Inaj.

Jack's eyes fell to the arrow on the ground. A smear of white-ish liquid coated it. "I thought it was supposed to be ingested?"

"Not necessarily. This version is new and improved." Nahele swung the bow over his back. "Either way, you should be dead."

"Perhaps it is the Mer blood in me. Poison doesn't work on them."

"Ah, I've heard more about them due to the more frequent Vanisher visits. Water creatures, right?" Nahele said. "Perhaps it is that." But his eyes gave no truth to his words. He saw something different. Jack *felt* something different. He needed to figure it out before Cyran, but his memories proved nothing except growing plants from his hands. He checked his watch and notified Jonathon.

"They've been using drones for recon over the land. They found pockets of ahnsa north of the Canbia range, and a ways east of there. It is being collected at the moment, but I'd get there before the Worldbreaker's scout do."

A clench of his jaw. Nahele jerked his head. The other Inaj lowered their bows, eyes hard on Jack, before they retreated.

Jonathon appeared, weary eyed but with more energy than the last time he saw him. Navee clung to Jonathon's arm. "I'm going with you."

Jack rubbed his jaw. "Yes, you are."

A triumphant sneer coated Navee's face before she released Jonathon and turned to Nahele. She bowed deeply. Nahele gave her a strange look and rolled his eyes. He opened his arms. "Come here."

Their hug was one of family and bond. Nahele kissed the top of her head. He pulled away to brush her face and a bright smile pulled at his lips. "I see it's official."

Navee shot a look behind her shoulder, absolutely beaming, and Jack caught the thin, black lines beginning at her hairline and meeting at a point above the middle of her brows. Another line followed the same pattern, both creating two V's against her pale green skin.

"Official?" Jack asked.

"My womanhood," Navee said, smiling, and Jack realized he rarely, if ever, had seen her smile. She had a small gap between her front teeth, and her gums slightly showed, but it was one of pure happiness.

The tattoo was slightly raw by the looks of it. "Did you just get it?"

"Finished minutes ago." Navee leaned into Nahele, giving one last hug. "I'm honored to have it."

"As you should be, now that we have the freedom to do so," Nahele said.

Jack pursed his lips, looking away to give them a moment. He absently brushed the top of his hand where a tattoo of a flower blossomed into the stars.

"Ready?" Jonathon interrupted.

Navee stepped back and bowed to Nahele once more. "I'll see you again."

Jack swore Nahele's eyes watered, but the general kept the tears at bay. "Or until the hills."

"Or until the hills," Navee repeated.

With that, Jack, Jonathon, and Navee vanished to Greed.

The moment they landed in Jack's room within the fortress, Jonathon stumbled, falling to his hands and knees. When Jack gripped his arm, he shook him off. "I'm fine."

"Nearly there," Jack said.

"I know."

A knock sounded on the door. Navee sprang to her place in the closet, shutting it softly. A Vanisher Watch member poked their head in, took one look at the men, and tapped on his tablet. He pressed his ear. "Captain Marin and Cadet Bolto's return confirmed." He took his finger off the com. "You do know to return to the world transfer deck, not your room, right?"

Jack motioned to Jonathan. "It took a toll, as you can see. I was going to offer him rest here."

The man's undereye bags seemed to grow darker. Jack would be stressed, too, if his job was to keep track of the nearly thousand Vanishers' comings and goings. "Don't let it happen again."

Jack gave a mock salute. "Roger that."

A flash of annoyance. "Commander Halco requests a debrief after your appointment at the Hybrid Tower. Be sure to eat something."

"Will do," Jack clipped.

The man flicked his gaze between them once more, lifting a brow, but wisely decided to shut the door.

"Thank fuck the bloodhounds don't prowl our quarters."

Distantly, Jack heard one's low growl. "No, only the hallways. How much time was that?"

"Eighty-seven seconds."

"Watches off now."

The metal thudded to the cream rug. Navee burst from the closet and grabbed onto Jack's arm. Jonathon stood, brushed himself off, and vanished them again. This time, they landed in an antique shop. Jack looked toward the door, checking the lock, the closed sign, and the curtains. Satisfied, he turned to the front desk where Varik nursed a cup of tea.

"You're late."

"I got shot," Jack replied. "Please give Jonathon a wellness serum."

"I'm not your liege," Varik complained.

Jack gave him a side-eye. "I said 'please.'"

Varik scoffed, but paraded to the back. He knocked before the curtain, and a moment later, two sets of footsteps ran downstairs and shoved through a hidden door. Rio beamed at Jack, a smile splitting his face, and ate up the floor to engulf Jack into a bone-crushing hug. The man had been eating well. His brown hair curled to his neck, skin extremely tan, and he seemed...less stressed. Over his shoulder, Jack locked gazes with an icy-faced Endolier.

"Oh, Jack, I've missed you," Rio said, squeezing harder. "Like *a lot*." He pulled away. "Hang with me. Save me. Because I'm about to kill her."

Another look at Anaya. "Bossing him around too much?"

"I don't trust you," Anaya said, straight to the point.

"I wouldn't either. But I was hoping this little offer might gain favor...just a small one."

Rio ruffled Jack's hair and then gasped when he saw Navee. "You? *You?*"

Navee blushed—*blushed*—and tucked a strand of hair behind her ear. "Surprise. I'm here to kill, but it is good to see you, too."

"Everyone is so bloodthirsty these days," Rio said.

Anaya stomped her way over, shoving Rio out of the way and raising her arm. Her fist came fast—and semi-camouflaged. Jack raised his hand, catching it—

Her other fist smacked into his jaw.

"*Skiv*," Anaya growled. "You were supposed to *stay* dead. Not become this."

He dropped her hand and massaged his jaw. Hard fucking hit. "I didn't have a choice."

"Then you stay *out* of our lives."

"Won't be around much longer, I'll promise you that."

But Anaya wasn't having it. "You didn't have to take your dick out and mess with her like that. It's not the same anymore. She knows that, but you just wanted something from her because she was *available*—"

Jack growled, "Don't you ever accuse me of using her. Not like that."

"That's what it looks like—"

He stepped forward, anger swarming his chest. Anaya held her stance. She wasn't afraid of him. She never will be. "I don't give a fuck what you think it is."

"Are you saying it's *love*?" she scoffed. "Don't bullshit me, Jack Marin. You're not capable of such a thing."

Jackie…Jackie…

Are we going home?

"No…" His voice was cold. "I'm not. But it doesn't mean I'm not capable of minding other's feelings."

Silence passed. Varik returned from the back to wrinkle his nose at the tension. Rio's eyes shifted between Anaya and Jack, and Jack didn't miss the way he stepped toward the Endolier. Jonathon was nodding off against a bookshelf. Navee picked something out from under her fingernail.

A flash of light marked Jodin's arrival. "I'm here for the girl," he said, nodding at Navee.

Navee's brows buckled. "Why?"

"You want to fight," Jack said. "Then you'll assist Violet and the others in freeing the Inaj children from the Residential School." He waved his hand, irritated and short. He wanted to be done with all of this. He would never admit aloud that Anaya's words hurt him, that Rio's wary gaze sliced into him. Whatever they had before was gone. Ruined. There was no fixing it.

But it certainly made the goodbyes easier.

Navee grabbed Jodin's forearm, and Jodin's hands lit up.

"Wait," Jack said.

Jodin sighed. Navee turned to him.

Jack held the Inaj's gaze. "Tell her…" His chest tumbled, but he righted it. "…that her fire will always, and forever, surprise me."

Confusion. Her mouth parted. But realization smoothed her face, and with sad eyes, she nodded. "Good luck, Jack."

He watched them vanish.

"Jack…" Rio began.

But Jack was already moving. He nudged Jonathon, who groaned. "What?"

"We have to go," Jack said. He glanced at the still-fuming Anaya over his shoulder. "You'll have a mission with Jonathon within the hour. Be prepared."

"I don't take orders from you."

"Then I'll find someone who does," Jack snapped back. "Envy is nice this time of year, right?"

Anaya gasped, then bared her teeth. "Don't play with me."

Jack rolled his eyes. He turned to Varik, who was fixing a serum drink for Jonathon. "One more question."

Varik raised a brow.

"Do you have room for a rather large cat?"

❀❀❀

Jonathon and Jack retrieved their watches. Jack took a couple shots of liquor when Masar burst into his room, stressed. Yeren followed behind.

"It's been chaos," Masar started. "The Order is in shreds. None of the higher-ups can be located."

"Zavar is shitting himself," Yeren said. "Pharos didn't have this capability."

Jack took another shot. "Must be horrible."

"The Order is a bunch of fuck-wits anyway, but His Master won't be pleased at the situation," Masar said.

"I'm sure he won't be pleased if his steak is cold, either."

Masar snorted. Yeren ignored Jack and nodded at Jonathan. "He okay?"

Jonathon was passed out on Jack's bed. Drool dripped onto the sheets. "He's all right. Long trip from Gluttony."

Jack caught Yeren stiffening in his peripheral vision. He went about changing his clothes, when the long-awaited question tugged at him. "This Mer Zavar captured…"

"Oh skies, Zavar is having loads of fun with that one," Masar said, crossing his arms. "Even Serwa is participating in the torture. Prince Renell is his name. Zavar's so pissed about the girl—"

"Masar," Yeren warned.

And with that, Jack turned. "I know she's alive. I know the other two are in Greed. It wasn't ever a secret."

Yeren cocked his head.

Masar shrugged. "It was news to us about a week ago."

"They don't have any signs of her?" Jack feigned.

"Nothing," Yeren said. "But you should not be asking about it. She's low on the priority list. Once Serwa returns from her assignments, the girl is next. And no one survives Serwa."

Jack strained to keep his emotionless expression in check. Yeren was watching him carefully. Masar strolled to the window. "Don't you have your appointment soon?"

"Soon," Jack said.

"Well, if you see the Mer, tell him I'm still holding to my promise."

Jack walked over to the bed and nudged Jonathon. "Your promise?"

"A man who assaults is a man who will hurt for the rest of his life," Masar said darkly. He looked like Lyla in that moment—scary and evil. "I keep my promises."

Jack's breath tightened, but he forced a nod, wondering what Masar meant by that. Once Jonathon was up, they left Masar and Yeren to Jack's liquor stash.

"We're early," Jonathon said as he looked out the window from the fourteenth floor of the small room Jack lounged in before and after his blood transfusions. It was barren and gray, with a singular couch that he had thrown up on the first few times after being drained.

"How much time do I have?" Jack asked.

Jonathon checked his watch. "Nine minutes, fifteen seconds."

"Your last assignment is to take a wellness shot from Varik and go to Envy." Jack ignored Jonathon's confused gaze. "Take the Endolier with you—she's your best navigation. And take this, too."

Jack held out the small vial of red. It was fairly difficult to make sure Violet stayed asleep in the caverns while he extracted her blood, but a little Aurien calmness certainly helped. He'd done her right that night.

"This will...?"

"Be our last little hope. Make sure your mother has her things packed. Your time under the Worldbreaker is done." Jack offered a soft smile. "It was nice to know you, Jonathon. Thank you for everything."

With that, Jack turned to the door and exited.

Jack felt a tiny bit lighter at each goodbye. His steps were soft as he walked the mostly empty, fluorescent-lit hallways. Five floors above was the blood room. Four floors below—the hybrid room. But right now, he was heading two floors below, to the hybrid supplier floor, where his gut told him he'd find a couple more answers.

Perhaps not true answers, but it would get him closer to the truth.

When Jack entered the elevator and scanned his wrist, breathing a sigh of relief that his clearance hadn't been restricted, a memory flashed in his head. His heart pounded at the sight of his mother.

She hummed in the kitchen as she stirred the pot over the lit flame.

Above her head, high on the shelf filled with spices, was the little jar of light green salt that looked peculiar. Jack stared at it a lot—he could have sworn it glowed a few times.

"What is it, Mama?" he asked. She turned her head and followed his gaze. Her pretty face paled slightly, but she was also with child, so she did that a lot.

"It's a piece of home."

Jack's brows furrowed. "I haven't seen it here."

"Your father swam very far to retrieve it," she mused. Her hand rubbed her round belly. "It is magical, like you—one little taste and you can fly."

Jack giggled. Mama laughed with him.

"I want to fly, Mama." He bounded from his reading work at the table. "Can you give me some?"

"It can only be for a special day, my love, when you see a golden light."

"A golden light?"

"That's when you know it is your time."

The elevator doors opened. Jack wiped his forehead of the cool sweat. Four guards greeted him in the supplier hallway. They bowed. "Captain."

He pressed the button on the elevator to halt it from going to other floors. He then waltzed forward, stuffing his hands in his pockets. "I'm looking for the new supplier. The Mer."

"You are not authorized to speak with any suppliers—"

Jack moved quickly. He drew the plasdagger from his pocket, ignited it, and jammed it into the throat of one guard. Blood sprayed. He flipped the dagger in his hand and stabbed the next. Both guards dropped. The others raised their guns, but Jack had already thrown the dagger in the skull of the third so hard it careened into the fourth.

He fixed his collar and smoothed his hair, then wiped the blood from his cheek. He barricaded the only stairwell door with an unheated plasblade from a guard. A moment later, he had a key in his hand and strutted down the hallway until he reached the Mer's cell. Scanning the key, Jack took a deep breath and entered. He shut the door softly behind him.

The Mer lounged on his chaise, hands tucked behind his head and bruises scattered across his cheekbones. Slivers of the city glow shined through the small window, the only thing lighting the dark room.

"You're not the lightning man."

"No, but I might be worse."

Renell's eyes dragged to Jack. "I don't know how the two fugitives got out of the world—"

"I don't care about that," Jack said lowly. He'd begun to piece things together…and this first question was a little more personal. He never forgot Violet's blatant lie when she said the cut on her arm was from her leaving Greed. He saw the truth there, but it didn't take Aurien abilities to catch the omittance. Jack knew what a deep, fingernail cut looked like. Healed like.

He had one scarred into the side of his neck.

He took a step forward. Renell stiffened. "I have to ask, though, did you ever encounter the girl?"

"The scaly one? Frightening little thing."

"No," Jack snarled softly. "The first one. Brown hair, blue eyes, breathtaking—the usual."

A scoff. "The first girl? I wouldn't say breathtaking, but I didn't get much of a look because the bitch stabbed me in the eye."

It was hard to see in the darkness, but from the angle, Jack spotted the pure white of his right eye, angered with scars and a mutilated brow. Healed, yes, but not smoothed over.

One thing Jack's skin didn't do—no, Jack didn't receive scars anymore. No mark was left.

Jack's eyes dipped. Renell's fingers were pointy, his thumbs the longest. "Why did she stab you?"

"I wouldn't let her escape."

"The shot to her hip was straight on. Same with your eye." Jack clenched his jaw. "Both could not happen at once."

A hoarse laugh. "Fine. I was trying to fuck her. Give me some shitty Vanisher babies for my world because she held some fucking weight to the Ruler. But the bitch didn't want it."

Ice. Jack only felt ice. Every muscle in his body grew taut as dark fury flowed beneath his skin. He didn't see red—he never did. Instead, he saw every artery, every place on a body that would produce the most blood or emit the loudest scream. He calculated the pain. He analyzed every aspect to become the biggest nightmare to his enemy before him.

Unfortunately, Jack couldn't allow Renell to scream.

Jack walked over to the bedside, yanked the Mer up by the neck, pried his jaw open, and ripped out his tongue in one swipe. The Mer didn't even realize what had happened, and then a gargled, breathless cry escaped. Jack clenched his hand, feeling the bones crack beneath. His cold ire danced. Renell's arms shot out, aimlessly hitting Jack, but he merely yanked the Mer's shoulder from its socket. Renell trembled in pain. His one working eye flared wide.

"Every woman in existence has someone who would kill for her. Mother, Sister, Father, Brother, Cousin, Friend, Lover." Jack dropped the Mer to the floor, where he shuddered, mouth leaking blood. "I am her protector. I am her reckoning. I am her killer. And for every place you touched her, I will make you feel a thousand degrees of pain until your eyes beg for death. And then I will do it all over again."

Renell cowered on the floor. Jack broke his kneecaps. His femurs. He took the bloodied plasdagger and dragged it down the Mer's forearms, and then when the Mer was a crumpled mess, Jack sliced his own wrist and dripped his healing blood into his mouth. He waited. Watched as the Mer steadily glowed and bones snapped back together. Watched as his mouth stopped leaking blood, and a bright pink tongue began to grow.

Then Jack did it all over again.

Just like he promised.

When the man was tortured enough for the fifth time, Jack gave him his blood, erasing all the injuries. He left Renell, whole again, on the floor.

Renell desperately crawled away. Full of fear. "You're not going to kill me?"

"You're not mine to kill," Jack drawled with a smile, following him. "I understand Mers have a healing ability."

Tears streamed down Renell's cheeks. He cowered in the corner of the room. "Only if submerged in water. If you're asking…what you did, I've never seen. We can't give our blood to heal others because Mer blood is the only poison that can harm us. Yours… yours is magic."

The understanding clicked inside of him. The dreams, the memories began to form. He remembered a word: Mezcla. Jack lifted a hand—

Renell cried, "Please—please, no more! I beg. I'm sorry. I shouldn't have touched her. She's yours."

Jack ended it with a threat…which was also another promise, "She'll finish you off."

He abandoned the Mer, and passed the stairwell door where a guard was trying the handle. He called something into his com as Jack gave him a wave behind the pane of glass. Jack picked up a round object from one of the dead guard's belts, along with a plasblade and gun, and moved back to the elevator. He hijacked it straight to the Hybrid floor. An alarm began to blare.

One of Mama's sayings slammed into his brain.

You want to win over people, Jack? You want to make a difference? Get to the end of the game. Let them think they've won. Let them think they've broken you.

Then when they bask in their glory. When they smile and laugh and turn their backs…

That is when you destroy them.

It was one of the last few sane things she'd said before her death. When chains wrapped his family's wrists, and his community was struck from their homes.

He camouflaged himself. When the doors opened to the Hybrid floor, he shot the six confused guards and stepped over their bodies. Medical cots lined the sleek linoleum. Drips hung at each one, filtering Jack's maroon blood into the bodies to help their successful transition. A hundred, maybe more, lay in deep sleep.

He took one last look at the hybrids before returning to the elevator. He pressed the button for the floor of his waiting room. At the last moment, he pulled the plasbomb from his pocket, pressed the button, and rolled it into the Hybrid room. The metal doors eased shut with a ding.

A breath later, an eruption shook the building. Jack stared ahead as the elevator vibrated, yet it continued its ascent. His breath sailed evenly. Calm filtered. The doors opened. He sauntered to his tiny waiting room and sat on the loveseat.

The building's alarm still blared. Boots pounded the hallway, drawing closer. He dragged a finger along the plasgun, before raising it to his temple.

"We're going home, Lily," he breathed. But when he tried to think of that girl, her bright green eyes turned blue. Jack hesitated, but this was the only way to win. It was the *only* way for Jack to not let Cyran get the upper hand.

"Go ahead. Shoot yourself."

Cold metal nudged his finger on the trigger. Pulled it. A deafening bang filled the room. The bullet grazed his skull. Jack's vision went black—blind. Wet, hot liquid poured down his face. A voice growled in his ear.

"But *Mezcla* are very hard to kill."

A bright, golden light pierced through the darkness. The shape of a hand. It collided with his chest, right over his heart.

And Jack Marin was Awakened.

32

ʀESIDENTIAL SCHOOL

VIOLET AND EMRYN TOOK THE body back to Meretta's hideout. At some point during individual prayers of well wishes, Emryn had wrapped her hand in Violet's. Squeezed hard. Violet's eyes watered, but she held the tears at bay.

She could have helped this girl. This girl who cried in a church. The girl named Eve.

They dressed quickly and quietly. Violet was covered in fighting leathers and gloves, a black mask on the lower half of her face, a braid down her back, by the time she fashioned her purple plasblade to her hip and swung her leg over the back of Emryn's bike.

"You know the drill," Bryce said to the seven of them waiting in Meretta's garage. The tension was tight in Violet's chest. "Kill any staff who fight. If their hands are up, stun them with your taser. There are three points where a Vanisher will meet you—in the church, outside the gates, and in the staff room. They have special wards elsewhere. Alarms will be triggered if there is a shift felt by a Vanisher, so it is your job to get your tally of kids to those locations so they can be transported safely. Understood?"

"Understood," everyone repeated back. Violet stayed quiet as Bryce's gaze lingered on her for a moment.

She pulled her visor down on her helmet.

"In and out." Bryce crossed their arms. "If any of you are injured, your partner is responsible for you. You two abandon the mission. Notify the rest in your coms. And remember, if the kids fight you, let them do that where they are safe."

Emryn gunned her bike, and the rest followed. Tamu was with another girl named Izzie—a longtime division leader, and deadly like the rest. Izzie bumped fists with the other team of girls on the third bike, and air-fived the solo girl—communications and security head, Polly—then nudged Violet. "Let's fuck these guys up."

Emryn reached for Tamu, and together they squeezed hands.

"Take care of her," Tamu said to Violet.

"She needs babysitting more than I do," Emryn teased. Meretta opened the garage doors with a button. "But we will be fine, baby. See you on the other side."

Tamu shut her visor. One by one they peeled out. Violet wrapped her arms around Emryn's waist.

A buzz filtered into Violet's ear. A voice—Izzie's. "This communication is encrypted, but still be careful. E and V, you are to meet with Vanisher One. Your objective is dormitories four through seven. T and I will cover one through three. B and Z will cover eight through ten, with their Vanisher appearing sporadically outside. P will have all eyes and ears on any outside communications. She'll alert us if something is off. You know the code words when we need to pause or abandon. There won't be time to regroup. If we fuck this up, there is no going back. They will double down on security. So there will be *no* fuck ups, got it?"

Emryn's loud laughter hit Violet's ear inside and out. "Got it, bitch."

Izzie returned the sentiment with a wild call of her own, and soon the rest of the girls followed. Violet channeled it—the call of women scorned was a powerful thing. But her mouth stayed closed.

They took a steep turn out of Navru. The Twin Cities glistened in its misty night. A moment later, the road dipped into a tunnel, and the world suctioned into the loud roar of engines. It was early morning, so the cars were few and far between. Emryn jammed the accelerator up more and padded Violet's wrist as a comfort. Violet didn't realize she was gripping so hard.

"We either die or save, babes," Emryn called into Violet's com. "That's what it has come down to."

"I just…have a feeling."

"Bad or good?"

"Sour."

"Pop a mint into your mouth and focus. We got this. We have trained for this. These kids won't have to suffer through the Order's brainwashing any longer."

Violet's jaw clenched, but she turned her thoughts to their earlier surveillance at the school when they found that boy with his pants down. He had since been relocated with an elder Inaj well-versed in decompressing trauma from trafficking victims. A select Inaj group were about to get a giant influx of their young ones, and according to Bryce, they were prepared. But it was Violet and the rest of the girls' duties to get them there.

Jack had completed his mission. She needed to do hers. Then she'd save her brother and get them the fuck out of here.

Emryn wove the bike through back alleys until the streets held the familiar ominous ambience of the Order. Its symbol was plastered on flags beneath eerie lamp posts. The Church District's gates were up ahead. Emryn silenced the bike as she steered into a back alley.

They parked their bikes far away from one another. Their prime mission was to stay separate, therefore keeping the other groups untouchable if one group was discovered and confronted.

Emryn and Violet hopped off the bike, sharing a silent glance with their helmets still on, visors still down. Violet listened carefully, but only the steady mist of rain and the occasional creak of a gutter met her ears. They waited. Listened again. Held their breath.

Emryn gave a signal. Violet removed her helmet, glimpsing the blonde strands of her hair as a glamour went up. They hid the bike as best they could under a mesh, mirrored tarp that made it mostly invisible, and then checked their weapons.

"Your hair looks good tonight," Emryn said.

Violet finished tucking it into a ponytail, before fixing her mask back on the lower half of her face. "Thanks, I used a new conditioner."

Emryn perked up. "Really?"

"No."

She scowled with a smile. "These kids will be frightened, but hopefully drowsy enough from sleep to not fight too much. I… when I was younger, if there was anyone who said something bad about the Order, I was trained to scream. To yell. To break things. To create enough commotion that an adult would find me, and whoever said something bad would…go away." Emryn rolled her eyes and cut her hand across her throat in a killing motion. "It was too frequent. They didn't want any of that talk in Hallow. But I grew up in the Order from birth, so it was ingrained. These kids might be learning, but they're also scared. They weren't blindly manipulated from birth. There is *some* memory that wasn't tainted by the Order. We just have to find it—"

Emryn paused. Violet heard the static of Bryce's voice in Emryn's com. It was a quick, quiet command, and Emryn's brown eyes bugged in surprise. "Our location?"

A short answer.

Violet furrowed her brows.

Emryn gave their coordinates, and after marking notable things within their landscape, Bryce hung up. Emryn scoffed. "A Vanisher is coming."

A moment later, a dim light flashed in the alley and Jodin appeared, looking slightly ragged. His trench coat wrinkled, stubble crowding his tense jawline. He yanked a smaller figure forward. "Your new assistant. She's cleared and assured us that she can care for herself."

Violet stumbled back in shock. Navee glared from Emryn to her, before squinting longer at Violet. "So, you *can* shape shift."

"*You*," Violet breathed. "What in the skivvin' world—"

"I helped your man with killing those ugly higher-ups in the Order, and now I want my people out of this school. Your man failed to convince Nahele to let me stay in my world, so here I am. These kids will need someone who looks like them."

"Jack suggested this?" Violet clenched her jaw. "I could have changed my skin color."

"You'll make it look ugly." Navee brushed at her face, whereas the rest of her tiny green body was hidden beneath black fighting clothes. She had numerous daggers strapped to her thighs and a long plaswhip wrapping her waist. "We will keep our pretty skin, thanks."

"You're a child."

Jodin sighed. "Can I go?"

"I'm not a child," Navee said, pointing to a new tattoo that adorned her forehead. Both girls ignoring Jodin. "These are my people, my children, and I will fight for them until my last breath. They will remember our language and culture. They *must*."

"Fine, it's not my decision, anyway." Violet wrinkled her nose. "But where is Jack?"

She didn't miss the flash of sadness on Jodin's face, but the Vanisher said nothing. Navee shrugged. "Dunno. He said he wanted to sleep. He had dealings in my world."

Panic flooded her. "In Glut—?"

"*Sagitta*," Navee corrected.

"Sagitta," Violet said, clenching her fists. "What was he doing there?"

"Returning me, but he failed. Ha!"

"He's safe, though?"

At that, Navee pursed her lips. "He's in this world. Safe for now."

Emryn checked her watch. "We have to get going. We can discuss this all later." She turned to Jodin. "You're dismissed."

Jodin gave a mock salute and vanished.

Navee's smile was savage as she patted each one of her knives. "Let's burn this school to the ground."

Arson ran through Navee's blood, it seemed.

※※※

After an agonizing five minutes squatting awkwardly behind a leaky gutter, Polly finally gave the clear. The plasma fence guarding the innards of the Church District hummed a distance away. Violet narrowed her eyes on an Order guard strutting into the mist behind, stocked to the brim with weapons, before Emryn made a hand signal. She pulled out the little black box she'd used last time, and after a second, tense listen, she pressed it into the fence. The reverse taser negated the plasma-wrought iron, and a pocket appeared.

"Go," Emryn commanded.

Both Navee and Violet nimbly climbed the fence and dropped to the other side. A beat later, Violet was holding the box, and Emryn landed lightly next to them. She pocketed the device, and gave a short update to Polly, "*Cleared.*"

"Got it," Polly immediately answered. The girl was hidden somewhere on the rooftops, in a tiny, mirrored tent that established a short radio frequency meant for their communication. At this point, she should have tapped into every Order com, checking on any odd notions, but an update made Violet's heart drop. "I want everyone to know that there's an odd static coming from the Order headquarters. They're scrambling it better than usual, so my assumption is that it is external—to some higher-tech place. I'll try to breach it as fast as I can, but if I sense danger, you pull out immediately."

Emryn rolled her eyes and pressed a finger to her ear. "Annoying of them. But got it."

They hurried down the slick streets amid a growing, pillowed fog. Bleak lampposts blared in the thick moisture, blinding their visuals. Emryn cursed, sweat already beading her brow, but she guided them on.

It was the same decrepit route to the depressing landscape of a school. Wrought-iron plasma fences, guards within even forty feet, cameras that are looping a misty, unalarmed background, and a kind of quiet that gnawed at Violet's nerves. She touched Gwen's new dagger stashed at her side.

They waited for a break in the guards and passed over the school's fence. Emryn dropped last, and all three of them ducked behind a trimmed rose bush.

"Cleared the fence," Emryn stated into her com.

"Okay. Wait for it…now," Polly commanded.

They watched a guard turn his back as the other drifted toward another set of bushes and unzipped his pants. Navee scoffed, rolling her eyes.

They bolted for the service door, and like last time, Emryn used a magnet to disable the alarm and unlock the bolt. They sidled into the white linoleum and barred hallways.

Violet's gaze flicked to the floor. She'd seen a crayon laying there last time. It was gone now. Spotless. Like no child had ever stepped foot here. Pressure grew in her lungs, but she tamped the anger down.

Emryn pulled out her fancy watch loaned specifically for this mission and tapped a few buttons. The display burst out of the face into long, curving lines of blue. The blueprint. She pointed to one of three glowing dots. "Our Vanisher," she whispered.

It was about three turns from the lines of dormitories they were to evacuate. They had calculated the time it would take to guide children there; max three minutes and thirty-six seconds to allow for any stragglers, minimum of two-forty if the kids were compliant.

Violet produced a towel, and they wiped their boots of dew. By the time they hurried toward their mission, their footsteps were soft. Soundless. Emryn checked around every corner. Navee kept a hand on the hilt of her plasdagger. Violet strained her ears for any sound.

They made their last turn, and Emryn halted, then pushed them back. They pressed against the wall as a portly woman with a white cloth on her head paraded by. A tie wrapped around her black robes. With squinted eyes, Violet noticed it was a plaswhip.

Navee seethed quietly, but stayed rooted in place.

Emryn motioned for them to go. A moment later, they slipped inside the first dormitory.

The giant room with square, barred windows held only metal bunkbeds and slabs of nearly twenty mattresses. No toys, no art, no color, no vision of a child lay within an inch. Thin blankets covered small, curled bodies. Soft snores and whimpers filled the space. A strange stench hung in the air, and Violet recognized it as stale urine. It lingered, stronger, to the point where Violet guessed accidents weren't cleaned up.

Emryn dug four small canisters from her bag and gently shook each one. She pointed to a small key that she twisted. A sucking sound emitted, and thin smoke sprayed out. "Semi-sedatives. Kind of like anxiety medication, but without being so strong to knock one out. It will help prevent panic. Drop one in each room and then meet back here."

Violet and Navee left to enter the other dormitories and proceeded to activate a canister in each one. It only took a minute for it to fill the room, then another minute to notice the calming of whimpers, the steady ease of breathing.

When they returned, Emryn turned to Navee. "Now it's on you to have them ready. I'll get the go-ahead from Polly, and then we will move the first group."

Navee gave a curt nod, but Violet saw the fire in her eyes. She nudged the girl in the shoulder and Navee pushed her back. "I got this."

"You better."

Emryn rolled her eyes as the timer in her watch went off.

"Hallway is clear," Polly said into their coms.

Emryn flicked on the lights. "All right, kiddos, time for a field trip."

One head popped up, followed by another. Soon enough, pale green faces stared blearily at them, some rubbing their eyes, some yawning, but there were some who showed fear. A trigger. Violet's heart sank.

Navee began her speech, *"Bienjah a vonaja, um Navee agia..."*

At that, an Inaj girl a few beds away burst into tears. She was older than some others, and she bolted out of her bed, sprinting into Navee's awaiting arms. Navee's eyes grew glossy, but she kept the rageful tears at bay. She kissed the girl's forehead and beckoned the rest, still speaking in Inaji.

Other kids whimpered, lazily crawling back due to the anxiety smoke. Some glanced at the cameras above. Navee motioned to them and shook her head. Another child cried.

But the painful part for the others, for Violet, for Emryn white-knuckling the door handle, was that most of the children's faces were blank. Emotionless.

Gone.

They gathered the first group, and with Navee's Inaji reassurance, each child clung to another and filed into a line. Emryn got the go-ahead from Polly, and they were off into the hallway. It was a tense few minutes, and Violet held her breath the entire time as she watched the back, the last child trembling in his blanket. He stopped, shaking his head and gasped with fear, but she gently nudged him along. Let him worry in the arms of an Inaj.

They reached a room labeled "Staff" in two languages, and Emryn unlocked the door with her special magnet. They filed all the kids into the room.

A lone figure stood dressed head to toe in black. Incognito. Violet glimpsed their brown eyes, but she didn't know the Vanisher. A small glow emitted at his palms beneath his gloves. "You're on time. First round confirmed, P."

Navee explained another thing in Inaj, clasping her own hands together and clenching them tightly. The children imitated.

The Vanisher took the hand of the elder, more eager child, and with a double check of interlocked hands, he nodded to Emryn and vanished. One by one, each child blinked out of the room in a soft light.

"Holy fuck," Emryn muttered. "It worked. I mean, we tested it, but it worked."

"On to the next one." Navee turned on her heel and paraded to the door. Her hand touched the knob—

"*Stop!*" Polly yelled in their ears.

They froze, breath held. Outside the staff door, in the hallway, soft footing walked down toward the dormitories, paused, sniffed, and then continued. They painfully waited for the footsteps to fade, before Emryn nodded and Navee turned the knob, poking her head out.

They moved on to dormitory two. Three hurried minutes and the next set of twenty kids were gone. The third set five minutes later, a severe lag because one kid tripped over the hem of his sleeping pants, knocking three others down, and they sprang to muffle their cries.

"The other teams are on their last room. Some delays for I."

Izzie's voice was a growl. "I swear to the shits, if I have one more kid puke on me..."

"Are you volleying them into the courtyard?" Emryn teased back.

"No, these just happen to be the ill ones—it's sad—their tummies can't handle the food, nor the water, but I am *covered* in little kid bile. They're certainly the more recent transfers. Thank fuck for the sedative smoke."

Tamu's voice was quiet, "No alerts, but the patrols left a while ago and haven't come back during their routine inspection."

"As long as everyone is done in the next ten minutes before hourly bed checks, we are good," Polly said. "I still can't figure out the static from that communication, but I swear I heard a dog bark—"

Violet froze.

Emryn slammed into her back. "Watch it!"

Violet's finger was on her com. "You said dog?"

"I could be mistaken…"

"On any other day, did they talk about increased security?"

"Well, yeah, but more patrols and cameras, not anything else… they did, however, talk about an absurd amount of food suddenly needed, which was weird for a human to consume… Oh, and…" Polly swallowed. "Water bowls."

"Water bowls?" Emryn whispered.

"I thought…" Polly said, her voice strained. "I've heard so many terrible things about this place—leashes for the kids months ago, food sources, plaswhips, all kinds of stuff…I thought it was just another horrible, degrading thing…"

Violet opened the staffroom door and pushed Navee into the hallway. "Go, get those kids in line and get them moving. Emryn and I will take a lap."

"I'll alert the distractors," Polly said. "Hold up. I've got movement on the front lawn—big truck—fuck. *Dogs?* Really?"

"Still burning this place to the ground," Navee snarled, then sprinted to the final dormitory.

Emryn unbuckled her plasblade. "I'll take the left-wing—"

"Oh—oh!" Izzie shouted into the com. "Patrols outside the windows—oh fuck!"

And in that static, gunshots blared. Glass shattered. A horrifying, gurgling sound bubbled, followed by a thump. A scream. A child cried.

"Gotcha, bitch," came a man's voice. "They've infiltrated! Release them!"

The horrible sound of barking screeched into Violet's ear, and then Izzie's com went out.

Silence. Emryn and Violet shared a look.

Then Polly's voice, "Izzie is down. Abandon mission. Get out of there *now*. I'm pulling the Vanishers—"

"No," Violet said quickly. "We can get this last group."

Tamu's voice, "Our assignment is finished. We can assist in backup. We are heading to Izzie's location—"

"Bryce said—" Polly started.

"We get all of the kids or none," Emryn snapped. "We save or we die. Be safe, Tamu, and the rest of you. Fight hard…and see you for a drink later."

"Love you," Tamu's voice came.

"Love you, too, baby," Emryn said, strained.

Violet released her purple plasblade. Navee opened the door to the last dormitory, and one by one, tiny little kids under the age of six filed out, blankets covering their heads and holding hands.

Navee spoke to them in Inaj, then she turned to Violet. "We are playing a game."

Navee yelled something, and each of the children blasted off into a sprint, following the line that held onto Navee's hand. They rushed toward the staff door, and Navee encouraged them through. The Vanisher was back.

"Hurry," Navee said to the Vanisher. She passed off the front child's hand to him.

He nodded, already exhausted. His limbs flickered with light, and then he dipped into the realm—

A shot rang out. A bullet whistled past Violet's ear.

The Vanisher jerked backward, bringing the front half of the kids' line with him, but splitting their hand connection. With a roaring scream, he flared with bright, Vanisher light and disappeared. Blood splattered the floor where he'd stood.

The seven remaining kids burst into screams. Violet slammed the door shut, blocking out the hallway as more patrols came, and the deep growls of dogs surrounded them. Navee yelled in Inaj. Every child dropped to the ground.

Then bullets rained through the walls. They covered the kids with their bodies.

Emryn grunted, "*Violet*, get us out of here!"

The bullets continued. "I don't know—"

"Or get us to the courtyard!"

"I…I…"

"*Now!*"

The urgency, the desperation in her voice activated in Violet's chest. Her glamour strings snapped, and her appearance flooded into her real one. She reached for Emryn's hand as a heat blossomed in her chest. She saw the door to the realm. She opened it. Her hands glowed. Tethers appeared around her in that glistening world. "Hold on to me!" she cried.

Hands reached. Clinging with desperation.

The door to the staff room opened, and teeth grazed her ankle—

She spied the closest one, a white one with a hint of blue in it. She understood white was locations in the current world, but blue…blue proved to be rare. With no time to ponder, Violet pulled on it.

They dropped on the stone, and the courtyard erupted with cries. Navee began to shush the kids. Emryn scrambled up. In the dark, harrowing night, the residential school surrounded them like a big, white cage. "Well, I meant to go outside the school—"

"You'll need a more competent Vanisher for that, right?"

Violet turned to the male voice. Jodin smirked. His eyes drifted to her burning, bloodied ankle. "They sent the dogs. Goodness."

Navee gathered the remaining kids, making sure the blanket still covered them, and guided the group to Jodin. "Get them out of here."

"Am I to come back for you guys?"

"I'm staying," Emryn said. "Tamu and the others need us."

Violet so desperately wanted to be selfish in that moment, but she huffed. "*Fine.*"

"I'm not going anywhere, either" Navee said.

Jodin shrugged. "Well, let's get you someplace warm, nuggets." With a wink, Jodin grabbed the hand of the first kid and vanished.

Emryn brought up the blueprints on her watch. "I have Tamu's location, follow me."

They sprinted through the lush courtyard, and blasted their way through a service door. Emryn guided them through the corridors, shouts growing louder, bullets still ringing out, and a frustrated scream followed by the whine and thump from a dog.

"Love her." Emryn smirked.

They ran up the stairs and turned down the hallway, where Tamu slashed another dog, dodged behind an overturned metal cart, and shot a guard between the eyes. The three dropped with her, and Tamu gave an exasperated sigh. "Izzie and Bailey are dead. Zaia went with the last group of kids because one wouldn't leave her. We still got two left—" Tamu's eyes darted to the nearby room—a broom closet. "Just waiting for the Vanisher to come back."

"When is he due?"

"Any moment."

Shots continued overhead. Navee disappeared into the closet to hush the children. Tamu fired another shot into the neck of a guard. Blood misted the wall. A dog bounded forward, teeth bared, and Violet swiped its head off in midair. Black hound blood sprayed over her shoulders.

"Ugh," she flicked some of it away. "I hate these things."

More guards poured from the far entrance. Dogs continued to lunge, but Tamu and Emryn shot them down.

"Where is that *fucking* Vanisher?" Emryn hissed behind the cart. She shot another. "I'm going to kill him after."

"I wish I could—" Violet started.

"You don't know the location," Emryn said.

Violet scowled as a bullet slammed into the wall, splattering debris and dust over them. She coughed, "I know that."

"Retreat!" one guard yelled. Boots clicked down the hallway, fading, until all were gone and all fell into silence.

Violet poked her head out. Emryn and Tamu followed. A lone dog sat, panting, with a ball in its mouth.

"Does it want to fucking play?" Emryn stood, waving her plasblade. "I'll baseball that thing straight into you, mutt."

The dog only bowed its head and dropped the ball to the ground.

It clinked—metal. It sparked—plasma.

"No!" Tamu reached for Emryn, who had stepped over the barricade.

The dog barked.
The ball flashed three times.
"Fuck," Emryn muttered.
And the plasbomb erupted.

33

Awakened

Jack woke with a start. He was on fire—he knew it. His skin burned hot; his heart raced. He blinked through the black inking his vision and glimpsed the snowy alps around him. Cold stone barely cooled the inferno. He lay on a rooftop high above the rest of the city, night arriving. Clouds swarmed, fogging the chilly air. A hint of smoke wafted his nose. The Hybrid Tower—confusion caved his forehead, but then he remembered the bomb. He sprung up—

"Not so fast," an unfamiliar voice said. A metal boot with ripples of black met Jack's chest and pushed him down.

A man—an older, gray-haired man with an eyepatch, a lip ring, and a bright, single green eye—tilted his head and sucked hard on the lollipop in his mouth. He was covered in wrinkled scars, evidence of war battles and not mere knife fights. A giant plasrifle hung across his back. Both thighs each had four daggers strapped, and to Jack's surprise, his entire right arm was robotic. Not the simple prosthetics like in Calesal, but an advanced, plasma-filled weaponry machine starting from his clavicle down to the five tips of metal fingers.

The man smiled. "You really do look Mezcla. Surprised Master never made the connection, but there were only supposed to be two of us left, and that was calculated for decades. So, you're a true surprise."

A pounding headache formed behind Jack's eye. He felt weird—rubbery and too fucking warm. Sweat licked his forehead, matting his curls.

"Name?" Jack gritted out.

"Commander Modav."

"Never seen you around."

"That's because this little world is a front, Mezcla. I live in the better one." He pulled the lollipop out and motioned to the mountains with it. "This one is dying."

"Dying?"

"All the corporations with their greed and need for resources have killed eighty-five percent of the planet. He'll give you the tour." Modav winked one eye.

"So…this fortress, this whole world of Greed, is just a game for everyone? It isn't real?"

A shrug. "Yes and no. The commanders know about it. This world is about tying up some loose strings, I suppose. But it's not *our* world. Our home base. It's too disgusting. So much smog and shit, and people praying to some dingy gold god. It's boring, really. The other world is better."

Jack rested his head back on the pavement, taking a slow, deep breath. "What did you do to me?"

"I Awakened you."

"You?"

"One of the two—well, three Mezcla left. Unless we count your lone brother in Veceras, then that's four. Nice little collateral with that one in case you try to off yourself again. But he'll be significantly less powerful than you or I."

Jack's headache grew stronger with every loud suck of the lollipop. He heard the words, but nothing registered.

"What is the point of this world?"

A scoff. "It *was* the home base, but the Sin is too stubborn here. Barely listens to His Master. From there, every species on this planet began to ruin the world. Right about now, people outside the city are greedy for uncontaminated food and water that isn't filled with micro acids." He finally bit the lollipop and flicked the soggy paper stem at Jack. It landed on his cheek and slowly slid to the stone. Jack made a promise to slowly kill Modav for that action alone.

Modav snorted, paused, looked to a particular spot, and bowed deeply. A soft light flashed. The Worldbreaker appeared.

Cyran looked, for some strange reason, well-rested. He waltzed over to Jack's body, his salty hair untouched in the wind, scars prominent along his neck, and icy eyes fixed on the boot still resting on Jack's chest.

Modav moved it without a word.

"You killed my subjects," Cyran said lowly.

"I was supposed to kill myself, but your insane sidekick stopped me."

"You wouldn't have succeeded, fortunately."

"How did you figure it out? Me being a…whatever a Mezcla is?"

Cyran remained stoic. "There was always an unsureness about you. You said you didn't know how you survived the species infusion, yet you weren't surprised by it. It was interesting, considering the first few subjects with your blood were so traumatized by the transformation, we had to ruin their consciousness completely. Obviously, I would have never realized such a thing until we produced another."

"So those subjects…"

"Would have merely been robots if they were transformed the same way you were. Their souls, their emotions, didn't handle the hybrid transition. After some changes, we made the transition less invasive, and the subjects had treatable trauma. You just so happened to kill the unviable robots."

Defeat flooded Jack's chest like gnawing poison.

Cyran jerked his chin. *Get up.* Modav nudged Jack with the metal-toed boot. Jack was on his feet with surprising ease. He wobbled, and his spine flared with unusual fire, but something felt more…stable inside of him. Like the last puzzle piece clicked into place. A confirmation of Cyran's observation; Jack was surprised by the sudden transformation months ago after his death, but he was never shocked by the fact he *survived* it.

In retrospect, Jack was never surprised he survived anything. He fought for his survival with claws and teeth and intelligence, but he never guessed that death would meet him on the other side. Pain and injury, yes, but death was foreign. He never tried to avoid it—no, it avoided *him*. He associated his dismissal of death with his blind ambition to avenge his past and his family, not that it was some unconscious, soul-changing reason.

"You're going to strap me down and force me to make you a hybrid army," Jack said matter-of-factly.

"Precisely that," Cyran answered.

Jack found it strange Cyran was being reasonable. No, not necessarily reasonable, but *reachable*. He existed as some god who traversed to this world every now and then to put down problems, but otherwise, he wasn't around. That checked out with Modav's admission of another home world, but a million other questions swarmed in Jack's skull, adding to the headache. "Do I get answers?"

"All the answers you want, give or take some. I'm sure Modav has explained some things to you."

Jack parted his lips. "What are you doing?"

A lifted white eyebrow. In the city light, there was a tinge of limestone to it. "In general? Creating my own universe."

Jack snorted, but Cyran simply stared at him. Modav crossed his metal arm with his natural one.

"How are you doing that?"

"Collecting powerful people and establishing my reign."

Perhaps Cyran did have a dry sense of humor, but there was full seriousness on his face. Jack opened his mouth, "What kinds of powerful people?"

Cyran's gaze brightened. "The four pillars of the universe. The Celestes."

A bright, prideful smile filled Modav's face.

"Vanishers…Mezcla…" Jack started.

"Vaelaurs and Kitsuyes," Cyran said. "Vanishers, however, have an ancient name, too: Airsai."

A long pause. Jack didn't know what the fuck a Kitsuye was, but his lips parted, mouth turning dry. "Zavar?"

"Let us go for a walk, Mezcla." Cyran turned to Modav. "Convene with Serwa and Cillian—I want the Order replenished with their higher-ups after this one murdered them all."

Jack stiffened, but Cyran wasn't angry. He didn't seem to care.

Modav bowed deeply. "Yes, Master." He then pulled out a small cylinder identical to the Iris, but with more glowing buttons, and lifted his eye patch. Where Jack thought a gaping skin-colored hole would be, there *was* an eye, but it glistened the same star-dusted silver as the Iris. He brought the device to the cyborg creation and looked through it like a telescope. He pushed a button. His body began to glow, not in a Vanisher way, but a synthesized way. It took longer for him to teleport, but a moment later, Modav was gone.

"There is no outer-world travel with that device. It only has pre-programmed drop locations for those who cannot Vanish."

Jack found himself gaping. He shut his mouth. "Like how one can transfer between worlds during the Sins?"

"That is a little more complicated than Modav's device, but essentially, yes. It will take any un-Awakened or non-Vanisher to the next world once it deems they won against the Sin three times."

Cyran offered his hand, his filigree lines beginning to glow, but Jack hesitated. "I want to know about these four powers. These… Celestes."

Annoyance twitched his face, but Cyran relented. "Similar to the four elements of fire, earth, water, and air that promote life, there are four grander elements that promote souls—aether. Something deeper than mere breathing and hydrating. The four pillars created the universe, and they can destroy the universe, as well. They are the beginning and the end, blessed by the four gods they descended from." Cyran waved his hand, as if it didn't matter. "As I mentioned, the Old Names are Airsai, Kitsuye, Mezcla, and Vaelaur."

Jack's chest grew tight.

A dark, feral look from Cyran. "Vanishers, Manipulators, Givers, and Slayers."

The burn in Jack's body did not feel so hot anymore.

"The Vanishers are blessed with the power to travel, the Manipulators the ability to control the earth of any world, the Givers privileged with the conception and sustenance of life, the Slayers the takers of it. These four abilities each stem from the aether of the gods—their souls—and they trickled into conscious species eons ago. From there, communities, worlds, galaxies, have been built around the four. They push and pull our very creation. But now that the gods are dead or in hiding, the universe is out of proper control, and the abilities have since mixed, creating ultra-powerful individuals who can rival the deities."

"You."

"Me." Cyran lifted his arms. One hand of the filigree glowed familiar silver—Vanisher. The other a purple. But then beneath Cyran's eyes in the two stripes, it was a golden light. Mezcla—the Givers.

"You're…like me?"

A glittering smile. "Not quite. Not a *born* Giver."

Jack searched the Worldbreaker's eyes, unable to find an answer. "The purple light?"

"Kitsuye—Manipulator."

Cyran motioned to his body. "It is different for each power, but the Vanisher is the most common to understand." Cyran adjusted his light to Vanisher silver. He pointed to the eye slits. "To see the realm." He held out his palms. "To flick through the tethers and then grab the one we desire." A scuff of a boot. "And then to step where we want to go. Now, take my arm."

Jack stood and reluctantly grabbed it. They vanished.

It wasn't the pop of sense Jack received when he transferred to a new world. He guessed they still remained in Greed, but the air simmered warm. They landed on the lip of a cliff, high above a stretch of land that filtered into a murky, churning sea.

A sea hardly filled with water. Well, it was water, but the wash of the waves rippled over mounds of trash that went as far as the blur of the horizon. He was high enough to gaze across the never-ending ocean, and while that tugged again at his heart and his past, this was nothing like the bright blue water bursting from his childhood memories. This was an ocean destroyed. Ruined. A sea of man's waste.

The air made Jack cough. His eyes burned. It wasn't air he was breathing, but the horrid stench of festering refuse. He turned from the cliff and looked over to where rocky valleys swarmed with more trash. It was all blurred in a smoky haze. In the distance, factories rivaled the height of the mountains, large smokestacks spewed rancid fumes. Buildings stood next to them. Streets flowed through the littering steppes. Small little bodies hiked and shifted through the filth.

Jack brought up his arm to cover his nose and mouth. "What is this place?"

"This is the result of earthly greed," said Cyran plainly, as if he were giving a scenic information tour.

The landscape went on forever. "Modav said this planet was dying."

"Thankfully, it isn't my planet."

"There are homes next to the trash mounds. Beneath them." A cough. "Do you do anything about it?"

"This has nothing to do with me." Cyran kicked a bit of plastic. "I gave them the Sin, they failed. The rest of the world doesn't know the dangers of this. I think with the current trajectory, this planet, or at least this part of it, has four years left."

"Is it reversible?"

"No."

Jack almost wanted to laugh. Cyran truly was some god looking down on a creation—no, an experiment, and merely observing how they fucked their own world over, even if the Sin exacerbated it. "So why do you live here?"

"I don't."

Jack's lips twitched. Modav wasn't a liar. "Another world?"

A satisfied look. "Another world."

"Why bother with this one?"

"It was a suffering world and the easiest one to infiltrate. They thought nothing of a new ruler. They loved the feeling of greed. They changed their beliefs for a dogma I created to benefit me and my power."

"You…" Jack turned to the Worldbreaker. "You made that up?"

"I embellished it. The Sin spiraled it. It was fascinating to watch millions of people turn against each other, kill each other, all because they craved more control."

Jack remained silent.

Fascinating to watch…

"I'm not responsible for the entire religion. I simply wanted to be a part of it, to take advantage, and when oral history blurs and original texts are burned, then re-written to fit a certain narrative, it doesn't become too difficult." His lips curved into an emotionless frown. "I was merely curious."

"Your curiosity made this world believe all of that?" Jack asked.

"Give them the threat of some horrible hell, a gracious voice in their head that speaks to their greed, and people will believe anything."

"You've created fear."

"And fear enables control."

Jack's lip twitched. "But not loyalty."

"Why would I want the loyalty of anyone who doesn't question basic things?"

"No…" Jack said. "No ruler would want that."

Cyran turned to him, procuring a simple blade from his pocket. He didn't hold it in a threatening way, but Jack tensed still, his heart thumping loudly. It was fear and excitement. Was the Worldbreaker going to fight him? Kill him?

It was a constant mind game to be a step ahead of the Worldbreaker, but Jack didn't know what steps Cyran took. He didn't know the full scale of what the man was capable of—

skies, what Cyran truly *wanted*. No Sin bothered him. The loss of a precious world didn't make him care. Back when Jack was sentenced to the Sins, Cyran happily murdered nearly half of the candidates in the sixth world, while at the same time, one lone candidate made it to the seventh.

He remembered that candidate's name: Darien Bones. Remembered the two minutes and thirteen seconds the man was in the notoriously fatal seventh world before he was killed.

By Cyran.

Why was that? Why was no one allowed into the world of Pride? Was it because it was easy to pass? Or because it was the last step before home?

Jack had always chalked it up to Cyran never wanting someone to break the curse, because that meant no more candidates for him, including potential Vanishers. The cycle would stop, and Veceras would finally be free from the torture of the Sins...

No.

It was all wrong.

Jack's gaze was dark, his heart a fretful beat, as he stared at the knife in his hand and remembered the way Cyran sliced off his own arm, therefore creating a respondent earthquake. It was a connection.

There was *no* curse. Nothing to break.

Because the droughts, the earthquakes, the growing storm, was merely *someone* being harmed that was connected to Veceras.

He lifted his gaze. Met the one who created it all.

Cyran grabbed Jack and vanished them back to the Twin Cities. They landed on the same rooftop. Jack sucked a lungful of semi-cleaner air and blinked the watery sting from his eyes. Night fully descended, the Cities a flicker of their usual luminosity.

"The only thing you need to know is there is no stopping me. There is no stopping any of this. I am immortal. I am powerful. I am a god. And who in this universe has ever killed a god?"

Wind whipped Cyran's hair. There was a rumble. His eyes dropped to the rooftop as a tiny sediment vibrated against his polished shoes. Confusion filtered over Cyran's expression as his gaze moved to Hallow, and south, to the gilded tips of the Church District.

A man surprised.

Even though Cyran held the power of gods, despite his access to the blood control of potential billions through a fabricated religion, despite that he could create robotic humans, animals, and the like, despite that it seemed no one could touch even a single hair on his head, and he proved to be the very threat to seven worlds imploding, Jack Marin knew one thing:

One wild girl could ruin them all.

We cannot be siblings in these games.

My sister is the only one who can stop him.

He. Doesn't. Know.

Jack knew that there was a small sliver of weakness to even the most powerful.

His was love.

Cyran's was a mistake.

And that very mistake, by the looks of it, was currently destroying the Church District.

Jack burst into laughter. Uncontrollable, high-pitched laughter. Flames buffeted in tiny explosions. A giant purple burst of light seared the distance, nearly blinding him at his spot. Buildings shuddered and crumbled. Screams bit through the breeze. Jack doubled over, in complete awe, as he blurted, "Did you fuck someone you shouldn't have?"

His laughter spasmed, as did his lungs. His spine snapped. Blood crawled up his throat and Jack gagged, spitting it out. His tongue swelled. Cyran's control spread to his wrists, where both snapped, but beyond the pain, Jack continued to laugh. Covered in blood and unable to breathe, his chuckles were a deep rumble.

Cyran's terrifying figure vanished, and so did the pain. Jack collapsed to his knees. A golden light began to ebb at his wrists. A breath later, the Worldbreaker returned with another limp figure. Reed.

He looked half-asleep, bleary, blinking his eyes open at the destruction before him. A drip line and needle hung from his arm—ripped from a medical room. Cyran held him by the throat, forcing him to look. He groaned before his eyes shot open and his light-brown skin paled. Reed exhaled, "No."

Cyran pulled at his hair. "Your love for her must be so strong it failed to show during your treatments. I asked you, over and over again, if there was another, if a little you existed somewhere that I mustn't know about. You were the one plan, but it seems a mistake was made along the way."

Reed's body limped. Tears streamed down his face. "I don't know. I don't know who—" Bones snapped. His back bent awkwardly. He released a blood-curdling scream.

Cyran's face was a mask of horrifying fury. "Every lie you give me now or have before, will be a scream from her. *Who is she?*"

"No, no no no—"

Cyran's control wormed its way to Jack's body. He bit his cry, doubling over, but Jack's body was already filling with bright, golden light. His Giver light fought it, humming beneath his skin against Cyran's cold, unnatural intrusion, until the golden rays healed and pushed and gave Jack his breath back. It fought the darkness, the control, and wrestled it out of his blood. Jack breathed a sigh of relief. He opened his eyes.

The Worldbreaker stared down at him, appalled. "Awakening you might have been a mistake, then." He snapped his fingers. Jack jerked, anticipating pain, but only the steady thrum of his healing light remained. Cyran's control could no longer touch him, because, it seemed, his true abilities wouldn't allow that kind of... manipulation.

The snap must have been for something else, because a breath later, Jodin appeared, slightly out of breath, but he stood rigid. Only Jack seemed to notice—Cyran didn't even look at his liege.

Jodin bowed deeply. "Master."

Cyran gave one command.

"Take them under the mountain. I'm going to deal with her."

34

JONATHON

JONATHON WAS TIRED. TIRED OF Jack's ridiculous plans with the promise of safety at the end of all of it. His mother was secure—according to Varik—ready for transport once he returned. But for now, his boots soaked in the mud of a world he'd never been to, surrounded by the biggest trees he'd ever seen, and smelling a scent so foul it made him gag. Whatever energy boost Varik gave him helped, but Jonathon was on his last leg. His chest felt unusually cold. But he needed this—for his mother. He needed to bring her to a peaceful life. Jack promised it, and Jack always kept his promises throughout the time Jonathon served him.

The tiny, scary Endolier finished hugging the tree, as she had been doing for the last ten minutes, and sighed deeply. "It's time now." She bent, worming her hand between gnarled roots, and plucked a big white flower. She plucked another, then stuffed them in her pockets. "For later."

Anaya uncorked the blood vial and waved it in the air. She turned to him with a sickly sweet smile.

Uttered words that sent a shiver throughout his body.

"Here, kitty kitty."

It was quiet for ten shallow, slightly panicked breaths. A cat. Jack said a cat. Jonathon's eyes dipped to the ground, searching for the small, furry creature—

Hot breath blasted him in the neck.

Anaya whirled, her smile doubling in size. "There you are pretty boy."

Jonathon turned and beheld the sight. "I thought you said a *cat*."

"Semantics."

He closed his eyes.

Semantics.

After some consoling from Anaya, the creature shifted down to the size of an *actual cat*. With a deep breath, Jonathon went into the Vanisher plane, the tethers to other worlds flickering with his last bit of energy. He yanked them back to Varik's. They landed—

The nauseating wrap of lightning slid around his neck.

"Traitors always lose," Captain Zavar's cold voice slithered into his mind. Anaya was nowhere to be seen, and Jonathon panicked for a moment, thinking he failed to vanish her back to Greed along with the cat, but he saw the tiny flick of a tail disappear behind a bookshelf.

Both Rio and Varik were unconscious on the floor. Zavar purred in Jonathon's ear, "Your demise will look worse, don't worry."

A moment later, Jonathon blacked out, the taste of his bile on his tongue.

35

The Hills

It felt like years had passed before Violet's back slammed into the linoleum. Her plasblade flew out of her hand, the hot material slicing her forearm in the process. Debris piled on top of her. A coarse, high-screeched pitch filled her ears while blood filled her mouth. Her tongue ached—she bit down on it. The blood flooded her nose and dripped to her lips, cycling through again, until it was all she tasted. Smelled. Felt. Blood. Blood.

Blood.

A bright flash. A light fixture swung from the ceiling and the wire snapped. It crashed above her head. Glass peppered her cheeks. Violet groaned and shifted to her side, spitting. She reached, trying to grasp for…her eyes peeled open.

For some odd reason, Violet thought she would see Jack there. She didn't know why—it bugged her that he came to her mind in this moment—but disgraced and injured in the school, bloodied and beaten, she thought he would…

Come to rescue her. Sweep through the premises and rid the world of enemies—of those trying to hurt her and her friends. But there was no Jack. Just a blown-through wall and a door that snapped in two pieces, and a pair of wide, dark eyes wrapped in pale green skin.

"Violet?" Navee whispered. Smoke flooded the space. Another piece of the wall crashed somewhere. Something crackled.

"Where…is Jack?"

Navee's brows crumpled. "Jack?"

"He needs to help," she rasped. "He should be here."

"Jack isn't coming."

A laugh bubbled. "He needs to come."

"I—" Navee shook her head. Two dark blobs of hair were tucked into her armpits. The Inaj children. "We need to leave."

"Jack will come."

"He can't…he…" Navee's expression distorted. "He—"

Panic jolted Violet's body. "Tell me."

The strong, rigid Inaj's face fell into fear.

"Where is Jack, Navee?"

Defeat flashed. "He said… 'Tell her that her fire will always, and forever, surprise me.'"

There was no word for the stab in her heart. Her lacerated fingertips reached across the broken floor. She tried to get up, to growl and find him and throttle him. A desperate moan filled her mouth, as if she could tell him *no, that's not how this ends.*

That's not how our story ends.

"Emryn!"

Tamu's shriek sounded as loud as the bomb. A clattering of metal dragged Violet's gaze. Amid the smoke, Tamu scrambled through the blown-apart hallway to a crumpled body. The shock jolted her. Jack wasn't coming. This was real. They were alone to fend for themselves. Emryn was blasted by a bloodhound's plasbomb ball.

"No! *No!*" Tamu screamed. She fell to her knees. "Emryn!"

A tiny cough emitted.

"She's alive! Help! Someone, help!" Tamu cried. A great, mournful moan escaped from her, and she slammed her fist into the floor. "Stay with me, stay with me!"

If not Jack then… "Jodin," Violet said hoarsely.

But the Vanisher didn't show. She didn't have his contact.

She picked herself off the floor, groaning as her knees cracked and more blood filled her mouth. She spat it to the side, wiped her lips, and turned to Navee. "Get them to the field. Do whatever you can. We are almost done, okay?"

Navee's usually rigid demeanor had softened, and Violet finally saw the child within. Barely fifteen years old, and battling in another world for her people, continuing her suffering that should have ended the moment the Farm exploded. Violet had no say in Navee's decisions, but moments like this made her think that everything she did was wrong. That it didn't need to go this far. She should have saved the girl from further torment.

"Clear the hallway," a rigid male voice said. Boots clicked. Navee ducked with the children, disappearing into the dust and shadows of the closet. Violet dropped herself to the ground. Played dead.

Tamu moaned, grieving. It bounced off the razed walls. Violet's eyes found the ceiling—the sky twirling through the shredded beams above.

A gunshot sounded. She jerked in shock. Opened her mouth. Let the blood pool out, along with a tear.

"No sign of movement," one guard said. Their boots kicked gravel. Small flashlights flickered, but she stared, unblinking, at the hazy sky. A black-clad guard flashed his light at her face and held it there, nearly burning Violet's eyes, but a breath later, he grunted and swung around. "Hallway is clear. Notify the headmaster and the fortress. They will need to do a sweep after this breach."

"Do we have a count on the immigrants?"

"Four children dead, the rest…gone."

"Pharos really stole them."

"Yes, sir. They've taken the children. We have men searching the city for their whereabouts, but we believe Vanishers were involved. We have notified the Tracker Station, and they will alert us of any outer-world movement."

"I want blood samples from select children sent out and given to the hounds—"

"That is out of bounds, sir. Captain Zavar strictly told us the hounds cannot leave the city."

"You believe they took the children out of the city?"

"I believe the children are lost."

A gunshot fired. The guard above her went down, landing with a heavy thump next to her. Violet took the moment to blink.

"Fuck the captain. We have his dogs. Send them out."

"Yes, sir," said a different guard.

And with that, the remaining guards left.

Violet waited until the chirping crickets and occasional drop of debris filled the space. Her throat coarse with dust, she rolled to her side. Navee's eyes were wide.

"They're gone," she said.

"The kids?" Violet croaked.

"Fine."

"Jodin will come back." Violet pushed herself to her elbows.

"I don't think anyone is coming."

"Then stay there and hide until someone does."

Navee dipped her chin, her eyes watering, but she furiously brushed them away. "Okay."

"I—" Violet started, but a bubbling cough bounced off the wreckage. She slowly turned her head, groaning at the ache in the back of her skull from the impact.

Two bodies lay beyond their small barricade. Dog skin and blood smattered the walls. A long, white tooth punctured the floor. Her eyes dipped back to the bodies. One shuddered.

"Emryn," Violet breathed. She began to crawl, cloying desperation overwhelming the pain in her bones. Her hands left bloody prints. Her mouth leaked. "Emryn."

Her partner, her colleague, her friend jolted, and blood sputtered out of her mouth. It coated her cleft lip. Violet groaned, her chest becoming cold and icy as she pulled herself to Emryn's side. The girl was obliterated. Blood leaked from hundreds of lacerations, the biggest across her chest, another to the bone on her thigh.

Violet reached her, nearly collapsing on her body. "I got you, I got you," Violet rasped, wrapping a hand around Emryn's jaw and turning her head to the side so she wouldn't choke.

"Tamu…" Emryn's voice was a bubbly whisper. Her glassy eyes stared, never finding Violet.

Violet's gaze drifted to the other body. A clean shot through the skull. Tamu's brown eyes lay unblinking, her mouth parted in shock. Her deadly plasblade buzzed against the floor, slowly melting it.

"Tamu," Emryn said again.

Lovers separated. Lovers lost. Violet desperately grabbed Emryn's hand and clung to it. "She's resting."

Tears pooled in Emryn's unseeing eyes. Her mouth split in anguish. She nodded, understanding. "Take her…somewhere nice."

Slowly, surely, tears leaked down Violet's cheeks. Silent and mourning. They dripped onto Emryn's chest as the girl weakly squeezed their hands. Her fingernails dug, and within her features, fear rose. Her throat bobbed as she tried to swallow, but she choked, and more blood leaked from the corners of her mouth. Emryn's eyes tried to find Violet, but they were growing milky, and bloodshot. "And me, too. Take me to somewhere nice. Where… where there is no more hatred."

"No," Violet said harshly. She clenched her teeth, trying to fight the tears so Emryn didn't know…so… "You're not dying. You— you're going to be okay. We just have to—"

Let her rest. She just needs rest…

Pain flared in Violet's chest so sharply that she wailed, long and low, as the current reality mixed with a visceral memory. Trees. Watchful mountains. A cold night. The thrashing of her pulse. The way the air stilled and the wind stopped, as if the world, the land itself allowed a break in its cycle to honor the dying Inaj before her. Blood, there was so much blood.

"No—we can cauterize her wounds. I can light a fire and heat a blade—"

"Violet."

"There's alcohol or some disinfectant…somewhere. Or I can make some. Then we can let her rest. She just needs rest—"

"Violet."

"And then it will all be okay—" She sobbed into Gwen's hand, turned her head, kissed it, that memory of Gwen kneeling with her, telling her she was loved. Wiping her tears like a mother would, teaching her how to find her own life, how to fight, how to be on her own and without another. This beautiful, strong Inaj who saved her from horror, risked her own life to protect her, and loved her.

"I can't—" She scrunched her face in anguish. "I love you. I can't do that."

Gwen looked at her deeply, "Do not let them...take me."

Violet squeezed her lids between her tears. The world did the same now; stilled. A gentle breeze brushed the rushing tears. A harsh sob drew from the belly of her heart. She clung to Emryn, who coughed and moaned, and Violet sucked a deep breath. Her grief, her torment, clouded her gaze. She snatched Emryn's other hand and threaded it through Tamu's, then she gently closed Tamu's eyes and mouth. She bent down and pressed a kiss to Tamu's forehead. Resting. She was resting. Another stab of agony. She brought her other bloodied hand to Emryn's face.

There was no healing this. Violet had learned from the last time she lost someone she'd loved. There was only brief moments of shallow breath, of weaving the last words before they faded into a dark bliss. She pressed her forehead with Emryn's. "It's going to be okay," she said gently. Emryn's lips peeled back, a sob erupting.

Comfort. Violet decided to bring Emryn to the hills and meadows. She whispered the words to a girl who fought with endless courage, who loved with her heart, who saved many for the sake of breaking the curse on her world. "There is a meadow in the next world. It sprawls endless, as far as you can see, until its green and blues and yellows and oranges become a blur. It's filled with millions of flowers, and they are infinite. The sky shines a bright blue, the wind gusts a crisp and fresh taste on the tongue. The sun warms your skin the longer you lay under it, like a soothing hug. The trees are giant and lusciously green. So, so green that it doesn't look real. It smells like fresh dirt and smokey mint. The mountains overhead curve to each other, like twins, capped with cold white snow and watching like goddesses."

Emryn's cough weakened. A small smile breached.

Violet squeezed their hands, fighting the wobble in her voice. "It is safe. It is wonderful. It is a land for the free."

A shaky breath.

"There, the fighters, the warriors, the ones who never give up, find peace. You can rest there, in that meadow, Emryn." A sniffle. "You can finally rest, Emryn. Underneath the balmy sun. You and Tamu. Do you see it? That meadow?"

"Yes," Emryn breathed. Her brown, broken eyes glittered. "It's beautiful."

"It is, like you. You and Tamu. You guys can be free there. You can build a cute cottage with a giant fire, and you can dance. You can cuddle during the chilly nights beneath a colorful blanket you wove. You can laugh and smile and twirl in whatever you want to wear and whoever you want to be. You can dance in the freedom of it all, Em."

"I…like dancing," she whispered.

"You can dance as much as you want. And then you can lie beneath the wide wonderful night sky filled with billions of stars."

Tears slid down Emryn's face. "With Tamu?"

"Tamu will be right next to you. You will live out your days in love." Violet's eyes were a waterfall. "You are so, so loved."

A small squeak escaped. Emryn's face slacked into one of peace. "Will you come, too, Vi?"

Violet forced a smile, brushing Emryn's forehead as Rio did for Gwen those worlds ago. "Yes, soon. I will be there soon. I have some things to do first."

"And the others?"

"We will all dance with you in the meadow, Emryn."

A ragged breath. "I want to dance, but…"

Violet pulled back, her eyes blurry, and she wiped the tears and snot with her arm. "But?"

"Kill them."

Violet stilled. The precious moment flickered with a hint of rage. Anger. Hate. The pain in her chest warmed as a tiny ember sputtered, growing bigger. The meadow combusted. A storm blossomed on the mountains. The screams of the dying, the hurt, roared in her ears.

"Kill them all, Violet," Emryn breathed. "And then we can dance. Together…"

Emryn shuddered. Blood leaked from her mouth. Her eyes found Violet's, and in the hazy, watery look of them, flashed defeat. Then rage. Then fear. Then peace. Until the girl who had suffered at the hands of a greedy Order, only to fight to save oppressed others, took her last breath.

Violet took a shaky inhale. Her tears ceased. Her eyes danced over Emryn's still face, before she closed them with a trembling hand. Emryn's fingers fell limp. Violet still clutched them, processing her words.

A deep, unnamable darkness formed in her chest, pushing, punching to get out. Her grief molded into fury. That smoldering ember, teased over worlds, blown out and rekindled again, blossomed into flame. Burned into a bonfire.

Unleashed into an inferno.

That door within swung open. Her arm tore into lines of filigree light. Her vision blinded silver with shimmering tethers and strings to other worlds, but then shifted into purple, where another set of eyes gazed down on the destruction of the school, the patrols marching the streets, the alarms blaring on rooftops, the rush of dogs, and the prickly haze of blood. She saw red as she looked down on the Church District like a god. The rational part of her lounged back, a smile forming on her face as the new, vengeful Violet took over.

Emryn's voice sounded in her head, meshed with a cold, dark, familiar one—Greed. *"Kill them all."*

"Violet, no."

Jodin's voice. It drifted in between the smog of rage.

Violet saw through two different visions—the mortal and the immortal. The immortal was made of two gods; one who could travel worlds, and one who could manipulate them. Destroy them.

The mortal felt the pain and rage and grief. The mortal stared at her comrades, bloodied and dead, destroyed by Sin.

"Come back," Jodin said, even more distant. She turned her mortal head while her immortal body took over. Her power flared with untouchable silver and purple light. It burned.

Bled.

Blinded.

Jodin covered his wide, frightful eyes with his forearm. Navee hovered behind him, the Inaj kids behind her. Violet knew what she looked like—she saw it from the god-vision above. It was her eyes that frightened. That glowed and glared with revenge.

She whirled a single finger.

Her power answered. Wind lashed through the school, nearly knocking over Jodin and the others. Screams filled in the entire district.

"Get out of here," she warned.

Jodin dared to take one step, holding his hand out. "You don't want to do this."

"Oh," Violet said with a humorless smile. "I want to do *exactly* this."

Jodin lunged for Navee and the kids, and with a panicked last look, he vanished.

Take, little Manipulator. Take what you want. Revel in it, take more, destroy more, become more, you are the heir—

"Shut up," Violet said, and in her endless, power-filled mind, she found that sliver of Greed's darkness and grabbed it. Snapped it. A small, muffled clink sounded on the floor, and her mortal body looked down, finding the Iris. Her bloodswearing mark burned. She picked up the cylinder and stuffed it into her pants pocket.

Violet's eyes raised to the sky. The beacon to the next world flared brightly within the far mountains, over the pulsing volcano. But she wasn't done yet.

Unleash, agia.

So Violet Sutton did.

36

Unleashed

Violet stood above her dead friends. Her lungs never seized, nor her muscles or her calculated rage. Purple seared the filigree lines, and through her higher eye, she found the Order troops closing in on the school. They crammed the streets, shut the plasma gates, attempting to hold her in, but no one could stop her.

Kill them all, rang an ancestral, powerful voice. Each word beat with her steady heart.

With a raised arm, Violet felt the stiff, cold beam of metal and willed it to crush. Half the wall crumbled. She whipped out her other hand. The other wall caved with just a flick of her finger. She cocked her head, face hard and eyes alight, as she began her destruction.

"Hey!" The voice was distant. Up ahead, a black-plated guard held a plasgun and shot it. The bullet met her hand, and the tinge of plasma simmered into her skin like a tickle. The guard paled, taking a step back, but continued firing. Violet sauntered toward him, pulled her plasblade from her back, and with one single stroke as he continued to pointlessly fire, she lobbed the man's head off.

Her immortal body saw the troops closing in on the demolished school. She waited. Turned once to glimpse the limp bodies of Emryn and Tamu. Rage poured. She flexed her fingers around the hilt. There was no remorse, no yielding, no morality thrumming within her pulse.

With half a thought from her immortal, manipulating eye, the remaining school walls caved to dust.

She continued through the wreckage as fire erupted around her, warming her cheeks. Licked her boots. It smoldered the same as her revenge. She swaggered through the school, slashing her plasblade at random beams and stray guards who tried to stop her. A hound barreled its way through the dusty haze, sharp teeth aiming for her throat, but she merely grabbed its muzzle with her fist and tossed it aside with god-like power.

She called upon the silver ability and vanished to the school's front lawn.

"Weapons up!" someone called. The clicks of hundreds of guns sounded. Lasers focused, finding her forehead, her heart, her knees. Her face stayed neutral.

"Vanisher," she heard one say. "Activate heat tracking! Use proper fire!"

Violet lifted her hands in a sign of surrender.

"Drop your weapon and get on your knees!" One guard advanced near her, gun raised. His laser blared in her eyes.

An enraged, sardonic smile. "Okay."

She threw her plasblade to him and vanished. Appeared in front of his black-clad body. Caught the hilt of the plasblade and whirled that simmering purple straight across his neck.

He collapsed to his knees before her.

"You first, though." She kicked him in the chest, toppling him to the ground.

Guns clicked.

Fired.

She crushed her palm into a fist.

Sinkholes opened beneath the roads. She flung her power into the buildings. They crumbled. Bodies flattened beneath rock. Screams rang. She rose to her immortal, all-seeing eyes and stomped. She lifted her arms, and the wind clamored through the space, sending people and guns flying. The light on her skin pulsed, and that ancestral power flowed through.

More. More. More.

A gas line exploded, taking an entire block with it. All the residents poured from the buildings, frightened, with children in their arms, barely making it a step before the fire consumed them. The troops reared back. Bombs were thrown at her, and she vanished to a main road where citizens fled. Destruction surrounded, war raged, but it was a certain cry that jolted through her bloody daze. She turned, unemotional, to stare at the small child clutching its blanket, tears streaming down the boy's face.

The cries of fear roared around her. Everyone ran away. Violet stood before the child, tilting her head. Morality wove its way back to her heart.

You've destroyed enough! A small, tiny part of her screamed. Blood scraped the boy's cheek. *Stop it. Stop it now—*

No, the immortal part of her demanded.

Her light flared again, and her power pushed back, wanting to be released. The fire burned too bright in her chest, then carried to the buildings around her. Triggered by her emotions. The boy began to cry, frightful eyes glancing to the ruins. Soldiers pounded down the streets. Gunfire rang. She shook her head, taking a step back, needing to distract it—

An arrow slammed into her shoulder. Through her internal fight, the pain flared enough that she gasped, bowing back. The child continued to screech into her ears. She fought for control.

The voice returned, *Kill them all.* Violet growled, distantly afraid of the sound she made. She felt her body twist, and watched her gaze narrow on a lone rooftop, but the ancient thing brought her up to a worldly gaze. Her foot jerked. *Stomp.*

"No," she breathed. There had to be a stopping point. Violet froze every single muscle, trying to regain control. People were running. Soldiers advanced. The city was in chaos. *Kill them all.* But only the ones who hurt, surely? Not everyone. She couldn't do that...

She spared the child one last look and vanished. Her abilities slipped. It was just enough for that door to fling open, and for the world to shudder around her. She landed atop Emryn and Tamu's bodies amidst the carnage of the school. They were untouched by the wreck, as she intended.

Violet became an inferno. A bright, uncontrollable purple light burst from her, shooting into the sky. What the light touched, it demolished. Each bit of destruction snagged at a heart string, making her lungs ache, bringing pain to her head, but she couldn't stop it. Violet Sutton became a small, tiny, cowering thing while the light took over. She watched herself incinerate everything within a visual radius.

Guards poured into the hallway, but they were snuffed out an instant later. An awful burning stench reached her nostrils, but Violet couldn't stop screaming. Her throat burned and lungs ached, but she kept going. Going and going and going. She was exploding. Her nerves zapped at every inch of her skin and caught fire. Whatever had slumbered inside of her awoke, laughing, cackling, telling her this was inevitable.

The ground shook beneath her.

Bodies crunched. Her immortal, all-seeing eyes watched as nearby buildings were razed with the rest of the destruction. Her light incinerated it. She covered her ears. Hot tears streamed down her cheeks. The light kept going—a beautiful, harrowing light melting everything in its path. But then there were thumps—near her, in the courtyard, out on the street. Too many thumps. Then screams. Cries for help. *Kill them all. Kill them all.* The light followed Emryn's orders, but Violet's sanity shrieked to a stop. She fumbled her control—

She bowed over her friend's bodies as the purple light took over, protecting them. "Please, please, please," Violet begged it, her sanity breaching. "Stop it! Stop it!"

She couldn't feel her heartbeat anymore. Her breath slowed. Her eyes shut but the light kept going, as if since the moment it was released, it was going to dredge every last bit of life out of her. She had held it in a prison, and now it was finally set free.

Before Violet collapsed, four figures slammed into the rubble around her. Commander Serwa was the first she recognized, followed by Captain Masar, Captain Yeren, then, to her disgust, Zavar. The wind drew closer to her, protecting her, but they motioned to each other and paraded forward.

"I'll kill you!" Violet warned.

Zavar was the one to brave the wind and light. His lightning flickered around him, some of it retreating from her ability, but as he entered her stronghold, his eyes began to widen. He wrinkled his nose at her perished friends.

"Stop it," Violet said, shaking her head. He took another step forward, pretty face neutral. He kept his mouth shut as his lightning steadily extended, touching her abilities. Nausea flared in her stomach. She wanted to lunge at him, kill him for touching her like that, but the mortal part of her retreated, afraid of this, wanting it to stop.

He knelt in front of her, rested one hand on her shoulder, and the other at the center of her chest. She wanted to recoil, but his grip said *don't think about it.*

His touch was frigid. Above her thrashing heart, his black power pushed, testing, and she jerked. While hers burned like fire, his was cool. Taming. Minty. With a hint of spice at the ends. She could taste it, feel it. It told her light to behave, go back, that it was safer there than burning down this world. Tears slicked her cheeks.

Zavar glared with glittering black eyes. His voice dominated the space, *"I command you to return to your home."*

Home?

"Return home."

The light paused. Stilled.

And rushed back into Violet.

She went flying backward, the same as when she was Awakened. The force of it slammed her back, sliding her body into the remains of the school. Splinters and blood littered her skin. She trembled. And when she beheld the ruins of what lay before her, she clamped a hand over her mouth.

Bodies everywhere. Charred and smoking. Every guard lay reduced to hunks of limbs, while the rest were cremated into ash. Fifteen blocks worth of city—razed.

Commander Serwa hovered. Her gaze flicked above, and she bowed deeply. "Master."

Other voices murmured the same. Cyran appeared overhead, fury writhing his face. He bent, grabbing Violet with a searing palm that burned hot, and vanished them.

He threw her to the ground. She skidded, her leathers torn from her abilities and plasgun shots.

"I will get my answers with you," he said. "But first, I will show you the real power."

They were on one of the three bridges connecting the Twin Cities. Water rushed beneath. The few cars ambling about honked, stopped, and abrasively reversed. Cyran held her eyes, and she held his, trying to bring back that fire so she wasn't swarmed by fear, but four separate bone-jolting crunches made her flinch, and fear won. He saw this. A satisfied glint met his eye. "That thing inside you wants to unleash. It is not you. It is an animal, meant to be controlled, and you let it control *you*. An emotional, pathetic thing."

Her eyes watered, smoke billowed around them. Four explosions. Violet didn't have to look to know those cars were burnt to smithereens just by a half-thought. She felt that power, did things both willingly and unwillingly, but with Cyran, it was all deliberate. He was showing her that his power did not come from his abilities, but from his choices with them.

Panic froze her body. She thought it was right—*kill them all.* But it was from another part of her that held no remorse. Two sides fought—the avenging one, and the loving one.

"This world is wasted by greed." His icy eyes turned to her. "Your world, your life, will be wasted by greed as well."

The ground trembled. The river below burst into flames. Lightning smacked the onyx skyscrapers in both Hallow and Hanhii. Glass exploded above. It rained, sharp and heavy, cutting her hands and creating a storm. People screamed. People ran. Bloodied. Fearful.

"All this greed is forgotten when one is reminded of their mortality." He cocked his head. "Because money, power, status does nothing for one buried in the wretched earth they destroyed. And these people…they destroyed their world. So as gods, it is our duty to put them to rest."

As gods.

"No—" She jolted forward, but he used his abilities to whip loose a chunk of brick, hitting her in the stomach. She collapsed into herself.

Cyran lifted his hands. Lightning struck again. Fire devoured a building, its flames then moving on to the next one. It ignited like an inferno, moving from the next to the next until her face burned hot. The soot and ash smeared with her tears. Everywhere she looked, fire burned, water flooded, and buildings crumbled. A snap of his fingers and a mountain nearby shuddered; an avalanche formed from coarse rock and paraded into the eastern side of Hanhii. A giant, heart-stopping boom. Buildings that once tasted the sky disappeared into dusty destruction.

Violet was projected back to the very moment when she ran onto that stage, desperate to return to her brother's arms, and sliced her hand into a vicious obsidian bowl. Her blood stained the world of her home, and six other worlds after that, but no matter the pain, the price paid for throwing herself to some semblance of freedom, a man stood before her. Not a man—a god.

And he destroyed this very world he built with a smile etched on his face.

A man who controlled people. Who could destroy seven worlds at will. Who started the games. Who breathed five-hundred years old and held magical, celestial powers that shouldn't exist. An army followed at his back. Weapons of mass destruction were at his disposal. Every sign pointed to downfall, and Violet was belittled in his presence. She thought she did something, she thought she could fight and bite and snarl, but she was an insect compared to this. She was nothing. Her dreams didn't matter. Her yearnings made her a fool. Her only hope lay in his hands.

The Worldbreaker.

The World Ruler.

The Creator of the Sins.

The Handler of Their Lives.

"The people left in this universe know nothing about us." He stepped toward her, each footfall shuddered the earth. She dug her hands into the broken road for stability. Glass bit her palms. The fires scorched her vision, but he continued, unbothered, like a true god with the background of his ruination. "There is no hope. No gods to save you. No skies to pray to. It is me. Only me. This game was your test, and you failed by surviving. Because no one who opposes me survives. So this is on you, little mistake. Each breath you take means the downfall of others, and yet you didn't believe me. Every moment you stay alive, more and more will die. And now look, I didn't even have to kill most of this city myself. You've done it for me."

"*No*," she moaned. It wasn't her. She just wanted revenge. Not to destroy it. That was her power. That was the parasite inside of her. "You did this to me."

Evil darkened his eyes. "Yes, you were Awakened, so that was my undoing. *My* mistake. Punishment must still be served for that."

Violet sobbed. Her face twisted in misery. *Mistake. Mistake. She's a mistake.* Her mother's words clanged in her head. A resounding explosion and she whirled—the demolition closed in on Navru. She jolted her legs, crawling toward it, but a whirl of wind wrapped her ankle and yanked her back.

"Rule number one of a Celeste," Cyran spat. "Do not play with what you do not know." A phantom hand gripped her head and forced her to look. Fire burned her eyes. Smoke misted the air. Cyran bent toward her ear, harshly whispering, "Watch, little Manipulator. This is the price of your survival."

Navru came crumbling down. Screams pierced her ears. She cried with them. Her tears poured into her grief-ridden shriek. Cyran laughed. Cackled.

The earth rumbled her shattering heart. Violet wished to bleed with them.

But Cyran wasn't done.

"Take it from me, though. If you try to be good, to care, to help, to save, the hurt won't ever go away. It's better to be the villain." A haughty sigh. "And you will make an excellent villain."

37

HE CAN'T DIE

"WAKE UP."

The voice riled Jack, vibrating within his ribcage. He had no recollection of his eyes shutting, nor being bound by burning plasma on his wrists and ankles. He peeled his lids open, and the first, lovely thing to appear was Zavar's always-flaring nostrils.

"You trimmed your nose hairs," Jack mumbled, his neck cracking as he drew his head up.

"And you sealed your death," Zavar clapped back.

"That was sealed the moment I was brought back from the first one."

Zavar raised his boot and kicked at the chair Jack sat on. Jack teetered, and with a whine of the wood, smacked into the floor. His neck jolted and a groan escaped. "That was rude."

He pulled Jack back up, lingering close to his face. "You made a fool of me."

"You put yourself in a position to be one."

"You knew she was in disguise," Zavar said. "The longer she stayed alive, I didn't count on you not figuring it out, but I thought you wouldn't *care*. That you'd accept her demise, but for some stupid fucking reason, the bitch made you turn, and now we are all in trouble for it. You played us."

Jack offered a sardonic smile. "I'm beginning to think you truly don't know me, Zavar."

It was a brief expression, but Jack caught it. His eyes dipped to Jack's lips. Hurt passed over his face. Betrayed.

Jack pulled at the plasma cuffs, wondering how many seconds it would take to subdue Zavar. Maybe just throttling Zavar would be enough, but Jack didn't want to test his survival against someone labeled a celestial Slayer. Jack guessed Zavar didn't know the full extent of what he was. Cyran was the sole one, and he wielded the knowledge like a weapon, pitting everyone against each other with falsities and half-truths.

In the giant cavern crested with stalactites and running lava overhead, Zavar owned his position as a dog to the Worldbreaker. His chin lifted. His ego flared. Lightning wound his knuckles. Jack would bet a lot of skivvin' money that Cyran withheld information to keep Zavar on a leash. If Zavar truly knew his power might match the Worldbreaker's, he'd be a severe threat. Better to tame the powerful than to risk giving them an advantage.

The massive chamber made light weak and spotty. Pockets of lava brightened certain places, plaslight flickered in others. He was surprised he wasn't a sweat ball, but then Jack noticed the vents above, and the cool air brushing his cheek. It was a ginormous space. Serwa, Yeren, Masar, Modav, Halco, and a few other commanders posted around, at ready, all looking venomous minus Yeren who seemed bored. His eyes lingered on a spot across the cavern. Jack twisted his head.

His heart dropped.

"You nearly made it to the finish line," Zavar said, following his gaze. "But others made it farther. You're not that special, nor are your friends."

Rio sat bound, gagged, and wide-eyed near a post complete with medical-grade equipment, a stretcher, and multiple bags filled with liquid. Jack couldn't decipher them from this far, but Rio's bugging doe eyes landed on his, panic flaring.

Jack smoothed his expression. No emotion. Just observation.

And with that observation, came two other bodies. Varik and Jonathon. Both caught.

Jack's eyes fell shut. He took a deep breath and his focus landed on Jonathon. The man had tears streaming down his face, and Jack pushed the ache in his chest away. He needed a means to an end. Jonathon was that, until he wasn't. Until Jack cared.

There will be no sorries. No goodbyes. Jonathon avoided his gaze. Varik appeared solemn next to him. Filled with acceptance.

A flash burst into the room, and Jodin materialized, dropping a body on the ground. Jack recognized it instantly—the head commander of Pharos. Bryce. He thought they were dead, but Jodin gave the leader a kick and Bryce groaned. Their face was bruised and bloody.

"Put up a fight, this one."

But Bryce wasn't the fighting type—Jack garnered that from their interaction. They were better with the mind than with fists. Jack noticed most of the injuries were from numerous angles. Unusual if it had been an actual fight. A couple of hits to one point would take an opponent down faster than scattered ones. It would hurt less, though, to scatter it if perhaps they planned where to punch…

Ah. Part of the bloodbonds Bryce made. Terms that have now come full circle. Bryce would go down, Jodin would keep his traitorous ways. Jodin wouldn't blatantly sign himself to protect Pharos—he'd need something in return, and that thing was a guarantee of his ass being saved. Handing over the leader of Pharos for death should do it.

Jack briefly recalled a conversation with Bryce. His eyes narrowed on Jodin.

"He joined rather abruptly, if not forcefully."

"Something motivated him."

"Something changed his mind," Bryce said. "He said the veil parted and he had something to fight for. He said he finally wanted it all to end, because if the Worldbreaker succeeded in solidifying his reign more than what it already was, we were doomed for eons."

Eons were farfetched in Jack's mind. Worlds collapsed, stars collided, and galaxies died in that time, yet Jodin seemingly proclaimed that Cyran would match the nature's trajectory. It was exaggerated, Jack had said.

"The desperation in his voice made it seem very, very real," Bryce muttered, and Jack noticed they absently rubbed the bandage on their palm. Then they spoke again, "It was funny, though. Interesting, actually." They took a steady sip. "I finally put some pieces together. The day that Jodin swore himself to me, to Pharos, was the same day Violet entered Greed."

"He's coming." A proud expression crossed Zavar's features. He, along with the commanders and captains in the room, began to bow deeply. A searing light momentarily blinded Jack, and a curse erupted next to him. He turned his head, curls falling in his face, as Reed sucked in a sob. The man was crying, bound to a similar chair like Jack.

He caught Jack's gaze. "I tried, Jack. I really did."

Reed's previous words slammed into him. *In some sick, twisted way, I thought letting her die was better than letting her live under the Worldbreaker.*

And it all became evident.

Cyran appeared, a hand fisted around Violet's neck as she gagged for breath. He threw her to the ground. She slammed, hard enough that her bones protested so loud it echoed off the brawny walls. Her inhale was a desperate wheeze. Saliva and blood dripped from her mouth. She tried to pull herself up, but she collapsed onto the floor.

She was shaking. Trembling. She didn't attempt to get up again, but instead, hugged her limbs to herself and rocked. Dried blood covered her exposed skin, but Jack caught no sign of wounds. His heart jolted, wanting to reach for her. He tried to catch her gaze.

Her typically ferocious blue eyes now lay empty. Tears stained the rock. Whatever fire existed in her, it had been snuffed out completely. Worry flushed through him. He teetered on breaking the plascuffs and going to her. He hadn't protected her enough. He miscalculated her care for the people in this city. Bryce had told him about Violet's mission with a couple of comrades at the

Residential School, and while he fretted over the danger, offering his help instead, the entire plan seemed flawless. Bryce assured him. They will be in and out, but there were always risks. Jack understood those risks. He always calculated them. What he didn't count on, though, nor anyone else for that matter, was Violet's fury resulting in the demolition of the Church District. Violet snapped. Power as confusing as Jack's lingered within, and she let her emotions run with it.

"This was a disappointment," Cyran began. His eyes swept around the room, landing on each defeated body. "I thought better for three candidates who made it this far, evading me to this degree, with two turning out to have immense powers that I've overlooked. And still, you're here. Contained. I expected more fun."

Zavar smirked. Serwa twirled her dagger. Masar glared at Jack unabashedly. Clearly betrayed. Jack didn't blame him. The man was a soldier, and he followed whoever was destined to win. Masar acted like Jack would do the same once he was sent to the Sins— siding with the Worldbreaker was the safest survival option. But Masar was cold-cut and narrow-sighted. Heart didn't play into it, and Jack's heart changed a lot of fucking plans.

His gaze flicked to Violet again. She didn't shift position.

Rio yelped, eyes widening as Yeren drew close. An uncharacteristic snarl erupted from Rio. Yeren raised a brow.

A minty realization flushed through him. He kept his expression complacent, but Jack noticed the tiny thing missing from the room.

Anaya.

The small devil was nowhere to be found. His eyes wanted to find Jonathon, to see if he could determine where the little shit was, but Jonathon's gaze was empty.

Jack was suddenly vaulted back into his memories.

Chained to the desk, he woke. Lucien was passed out next to him, as well as Lyla and Cairo. His closest team was unconscious. The door burst open, and Bronto was there, panting.

"Reed surrendered to Arvalo. He's turning you over to the Empire."

Traitorous rage flushed through Jack, but it was drowned with shame. Failure. He allowed himself to fail, even if he was drugged and strapped to his penthouse while Reed destroyed his reign. He failed the thousands of people who hoped he'd become a hero. Failed his family he turned vengeful for. Failed with every breath, every action. His dream crumbled around him.

Jack Marin had failed.

That same sensation washed over his skin. He slouched his head and curved his shoulders. He'd fail, and the decrepit world would move on. Anaya was no saving hope, as much as he wanted her to be. If she were smart, she'd find a way back to Lust or Sloth—deemed the safest worlds—and disappear.

"You, though, hold nothing." Jack's head snapped up. Cyran leered at Rio. Sweat licked Rio's forehead. He pleaded into his gag, but only a wet groan escaped. Two medics appeared from behind the machines. Commander Serwa stepped between them and lifted Rio underneath the shoulders. They worked on his binds quickly, re-strapping him to the stretcher and getting his vitals.

Jack's stomach dropped.

Zavar stepped before him, a needle in hand. "Only the freshest for your friend."

"No," Jack protested. "*No.* Not him—" He tried to jerk away, but Zavar snatched his forearm with ferocity, digging his nails. He shoved the needle in. Jack's blood flowed into the syringe, then followed a small tube to the bag at Zavar's hip. Two minutes and thirteen seconds was how long it took a bag to fill. Rio's quiet sobs echoed around, muffled by the gag.

Desperation stuffed Jack's voice. "Not him. I'll do anything—"

"You already did everything, Jack," Zavar said, his name sounding like a curse. "You ruined it all."

Jack didn't know if it was Cyran's operation, which was doubtful, their missions, or his and Zavar's troubled relationship.

Zavar brought the blood bag to the medics. They hooked it up to the machines. Cyran waltzed over, put on gloves, and accepted a case the medics offered him. He pulled three giant tubes; one filled with red, another with brown-red, and the last one a glowing blue—nothing like Jack had seen before—and smiled. "Perfect."

Jack started. "What is—"

A fist met his cheek, nearly knocking the chair over. Masar had wandered over, now sneering before him. "Shut up."

Jack still waited to break the plascuffs. He imagined they were all waiting for him to snap.

"Harmas steel hardening to protect him from killers, because he'll be very wanted for this. Droanian strength is useful as always. And the last…is a secret. It's from a world you don't know, and a magnificent species I only recently discovered. He'll be useful once he is fully transformed, as he will be accepted into their community and be extremely reliable in other capacities."

Tears streamed down Rio's face. He jerked away from the needles as the medics loaded them in. Cyran attached the tubes to three individual bags, while Jack's blood was loaded into a spinning component. Cyran connected it all in a middle container, and the medics jammed a giant needle into Rio's arm. He bellowed into the gag and shrieked his heart out. Violet never turned her head. Reed looked down at his boots. A loud whirring sound dragged through the room as Jack's blood began to mix with each of the three species. They connected a plascution patch to Rio, as well as stripped his chest and sanitized the bony space above his heart.

Jack's eyes moistened. He flinched at each screech from his friend. He had failed him.

Failed. Failed. Failed.

When the blended blood slowed, a medic loaded it into another massive syringe. The medic handed it to Cyran. They held Rio down as Cyran stepped over him, raising the thick needle above Rio's heart. Rio begged, shook his head, jingled the table, and screamed to a world that never looked out for him.

And Cyran smiled.

He stabbed the needle straight into Rio's heart.

A nauseating gurgle escaped from Rio's mouth. He slowed. Stilled. Violet traced patterns on the ground. Tears fell from Reed's face. Yeren stared at the wall. Serwa wrinkled her nose. Zavar's expression was unreadable. Masar looked disgusted.

Varik, on the strange hand, looked smug. He shared an exchange with Jodin. Jodin's eyes were alight. A friendly look, Jack recognized. The same look Lucien and him would share when they telepathically knew each other's thoughts.

Cyran pushed the remaining blood into Rio's chest and stepped back while Rio began to convulse. The seizure overtook him, but like the other subjects, a small, golden light shined beneath his skin. It flowed with his blood, healing, securing, creating new life, as Jack now understood.

"Remarkable," Modav said. "Pity my blood is poisoned. Then you wouldn't have to put up with him." Modav jerked his chin to Jack.

"That was your undoing." Cyran peeled off his gloves and threw them in a trash can.

A poisoned Giver…whatever that meant.

"In the meantime." Cyran waved his hand to Varik and Bryce. "Kill them."

Zavar took a step. "You don't want info—"

Serwa silenced him with a look. "The Twin Cities are destroyed. Pharos is meaningless. The antique shop owner merely harbored fugitives. Listen to His Master."

Zavar deflated in submission. Jack felt a tinge of pity, as he always did, for the man. Born as a dog, raised as a dog, Zavar only knew orders throughout his whole life. No freedom…

Lucien shouted. "Grab him!"

But Jack was sprinting down the beach with his opponent's flag, wet sand molding between his tiny toes. He ran with the breeze, pushed by the lapping waves. Avan was near, but the second eldest was the slowest of the brothers. Jack, despite being the youngest, was the fastest. He stretched his arms out as the sun peeked between the clouds. A smile breached his face.

"Go, Jack! Run! Win!" Father screamed, held back by Lucien.

Jack passed back into their territory. Avan threw a frustrated ball of sand. "You distracted us, Dad."

Jack collapsed in the shallow waters, and with a bright, bubbling laugh, he learned to love this feeling. It was euphoria. It was happiness. It was chasing the stars and wanting to catch them.

It was freedom.

Jack could have sworn he felt that same breeze on the back of his neck, but it was hotter. Humid. He stiffened. His eyes shot to Reed, but the man was still bowed over his knees.

He thought he caught movement in his peripheral vision, but no one was there. He turned his attention back to the scene.

Jonathon was the first. He slouched his head as Serwa strutted up to him. "A traitor."

"I'm sorry," Jonathon pleaded. "I'll do anything—"

Serwa slit his throat. Cold seeped into Jack's chest. Jonathon's body crumpled.

A look passed between Varik and Jodin. Varik gave the slightest, minimal nod that passed as exhaustion. Commander Halco—a buff, silver-dusted, black-skinned Aurien with pristine white hair and a fat mustache—held Varik in his muscled grip. Varik didn't fight. He lifted his chin as Serwa strutted forward and unleashed her plasblade.

"You'll lose," Varik said, turning to Cyran. "The only way you'll ever control a universe is if that universe was atop a pile of bones, you pathetic man—"

The plasblade whirled into Varik's neck. His decapitated head smacked onto the floor. Cyran frowned, but turned to the next. At this point, Bryce was stirring, soft groans puffing from their swollen lips. Yeren took a step toward the Pharos leader.

But Violet lunged first. In a burst of energy, she snatched a blade from Yeren's belt and sprinted. She dove atop Bryce and held it at their neck. "You knew we lost contact! You didn't help us! They *died*—"

Bryce's fist swung out and landed at Violet's nose. Blood leaked. Yeren bolted for them, tugging Violet off and twisting her arm so she dropped the blade. Violet's face spewed pure hatred, anger, and grief. Her hair stuck to her tears. Her motions were lethargic, but rage pushed her muscles. It was a messy, desperate fight. "You *promised!* And you used us! You used him!"

Jack froze. Oh, so she found out about his not-suicide plan.

"All you said was fucking *sorry*," Violet spat. "You actual skivvin' *conjua*."

Yeren flinched at the word. He looked at Violet as if she'd grown three heads, holding her at bay like she'd turn to bite him. His gaze landed on the coil at her ear, and he paled. Stunned.

A rock wall burst up and slammed into Violet. She volleyed to the side, smacking the ground. Cyran lowered his hand. "Don't worry, you're next."

Bryce's puffy, bloodied face was unrecognizable as they turned and locked eyes with Jack. They stared. Blinked. A tiny statement, *I'm sorry.*

Jack read between the lines.

I'm sorry, but the children are saved. We must suffer for their freedom.

Serwa's plasblade shoved into their chest. Bryce jolted. Then fell still. Violet scratched the floor from where she lay, a snarl plastered on her face, but it waned. She breathed through her teeth, crazed, before her eyes whipped to Jack. "Don't you *ever* say shit to me about my fire again. Not like that, you coward."

Violet was losing it. Jack's mouth thinned. She disregarded those around her. This wasn't some battering cage. She wouldn't see it as such. She wasn't…there. Her eyes said so. They shifted from Bryce, to Varik, to Rio, then to her hands. She huffed a laugh, but then her mouth twisted, and her laugh fractured into a wail. Her emotions were fighting. It was their last-ditch crazed effort to keep her alive.

Because at this point, sanity might not be an option.

"Shut her up," Cyran commanded.

Zavar strutted over to Violet and Jack jolted in his chair. "Don't you fucking—" Zavar held up a wad of cloth and, brushing her hair back, shoved it in her mouth. He tied it in the back. Violet was too lost to even fight it.

Cyran's eyes flickered over Rio. A medic muttered, "Vitals are good. Fresh blood produces more rapid progress."

Rio sagged on the table. His tongue lolled out of his mouth, his hand hung off the side—

Black rippling fur. A pale, pink tongue licked Rio's limp hand. Jack blinked—nothing was there. He swore he saw a cat. But between that and the hot wind…

Not wind. *Breath.*

"Now for you," Cyran strutted over the dead bodies and paraded to Reed. He fisted Reed's hair and dragged his face up. "I gave you everything, and you lied to me."

A corner of Reed's mouth turned up in a half smile. "I didn't *lie.*"

Cyran's white brows fell. "Excuse me?"

"I said I didn't lie." Reed's blue eyes flicked to Jack's. "I don't know her."

A full circle. It brought Jack back to his confrontation with Reed after the sex club. Reed had been so adamant about Violet's desires that he failed to see she'd changed.

"I know her more than you do."

"Actually, at this moment, you don't." Jack wiped his face and stood, shoving his hands in his pockets. "You don't know her anymore save for her dedication to you…"

Jack always knew Reed was too smart for his own good. He fooled the fucking Worldbreaker. Jack said multiple times that Reed didn't know Violet anymore, and Reed convinced himself enough that it didn't spark as a lie. It was the truth. The Violet who existed in these worlds was nothing like the one he'd raised in the South.

Cyran's palm smacked Reed's face. The slap bounced around the cavern. Jack took the moment, the sound, to snap his plascuffs.

He bit down on a hiss, wrists burnt, but healing already.

Violet went feral. Zavar tightened his grip on her, and it took every ounce of strength for Jack not to lose his advantage and rip Zavar's hands off. Violet screamed into her gag, bloodshot eyes on Cyran.

The Worldbreaker frowned. "But you…you may not be as much of a mystery as I thought."

Out of the corner of Jack's eye, he saw Jodin stiffen.

And behind Jodin, he saw a familiar white flower. Holding that white flower was a masked Anaya.

"There is only one explanation for you." Cyran bent before Violet and snatched her jaw. He turned Violet's face this way and that, studying her, then flicking his gaze back to Reed. "How… did I miss this? A remarkable foolery." His voice turned incredibly dark. "And the girl is the younger. A younger sibling is not supposed to exist."

Violet gave the biggest roll of her eyes. If Jack wasn't growing so panicked, he'd have snorted, but Anaya disappeared, and he heard the whine of metal. The groan of air pushing through. His eyes flicked to the vents.

The flower.

Violet's scream tore through the cavern, painful and piercing. Jack lunged, but Zavar was there, tackling him back. Pinning him to the ground. His lightning swarmed, and Jack fought the insistent urge to vomit. When Jack looked, Cyran's hand was on Violet's chest. The light at his palm flared brighter and brighter…

Horror washed over him.

He was *pulling* the light out of her.

Reed cried. He fought to get out of his chair. "No, no, no!"

The commanders swarmed. Jack flung a punch at Zavar, but he missed. Zavar growled. "It's better if she goes," he hissed. "There will only be pain for her."

"*Violet!*" Jack cried so desperately, and another memory slammed into him.

"Lily!"

The cold mud bit his toes. It was harder to run in than the sand, but he ran all the same. To the blood coating her tiny back. To the sheepish clothes barely clinging to her child body. He pushed his way through the mob and dove for her.

He was helpless. Watching another die—

A giant, black shadow blurred by. It dove straight into Commander Halco, who had his plasblade raised and chomped off half of his body.

Navo. The panther opened its mouth and roared. Spit flung, eyes a deadly gaze. Zavar paled, pulling back—

Jack tackled him and sent a punch flying into his face, hard enough to knock the man out.

"Fuck you, *skivs.*"

All heads turned up. Anaya hung from the rafters. She pointed the plasgun straight at Serwa and fired. It hit the commander in the shoulder with a blast, and she flew back. White-tinged air poured from the vents behind her, mask still over her the bottom half of her face.

Navo lunged for the Worldbreaker. A spear pierced the air, but the cat shifted back into a smaller form, agilely avoiding it, before transforming back into the massive, robotic beast. Cyran's surprised face lasted for a moment. His arm raised, and a blast of wind knocked the panther back. His other hand didn't release from Violet's chest. Violet's skin grayed, her body nearly hunched into Cyran. She gave halfhearted attempts to push him away, but her movements weakened.

Jack pulled off his shirt and wrapped it around his mouth as tightly as possible. He lunged for the spear. He turned it on one commander, smacking their plasblade out with a hit and stabbing them in the stomach. Jack twisted them to the floor, yanking the spear back, before volleying it into the head of another commander. Jack whirled, bounding for Cyran—

Modav was there. He lifted the plasblade.

Then faltered.

His brows drew together in confusion. He sniffed the air. A deep growl ripped through his throat, but he choked and collapsed back.

"Meeter flower! Nature's sedative!" Anaya cried from above. "Fuck you people!"

A jolt shook the earth. Serwa gasped. Yeren paled. Jack whirled.

Violet held the hilt of a dagger…and it stuck out of Cyran's neck. Red sputtered, pouring profusely in all directions—

"That's for my friends, skiv," Violet wheezed, Cyran's blood coating her cheek. Her eyes rolled into her head, and she crumpled backward.

"*No!*" Reed cried. "No! He can't *die*—"

The ground began to shake. Anaya dropped from above, landing expertly. She smacked the blunt, unlit end of a plasblade into Yeren's head as the rest of the captains, Serwa included, collapsed from the sedative. Anaya's eyes widened. Rocks began to fall from the ceiling. The lava grew hotter.

"The flower worked," she proclaimed. "But…"

"Get Rio. We need an Iris *now*. The portal is here." Jack vaulted for Violet, yanking her to his chest. His hand brushed her leg, and his brows furrowed. He pulled out the Iris from a pocket. "Well, fuck, that was convenient."

Jack's eyes darted back to Cyran. His blood sang. *Giver—Mezcla.* Gold light poured into filigree lines at his hands, pushing him…Jack shook his head.

"Save him!" Reed said, wobbling on his feet. He hastily ripped a piece of cloth from his loose shirt and wrapped it around his mouth. His eyes drooped, but he fought it. "Do it, Jack!"

It was the damnedest decision he'd ever had to make. Seven worlds for one man's life. But then it would all be over. No more suffering—no more anything. They'd be done.

Jack smacked his bright, golden palm onto the Worldbreaker's chest. Pushed the Giving power into him. Cyran's body rattled with it. The light soared to the center of his chest, and a moment later, the earthquake stopped. The lava returned to a casual simmer. A few more rocks fell from overhead, but all stilled.

"Jack!" Anaya called.

Jack wasted no more time thinking about his actions. He slashed Reed's binds and passed Violet's limp body to him. Reed cradled her closely. Jack then rushed over to Rio and flung him over his shoulders.

After Anaya unbolted the doors, they were running through the cavern's halls. They passed through one empty room, then the next, and then it exploded into a giant, massive hall under the volcano. Shelves upon shelves lined with vials of blood stretched for as far as the eye could see. Jack slid to a stop, but Anaya kicked at his shin. "I know, it's horrible, but keep going."

The Order's bloodswearing vault. He knew it. As they passed the last shelf, Jack turned, and with all his Droanian strength, pushed the ten-plus tiered thing over. It knocked into the next row. Vials of blood fell and shattered on the floor. The shelves stopped at only two, and he paused, wanting to finish the destruction that was sure to piss off Cyran's grand controlling plan, but Anaya barked, "Now, Jack!"

Navo turned back into a tiny cat, and with big green eyes, bounced stoically into Anaya's backpack. They breached another room, made one more turn, and the pedestal to the next world glimmered with a million heartbeats of hope. Reed held the Iris, and gripped Anaya's hand, while Anaya gripped Jack's.

Anaya looked back, "Watch out!"

Jack turned, eyes narrowed on the massive figure sprinting in his peripheral. Masar raised his plasblade, gaze set on the Iris—

Jack grabbed the humming blade with a free hand, crushed it, and threw it to the side. He put an iron grip on Masar's arm.

"Time to go say hi to your sister."

Serwa stumbled into the cave, holding her bloody, injured shoulder. She threw one last dagger, but Anaya cackled a high laugh as she ducked from it.

"Ciao, bitch," Anaya sneered, giving a middle finger.

Reed slammed the Iris down. The sixth world snuffed away.

38

THE SEVENTH SIN

A BARREN WORLD GREETED THEM.

Jack felt the salt pelting him first. It showered his bare cheekbones, stung wounds he didn't know he had, and barely caught him when he landed in a lush pile of it. Four bodies smacked next to him with thuds, followed by the tiny meow of a cat.

He coughed. Blew his nose out. It was everywhere. He tried to inhale, but it stabbed the back of his throat and he gagged. His neck was turned at an odd angle, and with a lurch, he drew himself up. Rio let out a soft groan as he slid off Jack.

Jack rubbed his eyes with his shirt, removing as much salt as he could. Only three other bodies roused—Anaya's low cursing, Reed's whimpering, and finally, Masar's bated breaths. Jack opened his eyes.

Shrouded in a salty, limestone haze, Pride expanded before them in an empty flat of land. That was all it was. Deserted. Lifeless. Devoid of—anything. Wind constantly whipped, bringing kernels of salt with it. There was no sky in sight, no sun, but there was light. Eternal dawn, he guessed. Jack slowly rose to his feet.

The gritty wind, dull light, and nothingness produced a haunting feeling.

Beside him Anaya vomited. Reed twisted every which way, mouth gaping. Masar lowered his sword and placed a hand over his heart.

Violet lay slumped, Reed still clutching her to his chest. Rio drooled.

"I should kill you," Masar turned his dark eyes to Jack. He rose to his feet, whipping his plasblade. It ignited brightly in the fog, nearly blinding. He held his chin up high, but a wariness lingered in his gaze. His eyes darted back over the plain. His face paled. "What is this place?"

"Do you feel that?" Reed's eyes scanned the expanse.

Violet whimpered, shaking her head. "No, no, *no*—"

"*Dead,*" Rio whispered. "They're dead."

And that was when Anaya's finger rose, pointing to a thing in the distance. Jack's eyes squinted. Reed cursed.

A bone.

Jack's arms fell to his sides. His shoulders slouched back. A strange thumping existed in his chest. Time slowed as his eyes drifted across the landscape. The more he *looked*, the more he saw. Bones littered the place; giant femurs, tiny fingers, pelvises, a clatter of collarbones.

He stepped back. His heel brushed something. He turned.

A skull, mouth agape, stared up at him. A symbol was etched on its forehead—a roguish star meeting the center of an ingrained halo.

His chest grew cold. Breath escaped him. Eyes watering, Jack could only faintly mutter; "Six minutes, twenty-seven seconds."

The group ignored him. He didn't care. His abilities flared in a golden light, whining, his heart a rapid, untamable beat in his chest.

"It's a graveyard…" Masar breathed. "Of candidates."

"Only forty candidates out of hundreds have reached the seventh world." Jack didn't think any candidate had that marking on its skull, regardless. There was more to these bodies, and it shivered his still-useful bones. "Pull out your weapons. Someone needs to beat Pride, *now*—"

A cold, deep voice vaulted into his head. His vision blacked. It was powerful. So, very powerful.

I have been waiting for your return, prince.

A headache cradled his temples. Jack turned every which way.

One of you, at least, to see if you would take back your land after we slaughtered it.

The vision of limestone salt in his mother's kitchen came back. All senses left him. The Sin of Pride swarmed in, grasping at the back of his neck and tilting his head up.

Far away, he heard everyone riling. Someone called his name.

Looks familiar, doesn't it?

The limestone jar, the limestone world.

His world.

Giver. Mezcla. It said. *But this is only a sliver of what you once ruled. One of many connecting worlds that breathed life before we took it all away.*

From there, Jack felt the ancestral pulse of his Awakened abilities. It dove through the soles of his feet into the graveyard of earth. He heard millions of screams, the boulder-cracking sounds of a destroyed planet, and flayed skin splattering rock. He felt the story, the bloodbath that had existed here.

You want to sit on a throne, don't you? You were born for one, prince. Bleed on this earth and take it back. You're better than the rest of them. You can destroy anyone who threatens you. Jack's chest inflated. *You are a survivor. You're the best. Even better than your brother—*

"*No,*" Jack hissed.

Better than your parents—

"No!"

An animalistic snarl ripped through his throat. He forced the Sin from his head. Years ago, it might have worked. But today, Jack was better than no one. His bloodsworn mark flared. The world fell back into his vision. Reed was in his face, pulling at his shoulders.

"He's coming!"

Pride's earth shook.

But the Sin was persistent. It opened the door to his mind with a mocking smile. *The Mezcla thought they were the best. Healing and giving life. You are part of them. You're better than the one who slaughtered them. You feel that? The puff in your chest? You love that feeling. They've always said you were destined for great things. Wouldn't you agree? Aren't you the best there ever was?*

"Yes," Jack breathed. A warm swirl filled his ribcage. The wind powered him. He didn't know what the fuck the Sin was talking about, but he knew it was right. Jack *was* the best. He succeeded on every part.

Failure will never touch you. Take my hand and I'll make sure—

"Jack!"

A familiar voice. One that yelled at him over and over from years ago. One that had once told him he was doing too much. He was going too far. His pride was blinding his actions—

Black coated Jack's vision, but Reed continued to yell his name, to call him back. "Jack! You're better than it! Fight it!"

Jack's pride burst with the Sin's words. A cruel smile pulled, and he laughed. "But I am better than all of you."

A slap landed across his face, followed by a hard, bone-cracking punch. Jack flew to the ground. His vision sharpened. The Sin swam away. His mark flared a second time.

Masar stood over him, pinning him down. "If you dragged me to this stupid last world, you're dragging me home. *Fight it*, Jack."

Jack opened his mind once more.

You want to be Emperor. You want to beat the Worldbreaker. You can. Feel it in your chest, fill your ego. You can get whoever you want, be whoever you want to be, kill your enemies and win your lovers—

"Fuck you," Jack spat to the Sin. "You made that too easy."

It *was* easy, because through six other worlds of Sin, Jack's ego deflated and his soul absorbed it. It wasn't pride that fueled him anymore. He had it stripped away on a stage before a city filled with his failures. From then on, Jack knew his worth, his hope, and his dream strived from those who stood by him in his darkest times, not those who praised him in his brightest.

In his mind, Jack ripped the remains of his old, abused pride, and the Sin of Pride, apart. His mark seared and he grunted in pain, but a smooth, metal cylinder fell into his hand. He blinked. Masar was beaming, "You did it, you skiv."

"How many minutes?"

"Four," Reed said.

Jack's eyes snapped to the beacon in the distance. "Let's run."

Rio was strapped across Masar's back. Jack took Violet—Reed was already lethargic and slow. His ankle held some injury, but he didn't complain. Violet sniffed at Jack's neck once, and her arms tightened around him. "Are we going home?"

His lips met her forehead. "Yes, sweetheart, we are going home."

Home sounded like a foreign word in his mouth. He ignored the bite of the salt around him. They kept their eyes up, ignoring the bones, sprinting for their salvation. The wind began to whip hard, the ground shaking beneath their feet, but they persisted. In the distance, the portal slowly appeared, a hopeful star buzzing the Iris in Jack's hand. A storm drew, and the wind became more wicked, cutting into Jack's cheeks. He pulled Violet in tight, shielding her.

A whistle cut through the air.

"Zig-zag!" Jack commanded.

Everyone obeyed. A spear sluiced through the salt storm and landed right where Jack's foot had been, jolting the ground. A disgruntled laugh tore through the space.

Reed faltered, looking back. "Fuck."

Jack spared a glance. Cyran was vanishing to certain spots, closer and closer, while throwing spears provided by Modav.

Violet gasped in Jack's arms, her eyes wide. "Fuck," she said, imitating her brother.

"Hurry!" Anaya called.

The portal drew nearer. Fifteen feet. A spear whistled and knocked near Masar, but he stayed standing. Jack held the Iris up and their hands all clambered together, grasping—

Cyran appeared before the portal, an evil smile pulling at the scars on his neck. "Good try." He threw his last spear into Reed's stomach. A horrific gurgle sounded. Reed doubled over, falling to his knees as the spear shredded his insides. He clutched the metal, shocked.

A scream tore through Violet. Light flared.

Jack's arms suddenly held air.

She had vanished and now stood in front of Reed.

Her voice darkened, "You do *not* touch my brother." She caught Cyran's outstretched hand, and with eyes of pure silver and purple light, she flung the Worldbreaker to the ground. He countered her, flinging her back with a whip of wind and pinning her down. Reed vomited blood. The portal was before them. Jack pulled at his plasblade—

With a furious, devilish look shot in their direction, Violet swiped her hand through the air, and a powerful wind jerked them all together. She cried through her gritted teeth, still holding Cyran down with one hand of power, while the other maneuvered them.

"Violet, no!" Anaya shrieked.

"Win!" Violet roared. One more whirl of her hand, and the Iris slammed into its notch.

Click.

The last world of the Sins swallowed his cry.

"Violet!"

❀❀❀

Everything bled dark. It stayed murky, but the most beautiful smell called to him—smoke, dust, shiva, and coffee. Jack opened his eyes. A portal twisted before him—one made of an iridescent, smoke-like substance that both beckoned and warned. He stood in a realm with no floor or ceiling. Only black; the same black that existed between the stars flickering in the night sky. He twisted his head; Rio, Anaya, and Masar stared, gaping, at the swirl of Calesal between the portal's hazy translucence. Navo poked his head from

Anaya's backpack, a trill sound stemming from his throat.

"Home," Rio breathed. Tears poured down his cheeks. "We made it home." He stumbled forward, Anaya holding him up, and with a widening, Rio-like grin, he limped with the Endolier to the swirling portal. The haze enveloped their bodies like a hug, until another step, and their forms disappeared. Jack heard the muffled car honks and alarms blaring in the night, then a yelp of relief.

Jack's heart was a slow, steady beat. Masar stepped up next to him. "Ready?"

Elation filled his chest, followed by despair. He looked back once again, but he saw no sign of her. She wasn't with them. She was *supposed* to be with them.

"She'll come," Masar said. "Go home, Jack, you deserve it."

Home was a weird word. Everything about Calesal felt like it, but at the same time, Jack found himself looking behind his shoulder. Not all of home was through that portal. Blue eyes flashed in his mind. Limestone salt coated his hair, his skin, his mouth. He took a step back, but Masar grabbed his arm. "There's no going back. Finish it, Jack. Let's finish this game."

"The game," Jack breathed, snorting slightly.

Masar pulled. Jack hesitated once more, but a sliver of his home lay beyond the iridescence. He knew it.

They stepped through the portal. The smoke was a smooth, crisp whorl caressing his skin, shoving itself as a breath. He exhaled on his next move, watching as the glittering fume transformed into a place he made home.

The world of Veceras, of the citadel of Calesal he had come to love, welcomed him. As well as a gun in his face. A horde of figures dressed in black stood around the Sky Arches and piled into the same daises Jack had walked so long ago. He recognized the material on the guards. The guns lowered, revealing familiar, shocked faces. Rio, at some point, collapsed on the ground, Anaya overtop him, snarling to Jack's gardia.

"Jack?"

That voice brought tears to his eyes. They fell freely. Jack turned to one figure in the group. They pulled their mask down, and his brother stared at him in disbelief.

"*Jack?*"

A smile curved on Jack's face. "Miss me?"

Lucien bolted forward. His brother's strong arms wrapped around him, and Jack sobbed. Sobbed for everything he went through in the Sins—the people he lost, the people he missed. He fell into his family's arms, at the same time falling apart. Lucien held him tightly. "It's okay, it's okay, you're home, Jack."

Home.

The word felt—incomplete.

39

ʀᴇᴛᴜʀɴᴇᴅ

Jᴇʟᴀɴ ꜰʟɪᴘᴘᴇᴅ ᴛʜᴇ ꜱᴡɪᴛᴄʜ ᴏɴ the neutralizing table and retracted the plasma. She buckled the bracelet around her wrist, double-checked it, and with a flick of her thumb against her ring finger, bright purple plasma blasted in a perfect circle at the edge of her left forearm. "And that's it."

She lifted her gaze. The three heads of Luka's plashield development team stared at her, dumbfounded. She had it all assembled in around three hours, and they had been watching every move meticulously. Luka leaned against the far door, arms crossed, amusement on his face at his employees.

She offered a strained smile and flicked her fingers again. The shield dissipated. "Any questions?"

All hands went up.

❀ ❀ ❀

Night descended in Calesal by the time she exited Plastech Industries via a backdoor and into a nondescript car. Luka slid his sunglasses on, wearing an unbuttoned shirt covered in a swirl of gray, followed by fitted black pants. He watched from the curb as security drove her away, yet Jelan found herself turning her head. He looked expensive, as always, with an air of untouchability. She stared at him, unabashedly, through the tinted windows of the car as he turned back into the building. On the other side, photographers were waiting to score an elusive image of the man.

When they turned out of view, she sighed back into her seat and twirled a braid around her finger. Antsy. A sour whorl crawled into her gut. Here she was, frolicking with the enemy and *liking* it. She hardly thought of Lucien, and suddenly Luka's brief glance and touch gave her more shivers than the sex with Lucien did.

And she felt *horrible* for it.

There was only one week left before their supposed trade, yet it became a clock counting down, and while past her wished the time sped up…now she wished it would slow down. Three weeks wasn't enough time. She did her duty and constructed the basic plashield for him, obviously leaving out the components for her developmental *plasshield* as Hira called it, and was left unscathed throughout the whole ordeal.

While she was still morally and loyally tied to the Marin gardia, she glimpsed the hurt of Arvalo's second eldest and wished to help. She straddled the blurred line of a traitor, and Jelan suddenly wished her life wasn't so complicated. Wished for the lack of aircon in her tiny dorm and went obediently to her plasma job. But this was her grandeur life filled with everything she could've asked for, and yet she…

Was sad to leave.

The driver whirled around the building and back on the main road. They crossed the front of Plastech Industries and the blaring flashes of cameras as Luka stepped out, lips tight and looking like the dreamy bachelor he was. People screamed for him, yearned for him, and reached for him, yet he kept a distance with a tipping head as acknowledgment.

The driver peeled away, and Luka's public eye went with it.

Jelan took the service elevator up to his apartment while swathed with two guards. She'd glimpsed two of Lucien's spies dining at the cafe across the street, and with a side-eye glance, they raised their glasses to her.

When she got back to the apartment, she collapsed on her bed. Her thoughts ran wild. She was supposed to hate everything about Luka, but instead, she pitied him. Another pawn in the game like the rest of them were.

Arvalo's game.

Her head picked up off the pillow. Yet with her plashield and a couple of right moves, Luka could position said game. Could right himself as the opponent.

Could commit checkmate.

She fell asleep after her plans exhausted her and woke to the beeping keypad at the door. Bags dropped on the kitchen island. Classical music played through the walls. Her heart picked up its beat as she blinked her eyes open.

Luka stood at the end of her bed, no expression on his face. "I'm making dinner. There's wine."

He left.

Jelan closed her gaping mouth as she heard him move about the kitchen. A knife slid against a cutting board, a pan sizzled, and the wonderful smell of caramelizing onions met her nostrils. She abandoned the bed and waltzed into the living space. A towel was flung over his shoulder and a giant, shiny blade finely chopped into a plethora of vegetables. Noodles simmered in a pot of water. A glass of pink wine sat on the counter, waiting for her.

His eyes dipped, studied her for a moment, before his stoic face went back to cooking. He lifted his own glass and took a long sip.

The tension slithered down her spine. She parted her lips, ready to cut through it—

The keypad beeped. Someone punched a number. Failed. Luka set the knife down, gaze hard at the front door. "Get in the bedroom."

His dark command slammed her into motion.

She hurried back into her dark room, shutting the door softly. Her pulse roared, but she stayed huddled against the wood, listening to the clink of the knife and soft steps draw to the front.

A click and a yawn.

"Brother," said an amused, casual voice. "You haven't been to parties in a while."

"What are you doing here, Park?"

"Joining you for…dinner apparently. Oh, look, you already have a glass of wine set out for me."

Jelan stilled. Her thoughts ran, trying to picture Park Arvalo. Thick dark hair, sensual eyes, a tall, thin frame, and quite the charmer, according to Lyla. He was harmless, they had said. Mostly a partier and drinker. "You've seen Mai around? Father's getting worried."

"After only two weeks? That's a surprise," Luka said. He sounded relaxed in Park's presence—perhaps they were close. "But no, I'm sure she's letting loose in the Mid away from our family chaos."

A darker, familiar voice. "Well, that certainly sounds like the little bitch."

"Bael." Jelan could hear the threat in Luka's voice, the tautness that formed the name. *Not* friends. "You've come to join, as well."

"Unwelcome, I can sense." Bael's cruel voice leeched into Jelan's room. Her guard went up. She remembered how he treated Mai at the party, and especially how he nearly shouldered his little sister out of pure spite.

He's an asshole. Worse than the others, believe it or not. Mai seemed scared around the eldest Arvalo. It wasn't a surprise Luka shared the same hatred for him. Jelan didn't need to be in the room to hear it in his voice. "You know to notify me when you want to see me."

"But with Park, he can come and go?" Bael growled.

"I am a normal, social individual, whereas you have a high kill count that no one wants to be around," Park said so blatantly, Jelan was surprised to hear it. "Do you know how many murders father has covered up for you? Luka doesn't invite you around because you'd kill the doorman if he looks at you wrong."

Bael was silent as Park's strained admission circled the three brothers. The sound of onions simmering filled the space. Metal banged—Luka went back to cooking.

But Bael apparently wanted to press, "There's a lot of food for only one person."

"He was expecting me," Park interjected.

False, obviously, but Jelan's chest inflated at Park's protection of Luka. The brothers weren't stupid and clearly held sides in their family.

"Fine but make me a plate. I'm starving. Where's the bathroom?"

"Down the hall." Luka's voice remained strained. Jelan held her breath. Bael lumbered, steps heavy, toward her. The guest bathroom lay in the hallway near her door. She slowly turned the lock on the bedroom, cursing herself when it clicked loudly.

Bael's steps paused. He sniffed. Grunted, and went into the bathroom. He turned on the loud fan. Jelan's eyes darted to the adjoining door to her bedroom and she rushed over to it, her fingers a sweaty mess as she tried to pivot the lock—

The door burst open. Bael stepped into the darkness, voice low. "I knew Luka was hiding something." His hand shot out, collaring her throat and slamming her into the wall. Her feet left the ground. Pure muscle rippled along his bare arm. Jelan's eyes locked on his hard ones, resplendent of Arvalo's cold, black eyes. "I don't see many hidden girls in here…" His gaze shot around the room, then snagged back on her face. Realization hit. "*You.*"

Jelan loosed her hidden dagger and slammed it into his bicep. He grunted as blood welled the wound, but he didn't drop her. Didn't seem fazed. She panicked, choking on the grip at her throat and unable to scream. Tears slicked down her face.

"You do not threaten the Arvalo family," Bael growled. "I should have killed you and your fat friend back at the club, but whatever plan you have ends here."

He yanked the dagger from his arm and pressed it against her chest, pushing—

The bedroom door burst off its hinges. Jelan's vision blacked in and out. A gleam of silver…

The cutting knife stabbed into Bael's neck. Blood misted her face, the walls, everywhere as his artery pulsed out. The tip stuck out the other end. Bael's grip released and she crumpled to the ground, choking for air.

Luka watched as his brother heaved a splash of blood on the floor. Jelan scurried away. Park stood at the door, shocked.

Bael dropped with a slam. He convulsed. A breath later, he stilled.

Luka's eyes stayed on her as he tugged the towel from his shoulder and wiped his hands. His expression was cold, hard. "Dinner's ready."

Park stared at his brother's body. "Honestly, about fucking time. I need another drink, though." His eyes shot to her. "You too, probably."

Jelan wheezed another breath. In and out. Her throat burned horribly. She wiped at her eyes and on shaking legs, darted out of the bedroom to the kitchen. She snatched the entire wine bottle and began to chug.

"Don't know who she is," Park mumbled as they exited. "But I approve."

She whirled, locking eyes with Luka.

His lips pursed, studying her as he always did before he took a step in her direction. She pulled the wine from her lips, her voice a rasp, "Why?"

"Because if we are meant to take down our father, we need to rid this city of his mutts, first." Luka shared a look with Park. "And just because we share his blood, doesn't mean we are loyal."

Just as Lyla and the rest of them predicted. A glimmer blossomed in Luka's silver as he beheld her. A new path formed, the chess game took a turn, and after nearly being choked to death, Jelan seemingly had both Arvalo brothers on her side.

Luka carefully ambled up to her until his breath danced across her face. He took the wine bottle, brought it to his full lips, and gulped. Beyond his shoulder, Park lifted his wine glass in a salute.

"Call Victor to bring the car around." Luka instructed his brother all the while staring at Jelan. His thumb grazed her chin and wiped a spot of blood. "We have one last mission, and then you…" He stared deeply into her eyes. "Are going back to Marin."

She didn't fight it. "Okay."

"Mai will stay there."

Park's brows shot up. "*Mai* is with Marin?"

"Temporarily," Luka said. "But if everything goes according to plan, she'll only be a pawn a little while longer."

Park sighed deeply. "I'll roll him up in the rug. You'll need a good stain remover, though." He exited the living room and called to Bael's body, "Damn, brother, I really wish you weren't so hulking now."

Luka continued to search her gaze. "Are you all right?"

"Yes," she said. "But…when did you…why are you turning?"

"Why? Because I'm tired. When?" He held the hint of a smile. "When I watched you best all of those old, despicable, greedy men in chess and I was *jealous*. Jealous of the way you secured checkmate so easily, jealous of your freedom, and especially jealous you turned your head and looked at Marin like he'd give you the praise you deserved."

Her breathing halted in her aching throat.

He crowded her into the counter, hands at either side of her hips. His hair slid from behind his ear and onto his cheek. "I realized I was willing to fight against my father when I watched this girl, so out of place, put the scheming rulers who governed the world to their knees. It was then that I discovered there was a possibility to win this war."

She straightened, pressing her front into him as heat warmed her cheeks and her core. Her scarred fingers hesitantly touched his waist and Luka's eyes fluttered at the contact. "You don't have to be a pawn, Luka."

He dipped his head, mouth nearly brushing hers. "I'll always be a pawn, but I want to be on the right side of the board this time." A wink. "Next to the queen."

Her chest fluttered. Stomach flipped. *Butterflies are bad*, her mother said in her head.

I'm not toning it down for you, mother. Never again.

His heady breath met her neck. This was wrong. *So* wrong. But Jelan was on fire. She was a flame and with every brush of his fingers, every small groan from him, every moment their eyes caught and knew this wouldn't end well, Jelan grew hotter.

Wanted more.

Luka closed his hand around her hip. "Please," he breathed against her lips. "Say yes."

Absolutely nothing made her hesitate. "Yes."

She lifted herself and crashed their lips together. He immediately pressed into her, as if a massive amount of restraint had been held taut for so long. She bit his lip and a small groan pulled out of him. His hands moved to her jaw, gently avoiding her neck, as his thumb stroked her skin. She moaned against him, into him, into the plushness of his lips and the skill as they molded with hers. He smelled of body wash and cologne, tasted like the ripest pomegranate, and warmed every inch of her skin.

A cough slashed through the moment. Luka pulled away, annoyance crossing his face as Park's voice carried, "When you guys are finished, I'd really appreciate help moving this thing. I'm a bit hungover and my tummy hurts."

A smile crawled to her lips.

❈ ❈ ❈

They loaded Bael's body into the back of a black van at Luka's apartment parking deck. Jelan spent the whole time pressed against the rolling door, wrinkling her nose at the smell of blood. The driver—Victor—said nothing. She assumed Luka or Park would pay him a handsome amount of money to stay quiet.

It was a silent ride to the Trollova River. Jelan glanced at Luka, who pressed against Park in the back of the van. They muttered to each other, a slosh of realization trickling over their expressions every now and then before their perfect Arvalo boy mask was fixed back in place. Park pounded on the side when they reached a secluded portion of the river filled with reeds and mud and lulling murky water. They piled out, and with a heave, Jelan helped roll Bael Arvalo wrapped in her bedroom carpet to the shoreline. Two black-clothing-clad men brought a dinghy up to the mud and helped them flip the eldest brother into the boat. Park and Luka stayed on the shore with her while the men pushed the boat into the water and began to row. They stood, staring, as the boat became a blur in the darkness. Bags of rocks were wrapped around Bael's body and it was pushed over the edge. The loud splash took a second to reach her ears, but it echoed through her bones. Her hand absently went to her throat.

Park raised a hand, cupping a flask. "To nearly killing me the time I made out with a girl he liked."

Luka snorted. "He wasn't right in the head."

"No, he wasn't. Scary bastard. Never thought he was a brother of mine." Park took a swig of the flask and held it out to Jelan. "And to you, hopefully helping to end it all."

Jelan hesitantly took the flask and swigged back the stab of liquor. She scrunched her face, coughing, but managed to swallow it to Park's teasing gaze.

"Come," Luka said stoically. "I need to get you back—"

A blaring alarm shrilled through the city, dancing over the river, and pulsing lights along the giant bridge before them. People began to scream out of their windows, clanging pots and metal and whatever they could find. Jelan whirled, staring at the bright burst of celebration cloying through the North. Fireworks sprung up from Mid, and smoke from the South.

Park drew out his phone, along with Luka. They tapped away, checking until Park's eyes bugged open. "Holy actual fucking shit."

"That bastard," Luka breathed, unbelieving.

The city breathed in chaos. It burst alive around her. She darted and snatched the phone out of Luka's hands. Her jaw dropped.

Jack Marin's name stood in the seventh world.

He…he was *alive.*

Elation bubbled to her lips and a smile grew. She had the urge to cheer with the rest of the city—the man, the myth, the ultimate golden boy of Calesal appeared in the seventh world, besting apparent death once again.

And the citadel cheered for him.

Her eyes dropped to the other names. *Violet Asher. Reed Sutton. Masar Donnal. Rio Gaverra.*

"Holy skies," she breathed.

Red dots blinked next to each name like her thunderous heartbeat. They stared on the shore as the city clamored its screams, urging them on, hoping for a break to the curse on their world.

"Go, go, go…" Park cheered as well, patting his flask. "Fucking do it, Marin."

The minutes passed. People swarmed the streets, waved flags from their balconies, and shrieked into the night. Jelan stared, hardly blinking at the small screen on Luka's phone. No one said a thing. Two minutes, three, four. The fifth slowly rolled into the sixth and that's when Jelan stopped breathing. No one made it to the seventh minute.

Her hope waned. The screams of the city bounced around her head. Park muttered Jack's name like a prayer. Luka held a glimmer in his eye.

The seventh-minute hit.

The city paused.

And then three names moved out of the seventh column.

Jelan witnessed pure history because for the first time, in over five-hundred years, an eighth column appeared.

Returned:

Jack Marin

Rio Gaverra

Masar Donnal

Tears streamed down her face. Fireworks smothered the sky. Screams of happiness, of joy, of utter elation, sprung through the streets as every resident celebrated the wild achievement.

They beat the Sins.

Park bounced up and down, howling across the river. A smile curved on Luka's face, the same as Jelan's, but when she processed the information, when she looked back, her heart stuck into her throat.

Reed and Violet were still in the seventh world.

"No," she pleaded. Stared at the screen with blurry tears. "No, please no no no—"

Eight minutes. Nine…

"We have to move," Luka warned, glancing at the blare of lights turning on in the Government Sector. "The Redders will be out to quell this."

A car pulled up at the edge of the bank, and the window rolled down, revealing Ashan. Jelan's heart jumped and she beelined over there. "Oh skies."

"Get in honey, this is about to be bad."

"But Violet—"

"She'll make it, but I need you to get in."

He beckoned her. Her fingers met the door handle, yet she whirled to Luka. His hands were shoved into his pockets, and without a word, he gave a command. A nod of his head. *Go.*

She pulled the handle.

Another nod. *Thank you.*

Park did cartwheels down in the mud, his flask sloshing alcohol everywhere. "To Jack *fucking* Marin!"

Luka slid his sunglasses on.

Jelan ducked into the car and shut the door.

Jack Marin had returned and with that, they all filed back into their regular positions, any freedom a secret dream.

And as Jelan settled into the seat, a bright, otherworldly flash seared the city.

One from the bridge.

40

PRIDE

VIOLET DID A LOT OF things irrationally. She bit a teacher's hand once because they asked about her dirty clothes. She stole things just because she could. She chased her brother across Souther rooftops barefoot because he snatched a bottle of shiva, which got her angry burns that didn't heal for weeks.

She let a girl abuse her for months because she gave good head.

She abandoned her only friend.

She cut a mark into her palm to enter herself into a death game.

But this…this took the cake. Her mouth hung open in a wretched wail that never sounded. Her fingertips dug into Reed's shoulders. Her hair whipped about in a dangerous storm. She stared. And stared. And stared. At the portal where her friends vanished.

On their way home.

A giant salt boulder smashed the portal into the ground. Cyran stood a distance away, having disrupted her control, and formed the man-made rock right as she shoved that Iris down for her friends. They would have been squashed a breath later.

She didn't remember doing it. She blacked out, partially, at that point. But she watched a desperate part of herself as she internally screamed, *bring them home.*

Bring them home.

BRING THEM HOME.

She heard his last distressed cry. It slammed into her heart and brought tears to her eyes.

Violet! A cry filled with shock, betrayal, and vexation. Jack was never going to forgive her for that. He was going to throttle her, then kiss her, then love her…

Love her.

The tears poured fast. Love. She did it out of love. She hated the word all of her life because her mother said it to Reed, but not her. Here Violet was now, acting on it, because she loved her friends and wanted the best for them.

And she also loved her brother.

Her head jerked down. Reed grew pale, slowly. Blood leaked from the sides of his mouth. His eyes were a bleak blue, staring up at the sky. She moved her hands from his shoulder and pressed the gaping wound at his belly. Time slammed back into her. Her voice felt entirely too small, too quiet, for this moment.

"Stay with me, Reed," she gritted through her teeth. Even though her body was ripe with exhaustion, adrenaline pumped. "You need to activate your powers. It will give you some healing—"

Reed squeezed his eyes shut. His Vanisher lines flashed feebly, but his hands, feet, and eye lines shot light to his wound. Then it winked out.

Violet waited. The bleeding slowed. She blew out a breath, lifted her head—

A plasgun barrel landed on her forehead. Modav held her there. "Commands, Master?"

Cyran stared at the mess that was the portal. Bludgeoned under the boulder, Violet's ticket home was scattered in a silver metal array across the salt. She tugged Reed closer to her body.

"Should I kill her?" Modav implored.

Cyran turned his head slightly, locking eyes with Modav. "No." He jutted his chin to Reed. "Give him your blood."

"No," Violet snapped. She covered Reed's body with hers. "No. Don't *touch* him."

"Vi," Reed groaned, whispering for only her. "When you can…
it's blue. Home is blue. Feel it."

Violet shook her head, confused at his words. "No…*no*, they
don't get to touch you. You'll be fine on your own—"

A gentle pinch at her neck. Violet's head dropped. Reed had a
soft smile on his face. "It's okay."

"He said his blood was poisoned," Violet snarled, twisting her
head to Modav. "Whatever it is—it's poisoned."

"It's the same blood that your lover has," Cyran stated plainly.
"His is just more potent. Modav's is poisoned because he killed his
own people." Cyran waved a hand, dismissive.

Modav kept his face straight, but with his mechanical arm,
his missing eye, and the general look of the man, Violet was not
trusting. She growled when he took a step. He rolled his eyes.

A block of wind slammed into her. She flung back into the salt.
It pinned her down, nearly drowned her as grain spilled into her
mouth. Her powers flared. She dragged her head up to see Modav
slashing his human arm and letting the blood fall aimlessly into
Reed's open mouth. Violet shrieked, fighting Cyran's power.

"Don't *touch* him!"

A laugh from Modav. "Your fire ends here, girl. Smother it."

Unleash, agia.

Win, agia.

The salt caressed her. The world beat its silent tune. She shoved
her fingers in, feeling it, and with force, she pushed all that she had
from the earth, aiming at Modav. Sharp, pelting salt slammed into
the man so hard, he hurtled nearly twenty feet and plummeted
farther. He failed to move again.

She broke Cyran's power with her own, rushing to Reed and
pulling out a hidden plasblade from her pants. She brushed Gwen's
dagger for strength, because when her eyes met Cyran's hot ones,
the wind grew. Salt circled them. Light flared at their hands. His
flashed, hers did the same. He roared, "Do *not* challenge me."

"I. Don't. Give. A. *Fuck*."

Violet fumbled into the Vanisher realm, desperately looking. She needed to get to another world. Get Reed out of here at all costs. Her energy waned, but tethers of white and orange and green flashed about.

Home is blue.

"You're not going anywhere." The plasblade flew out of her hand. Claw marks by the sand scraped her skin. Violet was yanked out of her daze. Her abilities pushed back on Cyran, always protecting her. It fought him, swiped at him, raged at the threat he posed. Their abilities mixed, swarming, and Violet's brows crumpled at the certain points where their lights met, it absorbed.

Cyran bellowed at the wind, sinking to his knees. She sank with him. A deadly scream tore through her throat. Dust whipped the air, the world churned as Cyran dipped within his power, his control over it, and wielded it.

The wind wrapped her wrists, thrusting her hands away and upturning them to the sky. The salt slashed lines along her skin. Blood poured.

"You are powerful." Cyran struggled to stand. He loomed over her, a smile twisting as he beheld her growing cuts. Another at her neck, another at her cheek. Needles of pain sparked all over her body, tears spilled down her cheeks. "You are all but a speck to my existence. I will rule, and you will fall. There will be no more mistakes such as yourself. Some unloved thing with writhing, sad pain inside—oh, how I pity you for thinking you are better than me, holding on to fool's hope." He leaned close. "I am immortal. I am the World's Ruler. I am the beginning, and I will be the end. A little girl—a mistake—will not be the fall of me. Nothing will."

His hand jutted out and gripped her throat. Her breath paused, burnt within her, screaming for release. His grip tightened. Her body began to betray her, ebbing away like dust unto the wind. On her knees, before him, she closed her eyes, and that warm embrace of death whispered in her ear.

She could give up. Wasn't this, all along, what she wanted? To fall into the curious lull of death and move on to a better, more promising life?

"Do it," she whispered. "Kill me."

"I will do much, much worse to you." His voice crawled into her ears. She choked when he squeezed harder. She clawed at his arms, and he laughed. "You don't know this power. You don't know this universe. You are a small, meaningless girl. You only know the pain of being human, and that pain hugs you. Comforts you. Because it is all life has ever given you. So, feel that pain, bask in it, because it will be all you feel for the rest of your pathetic existence."

He wasn't killing her with his choking. No, he wanted her to beg for death from him. He wanted the decision to be hers because it would be too easy to kill her and be done with it. He wanted to know if she would fear him and fear death by his hand, and if she didn't, he would lose a part of that terror that cuffed to him like armor.

And in this world, that hurt his pride.

"Someone like you is too worthwhile to die, but no part of you deserves to be free."

Free.

Free.

Free…

The bright green of Sagitta. The crisp air in her lungs as she ran through the meadows. The smiles from her friends. The protective gaze of a lover. The pinch of her brother. The scarred hands of comfort.

Some burst of energy seared through her. Her eyes opened. Met his. Those icy gray, burning into her with five-hundred years of hatred—

Something flickered behind it.

Fear.

The world around them faded away, and that transcendental plane of colored tethers appeared.

On that plane, she reached. One hand was lined with silver, the other lined with purple. Something pushed her to. It felt right, whole. As if a part of her soul beckoned it.

Welcome, child of the stars.

Her eyes turned from the millions of worlds, of spaces she could go, and snagged at the bright, glowing one that seared from Cyran's chest. It rooted into the ground of Pride, sprayed up like branches of a tree, and Cyran was the center of it. His connection. His control.

She reached her purple hand to the bursting white at the center of Cyran's chest and yanked it.

She panicked. Held it. Squeezed it. Cyran buckled over, roaring. He fought her. Wind slammed her. The light she held, forming into a cylinder mold such as the Iris, fractured in two. One piece flung to the salt plain and it pulsed. Pride's earth trembled.

And the other piece…

Immersed into the center of her chest. Her heart.

Her soul.

There was heat along her scalp. Blinding radiance. Her senses were gone for a moment, and then slammed back into her, sending her flying.

She landed. Delirious, she lifted her head. Cyran lay sprawled a distance from her, struggling to rise. She scrambled up and raced for the discarded plasblade. At a thought, the weapon flew to her hand and she ignited it, whirling on him—

He met her blade. Plasma flashed.

Her eyes widened at the sight of him. His white hair leaked color, dusting the wind, and gray slithered up from his scalp, replacing it.

"No," he gaped at her own head, following her hair as it whipped around her. "*No!*" Fear barreled through him. He stumbled back, his hand wavering on the blade. "It can't be. You couldn't have done that."

Her heart was a flutter in her chest, dancing, twirling with power. Something next to it burned for the very first time.

This was her threat, and there was that fear, riddling his eyes. She growled and jabbed the plasblade again, but he twisted.

Call us, Master.

At the wave of her hand, the ground shook beneath their feet. Fissures cracked through the earth, splitting the limestone. What was one power bled into the control of another natural one. Wind whipped at him, around him. She willed it to choke him. He fell to his knees before her. The dust swirled and glistened, locking him tight. His plasblade fell.

She drew her own to his neck.

Cyran bristled at the heated contact. His emotions clawed within him, evident across his face. His new, gray hair twisted like greasy tendrils.

"I am no mistake!" she cried, to him, to the world, to herself.

"You—you took it."

"I took your world," she admitted. A separate heartbeat fluttered within her. The top of her head seared.

He boggled at her, and then a smile twisted, and he laughed. "You will die from that, *daughter.*"

Dread sucked all the air out of her lungs. She shook her head. She slashed the plasblade, nicking the side of his neck. He wasn't fazed.

Violet stumbled back. Her energy faltered. Knees shook. Vision dotted. Cyran laughed, his bindings releasing, "Everything you do matches me. That blood in your veins is *mine,* even when it shouldn't be. You're destined for *me*—"

"*Never!*" Anger swelled. The wind whipped him so hard that he toppled over.

That was the last of her energy. Her hands shook, her cuts reopening. The world's heart beat within her, a frenzy full of pain. Reed's unconscious figure caught her gaze and she hurried to him.

Footsteps pounded after her. "You will die!"

She whipped out another gust of wind, and Cyran flew back. Her heart—her own—was beating so fast she thought it'd explode out of her chest. Her senses were slipping, her vision growing hazy. "Reed! Reed! I need you to get up!"

"Vi…" He groaned.

The world trembled. Two hearts that could not separate. Heat built inside of her—she—they had to leave. She dove for Reed, wrapping her hand around his arm, and pulled with every bit of strength she had into the Vanisher realm.

Home is blue. Made sense now. She looked at the thousands of tethers before her. Panic flared, there were tens of blues, one a vast field of purple flowers, another a medical room, where a long jacket was flung over a chair—

Feel it.

"Home," she called.

Her eyes drifted to a certain one. She glimpsed a familiar bridge. Her breaths were short.

"*No!*" Cyran's voice cried. Pain flared in her arms, but she saw it. Home. Home.

Reed squeezed her hand. His eyes were on her—on her head. "Your hair…"

She yanked the blue tether.

The last world blinked away, and Pride said its goodbye.

Violet Sutton brought her brother home.

PART III

THE BETRAYAL

41

BROTHER

JACK'S LUNGS SEIZED. HIS STOMACH roiled and he vomited into the bucket. Sprawled in the backseat of a weaponized high-roofed car, his brother stared at him, rubbed his face, then stared again.

"I'm here," Jack grumbled.

"No one was even meant to come out of those games," Lucien said plainly.

"There's a reason for that."

"Take as much time as you need to rest. I called all security—"

"We have to go back," Jack cut him off.

Lucien's lips morphed into a scowl. "You need to go into hiding, Jack. The whole city will be after you, even Arvalo—who, mind you, is now *Emperor.*"

"I know," Jack said softly. "I heard."

Lucien's eyes bugged. "You *heard?*"

"I'll debrief you." Jack put the bucket down and wiped the sweat from his forehead. Lucien felt unreal. One moment Jack was fighting for his life against the ruler of the Sins, and now his brother was nagging him yet again. Jack snorted and opened a compartment where four bottles of very expensive liquor stared at him. He balked. "No shiva?"

"Since when…" Lucien sighed deeply. "I'll get shiva. Don't debrief me, Jack. The Sins wasn't a mission. And who do we have to—"

Jack wasn't listening, he pressed a remote and a plascreen descended from behind the driver's seat. He flicked through the channels until the Sins Screen appeared. His heart pounded too hard, his throat closed too much. Nausea breached his stomach, and he yanked the bucket again. "Fuck."

Violet's name glowed in the seventh panel. And above her name, Reed's. Two red dots blinked next to them.

"She's still there?" Lucien checked the time. "It's been ten minutes…"

"Xavier! Turn the car around. Back to the Aariva," Jack commanded. He fumbled with the door, wanting to open it already because she is going to return soon, and he needed to be there for whatever state she was in.

Lucien pulled Jack's hand away. "What in the world are you doing? I'll keep security there."

"*Security* is not enough," Jack spat, his teeth bared. His canines hurt. He hurriedly shut his mouth, but Lucien lunged, prying his jaw open.

"What in the actual fuck." Lucien blinked once. Twice. "Jack…"

"I'll give you a *damn* debrief once she is safe with me again," Jack snarled hard enough that Lucien slid back on his seat, stunned. "Now turn the fucking car around and unleash Anaya."

Everything made sense to Jack in that moment. Anaya would take care of any enemies and Masar could help. He didn't know when the Worldbreaker would be arriving…

"Jack!"

But he knew that Zavar wasn't far behind. He twisted in his seat, looking up to the sky, searching for an incoming storm that signaled the end of his world. He paused. His thoughts ran rampant…

"*Jack.*"

A slap slammed across his cheek. Hands grabbed his shoulders. Brown concerned eyes—their mother's—searched his.

Sound returned. A loud, shrieking siren blared outside the car's bulletproof windows.

The driver began to slow in the back alleys. "We have to go on the main streets, sir."

"No," Lucien said. "Stop here."

Traffic lights flashed red. Cars stopped. One of the main streets that cut through the North was packed with people. They cheered, smiled, but those smiles dropped when the city's emergency bells flashed.

When the alarms grew louder.

When panic settled in.

People began to run everywhere. The abandoned streets then filled with Redders.

"Arvalo is shutting down the city. There's a manhunt for you." Lucien caught Jack's gaze. "No one comes out of the Sins, Jack. *No one*. But *you* did."

"Violet," he breathed. "She will, too."

"Yes, she will, however she does it, but right now you need to be protected from the others and hidden. Arvalo will either flaunt you or kill you."

A loud, ringing bell sounded from the screen.

Jack's head twisted.

Violet and Reed's names weren't in the seventh world anymore.

He lunged for the door. "Turn back to the Aariva, *now!*"

Jack's overwhelming panic snapped to Lucien's personal radio. Lyla's voice trickled in, confused and commanding, "There's unrest at the bridge. No sign of the duo at the Aariva, and oh…oh, my skies." Lyla paused, then screamed at her troops, "*Get to the bridge now!*" Lyla's voice came through clearer. "Commander, she's at the bridge. It's…there's a copter. Her brother…a lot of blood. I have the Firsts running to secure the spot, one minute away. My team is four behind, but these damned people won't *move*." The sound of a bike revving filled the car.

"The bridge?" Lucien said.

Jack swallowed. He rasped, "She…vanished herself here."

At that, Lucien stopped, confusion twisting his face. He gave one jerk of his chin. "I trust you, Jack, but trust us to get her. We *will* get her."

Jack couldn't sit still and wait. He eyed the driver. Lucien followed his gaze and said, "I will strap you down if I have to."

Lucien's radio roused with static. Multiple voices crackled in and out, but the most noticeable was a low whine, *"Anaya, you're on my shoulder."*

Rio.

A couple more indiscernible words, and Anaya's voice was there. "She's back. She's fought all this way to get here, after nearly sacrificing herself to get *us* here. We'll get her back, Jack." Anaya yelled at someone else. *"Turn this car to the bridge, skiv."*

"Who is this girl?"

"A foreigner," Rio said. *"A stray we found. Untamable, though. But—Anaya! No! Put the gun down!"*

"I said, turn this skivvin' car around, twat." Chaos erupted. A growl. Rio's panicked screams. A car screeched. There was a ding of metal and Anaya's roar.

Rio cried, *"Anaya! You can't drive!"*

"I'm getting the fucking girl, whether you like it or not."

The radio went silent.

A hush descended in the car. Lucien's eyes bore into Jack. "Don't do it," Lucien said quietly.

Jack gave him a solemn look. "Too much has happened to us not to fight for each other."

Jack's hand wrapped the door handle, and his muscles bunched, ready to rip through the door and make his brother properly shit his pants, but he hesitated. Then he took a breath. He sat back in the seat and ripped one of the liquor bottles open. "You're right."

Lucien let out a breath, one he clearly had been holding. "She's here, in this world. By whatever power you *all* are. If you go on those streets, one bullet will kill you."

Not likely, Jack wanted to say. His heart hammered too hard, if he went out there to tear the bridge down and save Violet, his efforts would be futile. Exhaustion made his limbs heavy. A split, emotionally made decision could put her more at risk than Lyla, who was an expert at deadly situations, and quite possibly the most dangerous person, even in all the worlds, to come across. Anaya *might* rival her, Masar would definitely be a good match, but Lyla had a head about her. She never revealed her emotions. She kept it cool, calm, even while she tortured and slit throats.

"The penthouse, Xavier," Jack said.

"Yes, Commander."

Jack took Lucien's radio. "Anaya hands down."

A beat of silence. A scramble for the radio. "*Excuse me?*"

"They've got her." Jack pressed another button. "Right, Lyla?"

A moment. "I have her in sight. Bloody thing. Get the surgeons ready, this will be a hard one. Commander, can I call for backup?"

"As much as you want," Jack ordered. "But you bring her to me, Lyla. She is the only reason I ever made it."

"Of course, Commander."

Jack set the radio down and turned to Lucien. "There's a lot we need to talk about."

"I know, Jack." Lucien took the bottle from him and chugged deeply. "I know."

42

MARKED

REED AND VIOLET TUMBLED TO the asphalt. She shoved him behind her, wanting to take the fall, but it meant he slammed straight into her back. Her spine cracked awkwardly, but she bit her cry and twisted underneath him. "Reed, *Reed.*"

Her eyes danced. A bridge. Plaslights. The smell of smoke and algae water. Violet squeezed her lids shut. It couldn't be—could it? Did she do it? Her gaze lifted to the towering metal shoots that crisscrossed, creating the famous bridge landmark in Calesal.

Tears welled. She pulled her brother to her chest. "We made it, Reed. We're home."

"Home?" Reed muttered. She turned him to his back and crawled atop, pressing her hands to his wound. The spear disintegrated at some point—whether it was from Reed's powers, or her own, she didn't know. Her muscles whined at every movement. Her chest felt empty, but that sickly, second beat pounded out of sync with her feeble heart. Fingers pinched her neck.

"You did good, Vi." Reed looked at her bleakly with a soft smile. Blood gathered in the crevices of his teeth. "You brought us home."

A sob burst from her mouth. She dipped, hugging her brother tightly. "We're home. We are home." She repeated it into his neck as her tears slid onto his skin.

He squeezed her weakly. "I'm so proud of you."

"But…" Violet lifted her head. She stared to one side at the flickering hill of the Government Sector, and the giant wall towering behind it. Her head turned—the North's skyrises. Their lights blurred in her vision. "I don't know where to go."

"Jack will…"

Her heart jumped at his name. He was here. He should *be* here. But she didn't land at the Sky Arches where they would have exited. Her eyes flashed back to the Government Sector. Maybe… they would provide a haven. They'd survived the Sins. They'd—

A horrifying whipping sound vibrated through the air, growing stronger, until it filled her chest. Her gaze lifted, searching the sky.

Red lights began flashing on the bridge. *"Breach. Breach."* An alarm blared, piercing her ears. It shrilled and shrilled, until the Redders at either end of the bridge turned their attention to the center, where Violet lay next to her collapsed brother.

The whirring came with a gust of wind. Lights flashed in the dark light, and then a bright, blinding spotlight seared their position from above.

"Reed," Violet warned.

The Redders held their guns up, running toward them. They signaled others. From the Government Sector, cars began to roll out.

"I'm out," Violet said, distressed. She tugged at Reed's shirt. "I don't think…"

"Go, Vi—"

"Come on," she whispered, looking back to the North. The Redders did not appear helpful—not that she ever thought they were, but with the cars, the giant guns, the plasblades, the troops rolling out to grab them, then the copter…

Enemies.

Her body screamed. Her movements were lethargic. She wanted to close her eyes, pretend it was all a dream, but she was so close, and Reed was losing blood—

"Hands up—get your fucking hands up!" they began to shout. "Stun them!"

"No!" Violet cried, attempting to stand. She wobbled, but her hand yanked Gwen's dagger and she held it out. "Don't you touch him!"

A boom. She looked at the copter. It burst into flames. A black-clad figure jumped from it, flipping once, before two grapples shot into one of the bridge's towers and they flew, dragged by the cables. They bounced, held out a plasgun, and drilled a fast round of shots at the first group of Redders.

A horde of other figures descended from the North side, above the Redders, flying through the air via cables. Engines revved. Plasbikes roared from the street. The Redders flung themselves away, firing desperately, but the group took them down. Two plasbikes zoomed through the chaos, aiming for Violet and Reed.

Her breath halted. They accelerated past her, leaning to the side hard enough that the bikes slid from under them, and the riders fell to the road. The momentum catapulted the bikes into the army on the Government side. Both the riders stood, guns ready, a black box held in their hands. A second later, the bikes exploded.

The bridge jolted. Metal and pavement flung into the sky. It barricaded the Government Sector. Violet's jaw slacked. The two riders held that side. She whirled to the North, where the insurrection occurred, Redders trying to fight off the new arrivals.

The same figure who dropped out of the copter slammed into the bridge. A woman. She twisted her dual plasguns and shot at four Redders, sinking bullets into their necks. They collapsed. She drew her grapple back to the mechanics at her shoulders. When her boots finished skidding, she flicked her ring finger with her thumb, and a bright orange burst of plasma erupted into a three-foot circle from her wrist.

Guns fired into the shield, but the orange held. The woman crouched, protecting them. With her arm, she lifted the visor on her helmet and cold eyes studied Violet. "Stay down."

A command. An order.

Some of the same fighters from her group flew overhead, grappling to the bridge columns, and landing on the other side of Violet. They created a perimeter, protecting her. An elite squad with impeccable skill.

She noticed the small red emblem engraved into the back of their fighting gear. Relief spilled into an outward gasp. A mess of snakes, two arrows, engulfed in a circle of roaring water. A mark she used to hate. "Jack," she breathed.

"Ordered by him, yes," the woman with the shield said. "So keep your head down. You need to run with us. We will hold them off long enough to clear a path. One of my men will grab your brother."

Violet's hand squeezed Reed's. It took her a moment to react. The woman gave an icy smirk. "He's waiting for you, darling. Let's get you both home safely. We will take it from here. Trust us."

Violet nodded aimlessly.

One of the figures broke the perimeter and rushed at her. Within moments, they had Reed's shirt ripped off, and a healing patch slapped over his gaping wound. A portable drip line was installed. Then Reed was flung over their shoulders. "Ready, General."

The woman—the general—signaled to the others. "Hold them off!" She pressed her ear. "Make room on the roads. Have the cars ready. Both are secured."

A group of her men took down the remaining Redders. At the end of the bridge, more poured from the North, but horns resounded, and giant, black cars dominated the streets. Figures hovered on the rooftops. The general's troops surrounded the city. Guns pointed. Shot. Redder's fell. A hand was at Violet's back. A masked man. "You okay to run, honey?"

Everything hurt, but she gave a weak nod. "I think—"

Pain slammed into her shoulder. She choked a cry. Her muscles seized, going numb. Shocked. Plascuted.

"She's down! Cover her!"

She began to fall, but one of the soldiers swooped her up in his arms. "He's gonna kill us for this."

More shots were fired at the Government Sector. "They're breaching!"

"Get them out of here," the woman snarled. "I want my damned drink and our Commander's girl *not* shot. Get more medics ready. *Now!*"

Violet's head bumped the soldier's shoulder. They began running. Guns lifted. She couldn't feel her toes. Her vision blacked in and out. This close to a com, she could hear a familiar, growling voice, "She got *shot?*"

"She's fine, sir. We got her."

"He's pacing," the woman said. "It's not good when he paces!"

Jack's voice became clearer. There was a protest from someone in the back, but his ivory voice sent a chill down her spine. "It's a tracker. Take a different car and have it removed."

"No," Violet gasped. "I want…Reed—"

"Violet, *not now*," Jack snarled.

She scowled, her face not moving much from the muscle spasms.

"Yes, sir," the woman obeyed.

"Get her to me, Lyla."

"Of course, sir."

Lyla—the woman—held up that swirling orange shield to disrupt the plasgun fire, and within moments, she was signaling the black cars at the end of the bridge. Redder bodies littered the area. Violet was shoved through one of the doors, and then immediately laid belly down on the car's floor. The driver gunned it. Nausea overwhelmed her. "Reed, Reed."

"Hold still." Lyla straddled her lower back, ripping Violet's shirt off. Pain pinched her upper shoulder. She cried out. Metal dug in. "This fucker. Come on, damnit."

Violet screamed. Her shoulder flared hot, burning. Lyla dug into her skin with tweezers or nails or a literal screwdriver—either way, it hurt like shit. With a pop, a small metal bead glistened between her fingers.

The window opened. Lyla tossed the tracker onto the street. A cooling sensation met Violet's shoulder. It slithered along her neck, to the backs of her eyes, and a moment later, she blacked out. Words and sensations came and went. She rolled as the car turned. Then stopped. A door opened. She felt her body move. Be heaved up.

"*She's fine?*" Lyla asked.

"*Vitals are unstable, set her up on a drip line,*" a medical voice.

"*Tell me she's fine.*" Panic rose in Lyla's voice. They moved, bouncing. A ding of an elevator. Hands released her. Cool metal smothered her back. A door burst open. Lyla again, "*Commander.*"

"*Vi.*" Panic. Demand. Hands cupped her cheeks. "*What did he do to you?*"

"*There are so many cuts, I can't get a proper look. We need scans. Strip her.*"

Cool air met her skin. She shivered. Her consciousness cowered away, protecting her. A prick at her arm. Those warm hands moved from her face to brush her hair back, and then they were gone.

"*What's on her hair?*" Anaya's voice.

A gentle tug. "*It's…blonde. Half of it is blonde.*"

"*What does that mean?*"

"*It looks like…*his *hair.*"

Silence. Violet was stripped. A warm blanket covered her.

"*I'm going to put her to sleep, Commander. I'll need you to let her go. We'll be quick.*"

Reluctant hands paused, then left her skin, leaving ice in their wake.

An unbearable heat replaced the cold. She moved around, shaking, reaching for cold air or a snow pile or *something* because internally, she was combusting. Her heart thrummed at a chaotic pace.

"*Steady. Let her seize.*"

"*Violet! Come on, stay here. Stay here, please—*"

"*Commander, I need you to step back.*"

"*No—help her—*"

"We are doing everything we can."

A throat-tearing, blood-curdling scream ripped from her. Her insides were shredding. Fire erupted. It coursed from the tips of her toes to a raging firestorm in her mind. She screamed so hard her ears screeched with a high-pitched sound. It was devastation. It was horror.

It was torture.

"What is going on, Doctor? She's on fire. Her skin…"

"Her hair."

"It's him."

Him. Cyran. The tether she took from him. The comments on her hair. The second heartbeat. A bomb exploded in her eardrums as it erupted beneath her skin. Violet could feel him roaring within.

Then nothing. Her body thrummed with dwelling heat, but the inferno stopped.

And in her mind, in her heart, she heard a roar. His roar. The Worldbreaker's. He dug into the soul of the world she took from him, and he screamed.

Then silence.

A quiet sob escaped her. Tears streamed down her cheeks. Hands were brushing her head, particularly on one side.

Jack's broken voice breached the agonizing void, *"What did he do to you, Vi?"*

She blacked out completely.

43

NORMAL

VIOLET WOKE TO A TINY, but impeccable, apartment. Everything was smooth and modern—spotless, with a few plants and ornate artwork for decoration. No sound echoed in the hallway, no whisper of voices, just the steadily beating monitor that marked her heart rate, the whir of her drip line, and her shallow breaths.

Night swarmed outside. She didn't know the time, nor the day, nor the place. All she felt was a lingering heat within, like a tripwire waiting to fuse and burst. The familiar lull of her city calmed her nerves, but the sheets still felt too tight. Her scalp burned.

She pulled the covers off, hating the sweat stuck to her, and gently tugged out the drip line. While scurrying to the door, she realized she was naked. She whirled and found a stack of sweatpants and a sweater folded neatly on a chair. She tugged them on and opened the door.

Her eyes strained to adjust to the lack of light. She guessed it was early morning, before the sun rose. It was a two-bedroom place that immediately expanded into a gracious sitting room and connected kitchen. A quaint, small place in the North. A balcony faced the entire city of Calesal, and her feet padded that way. It took a concerning amount of energy to open the sliding door, but she stepped out, gasping for breath. Her hand went to her heart. The second beat was there. Fear flooded.

She dropped her hand.

Bare feet met the soft stone. The wind chilled her forehead. She gazed out at her city; the view a tumbling landscape through the North, into the Mid, and glistened to the very edge of the South, a blip in the distance, until the walls crawled up.

Her hands slid onto the thick railing. Her eyes welled with silent grief.

She brought her brother back. She found friends. She lost people she loved. She returned home.

And yet Violet Sutton felt as broken as she did before slicing her hand.

A tear slipped down her cheek. It dropped off the balcony, falling the fifty or so floors below.

She didn't get her freedom. She didn't get her peace. Suddenly, her hands were fisting the railing and she hauled herself up. Her toes curled over the lip. Her knees cracked as she stood. Her arms wobbled and her chin lifted. The wind played with her ruined hair.

Violet missed everything about home. She missed the streets, the shiva, the laughs with Jelan, the stupors, the constant wondering of what she was going to eat the next day. She missed it because it seemed more normal, more okay of a life, than the one she lived in now. This shell of a girl who had incomprehensible abilities, who faced a to-be god and stole something from him, who had the soul of a world beating in her chest because said abilities made it possible, and who was still *fucking* broken.

The tears slipped into the abyss of the North. They slammed into the pavement far below, where celebrations flowed to her ears, and the cries of joy were heard. *Candidates came back. They beat the Sins. The curse is gone*, she imagined them saying. Violet wavered atop the railing, basking in beautiful lights. The sirens howled and smoke crawled. Another tear slipped.

As her home carried on, she numbed further. She looked down. The height didn't scare her. One step…one singular gush of wind would knock her off balance and send her tumbling to her world below. She used to love testing death, loved the taunt of it whispering in her ear, teasing her. She used to even be afraid of it at one point. She wondered about its purpose. Other than taking loved ones away or creating a sick sense of peace. But now she knew it.

Death was a blessing. It was a reprieve. It was the world, the soul, the universe, turning a new page and starting another journey. Perhaps this was Violet's end. Perhaps she should shut the entire book and burn it. Start over. Where the word "mistake" didn't bounce around her head, where a powerful man didn't slice into her and make her screams unrecognizable. Where she didn't have to worry if the people she loved were alive. Violet's toes curled again. Her stance swayed. Home fell to her.

But a soft voice caught her.

"You're awake."

She didn't turn. She lifted her gaze back to the city, though. She rooted her legs firmly. His voice dumped a cool bucket of water over her, snaking easily through the chaos of her thoughts. They slowed. Stopped.

Jack's footsteps were soft, stopping behind her. His hands came to rest next to her feet. Never touching her. "Are you going to jump?"

"And if I did?"

"Then I would trust you to vanish us away before we hit the ground. We would make a messy splat, I'm sure."

Vanisher. That wasn't supposed to exist here, at home. Everything felt warped and wrong, different as if she plopped into just another world, and all she was waiting for was a Sin to whisper in her mind and drag her into the dark.

"But don't do it, Vi." His thumb stroked the side of her foot. "It won't fix anything."

"What will?"

"Time."

"It doesn't feel real." She parted her chapped lips. "Any of what happened."

"In those last moments…" His voice cracked as if it broke him to ask. "What *did* happen?"

Cyran's hands all over her. The clench at her neck. The slices along her arms. The bright burst of flame at the center of her chest.

"Someone like you is too worthwhile to die, but no part of you deserves to be free."

"I fought him," she said bleakly. "And I took his Pride. I took the world. I...I don't know how. I just saw it, and I was desperate. But instead of freeing the soul, I took some of it. Put it in my own chest." Her fingers rose and aimlessly touched her hair on the right side. "Now it's inside of me. I can feel it beating. Then I think...I think he bombed it. That was the fire. All I remember was feeling like I'd been lit on fire."

You will die from that, daughter.

Daughter...there was little proof other than sharing similar abilities. Even then, he was much more aware and powerful than she had yet to discover.

"I thought I'd lost you when you sent us...home." His forehead pressed against her thigh. His hands rose to grip her shins. "Then when you returned, and you were with the medics, I thought you died. Your skin...the veins beneath...they were...inflamed."

Her voice was still hoarse from the screams. It was Jack who had to witness that, and her heart numbed even more.

"Come down, Violet."

"Where's Reed?" she croaked.

"He's still in the hospital. He just got out of surgery, so we are waiting on the verdict of his back. He's safe, though. I have guards posted. The hospital is mine, so I don't suspect anyone will be after him or attempt to trespass, but I'll treat the situation as if someone will." She heard him swallow. He pleaded, "Please come down. Come and eat something with me."

"I'm not hungry."

"And the sky is blue. I'm not fighting you on this. I will straddle you and force you to chew whatever I shove in your mouth."

Her fingers relaxed. There—that was familiar. "How long has it been?"

"Four days. I've slept most of the time, too. We all have. The others are decompressing in different apartments. This will be a difficult transition, but I thought holding us up without anyone else would help. Anaya and Rio are in another, Masar is with Lyla, his sister, who saved you. Navo is seen as Anaya's little black cat. No one knows, but I plan on a debrief soon. The world is very confused right now."

Her eyes dipped to the sirens and beats of music below. "They're celebrating your return."

"Apparently, the moment we made it to the seventh world, the streets were packed. It was chaos. Turns out nearly everyone in Calesal was rooting for us."

"And we made it," Violet said. "But they don't know that it was never a game."

"They will have to know. Arvalo, who is now Emperor, is doing a lot to squash the media about the whole thing."

"How do you convince a world that a monster like the Worldbreaker exists?"

"You don't. You simply fight for them, instead."

She turned her head. Jack's eyes were on the city. His grip tightened on her shins. The lights of Calesal slashed through the strong edge of his jaw, his high cheekbones, and his straight nose. He still looked tired, but there was a brightness to his eyes. They locked gazes. Her breaths slowed, her shoulders relaxed.

"Come," he breathed.

She stepped back. He caught her around the waist and gently lowered her to the balcony. His body surrounded her, along with a musky, delicious scent that she believed was his body wash. He stepped back, giving her space, studying her. His eyes involuntarily flicked to her hair, but he shifted them to her neck. His jaw clenched, angered, but he made no move. "Take it one day at a time, but know that I'm here, and I will help you."

"And you?" Violet asked. "Are you okay?"

A twitch of the lips. "Sleep helps. My brother saw my canines, though."

"Wait 'til he sees you break a doorknob with a mere touch, that'll get him."

"You want to know something funny?" Jack bit his lip, looking incredibly boyish. Her heart thumped—in a good way. "Your friend, Jelan, and Lucien have been…seeing each other. How scandalous."

The sound of Jelan's name brought a smile to her face. Jack's expression brightened, his eyes dipping. She licked her lips, teasing, "Maybe the older Marin brother is the true catch."

His eyes drifted down her body. "I have a lot of ways I can prove that wrong."

She replied with a jut of her chin. "Then do it."

He took a step in, crowding her. Her back pressed the railing. "You're recovering, Violet. I'm not—"

Violet leaned up and captured his lips, shutting him off. His hands immediately snaked around her waist, pulling her closer. A soft groan escaped him. He patted her behind and she jumped, gasping as he ground into her, showing how ready he was.

She needed this. She needed him. To prove that she wasn't broken, to fill the emptiness in her—

"Lean back," he said. Her bottom was on the railing. He gripped her hips. "Remember you are *alive*."

Her brows drew together. The world grew louder. The green was so bright in his eyes, but she trusted them. She began to fall back, her head lolling over the balcony. With effort, she spread her arms. A gush of wind flowed, and a smile breached her face. He held on to her, tightly, supporting her, holding her…

"He's not winning," Jack said. "Get out of your head. You're not broken. You're recovering. You're healing. You went through shit, and you made it back. You saved all of us. You brought your brother home. The game might have only just begun, but you are not alone, Violet. Even if this world—your home—feels foreign now, over time the pain will lessen. And when Cyran comes, we will *all* fight whatever happens next."

They were harsh words to hear, and Violet half-heartedly took them in. She breathed, though. Breathed her home in and felt that pinprick of her past self. They went through seven different worlds, fought and lost and loved and laughed. Even if this was their only moment to feel the same, to feel stripped and bare, she'd take it.

"Please," she breathed, pulling her head up to look at him. "Touch me."

His eyes roamed her, lips pursing. Debating. "Are you sure?"

"Please, Jack." She leaned so their foreheads met, lips brushing. "Please, let us exist, just us, before it's all ripped away again."

He paused, and Violet knew she created a millimeter of distance with those words, but she meant it. It wasn't going to last long. He could put her back together like a puzzle, but they were only buying time before it was destroyed. She pleaded with her face, her voice above a whisper. "We both want it."

He clearly fought within himself, but she glimpsed the flare of his eyes, the same need that matched hers. Maybe it was selfish to give in, but Jack wasn't dumb enough to be manipulated by her.

His hands wrapped around the back of her head, and he pulled her into a bruising kiss. Their teeth met, their tongues clashed, and Violet pushed everything new and wrong and painful to the back of her mind. Right now, they were in the bellies of Lust, wanting to have fun and explore. She tried to convince herself it was fine, but when his hands skimmed the waistband of her pants, when she cupped him through his own, the tears welled. Her gasps turned into sobs. Jack released a broken sigh and pulled her into his chest. He held her like he shielded the world.

"It's okay," Jack murmured on her head. "I know it hurts, but you're safe now. Nothing will happen to you. Not with me."

At some point during her breakdown, he cradled her and brought her back into the apartment. Then they were in his room, across from hers, but instead of going to the bed, he turned her to the bathroom. A towel already lay draped over the mirror.

In mutual silence, Jack helped her strip, his own eyes growing watery as he took in the damage from Cyran. She merely pulled him close, gently taking his clothes off, as well, until they were both naked. Jack turned the shower on. He sat her down on the tile, shutting the door, and crawled behind her. With tender fingers, he washed her hair. She noticed he was careful about keeping it out of eyesight. He soaped her body, and when he was done, he kissed her neck. She turned to him and did all the same things. Bathing him, caressing him, kissing him on the tattoos that were foreign to this world, at the places where he hurt. The tears stopped at some point, and when she lifted her gaze, he nodded. She nodded.

In the steamed room, under a spray of hot water, with a covered mirror and silence filled with understanding, they made love. When they finished, he scooped her up in a towel and carried her to the bed.

Nestled together, both recovering fighters of the Sins fell asleep.

The next morning, Jack brought her coffee. She numbly accepted it, and they sipped in silence. He left at some point to take a call with Lucien, and that's when Violet felt a sense of courage.

Throughout the night, she felt Jack's hands on her head, every now and then pulling the right part of her hair away. Her heart fluttered at the intention, but she didn't want him protecting her like that anymore. She needed to get over it.

After another shower, she stood before the covered mirror in the bathroom. She tugged the towel off and rubbed the steam away.

Bleak, broken eyes bagged by dark circles stared back. Sallow cheeks. Pale, cracked lips. She looked abnormally sick—weaker, thinner, as if something was draining her. All the power she used might have been the culprit.

Her eyes finally flicked to her hair. Parted down the middle, the entire right side of her head was stark white, from root to tip, almost blinding in the daylight. Her fingers trembled as she touched the ends, tracing it, convinced that it was going to burn her.

She was a beacon. There was no way to blend in with this. She hated everything about it. It was *him*. Bruises still marked her neck from where he had pinned her down, screamed at her for all the horrid things he was going to do. She was the mistake, and in that desperate moment when he was tearing her apart without even laying a finger on her, she flashed into the other realm and stole a world.

A whole skivvin' world.

It marked her like a gruesome scar. It wasn't hers. It shouldn't be on her, it shouldn't be *in* her.

Pride.

She dropped down to the sink, rummaging. A brown dye bottle hovered in the back, one for gray hairs, and she fished it out. Not Jack's, she presumed. Unless he managed to secretly dye his hair during their rustic ten months in the Sins. Her fingers fumbled with the packets and bowls until she had it mixed. She didn't care if it looked like total shit. She wanted it gone.

She stained her fingers brown as she painted. She eventually dropped the brush in the sink and scooped a handful of gooey dye, clumping the white side, until it covered every reminder of what lived inside that *did not belong to her*.

The bathtub was a cool relief as she waited, eyes on the clock above the open door, watching each tick of the minute hand. At the end of the countdown, she hurried to the sink and flipped her hair in, rinsing the dye out as best as she could. Brown splatters stained the white tile floor. She flipped back up. Her hair hit her spine with a wet slap. Her stomach dropped as she gazed in the mirror.

"*No*," she breathed.

Her eyes flicked to the dye as it rinsed down the sink. All of it. Not a single strand on that side of her head was brown. None of it stuck. That blinding wet white shined even brighter.

"No!" She reached for the leftover goop still in the bowl. She painted her hair again in a frenzy. "Come on! Please—oh, skies, no!"

Rinsed. Nothing. Painted again, rinsed. Nothing. She was left with white.

An anguished noise left her throat. With a flash of fury, she slapped the bowl of dye off the counter and let it smack against the wall. The pristine bathroom now looked like someone had shat all over it—but her hair was still *white*.

Tears raced and she finally released a wail that had been bubbling. It echoed in the giant bathroom.

The bedroom door slammed open, and Jack stepped into view. He gazed around the room, gaping, and within a heartbeat, he was reaching for her, "Violet—"

"It won't work!" She pulled at the white hair. "It won't go away—why won't it go away?"

"Hey, hey, it's okay—"

"It's *not* okay!" She swatted his hands away. "It's foreign! It's… It's a parasite! Look at me. I'm being sucked *dry*."

He frowned.

"It's in me. I can feel it like a heart beating next to my own." She rubbed at her chest. "I don't want it. I don't want any of this."

Jack huffed and replaced the towel on the mirror. "Let's get you another drip line, and *also* get you something to eat."

No appetite had come to her, but Violet nodded weakly. Being left alone seemed like a time bomb, and by Jack's grimace, he thought so, too. He tugged her out of his room, toward the kitchen. Breakfast was already prepared; basic, bland things like toast and butter, but also a bowl of pomegranate seeds—her favorite. She never remembered telling him that, so she turned to him quizzically, but he only tapped his temple. "I know everything."

She sat, her mouth going drier the more she looked at the food, but for Jack's sake and his watchful gaze, she made a small plate.

"When do you want the medic to come?"

"Don't you have things to do?" she asked, forcing the corner of toast between her lips.

"I could have a million things to do or none at all, perks of being on vacation mode still," he said dryly. "Stop avoiding my questions. You can either prepare a time for them to come, or they'll barge in whenever."

"Barge in whenever," she said. "Do you have a hat?"

His eyes flicked up. "Yes."

"Can I have it?"

"What color?"

"I can have any color?"

"I can order it emerald-studded if you'd like to match my stunning eyes."

"Skies, I guess you are rich."

"Very." He smirked and pointed to her plate. "Eat." He turned back to his room, padding away...

"Yes, Daddy."

He stilled. Slowly turned his head, and with narrowed, commanding eyes, he said, "Absolutely not."

Violet jerked her thumb to the large windows displaying the city. "I bet that's what they all call you now, beating the Sins and all."

"I—" Jack blew out a breath. "No...well—maybe, I don't know. But *you* are not calling me that."

He continued, and with higher spirits, Violet ate a bigger bite of her toast. Moments later, Jack came back with a bright orange beanie. "This was all I had right now."

"Ah, just the color I wanted. So, I can costume play as a traffic cone."

He snorted.

She took it, a moment later frowning. Her mouth soured, and she put down the toast. Her chest hurt again.

Jack studied her but said nothing. He merely waited. She rubbed her thumb over the different material, blowing out a breath, "I wonder if they're dead."

"Who?"

"All those in Pharos. Or at least the ones remaining in the city when Cyran destroyed it. I…one of the young girls made me a hat. It had purple flowers. It's back in Greed, with my bag of other things."

Jack frowned. "I'm sure they survived."

"But Bryce didn't."

"Well, that…" Jack stopped himself.

She perked up. "What?"

He leaned over the counter, looking somber. "I think Bryce *had* to die. It's only my theory. But I think Jodin made a bloodbond with them. It would be the only way for saving his ass—turning over the leader. Jodin was forced to provide some kind of win."

Her mouth dropped. "You gathered all of that?"

"I'm observant."

She thought of Meretta, Grace, and Bunny. She…she wished she had done more to help them, but now she was here, in this spacious apartment, safe and sound, and their city was destroyed because of *her*.

Violet pushed the plate away. All the memories felt like dreams, but the emotions were visceral. She hated that they were memories now that the games were over, and she supposedly *won*. They had to continue fighting, yet in everyone else's eyes, Violet was done. Her fight finished.

"I need to talk to Reed," she said. "He'll have answers to… things."

"As do I, but Reed is still in a coma. He's in no state to be conscious right now. His body will fail him."

"When can I see the others?"

Jack glanced at the clock. "Whenever you want. They are in this building."

She perked up. "Jelan is?"

"With a friend, Hira, Lucien, some of my team…and your guardian."

Violet turned to stone. "Meema?" she said, a waver in her voice.

"She's been living in my penthouse all this time. I thought I told you."

"You did but…" Violet shook her head. "She's going to kill me."

A smirk. "She's a little peeved."

"You've met her?"

"No, just what Lucien tells me. Oh and…that man you saved. Your lover. He's there." Jack waved his hand, as if he were talking about a bowl, and lost his playful expression.

Violet bit the inside of her cheek, holding in her laugh at Jack's slight jealousy. "Are you mad I didn't save you, instead?"

"I'm sure you were happy to see me go into the Sins."

"I hated you."

A raised brow and flickering eyes. "Part of me thinks you still do."

"I think you're overbearing."

"Not a flaw."

"And a smartass."

"Comes with the trauma."

"And annoying to look at."

"*That* is a mutual feeling." He eyed her, up and down. "I can always provide a blindfold."

Violet stood and flicked his bare arm. "Maybe some earplugs, too. Then I'll get real peace."

Jack whirled, looking playfully offended. "*You* snore, Violet. Not me."

Her cheeks heated. She shoved the beanie on her head and tucked all her hair in. "I do not."

"Sometimes I wake up in the night to make sure you're still there, still breathing, and nope—no need to check. Your snores nearly vibrate the entire bed."

Her mouth dropped. Jack barked a laugh, loud and teasing, before strutting over to her. He fixed her beanie and kissed her cheek. "I'm kidding, it's cute. You also make a great traffic cone." He sidled past her. "Get dressed. Let's go see some people."

❊❊❊

Violet's knees wouldn't stop shaking as the elevator rose to the top floor. Jack lounged against the golden interior, one foot up, as he fussed with his pocket and eventually pulled out a pack of smokes. He was acting casually in an effort to calm her down, she knew that, and it *did* help lessen the nerves. It was the anticipation.

Violet double-checked the beanie. Jack lit his smoke. Her eyes darted to it. He stared at her through heavy lids, and reluctantly passed it. She took a hit, delighted.

Jack snatched it back when the doors opened. "I'm having shiva delivered to the apartment today."

"So, we are both ensuring our bad habits."

He winked and squeezed her behind. "Everything in moderation, sweetheart."

Jack walked in all boyish and at-home. Because it *was* his home, but Violet was stunned at the architecture, the amounts of marble and plants, and the mix of ridiculous expenditures and comforting adornments. One of his guards—Ashan, the one from the party long ago who threatened to kill her—clasped hands with Jack and pulled him in. "You dog. You really did it."

"A walk in the park," Jack said easily. He motioned to Violet, who trailed behind. "All thanks to this one. Good thing that ring wasn't sentimental."

Ashan snorted. Violet was slightly shocked Jack remembered the interaction. All before they were sentenced to the Sins, Jack had been partying his last free night away, and Violet had been drunk and avoiding Mai. Jack eyed her, taking her back to the moment he caught her stealing from him. Ashan's knife had nearly gone through her spine.

Jack still let her keep the ring.

And she had given it to Meema.

Her palms were sweaty. Jack's arm wrapped over her shoulders and tugged her close. He flashed a smile to Ashan. "We'll catch up."

It was quiet in the apartment, but Jack's voice called out to a few people. Servants and maids who had glistening eyes as they clapped for him. Jack squeezed Violet's shoulder and went to hug each and every one of them. An older lady sobbed into his chest, and Violet swore there was a glassy look in his eyes when he pulled away. He turned, pausing when he looked down one of the hallways. Every bit of Jack's mask slithered away, revealing a relieved man who had returned home.

Lucien Marin was a bulkier, brown-eyed version of his brother. He walked with steady confidence rather than Jack's swagger. Lucien's tired face brightened, and even though Violet believed they had caught up already, it was like witnessing a reunion all over again.

"It is nice to meet you, finally, Violet." Lucien's voice was deep, sturdy. He was definitely Jelan's type. "Or should I say, *Sin Savior*."

She stiffened. "What?"

"It's what they're calling you. The last one to bloodswear themselves and survive every world." Lucien jutted his chin to Jack. "This one apparently skipped the fifth. We didn't even know he was alive until his name reappeared a week ago."

Jack gave a heartless laugh. "Wasn't my choice."

"I'm no savior," Violet said. "I just…"

"Was bored?" Jack teased.

Lucien shrugged. "You went through all seven worlds in record time, and exited…although, not through the arches." A raised brow. "I'm sure I'll hear about that later."

Her stomach turned sour. She didn't like the name, nor the fact people were talking about her. She didn't like Lucien's inquisitive gaze, or Jack's constant concern. Not when *she* didn't even know what was going on. She had kept moving, kept going through those worlds, and now that her life finally slowed, and she didn't have another game to play, it all felt entirely worse.

She stepped back, turning on her heel—

Jelan stood in the threshold of the kitchen. Coffee cup loose in her hand. Jaw open. Warm, watery eyes on her face.

"Violet," she exhaled.

Violet sagged. Her eyes welled as she blubbered the only words that came to her tongue, "I'm sorry."

Jelan shook her head, putting the cup down. "Vi—"

"I'm *sorry*," Violet sobbed. "I'm sorry. I'm sorry."

Jelan caught her friend in a hug, pulling her tight. Violet buried her face into Jelan's neck as she muttered, over and over, "I'm sorry. I'm sorry. I'm sorry."

"You don't have to be sorry," Jelan whispered. "You never have to be sorry."

"I left you."

"And I turned out just fine."

Violet clung to Jelan. It was the most they'd ever touched, but Violet wanted nothing more than to sink into her longtime friend's arms. She'd missed Jelan's vanilla mixed with detergent scent. The tears were slow, but they fell onto her friend, a thousand apologies lingering within. She left Jelan all alone and—

"Stop," Jelan said, rubbing Violet's back. "It sucked, it did. But I get it. I do. And I would have never been the sole reason for you to stay." She pulled Violet away. "You brought him back, Vi. You did it. You won."

Win, agia.

Being back in Jelan's presence certainly felt like a win. It was a blissful, happy moment in Violet's cloudy haze. She studied her friend. Jelan looked…brighter. Stood straighter. There was more expression to her features, instead of the stoic look she always flashed. Violet's lips split into a smile, and Jelan beamed back. They laughed and hugged again. Jelan glanced behind, going slightly rigid. Violet turned.

"Hi, I'm Jack." He held his hand out. Jelan swallowed, staring at it, before she shook his.

"Jelan."

"Inventor of the Plashield."

Violet whipped her head, remembering Lyla's orange shield from the other night. "You did it?"

Jelan's smile brightened. "I did it." She pointed to Lucien. "He actually found one of the drawings in…a *book*."

Violet put a hand on her hip. "A book?"

"One of your books. From…your neighbor."

It took her a moment, but suddenly Violet's eyes bugged, and she whirled to Lucien. "You went through my stuff?"

Jack snorted, wisely moving out of the way.

Lucien's mouth slacked. "Well…I had orders…"

Jack froze, shooting Lucien a glare. Violet looked at him. "You *ordered* him to go through my stuff?"

"Technically, your stuff went to your guardian, who…legally went to me once you entered the Sins." Jack raised his hands. "I didn't ask him to read your romance books. Lucien's hopeless about that."

Lucien gave Jack an incredulous look, "I'm not *hopeless*—"

"Regardless," Jelan popped in. "He found the drawing, hired me, and we stopped Arvalo from blowing up the Sky Arches while he held collateral over the past Emperor. Arvalo then killed him, and is now Emperor, while we figure out how to stop weapons being shipped off to Greed—that's all we know—and well…" Jelan's eyes darted to the sitting room. Violet followed her gaze. "We have visitors."

A man sat, legs spread and ego showing, on one of the many couches, wearing a tight blindfold, yet still looking as comfortable as ever. Violet noticed the plugs in his ears, and three guards hovering behind him.

Then she noticed the thick, brown-skinned girl with long black hair sitting across from him, flicking through channels and shoving popcorn into her mouth.

Jelan cleared her throat. "Precautions."

"The guards, the blindfold, or the girl?"

"My name is Hira, skiv."

Hira only spared a quick wink in Violet's direction. Violet's brows dropped, a scowl crossing her face. "I see the precaution now. The dude?"

Violet was quick to notice how Jelan put her hands behind her back—a very small sign that meant there was something to hide. "Luka Arvalo."

Violet's mouth dropped. "The pretty one?"

Jack's jaw clicked.

"It's inconvenient to have him here," Lucien said. "But seeing as none of us can leave without possibly getting shot or bombarded, this was the only way to handle the trade."

"Can I take these out yet?" Luka's velvety voice lulled from the room. "They're not allowing me to eavesdrop."

Jack's face was moody, if not sour on Lucien. "This was a stupid plan."

"Then let's get it all over with," Lucien sighed and beckoned his brother to the living room. Jack studied Jelan, looked back to Lucien, and followed.

The entry room emptied, and Jelan lingered, hands still behind her back, she swallowed deeply. "It's this…whole thing."

Violet crossed her arms as the guards removed Luka's blindfold and earplugs. His sharp gaze flicked around the room, before landing on Jack. He sneered deeply, Jack no happier to be in the man's presence as well.

"My sister?" Luka drawled.

Violet stilled. Footsteps echoed. Two guards led an unblindfolded Mai out of a hallway. She sulked, but the moment her eyes fell on Violet, she steeled her spine.

"What in the actual fuck," Violet seethed. "*You.*"

Jelan's hand wrapped her forearm. "She's leaving."

"She's been *living with you?*" Violet tried to shove forward, but Jelan held her grip. "Excuse me? Is this some kind of joke?"

Mai's mouth twisted, and Jack flashed an exasperated look from the sitting room, where Mai hadn't seen him yet.

"Ah, the trials and tribulations of young love," Ashan said.

"Wasn't love," Mai sneered.

Violet gave her the middle finger.

Jack stepped out and beckoned the guards, along with Mai. "No, it was more like bullying her because you lacked affection in your life and had *severe* daddy issues." Jack slid his hands into his pockets. "Let's get this over with."

Mai shrunk. *Shrunk* into the guards behind her. Everything about her anger and entitlement was chopped up and thrown down the garbage disposal once Jack's eyes landed on her. She was a tiny, little piece of prey in a predator's gaze.

Her hands trembled. "You really are back."

"Little Arvalo," Jack mused, power thrumming off him.

"I've been cooperating," Mai blurted. "I—I haven't done anything wrong." Her gaze snagged on Jelan. "Tell him I haven't acted out. I've been good, tell him—"

"No one will touch you," Jack said, holding up a finger to Violet, who stepped forward to protest.

Rage flowed through Violet. She wanted to throttle the girl. Jack stared at her as Mai was hustled into the sitting room. His body blocked her.

"Get her *out*." Violet snarled. "She's the damn reason I went in—"

"It's going to be over soon," Jack said. "None of this excuses her behavior, but her trauma isn't invalid."

Smothered. Shut down. Violet closed her mouth. Overruled. Jack held her gaze, and she read it, *"Tame yourself."* It was a cold slap across the face. She shrunk within her mind. Jack had his commander mode on. He didn't touch her. Didn't kiss her forehead. He created a bit of distance to maintain an image in front of enemies and comrades, but it twisted her heart no matter how rational it was. He looked down at her. "Keep it together." Then he turned around and joined the rest.

Jelan squeezed her arm. "She's upstairs. Second bedroom. She's been asking about you."

Jelan followed Jack into the sitting room. Violet took a step, wanting to trail—

Two guards blocked her. Jelan turned around, frowning an apology, but she pointed a finger upstairs.

Shut out.

Violet twisted behind her. Looked back. No one regarded her. The murmurs were soft. She didn't know the guards. Slowly, the room, the place, and the…people felt more foreign. Her gaze drifted up the grand staircase, and she let her body move, called by another.

When she reached the second bedroom, she didn't bother knocking. She opened the door without a sound, slipping through the crack, and gently shutting it behind her.

Her guardian sat in a plush chair facing the window. A teacup perched next to her, along with a puzzle, a book, and a strewn box of records. Violet watched as Meema breathed. As she existed. And she remembered the moment Meema began to cook dinner for Reed and her—when she realized their mother was failing them and she needed to step in. Violet's mouth twisted into a frown.

She remembered the last time she'd seen Meema. Her memory went through phases, and for a couple of minutes, she thought Violet was her mother. She thought Violet was younger. She then thought Reed was just missing in the South and needed to come home for dinner.

"Whoever gives you a bad day, you tell 'em to fuck off. No matter what, you keep going, baby girl."

She broke. Her heart twisted. "Okay."

"You promise?"

"I promise."

"Good." She wiped her tears. "Now, off you go. And bring your damned brother home!"

Violet's legs jellied. She did it. She brought her brother home, but…

In some heartbreaking way, Violet didn't think she brought *herself* home. No matter the little instances with her friends, with Jack, it all falsely filled an empty space that died. Decayed. It provided temporary comforts to a withering girl.

Emotion slipped away. It was so easy to do—the smiles, the jokes, the mask she was used to—but that darkness never left. It expanded with Gwen…Emryn…Tamu…everyone who had existed in a *game*. Her legs straightened. Violet took a step—

Meema turned.

Violet caught her empty gray eyes. She waited. Gave it a couple of minutes. Jack mentioned she was on medication to help…

Meema exhaled like she'd been holding her breath far too long, "Wildflower."

Violet crumpled, the last bits of her that the darkness hadn't reached wallowed, bringing tears as she stretched her arms to her guardian. Meema's eyes watered. A sob tore through the hardy woman. "You made it home. You did it, baby girl." She caressed Violet's face. "You brought him home."

Violet sobbed. It was all anyone was ever saying. It was the praise, the happiness, that *they* were complete and yet she…she… she was still *so broken*—

"I'm sorry," she sniffled. "I'm sorry I left you. But this place looks cozy."

"Annoying ass people who care about my wellbeing—*that's* what it's filled with. They limit my shiva. But oh, how are you? Are you recovering? How did you do it? Did you meet others? You dragged quite a few out with you."

Violet smiled through the tears. It was familiarity at its core. The woman who paid attention to her when no one else did, whether it was as a child or as she was now. "I met a *lot* of cool people, and I fought other bad ones, too. I did it because I wanted your brownies again—"

"The ones with the mint?"

"Those," Violet said. She took in Meema's gray hair, the frown wrinkles, and the two moles on her chin. "I missed those a lot. I thought about them every day."

"What's with the hat?" Meema wrinkled her nose, tugging Violet closer with a strong grip. "It's ugly."

"Oh, my head…"

Meema ripped it off. Her hair tumbled out, and Violet caught the white part in her peripheral. Meema's mouth parted. She touched it. Tugged on it. "Did you bleach it?"

Violet wrenched herself away and stumbled across the carpet. Terror flooded. Meema reached, confused, but Violet shook her head feverishly. Sweat crawled down her back. Her breaths became shorter. "No…I…"

Meema's brows crumpled. Her eyes went distant. They switched, and anger poured in. Meema tried to rise from her chair, but her hips cracked, and she sank back down. She pointed a furious finger. "Mariana, did you hurt her?"

Violet stilled. She stumbled farther away. Her gaze grew black, then red. Dizzy.

"I'm—I have to go—" A familiar burning stirred in her chest. She ripped the door open. Meema called after her.

Her insides blistered.

A distant, internal roar. Cyran's roar.

Then fire.

Then pain.

44

STORY

JELAN PRESSED THE BUTTON ON the camera to stop the recording.

Jack sighed. His expression fell and his face dropped into his hands. Lucien had silent tears wallowing in his eyes. Jelan's mouth was parted. Shocked. Utterly shocked. She looked at the time on the video.

Six hours and seventeen minutes.

"And that's the story," Jack said, his words a mumble in his palms.

By Jack's expression, there was more to said story, but Jelan's presence started it all off rather…plainly. Beat by beat. Minute by minute. World by world. Until they reached the fourth—Lust—and Jack began to veer off. He skipped graciously over the details of what he did to Violet, but the insinuation of their week of bed-laying was there. When he reached the end of that world, when this Worldbreaker—Cyran—appeared, along with a man who could zap lightning and people, *their* people, that had secret teleporting powers. That's when the emotion took its toll. Jack paused numerous times. Caught his breath. Straightened his spine, but as the words spilled, he'd slack again, showing the burden of everything he'd been through.

Jelan's mouth was dry from her jaw-dropping the moment he began displaying his newfound abilities given unwillingly by Cyran. She didn't blink when he crushed a spoon in half, and then the rest to tiny fragments. Didn't breathe when he showed his enlarged canines or demonstrated his camouflage invisibility. Then there was the mind-reading he did on Jelan, in which she panicked within his intense gaze as she read off meaningless sentences she was instructed to write beforehand.

Her heart palpitated at each one.

She'd think, *I'm not a big fan of mungoes because the Souther stalls and bodegas make them too salty.*

Jack agreed. Repeated it back.

Violet was actually very good at sciences. Biology, to be honest. Although I think she's forgotten most of what she learned.

He was surprised at that one. "Tell me another thing about her, off paper."

She… His gaze had been too much, but Jelan couldn't blink or look away if she tried. She *did* try, because it made her uncomfortable, but Jack pressed and she thought, *Violet gave herself a middle name: Asher.*

"Another thing."

She likes picking clovers.

"Something deeper—"

Faroh… But Jelan stopped herself. Jack's brow raised. Jelan immediately began thinking about oranges so much that she tasted it on her tongue.

"Faroh?" Jack had asked.

Lucien's brows had drawn together. "Faroh?"

"No," Jelan had breathed. "Let me go. That's…enough. Ask her if you want."

Jack's gaze went cold, but he cut their eye contact. His jaw ticked. Jelan sucked a deep inhale, suddenly exhausted. She put a hand on her chest.

But then they had moved into the Worldbreaker. About what he did with Greed, the Order, his legion, and that there was another world existing as his true home base. Jelan's brain was fuzzy, her thoughts incoherent. She stood.

"Lucien." Jack picked his head from his hands. "There's…one more thing. But it's private."

Jelan understood that cue. She picked up the video camera and turned it off, exiting quietly into the main floor of the penthouse. She immediately went to another room, followed by a guard to make sure the camera touched no hands other than hers or Hira's and punched a keycode for a private door. It beeped open. She stuck her head in. "Jack is ready. Meeting is soon."

Hira sighed back in the desk chair, surrounded by three video-editing screens. "I've already set up his template. The software will format it for me. Should be done in the next fifteen."

"Who knew you were a whiz with computers."

"I'm not." Hira plucked something from between her teeth. "I just know how to read instructions."

"Who knew you learned how to read."

Hira scowled, snatched the camera, and slammed the door on Jelan's grinning face.

She wandered to the kitchen to pour another cup of coffee but paused at the threshold. Violet bent over a plate of toast, stabbing small bits with her fingernail. She put a small piece into her mouth. Chewed, scrunched up her face, and spit it out.

Rio sat at the dining table and watched her carefully. Frown lines formed around his mouth. Jelan now learned that he had been injected with something, as well, but for the most part he said he didn't feel much different. Heavier was his only description. His brain felt heavy, his arms, too, and every now and then, his fingernails would turn a steel color, or he would bend his fork without meaning to. She witnessed it a couple of times, but she knew Jack's explanation was coming, so she kept quiet.

Her gaze returned to Violet. Her collarbone protruded from her giant sweater. Her lips were pale. Her jawline cut sharp and cheeks hollow. The blue in her eyes was lackluster. Faint. She had another interaction with Meema, but it went bad. Violet looked so painfully un-Violet that her guardian failed to recognize her. Jelan wanted to give Violet a reason—the drugs were reaching a plateau, so Meema's memory was stagnant and halted at returning—but it didn't matter. Jelan's eyes flicked to the orange beanie still covering her hair.

It's killing her, Jelan thought. Her brain hurt from all that Jack confessed, but it sagged when it came to Violet's situation. She took a world and meshed its soul with her own, along with also discovering abilities, having an indistinct tie to the villain, and nearly losing her brother in the process.

Jelan's heart hurt. Jack had to tell Violet she couldn't leave the apartment building. Violet hardly put up a fight. She was too tired to even attempt it. The girl had trouble standing for long periods of time, she could barely keep her eyes open. A drip line was attached to her constantly, along with Jack's paranoia. He said he wanted to take her outside, but he couldn't. It was too unsafe.

"Commanders are arriving soon." Bronto appeared behind Jelan, announcing to the kitchen.

"Got it," Jelan said. Rio stood, knocked on the glass and walked over to Violet. His hands were gentle as he stabilized her, and with effort, Violet stepped away.

Anaya—the scaly Endolier with a killer expression—opened the door to the veranda and silently took one of Violet's hands. She flashed a protective look at Jelan, then Bronto, and slid the door shut behind them.

"They're a bright bunch," Bronto mumbled.

Jelan turned. "They nearly died a thousand times." She spotted Lyla and Cairo already walking toward the office. "Cut them slack."

Jelan got herself a coffee, downed it, and followed the generals to the meeting. She took a spot toward the back, standing in a shadowed corner away from the windows. Lyla and Cairo were already shifting through their notes. Jack and Lucien entered a couple of minutes later, looking rather exhausted as she felt. Lucien's eyes were red. She straightened, wanting to catch his gaze, but he merely took a seat at the table and poured himself a glass of liquor. Jack's expression was hard, content. He took a deep breath and glanced at the clock. A few others joined, generals and legions of Jack's, but people whom Jelan hardly saw. Jenkins wasn't joining, unfortunately. He'd lift the depressing nature of the situation.

Once Jack's core team of seven settled at the table, allowing three extra spaces, he cleared his throat. His fingers dragged over the documents in front of him.

"Arvalo has always been a…pain. I should have killed him when I had the chance. Yet after the Sins, I realized we are fighting for more than control of this city. It is for this country and this world. The superior threat to all of us lies worlds away. We don't know when he is going to act or in what way, but from what I suspect about his plans—which mind you, he only shares with those *bound* to him. Heart, soul, everything." At the widening eyes and lifted brows, Jack merely frowned. "I have a lot to explain to you. But I have you here because you never abandoned me after the wars, and despite all that I have done."

Cairo was the first to stand. "You do not need to apologize, Commander. I will not accept it." He put his fist to his chest. "Whoever threatens our fight for freedom, we will take him."

Jack nodded. "I thank you, Cairo. You have always been loyal."

"Of course, Commander."

"We will navigate this with you," Lyla said, twirling a pen. "I trust that the interview went well."

"Well enough," Jack said.

The door opened.

Masar appeared, looking rather…uncomfortable, and bulky for the room. His gaze shifted to Lyla and he grunted a hello, taking a step toward the empty chair next to her. Lyla looked surprised, "My brother?"

"He has information, and I'd rather we ask it favorably, all together, than for me or you to interrogate him." Jack brushed his curls back.

Next through the room was Covokai. The Commander of Public Works and Rescue had an old-fashioned clipboard under his arm, and as much of an exhausted face as everyone else. He locked eyes with Jack, pursed his lips, and sauntered around the table. They clasped arms. "It's…good to see you again, Marin."

Jack held a smidge of fondness in his gaze. Covokai was a legend among the Commanders. He's held his position for forty years and was well respected within the city. By that look, Jelan would take a large guess that Covokai helped Jack when he rose to power. They released arms and Covokai took his seat.

A door slammed and a loud clacking of heels sliced through the tense welcome. "Move, Bronto. You're taking up space."

A smirk rose to Jack's face. "Always fashionably late."

Lyla snorted.

Guards piled through the door, followed by the famous, sharp-looking woman. Jelan lifted her chin as Alexia Javez took in the room. Her wine-red nails tapped a plastablet. Her deep-brown eyes studied Jack.

"Of course, it's you who finally beats the fucking Sins." She angled her head, sharp jawline cutting through the tension in the room. "You really screwed a lot of things up when you left this citadel."

"Nice to see you, too, Alexia," Jack drawled, a sparkle in his eye. If Alexia wasn't atrociously gay and tied at the hip with her wife, that one look would have told Jelan that they definitely hate-fucked a few times. Perhaps it's a possibility. "How's darling Venara?"

Alexia scowled. "Cursing the world now that you're back in it."

"She likes me, you know that."

"You made a big show when you left this city, and now it is on lockdown because you are back. Arvalo is having a fit. Sorry, *Emperor* Arvalo is."

"Do you need a refreshment?" Jack asked politely, motioning to the coffee and liquor cart along the wall.

"Yes, *please.*" Alexia plopped in her chair and crossed her legs. She noticed Masar, and as a servant placed red wine in front of her, she waggled her finger at him. "What a surprise. You brought back another threat, too?"

Jack pressed a button for a remote. Jelan sat in her chair along the wall. This was about to be a long meeting. "I forced him to come back since he missed his sister so dearly."

"How sweet." Alexia sipped her wine. "So how long is this video?"

"Five hours and three minutes," Lucien said, taking a drink. "Get settled. Lounge on one of the loveseats if you want. This will be a long meeting."

Jack pressed play on the screen. Bronto locked the door. An adjacent bathroom would provide relief, but for the duration of the meeting, no one was leaving the room.

Alexia took a deep sip of her wine. "Fucking skies."

And then the video started. *"Hello, I'm sure you've missed me. My name is Jack Marin…"*

Then it cut to another face. *"My name is Anaya…"*

"My name is Rio Gaverra… I am twenty-two years old."

"I'm twenty-six years old," Jack said.

"I am eighteen," Anaya winked.

"And this is my story…"

Fourteen hours of grueling storytelling, all edited by Jelan and Hira in an offline, privately secured and monitored, automated splicing system that cut out the silent portions, the redundant words, and organized each story by the worlds. It was why Jelan was so tired from the last two days, but it was necessary. This information needed to get to the right ears fast, and it needed to be as authentic as possible. Rio and Anaya confirmed that they didn't want to be in the room when it was delivered to the heads of the city—minus Pofer and Luka. Violet was supposed to testify, but it was hard dragging her out of bed as it was, and Jack was worried it would trigger too much. She'd have to talk about this Gwen, and that was only in the second world. Violet was still sensitive about it. She carried around a turquoise-black blade that apparently came from the person.

The worlds passed. Wrath, Gluttony—everyone looked variations of sick at the cannibal part—Envy, when Anaya came in. She talked about Navo—which Jelan had thought was just a nice little pet, but instead was a full-blown conscious robotic panther, snake, and other hybrid things. The cat licked its paws in the window most days, until Anaya beckoned Navo to transform. Jelan caught it on video.

On the screen, its full, terrifying form took most of the sitting room.

"I need to see that in real-time," Cairo muttered in awe. Covokai agreed with him.

Alexia looked like she just got proposed to. *"Amazing."*

Then there was Lust. The moment Jack and Violet gave in. At the end of Lust, things changed. The Worldbreaker—Cyran—arrived. Rio and Anaya's were the only accounts for Sloth. Greed took the longest, though. Over two hours of Jack's recount alone was Greed. He talked about dying. About dreaming of his family. About waking up in a bare room to test new abilities, and then he displayed them. Jelan heard her gasps in the video.

As the video played, Jelan's mind returned to a certain moment during Jack's interview. He paused long and hard before admitting it, but he looked straight at her while he said it, *"And as the Worldbreaker tortured me and Reed...I watched her destroy part of the city. I watched...buildings crumble from her inexplicable power. It was a massacre in any moral person's eye, but I watched her finally unravel into something that seemed cathartic. Something she's wanted to do for a long time, and I'll admit...it terrified me."*

When they reached that part, Masar stood and walked to the window. He gazed out, hands behind his back, pure pain marking his expression. "It's true. Skies, it's all true." The man placed his forehead on the glass, his mouth twisting in a sob. Tears poured down his face. "And I...I thought it was *right*. Part of me still thinks so. Part of me hates that I left him. He was supposed to provide me *everything* but...that was part of his control."

Everyone else was silent at Masar's confession. His sister got up and whispered something in his ear, while also handing him a shot of liquor.

Thirty minutes later, after the desperate fight through Pride—the last world—they came back. The only thing missing was the minutes when Violet and Reed fought Cyran. When Violet took a world.

Lucien stared at Jack for a while. It was silent for a very long time after the video ended. Jack downed two shots worth of alcohol.

Alexia stared at him, mouth agape. "Even the most impressive people can't bullshit for five hours."

"So…a Worldbreaker? The creator of the Sins? A man who is over five-hundred years old and has control of seven—now six— worlds?" Covokai started. "Is that the reason for his immortality?"

"I imagine so," Cairo said. "But it connects to the one thing we found in those plasma plans back when Arvalo tried to destroy the Arches. *Aether.* We didn't know what it was. But it's soul energy. It's…in the mechanics of the blueprints. It makes sense that soul energy exists both in live species, and in the world that provides life. And all of this has been manipulated by one person." A swallow. "One person who created a *game* with it."

"Let's see them." Covokai nodded at Jack. "The Sin Savior, the Endolier, and your abilities."

"Which one do you want to see first?" Jack asked.

The Gardia Commanders glanced toward each other before Alexia leaned in. "Sin Savior."

At that, Jack's smile tightened. "Good choice." He nodded to Jelan and she swiftly left the room.

Violet lounged on the balcony, a plate of pomegranate seeds on her stomach as she stared blankly toward the city—the South. Her beanie was pulled down to her eyebrows.

She glanced toward Jelan with a passive gaze, then frowned at her plate, fingers stained dark pink from the juices. "Am I being summoned now?"

"Yes. Then they will want to see Anaya after you."

"She's in the training room." Violet waved her hand, popping more pomegranates. "I'll come, don't wait for me."

Jelan flashed her an incredulous look. "Violet, there are literal commanders in the penthouse."

"He just needs to prove you've done something… otherworldly," said Rio from the lounge chair across. "Stop biting his ass, Vi."

"I'm not biting his ass."

"Well, then take off that stupid hat and follow Jelan." Rio reached over and plucked the plate away, settling back to throw a handful in his mouth. "Get in there before Jackie has a tantrum."

She huffed but swung her legs over the edge of the chair and stood. "What am I supposed to say to them?"

"You don't have to say anything. They have enough of a story." Jelan tugged the hat off, and Violet's duo-toned hair spilled out. "Just show them that."

Violet flinched when the white strands fell on her shoulder. She glanced down, then quickly back up, paling. Her hand rose to the center of her chest where she clutched her shirt. Jack had said she felt a heartbeat that wasn't her own. Sometimes beating in rhythm, but other times beating out. Like another being was stuck inside of her, living off her life.

A parasite, Jack called it.

Rio frowned at Violet. Her normally golden skin, that fire behind her eyes, was leeched. It broke Jelan's heart.

"Come on," Jelan beckoned. Violet ignored her outstretched hand and passed through the glass doors back into the apartment. She didn't swagger or stomp her way in, no, she trudged along, walking like it took energy, sighing like she wanted nothing more than to crawl into bed.

It was no wonder Jack hovered around her, kept her close to him most of the time even when he was dealing with city business, gang business, or Arvalo. Above all of that, Violet's state was what stressed him the most.

Unless there were some forgotten texts on Vanishers lying around in the Government Sector, the quickest answer would be the Worldbreaker. He held six worlds within his body, but wasn't withering from the weight of them. He was healthy-ish. Alive. Immortal.

Rio muttered once that Violet might not last the next week. She lost ten percent of her weight in two days.

The guards moved aside as they reached the office door. Before Jelan entered, a hand brushed her elbow and gripped. She turned her head to meet Violet's hollow gaze, nodding once. Forward. But her grip never released.

Jelan led her into the room and the conversation hushed.

Jack's face softened for the slightest of seconds before it went back into his contempt mask. "The Sin Savior. Violet Sutton."

All eyes turned. Violet never released her grip, hovering close. She gazed at each person, but again, there was a lack of fire. A lack of challenge.

"This is the girl who did it all?" Alexia sat back in her chair. "*This* girl?"

"Her, her brother, and Rio, completed all seven worlds. But *this* is the woman who came back with something… extra. As you can see, her hair is marked with the essence of another world."

Violet's grip tightened so much that her nails began to dig into Jelan's skin. Lucien and Jack both noticed, but Jelan merely shook her head.

"How do you take a world with…your abilities?" Covokai asked.

"There were four forms of soul elements that existed long ago. Vanishers—which are the most common and seem to live dormant in a lot of Calesal residents. Then Slayers—only one still in existence. The man named Zavar." Jack smirked at that, but it fell slightly as he continued. "Givers. And then Manipulators. The Worldbreaker is a Vanisher *and* Manipulator… I believe Violet is the same."

At this point, Violet's face was nestled in Jelan's arm.

"So the white on her hair…is a world?" Lyla's head tilted to the side.

"Pride," Jack's eyes flicked to Violet. "The Worldbreaker's hair was the same color, until she took it. She says his switched back to gray."

"This is… beyond me, Marin," Covokai scoffed. "We already live in a state of unrest. Arvalo wants to open our borders to nations we don't even know. He might be creating a current world war as we speak, and then there's…a *Worlds' War?*"

"Our biggest threat right now is Arvalo," one of Jack's generals said. "Him *acting* as Emperor has destroyed our city. He has upped the taxes against us to weed out control of the gardia over our industries. Most of the money is going into Plastech. Food production has been lacking—people are starving in this city. We must worry about here first, Commander."

"While I agree Arvalo needs to be dealt with." Alexia twirled her black hair. "We need to secure Veceras as a whole before dealing with him."

Jack's eyes flicked to Violet every now and then.

"The only way I'm sparing my gardia, beyond what I already have to deal with right now, is to usurp Arvalo. He needs to be challenged." Covokai gave Jack a pointed look. "And his number one priority, besides destroying our city, is finding you and killing you."

"I'm not concerned about that," Jack said.

"But you're concerned about an imaginary war?" Alexia asked sharply. "These priorities aren't straight, Jack. How long do we have to prepare? We don't have armies, we have loyal gangs. We don't even know what is outside the damn walls. You always had these grand ideas, but I might have to agree with Hunt on this. You went through the Sins, you finally made it out, but you say there's some *Worldbreaker* controlling the game and wanting to bring it to Veceras? The abilities thing is wild, something clearly happened to all of you, but this is…more than I can handle." Alexia pointed to Violet. "Can she vanish for us? Prove it?"

"She's…struggling." Jack paused for a moment, jaw tensing. "I understand about Arvalo and Pofer as his backup, but this is worse. Cyran has six worlds under his skin, he can make them do whatever he wants. They mark him with scars and burns like the one had marked Violet—"

"We've never seen him!" Covokai all but laughed. "You just love starting wars, is that it, Marin?"

Violet bristled at that. By this point, Jelan was numbed to the pain of her grip, but she released, if only for an instant to lean forward.

They didn't notice her.

Jack's look was icy as he glared at Covokai. "Watch what you say about me while you're in my home."

"It's simple, Jack," Alexia said. "We're on your side about Arvalo. We want him gone. But another war… we are only a city."

"*He will kill you…*" Violet whispered. Jelan finally turned to see her eyes glazed. Fighting back tears.

Jelan glanced at Lucien, who looked ready to pounce to defend his brother. Tension rose. Violet trembled against her.

The commanders bickered, growing louder. Alexia stood. Lyla squared up with her—

"Oh, skies," Violet clutched at her heart. "He's—"

But she dropped to the ground, and a blood-curdling scream tore from her throat.

All heads whipped to her. Jack sprung out of his seat in an instant, diving for Violet. "Hey—hey, it's okay. Breathe through it. He will be done soon."

Alexia was reduced to silence and wide eyes. Covokai the same.

Violet sobbed as her body bent and twisted, skin paling at a rapid rate. Jack let her seize, let her scream, brushing back the tears from her face.

"You'll see," was all he said, voice cracking.

Jelan's heart broke for him.

"Stop it! Stop it!" Violet wailed. "*Please! Stop!*"

"We need to get her to an infirmary." Alexia stood. "Bronto—"

"No!" Jack growled. "This is *him*. This *is* the Worldbreaker. He goes into the world she took from him—Pride—and tortures it. Bombs it. That's how it works. She gives a part of herself for a part of the world. If drastic, horrible things happen to the world, it can be enough for her to feel them. On the contrary, via the connection, if she dies, the world dies."

Violet was still sobbing, eyes shut tight, body arching—trembling.

"So, she is feeling—?" A general gaped.

"*Fire!*" Vi cried.

Her skin blazed from the inside, deep rivulets of red and orange lines thrumming underneath as if her veins were formed of fire. A bright light grew from the center of her chest, peaking, igniting, before it slithered to her fingers and toes, where it winked out.

Like how it started, it simply stopped.

She curled into herself, whimpering. Jelan could have sworn smoke billowed out of her mouth.

Hand-checking her pulse, Jack lifted his head to Bronto. "I want the doctor here, a burn specialist, and whatever else she needs. *Now.*"

Bronto nodded and Ashan stepped forward, arms open—

Rio brushed past him, followed by a sweaty, yet concerned-looking Anaya.

"Another one?" Rio said softly, frowning at Violet.

"Yes," Jack borderline growled.

"Get her." Anaya nudged Rio. "We'll take her up to her room and stay with her."

Jack merely nodded. His hands trembled as he touched Violet's skin. Rio stepped forward and placed a hand on his shoulder. "We will find a way, Jack."

"I know," he whispered.

Rio gently slid his arms underneath Violet and hoisted her up. "Come on, little flower. It's alright now. He's done. It's over."

She whimpered again, curling into Rio's chest.

Anaya shot a pointed look at the guards, who flattened themselves on the wall to let their small group pass.

Jelan wondered if she should go after them. Blood dotted her arms where Violet's nails had broken skin. She decided to stay put, thinning her mouth as the Commanders looked at each other, then out the window at the city.

Silence pressed into the room. Jack stood, rubbing at his face.

"You would go to war for her," Alexia said softly.

Bleary-eyed, Jack turned to face his fellow commanders. "I *will* go to war for her. I only ask that you join me in this fight, to prevent what's happening to her from happening to anyone else. I fear that was his way of taunting her, punishing her for defying him. Imagine what he would do when he truly wants something gone. What we know about the Sins, and the catastrophes that come when blood isn't given to the bowl, isn't true. It's not a curse. It's *him*. He controls it all; the earthquakes, the droughts, everything, because…well, I imagine it is him…but because he's connected to Veceras as she's connected to Pride."

Alexia jutted her chin, standing. "If someone did that to Venara, I would slaughter anyone responsible." She stepped up, a hand sliding to Jack's shoulders. Squeezing. "My gardia is with you, Jack."

Jack looked positively defeated, his usual grace and charming attitude gone, sucked away after seeing Violet like that. But still, he shifted a smile on his face, "Thank you."

"I want more information about this Worldbreaker. I'll have my laureates looking into more information about Vanishers." Covokai walked around the table and clapped hands with Jack. "You have my gardia, Marin. But get rid of Arvalo *first*."

"Thank you," Jack said, nodding gracefully. "I appreciate your support. Thank you—all of you. I need to go see—"

"Be with her. She needs you," Alexia said. "We will see ourselves out."

"We will reconvene with our heads of intelligence in three days' time to discuss Arvalo." Lucien nodded at his brother. Jack exited the room, and on the way out said, "Get home safely."

Jelan slipped out that night, a headache breaching her temples.

After Violet was tucked back into bed, and the entire penthouse was still reeling from the day, Jelan managed to convince Bronto that she needed to go on a walk. They had their routine from earlier—three blocks down, a certain alleyway that Jelan sat in by herself to stare at the wall and let her mind run—then three blocks back around. It was dangerous to ask him, but by Bronto's quick, grunted agreement, it was clear they both needed fresh air.

When Jelan turned into her alley for peace, walking far enough down to be out of Bronto's earshot, another figure met her.

"I got your message," Jelan muttered. "You said it was urgent?"

Luka lingered in the shadows. He tapped a slender finger on the wall, thinking.

"This is a warning," he began.

"Aren't you supposed to be in the Government Sector?"

His face paled. He pressed off the opposite wall and crowded around her. "It's bad."

She huffed. "What is it?"

"The wall is coming down, Jelan." Luka squeezed her shoulders, urgency in his gaze. "Tonight."

Her chest constricted. "What?"

"Jack Marin has returned. He is Arvalo's only threat—"

"No," Jelan said. "*You* are."

"I am a pawn, Jelan." His thumb rubbed over her bottom lip. Heat flushed her cheeks. "I was born one, and I will die one. I'll pull as many strings as I can on my own in the process. This is one of them. If Marin wants to make his move, it has to be now."

A dull roar filled her ears. *The wall is coming down.* It was Arvalo's last, desperate attempt. He knew Jack would challenge him, and if the wall came down...and Jack won...they'd have even more chaos to deal with. Who knew what lingered outside the borders of Veceras? Luka and her had only glimpsed the beginning when they searched the sewers and found the grate beyond the wall, but the secrets were tenfold.

"Interesting," came a drawl.

Jack pulled the smoke out of his mouth and crushed it into the brick wall. He swaggered, lights at his back, looking like a menacing silhouette. Bronto lingered behind. Jelan side-eyed him. She was hoping for a little more time before he notified Jack, but the man had loyalty to his commander. She'd given Bronto the message—the only one who knew—and Bronto reluctantly agreed to her little plan. She needed someone to see her interaction with Luka. To see he wasn't a threat…

"You told," Luka said. Jelan opened her mouth, but he held up a finger, "As you should. I just thought it'd be the *other* one."

"You flatter me. I'm blushing," Jack deadpanned. He pointed the burnt end of his cigarette from Jelan to Luka, and then back. "I will keep whatever *this* is out of my mouth."

Jelan started. "Please—"

But Jack held up a finger. Just one finger and it felt like her whole world was complicit to the digit. His lips quirked. Jelan saw the lack of fucks given—his girl was dying, his city was crumbling, he was trying to both save it and himself and everything around him, and he was collectively agreed to be the only one to take Arvalo down. This news paved Jack's red carpet straight to the Emperor's mansion. "Give me every bit of information you have. Don't compromise yourself. I'll make sure you pass the bridge safely. *But* that wall cannot come down, do you understand?"

"I'm not a child," Luka said. "I'm two years older than you."

"Then grow your own pair and get off your father's," Jack challenged with a slight growl. "Because I'm about to chop them off. Might as well run for cover in case you want to continue"—he motioned again between them—"this."

That was not what Jelan wanted Jack to see. Luka and she kissed once. It was a mistake. A very…hot, passionate, desperate mistake.

"Tell me everything," Jack commanded, leaning against the brick and crossing his arms.

Luka matched his height. "Well, first, you'll use Mai…"

Jack smiled, like the two men had been thinking the exact same thing, the entire time.

45

NALA

JACK LEANED DOWN WITH HEAVY lids, elbows on the desk, fighting the depravity of sleep. He hadn't seen it in the last two days. Stress weighed heavily on his shoulders, and he desperately wanted to lie his head among the sheets of reports, the plastablets, and the constant stream of radio communications between scouts monitoring Arvalo. He wanted to throttle Luka Arvalo. And he wanted to be in *bed*, but after the chaos of the last week, he knew his little paradise with Violet was shortsighted.

Even then, it was only a matter of time before the world came crashing down. Literally. Jack played it quiet, not wanting to give Arvalo any reason to attack him. There had been no message from the Empire since Jack's return, yet the city was on edge. Buzzing. Riots were brimming in the South, the North was retaliating and abandoning the Empire. Businesses were shutting, the Mid was on a strict curfew.

He left his desk, slipping quietly through the corridor and the foyer, until the elevator opened, where a surprising sight greeted him.

"Tivra," he breathed.

His wonderful friend beamed at him. Her brown skin held a glow, caressing her round cheekbones and emitting from her warm gaze. Her black hair was tied back into a braid. A guard lingered to her right, alert. Jack's gaze flicked to the plasblade bulge at his hip, the carrier in his hand… A smile drew to his face. A scuff of a boot behind him and Ashan appeared in Jack's peripheral.

"Welcome home, Jack." Tivra's light, airy voice was a nostalgic hug itself. She burst toward him, wrapping him tightly in an embrace. Jack's arms tugged her closer as his head buried into her neck. Tivra was a dear friend, a confidant he met through a celebrity party and flirted heavily with until she flashed the ring on her finger, announcing her very recent engagement to her now-wife. They used to laugh about it all the time, and since then, Tivra has been a steady rock to rely on.

He pulled back, warmth filling his chest, but a pit of dread dropped in his stomach. "You…shouldn't be here."

"I don't care, Jack. You nor your enemies don't scare me." Her eyes alighted and she stroked his cheek, doting like a mother. "I needed to see you for myself. I was hoping night would be quieter—seems like it is." She flashed a bright smile. "And you deserve to meet your goddaughter."

Her guard placed the baby carrier on the ground, and Tivra bent in her massive stilettos. She pulled off the cover, revealing a beautiful baby with puckered lips and dozy eyes that slowly opened. "Hi, sweetie pie." She picked the baby out, cradling her. "This is Jack, your godfather, and Jack." She turned the baby to him. "This is Nala."

"Nala," Jack repeated.

Tivra nodded. "Thanks to you, she's the most spoiled little girl ever, and she loves looking at flowers."

"You got them all?" Jack asked, not taking his gaze off Nala as she blinked her big, brown eyes at him. Long, dark lashes were soft against her cheeks, and after a moment of staring back at Jack, a chortle burst from her. She reached a tiny hand out to him.

"Every one. Made me cry, thank you so much. You know I don't like ruining my mascara."

"I should have sent ugly flowers, then," Jack said.

Tivra chuckled, stepping closer. "Do you want to hold her?"

Jack swallowed, unbelieving of this moment. He remembered

the long conversations with Tivra about wanting families and having futures. Jack abandoned a lot of that when he took on his City Commander role—it just wasn't safe, especially with his… fame. Tivra, on the other hand, had the world lifting her up. She was a renowned artist in the North now, having painted in a small apartment in the Mid most of her life before recognition that built from Jack purchasing most of her work. It filled the penthouse. Tivra would talk about all the babies she wanted, but it was difficult for two women to get pregnant—difficult and expensive. When Jack proposed that he help them, it was the first time he'd ever seen Tivra cry.

"Yes," he answered finally. He *did* babysit quite a lot while he was on lockdown, so being around an infant wasn't unusual, but seeing Tivra meet the first of her many dreams, his eyes grew watery. "She's absolutely beautiful."

"She was the easiest thing, I swear. My water broke and then boom, she was there four hours later, all healthy and screaming. But here…" Tivra gently tucked the cooing babe in his arms, who immediately reached up toward Jack's face. "Say hi, Jack."

"I'm going to spoil you even more now," Jack said in a higher-pitched voice, a soft smile on his lips. Nala giggled. He looked back at Tivra. "Ready for the next one?"

"Maybe in a year." She waved her hand, her beaming smile dropping as her eyes roamed his face again. "I…the last few months were tough. Depression got to me, especially thinking you were gone. I couldn't wrap my head around you never getting to meet her." Her eyes watered and she sniffed, lifting her chin. "I'm glad you aren't dead, Jack Marin."

"Me, too." Jack wrapped an arm around Tivra's shoulders and pulled her close. He kissed the top of her head. "I'll fill you in another time, but you should—"

"Is that a baby?"

Jack turned at her voice, chest caving at how raspy and empty it sounded now. Violet stood in the kitchen. He glimpsed Rio out on the balcony, watching her carefully, while Anaya was passed out on one of the lounges. When Jack wasn't around, all three preferred to sleep on the spacious veranda, clearly uncomfortable with being cooped up.

Tivra stepped back, offering one of her warm smiles. "This is Nala. Jack is…"

"I'm her godfather," he said proudly to Violet, and then to Tivra, "This is Violet—"

"*Her?*" Tivra's jaw dropped. Her heels clacked as she walked over to Violet. Jack hissed slightly, and Tivra reared back, controlling herself. Violet was clearly grateful the woman didn't touch her. "It's an *honor* to meet you." Tivra glanced back at Jack, beckoning him. "You…all seven worlds in such a short time? Everyone in the city is talking about it. The girl who sacrificed herself, finishing the Sins… How did you—"

"Not now," Jack clipped. Tivra shut her mouth, turning back to Violet. She stiffened a bit, her allure faltering as Violet's expression went blank. Dead.

Tivra's smile became strained, but she gestured to Nala. "Do you want to meet her?"

"I don't…" Violet tugged her orange beanie down farther, but a lock of blonde hair slipped out. She didn't notice. "I mean…if you don't mind."

"Not at all," Tivra said tightly. She was turning motherly. Protective. Violet was giving off a threatening energy. Jack opened his mouth, ready to protest—

Violet leaned down to baby Nala, who cooed and caught the blonde part of her hair in a tiny fist. Violet flinched, pulling away slightly and tugging the hair back.

She blinked rapidly, as if she'd just woken up, but then her gaze shifted to a far, glassy-eyed, wide, and lost look. A strange smile breached her face.

"Don't grow up, little Nala," Violet said, voice even. Jack clutched the baby tighter. Violet didn't seem to notice. "It's all a trap."

Tivra cleared her throat and plucked the baby from Jack's arms, giving him an apologetic look. "It's past her bedtime. But it was good to see you. You're looking well." She gave Jack a quick kiss on the cheek. "It was nice to meet you, Violet." She placed Nala back in her carrier and motioned to her guard. They walked to the elevator.

"I'll see you out," Jack said, hurrying after them. He turned his head to Violet, who stood motionless. "Stay there."

He slipped into the elevator as Tivra pressed the button for the bottom floor. When the doors shut, she sighed deeply and clenched her manicured fists. "That girl is *not* okay."

"She's not."

"Something is off about her."

"She…" The elevator descended fast. There wasn't enough time. "She's been through it. We all have. I'm working on it."

"No…Jack." Tivra grasped his arm, worry in her eyes. "She's not *there*. I see a dead girl. I *don't* see the girl who stormed that stage, and with every emotion, sliced her hand. But that girl isn't there anymore. Whoever stood there…something is wrong."

Everything is wrong with Violet, but Jack was entirely helpless to it. They nearly reached the bottom floor. "I'm so good at everything, but I'm failing, Tivra. I can't…I can't help her."

The elevator dinged. The doors opened. Her guard stepped out. Tivra lingered.

"You don't have to be the best, Jack." She stroked his cheek. "You only have to give your best."

With that, Tivra's heels clacked away, and the doors shut. The elevator didn't move. Jack sagged to the wall, squeezing his eyes closed. Cyran had tortured Violet twice more in the span of twenty-four hours. She was as empty as Tivra claimed, yet Jack convinced himself not to see it. After minutes alone in the small box, he pressed the button to go back to the top floor.

When the doors opened, Lucien stood in full gear. "It's time."

"Now?"

Lucien gestured to the plascreen, where a concealed camera from one of his spies caught the tanks rolling to the marked points along the walls. "Arvalo put a halt on all trade. The city has been ordered into lockdown. All officials have been called to the Government Sector." Lucien sighed and closed his eyes. "It's a trap, Jack. You can't believe the spawn."

"It needs to happen anyway." Jack rolled his shoulders. "Ashan, get me my clothes."

Ten minutes later, Jack stood in front of his brother, dressed in fighting clothes. Jelan lingered behind Lucien, dressed similarly. Jack didn't necessarily enjoy seeing them in close proximity after witnessing whatever the fuck happened between her and Luka, but he didn't care enough to give it any further thought. It was a minuscule issue. Otherwise, he liked Violet's old friend. Ashan wrestled Mai from one of the guest rooms in the far back where she's been staying. She met Jack's gaze and flinched.

"Save it," he commanded.

"Are you going to kill my father?"

Jack gave her a lazy look. "Do you want me to?"

Her nostrils flared. "Yes."

"Say it like you mean it, little Arvalo."

"I want him dead." She lifted her chin, eyes dark. "I want him gone for good."

"So be it." Jack fixed his glove and turned to the balcony.

"Two minutes," Lucien said. "Lyla's ready with her fighters. The minute you chop his head off, they'll kill each of the Redders at the walls. If you fail, we will do it anyway."

"There's no failing this time," Jack said, walking to the balcony door. He slid it open.

Rio's head perked up. Anaya took a long drag of her smoke, blowing it toward him. "You're going?"

"Yes."

Violet was a tiny ball on the patio couch between them. No amount of guards could match the protection they had for Violet, nor the trust Jack had for them. He knelt before her, stroking her cheek gently. Her eyes remained shut. She passed out in spurts. Her body could barely handle the parasite.

"I will win," Jack whispered against the wisps of her eyelashes. "And when I do, I will bend this cruel world to your favor."

Three words hovered on his lips, but he pressed them together, refusing to say it. Those words were fractured at the moment, and they meant nothing. "Keep her close. No one leaves the penthouse. This will be over by the time the sun rises." It was nearly midnight at this point. The city glistened around them. Jack sucked in a deep breath and stood.

Jack's pride was there, but it was dulled. This wasn't for his gain or to prove to the world that he was the best. That he could conquer the country that took it all away from him. He left those dreams in Pride. He abandoned the idea of ego in the strive for being the *only* one who could ever challenge Cyran and win. Arvalo was a minimal player. There was a war coming, and Jack needed this city in his hands to best protect it.

To protect what the walls stood for.

To protect those he loved.

His gaze flicked to Violet. Rio draped a blanket over her and stood. His tired eyes lifted. "Do it, Jack. Finish your dream."

And with that, Lucien pulled Mai with him and tied her hands behind her back. A blindfold went over her eyes. She pouted, a slight shake in her limbs, but she remained quiet.

They headed out, but a gaze burned into his neck. He turned, and just as the elevator doors closed, he caught Violet's shining blue eyes. A glimpse of her in them.

The doors shut. The elevator descended.

They piled into multiple cars. They drove to the bridge. Redders brought their guns up. Cameras focused on Jack. He turned to Mai, ice slithering into him as he prepared every muscle for this. "You ready?"

"Don't be gentle," she growled, deep and low.

Jack wrapped his fist in her bindings and yanked her close. He pulled out his plasgun, clocked it, and pressed it to her temple. "Don't need to tell me twice."

They exited the car, and the minute the nearest Redders caught sight of his threat to Mai, a commander yelled, "Halt your weapons! Eyes on the Emperor's daughter!"

Jack knew the barrel was bruising on her temple. He tugged Mai close, roaring to the Redders, "You will not lay a single hand on my comrades. You will let us pass this bridge and let me challenge the Emperor to a death combat vying for the Throne of Veceras. If not"—Jack pointed the plasgun to the pavement right before the bridge and fired. Stone buffeted up. Dust swirled. He placed the barrel back on Mai's cheek—"his only daughter dies."

He held his breath. A government official appeared behind the horde of Redders with his hand raised in a signal. His other hand rested on the com at his ear. He waited. They all did.

Then a cold voice slithered through the silence.

"Let him in."

Jack could hear the smile in Arvalo's voice.

"I accept your challenge, Jack Marin."

46

The Final Fight

The Emperor's Circle was an ancient battleground. Located in the Government Sector, surrounded by pristine white buildings and the looming wall a way away, a dried, dirt courtyard untouched by any except those who fight and kill, spread before her. Columns of metal and stone towered with stark white plaslights. Veceras's emblem hung on flags all around.

Jelan wore Jack's gardia insignia proudly, standing to the left of Lucien who continued to suck in sharp breaths and failed to exhale properly. Lyla scowled to Lucien's right, Cairo to the right of her, and then beyond a gold rope and mill of Redders, the Arvalo family gathered. Rivals. Yet Jelan couldn't help spare a glance to the family—Mai, who was fussed over by servants, Luka, who stood rigid and glaring at the Circle, and Park, who clearly had quite a few drinks.

Bael, unfortunately, couldn't make it, as his body lay with the acid algae at the bottom of the Trollova River. Jelan absently rubbed her neck, hating the memory of his hands around it.

Delighted, though, in the memory of his body collapsing, and Luka's unremorseful gaze staying only on her.

The rest of the City Commanders and other Empire officials crowded another stand. Alexia had her signature glass of red wine, clearly on edge by the way she gripped it, while Covokai talked into her ear. She nodded absently.

"It's time," Lucien said, jutting his chin to the Circle.

Jelan steeled her spine and turned her gaze to the desolate stretch of land. The wind blew, bringing the scent of mud and old blood. Redders formed a perimeter—the Circle itself—and would prevent either Jack or Arvalo from ever leaving it until one lay dead.

"Are you okay?" Jelan muttered to Lucien, not daring to look at him.

"Fine."

"Fine…" Jelan let the word roll between her teeth and lip. "Just another day, right?"

His grunt was the lone answer.

She cringed. Things were…butchered between Lucien and her. Ever since she arrived back from Luka's clutches after her father was admitted to rehab and Jack's name reappeared on the Sins Screen, Lucien became distant. Not with just her, everyone, for the most part. A wall stacked over his emotions, and he hid behind it, fortifying it with clipped words and passing glances. She accepted it, but she couldn't help but feel he knew about Luka. She didn't trust Jack to keep his word, not that she even deserved the secrecy, either.

Redders parted at opposite ends of the Circle. From beneath the stands, Jack and Arvalo sauntered out, dressed in only what was archaically allowed: a long-sleeve black shirt, pants, and leather boots. They were provided with one plasma weapon of choice that was updated to the era: a blade or an axe. Jelan thought guns would be a lot less messy, but Veceras was a bloody country, and from the history of battles within the Emperor's Circle, people liked a true fight.

Jack's curls tussled in the breeze. He lifted his chin as he passed between the Redders and into the Circle. He clutched the plasblade hilt and activated the heat. It simmered green. Lucien exhaled another uneven breath.

Arvalo hesitated outside of it. Stared at Jack and his weapon, then at the stands. A look of unease crossed his face, but he righted himself and stepped through. A cruel smile pulled. "You're looking well for traversing seven sins."

"That's flattering," Jack said, humorless. "I made sure I got my beauty sleep."

"You broke the curse and yet you want to fight me when you can have all of the grandeur in the world?"

"The Sins weren't my dream." Jack cocked his head. The Redders closed the Circle. They slowly walked around each other. Arvalo produced his plasblade and it gleamed red. "My dream was to kill you."

"Flattering," Arvalo mocked. "I was hoping you'd stay dead."

"You and a massive amount of other people, but I always liked to prove others wrong."

Their taunting slashed tension through the space. Jelan had no doubt Jack was going to win, but her gut gnawed, flipped, and alerted her to something else. She couldn't quite put a finger on it.

Arvalo willingly accepted Jack's request for battle, as if he… knew. Knew his demise was to come. But while they flashed their weapons, Jelan's eyes lifted beyond the Circle. Searching. She didn't know what for; a trick up Arvalo's sleeve? She glanced to the surrounding rooftops—would Arvalo dare disrupt the centuries-old law by sniping Jack? No, he wouldn't. The Empire had people in place to manage this, and they only abided by the written law, not any word from any Emperor.

Her gaze flicked to the wall. She narrowed her eyes, tracking any movement—

Arvalo launched himself at Jack, swinging. Their blades met in a flash of red and green plasma. She fixed her gaze on them, hardly blinking as they both danced around each other, moving quickly, like blurs. Jack's jaw clenched as Arvalo revealed himself to be a competent opponent. She wondered if Jack would cheat, technically, by using his bestowed powers.

Arvalo dipped under Jack's blade and managed to slice Jack's arm. Jack hissed, but a smile formed. Lucien flinched next to her.

"Oof, you managed to touch me. A round of applause for that—"

Arvalo snarled at Jack's teasing and lunged again, swinging on the offensive. Jack parried with ease. Arvalo's voice was dark, "You're nothing but a rat from the streets, living next to trash with your brother. Who are you to think you can equal me? Equal an Emperor? You might have made history by beating the Sins, but I'm sure that was pure luck from the *real* ruler."

Jack paused. His face fell. Jelan's heart thumped. *Real* ruler. Arvalo smiled and took advantage, arcing his blade to Jack's face—

Jack's hand grabbed the weapon, plasma and all.

Jelan's gasp filled the space, along with a few others. Jack was touching…straight *plasma*. Her hands burned, phantomlike from long ago.

"I was going to give you some leisure time for our audience, but now I'm mad." Jack wrenched the plasblade from Arvalo and chucked it past the Redder's perimeter. Jelan's eyes bugged. She couldn't believe it. Arvalo paled ten shades, gaze on Jack's blistering hand, but Jack seemed entirely unbothered.

"You…" Arvalo shook his head.

Jack wove his weapon and sliced one of Arvalo's hands off. "For every girl you touched, and then for all the times you thrust your daughter into the arms of despicable men."

A glance at Mai. Tears streamed down her face. Luka's hand lightly brushed his sister's back, comforting.

Arvalo choked on his cry, unbelieving. Jack amputated Arvalo's leg at the knee. It burned with a gagging crunch. Arvalo wobbled on his still-good leg. His wail bit air.

Jack seethed, "For every lesser person you've kicked down to secure your evil role."

Arvalo's other arm thumped the dirt.

"For those you've killed both by your own hand and by proxy."

The searing, bloodied slash at Arvalo's last limb. "And for ever stepping foot into my life, turning me over, ruining this country, and because I think you're ugly."

Arvalo collapsed to the ground, mouth hung open, face plastered in shock. Blood spurted from each of his limbs. The crowd stayed quiet.

"You—you—"

"*Me*," Jack snarled a dangerous, primal smile. Jack lifted his chin, his arms to the crowd around them. His gaze found the video camera displaying this live to the city. "My name is Jack Shayan Marin, and I was born on the coast of Veceras to Sima and Roman Marin."

Lucien grappled for the railing, squeezing it so hard his knuckles whitened. Lucien's brown eyes were warm and shiny as they gazed upon his younger brother. She was too stunned. She had no idea...

"I was six when my home was annihilated by this very Empire. I was seven when my mother died from childbirth while we lived as slaves at the Port of Fenpor. I was thirteen when a Redder whipped my little sister to death. I was eighteen when I killed Theo and became City Commander of Trade. I was twenty-five when I went into the Sins."

Jack pointed the tip of his plasblade into Arvalo's neck.

"And I was twenty-six when I killed you and became Emperor of Veceras."

A gurgled cry escaped from Arvalo as Jack pushed the blade in, stabbing it into the ground, and watched as the heat melted Arvalo's skin, shredding itself at the neck. The old Emperor's face withered away. Jack bent down, fisted Arvalo's hair, and with inhuman strength, decapitated him.

Silence descended.

Jelan held her breath. Lucien's knuckles gripped the railing. He turned, hurdling himself down the stairs and near the brim of the circle where Jack dropped the head of Arvalo and ran to him. An emotional conversation erupted, surrounded by the cheers of the Empire, and the cries of praise. Even Park lazily clapped.

"I now present you, newly crowned Emperor of Veceras, Jack Marin!"

Jack's roar of victory filled her chest. Tears sprang. She turned, glancing across the rivalry barrier and locking eyes with Luka. The corner of his mouth pulled, and with a hand still resting on Mai's shoulder, he inclined his head.

Good game.

She flicked her gaze back and her breath halted. Lucien stared at her. Then Luka. Between them. His lips pulled into a frown. His mouth opened, turned, but Jack's eyes caught on something—someone—beneath the stands.

Jelan bent over, searching…

Rio appeared, utterly distraught. Rage tore across Jack's face. He prowled to Rio, snarling words Jelan couldn't hear amid the clamor.

High above the history, a blip of black caught her eye. It ran along the wall—not a person, but a drone. Against the rising sun, it flashed green. A signal.

"No!" she screamed.

But the same flash she'd protected with her shield months ago in the Aariva, now occurred in full. She wasn't there to stop it. It grew brighter than the birthing sun atop the wall, blinding her. The crowd screamed. Jack whirled.

The boom smacked into her ears. She cried, covering them. The ground shook. Beyond her watery gaze, she watched the wall surrounding the Government Sector surrender to the plasbombs. Sand-colored rock tumbled in the eerie, history-altering night. And they all watched. Watched with gaping mouths and shattered hearts, as their protection, their cage, their reckoning deteriorated.

Jack Marin won.

But the Citadel of Calesal still fell.

47

Emperor

Blood, wet and thick, slid down his cheek as he rose.

Jack dropped his plasblade to the floor, turned to the stands, and roared a victory cry.

The crowd's screams of triumph shook the earth and his bones.

A smile tore at his face, one that crushed his eyes and lifted his soul. This, *this* was what he had been fighting for all this time. Tears burned.

He turned toward his brother, who barreled his way down from the stands and onto the dirt. His face was swathed with emotion, a dream that was now achieved. One they whispered about in the alleys, along the streets, homeless and hoping.

Jack tossed Arvalo's head to the ground and ran to his brother. "This is for her." *For Lily.* "This is all for her."

"She is looking down on us now." Lucien buried his head in Jack's neck. "You did it, brother. They would be so proud of you."

Jack pulled back and took in Lucien's brown eyes. "They are proud of you, too. I know it." Tears slid down Jack's face. "Now we show them a better world."

Jack turned to the rest of his cadre in the stands. Lyla, Cairo, Jelan, and Rio—

He halted as he took in Rio's expression, so different from the beaming smiles on everyone else. Jack's own grin faltered. He shook his head in disbelief as Rio's frown deepened.

His breath was a whisper, "Where is she?"

Rio's face twisted with grief. "I failed," Rio said.

"Where *is* she," Jack growled. Lucien attempted to hold him back, but Jack stomped through the dirt and disassembled Redders, blood boiling.

"Gone," sobbed Rio. "She's gone, Jack. She went back. I tried—I *tried* to stop it, but she was screaming and crying. She teleported us to the South and she just ran. Ran and ran until she got to the Square and then she vanished." Rio's breath shuddered. "From this world."

Jack's chest contracted, tightened, and he brought a hand to the center of it where some invisible blade pierced. "No." His eyes flicked up. "*No.*"

A scream. Jelan's scream. She pointed from the stands. The ground shook. He whirled.

The wall behind the Government Sector came crumbling down. Arvalo's final act.

And Jack Marin fell to his knees before the city he had dreamed of conquering. This moment had flashed in his head a thousand times. But the elation he thought he would feel, the pride, the splendor of knowing he could finally change things, improve them, abolish the slavery on the coasts, and simply help this country that had never helped him, wasn't there. The wall crumbled, their cage opened to disastrous opportunities, and Jack still failed.

His heart broke. Fractured within his chest. That wretched thing he had spent so long protecting shattered into pieces. His world slowed. People screamed. Ran. The bombs continued, but stopped before the Trollova River. Dust plumed, and then silence.

A heavy item was placed on his head.

His diadem. The Emperor's crown.

But as the crowd roared his name, cheered for a better world, his mind slowly shut down. Numbed to that horrific pain gripping him.

He failed.

The wall came down.

And she was…
Gone.
She's gone.
And Jack realized that no dream mattered if the ones you love aren't there for it. Or maybe, after their journey, this dream had changed entirely.

A dream who was gone.

48

SOUTHER

VIOLET DIDN'T FEEL THINGS ANYMORE. Her vision hazed, her breaths rattled in her lungs, and her ears screeched at random times. It took an effort to keep her head up—it's why she preferred to spend most of her time horizontal, slowly decaying on the patio couch while she blankly stared toward the South. To distract from the emptiness, she mapped the South's streets in her head. She ran them. She breathed in the smoke and oil and piss. She held a dusty, unmarked bottle of shiva in her hand. A smoke lingered in the other. And even when she would pass out on rooftops with her arm as a pillow, it was a better escape than her current reality. She stared and stared, her heart a feeble beat as it yearned for a hollow simplicity that weaved like a dream.

She was so desperate for the chaotic sense of freedom that a couple times before, she found herself jolting up, opening her mouth, ready to drink and sit in Souther's Square to watch her brother's tracker. Delusional. It took effort to remember that he was back in this world—her, too. None of it felt real. She merely existed.

And it was a pathetic existence.

The heartbeat of Pride drummed next to the patter of her actual one. Every now and then, she'd sink more into herself and imagine that adrenaline-filled power slumbered below in a ball. She poked it. It would flare. Some energy would push, cooing in response.

Her vision cleared and her mind would crystalize. A weak attempt at keeping her alive, but prodding the immortal, godly ability within helped her pass the time. It would give her just enough energy to use the bathroom or eat a bite of toast.

The flare happened enough for her to creep to the elevator and watch Jack leave for his fight in the Emperor's Circle. She wanted to race to him—to give him a proper send-off, but her knees ached at the act of standing. She caught his eye and hoped that he saw her true well wishes.

Anaya hummed next to her. Meema was upstairs, asleep. Few lingered in the penthouse. Rio tore himself from the sliding door. He refused to step in—they'd already replaced the handle to the door four times since he would fracture it.

They quickly realized the unnatural abilities Cyran pumped him with were muddled and diluted. He couldn't crush things as harshly as Jack could. His Harmas hardening would only appear if he were about to ram his knee into something or scrape a knuckle, but otherwise, Rio was Rio. He yearned to see his family, but Lucien confirmed that a swarm of incognito Redders lingered around Rio's home and followed his siblings, even once harassing his mother. He cried about it for a while, but he would join Violet and they would silently stare at their wild home, wishing for the ease of what it once provided.

"Do you want to watch—" Rio started.

"No," Anaya answered, picking something out of her teeth.

Violet silently agreed.

Rio sighed and padded over to the railing. He clenched his fists. "I hate being cooped up here."

"How many guards?" Anaya asked.

"Four. Bronto is here."

Violet reached inside and poked that power. She sat up, groaning. "I want to leave."

"We can't—"

"I'm going to leave." She poked that power again, tasting shiva on her lips. "I need to see my brother on the Sins Screen."

"He's not…" Rio's brows crumpled. "He's in the hospital. He hasn't woken up. Jack said it was too dangerous."

"He's here, Vi," Anaya said.

Blackness scoured her vision. The air, the smell. She needed to see her brother—

She remembered his blood. The spear going through it. *Feel it. Feel for home.* But this wasn't home. She avoided their concerned gazes and turned to the balcony door, "I'm going to the bathroom."

Eyes burned her back as she struggled to slide the door open, but with a heave, it budged enough to fit her foreign body though. Her bones cracked as she walked through the kitchen and into the foyer. Bronto looked up from his newspaper and watched her carefully.

"Going somewhere?" Bronto asked.

"Bathroom."

He huffed.

She continued, and when she reached the tiled room, she shut the door without locking it. Then she slid to the floor and rested her head against the wall. The lights remained off. She didn't want to see the four walls enclosing her and bring panic, but her heart still beat at the fear involuntarily, picking up to a deadly pace. She knew she was dying. She could feel every bit of energy leeching from her, the most fading when Cyran burned her beneath skin. She buried her head into her knees, hating the enclosure. The trap. The idea of this whole fucking place.

This world thought she was something to celebrate. Violet dragged the beanie down farther. She squeezed her eyes shut, her mouth twisting into a sob. This penthouse suffocated her, closing in and in and in.

But Jack said to stay. He told her she couldn't leave…

Violet couldn't breathe. Her chest moved quickly. Her pulse pounded in her ears. She poked at her power. It flared in response, a bit brighter than before.

A soft knock. The handle moved.

Rio and Anaya poked their heads in. Rio turned to Anaya, "See, I told you she didn't need to go. She hardly drinks water."

"I need to get out of here," Violet whispered into her knees. "Get me *out* of here. It's…I can't breathe." She panicked, gripping her chest. "I can't…I can't…I have to…" She lifted her head; black, ink, nothing. She couldn't see her friends. There was a brief flare of light in the room. A gasp sounded. Her clamors for air roared in her ears. Heat flared. No… No….

"No,"she said. The fire blazed. He was in Pride. He was lighting a bomb. He was laughing. Roaring. Beckoning her. Mocking her. She wasn't in the bathroom anymore. She was alone in the darkness, with a brief speck of light sparkling.

The fire grew hotter. Her lungs burned. From a distance, she heard her panicked pleas for relief. Hands met her skin and she flinched. The darkness continued to swarm.

That light seared in the distance.

She couldn't breathe.

In desperation, she ran for the glow. Someone yelled her name. She reached out—it was a tether. She needed to escape his torture. Fire burned at her heels. She ran. Ran and ran and reached for that tether—for something that could comfort her, for whatever would protect her. She yanked.

Two hands latched onto her ankles at the last moment. A siren shrieked. Violet's power ignited. Familiar air slammed into her. Bare feet met dusty cobblestones. She opened her eyes to reality and not the darkness. Her beanie slid off and her scalp warmed under the glistening, bright plaslights of a South street. Tapestries hung above, bottles clinked, Southers moved, solemn-faced and infrequent. Smoke cloyed the air. Children rushed across the street, playing with empty glass bottles and deflated balls. Drunks stumbled.

Home.

A smile breached her face, bright and wide. She stumbled forward. She needed to see her brother. She could run. She was always good at running.

Arms enclosed her waist.

"Violet! No! We have to go back," Rio panicked, pulling at her. Anaya bristled, shocked by the street and the growing crowd.

But Violet ripped his sweaty hands off her. Tepid pavement filled her soles. Light flared at her feet. Fire warmed her core—no, no, no. He was coming. She needed to see her brother first. She pushed against Rio, growling, "Let me *go*."

She burst free and Violet Sutton ran. Her hair flew behind her, duo-toned and foreign to this world, but the smile didn't stop.

Suddenly, Violet was a small child, barefoot and bright-eyed with missing teeth and whirling through the crowd while other children yapped at her heels. She was always the fastest. She could race many streets and never tire. The others couldn't keep up with her. She veered around the drunks, the broken glass, the smoke clouds and piss puddles. People waved to her from their stoops. Others stared through dusty windows. Violet was a child again— back home where she belonged.

She laughed loudly and looked over her shoulder. Rio and Anaya sprinted after her. Her friends—this was so fun. They were chasing her. But she was faster.

She needed to see her brother.

The past and present meshed together. Every year she spent dashing these streets rolled through her mind. Violet, age ten, after stealing smokes for Meema with angry shop owners waving their crowbars and bats. Violet, age fifteen, losing Reed in the crowd when he caught her kissing someone. Violet, age seventeen, when she heard the devastating news that Reed was sentenced to the Sins.

Violet, age twenty, the Sin Savior who completed the game and helped break the curse. She tore down the same street she did all those different times, until each memory bled into one, and she became the wild, wicked mess she always was. She shoved Southers out of the way, sucking her home's air into her lungs. The dried tip of a fountain gleamed like a beacon. Reed was sentenced to the Sins. Agony speared through her. Her memory whiplashed, and now she was running from the torturous fire splayed by Cyran. Back to another memory—sitting at the fountain with Jelan, nearly drinking herself silly while they watched the Screen.

While Reed's name flashed with a red dot.

A different memory. She clasped her chest, heart thrashing within. Both hearts. Horror flooded through her. Was he okay? Reed—Reed. He left her. She was all alone on these streets. She continued to run. Familiar voices screeched behind her. Redders caught sight of her. They sprinted, flicking their whips against the dusty stone.

Reed was in danger. She needed to see. She needed her family back. She needed peace. She needed to leave this never-ending darkness and reach the light.

Her legs pumped and the wind coursed through her hair. The fountain drew closer, and Violet squinted her eyes at the blinding, giant plascreen hugging multiple buildings. She vaulted over children and darted through the mess of Souther's Square. People yelled. Pointed. She didn't care.

She needed Reed.

She drew close enough to see the names, and she desperately searched the sixth column. His name wasn't there. She slowed— she knew she couldn't slow, because if she stopped running, the fire and darkness would reach her.

Her eyes flicked. Her skin grew hotter. A pained gasp left her lips and she fell to her knees, scraping them. She couldn't find Reed's name. Her vision turned red. She could hear the monster's call.

Where was her brother? He would know what to do. He could save her—

Her vision erupted into flames. A scream tore from her throat. No—*no*—he found her. He was going to hurt her—

The light was blinding. Her throat scratched on her cries. She reached toward that screen, toward a bit of hope, but the darkness and the fire and the light and the pain consumed her. Her power thinly flared, called by another. All those tethers flashed before her eyes.

A voice yelled.

"Violet! Violet!" Rio. Anaya. She turned. She couldn't see anything. Only the tethers. One shined the brightest. She glimpsed a familiar world within—one of limestone and salt. It beat hard in her chest.

But it hurt. It burned. She was on fire. She was going to die.

Take it.

Gray hair showed within that tether.

Grab it.

Another explosion of fire withered her body, cracking bones and boiling her blood, and at her last scream, out of desperation, she grabbed that blue tether. She needed to save it. She needed hope. She needed to be free of all this darkness and pain. She needed to find her brother.

She tugged it.

And shot toward another world.

The moment she slammed on a pile of harsh glass-like salt, she was shifting in and out of consciousness. Arms were pulled behind her back. A cold patch met her neck. It slithered down her spine, lulling her into the darkness. Her jaw was grabbed. Fingers stroked her cheek.

"You fought it longer than I expected, little one," a cold voice said. "You can rest now."

Rest. Yes, she would love that. The fire stopped and the cold patch swarmed her nerves. Arms picked her up. She blinked through blurring vision to stare up at black, mono-lid eyes, dark hair, and a scar that slashed across a pale cheek. Onyx lightning surrounded him.

That cold voice, which promised rest, said once more,

"Take her to Eterna."

49

MONSTER

LIQUID STREAMED DOWN VIOLET'S THROAT. It tickled the back and she choked, gagging. Her eyes burst open. She leaned over the edge of a cold metal table and heaved. Her vomit slapped a pair of boots.

"You'll need to keep that down if you want to recover faster."

Hair plastered to her sweaty face, Violet's eyes lifted. A male medic stood over her, half a bottle of green liquid in his hand, the other holding a capped syringe. "It works better if you swallow it, but if you vomit again, I'll be forced to inject it. Burns more that way, unfortunately." His features formed an aggravated expression. "And I'm sure you don't want any more burning sensations after what His Master did to you."

"Did…to me…" Her voice was a mere rasp. She swiped her hair from her face, barely catching the hint of platinum. Her eyes flickered around the room—but there was no tell of where she was. It was a windowless examination room. Four gray walls, a table, chains hanging from above, and Zavar leaning against the doorjamb, blocking her only escape. Black tendrils hung over his half-lidded gaze that stared intensely. His arms were crossed.

She touched her forehead.

So, she did it.

She went back to Cyran.

Her recent memories were a complete blur. She cuddled with Jack in a bed a few times, and then the Calesal wind on her face… then the firestorm beneath her skin…then…

Running.

Running through the South.

She covered her mouth. Tears welled in her eyes. Her gaze snapped to Zavar, who was still as stone, then to a medic.

She lunged. The medic yelped. She tackled him and snatched the syringe. Lightning scoured her skin and nausea slammed into her. A hand wrapped her hair, yanking harshly. Zavar appeared above, looking bored.

"That was stupid—"

Violet jammed the syringe of cayna into her thigh. Zavar's mouth thinned. He shoved her back to the ground as a great, cold fire burst from the prick. She gasped on her breath, whining as she clutched her leg desperately. It was going to fall off—she was convinced of it. It burned and burned. She ground her teeth together and moaned through the onslaught. The medic rolled from under her, hurrying out the door. Zavar stepped in front of him, brow raised. "Fucking try me—"

The cayna worked. Energy blasted through her veins and Violet pounced for the Vaelaur. He dodged with a teasing smile. She rose, but lightning smacked and she doubled over, vomiting. Blood mixed with it. She coughed, heaving, as boots strutted toward her and Zavar grabbed her by the arm. "Since you wanted to speed up the process, His Master awaits you."

"No." She tugged away, but Zavar maintained a firm grip. She fought the entire time he dragged her out. She was only dressed in a short-sleeve slip, bare feet snagging on the tile. This world was not Greed—she racked her brain. She knew they mentioned it. Knew that Cyran didn't base his home out of the Twin Cities— which were now destroyed, regardless, because of her. She whipped her head, but it was a long, windless hallway. They had to be underground.

She tried to kick at Zavar's ankles, but he merely stepped out of reach, as if anticipating her moves. She snarled. He laughed. "It's like a wild cat. Untamed, but predictable." A flicker crossed his gaze as he stared at her down his nose. "That's about to change."

She tried to reach for that power, but an empty, gaping hole filled her chest. She thought the well was endless, but now it was capped and sealed. She couldn't reach it. A drug, perhaps. Something that subdued her to human.

Zavar seemed to follow her thoughts. "Your abilities are there, but you nearly exhausted them when you vanished to Pride. They'll remain invisible until their host gets her energy back. Your powers don't exist at your beck and call." His grip was going to leave bruises. "It protects, assists, but if the host abuses it like you did the last two weeks, it goes away. There's no leaving here, Sutton."

She slowly stopped struggling and instead found footing. Zavar didn't let her go as she walked next to him. She searched his person, but no secret weapon sprouted. With that deadly lightning, most weapons were probably just for show.

They turned to a different room. Little else gave way to her situation—a sitting room of red and gray, filled with a carpet and a roaring fire. Cyran glanced up from a book, icy gray eyes narrowing on her.

Violet knew she wasn't going to permanently escape the man in this lifetime, but gazing at his gray hair, the scars along his neck, the faded burns at his knuckles, and the manicured suit he put on, she didn't think she'd return this soon. She didn't think she'd drag *herself* here, whether it was through life-threatening desperation or not. He twirled a glass of dark liquid in his hand. A plastablet flashed on the desk. She couldn't see its contents.

"You're awake." Cyran's eyes drifted over her. "And energized."

"Fuck you," she growled. "You tricked me."

"You were dying, Violet Sutton. By the time you came to me, you might have had twenty-four hours left. You saved yourself; you and your abilities, that is." A lifted brow. "Or else you would have only breathed long enough to see your lover sit on his newly acquired throne."

She stopped breathing. Jack. *Jack.* She shook her head. "He won?"

Cyran gave her an incredulous look. "Of course, he won. What specimen like him doesn't win?"

She closed her mouth.

"I created the man who now sits as the Emperor of Veceras."

Zavar released her arm and sidled to the side.

"I built his physicality. He was too strong mentally to ever break in the way I wanted him to. But I am the sole reason he has the throne. He delivered quite a…Droanian blow at the end, didn't he?"

Violet's eyes fell.

"No, you didn't watch. You didn't care. You were hurting, and you wanted peace. You ran through that city like it might offer you something—but the Original City doesn't offer anything." He brought the cup up to his lips and sipped deeply. Its contents looked like blood. "It doesn't save. One must give to receive something in return. Emperor Jack Marin gave up his lover to get his dream—power."

Her mouth twisted. "No."

Cyran stood from the armchair and placed the cup gently on the side table. He gracefully walked to her. His polished boots filled her vision. Cold hands grabbed her chin and yanked it up.

"Veceras gets one Celeste, and I get another." A satisfied smile played on his face. "Now, how about we stop wasting time?"

Her brows crumpled.

"Bring him in," he said, eyes still boring into hers. Zavar bowed in her peripheral and vanished, returning a second later with a limp man—a Vanisher by the glance of his Fringe headband. The Vanisher dropped to his knees in respect.

Cyran stroked her cheek with his scarred thumb. "I am going to break you." A horrifying shiver slithered down her spine. "Then I am going to mold you. You are mine now, Violet Sutton. There is no escaping. Your abilities, your person, *everything* is mine. A Manipulator. One of a strong bloodline." His devilish smirk grew. "You will forget every bit of your being for the new person I will make you into. Because you are *weak*."

The slap came hard and fast. He backhanded her into the ground. Her jaw rattled. Pain flared across her nose.

Violet clutched her throbbing cheek. Tears sprung in her eyes. Cyran stepped up to the long desk and she noticed the simplistic black box that lay there. He opened it.

The Bloodswearing Blade.

No, not the one from Calesal. Instead of the night incarnate blade that slashed the hands of candidates, this one was pure white. Both the metal and the hilt. Ancient. She shivered before it, haunted by its bleaching glare. Internal fear roiled inside her and she scrambled up, then back, hating it. Frightful of it.

Zavar shoved her to her knees. "Don't worry, you'll get used to it," he said as if it were routine.

"Make it quick," Cyran ordered.

Zavar strutted to the white blade and, with a slight tremor in his hand, picked it up. He seemed…adverse to the object, as well. The retrieved Vanisher lifted his gaze from next to her, and the moment his eyes locked on the weapon, he paled tenfold. "No."

It drew an intrinsic dread from every person in the room—except Cyran. She didn't need to guess that there were evil properties at work.

"Your time with the Fringe has come to an end," Zavar said boringly. "Thanks—ah, whatever. I don't care enough."

He stabbed the blade into the heart of the Vanisher.

A soft, silver glow emitted beneath the Vanisher's skin. It traveled along his veins, pulsing with his fretful heartbeat, until his filigree lines formed. Then slowly, they began to fade from the tips of his fingers, the slashes under his eyes, the soles of his feet, as if the blade sucked the very power from him. His cheeks suddenly hollowed. His lips purpled. *Life* was leeched. It simmered through his blood until it all piled into the dagger, absorbing his luminous silver glow. Zavar yanked it out.

The Vanisher collapsed. Blood welled at the wound over his chest. The blade continued to glimmer. Violet wrenched herself away from it, eyes bugging and pulse roaring.

Cyran stepped to her and shoved his hands in her hair, forcing her down. "You'll take it, because this is the only way to feed the monster."

Zavar's gaze displayed no mercy as he shoved that dagger into *her* heart.

It embedded smoothly, slipping past the bones of her ribs. The light brought warmth—a soft, sparkling hug that shot underneath her skin and dragged a gasp from her lips. Substance filled her. Breath came easier. The constant blur of her vision cleared. The power flowed and poured into the empty well of her own, adding to it.

"This is how you sustain your control." Cyran petted the platinum side of her hair. "It lasts for a month." A dark smile. "For one world."

Her jaw dropped. So *this* was how Cyran stayed alive instead of succumbing to the parasitic power.

"Now, young one, as long as you hold onto Pride, you will live as long as the planet does."

And that was how he remained immortal. Unkillable.

A god.

Once the stolen power simmered from the blade and into her, Zavar pulled it out. Violet groaned, falling to her hands as her blood dripped onto the hardwood. A soft tingle skittered where the blade had pierced, and when she looked down, she noticed a golden light closing over it.

"The Dusk Blade heals after it gives," Cyran said. "It destroys after it takes."

Violet's lip wobbled as she glanced at the nearly decayed Vanisher. Numbness overtook her morals, protecting what was left to break. His life ended for a month of boosted energy. To sustain something she mistakenly took in the first place.

"And that golden light? That will aid you." Cyran's finger tapped her spine. "It will heal you like it does your lover. However, it will not be as powerful compared to a true Giver celeste. But since you hold the earthly aether of one of the Mezcla planet systems, you will be able to heal in fractions your other abilities couldn't. Now, take her."

Zavar's warm hands yanked her up and jerked her back into the hallway. Her head hung low. Blood sluiced out of her nostrils. Her toes dragged, but Zavar only offered a scoff. Another room.

"Ready?" he called. Violet looked up blearily. Two men managed a control system before a glass-paned window. It faced a room with thick stone walls, but two walls looked awfully bigger than the rest. She turned, confused, but Cyran soon entered and slammed the door.

"Place her."

Zavar carried her into the stone room and dropped her on the floor. She scooted away from him immediately, hand rising to caress her chest. He merely turned his back and walked out, shutting the door to the control room.

Small. Small. Small.

The room glared at her.

"Begin," came Cyran's cold voice through a speaker.

The room shuddered. Stone scraped against stone, and to her horror, the two thicker walls began to move. Inward.

She crawled to the center, panic gripping her throat. Her breaths stopped. Her hair a mess around her face, creating a curtain as she glimpsed the impending crush of rock. The scuffle bounced around her skull. Her mouth twisted as a desperate sob left. No escape. No relief. The walls drew closer, looming. Crushing.

"No!" she cried, throat tearing. "Stop it—stop it!"

Fear—pure, unrelenting fear—washed over her, and she lunged for one wall, pushing on it to halt it. To stop. Her muscles strained as she dug her heels into the ground, but strength evaded her. They continued, and so she slid with them, until she cast a glance over her shoulder and noticed the other wall was less than her body length away.

She struck out her hand against it. Screamed as the walls pressed in on her elbows, grinding her bones. Her wails bounced. Her elbows gave away. She sank to her knees, another cry clawing. "Stop! *Stop! Please!*" Twisting her body, she planted her feet on one wall, back on another and pushed with all her might, but they still shifted together, bending her knees into her chest until she was forced to drop to the floor. One flattened her cheek, the other her shoulder, unyielding—

The groaning stopped.

There was no relief. Not as they towered and left little room to even expand her chest in a fearful breath. Her mouth opened, soft whimpers mixed with the tears sliding down her face.

Loud groaning signaled the walls' shifting. She dropped into a fetal position the moment they birthed enough room. The rumbling snuffed up sound as they retreated to their original position. The metal door opened.

"Get up," Cyran said, emotionless.

She barely blinked at his words. Fear plastered her into herself. He sighed, annoyed, and his foot shifted against the gravel. He turned away. "Bring her to her room."

"Yes, Master." Zavar's voice rang deep. His pounding steps drew closer. Her mind told her to flinch away, but she was so exhausted, so protective of herself that she merely fell limp when his arms scooped behind her neck and underneath her knees. He hoisted her against his hard chest, scoffing, "Of all the fears, yours is tight spaces?"

Her head lolled against his shoulder, arms tucked.

He snorted at her silence. She could feel his dark eyes along her skin, burning her. He said nothing else as he carried her through the halls. She was a shell of a girl. Her only rebellious act now was to keep breathing. In and out.

Zavar kicked open a door and dropped her on the floor. He chained her ankles to her wrists. Only a bucket sat in the corner, along with a thread-bare blanket. She blinked her eyes open to him sneering down at her.

"Pathetic." He moved toward the door, dark hair shifting. "It hurts less if you bend to his will. Because he *will* break you. Multiple ways, not just with some moving walls. So prepare yourself, girl, because that was nothing." He smirked. "I would know."

He slammed the door after he left. She blinked at the chains and lay back down.

She was placed in the moving-wall room seven more times until she reached for Zavar once the rumbling ended, a subconscious association that his touch meant it was over. Then Cyran placed her in a casket-like iron box and steamed it hot. Zavar would pull her out with a cool towel, until over and over, she would scream his name, begging him to save her. His touch became a safe place.

Until she was chained to a wall, all four limbs stretched like a star, and people began to appear. They touched her, said insulting things, but when Cyran or Zavar appeared, she was trained to relax. To trust. To obey them and the reprieve that came with their presence. No matter her recognition of it, when a stranger reached toward her, she would snap. Bite at them, snarl, cower, then fight. She'd rattle the chains and her power would flare until any face that wasn't Zavar or Cyran would become an enemy. If they dared to touch her, if she *let* them touch her, a plasmic shock would sear beneath her skin. She vomited the first couple of times, but before long, the pain became a sliver of sanity.

Yarrow appeared once, then Jodin, and then them together. Yarrow's eyes remained hard, scowling, as he entered the room and took her in.

"Give her a hug," Cyran commanded.

Violet's gaze flicked to Zavar in the corner, fear pushing her back into the wall. No, no, Yarrow would hurt her. He would slice her, even though he Awakened her. The same thoughts ran through her mind as Yarrow approached, some sort of hatred on his face that she couldn't place. Of course, he hated her—she'd hate him right back. But chained to the wall, she had no other option than to suffer through the minty scent of his breath, the cool touch of his fingers, and the quick, plain hug he gave her. She waited. Yearned for the plascution.

But it never came.

Jodin did the same. No part of their past arrived in her mind—she'd already begun to forget. Zavar remained silent, always studying her closely.

Cyran stepped from the door's threshold of the control room. "Only four. Only four will make you safe. The rest will die if they touch you because if you let them, they will kill you. Us four will provide everything you need. Understand that."

The next day, a plain dagger was placed in her palm and the chains remained limp. She was free.

And through Cyran's manipulation, she killed each person who entered. When Jodin stepped through, she halted. Put her hands behind her back. Over and over, he drilled it into her, and over and over, Violet accepted it.

It was two weeks of this. One night Violet curled into herself. Sleep nearly claimed her, but the door opened, and a hot, wet tongue slobbered her face. She jerked, knowing she didn't have a weapon, so her hands reached—

"Animals are fine." Zavar's voice. She calmed instantly. Her vision was filled with white and brown fur, pointed ears, and a black snout. She pulled back. A dog. *The* dog. The one she gave Jack.

"Her name is Minji." She snapped her head up. Zavar held the door open. "She's too distracting for my dogs."

"She's…" Violet tentatively ran her fingers through Minji's fur. "Not as dirty. Or skinny."

"I can't have ungroomed dogs lingering around mine." His dark gaze dipped. "Nor starving ones. She makes a mess. I'll have them bring up supplies and…" Zavar sighed deeply, nostrils flaring. "Her ball."

"Her ball?"

"Yes. It's a disgusting pink."

A smirk crossed her face. "Did you give—?"

Zavar slammed the door.

As the tests continued, Violet found herself finding solace in Zavar and Cyran's touch more and more. The Worldbreaker dined with her, then tortured her, then wiped her tears. Zavar undressed her, placed her in the shower with a gentleness she was unused to, and let her bathe. No one was allowed to approach her. In some tests, they'd have other men and women try—ones who would run up, but her instincts were morphed. She saw them as threats, and slowly, day by day, Violet injured or killed anyone who wasn't the Master, Captain Zavar, Jodin, or Yarrow. She was given a wide berth as she walked around and was allowed more freedom. Minji followed her everywhere, cuddled her at night, and was the only non-human companion she allowed next to her.

When she was placed in another room, one that wasn't associated with the torture, she nearly fainted.

Jack stood by the fireplace.

Zavar gently took her hand and placed a dagger in it. Then shut the door on her, closing her in. She knew Cyran was watching from some little hole, some video camera, but her thoughts vanished as she took in Jack's tattooed, black-clothed body, and his hair pulled neatly into a bun. Green eyes flashed teasingly.

"Hello, Vi."

His velvety voice simmered over her skin, drawing goosebumps. Her palm grew tighter on the blade. He wasn't one of the four. He can't get near her.

But a tiny voice in her head blared, *he shouldn't be here.*

"Our story is a broken one, isn't it?" he drawled and stuffed his hands in his pockets. "Seems like you broke it further by abandoning me."

"I…" She rasped, unable to find her voice. Heat raced across her cheeks. Her eyes flickered around. Where was Zavar? Cyran? Even Jodin or Yarrow? She needed to know if this was okay. Or else…

Her hand twitched with the dagger. She gritted her teeth and kept it by her side.

"How does it feel to know you abandoned those who loved you?"

Her eyes watered. "Stop that."

"You *left* us. Fled right into his arms—"

"I was hurting—"

"We *all* were hurting." The green flashed. "And you want to make it about you? It's always been about you, right? None of us matter, right?"

"No," Violet breathed. A choking sound. "I…I couldn't feel things."

"You're no Sin Savior." Jack's nostrils flared. "You're merely a selfish, monstrous betrayer."

Violet lunged. Jack didn't flinch. She raised the dagger and sliced it across his neck, and there… she felt it stop before the skin. A breeze blew from the movement—an occurrence that never happened. She cried, pain ripping through her, uncaring. She flung the dagger into the wall in frustration, and it stuck, ringing into the silence.

Her feelings overwhelmed her. There was pain. So much pain bloomed from her chest, and it made her want to claw at her skin. His words slapped her coldly.

"Violet."

"*Do not say my name,*" she snarled. Fury rose. "You don't get to say my name. Not like that. Not in the way that you do when you accuse me of being a monster."

He cocked his head in the stupid way he always did. When he thought he was better than everyone. When he ruled the room. "Aren't you, though?"

She remembered the darkness inside of her that cooed with the ancient power. Her hands shook as she thought of the crumbling buildings and the screams of innocents and the blood slicking the streets as she destroyed the Church District. Her eyes searched his, looking for his tease or the blossom of his dimple that proved he was messing with her. She begged silently.

That dimple did show. "Even I'm not as horrible of a monster as you are."

Another backhand. Ice slithered through her veins. Her mouth popped open, stunned. Her heart twisted and she stepped back, clutching it with a shake of her head. "What did you do to me?" she muttered, on the verge of tears at the incredible pain. He opened his palm. Her gaze snagged on their bloodbond scar.

"Did you think this meant I'd have to care about you?" His frosty words dumped over her. "Did you think this bond made you…special to me?"

"No—" she begged. "Please, don't say that—"

"Are you in love with me?" he said, his voice so, so soft.

Her heart caved. "Of course, I am in love with you!" She stepped back, shaking her head. "Are you that dumb? To think after all this time it meant *nothing* to you? And you meant nothing to me? I started this world vulnerable—I was lost, hopeless, looking for life. You were there…"

She looked at him, but she wasn't seeing him. All their memories together flashed before her eyes. His hands, his lips, his words. She let herself fall for him. She let herself, even then, broken and all, believe she could be loved in return.

"They always fall in love with me." Jack shrugged. "You were just one of many." He walked to the door, pausing, not meeting her eyes. "Maybe in another life."

"Liar!" She rushed for the blade, yanked it out of the wall and whipped it toward him. But with a loud crack, it embedded into the shut door.

She wailed into the air.

And like that, Violet's heart shattered into not pieces, but dust. Unfixable.

Destroyed.

The door opened. Cyran stepped through wearing the same clothes as Jack had been. Her brows crumpled as tears stained her vision. She waited for his hug, his warm touch, the comfort he was supposed to provide…

"You loved him."

"*Make it stop*," she sobbed. "Please, make it end. I can't… this pain." She pressed her palms to her cheeks. "I should have never—"

"Love will only destroy you, Violet," Cyran drawled. He glanced to where Jack had stood. A part of her knew that Jack wasn't real and Cyran glamoured himself, but she was hurt all the same. "You must let it go."

"He called me a monster," she exhaled. Her tearful gaze lifted. "Is that what I am? Is that…is that what I'm meant to be?"

He stood before her, lifting his hand. His fingertips grazed her chin. A solemn look. "The power to be a monster lies within you. You can rule this universe if you chose. You can cut down anyone like him who makes you feel small, and show them all the prevailing, god-like girl beneath. If you so choose."

It was four more days of being called a monster by each of her friends. Anaya, Rio, Reed, Jack again. They circled, and at some point, their harsh words bounced off her chilly, dark heart.

Zavar saved her from them one day. He asked a simple question, "Are you ready? To become everything they hate about you?"

Her eyes were dry. Rio rippled into Cyran. She was thankful for it.

"I'm ready."

❈❈❈

A week later, in the two-planet and chromatic realm of Eterna, Violet stood on the dais below the Master. The wind blew. A glass and onyx palace ascended behind him, and the beautiful gardens of Cyran's endless realm stretched at her back, before expanding into a sprawling, advanced city, unlike anything she'd laid eyes on.

"Look at me, my child," the Master called.

Blood dripped from her hand as her eyes left the body of the traitor she'd killed. She stood. Her heartbeat steady—serenity washed over her. A smirk grew. She could taste the blood on her lips and the killing calm ricocheted beneath her skin. It pulsed in desire, for more. More vengeance. More power.

"Come to me," Cyran commanded.

Her fear-provoking eyes met his proud ones. She drifted slowly, bones creaking, but she fell to a kneel in front of him.

His hand petted the white side of her hair. A world that lay within her. She relished in the thought of that power. It flowed through her veins, pounded against her heart, just as her blood flowed through its.

"Swear to me, Violet Asher, to serve me until your last breath. Swear to protect the promise of joining the worlds and ruling the universe together. My child, swear yourself to me and my Empire, and then rise to meet your home."

A ritualistic dagger appeared on a pillow. Zavar's ring-clad fingers held it. When she glanced at him, his black eyes sparkled proudly.

Violet took the blade and slashed her palm, right over her bloodbond to a man worlds away. A dead man. She almost laughed at the woman she had been with him—yearning, desperate, in love. She pitied the weak girl now left in a buried grave.

"I swear, my Emperor, to serve, to protect, and to conquer these worlds with you. I swear to serve you until my last breath of this life." She lifted her head and looked into his eyes. "As Violet Asher, I swear myself to you."

Cyran carved his own palm and clasped hands with hers.

The blood between them warmed. And then sang. The earth trembled and she could feel, within her bones, the power in her veins, that it worked.

She rose from her knees. Cyran nodded at her, a smile lingering on his lips. She returned the smirk as he let her hand go and she took her place at his left.

To the realm, to the army at her back, to the Fringe gracing the steps, and to his world—their world—and all the realms beyond, Cyran bellowed, "Bow, my servants, for before you is the last of my line. The last of my dynasty. The power in her trembles the worlds we have conquered. Those who fight us, oppose us, wish to destroy us will fall by the edge of her blade. The last of my bloodline, meant for death but found a home, a family with me. *Bow*!"

Her smile didn't falter.

Obsidian draped her. Thick leather strapped knives to her thighs, needles the size of her fingers to her chest. A silver whip coiled around her left arm. Her clothing hugged every bit of her body—moveable, breathable. Her toes curled in her boots. She lifted her chin against the collar of her armor, her braid tight against her scalp, thin strips of silver plaswire woven into it.

The world bowed to her. To the blood in her veins.

She was death. She was shadow. She was sinful.

She was the descendant of a monster.

So, she would become one.

Acknowledgments

First and foremost my biggest thanks to my wonderful editor, Marie Still, who was extremely patient with me as I wrote and re-wrote this story, and gave me invaluable feedback in the end. You're truly a skiv for dealing with me.

Big thanks to Nat from Miss Nat Mack for her beautiful cover as always!! I am in awe of your talent and harnessing my LOVE of color.

To Elaine from Allusion Graphics for proofreading this massive work, you are truly a superstar!

To Sam. Samantha. You were a lovely first reader and now one of my closest friends. Thank you for both popping your webussy on my bomb ass website and also helping carry my dead cat out of my apartment on the second day of us hanging. You a real one.

To my other wonderful friends: Lili, Suitcase, Meghan, Ashley, Kirenjot, Caitlyn, Eryn, Michaela, Alexis, Karin, Finn, and all my other darling supporters—I love you guys!! I'm sorry I'm keeping this short but ya'll know I'm tired of writing lol.

To Kelsea, my amazing roomcuz, thank you for randomly moving to Charlotte with me (and soon Chicago!!) being okay with the massive amount of post-its in our apartment that still never helped me figure out this damn plot, listening to me rant about bad reviewers, reading little snippets and giving me the best support, and of course, getting used to my enthusiastic jumping and pacing when I wrote a good scene.

To my cat, Maggie, you are the best little Navo there is. Too bad you can't hear me say it.

To my family; Mom, Dad, Justin—my forever support team. Whether it is a dream or a true reality, I know I have you all by my side. Here's to another completion of one of my many dreams.

And lastly, to my wonderful readers who, while a small family, still support me through it all and keep me going word by word. I love reading your messages, your reactions, and about all the therapy you need after what I put you through :)

You all rock.

Thank you from the bottom of my cold heart.

www.ingramcontent.com/pod-product-compliance
Lightning Source LLC
Chambersburg PA
CBHW020345220726
48290CB00014B/1012